# The
# Glass House

# The
# Glass House

## MONIQUE CHARLESWORTH

Hamish Hamilton
London

First published in Great Britain 1986
by Hamish Hamilton Ltd
27 Wrights Lane London W8 5TZ

Copyright © 1986 by Monique Charlesworth

British Library Cataloguing in Publication Data

Charlesworth, Monique
  The glasshouse.
  I. Title
  823'.914[F]        PR6053.H372/

  ISBN 0-241-11906-5

Typeset at The Spartan Press Limited,
Lymington, Hants
Printed in Great Britain by
St Edmundsbury Press, Bury St. Edmunds, Suffolk

*For my mother*

# Chapter 1

Victor had had the oddest feeling for some time. It was the sensation of being followed, of being watched. Even in the dark underground garage, as he climbed into the big Mercedes and sniffed the aromatic new leather, he felt impelled to look over his shoulder. There was nobody there; no other car but Herr Wachtel's dark green Jaguar. Nobody sprang from the shadows to menace him. And yet he looked and every time shook his head at the absurdity of it. Victor was not a nervous man, nor was he fanciful.

Another thing: in the streets, the placid, well-ordered, elegant thoroughfares of his city, he had begun to notice something he had never seen before. Children; the odd small boy walking purposefully across the Alster/Kennedy-Brücke, head bowed, trudging along with no mother or elder brother in sight. Two or three of them loitered near the flag poles on the Jungfernstieg. In summer, the tourists queued there for excursions on white, glass-topped motor boats, but now the wind was chill and he wondered, on his morning walk, that they should choose such an exposed position for their games. A child of ten or eleven, a boy who surely must have been playing truant from school, had stopped him yesterday, asked the time politely and then run away before he could reply. Victor, a courteous and good citizen, would never refuse such a request.

I

A whole tribe of them had preceded him on the way to the bank, dodging in and out of doorways, springing noiselessly on thick-soled sports shoes which seemed far too large for their spindly legs. They were thirteen or fourteen, that awkward gangling age, with that faintly threatening air such juveniles had when out in packs, causing the mid-morning lady shoppers to clutch their bags a little closer. They did not shout or call to each other, but wheeled and swept among the pedestrians like bats using radar to swoop and turn, never quite touching anyone. Then all, as upon a signal, had suddenly raced away around the corner. They would have bats' voices, he thought, angry adolescent squeaks, and wondered why he had never noticed them before.

Unmarried and childless, Victor had little interest in the younger generation beyond the show of tolerant benevolence expected of uncles. He held this honorary position in a dozen households and his arrival always caused a certain amount of jostling and thrusting, a certain smiling eagerness to be the first to greet him. Like all good uncles, he generally had some small present in his pocket, something to keep the children quiet while the parents sipped an aperitif. He did not like or dislike children, and, being quite unmoved, knew exactly how to deal with them.

These adults-to-be kept impinging upon his consciousness. There they were again, three boys at the zebra crossing as the big motor idled. They did not cross and one of them stared impudently at him through the tinted glass. He was old enough to have a child the age of this adolescent with his arrogant stare, his shoulders hunched in the dark blue anorak, delicate pink ears protected from the cold only by the long, fair, girlish curls tucked behind them. A pretty boy, a profile as delicate as a girl's, smooth cheeks unblemished by a pimple or hint of a beard. There was something uncanny about that unblinking gaze that sought Victor out; something familiar. The car glided away and it was not until he reached the dual carriageway that the faint twinge of recognition fixed itself more exactly. Of course, Victor thought, that is how I looked as a boy. Those effeminate curls were the colour of his own military crop, except that the stubble over his ears was

2

whitening. He had seen that piercing look, that vague, sulky defiance long ago in an old photograph album. He had stood thus, now sharp, now staring sullenly at the camera, but he had been younger. Nine, ten at most.

That album, like all the rest, had not survived. Victor had no family treasures, no yellowing snapshots on his lacquer sideboard. He saw again the heavy brown leather book with its delicate, interleaved pages which crackled as they were turned. How odd, he thought, for such a memory to surface from the void. Perhaps he was getting old. He smiled at the notion of an old, toothless Victor mumbling on about boyhood days. Unthinkable, impossible, for Herr Genscher, so much a man of today, ever to degenerate to such senility.

Victor never spoke or thought about his past. It was like a country he had visited once and disliked, a cardboard stage-setting peopled with unpleasant characters. Not for him the tearful reunions of old Kumpeln or the back-slapping Bierfest with strangers who once carved their initials at the next desk. There was no scrap of nostalgia in him for that common fabrication, the childhood idyll. He observed the children of his friends, who seemed to inhabit a sunny, false fantasy world of books and games, a jolly fairy-tale of princesses and talking animals, which seemed as unreal and distant to him as the dark wastelands of his childhood. They seemed to him to play at innocence, to pretend a naïvety that only story-book children had. He, playing the friendly uncle, credited them with more sense and saw the sly looks behind the dutiful Knicks and proffered hands. His friends might sigh for their lost youth, but Victor would not have been a child again for anything in the world.

These street-corner kids, alert and prematurely wise, looked as though they belonged to the real, the darker realm, he thought. And then, hooting down and humbling an upstart Karmann Ghia, he shrugged off these absurd notions. Only old men brooded about their youth, he thought, and it was for old women, grown nervous, to see a threat in every shadow. He was at the very prime of life.

There was no denying a touch of vanity in Victor. Not, heaven forbid, the preening ways of the dandy, whose comb

3

was forever leaping from the back pocket into the hand; not the anxious, frowning looks that middle-aged men gave themselves when they passed those huge mirrored wardrobes in Bornhold's splendid display, that quick turn and reassessment of the thinning patch. He did not need to indulge in that dip and bob of the head. Victor's was an above-averagely handsome face; his suits, of fine English worsted, were not, yet, cut to conceal a paunch. He saw himself pleasantly reflected in the plate-glass doors of the restaurant and in the smile of the lady manageress. She tilted her head flirtatiously, leading him to Herr Walther. He belonged to the secret society of the attractive, who acknowledged each other with glances as unmistakable as a Masonic handshake. Pretty women, meeting Victor, inevitably examined his right hand and, noting the absence of a ring, always smiled in a certain way. They were his milieu, not these hitherto invisible half-people, these gangs of baby thugs so unaccountably roaming the city centre.

'Grüss Gott!'

There he sat, stout and jovial, nicely wedged into the plush green alcove, the bottle already uncorked, one pudgy hand outstretched with an apologetic smile as if to say I would get up, but you see how difficult it is for me.

'We must hurry,' he said. 'Unfortunately I fly this afternoon to Bonn, more verdammte Ostpolitik. Can you see old Adenauer turning in his grave?' and he chuckled at the thought. 'It's an interesting moment to get into this game, my friend, I think that I shall miss it in my little house in the woods with only little birds and animals to shoot at and no humans,' and he let out a breath of premature nostalgia, looking hard at Victor over the rim of his glass.

He had round, rosy little cheeks like a doll's, a gleaming egg of a head which shone under the green-shaded lights, and a Humpty-Dumpty body, but with no hint of fragility. His round stomach was unfashionably circled by the dark cloth of enormously high-waisted trousers, further supported by braces, which gave him the air of a Tyrolean on his Sunday off. His comfortably spread legs, like the rest of him, had long forgotten the sensation of being crossed.

4

'Ah, but you'll spare the wildlife for six months, won't you, if the deal goes through?' Victor said amiably. 'I shall need an adviser, a consultant for a time. Let the pheasants fatten for a season. It will be worth your while.'

Herr Walther nodded his head; he was pleased, but wouldn't show it. He made a point of bestowing even the inevitable as a favour. He never took his round little eyes from Victor's face.

'First the deal must go through. The half-year figures are a disaster, circulation's down fourteen per cent and everybody is nervous. This time I think the journalists will accept a package even if it loosens their control, especially if the alternative is, Gott behüte uns, Herr Springer.'

He aimed a mocking smile at Victor, who smiled back. His was a privileged initiation into the rites of his chosen world; a view from the top. He noted the newspaper man's pleasure in hyperbole as characteristic of his type. Victor was going to learn to play with the unfamiliar vocabulary and alternately to abuse and placate a difficult, but gifted staff.

'Your advantage, Herr Genscher, is one of surprise. We will present you as a non-political proprietor, an old-fashioned liberal of the old school. He's a businessman, we'll say, one with impeccable credentials. Even so, it won't be easy. You understand, of course, that the editorial board alone can select the new editor?'

Herr Walther had a brisk and confident manner, exuding authority, just as his solid bulk denoted a massive strength. He was not the sort of man who cared to be contradicted. He had the unyielding heart and all the stony impenetrability of a rent-collector in a bad district; he would get his money, whatever happened. He was unstoppable. Victor, loth to interrupt, agreed with his statements by nodding. He gave him full rein.

'Good, good, that's impossible to change, you see. Now the crux of the matter is the initial share purchase. You must have my ten per cent, as quickly as possible, we cannot move too fast.'

'Today, if you like,' Victor said mildly and the fat man gave him a beaming smile in which gold teeth glinted. He held a

5

small piece of paper, but seemed not to need to refer to it.

'Excellent. Now, you take an option to buy the new rights issue, and when you put that together with my modest holding, the editorial staff's percentage goes down by ten per cent to just under thirty. Of course my ten per cent is then reduced to about six, but you then hold 31, which gives you control. Done! And you have the cash to relaunch, even to begin to modernise production. And you still have the lease-back on the building to negotiate. That's your business of course. I shall merely be your honoured consultant,' and he raised his glass to that notion. They toasted the new empire.

'Yes, good, it's very acceptable,' Herr Walther said, easing himself further into his niche. 'I think we can persuade them. I flatter myself I have a little influence,' and he smiled modestly. 'Now the ticklish bits are the redundancies and the wage agreement, that's where your real problems begin,' and, looking round him, but discovering nothing more threatening than a waitress in a bright red and green dirndl, he lowered his voice to a confidential tone. Security was one of Herr Walther's favourite words.

'We present the package at a surprise general meeting. No speculation before hand and a week for them to decide. Boum!' and a fist thumped down on the grass-green table-cloth.

Now it was time to order. Herr Walther asked for fried pork chops, fried potatoes and the token salad his wife always insisted upon; he would follow this with a plate of Salzburger Nockerln and soft, Limburger cheese. Fats were his passion; fed on pork, Wurst and salami, rich gravy, butter and melting cheeses, he had acquired a permanent, slightly greasy sheen. His wife thought that his huge, pale buttocks and almost hairless, tapering legs looked just like a pig's, an obscene comparison she tried to avoid making by dint of turning her back, always, as he undressed.

'I don't see how, with the right management, it can fail,' he went on, wiping his mouth. 'Not if you have my shares and the cash in your hand. I, of course, shall introduce you. A little speech, I think, stressing the inviolable nature of editorial integrity, that sort of thing. Here, I've prepared this. Rather a

6

persuasive little word, tell me what you think.' Conspiratori-
ally, he slipped a piece of paper across the table. He smiled
through bulging cheeks when Victor did, scanning the lines.

'Pop!' Herr Walther said, leaning back to aim an imaginary
weapon at his jouranlistic adversaries. 'We'll hit them right in
the pocket, where it counts.'

Victor came as a godsend to this greedy man. Behind his
bonhomie, this tough old bird was truly delighted with the
solution he believed he had manufactured personally to solve
his problems. Victor had his measure; he had had him bagged
for a long time. He slipped the paper into his pocket before
calling for another bottle and a fingertip just grazed something
there: a small, rectangular card.

The white car wended its way through the afternoon traffic
heading towards the Ost-Weststrasse and Victor was glad to
turn off at Holstenwall, where it eased a little. He was a
confident man, a man on the brink of achieving an ambition, a
man quite without nerves. And yet: there was one little thing.
A trifle, an oddity, the regular daily appearance in his postbox
of a small printed card. It was the cheapest kind of business
card, vaunting the prowess of a martial arts specialist, offering
lessons in the grubby backstreets of Altona. A joke, of course,
on the part of one of Victor's sporting pals, one that no longer
raised a smile when, day after day, the card insinuated itself
into his pile of letters. Victor's postbox did not only contain
business items; he was accustomed to find pale, pastel-tinted
faintly scented letters there, but these were the only aberration
he tolerated.

This card bore a name, of sorts: Meister Judo. It offered a
telephone number, an address and a crude sketch of a man
sitting cross-legged. He wore the loose white coat and pyjama
trousers of his calling and from his mouth issued the words,
'Self-defence the only defence! For sport, for recreation, for
your security, learn with Meister Judo. Ages 8 to 80 accepted,
private tuition available.'

This card did not find its way into Rommer's box, nor into
that of Herr Frisch; its offer was made to Victor alone.
Wheezing, mumbling, faintly annoyed and apologetic, the old
caretaker had shrugged his shoulders at it. Perhaps, when he

7

took the rubbish down, somebody slipped in; he could not, after all, inhabit his glass box all day without a break. There were chores to do. Disagreeably conscious of failing his employer, while loth to exert himself in any way, Herr Frisch had promised to keep a lookout. His hunched, retreating back adopted an attitude of defeat before the event, and sure enough, no card-dropping miscreant had been spotted.

Something about this card made Victor uneasy. He took it from his pocket now, a slip of pasteboard which arrived grubby, with curling edges flaking into their separate parts, as though it had been used to clean a particularly filthy set of fingernails. Later in the day, Herr Tiedemann noticed it in the waste-paper basket, picked it up and examined it with his habitual curiosity before he, too, discarded it.

Herr Tiedemann was an upstanding, thorough, precise, conscientious old gentleman, letting no detail escape his careful attention. Whatever interested Herr Genscher necessarily enthralled his venerable, albeit junior colleague; all the more so since his employer had taken to leaving the office for two to three hours to transact unknown business elsewhere. For it was business; even Herr Genscher's relaxed and congenial lunches with acquaintances turned out to be business, sooner or later. Was he taking judo lessons? Herr Tiedemann could hardly believe that this was the case but, just to be certain, made an excuse to enter the inner sanctum and examined his boss's features sharply and in vain for any signs of recent exertion.

Nobody worked late at Rommer's. On the dot of six there was a click as Fräulein Schmidt turned off her machine and covered it carefully, rearranging the mighty Olympia on its thick felt mat in the exact centre of her desk which she then locked, departing carrying her wastepaper basket which she aligned at the door in a suitably inferior relationship to those of Herr Brinckmann and Herr Goldberg. She had the small pleasure of wishing Herrn Genscher, who descended the stairs with her, a pleasant evening.

Herr Tiedemann, who had dawdled busily through another day, was already walking smartly towards the Hauptbahnhof, his daily constitutional flushing his sallow cheeks, and Victor, who had forgotten his briefcase, leant to unlock the boot of his car.

Against the dark, carpeted interior, the white was at first glance a startling contrast. Somebody had scattered dozens of the cards inside; they had even found their way into his leather case. He straightened in stiff-backed anger, the shiny new anti-theft key dangling in his hand. Now this was a violation. He would throttle the intrusive bugger, den beschissenen Judomeister.

He left the busy brightness of the Königstrasse as it hurried through Altona aiming with all possible speed for the salubrious suburbs, and drove slowly down the Beckerstrasse. It was one of those narrow, straight side streets where the houses formed one long row in the same dirty grey stone, the symmetrical lines of windows staring unsympathetically at their counterparts broken only by the intermittent claims of Astra, Stella Maris and Pilsener Jever.

It was twenty past six and yet few windows were lit behind their net curtains and there were still a number of urchins idling in doorways, the sort who liked to run a key down the sides of cars, especially if they were new, making their mark in anticipation of owning something rather similar when they grew up to be hoodlums. Victor parked under a street-lamp two streets away and walked back, leather soles skidding slightly on the icy tarmac.

The judo school was next to a taxicab business, where a number of men lounged on old armchairs half-reading sporting papers while they eyed the faded blonde who worked the switchboard. Meister Judo, the window proclaimed in see-through angular capitals, the remainder of the glass being sprayed black. An amateur had executed this legend in tape which had left long white snail marks and further gleams of light seeped through small scratches and spots where the colour had worn off. A bell jangled distantly as Victor opened the door and stumbled on the unforeseen step.

It was a kind of anteroom, a narrow corridor no more than two metres wide with half a dozen chairs against the wall opposite. A large framed testimonial of some sort hung on the plastic which was pretending to be wood, the large red seal

9

flattened against the glass. The door at the far end opened and an old woman shuffled out and thumped herself down on the chair behind a small table there.

'You're late,' she announced severely. 'The lesson has begun,' which was already clear to Victor from the loud thumps and shrieks which had accompanied her through the doorway.

'I am thinking of taking a course,' he said mildly and she looked him over, assessing the rich fabric of his coat through cunning old tortoise eyes which had a whitish rim around the iris and which struggled against the further handicap of overhanging pouchy eyelids.

'Private of course,' she said. 'You'll be wanting a private course at your age. Beginner?' and she drew from the desk a faint Gestetnered sheet, containing information which had left the page at the bottom, the whole surmounted by the familiar sketch, also askew, so Meister Judo looked as if he was toppling over. She fished spectacles out of a pocket and peered at it.

'Two hundred Deutschmark the beginner's course, private,' she said, jabbing with one stubby finger at a number on the page. When this met no protest she rose, with an effort, pushing the yellow heels of her hands hard against the table. 'Well, follow me,' she said. 'He won't take just anybody,' and then, over her shoulder, 'But you'll do, I can see you're the sporty type, Herr?' and Victor, who could not help smiling at the ingratiating slant she gave her insolence, said 'Genscher' and followed her into a room which seemed vast by contrast.

Children; the place was awash with them. The entire floor was covered by a white mat on which two rows of little boys were sitting cross-legged watching one of their number being held in a stranglehold by a slightly older lad. Nearby, half a dozen bigger boys tussled and tumbled about in pairs, uttering loud shrieks as they hit the floor, cries which were satisfyingly melodramatic and theatrical. The old woman threaded her way through them towards a group of adults in the far corner, who sat watching two men circling each other.

'Da ist er,' she said. 'Herr Levison! Ein Moment mal,' and in the same breath, 'Off in here, shoes off,' and indeed she had kicked off her sagging specimens, but Victor had not noticed. His eyes were on the smaller of the two men, the one whose skinny legs seemed lost in the baggy trousers who, while they watched, darted forwards, whirled his hefty opponent through the air and in the work of a second had him spread-eagled on the mat, with one arm locked behind and the other thumping away for mercy. Only then did Meister Judo look up. As the dark eyes fixed upon Victor's face, the mouth slowly opened in a ghastly rictus of a smile. The teeth were jagged, uneven and of varied colours; one was even black against a long canine, the pointy yellow fang of a dog, and the man displayed his broken mouth to Victor in umistakable pleasure and did not take his eyes from his face, not even when he rose, executed a sideways bow of the head at the fellow gasping on the mat and walked towards his new pupil.

# Chapter 2

Tuesday, December 2, 1971

I was seventeen and madly in love with Victor. I'd loved him all my life but had never imagined anything would come of it. It was an unreciprocated grand passion, a folie de jeunesse. I was torn between appearing frail and consumptive, the pale young maiden nurturing a secret sorrow, and the often stronger urge to tell Oma, who irritatingly never noticed anything amiss. Linda knew, but she was the most un-satisfactory confidante and would mock my tragic passion whenever I was stupid enough to confide in her. I was literally struck dumb when Victor asked me to become his wife.

Opa had been dead four days and Victor was helping us with all the formalities. He had gone out with Oma to help her choose a granite slab. It would be very simple, he said, with three rows cleanly chiselled. 'Eduard Luther Rommer' above and beneath 'Geb. 11.4.1893', below that 'Gest. 10.3.1967'. No encomiums, no Latin tags, merely the facts in his mother tongue, precisely the sort of simple directness Opa would have approved of. In fact this bleakness would appear romantic and mysterious, later, in St Luke's churchyard.

Victor came to tell me about it and then he moved in for the kill. He took my hand and said, rather quickly, for Oma and Susannah were rattling about with plates in the kitchen and could return at any moment, that it pained him to speak at such a moment, when I was naturally upset, but that he couldn't leave England without knowing something. He loved me, he wanted to marry me, was there any hope for him?

I was completely taken aback. Dreams were one thing; the physical reality quite another, coming as it did in a wave of lemon scent and in a soft, special voice I'd not heard before. I gawped. My cheeks went beetroot.

'Do you think I'm too old?' he said. His charming smile appeared and, I suspect, a certain amusement in his eyes. I finally muttered something or other, enough for him to deduce that there was indeed hope, and very wisely he left the room and left me to my amazement. How I longed for an action replay, so I could acquit myself more creditably. But the deed was done and we seemed to have made some sort of promise to each other which, because of my youth, was to be kept secret. For seventeen I was staggeringly mature; beneath the schoolgirl exterior lay a throbbing, passionate and witty woman of the world and so I took it for granted that Victor had seen through that shame-faced façade to the glorious creature underneath.

What, indeed, did Victor want? What could he have thought? I didn't exercise my brain on the problem at all, for it was fully occupied with dreams of future glory. I failed to address the issue, as Prof. Schiller would say, for years to come. In my essays I do the same, rambling instead obliquely round the subject in the hope of hitting by chance upon some telling point which will let me off the manifest absurdity of the subject. Victor and matrimony was a preposterous theme, particularly with J. Rommer as child-bride heroine, that much was obvious to anyone but me. I had cherished this notion secretly for so many years that it seemed neither ridiculous nor unachievable.

I address the problem now. Not because I have even the faintest hope of resuscitating those dreams, but because the question remains, hanging in my head, getting in the way. I would like to acquit him of actual malice in order to acquit myself of dumb credulity, of being such a nerd. He made a fool of me; am I therefore a fool? How could I have made such a fundamental mistake? Something was clearly very wrong with said Rommer's perceptions, but are they any different now? The proposition: to analyse events, dispassionately, naturally, and acquit self.

First question: was the whole romance a farce? The evidence for the prosecution is plentiful, for Herr Genscher and I go back a long way. When he first started coming to England to report to Opa on the business, he brought toys for my five-year-old self. The first was a tiny raggedy hedgehog doll, a parcel which appeared magically in his hand. He explained that this was the Steiff trademark toy. All the little animals had the Knopf im Ohr, the button in the ear. It didn't hurt them, they were proud of it, it meant that they came from a great house, as I did. I accepted that compliment with the innocent awareness of the very young, who think they know their place and like it. Every subsequent visit brought a little friend until I had a whole gallery of the charming furry creatures to remember him by. Sentimental fool that I was, I brought that first one to Hamburg with me. It sits on my desk now with its beaming smile between apple-red round plastic cheeks. The German gargoyle equivalent of the madeleine, but quite inedible, and I don't need an aide-mémoire. First of all I have an appallingly exact memory and secondly a numbing tendency to replay events, making them unforgettable.

How, in any case, could I ever forget Victor? For a start he was always striking among my grandparents' friends for his youth, his charm and elegance. Their friends came to play canasta and to eat huge, old-fashioned dinners at which Susannah officiated in a black frock with white collar and cuffs, having moaned over the job of buffing up the best silver all afternoon. This was for the benefit of the bank manager, lawyer, accountant and sundry professional neighbours, all very proper and English. They frightened me until I was old enough to participate and discover that all they did was drone on about golf, or gossip about matters in the city, which they pretended to know intimately from the safe distance of quiet

Hampstead offices. Now and then they bored on instead about vintage wines or the shocking cost of private education, one or the other being the socially acceptable method of draining their fat purses as fast as their overpaid exertions filled them up. It was acceptable, just, to talk about money, providing you never told, or asked, what people actually earned.

The real friends, the German-speaking ones who often, confusingly, turned out to be Hungarians or Poles, were much more amusing. Compatriots in exile, they always laughed a lot; but still, they were shockingly, dreadfully old. For all their elegance, the ladies generally sported a little wave over the ears to conceal the tuck marks; the red-faced gentlemen would flirt outrageously over glasses of Russian vodka, but clearly hoped they would never be called upon to act out their extravagant promises. Some lucky girls at school had parents still in their thirties, who moved in the heady worlds of PR and the garment business, get-rich-quick commodities and property deals. In their fox fur coats, the ladies generally in couture leather suits, they had unspeakable glamour. Alas, they never were invited to the house; no competition for Victor at all, who was even younger than they were. When Victor proposed, he was exactly twice my age.

An interruption: a telephone call from Tante Mausi, who says she's bringing Ingrid to visit me as they're coming to Hamburg for the weekend. Obviously Oma has written. Poor Tante Mausi, she's so transparent. She'll eat too much cake, complaining all the while that she must diet, and Ingrid will cast her eyes to heaven in that unpleasant way she has and correct my grammar. She's like a paler replica of her mother, with added spite: dreary flaxen plaits and those large, prominent light-coloured eyes that stare out so arrogantly. Though Ingrid and I have never liked each other, we preserve the convenient family fiction of friendship, cousinship.

Tante Mausi looks older, though she has tinted her fading hair a brilliant yellow, a colour that clashes with the pale greenish strands of Ingrid's hair. Ingrid has had hers cut into a short, neat bob. They merged impeccably into the luxurious quiet of the Alsterpavillon, rose-tinted retreat of well-to-do wives exhausted by the morning's search for the perfect

English cashmere or the adorable little silk scarf. We all touched cheeks and Tante Mausi sank with satisfaction onto her chair, her blue troubled gaze that really meant to look my way sliding instead in the direction of the cake trolley, nose following the rich aroma of Kaffee mit Schlag. The Alster-pavillon even looks like a cake, like a meringue with cream inside. Ingrid was fussing with her camel-hair coat; too good to lie on a chair it had to be taken away and hung up — properly, mind you — by one of the waiters. It was the sort that, like a fur, had a little chain inside, that she said mustn't be used. The Germans have an excellent word for Ingrid: damenhaft.

You look well, she said, eyeing askance my regulation student gear, which suits me better than Ingrid's clothes ever could, her sober, well-cut uniform as sported by the daughters of the bourgeoisie. Ingrid thinks too-short skirts are irredeem-ably vulgar. And so do you. Ingrid smirked, fiddling with coffee cups in order to parade a diamond ring resting on her long, pale finger. And I flattered myself that this visit was on my behalf. Ingrid has secured a banker and tomorrow night I am to have dinner with the two happy families to celebrate. Worse; he lives in Hamburg and so will she.

I suspect that Tante Mausi, vague behind the poised fork of Sachertorte, is relieved to be rid of bossyboots. Ingrid has always held the Bock household in thrall. With her out of the way, Uncle Hansi will be allowed to belch, eat salami sandwiches and drink beer for supper and Tante Mausi will guiltily slip into the old housecoats her daughter despises. She kept offering cakes, worried that I wasn't eating properly. Her concern reminded me of Oma and made me feel homesick. Without the heavy make-up she diligently applies as her salute to the Bock family fortune, she even looks a little like her. As usual, she brought a whole case of the stuff for me and I feigned pleasure. She is a dear, really, and the little black zip cases are useful. I keep my diaries in them. That's another reason for preferring to meet them in town: the diaries and papers all over the flat. Ingrid would sneer; worse, she's capable of reading them behind my back. She does offer one benefit, though. She has a salutary effect on my student slang and sloppy ways and I didn't mess up a single phrase, not even a pluperfect subjunctive, under the critical gleam of her schoolmarm eye. Her eyes really do protrude; you can almost squint sideways through the pale discs, but that would mean seeing things in Ingrid's steely light.

Coming home in the S-Bahn, something horrible happened. A man exposed himself to me. He was hidden behind the *Bildzeitung* but even above the roar of the train there were rustlings and I saw movements of his woolly, rust-red suit, then he lifted the paper high so I could see what lay beneath. One bleary eye peeped through a round eye in the paper to enjoy my reaction. I got up at once and rushed to the door, trembling with rage, and at Altona looked for the guard. He was kind, but said they could do nothing. He'll be put together again by the next stop, he said in his flat Platt, and that it was best to travel in second-class when the trains aren't full. Hurrying down the narrow winding road home I started, then, to imagine I was being followed, but when I turned there was nothing, just the flicker of the old-fashioned street lamp turning on to light the last tumbling flight of steps.

It's easy to get nervous moving through this schizophrenic city. The elegant lady on the Jungfernstieg and the worldly matron on the Neuer Wall could be St Pauli whores in their day dresses. When it's dark, strange creatures parade along the neon boulevards and backstreets, the Grosse and Kleine Freiheiten. In the iron-gated Herbertstrasse the ladies of the night lounge behind their windowpanes; the less favoured shiver at street corners. Leather-jacketed louts and US marines lurk about everywhere while respectable paters with their ladies stroll past or sip white wine in cafés to admire from a safe distance the shifting cabaret of erotic endeavour. The clubs shrink from nothing; no act too ridiculous or too bestial, and I have seen a man play the violin while he has sex with a grinning, eager puppet of a woman. The audience is often so respectable and so expense account-oriented that it's hard to believe these things are going on on stage. In the less reputable places there are apparently dogs and worse. Oma would be aghast and so would I. She worries about me and sometimes I get scared or lonely and immediately write her a long cheerful letter to reassure us both.

Four thirty and it's already dark. The coffee machine is slowly filtering its black drops which sizzle on the hot glass; the old walls are losing some of their chill. I sit on cushions with my huge fur rug wrapped around my legs and write on the low table. I mean to exorcise Victor, to take him out of my head where he fills too much space and put him down on paper where I can dissect and be done with him in careful, consecutive paragraphs.

The first question to address: which approach? In our literature essays we're always told exactly what line to take, which social influence to analyse, which dialectic. I have been told today to prepare a paper which discusses the poems of Hartmann von Aue as an expression of the lowly troubadour's quest for social advancement. The poems are irrelevant to the theory; it's words we concentrate on, to show the socio-economic forces of the time, picking out those which refer to riches, power or, 'lady', to class, and waving them triumphantly as proof. Our long, dull tracts vindicate the approach endlessly. Lyricism is passé. To talk about poems of love or despair is to excite ridicule, to miss the point. I am severely censured for my old-fashioned, romantic, rambling approach. Too many digressions, as here.

So: Victor as socio-economic force. Perhaps it's not inappropriate. Opa always called him the mainstay of the house of Rommer. He attributed much of our recent affluence to his energy, his uncanny way of anticipating rises and falls in the market, sniffing out deals and cheap cargoes to be picked up and unloaded at a profit, his shrewd purchases of land and stocks and shares. He was a worthy successor; winking at me, Opa would add that he was also the only possible one; that was why, shortly before he died, Opa sold half the shares to him.

He had actually left Hamburg fourteen years before he sold out, when he was sixty. He called it retirement, but it was no such thing. Victor was only twenty-four then and had been with the firm several years; he was very junior, but already beginning to try out a few ideas of his own. These were generally pooh-poohed by Otto Tiedemann, Opa's right-hand man.

Otto was theoretically in charge; but it became clear that he was not the entrepreneur who upped the dividends. Old-fashioned, prim and proper, he's a stickler for tradition and the correct way. I swear he clicks his heels at me. Once I was bold enough to smoke a cigarette in his office, stubbing it out in the hollow brass anchor on his desk which could never have been defiled before. He became quite red in the face, rushing out with the nasty dirty thing as soon as I'd finished. If I weren't Fräulein Rommer and half-heiress, I think he would have thrown me out. He's seventy now and gives no hint of retiring; he believes, quite wrongly, that he doesn't look his age. Opa promised him he could stay on as long as he wants to, so he remains in the big office, the huge desk distressingly clear of papers, for Victor makes all the decisions. Through his glass wall he is the scourge of junior clerks and terroriser of messenger boys, given to appearing suddenly behind the poor woman who operates the telex and making her jump. Nobody is allowed to smoke, except for me, and I only do it to annoy. It's always Herr Tiedemann I see whenever I go to collect my allowance or to sign papers; Victor is never to be seen. Perhaps he's warned to stay in his office; I don't know. I don't ask.

Rommer Import-Export own their dignified old stucco building in the Esplanade, a stone's throw from the Steinway Haus. As ever, in Hamburg, culture and business go hand in hand. It was a blackened ruin after the war. Opa rebuilt it and he and Oma made a flat on the top floor, which Victor ascended to in due course.

In the brilliant, troubled summer of our engagement while in Paris students ripped up the streets to build barricades, I thought I was storming Victor's. He ushered me round the newly-renovated glories of the flat. He had had new cupboards put in for the endless clothes, the summer and winter suits, the piles of monogrammed shirts. He had new glass sliding doors onto the balcony and had opened up the inside to make one large space. It is desperately elegant, modern sleek furniture, leather and chrome, mixed up with exotica, Korean chests, old Chinese scrolls and art deco screens. Every object is carefully placed at the correct angle to its neighbour and the furniture has little cups under the feet, so the carpet won't mark. Expensive hi-fi and a baby Steinway grand near the open hearth, though he can't play, and everywhere mirrors, walls of them and grand gilt ones and one ornate matching pair with a tiny fisherman in a Chinese hat dangling his rod at the top, his wife bowing humbly in its counterpart. They made me nervous; all those reflections and the shiny, perfect surfaces.

It breathes the bachelor of cultivated tastes, as though he'd briefed a fashionable interior designer. No old photographs or souvenirs, no teddy bears, nothing shabby. It's a statement, sotto voce, of culture and taste, a careful, anonymous mingling of the two with money to burn. It wasn't a Hamburger's flat; no ship's models, not a single clipper in oil, no sea captain's dogs or maritime bric-a-brac, none of the things which clutter our house. He could see that it intimidated me. I couldn't see myself elegantly bending over to place the Japanese place mats at the perfect angle on the mahogany dining table. And yet we lay on one of those leather sofas once, while Mahler, poignant and sentimental, surged and swirled in the warm air. I can't hear it now without thinking of him, that lemony smell on his warm, elegant body. Sometimes I sniff it in the street and my heart turns over.

More digressions, how Schiller would scowl. 'To the point! Fräulein Rommer, get to the point!' He saves his most plangent comments for me, striking up obsequious echoes in my co-seminarees. That weedy clever little worm Behring pointedly puts his pencil away, though not his sharper tongue, when I start to read my papers.

Victor's past: where did he acquire those tastes? His was a humble background, I know that (source: E. Rommer) though Victor never spoke of the past. An autodidact, he also went to night school, swallowing up texts, learning late into the night 'wie ein Mann besessen', Opa said. He would be at work on his ledgers by 7 a.m. and always in before Herr Tiedemann, who is a stickler for punctuality. How that must have needled the old man, especially when Opa was seen to admire that restless energy. Victor must have picked up culture somewhere along the way, though it wasn't part of his apprenticeship.

Victor is an orphan, like me. It was an unspoken point of mutual sympathy. I should cross that out. How I keep on creeping in, as though V. Genscher can't exist without J. Rommer putting her grubby thumbprint on the picture.

Victor is an orphan. He survived the Berlin bombings and at the age of twelve was living on the streets, quite alone, when the Red Army launched their final attack. He survived on his wits and, later, on GI handouts. When he left Berlin, it was in order to go to sea. Was he a romantic boy, with visions of tropical islands lapped by blue lagoons? He saw the world through the portholes of greasy galleys in dirty cargo ships or rather, like that silly song, he saw the sea. He was only sixteen but precocious, of course, and tall for his age and strong and nobody asked questions. Finishing school afloat, Opa called it, from which he matriculated at eighteen. A genteel establishment to be sure and it certainly finished off those romantic dreams, because he couldn't wait to get ashore again.

It was 1951 then, the start of the boom years, empires rising from the ashes and J. Rommer in nappies. He chugged in on one of the dozens of cargo ships flowing into the great harbour. They'd cleared away the burnt-out hulls by then and propped up the ruins of the Michaeliskirche. There was lots of money around, the real stuff, American dollars which couldn't be spent on defence. The city fathers were rebuilding their bombed-out city, though in all humility they left some of it, like St Nikolai, 'eine Mahnung für kommende Geschlechte'.

Opa had already restored his façade; he was busy giving the business a new core. My great-grandfather started Rommer's, trading in rubber, jute, tea and tobacco, crops nobody wanted any more grown on plantations that had been abandoned or destroyed. Opa wasn't about to neglect the shipping side, but he saw there was money to be made nearer home, in land, new apartment houses and stores as well as in ships. Rommer's advertised for a junior clerk (trainee) and two dozen young men turned up ready to make their fortunes. Victor, at eighteen, looked like a man. Equipped with a 'knowledge' of merchant shipping and a smattering of half a dozen languages, he crammed those broad shoulders into a borrowed suit and came, cap in hand, to learn. He said he was ready to start that

21

minute. Opa was always proud that he took him on in the teeth of Herr Tiedemann's disapproval and no doubt he enjoyed discomfiting that sober citizen. Ah, but I saw his worth at once, he liked to say.

Victor survived Herr Tiedemann's petty tyranny; he annulled it with his charm. He mastered the work with ease, for he had a naturally good business head and an eye for an opening and he impressed people. An old head on young shoulders, Opa used to say. Is it my fault I fell in love, when we talked about him so often? Opa described him as the sort of man who, lost in the jungle, would be discovered king of the cannibals ten years on. Of course he meant that as a compliment.

Other clever young men came; turnover doubled in a year, then it doubled again. Opa began to talk about retiring. He'd had a hard war and said it was time for a rest. Of course he had no intention of letting go. He had good old Otto to oversee things and he meant to enjoy himself. He moved country, but it didn't stop him interfering and directing matters long-distance, the inevitable dissension ignored, the counter-advice overruled. The sound of my childhood is the chattering telex in Opa's study. It would stop and then there would be the rip of paper being torn off and discarded as, once again, Herr Tiedemann urged caution and was ignored.

I was the ostensible reason for the move. In reality, Opa was a terrific Anglophile as all the old Hamburgers used to be. He relished the snobbery, the men's clubs, the good tailors and the Ritz, cruising in black taxis to get a new pipe at Dunhill's or have tea at Fortnum and Mason's. He claimed the weather was actually better and he didn't mind the bad cooking, for he had Oma. The queen of the Auflauf, he called her. She makes delicious Sauerbraten, inspired dumplings and always, on my birthday, fragrant lemony cheesecake in a rich pastry crust. And of course there was always Uncle Victor, the bearer of goodwill parcels which were always greeted with surprised delight, even though the contents had been telexed through as an order. He brought us Niederegger marzipan and crusty Zwiebelbrot, unsalted butter and a selection of sausages. Opa liked knobbly hard salami, the sort with wine-red mottled skin which Oma sliced into perfect, thin, densely packed circles, each slice exuding the faint tang of garlic, some with that exiguous desirable dot of pale green peppercorn. I pitied English girls for their soggy egg and tomato sandwiches. Oma's sandwiches were a feast, the dark peppery slices laid on cool lettuce over thickly buttered dense bread, which had crisp onions on top, more succulent fleshy pieces inside.

We didn't really go native at all. We settled in Hampstead in a large house which Opa always described as Rissen-Vorkrieg, so for ages I thought that was the name of the place. We were in the middle of the European-Jewish community, where in shops people spoke German, where Anna Freud had a children's clinic and cafés had real coffee and understood what Schlag was. Just as important, we were inconveniently placed for my mother's parents in Yorkshire. They were to be granted their wish for an English granddaughter without having the opportunity to see me often and to influence me in the slightest degree. I always visited them in school holidays. They are kind and slightly incomprehensible and eat salads of fatty, thick ham, lettuce and tomato with half a hard-boiled egg. Once I told Granny you could make a nicer salad with white cabbage and caraway seeds, oil and lemon, and she laughed for fifteen minutes. Grandaddy, who hardly ever opens his mouth, and looks at me with puzzlement and faint pride, sees me as a not unpleasant foreign element, an exotic flower among the prize dahlias. I never could understand how they ever produced a child as adventurous as my mother. They don't hold with foreign ways at all. While they were relieved I'd grow up speaking English, they lamented the choice of London, which was almost as bad as abroad. It turned out even worse than they anticipated, for we lived like colonials, always nostalgic for the old country and recreating it in the way we ate and dressed and in our pastimes. We dressed up on Sundays when our neighbours washed cars, went to spa resorts when they headed for beaches and skied when they stayed at home.

There's J. Rommer, centre-stage as usual. It may be Victor's life, but it's mine too. I can't separate him from my childhood and adolescence and just cut him out of my life, though that is exactly what I have pretended to do. We all carry our past around with us, permanent and heavy baggage, even if sometimes it hardly seems to weigh at all, even if we don't always choose to unlock the trunk and forage. I wish I could get inside Victor's box, Louis Vuitton to be sure and covered with first class stickers, and fathom his secrets. Then perhaps I wouldn't have to trail him around with me wrapped up in that horrid black bundle of regrets and sad misunderstandings that weighs so much I feel permanently bowed.

# Chapter 3

They sat in a small room decorated with sporting calendars so long out of date, so oddly placed, that they had, surely, to be covering eyesores on the florid, mosaic-patterned walls. A rust-rimmed filing cabinet disgorged a mess of papers near the door, an office desk was flanked by two leatherette swivelling chairs that tipped alarmingly. A white-painted cupboard let into the wall had doors held together with twisted wire. This room, jutting out at the back of the house, had previously been a kitchen or scullery. A thick, deep old-fashioned stone basin spanned one corner; one tap, from which the chrome had long flaked away, protruded drunkenly from the wall. Above it was nailed a pink plastic rack on which a cup sat and a plate and a delicate porcelain tea pot quite out of tune with its surroundings. A frayed towel hung stiffly above on a string; this and a cake of white soap suggested that Ludwig carried out his toilette here.

From the look of the bundle in the corner lassooed with string, which resembled the sort of sleeping bag explorers were said to prefer in rough terrain, Victor deduced that this miserable room could also be Ludwig's bedroom. He looked all around, observed everything, the chair anticipating his movements while the dark man sat perfectly still and watched him.

It was curiously, oppressively hot. The paper bubbled and crept away from the walls and rivulets streaked down onto the dirty window-sill; a damp, crumbling place below showed where these tributaries combined and had eroded a route to the spongy lino strip. The heat did not even seem to have a source, for there was no radiator, not even a gas fire in front of the boarded-up fireplace. Sweat was beading on Victor's forehead, but he remained encased in his coat, reluctant to make any gesture which might indicate a willingness to be there. He spoke with a certain amused nonchalance. 'Interesting,' he said at last, 'that it should be you. I should have guessed it. Still hiding in dark corners, I see,' and he let a contemptuous glance stray around the room. 'Well, what do you want? I'm a busy man, I have no time to waste.'

The other frowned slightly. He sat perfectly motionless, seemingly oblivious to the sounds that resonated through the door and quite at his ease, his palms turned up on thin thighs. He drank in the face opposite greedily, with the air of one who had waited a long time for this.

'My dear Victor, this is a pleasure I hardly dared hope for. Let me savour it.' His Berlin accent was strong; his was the sharp and mocking tone of the old Ku'damm bully-boys. 'You, such a busy man, here in my little office,' and he smiled jaggedly. 'How many years is it? And look how smoothly they've flowed past you, for you've not changed a bit. But so very smart. How well you look in your fine coat. Ein teueres Fädchen,' and he made as though to touch it. Victor, who could not return the compliment, sat rigidly and suffered the approach of a dirty fingernail. There was a tingling sensation at the base of his spine which made his buttocks clench involuntarily and the chair lurch a little. He could not keep his gaze from the mouth, any more than a motorist could help staring at a gruesome roadside accident. He knew that smile from earlier days, from unblemished times, when it used to flash out for pleasure, not in this sly, knowing way. This smile was an ugly accusation waiting to be made. There was altogether a knowing look on Ludwig's face, a consciousness of the effect he was having and Victor saw now that he must have rehearsed this encounter often. For all his calmness, the small body held its upright position with a certain effort.

'Don't play games with me,' Victor said. 'What do you want?'

'How suspicious you are,' said the sly voice. 'I remember as a boy you had that look; knowing you'd been caught out, waiting for punishment and still hoping to evade it.' He laughed, a mirthless rictus. 'Yes, it's the same expression exactly,' and the dark eyes stared unblinkingly at him. 'And here I am, waiting for you. I knew you'd come. You were curious, weren't you? But I have changed,' he laughed, a strange gulping sound and then spread his thumbs at right angles to the long fingers and framed his face with these bony right angles, like a picture. 'Oh, don't you like it? But it's not the packaging that counts, my dear Victor, even a fine and costly one. Inside we are both the same,' and he beat melodramatically at his bony breast.

Victor's eyes slid, for relief, from the grinning puppet. 'Or is it the room you don't like? My apologies, Herr Genscher, for the disarray. It's not what you're used to, I'm sure. But you were not always so fine,' and he pushed his head forwards on an elongated, endless neck in which the Adam's apple bobbed and danced. 'This is where you started your career, my dear Victor, take a good look at your handiwork.'

Victor controlled a movement of revulsion and impatience. 'You will leave me alone, do you understand?' he said in soft, measured tones. 'Keep away from me, or I shall take action to ensure that you do.'

The little man was silent for a long moment, staring hard at Victor, testing him with his unblinking gaze. He nodded, then, as though satisfied.

'Action,' he said in a level tone. 'Of course, that was always your way, to strike first. But no, I think not. How is the eminent Herr Genscher to take action, let me see, will he perhaps call the police?' and he was mocking again, his face drawn into a long expressive O of disbelief. 'My poor Victor. It's not always pleasant to look back and see your shadow. How it sticks to the heels and won't let go, even on the darkest days it only pretends to disappear. A little ray of light and, hupla, it's back again. How can it leave you?'

27

'You have heard me, you understand. Be very careful, Ludwig,' and Victor stood up, sickened with the unhealthy atmosphere of the place and Ludwig made a pretence of starting back, as though in fear.

'You mean to wrestle it perhaps, to take a knife and cut it away?' His eyes were alight with some strange pleasure; he curled back his lips like a dog to show his fangs. 'Now we approach the heart of the matter. What are you going to do about me? But you're nervous, Victor, now that surprises me, I can see that you are. But I know that you have it in your power to be — shall we say, accommodating? You can make a choice. Think of the old days, my dear Victor,' he whispered caressingly. 'Think of old times. Why should I mean you harm, unless you will it?'

He caught up with him at the door, he laid his long hand on Victor's sleeve and gripped it with a force that made muscles bunch on his wiry arms.

'You are a worried man, a discontented man,' he said, his fetid breath warm on Victor's face. 'The higher you climb, the further to fall, my dear Victor, yes, I can see you falling, down, down,' and the other hand raised itself high and thumped down on the door with a sudden, loud report. They stared at each other. 'A pity there is no time now when we have so much to discuss,' he went on, briskly, disengaging himself, 'I don't close at six. We're not in the smart quarter here,' and brushing past him he went into the large room, with Victor following. The mob of children hushed as he entered and separated into rows, all faces turned in their direction.

Ludwig stopped, then turned, blocking him into the corner. 'Listen,' he said very quietly. 'What you see here is the curiosity of a child. Are they looking? Are they staring at you?' And, over his head, a procession of eyes, some blank, some curiously alert, were indeed fixed upon them. 'The need to know, to comprehend, is quite involuntary, as automatic as breathing. What has happened to you, to make you lose it? It's the very process of life, the reason for existence. A man is dead when he ceases to learn.'

The head, under its thin fur of hair, was bumpy. A small crater, a space to balance an egg in, lay in the centre of the cranium. Although the boys could not possibly hear the man's whisper, Victor had the bizarre impression that the eyes were absorbing each word, reflecting back the hypnotic murmur. 'You are perfectly inert, do you realise that? A walking, dead mass. I am offering you a voyage into yourself, to comprehend the cause and effect, to see the pattern so that you can free yourself of it. When the nerves are dead, numbed, it hurts to bring them alive again. The realisation of self is painful, but you must perceive yourself to comprehend life. And then, Victor, we shall remake history together.'

The pink-faced boy was sitting there; recognising him, Victor took a step forwards and the boy averted his gaze. He crossed the room, feet sinking into the mat like a man walking on sand, and was conscious that the heads turned; as he reached the door they all, upon an unseen signal, scrambled to their feet.

The lesson was over at eight o'clock and for a quarter of an hour there was a scurrying about as the little boys got dressed again and crumpled their kits into nylon bags; as those who hired their outfits scrimmaged in the corner for coat-hangers, for Herr Levison was most particular about the way everything was left and not a few of them were afraid of him. The adolescents jostled for a view of themselves in the small cracked mirror where they combed back sweat-darkened hair and eyed the unappealing skin eruptions that characterised that age.

Meister Judo did not offer the convenience of showers or a locker room. There was a lavatory two flights up a rickety wooden stair sufficiently unappealing and badly-lit to provide a small boy with a useful schooling in bladder control. It was not generally known at the school, but one or two of the older boys had been permitted to use Herr Levison's private shower under particular circumstances, circumstances which did not generally apply and which were not the sort that got talked about. A certain boy hung back now, a boy with long, fair hair who was tall for his age; but when he received no encouragement he went with the rest, pushing through the crowd of little kids whose mothers crowded the anteroom, pushing their protesting offspring into thick jackets and gloves, pulling thick, woolly hats down over flushed little faces. It was surprising how many smart cars were to be seen pulled up onto the kerb of the Beckerstrasse, chauffeured by doting mothers from as far afield as Hammersbrook, as Bergedorf even, such was the renown of Meister Judo.

Frau Liebmann trudged about, rolling up the little boys' white belts and returning them to their niches in a resigned manner. This, the odd, desultory flick of a feather duster, the replacement of the toilet roll and her public role as receptionist made up the extent of her employment, for which favours the old woman received lodgings, a small salary and the constant company of children, whom she abhorred. Pleased to see the back of them, she thumped the front door shut, drew across a large bolt and, flicking off the lights with a practised gesture as she went, retired to the more congenial company of her television and a pair of knitting needles. She used these both to manufacture a succession of undergarments and to jab at the dials of the set.

Almost everything annoyed Frau Liebmann, most of all the idea that Herr Levison might think he was doing her a favour by employing her, since she was past retirement age. She treated him accordingly with curtness but also, since this looked like being her last possible job, did what he asked of her, never interfered or pried. Neither of them asked for, nor expected, any warmer human contact. She thought herself invaluable and, in a way, she was.

Listening for the thump of her feet pursuing their erratic path up the stairs, for the bang of her door and the noise of the inner bolt being drawn, for Frau Liebmann considered herself safe from no man, Ludwig awaited the moment when he could enter upon his rightful kingdom.

Meister Judo's acute hearing made out the sound of voices, a snatch of music from above and, abandoning the thick white jacket and trousers, he circled the large room, feinting at an imaginary opponent. For twenty minutes he skipped, finally slowing down and lowering himself to the floor where he sat cross-legged and still, a small blur in the faint light coming from under his office door; a dark yogi on a sea of white. Rising, he padded over to the office and carefully undid the loop of wire on the cupboard door, which swung open letting in a wave of moist, warm, pungent air. He breathed in the heady aroma of damp earth and greenery, the sweet scent of flowers mixed with the acrid odour of decomposing leaves.

A large conservatory lay beyond the door, a great glassed-in space which half a dozen heaters kept at tropical temperatures. This was Ludwig's secret garden, surrounded on the outside by high brick walls with sharp fragments of glass embedded in concrete. It left the house at an oblique angle and was almost perfectly concealed behind the brick box that constituted his office. Part of this structure could be seen from the windows directly above, Ludwig's and Frau Liebmann's, but it was impossible to see through the moisture-dewed dirty panels of glass, which were always filthy two days after Ludwig had cleaned them. Frau Liebmann, in any case, never bothered to look. It wasn't any of her business what he got up to in there. Naked but for a jock strap, Ludwig bent over a bank of flowers and crumbled the soft earth with hands that soon acquired a delicate black tracery over the palms. His skin rapidly turned warm and damp. He trod softly, delicately along the duck-boards, feet pointing slightly outwards, toes descending first, like a mannequin's. His ribs were countable, his belly had a concave curve and his knees seemed exceptionally large-jointed because the thighs and calves were so slender, yet strong muscles pulsed on them as he walked. He was conscious of a fine film of sweat on his body as he worked and relished the trickle that occasionally found its path down his narrow back.

As he went, he bent to pick off dead leaves and examined each plant minutely for signs of blight or disease. He sprayed the leaves with a fine mist from a brass can and took earthworms from a tin, laying them gently on the damp soil. His pupils knew that he would pay a good price for a tin of worms and would dig illicitly in the park for their squirming offerings. They speculated behind his back that he ate them live or distilled them into a potent drink to restore his strength: pleasurable horrors, which did nothing to lessen his prestige. He weeded and cleaned and, at last, walked to the central trough with the newest and rarest of specimens, the young, struggling plants, and examined their tender furling leaves. Carefully, he cleared tiny clumps of earth from new, almost invisible, pale seedlings.

Late on summer nights, he liked to stand in the darkness and look up at the stars. But for the absence of secret animal rustlings and strange cries, he could fancy himself in the jungles of Sarawak or Borneo. Now the winter mists swirled and there was nothing to be seen but the distant orange fuzz of a street-lamp, its glow diffused through the blurred glass streaked with brighter stripes where the condensation ran down. In the summer, birds spotting the luxuriant oasis among grey stone tried to fly into the foliage and often broke their necks on the glass. Only Ludwig was permitted to enter the sanctuary; he almost believed he heard a sigh, when the cupboard door closed behind him; the murmur of a thousand leaves turning in the warm air, of blossom heads dipping in salute. He loved this place; for the heat and silence, the simplicity of growth and decay, rot and rebirth. The glass house was a refuge, which also offered an exquisite form of deferred gratification, for nothing was ever finished. It imposed its disciplines and that, too, he loved. In this place he left behind the petty discomforts of the crumbling, chilly house and forgot that rough, barren streets surrounded him. It was his personal miracle, that such flowers blossomed in Altona.

The school was an imperfect counterpart. Though Ludwig was a good teacher, never bored with the constant repetition, always soothed by the familiarity of the timetable, his boys were not as responsive to his careful nurturing. True discipline and order existed only in his private kingdom. His poor means provided an oasis for the poor, the under-privileged, the kids with no one else to turn to as well as those who paid the full price. He gave them all strength and order and rules to live by and the process used him up, tired and exhausted him. He was often frustrated by their stupidity, their resistance, their failure to understand; it was too much for one man, alone.

Tonight, though, he was happy. He knew how to make a particularly shrill sound through one of the gaps in his teeth: a startlingly loud whistle for which he hardly needed to purse his lips, which came in useful when summoning small boys. Now, while he worked, he drew in a breath and let out this steam-kettle of a noise for sheer pleasure at the prosperous turn his affairs were taking.

At ten o'clock he slipped up the stairs and into the first floor rooms he inhabited; Ludwig's bedroom was a severe space equipped with two futons and an adjoining bathroom. For twenty minutes he soaped and scrubbed himself and scraped out the dirt from under his fingernails. He lathered off the sensual film of dampness and the erotic, mossy smell that clung to the hair, as a man might shower after leaving his mistress, for fear that his wife would detect her distinctive, cloying scent.

Emerging naked from the brightness, it took a moment for him to see the figure lying on the bed, which sat up, blond hair bright in the gloom, tucking long curls behind the ears.

'How did you get in?'

'The window's open downstairs. You've been avoiding me, you've been so cold. What did I do? I did everything, just like you said, don't send me away.' The eyes pleaded. 'My father's away, no one will know.'

Wordlessly, Ludwig lay down. Bernd carefully poured oil into his small hand; inexpertly it began to massage his master's body. His flesh, in the chill air, was covered with goose pimples. 'I'll warm you,' the boy whispered. 'Is this right, am I doing what you said?'

'Be quiet, can't you?' but the body was responding. This boy had a small power over him which Ludwig was loth to acknowledge. Through half-shut eyes he could see another face on the young bright head; in a moment, he knew that some trick of the light, some accidental movement of the pale limbs would provoke, with the sweetness of sudden memory, an immediate ejaculation. But for this extraordinary resemblance, this unconscious ability of his, the boy would long since have been banished. He was such a willing lad; so very able and useful that the judo master could not, quite, do without him.

In another moment, with closed eyes, his body was shuddering in rapture. The boy stared at him through the

33

gloom; he did not expect any caresses in return. A moment later Ludwig turned over; soon he would be asleep. Carefully, Bernd slid under the covers and lay still, eyes wide open. Ludwig never spoke, afterwards. He slid into oblivion as quickly as possible; he would feel sickened in the morning, but now he slept, his breathing regular against the faint, familiar rhythms of Frau Liebmann's box of tricks. Upstairs, the old woman's needles were for once quite still as she peered in slight confusion at the baffling succession of dramatic events which made up Francis Durbridge's latest Krimi. The pink baby wool lay loosely round her swollen finger joints as she thought that perhaps, if it had been in colour, she might have understood it.

The boy spoke in the faintest of whispers into the dark. 'Why don't you care for me? Don't you love me a little bit?'

It was an unpleasant night to be out. A dank misty chill turning to frost made an ice-rink of the streets. The white Mercedes purred along the Elbchaussee keeping a few kilometres within the speed limit. Now and then it overtook an empty taxi, cruising slowly back into the centre. Victor was returning from Wedel. He had remembered the Fährhaus Schulau, where ships of every country were greeted with a blast of their national anthem, a place of official welcome, merry, hot and noisy and always crammed with tourists jostling for tables. It had not occurred to him that there was a season for welcomes, as there was for everything else. As he had entered the main room its solitary occupant, an old man, had put down his glass carefully, the better to observe the phenomenon of late entrance and retreat, the grey head swivelling with the mildly speculative curiosity of vacant old age.

It soothed Victor a little to control this big, efficient machine. He had not yet outgrown the pleasure of owning such an expensive toy. He had developed the habit of thinking through problems while on the move. He made better decisions on the ski slopes or the tennis court than in the oppressive seclusion of his office, that dependable yet stultifying environment where paper clips were counted and letters containing even one error retyped. But on this long loop of a joy-ride, as if to mock him, his thoughts circled vacantly.

Since the Reeperbahn was crowded at this hour, he chose the route through Pinnasberg, up and down the hilly little streets to the Landungsbrücke, up past the Bismarckdenkmal and across the Ost-Weststrasse to St Nikolai. He knew all the side streets; he had made this city his own. The motor idled at the traffic lights and a VW drew up alongside. With slow precision, Victor turned his head, but it was only a young couple who profited from the moment to kiss. The boy's eyes, open above the curly head he gripped so fiercely with both hands, looked defiance at the rich man.

Verwöhnt, verstört, verdorben. The spoilt generation. Victor was not alone in finding them incomprehensible, unspeakably alien. And yet they were the ones who claimed alienation and smashed up their parents' cars; they decamped to dirty communes, remembering to take their stereos and colour televisions. They grew their hair, took drugs and would not eat; they let the orthodontic miracles in their mouths decay to spite the years of enforced care. Indulged and full of hatred, children of the bourgeoisie, they studied anarchy and disaffection at their parents' expense and grumbled if lack of money obliged them to take their frightening, almost unrecognisable selves home on a ritual visit.

And, he thought, those parents could consider themselves lucky. He had often spent weekends in the houses, now grown too large, of charming, cultivated friends. Sitting in the rustic Frühstücksecke over a second cup of Kaffee Haag they would confide in him as if he, lacking that experience, were somehow wiser. They would sigh over the names of darling little children, Udo and Peter, or Ingrid's girl, or did he remember Friedrich's boy, Jürgen, children who had grown up to accuse their parents of spiritual poverty. There was a whole generation that was altogether lost, roaming India or Afghanistan barefoot. Now and then they would send home postcards which babbled in broken capitals the name of some guru. The youth of today: the product of affluent, carefully nurtured

35

childhood years. His friends were right; it was a comedy so black and sharp that only the childless could appreciate it.

Many of Victor's friends had been old enough to fight; they all remembered hardships. Of course they could not understand it. The boyhood of Victor Genscher could have been a film, one he would certainly have walked out of. It would, he thought, have been a low-budget jerky thriller for a Geissendörfer or a Fassbinder to make. A tale of low life, violence and betrayal among misfits and outcasts. Ludwig could even play his own part, the Ludwig Levi he was then, but for that dreadful mouth. Not Victor. He was transformed, a success, and he had atoned in his blameless, productive and valuable existence for the sins of that boy. The boy did not even exist; he had been suppressed into blackness, where he would remain.

Ludwig had long since been banished to that oblivion. Victor had not given him a thought for fifteen years or more. Before then, if some chance word brought back his image, he had told himself that he was dead, or as good as, lost forever behind the wall. That long-gone boy had known him well, too well, had feared him and yet they had called themselves friends, for lack of a better word, in those starving, scavenging years.

Ludwig had always been an oddity. His father was a Jew, his mother a committed Catholic, and he carried within him the inheritance of their irreconcilable differences. His was a legacy of clashing superstitions, fuelled by stories on the one hand of heretics and martyrs, saints who severed limbs and practised bloody self-mutilation for the glory of God and, on the other, by tales of centuries of oppression, of pogroms and massacres, of the sufferings of this life meekly borne with no hope of redemption in the next. He had told Victor all these things, had held nothing back. A communion of souls; that was the term Ludwig, the professed atheist, had used to describe these one-sided discussions.

These bitter parents had vied for supremacy in suffering, had countered each other's afflictions with a worse tale of God-given fury and had brought up a boy who could believe in nothing and in nobody; who readily denied them both. A twisted, complex devil of a boy had sprung from these two, a boy who burned on this fuel and forged in these flames a religion of his own, a cosmology with Ludwig at its fiery heart. He had believed in himself as a saviour of souls. He had set himself up in a little 'mission' and gathered about himself a little tribe of lost children over whom he ruled.

He used to scour the bombed-out streets and half-ruined houses to gather in the abandoned children of Berlin, those who ran wild. There was no one to care whether they lived or died; the more fortunate had long been evacuated to relatives in the countryside. The pinched, white faces of those who remained could be seen among the rubble, digging for an oven which, cleaned up, could be bartered for food. Or, sharp-eyed Kippensammler, they knew how to make a cigarette with seven butts, enough to set up a juvenile entrepreneur in business. For cigarettes, it was possible to get potatoes or even the odd scrap of pork fat. The winters, bitter and long, brought Ludwig the best harvest, for his human merchandise was half-frozen, only too happy to exchange the constant insecurity of the streets for the promise of warmth and shelter. They had survivors' skills: hunger had honed brains under hair crawling with nits. They were portable assets and Ludwig claimed ration cards for the keep of each one.

Victor could still conjure up the humble, triumphant, seemingly self-sacrificing manner in which Ludwig had brought each new inmate home, as though he did not profit from them. And yet this was not the most sinister aspect; worse was the way in which he had exacted tribute from them, in body and soul.

Ludwig had cast off his parents; he knew allegiance to no gods and made himself instead the god of those boys. He ruled them sternly: he demanded from his small followers the physical courage of the martyrs, the patience and endurance of the oppressed. He expected gratitude, he expected love, because he fed them and kept them safe, and yet no parent could have imposed stricter discipline. They used to huddle together in the deep cellar as the earth rocked around them. When the sirens ceased their shrieking wail, which they could imitate to perfection, he would send them out to pick through

37

the rubble. They brought him their daily offerings, a clearing-out of pockets which should have contained marbles, or conkers, or schoolboy treasures. A small god of chaos, what would he not achieve when the world established a new order? How he used to talk and boast and tell them that they needed him, that without him they would all be dead and gone.

Victor had been a favourite, a disciple bound by the needs of survival and unquestioning in his acceptance of the young man's authority. The boy depended upon him and feared him. Yet there had also been a kind of affection, moments of humour and simple kindness. Victor had been bound up in him in the way that a child chooses to remain with a cruel parent, any attachment being better than none. After a year in the streets he had forgotten what his parents had looked like, for there had been no memento to salvage from the blazing flat; he had thought, with a stab of fear, that he would not have recognised them in the street. What would he have done without Ludwig, whose rude caresses offered affection, of a sort? Victor remembered sitting at a campfire in the ruins, one of a small crew of ragamuffins, and the sudden warmth of Ludwig's arm around his shoulders. He had gone home with him, that night; Ludwig had gone out again to get clothes for him. He remembered that he had sobbed with gratitude, for he had thought that he was saved.

It was a miracle, in the final stages of the war, that they had survived at all; one for which Ludwig drew all the credit. Survivors, against the odds, in cold-hearted Berlin, grown prematurely wise, they had developed a pride in their parentless existence. Ludwig, who described himself as a father to all these boys, encouraged them to believe that they were indeed happier and better off with him than with those half-remembered parental ghosts.

Peace, when it came, had not changed the order of things. The devastated city, ruled from sector to sector by a different, yet always summary form of justice, obeyed above all the laws of survival. There were rules, which they had learnt to flout. They were invisible: a ragged tribe of abandoned kids who hopped between sectors in juvenile disregard of authority, at one in despising the poor tricks of the adults who froze on the starvation diet and still queued, dispirited and bitter, for half a loaf of bread. They, who knew better, stole GI petrol, coal and spam; with goods scavenged, looted and bartered, they fed and warmed this monstrous household. Later, Ludwig extracted whole cartons of foodstuffs from the soft-hearted Americans for the unfortunate orphan children. He, who had no schooling of his own, would be found presiding over 'lessons' when such goods arrived.

Herr Genscher drove his splendid car around the city centre, encircling the scene of his triumphs, and saw, in acid counterpoint, the scenes of all his failures. These ugly images would keep coming back; they crept out of some dark recess and forced themselves upon him. Ludwig had cast out a line and Victor could feel it twisting tight around his neck; a little string that connected him to his past.

He set himself, with an effort, to see the Ludwig of today. In every sense a little man. A poor man. A creature who still scavenged in back streets; who still tyrannised little boys. The boy Victor might have feared such a creature, but the man could not. He told himself that the boy was truly dead and could not be resuscitated. He would not permit this past to divert the clear course of his successful life. The monster shrank down to its true proportions and, there, it was only a hobgoblin that played his tricks on him, no devil for a child to fear.

What was it that Ludwig wanted from him? Why come to haunt him now? Seeing, now, that he had come full circle, he turned off and traversed the narrow streets and the car slid underground, lighting up the grey concrete walls. The garage was, as usual, quite empty but for Herr Wachtel's car. It was absurd that Victor should even think to look.

# Chapter 4

Wednesday, December 3, 1971

I overslept again this morning, having stayed up too late writing. It's a long way from Blankenese to the university and sometimes, when Kröger's Treppe is iced up or I stand and wait for the little bus, I regret choosing to live here, despite the beauty of the little villas, ochre and pink and beige blending as they climb up the hill over each other's gardens to the Süllberg. Oma wanted me to live in Pöseldorf, the 'snob' English quarter, and precisely because it is that and because of its touristy preciousness, I was put off, though I could have walked from there to lectures. But I do love the Elbe and all my windows look onto the river, so I can watch the huge container ships slide from the kitchen into the sitting room and on into the bedroom. I am right opposite the rocky little beach. It will be charming in the summer, but it's melancholy now. The wind howls and the foghorns boom across the icy water.

For such an affluent suburb, Blankenese has its oddities. A tall, thin, pimply youth in a raincoat with enormously flapping bell-bottoms, who didn't even have gloves and must have been freezing, sat behind me in the bus. He was just in front of me in the train and lurked all the way from Dammtor to the university, his red-chapped face bobbing along the Rothenbaumchaussee. He was unmistakable, with orangey-red hair that stuck up in whorls. He couldn't possibly have been a student, his weirdness being a different sort altogether, but he followed me right into the building. He didn't venture into Aula II when, horribly late for Dr Heinrich's lecture on phonemes, I tiptoed in. That at least was understandable. Now, in the natural German academic response to ex-cruciating boredom, I hear they've made his course obligat-ory. Normally it's Turks who follow me, scenting the foreignness, and offering drinks in bars in their funny accents spiced with rich colloquialisms.

I feel happy today and of course Victor is at the back of it. I had news of him unexpectedly at dinner in the Ratsweinkeller. Tante Mausi thought that was a suitable place for her little celebration of Ingrid's engagement as it's so traditional. The fiancé is called Peter Schwantz, which is a bit of a joke as it generally means prick. Poor Ingrid. She's always despised the beery connotations of her name and hoped for a von. Despite this drawback, he's perfect for her: tall, Teutonic, precise, worthy, well-to-do and incredibly dull. They will have three blond children for her to dragoon. I expect they'll give proper dinner parties with fine displays of their wedding present silver and Ingrid will keep a little book recording what she wore and what they ate. Ingrid was a middle-aged baby and her young years weigh heavily on her; she can't wait to become a respectable matron.

It was the best-man-to-be who knew Victor, a youngish banking colleague whose ears pricked up when he heard the name Rommer. He drifted over to ask half-heartedly whether I was related to 'the' Rommers. With my 'wild hippie hair' to quote Ingrid's endearingly frank words – ah, Ingrid's charm! – and the English accent I never quite disguise, he clearly expected me to say no. He's called Uwe Schenck and had on a desperately sober dark grey suit, his stripy tie regimented by a horse's head pin; a laughing nag with a nagging laugh. Now if he'd really known Ingrid, he'd have been fully informed about us. He wasn't the sort, though, to know anyone, not

41

even Peter, whose depths could easily be plumbed with a shortish bit of string. I saw it all; they must have gone together to the baby banker training school and, being Schs, sat together, and Peter will have noted Uwe's thin old silver cuff links with a crest on them and known he was okay. Then real intimacy developed; they will have shared sandwiches and had a beer together and borrowed each other's slide-rules and furled black umbrellas.

Uwe had, however, the redeeming virtue of being most interested in Victor. He has been meeting with him, in some junior capacity, over a vast loan Victor's getting from his bank. He said he had a 'verblüffende Intelligenz' and laughed, as though that was a joke; very disconcerting until it became clear that he laughs at everything he says. He throws back his head to let out his mirth presenting a fine expanse of double chin, beautifully smooth pink skin it was too. He told me all about Victor's interesting mind, his interesting travels and how interesting it was that he was also a good sportsman. I, of course, agreed. By contrast, in fact simply by failing to smile much, the prick appeared very erudite. A solemn young man and just the thing for Ingrid. I stuck by Uwe for a bit, even this crumb being a feast to me. Old Tiedemann tells me nothing; he's under Oma's thumb.

Peter, Ingrid and Uwe suit each other. They are kindred souls. They have neatly ordered lives in which everything happens according to plan; perfect banker material and Ingrid a tailor-made wife. She always wanted to marry young and next year when she's twenty-two it will be high time to start the baby programme, at a correct and decent interval after the wedding, naturally. Poor Uncle Hansi. She'll have him in tails and a top hat in which he'll look ridiculous. She will ask me to be maid of honour, in pink or yellow shiny material, and take care to throw her bouquet at me in a conscious, pitying way after the ceremony with a kind smile.

The evening had its moments. The clear oxtail soup was horrible, but the pheasant delicious, Ingrid's full of shot which she bit upon to her outrage, for her perfect front teeth are all capped. It was a study to see her fiancé's face while she gave the waiter a drubbing. The poor old man explained courteously that this was inevitable with game, provoking an imagined loss of face which made her all the more viperish. She turned up her nose, insofar as that is possible, at the bombe with flambé'd cherries. Too cold for the delicate dentures I suppose; not appropriate for a winter's dessert, she said snottily.

Peter's parents, an unassuming couple, pretended not to hear any of this while Tante Mausi blushed and twittered. Uncle Hansi with his strong Rhineland accent hardly dared utter a word the whole evening. We agreed to meet secretly for a beer before they go home. I know a little Kneipe near the university which is just right and Linda'll be here by then. He'll like her. The archetypal English rose, plump and pink and accommodating and underneath quite savagely determined to get her own way. Uncle Hansi likes to like everyone; he loves to be comfortable and wants everyone to be happy. Nothing daunts him, only misery makes him miserable, particularly the tight-lipped martyrish sort Ingrid has in such abundance.

I still call him Uncle, it sounds natural, though he says with a great sigh that it makes him feel old and since Mausi's a half-aunt he's only half an uncle and that the other half feels so much younger. Incredibly, I called Victor Uncle until Opa died. Uncle, Uncle, Uncle, his title hops across the round childish script and the later, italic affectations of my childhood diaries. I still have them, dozens of exercise books, half of them elegant hard-back ones with swirly pink and blue marbled end-sheets. I used to beg him to bring me those from Germany. I wonder if he knew why I wanted them so badly? I credit him with sufficient prescience. There's the word at the back, in a long list of vocabulary with definitions. I used to try and learn grown-up words to impress him, chanting the definitions until I knew them by heart. Pabulum, excoriate, hegemony, what fascinating conversations I must have offered.

My bouts of intensive self-improvement coincided, naturally, with Victor's visits; then there were our trips abroad, which often seemed to go through Hamburg. He never would stay with us, despite Oma's insistent, kind invitations, preferring independence in grubby little hotels. Later he graduated to first-class establishments. We all looked forward to Victor; Oma for the gossip and women's magazines she, ever frugal, would never have bought for herself; Opa for the long lunches in expensive, men-only places. He marked these occasions by taking his best pipe and putting on his heavy gold cufflinks. I would see Victor at least twice; once when he came and paid his respects to Oma and then at the family dinner in town. Victor would ask politely after school and listen attentively to my inane, vague replies, for I could never think of anything at all witty or interesting to say, for all the hours of rehearsals beforehand. They all conspired to keep me a schoolgirl. I longed to wear stockings instead of the socks Oma considered proper. The dinners were rendered tasteless and joyless in advance because of the awfulness of the little tartan dresses with white collars and cuffs and the socks and flat shoes. In Linda's bedroom we would try on her mother's outfits with nylons, applying thick twigs of eyeliner and pale lipstick, our hair dampened into straightness, so we looked like middle-aged Cathy McGowans. We were always staggered by our sophistication and elegance, though the suspender belts hurt and we couldn't walk in heels without twisting an ankle. How I longed for Victor to see this transformed, adult me.

As each unsatisfactory visit ended, undaunted I started to tick off the days until the next. I learnt to ski at the resorts Victor recommended and sometimes at St Moritz or Ulm I would see him. I have the entry for the appalling Christmas when I bumped drearily down the moguls behind him and an elegant woman whose thick, fashionable Norwegian sweaters emphasised her large breasts. Despite her natural imbalance, she never fell down, as I so often did. A gawky, underdeveloped thirteen-year-old, thin and spindly, I loitered and pretended my sulks related to scrapes and bruises.

'Today Uncle Victor did the Olympic run twice with Inge. They are going dancing tonight. He said he would call in for hot grog but never came.'

'Today I saw Uncle Victor on the toboggans. Opa says they are too dangerous for me. Uncle Victor agreed but he said we would go skating together.'

'Today Uncle Victor came to say good-bye. He has to go back to the office early. He said he was sorry about the skating and another time, but it will be a year before we come back here. Oma said I was rude and should try to be more polished. Look at Inge, she said, she's smiling yet her holiday is ruined.'

That page is blotted with passionate, selfish tears. My diary entries were kept carefully neutral, for fear of spies, but they are as transparent as I was. Not only did I anticipate his visits with joy, lapsing into sorrows and sulks when he left, I also forced myself upon him. I would sit right in the centre of the back seat of the Mercedes when he drove, staring at his blue eyes in the driving mirror for long, rapturous moments. It never occurred to me that the mirror worked both ways, a realisation that at the time of my first driving lessons drew waves of inexplicable blushes.

Uncle Victor never embarrassed me; he showed no awareness of this smouldering, schoolgirl crush. While I longed for some sign, I was also relieved. There was a kind of a rapport, though, a hint of a look, suggesting friendly complicity, that told me he was aware of me in a way that seemed both adult and safe. He knew, of course, that I was ready to fall into his arms. Humiliatingly willing and ready. I never questioned that he loved me; it was enough that he said he did. I would no more have doubted the laws of gravity.

At seventeen I was quite corrupted by love. Not physically, but mentally. I was ready to practise deceit, not to tell Oma, knowing that much as she liked and depended upon Victor, she would never approve of him for me. I assumed that she would always carry on looking after me and wanting the best for me and meanwhile I mentally shuffled her off to the wings in order for Victor to occupy centre-stage. In fact he needed Oma far more than he needed me; I am the interlude in Victor's story that turned out to be dispensable.

At seventeen, I saw nothing. I had my eyes screwed tightly shut. Love, in my case, was not just blind, but deaf and dumb and stupid to boot. I had decided that we were two souls pre-destined for each other, it was Kismet, fate, all that crap. In that last A-level year I was repellent, day-dreaming, wandering around with a sickening smile in love's young dream. In

45

Victor's absence, I cast around for an acceptable bit of literature to moon over and thought I'd got it in *Wahlverwandt-schaften*. The theory was made for me: that people, like chemical elements, are irresistibly attracted to new partners when they touch, as though it were pre-ordained. Elective affinities when bound pairs of elements interchange: Johanna/grandparents + Victor = Johanna/Victor + grandparents.

The theory was laid out in the book with simple illustrations which we schoolgirl chemists tittered at patronisingly. Calcium oxide + sulphuric acid = calcium sulphate + oxides – though Goethe poetically called them tragic, abandoned vapours. How our hands shot up in class. He's forgotten about $H_2o$, we said, little clever-clogses, as though that put us one up on genius. The story ended badly, but I ignored the bits that didn't fit. Goethe was gospel for my German love; proof, as though I needed it, that literature and life skipped along hand in hand. I was going to have the happy ending, even though I was old enough to realise that the best books, unlike Mills and Boon, went miles out of their way to avoid that.

At that time, I not only believed practically everything I read, but preferred books by far to any actual experience. Who would want to snog with some pimply youth, his breath reeking of beer, to suffer his unpleasant fumblings as the penalty for boasting of a boyfriend, when there was real love and life right there on the library shelves? Linda would drag me out, but I preferred to spend Saturday nights at home, in Rome with Daisy Miller or in Paris wearing a white gardenia. Undiscriminating, but always trying to be literary, with Lorca and Lawrence, Mailer and Molière, the whole mixed-up stew of pretentious adolescence, set books and secret ones sweetened with furtive, saccharine drops: Jean Plaidy and Georgette Heyer. There was nothing in my North London reality to compare with those books; nobody in the juvenile mob, so proud of their first cars, notching up the number of times, they'd got off with somebody or furtively losing their virginity in their parents' bedroom on a Saturday night, who could attract me. I was, instead, defiantly intellectual. A swot with all the answers. Above all, I considered myself a German. It was at my insistence that we spoke only German at home, for I was preparing myself for Victor. My intended was the very stuff from which great German heroes were made.

It couldn't possibly go wrong; not when I had all those authors crammed into my head, not to mention the lists of words, the conjugating and declining, the strong and weak verbs and the pluperfect subjunctive. He, clearly, had not been able to resist all those concentrated hours of yearning, dreams and fantasies beamed at his unprotected head. I had willed Victor to happen; the shock of it having, miraculously, worked, was soon succeeded by blasé acceptance of my powers. Years of effort went into Victor and me, ce couple inouï. I got quite an education courtesy of Victor. Never in the sense of being prepared for life, but book-learning; I owe Messrs Schiller, Burger, Heinrich et al to my Uncle Victor. A dubious heritage.

The strangest thing has just happened. I am going to write it down very calmly. It's just an odd little incident, one of those bizarre things that happen abroad and never in England.

It is very late, nearly three in the morning. The melancholy mourning of a foghorn on the river just drew me to the curtains. I leave them open to let in the night lights and to hell with the draughts. That pimply boy was in the road, standing under the street lamp opposite and looking straight up at my window, as though he was waiting for me. He gave a tremendous jump when he saw me and darted across the street. He might not have gone away. He might just have taken cover where I can't see him.

I saw him distinctly, it gave me such a shock. He is unmistakable. I pulled the curtains to at once and ran to the door, which is double locked, and then I checked the window locks, as though he were a monkey who could climb up to the second floor to frighten me. With the curtains drawn, I'm frightened to look out, which I know is stupid of me. There's something horrible about the idea of leaning out and seeing him looking up just below.

There, I've written the number of the police station in the margin here. It would take them two minutes to get here at this time of night, probably less. I'm quite safe, the door is bolted on the inside and it has a chain, so there's no need for my heart to go on thumping so fast in this pathetic way. He must be some kind of loony. Adolescents are always freaking out and doing weird things, especially German kids who are affluent and snotty and hate everyone and know everything. It's just that at night everything seems sinister when you're alone. I'm going to look out now. It's stupid to be frightened and sit here in a panic when he's probably gone away.

# Chapter 5

The boy had been running and was still panting. His loose trouser bottoms were wet and trailed damp threads on the mat. He bent and a drop fell from the pink nose as he laboriously untied his shoelaces.

'She saw me,' he said. 'Yesterday I thought she had and then early this morning she looked out of the fucking window. Stayed too long, didn't I,' and pulling off the shoes and damp, black-toed socks, he seated himself heavily and rested his head in giant's hands. 'I'm done in,' he said and still dared not meet Ludwig's eye. 'Got any booze?'

It was five o'clock in the morning. Rocking on the smooth soles of his feet, Ludwig looked at this poor speciment with pity and distaste. There were curling tufts of red hair on each of the grubby big toes. He was barely seventeen, but it was hard to find any trace of the interesting pallor of three years ago under the stubble on the raw cheeks.

'Jasmine tea,' Ludwig said. Georg knew he didn't drink; that was his poor piece of self-assertiveness. 'I'll make it while you tell me about it. She saw you twice? A beacon, that's what you are, with that hair,' and he clapped him on the back and led him off into the back room, as the trainer leads the tamed beast twice his size. He extracted the meagre details while the great red hands warmed themselves on the tiny porcelain cup.

The lad breathed in the steam like an asthmatic.

The tart sat up late, Georg said, and how was he to know she'd look out and catch him there? He expressed scorn for the fancy suburb. Yes, he knew he'd fucked it up and he darted another glance at Ludwig and started to tell it all over again with emphasis on the misdemeanours of the fucking tart. He had an adult, swaggering vocabulary, an obscene set of phrases whereby each woman was a cunt, each man a prick, every person reduced to their reproductive element, though he of course had no experience of that form of conjugation. What self-respecting girl would waste her time with a creature like this? He did not have the money for the other kind. Ludwig was the only person who had ever squandered a little kindness on the poor brute and that was why, for all his vehemence, he kept looking anxiously at his protector, conscious of another little failure to add to the huge catalogue of errors that made up his short life.

Ludwig was kind to him. He gave him money; he pointed him towards the mat. 'You have to go at eight,' he said, 'before the old woman comes down,' and the boy curled up like a dog and thought himself lucky. Georg had not dared let on about the police and anyway the fucking pigs didn't get him, did they? Soon he slept; Ludwig lay upstairs and thought that they were right, the people who said that nothing could be done with Georg. He did not blame him for inadequacies he could not help; boys with possibilities were treated far more severely. This one was a hopeless case, who passed his days in amusement arcades when he had money. Drop-out from a special school which had defined him as unreachable, off-spring of a mother who, despite her age, still plied her trade down in the docks, he was not welcome home at night. He had been taught by his mother to drink for pleasure, as another might have encouraged reading or chess, and he sniffed around for alcohol. He was happiest in the late-night dock-side Kneipen where he joined in the laughter. There regulars sometimes bought him a drink for the amusement of seeing him gulp at it so eagerly and of bursting into laughter when they did.

Ludwig lay on his back. He tensed and then relaxed one

muscle after another until his body lay heavy and inert, as though a great weight were pressing on it. Still sleep did not come. A car door slammed; footsteps then laughter and a scuffling, running noise. He heard them all with exceptional acuity. Georg was snoring; an occasional grunting inhalation rumbled up the stairs. He wished him gone. Then he could have gone downstairs to meditate. He had no other way to release himself from the ceaseless ticking away of his thoughts.

Why could he not meditate in this room? He wanted to try, now, but the heavy body refused to move. It wanted the space, the familiar faint smell of sweat in the big room; it wanted the mat. Denied these, it would oblige him to wait for the grey morning light. What power this sack of flesh had over him and yet he never let it alone. He worked it and starved it; he would not have treated an animal so badly. He wondered whether other people, who pampered and over-fed themselves, found their flesh so stubborn. He could labour all day without tiring, could sit for hours in perfect stillness, but his body was a beast, well-trained but secretly rebellious. He ached, now, for release from it and it asserted itself with a cramping of muscles which contorted his cold feet into sharp, painful arcs. He did not move; he would not pander to it.

The old judoka who had taught him about zen had had the ability to master men of half his age and twice his strength. As frail-looking and bleached as brittle driftwood, he used to stand and wait for his opponent to make a move. They, approaching him, seemed to propel themselves onto the mat; his motions were so effortless, so spry and swift, that it was almost impossible to see how he had thrown them. He had explained to Ludwig that he released his mind; that dull-witted thing that thought too slowly and made mistakes, thus liberating his body. The body knew what to do. Its movements, trained by hundreds of thousands of repetitions, were perfect, quite automatic; the body responded faster than the brain could tell it to. He had grinned at Ludwig from his clever old face in which a scarcity of teeth bore witness to a childhood of malnutrition. The old man liked himself; he was pleased with himself in a simple, naïve way and, as he bowed in the correct manner, showing humility in victory, the slitted eyes gleamed with secret happiness. His had seemed to Ludwig a life enviably simple and satisfying: a life concentrated down to the purest possible elements. The body was trained and hardy and the mind released, to soar.

Ludwig, who had thought then that he would be a champion, now knew that he lacked the simplicity which he strove so hard to attain. He was too Western, too complicated; he was a disappointed man. When he explained the notion of zen to the advanced pupils, they thought he was initiating them into a secret how-to-win technique. They would listen very hard, the effort of understanding visible in strained faces. He felt sympathy for them then; pity and understanding of them, so rooted in their coarse-boned bodies and adolescent minds. How could they comprehend? They did not even have conventional religious beliefs; they did not even realise that they had nothing and laboured in a void.

The art could only be mastered in a perfect environment. It had to be a school where the boys lived, where the harmony of surroundings and their simplicity gave the lesson more vividly than any amount of talking. A home for the needy and lost, for the abandoned children of the city, an oasis of rigorous, yet elegant schooling. He could see its white-washed walls and a garden in which nature gathered its most exquisite creations and he tended the young, growing things.

The first steely light shone upon a rigid body and dry-eyed, calculating face. He could not rest when there were so many matters still to be resolved. He cursed his own slowness in failing to find a simple solution to the problem of this girl, and he refused himself the hot tea which made the early mornings pleasant.

He was sharp that day, alarmingly alert, and he terrorised the little boys in the ten o'clock class with his cunning feints and appalling swiftness. Georg had left a dirty mark upon the mat which a grudging Frau Liebmann was set upon to scrub, for it was expensive and not to be replaced in a hurry. She stared accusingly into each face looking for the perpetrator of this filth and her cry of 'Schuhe abziehen!' grew particularly shrill as a result.

Small heads bowed solemnly before each session of Randori; little bodies thumped down. Ludwig thought about the piece to fit this jig-saw. Bit by bit, he had assembled the outline of a worthless, self-seeking life, a picture by numbers which took on tone and shade as the little blobs were coloured in. He did not know how large an expanse of white space Fräulein Rommer occupied.

Ludwig had found his golden boy by chance. By the merest fluke, he had glanced at a copy of *Der Abend* which Frau Liebmann, clucking angrily, had worked out from behind two pipes on the first floor landing. He thought it remarkable that Victor should be enmeshed in the very fabric of his house. Ludwig, who always discarded such trash and never wasted his money on a newspaper, was destined to open it, idly, as he did. He was intended to see the photograph now taped to the drawer inside his desk.

'Prominenten am Spiel', the column was called, with pictures of pop singers and politicians, captains of industry and patrons of the arts, all smirking and drinking too much at parties and nightclubs; caught out with the wrong company or the wrong expression on their stupid faces. And there, where he had no place to be, not possessing a famous name, had stood Victor, edge to edge with the heir to a tobacco fortune and a playboy millionaire turned racing-driver. Victor, unmistakable, with a fatuous smile on his face and one arm round a ripe teetering blonde. Steering a new course? it said. Victor Genscher of Rommer Reederei escorts Miss Nordrhein-Westphalen at the seamen's charity ball.

The shock had set a loud pulse drumming at his temple; then drained blood from his head and sent the excess throbbing round his body. It had never occurred to him that Victor might have survived; he was so clearly the sort to come to a bad end. That he could have prospered was staggering, inconceivable. Ludwig had thought about him every day of his life with sadness, with regret, with the poignancy of desire for lost beauty and youth. It was not lost at all; the handsome face fulfilled that promise at least.

He had known at once that something would happen, but for a long time did nothing. For months the cutting lay in his drawer to be fingered and re-read until the words took on a new and cryptic significance. He was not a man to undertake anything rashly; he would never have embarked upon such a protracted and difficult exercise had he not first convinced himself of its righteousness. He saw, then, that Victor was his purpose. Ludwig had been ripe for a cause and this one was irresistible.

Ludwig's golden age, his time of plenty and benevolent exercise of power, had come to an abrupt end because of Victor. They had formed an invisible and self-sufficient community; now the punitive boot of the Allied Occupation stamped down hard on them. The entire nation bartered to survive, GIs made fortunes from their sufferings and ex-Nazis, denied employment, were growing fat on the black market. Ludwig, who had succoured the needy, was selected for punishment. They had requisitioned his house, taken away the children and imprisoned him. Youths over fourteen were set to salvaging the rubble, brick by brick; the German nation was collectively guilty and should suffer, that was the penalty imposed by the peace-loving nations which had conquered them. Ludwig, who had lost all that he possessed, was a marked man, a criminal. All this was the result of Victor's violence, and for years Ludwig had blamed and regretted him and asked himself where he had gone wrong. Necessity had obliged him to create a living from his hobby and he who, however depressed, was never a defeatist, had made the best of it. He had never ceased to mourn Victor. He had yearned, often, for the impossible: to have that time again.

In due course Ludwig had achieved an uneasy compromise with himself. He had accepted his way of life with its insecurities; he had a constant, irrepressible fear that this, too, could be taken away from him. He was not a happy man, that capacity mislaid alongside his sense of purpose. The unexpected, the sudden advent of Victor, so confident and unrepentant that he had not even bothered to change his name, had brought a small measure of joy into Ludwig's life. He had abruptly ceased to regret any of it; the past had retreated to its proper place as a necessary preamble for the events to follow.

As all this clarified, he had set himself to the work of

discovering what he could about Victor Genscher. It had been easy to find the imposing office building; no trouble to discover where the great man lived, nor to locate the garage where he parked his expensive cars. He had found out what he could about the business, seemingly successful and typical of its type. He had watched old Tiedemann all the way to his leafy suburb; accompanied the prim, tight-arsed secretary with her bag of crochet to Barmbek; tracked the Jewish one to his basement flat in Eimsbüttel. He had struck up a conversation once with the other man in a Kneipe, a halting desultory sort of a conversation over a Berliner Weisse, to do with the weather and the shocking state of football. The man was ill-at-ease, unwilling to be talked to, stiff-necked and taciturn and unfriendly to strangers as Hamburgers often were. Ludwig went back another night, and another, but did not see the man again. He knew better than to try the spinster living with her old mother, knew the effect of his pleasant smile upon impressionable females.

Exhausting these avenues, he had pursued a more fruitful course: a foray into the past. Writing did not come easily to Ludwig and he laboured for many nights on his document, his record of the Prominenten's not-so-respectable past. It was quite a work of art, tied up in green ribbon, one copy safely deposited with a solicitor.

Ludwig did not think or speak in long words. When it came to writing something down, he fell into a curious style. This mixed the sort of words he remembered from the wooden benches of Sunday school all those years ago with what he felt was a legal touch; there was something in it of the Volksschule schoolmaster he might, in other circumstances, have become. He wrote with tremendous effort and very slowly, weighing each word and putting it down with heavy pressure on the paper. Later, typing it out on the old machine, he had found his words strangely impressive.

It was a long piece of work which ran to fifty typewritten pages, executed with the utmost care by two of his bony fingers. He had typed so late into the night that Frau Liebmann had accused him, at one point, of writing a book. This idea, so worthy of derision in her mind, had given rise to her choking snort of a laugh.

Herr Meister Judo had produced a detailed, cunning document. His memory was excellent and he had spun out of it a web of intricate detail. As triumphant dénouement, he had added an appendix. This was the damning testimony, as it were – for Ludwig saw this document as a trial which simultaneously examined, judged and sentenced the accused – of a certain Frau Meyer. She was a very old lady now and he had had the good fortune to find her in Berlin. The truth itself was harsh; he had not shrunk from it, nor had he completely exonerated himself. To achieve his aims he needed a strong weapon. Frau Meyer's words gave him a blunt, hard club to beat a man into a new form.

The trip had been expensive. He came close to cancelling it a dozen times and put it off almost half as often, for he was close with money and hated unnecessary expense. He had gone, grudgingly, certain it would be futile, six months before. He had chosen a time when a great number of children were on summer holidays and when classes had shrunk to the die-hards, local kids who paid a reduced rate and were so often absent from school that holidays made practically no difference to their small calendar of events. So he had closed the school for three days for the first time; it could not be longer for he did not trust Frau Liebmann in the conservatory, indeed access was strictly denied her, and who was to water his leafy jungle?

The old street still stood. There, by a miracle, sat the old lady in the same apartment, ancient and arthritic, half-blind, willing to talk to anyone who said he remembered her boy and still able to squeeze tears out of her rheumy eyes. She could not quite make out Ludwig's face but half-thought she remembered what she saw of it. Certainly, she recognised her son from his description of a young life, needlessly wasted, a flower snapped in full bloom. She thought, without knowing exactly why, for Ludwig had put the idea into her head, that he came in some official capacity. She thought that the state would, at last, be erecting some suitable memorial or, at the very least, rewarding her for years of suffering with a handsome pension. He did not disillusion her; no doubt she

56

waited still for the fat manila envelope bearing the glad tidings to come through the door.

Ludwig had asked Frau Meyer a good number of searching questions. Discovering that she knew very little of the truth, he evolved a story by degrees, one not far distant from the reality of events that were, after all, over twenty years ago. She smiled as he refreshed her memory; he listened while she brought out old tales of the clever little boy, born to delight her in early middle age, stories of his many talents and promise. And, in the end, over a bottle of cognac he had had the foresight to provide, he had got her to dictate these details to her neighbour, for she could not write with her shaky old hand. He had thought, too, to get another neighbour in to append her round signature to the whole. It had been quite an event in the neighbourhood and for many months to come these three would recall the visit of the pleasant official and wonder when the pension would come and say a hundred times that these things took time, for hadn't it taken years for the case to be looked at at all? The old lady was soon convinced that she had initiated the whole thing herself and would congratulate herself on her persistence in never giving up the memory of her Wilfried, no, never, not while there was a breath to draw in her old body.

Perhaps it was an act of charity that Ludwig had carried out. His visit had quite cleared away from her mind any lingering memories she had that her boy had not always been so good; that he had fallen into evil ways and indeed that she had told him he would go to the devil a thousand times. She remembered, now, a young man so good, so noble and generous that he'd have been driving her around in a big car, had he lived, for he loved his old mother so, and feasting her just as she intended to treat her kind neighbours the day her boat came in.

Ludwig had had this document safe for some time and yet held back, waiting for his moment. Meanwhile Victor grew a number of dark shadows, who followed him in expensive taxis around his evening haunts and hung around outside for a glimpse of the well-dressed gentleman with his latest inamorata on his arm.

57

A time had come when Ludwig detected change. Victor began absenting himself from the office, paying frequent visits to the bank and neglecting his expensive, fancy women. Ludwig, sensing disarray, obliged him into the long-awaited meeting. It had disturbed him that the man proved so fortified, so hidden and unmoved, that he could not gauge his reaction. He, who knew everything, had counted on the effect of shock to reveal yet more. Because he could not afford a rejection, he found himself growing anxious. Here was a man without close friends, with women in abundance whom he took to hotels, like whores; a man who believed himself secure. That was what made the Rommer girl important. Her position had to make her a lever to move him; a chink in the façade. What young girl was not malleable, susceptible, gossipy? He would find a way to use her.

It was a pity that his special boys were so young. Ludwig had raised these urchins from the gutter and taught them to master pain and endure setbacks, to be modest in their occasional triumphs. He gave talks in local schools on the character-forming aspects of the sport and never failed to attract new pupils, drawn initially by the attractive notion of a small expert easily defeating a larger foe. When the bullies had been weeded out, a gratifying percentage remained. The more intelligent of these formed an inner circle, a small, trained battalion that he could deploy.

Bernd, who aspired to leadership, who had an unquench-able enthusiasm for taking the initiative, had taken it upon himself to follow the girl home, returning triumphant with the revelation that this occasional visitor to the office was J. Rommer. He wished it had been anybody but Bernd. He could not help feeling aversion for the boy for besmirching him, for his evident incomprehension and pale, silently accusing face, for his never ceasing to try and attach him.

Ludwig reviewed the young men of his acquaintance. He did this while, mechanically, taking a group of twelve-year-olds through Osoto-gari. A simple throw, unusual in sending the opponent backwards onto the mat. He kept advancing, right leg forwards, towards young Piepe, who failed each time to use the opening.

'Use your head, Piepe, if you have that ability.' The other boys smiled; Piepe kept on hooking feebly, ineffectually, with his chubby right leg.

'Clearly not,' he said. 'As a child could see, my dear Piepe, you also need to use your right arm. Watch,' and he beckoned forwards Schultz. Teacher's pet.

Schultz, with his bullet-headed obstinacy, would never join the inner circle, but he had a natural talent for the sport. Ludwig knew that a good teacher had to dazzle a little, when the kids began to lose interest, when they were starting to get tired and frustrated. There was no horseplay in the Beckerstrasse, no boisterous larking about, none of the neck-lock strangleholds that could be observed in supposedly better establishments.

Schultz neatly went over backwards for the second time and came up smiling. The mechanics of judo were simple enough. The opponent had to be caught off balance, so he could be thrown along his weak direction of posture, force used against itself. As Piepe tried again, Ludwig said to himself that, yes, Victor was indeed off balance. Roughly, for he would not learn, he threw the boy, who was clutching ineffectually at his jacket.

The lesson was ending and the roomful of boys lined up in the approved manner, sitting on their heels in order of rank.

'Sensei ni Rei!' A gruff shout from Kiechle, the senior student present, who for some moments now had been clearing his throat in anticipation of the honour and in dread of that post-pubescent squeak that sometimes betrayed him and made the little boys snigger. They all bowed; Ludwig bowed back.

The rabble of little boys scurried around, throwing off jackets, scuffling around for shoes and socks and breaking into an enervating chatter. A tall, dark youth standing in the doorway was watching the scene with a faint sneer. Seeing Ludwig observing him, he nodded at him, as one man to another, and leant back against the wall, crossing bony legs with studied nonchalance to show off high-heeled Cuban boots, an object of aspiration for every passing boy.

Now that he was fifteen, Wolfgang Schmidt considered

himself a man, that maturity signalled by the acquisition of such badges of manhood as boots and a short black jacket with an elasticated waist. This had a leather grain imprinted on its shiny surface and evidently he believed that it could pass for the real thing. Though not a pupil, he spent much of his time hanging around the school waiting for Bernd and his other friend, Heini. Ludwig looked at him and, suddenly, remembering, he smiled.

Wolf's brother was in his entirety an object of the deepest envy for the small fry, who dispersed, however, too soon to glimpse the paragon's arrival. Tall, well-built, in an expensive black leather jacket, he had a face so Italian, so patrician, that nobody would have taken him for the Hanseatic he undoubtedly was. He had, too, that Mediterranean self-assurance and air of grooming. An angular bump in the polo-neck sweater showed where some pendant, a medallion or tribal token dangled. This had to be assumed to be gold, such was the expense of his appearance.

'Incredible,' he said, dark eyes swivelling in slow derision. 'It's all the same. It's like a time warp in here.' Change was clearly a highly desirable phenomenon in his eyes. Unbidden, he threw himself onto a chair, nearly toppling it.

Ludwig, still wearing his thick white jacket and trousers, sat cross-legged on the narrow chair in delicate balance and smiled affably at the renegade.

'I preserve everything,' he said. 'What's this but continuity, of a kind, a museum to a thousand boyhoods? Why should I change it? It's only the young who must have everything new all the time. Now, don't you feel nostalgia, sitting here?' and he smiled at the expression on Sigi's face. 'How much more difficult life is outside, eh, Sigi?' and he went on, flippant and accusing, 'Your brother tells me you're still out of a job and when I think – oh I do think about you dear boy – of your poor old mother still slaving away – what a very nice jacket you have. What a fine skin,' and he reached out a hand and laughed when the young man drew away.

'Lay off,' Sigi said unpleasantly and extracted a packet of cigarettes from an inner pocket, puffing out the smoke in Ludwig's direction. 'Wolf said you had an interesting proposition to make. That's the only reason for my coming.'

How blunt he was, direct and confident. Sigi was not just typical of his kind, he was the very archetype. That was what made him such an inspired choice.

'Let me think now,' he said slowly, as though he was considering it. 'A proposal, yes. You see me here in an unusual role, my dear boy. So very unusual that I can hardly believe it myself. Can you see me as a matchmaker? But that's what I am, just for you. I have a delightful proposition, a young, rich girl, living alone in a most select neighbourhood. The girl of your dreams, the sort you, dear boy, would never meet. And I am going to introduce you to this marvel, no – don't thank me yet – ' the young man, who had not opened his mouth, was staring at him with the most curious expression – 'later you can express your gratitude. When you have, how shall I put it, examined the merchandise.'

'You're a cold-blooded swine, do you know that Ludwig?' Sigi was stung, defensive. 'I know your merchandise, it's not the kind I like,' and a speck of ash dropped onto one gleaming black shoe, a loafer with a gilt chain, and was flicked away irritably.

'Not so hasty dear boy,' and Ludwig made a show of locating, after some rifling through the bottom drawer of the desk, a small rag which he offered solicitously and which was refused. 'There's even money in it – now leave that shoe alone, won't you? Oh, does it mar your beauty? A lot of money. In return for which I expect only information, of a particular kind, the sort of little details you young people tell each other when you're like that,' and he held up two crossed fingers and stroked them, leering, with the digit of the other hand. 'Five thousand, Sigi, what do you say to that?'

'Five thousand?' The young man's tone was incredulous. 'There's something very – ' and he searched in vain for the word.

'I see. Nice of you to come, my dear boy. I've got a business to run. If you're not interested, you can go,' and Ludwig picked a paper out of the pile on the desk and scanned it. He waved a hand at the young man. 'Shoo, go away, can't you see I'm busy?'

Sigi ground his cigarette out on the floor with an unnecessarily vicious twist of the foot.

'What are you after? What's it all about? Come on, Ludwig, you've got to explain.'

Clearly, the bait was so large that the little fish had trouble swallowing it. Ludwig sat back, watching the hot brown eyes which cupidity had sharpened.

'Shall I tell you a little story? Once upon a time, my dear Sigi, when I was young and foolish – no, never that, but shall we say more credulous, I lent a large sum to a man who never repaid it. Who disappeared. Now you mustn't cry too much for me, for I've come across him again. He's wealthy now, he can easily afford it, but he refuses. He acknowledges his debt, but he doesn't want to pay. I'm a poor man and he thinks he can play with me. Now if I were rich and had influential friends, he'd have paid up at once, so you see what a sham morality his is. Now of course he won't be let off so easily.' Sigi was twisting about in his chair; now he took his jacket off and folded it carefully over his knees.

'Oh, am I boring you?' he asked solicitously. 'Another moment and I'm done, do you think you can manage that?'

The brown eyes expressed resentment, but Sigi smiled, an easy, winning smile. He was extraordinarily handsome.

'The girl, my dear Sigi, is a kind of relation of his. She doesn't know about this debt, but she knows him, she's involved in his business. I want information on that, on his private life, anything. I shall make use of it merely to approach him. Do you begin to understand? Are you following? Good.' The young man listened intently; he had, at least, the wit not to interrupt. 'A spy in the enemy camp, that is your part. You have nothing more arduous to do than to take her out and ask questions in your artless way. Your legendary charm, my dear Sigi, is what I require, for I think even you can see that the young lady will be more, shall we say, accessible, to you than to me.'

Sigi was silent for a few minutes, then, speaking slowly, he said, 'I won't help you blackmail anybody.'

Ludwig laughed; he made a show of wiping tears from his eyes. 'How crude you are. It's not illegal, talking to a girl. I don't expect you to find anything disreputable, quite the reverse. You will snoop, my friend, in a good cause, remember that. Not just for my benefit, my dear Sigi. If a man doesn't pay his debts to society, he's locked up, isn't he? This man has imprisoned himself; he is the victim of his misdeeds. To pay a price – a very small price – will release him.' He gazed at the uncomprehending face. 'I will pay all your expenses in taking her out, you will collect your money when I do. And if I don't get my money, well, neither do you. You will have to content yourself with having had a charming experience. You must take a small risk, my dear Sigi, for the greater gain, as I do. That will be a little incentive for you to do well.'

The young man, frowning slightly, was now contemplating his polished shoes.

'Here, she's not deformed is she?'

Ludwig's mirth, now, was scarcely containable. 'No, no, what a strange fellow you are, Sigi. Nothing wrong with her. Not bad-looking at all. She might think there's something wrong with you, of course. Have you thought of that? No, I suppose not, you are so very – successful in the field, aren't you, my dear boy?'

'Very well,' Sigi said. 'I know what you want. It's a very – no, never mind. I could do with the money, but not enough to do anything illegal, do you understand? If you've lied to me, I'll make sure you get dropped in it, not me,' and he put on his little show of bravado, his small display of self-respect in a hard voice. 'What's her name? What's the man's name, the one that owes you?'

'No details yet, my dear boy. I'll tell you what you need to know later. When I've found a way for you to meet her, by chance, I think. And I'll simply have to rely on you to do your best, won't I, Sigi?' and he smiled to himself, the smile of a man relishing a private joke too good to share.


Otto Tiedemann glanced at his watch as Victor sauntered into the office, an irritating habit he had which was inappropriate when connected to the arrivals and exits of his employer, who scarcely glanced in his direction. He knew he shouldn't do it; he knew it did him no good and was not a gesture inspired to win the confidences he so fervently desired, but there, it had happened again. His mouth tightened for a moment before relapsing into its customary bleak look.

Herr Tiedemann did himself far too much credit in imagining that Herr Genscher had noticed this gesture of his. Indeed that general self-importance of his, a fault he altogether failed to perceive, did him more harm than any of his old gentleman's tics. Victor had not seen him. He had other matters on his mind and proceeded into his office with no thought in his head beyond his personal affairs.

The post had brought him no card yesterday; no card today; nothing in fact but a missive from Heidi bemoaning the days that would intervene before she had the pleasure of seeing him again. He, too, was counting the days, but not for that young woman's benefit. Walther wanted to wait a month before presenting his fait accompli to the newspaper's staff, would not be budged from this decision and insisted that nothing could be done before Christmas, even less when staff were away on holiday and that January, when their pockets were emptiest, was the most telling moment to strike. It irked Victor and yet there was not a thing he could do to move the man. He saw that he would have to abide by this decision. He hated to wait; he liked to move things along at a brisk trot. Trivia bored him; the kind of pernickety examination of detail which appealed to conscientious Otto irritated him. A hundred, no a thousand, times, he had suppressed the urge to tell the old man to get on with it, or to shoo him away as he stepped purposefully into the inner office with yet another folder full of carefully docketed slips of paper.

Otto Tiedemann, over years of careful economy, had formed the habit of writing on odd scraps of paper or the backs of envelopes which he first cut into neat rectangles, attaching these crabbed annotations to the documents in question with a special, removable tape. He went out to buy this himself, an operation which necessitated the creation of another careful little note for Fräulein Schmidt to put in her petty cash box. These pieces of paper were as irritating to Victor as an itch. He had often wished him retired, gone, anywhere; he would have despatched him to look after the firm's business in South America or Africa if there had been the slightest chance of his being useful there. Instead he kept him here. It was not so much because of Eduard Rommer's promise to the old boy, but because he was so very finicky, so very conscious of the past glory and present honour of Rommer's that he did have some small usefulness at times, even if it was only as a walking memory bank or as a thorough checker of figures. There was a further reason Victor did not so readily admit to himself. Tiedemann had always been a fixture in the office. He represented all that Victor once aspired to; the solidity of position. He needed him there to prove daily that he had indeed surpassed his wildest ambitions; as witness to the reality of the present.

His distinctive knock at the door, a rat-a-tat-tat, purposeful in a military way, now roused Victor from his reverie. He made himself smile; he had been irritated, too, all that day and all the previous one with the need to do something about Ludwig.

Curiously enough, Herr Tiedemann looked almost apologetic. 'Störe ich?' he said and for once did not glance at the empty desk in innocent sarcasm. He had something on his mind, just a small affair (what else?) and wished to impart this (of course) to Herr Genscher. The sort of unpleasant little incident that was so regrettably a feature of present-day life (get to the point, old fool). He was an old man, he knew, and old-fashioned in his ways and it disturbed him to think of a young girl, alone and unprotected in the city, being subjected to that sort of thing. Oh, Herr Genscher need not alarm himself, it was nothing more sinister than one youth – loitering with intent, he believed was the expression – and with no more circumlocutions the old man finally got to the point and discovered that he had an unusually attentive audience.

# Chapter 6

Thursday, December 4, 1971

The policeman's gone now and old Frau Beckmann is fussing around, clicking her tongue, making her panacea for all evils, a good strong cup of coffee. She vouched for my good character to the police detective, unsolicited and in her usual shout, and he treated me with the utmost suspicion. Later I have to go and make another report, a written one, at the police station. His attitude made it quite clear that this was a formality, a necessity for their files, and not because he thought for an instant that there was any point to it. I think Frau Beckmann has a soft spot for me. She called me a young girl 'aus gutem Haus' and an exemplary lodger; she is convinced that the loiterer must be a would-be rapist.

She is muttering to herself about the wickedness of the Lumpen who hold up cars in broad daylight, lifting up the side of a huge, heavy Mercedes until the terrified woman driver hands over her fat Gucci purse or, she whispers – that being anybody else's normal volume of speech – worse. She reads the *Bildzeitung* daily from cover to cover, devouring the muggings, sex scandals, the occasional murder and the incestuous crimes from the dull flatlands of Schleswig-

66

Holstein. She admires my composure, which is entirely due to her reassuring presence, the comforting shelf of bosom encased in the dark suit she must have had made thirty years ago, the prim little white collar and short bootees.

She believed me, but the policeman evidently thought I was neurotic and had invented the incident to make myself interesting. He eyed my Hasselblad enviously, asked about jewellery and suggested finally in a quarter-hearted way that it might have been a burglar on the look-out. A boy, he said, and smiled sardonically and spouted statistics on youthful crime. 'You'd be surprised how often they come from good families round here,' he said and gave me a look as though I had at least a dozen skeletons in my closets. I suspect the reason for this second visit, in broad daylight, was to have a better look at me, for there could be nothing to add to what I told them last night. It's probably a crime to waste police time and they'll whisk me off to jail if I'm not careful. The fact that the youth beat such a hasty retreat when the police car showed up makes him guilty to me, but invisible and probably imaginary as far as the Polizei are concerned.

For a reason I can't begin to defend, in the small hope that news of this would percolate to Victor and disturb him, I called Herr Tiedemann. He, predictably, hummed and ha'ed at first, then got very excited and concerned and told me I should come and stay with them, that the driver would collect me in forty minutes, he and his wife would be honoured and so on. I suppose it serves me right. I could dissuade him only by letting him know that Linda is coming to stay, so I shan't be alone. It's true; she arrives from Harwich tomorrow at the St Pauli Landungsbrücke and no doubt she'll have some young man in tow who thinks carrying her baggage will advance his cause. I'll be well repaid for that piece of stupidity if the old man writes to Oma and worries her unnecessarily.

Monday, December 8, 1971

Linda is asleep, exhausted by her evening's exertions. Victor's letter has been in my pocket for half an hour, waiting for her to conclude her post mortem on the charms of Sigi. Herr Tiedemann clearly panicked sufficiently to tell him, for all the good that does. Epistolary Victor is a disappointment. Worse. He doesn't rate analysis.

> My dear Johanna,
> Please do not concern yourself too much about this unpleasant incident. Such things, regrettably, can happen in our city [as though I came from a cottage and had straw in my hair]. It is good to hear that you have your girlfriend to stay with you. Please contact me immediately if you require my assistance. With my best wishes for the festive season – your Victor.

And happy Christmas to you. As bland as butter, an old man's short dull letter. No breath of interest in my adventure; no hint of passion. No hint of anything. He can't remember Linda if he thinks she'll protect me.

The writing slopes downhill a little on the creamy paper; sign of a dilatory, melancholy character. Miserable, uncaring Victor who has not called me. There's no stamp, but he can't have come here. I expect I was another errand in the driver's busy day; I expect he complained at having to come so far. I have read it five, six, ten times, uncomprehending, as though a real message lay behind the round vowels, the n's that look like u's, the w that looks like an m, the over-sized capitals. How my little heart pounded when I recognised the writing. Victor's letters were never like that, they were pacy and charming and full of fun, not this old uncle's tract. I would get them out now but Linda's asleep in the sitting room and the desk drawer creaks. Perhaps we will hold a post mortem on Victor tomorrow. The sympathy in those big round eyes will be tempered by her not very well-hidden antipathy to my 'uncle'; now she believes that she was prescient, if anybody was.

Linda will hint that it's all to the good and ask me if I liked

68

whatshisname. Linda has already acquired her throng of admirers: three including Uncle Hansi. Before meeting him we went to an afternoon's labour on *Ulysses* in Aula I. An English lecture seemed a good idea as her German is so rusty, and besides it's fun: two hundred heads bowed by the symbolic significance of the text, dissecting Bloom's Dublin day on neat charts. Plotting a cyclops on cellophane, siting sirens on street-maps. The English department likes to dissect and draw graphs: their perfect analysis of a work of literature would come on long paper readouts, in a mountain range of different inks. Blue blocks for the most-used words: green waves for the rhythm of the text; red crests when a character rises up, to fall back again. In short, all the characteristics of a madman's encephalogram. Linda stifled her laughter in the back row while the note-takers ruled lines and carefully placed their little red dots.

Uncle Hansi was conspicuous in the little pub as the only non-student, his silly hat with the feather on the bench beside him. He was drinking one of those huge glasses of Berliner Weisse which he insisted on us trying; raspberry cordial and beer in foaming, diuretic masses. He warmed at once to Linda's noble attempts with the language, admiring her pink cheeks and what he called her English rose charm. What he meant was her voluptuousness, the long blonde curls and blue eyes rimmed with flaky mascara. I could see him making a mental note to send her a trunk of Bock products. She won't disappoint him; she scorns no aid to beauty and travels with a heavy bag of lotions and potions, two hairdryers just in case, heated rollers and an outfit for every occasion.

I do love Linda; she's a clever girl with no respect for anything intellectual. She wants to have as much fun as possible, to live life in the fast lane. Underneath the giggling and the batting eyelids, she's a dreadful tease, an inspired mimic and ruthless at getting her own way. She never mopes, not ever, and she always enjoys herself hugely. She arrived with a tiny suede bag swinging and behind her a young monk balancing her vast case on his shaven pate. The handle broke, she said blithely, and he leapt to the rescue. She was artlessly giving wrong telephone numbers to a middle-aged man in a mac when I caught up with her, the monk bobbing and bowing in front and waiting his turn. He must have been absolutely freezing; a woolly sweater half-covered his saffron robes and his bare legs were goose-pimply. She says he's going to take her to visit his temple.

I suppose she picked Sigi up too, but it was one of her subtler manoeuvres. She bumped into him in the doorway of the Kneipe; apologised – 'Ent-schul-dy-gung' – and he not surprisingly said was she English? and she gave him her most bewitching smile and hey presto he was at the next table sending over a gin and tonic for die nette kleine Engländerin, and what would I like? It took a further half a minute for him to join us at our table.

He is called Sigismund Schmidt, known as Sigi and quite good-looking if you care for dark men. Linda does; she was doing her best to transfix him with her killer orbs. I suppose it will be a flaming romance. He seemed quite amazed, indeed flabbergasted, that I was English too and paid me all sorts of fulsome compliments on my command of the language but I wasn't fooled one bit. He's young, I think our age, and I suppose he is rather handsome. Well-dressed in a flashy way with one of those awful gold chains nestling on his hairy chest, the shirt buttons undone to reveal it, which always makes me want to shriek. He's muscly, or, to use Linda's phrase, a hunk. Not a student; too flash and brash for that. I don't know what he does, but he's a smooth operator and winkled our number out of Linda in five minutes, volunteering to show us round Hamburg. When I said I could do that, she kicked me quite sharply, under the table.

I could see Hansi was having a good time. Out came the old jokes about 'Noch ein Bock für Herrn Bock' and he ate Bratwurst and chips in outright defiance of the dinner date with the fiancé's sober family and sighed for his lost youth and the student freedoms he never had and suspects me of – free love being wasted on the young and so on. Linda said crossly when I got home that I sat there like a prune, radiating pale waves of superiority. I suppose she is right. I don't like the picture of myself as a martyred, superior little madam. Tomorrow I shall be outrageous and flirt.

Linda is not a girl to languish by the phone. Just in case Sigi was thinking of changing his mind, she had the outing organised ten minutes after he'd moved to our table. A walk on the frozen Alster and down the Reeperbahn to see the sights. What a shame, he said, falsely, that Herr Bock wouldn't be able to come, for they're off home tomorrow.

Yesterday Linda insisted upon a trip to the Hare Krishna temple, which is just like a Girl Guides hut, one of those cheerless barracks which has one large room and a small adjoining one, the whole covered by an icy, corrugated iron roof with rusting pipes fighting to get away from the brickwork. You can't see in for the multi-coloured pictures of inscrutable goddesses and pugnacious gods waving their hundreds of arms in the window, their brightness dimmed by a matt layer of dirt. There was a faint humming noise, the sound of the acolytes at their prayers. One of them let us in with a broad beaming smile and hurried us into the big room, hot and noisy, a swaying mass of saffron in front under the pall of incense hanging in the rafters.

The streets are pervaded by these monks and monkesses, chanting and hopping around and thrusting their begging bowls at scandalised matrons. The burgers don't understand at all and certainly don't approve. Looking closer, they can see these aren't starving Indians at all, but European kids, their shaven heads, strange clothing and bare legs epitomising everything they don't want their sons and daughters to become. They cross the road when they see them coming; hide their hands behind their backs rather than accept one of their pamphlets. I don't know how the monks survive, but they are here in strength. They all smile so charmingly when anybody gives them anything or shows the slightest interest.

The girls have long hair and wear saris in the same orangey fabric and they too smile and smile; they seem as happy as it is possible to be, the most convinced religious fruitcakes ever, untiring in their efforts to explain their beliefs. Linda says they live together as brother and sister; that they never sleep together unless the master ordains and that then it is for procreation only and with the partner the master selects. If there was a master there, we didn't see him.

The room was draped with all sorts of hangings and sheets

71

dyed in shades of red, even the incense sticks are red. It looked as though we were worshipping another set of gaudy pictures, at any rate the frothy wave of real believers at the front were, lifting up their arms and swaying while they chanted. Behind them the hoi polloi, the cynical student body, mumbled along. Hare Krishna, hare Krishna, it's hypnotic and rhythmic and we knew the words in a second and a half. The reason for the packed house on Sundays is not that the kids have heard the word. The monks produce a lunch, the most delicious vegetarian food, for only DM5.– and half an hour's prayer. There are various messes, also delicious rice things and puddings that are small sweet balls, cream and pink and pistachio green with a nutty, tangy flavour. Linda cornered a plateful of those and the monk of her voyage, engaging both in serious investigation. He's a beautiful blue-eyed boy, an American, his blond hair razored to reveal all sorts of interesting little bumps and craters with a long tuft à la Mohican at the back. Linda claims that it is to pull them up to heaven. After the sweetness, the sell: plates replaced by leaflets and the monks close in to harvest souls among the well-fed unbelievers, who all started doing a backwards shuffle towards the exit.

I went in search of the loo, but there wasn't one. What do the monks do? I was looking at the back of the big room and had the feeling there was somebody behind me and turned around, but it was quite empty. There were no doors there so I collected Linda and we started for Altona Station and I had the same feeling, that we were being followed, and spun round. I got the merest glimpse of a man, a shortish man in an overcoat, ducking into a doorway. We went on, faster, and stopped round the corner and waited, but nobody came apart from a bunch of kids who'd been in the temple, laughing and singing the tune. It was getting dark by then; that awkward time on a Sunday when anyone with any sense is home in the warm, the streets practically empty, so we hurried on and I could just hear from behind the click of somebody walking at the same speed as us and when we stopped, he stopped. It made my blood run cold; an expression which is very exact anatomically and not figurative at all. We ran, then, for the station and hurtled across the large gloomy forecourt and straight into the ladies' loo which nobody can possibly have thought welcoming before, as it is glacial and stinks of piss. We stayed in there a good twenty minutes and then got our tickets and saw nobody, or at any rate nobody who paid us any attention. We chose the fullest compartment in the train, stuffed with at least fifty schoolchildren going home to Rissen from some excursion and were glad to be obliged to listen to their puerile shrieks. We were both unnerved. We even took a taxi from the S-Bahn, remembering the boy on the bus.


Wednesday, December 10, 1971


No doubt about it, Linda's in a huff. Sigi kept making advances to me, leaving poor Linda in the unusual position of lemon of the party. It was mystifying to both of us; we're under no illusions when it comes to her feminine charms and how they rate against mine. I must say there's never exactly been a competition before, indeed there isn't now, as he's not at all my type. He didn't precisely ignore her, but seemed strangely unconscious of her charms; if it's a cunning ploy to gain her attention, he's certainly succeeding.

The Alster was beautiful, full of little groups of walkers and skaters all bundled up like Breughel figures, black on the scoured ice, which the setting sun turned gold. We walked and slithered round the edges and Sigi pointed out various landmarks, most of which he got wrong. I skated a bit and Sigi kept slipping on his thin leather soles and shivering in his showy leather jacket, but we were merciless and walked for an hour.

He offered hot grog in one of those little wooden huts at the far end of the lake. It was sweet and alcoholic and we had three glasses each. While Linda delicately nipped the peel from our lemon slices, he raised his glass to mine in the silliest way, as though we were drinking Brüderschaft, except of course everybody says 'du' straight away. It's universal among students and always makes me want to 'siezen' them. Germany always makes me feel very proper and English, it's definition by contrast.

73

He asked me about Rommer's as the third round came; I denied the connection. I thought he looked at me rather strangely, but Linda, ever quick on the uptake, chipped in with her execrable accent that I'm sick of being asked that. Getting her own back. 'Es ist dur Zu-vall,' she said, that I have the same name, for she knows I hate that kind of categorisation. Is he in our business, I wonder? He doesn't look the part.

At his insistence we got a cab to the top of the Reeperbahn. He's at home there and no mistake; he knows every corner. I bet he's right in the middle of an enjoyable misspent youth. At the second set of traffic lights he suddenly grabbed my arm and pulled me into a phone box, flicking through a dog-eared directory and finally showing me a page with Greek symbols marked next to a name: gamma, alpha, Levison L. It didn't mean a think to me. He gave me a long stare then moved on. 'Guck mal,' he said and there at the next phone box were other symbols under that name and a page number. The next kiosk would continue the message, he said; this was how spies communicated with each other and he laughed hugely when I asked what happened if somebody tore a page out and would that ruin the whole thing? I suppose he was joking. I had the bizarre notion that he'd prepared those pages specially for me. He was most odd. He took my arm, again, and whispered don't tell your friend and then led me back to Linda. I kept having to unwind that arm, which went on snaking round my shoulders as though it had a life of its own.

We were outside a discotheque and Linda perked up somewhat. He got a great roll of money out of his pocket and pointed out another phone box, nodding seriously as if to say, you know. I had a vision of a latticework of phone booths lurking at street corners, absorbing the city with their electronic ears and linking up illicitly to transmit their messages out while the good burgers snore. Either he's not quite right in the head – nicht alle Tassen im Schrank, as Oma would say, or he's got an arcane sense of humour. I wouldn't let him pay as I loathe feeling beholden and that really bugged him, as it were, heaven knows why.

It was the usual place. Dark, dirty, loud, with flashing lights and a wooden floor throbbing to the bass notes of heavy rock.

German youth adores Frank Zappa, King Crimson and Led Zeppelin. All the Abitur failures who couldn't buy a train ticket to Ramsgate to save their lives know the words of 'Twenty-first Century Schizoid Man' and offer their moaning accompaniment to 'Blood rack/Barbed wire/Politicians' funeral pyre' while they conduct their drug deals at the back. Hamburg's musical tastes divide neatly between rock freaks; fans of the city's own golden boy, James Last, the bearded purveyor of folk songs-a-gogo; and the opera buffs. German students being what they are, rock lyrics have reputedly been subjected to Marxist analysis, though I've never found that mythical avant-garde seminar where they take the scalpel to Zappa. I'd like to offer them my new Jefferson Airplane L.P. It has an amusing gobbledy-gook German number called 'Never argue with a German if you're tired'.

There was not much in the way of pleasure in the disco. People clustered round the back eyeing each other and a few exhibitionists strutted on a wooden platform like a boxing ring a couple of metres high. I wouldn't dance, for I hate it, but Linda soon joined them, her bottom gyrating expertly opposite some man's large clenched buttocks as he jiggled from one foot to the other and shouted inaudible pleasantries. He was soon ousted by an audacious and extremely handsome Turk, a Che Guevara with hair-oil, who twitched his bulging pelvis suggestively.

I winkled Linda out at one in the morning, disappointing both the Levantine and the other wretched man, who had by then spent ages nursing a beer and staring gloomily up at her while Sigi and I shrieked meaningless remarks over the din and he kept trying to make me dance, and I kept refusing, and very dull it was too, for he wouldn't dance with anybody else. I amused myself by imagining I recognised fellow phoneme-sufferers frozen in contorted poses, grimacing faces painted pink and blue by the harsh lights.

The Turk followed Linda out and slobbered over her in the street, to be repulsed with some brutality. Sigi got us a cab and looked as if he had half a mind to jump in himself, but wasn't invited. Linda fell asleep at once, only waking up when we got home to remark, while scrubbing her face, that Sigi was probably a bad lot. Look at the funny way he stuck to you, she said as proof positive. False modesty was never one of her attributes.

Linda's presence is very reassuring somehow, even still asleep in her black pyjamas. Comforting in a naughty sort of way, for she's just the girl to lead someone astray. There's room for a great deal more of that joie de vivre in the person of J. Rommer, swot and superior little madam. When I think of our long association, I have the mournful impression that one of us has consistently and enjoyably been up to no good and the other, ever a non-combatant, has been content to observe and get on with something worthy, like an essay or cleaning shoes. It's not much of an epitaph.

> Here lies J. Rommer, a dreadful swot,
> Who polished shoes and mooned around a lot.
> She gave but little pleasure,
> And as she gave, she got.

Linda and I chose each other from the very first day at school. We were wealthy, but it was fashionable to be highbrow; it was mutual adversity which attracted us. I remember that we all had to say what our parents did, a piece of snooping disguised as general interest, and there among the doctors and lawyers and bankers, the architects and authors and MPs, were my parents, dead, and Linda's father a builder-developer, which was arguably worse. Ours was the attraction of compatible but differing characteristics, more of those elective affinities. She would never swot, producing the briefest and skimpiest of misspelt essays in the back of the car on the way to school. She applied herself fully to the composition of elaborate, inventive excuse notes, which deserved As for imagination and calligraphy. She acquired an intimate knowledge of the library's shelves from the dreary hours spent in detention after school, supposedly writing lines or doing prep, but mostly spent staring vacantly ahead among the sniffling, remorseful juniors. Eventually she was spared this humiliation by virtue only of her age.

Linda's love life was always thrilling. While I brooded hopelessly over my secret passion, Linda commanded the vanguard of juvenile romance. At morning break we would sit enthralled, a circle of knees quivering under our box-pleated skirts, breathless under our green-striped blouses, while Linda munched a biscuit and gave us the highlights of her amorous adventurings, one sweet mouthful after another. And then he – and then I – and then I took my top off. Oh Linda, you didn't. Yes I did. And my bra. She would smile enigmatically through bulging cheeks as the bell went and savour her cliffhanger.

When we got into the sixth form, her large audience for episodic romance was banished and I became sole confidante. Let them read Kinsey for their sexual field-work, she said dismissively. We were all virgins except for Linda, her initiation an event she planned with much care and which nevertheless so disappointed her that for a long time she forswore a repetition. She dragged me to parties and chose clothes for me, which I then concealed from Oma; I did her French proses, subtly altering my version to elude discovery. We did the same A-levels. It's the only practical choice, Linda said, blithely abandoning history, at which she could have excelled, in favour of my fluency in German. Her reports stock-piled the clichés of the non-achiever in tautological columns. Could try harder. Linda does not do justice to her intelligence. Linda must work much harder to develop her natural abilities if she is to succeed. Once again Linda's laziness has betrayed her talents. Their urgings never had the slightest effect. Linda's natural abilities are exactly that: they are manifest as a degree could never have been.

My diary for our A-level year records Linda's driving lessons and the instructor who tried to lure her into the back seat; her triumphant gravel-scattering occupation of the headmistress's parking space in her new MG and consequent disgrace; Linda ironing her hair and singeing it; Linda getting an A for her mock orals because the external examiner fell for her madly and she promised to meet him in the pub afterwards and did. There was the shocking episode when 'one of our girls' brought shame upon the school by smuggling two boys into the Sixth Form Common Room during the school dance, the culprits escaping by vertiginous flight over the rooftops. The PE mistress refused adamantly to climb up and catch them, pleading fear of heights, and thus precipitated open rebellion from gym among lower-school minxes, already deflowered, debauched and despicable. The times they were a-changing and Linda led the vanguard.

They couldn't expel the whole lower school so she, conspicuous in the timid sixth form, bore the brunt. She was caught both smoking and snogging at the school gates, grounds for expulsion in those innocent days. Miss Dalrymple was loth to know which crime appalled more; her lean spinster's soul revolted at such escapades while her canny Lowlands brain computed their possible worth. 'After prayers, Dullrumple announced the most generous contribution to the New Sciences Wing by Mr Davenport. Her moustache twitched at Linda in a grimace. It's now going to be called the Davenport Sciences Block, she said and there was a definite gargling noise as the old bat spat the words out. Linda bent her head modestly, she nearly choked. Dullrumple looked quite approvingly for once. I do believe she thought she was blushing for shame, for what she likes to call proper, maidenly modesty.'

And yet, for all her perspicacity, Linda never liked Victor and did not approve of him. Foreigners were in then. Everybody was conducting a long-distance romance in parroted French or garbled Spanish with a holiday fling. The common room was a morning Tower of Babel as we puzzled out each other's love letters, passing the best bits round, and scanning our A-level texts for flowery bits to incorporate in our replies. Linda combined her more earthy English amours with undying passion for a romantic Frenchman who sent her beautiful poems which turned out to be straight lifts from Verlaine. There was a Spanish beach boy who also wrote to her, sending countless pictures of himself in bronzed, muscly poses for two devoted years after their brief Minorcan romance. He was a waiter and eventually, much to her horror, turned up on her doorstep, pallid but still passionate, shivering in his uniform of thin black trousers and white shirt and fully expecting her to elope with him. When Mr Davenport packed him off, he sent her as his parting shot a particularly unflattering photo of her pulling a face and bulging out of her bikini with 'Muy gorda, muy gorda' written on the back. It joined a collage of his rampant struttings which we used as a dartsboard for a while.

Out of all these nonsensically unsuitable paramours, Victor alone – he the only serious, professional, mature lover – met with her disapproval. I treasured his letters too much to profane them by handing them around, but would condescend to read her the wittier bits. She set her face stubbornly against him. A smoothie, she said, and too old, too sure of himself and she didn't believe in marriage anyway. Had they but known it, she and Oma were for once in perfect accord. I introduced her to him and she refused to be charmed, conducting an uncharacteristically stilted drawing-room conversation about the weather, resonant with unspoken dislike. She found fault with all the unarguable points, such as his advanced age. Victor unappreciated: it was an unpleasant, incomprehensible novelty.

And he liked her, it was obvious that he admired her good looks. He kept on saying flattering things which she ignored. Lush blondes, as Oma has hinted more than once, are Victor's preferred type. Victor's blondes: a subject to consider at length, but one I have always avoided. Because the next subject would have to be why did he propose to me? I remember saying to Linda at the time that she could be more graceful, since she benefited after all from my passion for German and ceaseless strivings to master it, all to make me worthy of him. You were always a swot, she said baldly. He focusses it, that's all. It was the swot in me she disliked, though she deigned to copy my notes whenever necessary. She made it clear that I was her friend in spite of an overstudious bent and that she did me the favour of overlooking it.

I think she saw Victor as another character fault, an aberration she put up with. She's never been in love. Plenty of flings, crushes and mad yearnings, but never for an instant the desire to tie herself down. She approaches men with the sort of clinical detachment they are reputed to use when pursuing us, the same profound disrespect for the softer emotions, the same scorn of soppiness and tears. All the characteristics that I suppose Victor showed. I hope some of her rubs off on me. I could do with a good, thick layer of indifference right now. I must wake her soon. Today we are going to town to collect my allowance: another session outside the inviolable closed door of Victor's room, the place where he sits to write his horrid little notes.

# Chapter 7

A neat little man was following two girls in the street as they proceeded from Dammtor Station up the Rothenbaumchaussee and into the modern part of the University complex. He loitered in the chilly spaces, rocking on the cobbles, each hillock making its personal impress upon the balls of his feet. They didn't spare him a glance when they emerged, warmly wrapped, the pretty one's bright blue jacket and mane of blonde hair unmissable. Back they went and down the bridge under Dammtor and on into the Stefansplatz. At Esplanade they crossed to the right-hand side and he slowed down, loitering, even indulging in the contemplation of his dapper self in the shining windows of the gentleman's outfitters, for he reckoned he knew where they were going.

He toiled up the grey-painted back stairs, panting a little, meeting an emaciated woman swooshing the upper landing with her wet mop, the shiny aluminium bucket of hot suds leaving rings on the vinyl tiles. They exchanged a ritual 'Tag', her suspicious little sharp-nosed face peering at him as he laboured on and up, the tip-tap of his ascent echoing into the upper regions, and then the woman let out an angry 'Huch'. He had stepped in dog shit and was carrying up with him a soft little lump of turd, neatly stamping the same malodorous brown fleck on each alternate riser.

Poor Frau Meier; she listened and heard he was going right up to Herr Genscher's apartment. She would have to lift the heavy bucket again and drag it up another three flights, taking care not to slop it for that would again double her work. She had mopped the whole lot once already, in loving servitude to Herr Genscher who tripped so lightly up and down her shiny floors with his friendly greeting and pleasant smile, never too proud to say hello or remark how immaculately kept his 'escape stairs' were. She then thought the man might trek that filthy lump, wedged between that pretentious Cuban heel and sole, over the beautiful cream carpet upstairs, which she shampooed only last week. Clenching her pink rubber glove, Frau Meier shook it silently at the ceiling and decided that, since it was nearly eleven, she would go down now for her second breakfast in the snug caretaker's room and leave the floor until he had done his worst. Shaking her head, she went down to bemoan her lot to Herr Frisch, who thought for the hundredth time that she was a decent woman and, were it not from the two teeth missing at the front, almost attractive.

Upstairs the man knocked three times at the kitchen door and was admitted at once.

'I know, they're here,' Victor said mildly before he could open his mouth. The man raised his shoulders in assent and watched his boss. It wasn't much of a job, the shoulders implied, if this was all it amounted to, but he didn't complain. He sat stoically, looking around.

'Uni then here,' he finally said, laconic.

'And nobody followed them? No boys or children?'

He shook his head without curiosity, for what business was it of his?

'All right,' Victor said after a long silence spent looking into his vacant face. 'Keep with them, Herr Bruch. Report back to me tomorrow evening about seven.'

He nodded, rising, and left without another word, his footsteps echoing down to Frau Meier. She bit into her Rollmopsbrötchen with the left side of her mouth, that being the preferred cutting edge, and, mumbling through her herring, told Herr Frisch to help himself, go on, take one, while he could not stop staring at the silvery grey morsel of fish winking at him through its white enamel net.

Downstairs behind the sanctity of the glass wall, the girls watched Herr Tiedemann count out notes, which he then placed in an envelope to render them invisible for the delicate transaction of handing them over to Fräulein Rommer. He accompanied them to the door. Pressing their reluctant hands in farewell, he insisted that they must come to tea with him and his wife, her damp seedcake the punishment concomitant with the introduction of the charming Engländerin.

Herr Tiedemann longed for greater intimacy, for more confidences. He wrote regularly to Frau Rommer, addressing her with the utmost respect. He managed to convey through the expression of his vorzüglichste Hochachtung that he, her least worthy and ergebenster Diener, was also her most reliable and faithful. Punctiliously he imparted those scraps of news he had managed to acquire, receiving in due course replies which began Mein lieber Otto and which thanked him politely for taking the trouble to let her know how her granddaughter was. Old busybody, Frau Rommer always thought, as she addressed the envelope in her best hand, as though Johanna couldn't and didn't write herself; she would, however, have been alarmed, had his letters ceased.

Herr Tiedemann always spoke fondly of Frau Rommer. The days of her participation had been his most glorious. There were few people still alive who could recall that they used to call him Hamburg's jute king, der Jutekönig. Frau Rommer remembered the halcyon days of the old world, when the lowliest worker in the Calcutta gunny works knew him and bowed to the glistening face, then pink and round, under its sola topi.

'Sunday, then, at three o'clock?' he said and bowed stiffly, heels drumming a faint staccato tattoo. 'My wife and I are looking forward to it very much.'

It was one of the many small tragedies of Herr Tiedemann's life that he, Herr Rommer's right-hand man, retained this position with Rommer's successor only by a humbling reversal of his former self. Herr Genscher required not initiative, but unquestioning obedience; not authority, but subservience.

The messenger boy probably knew more than he did. He was a doorman guarding the inner sanctum, an occasional teller of small sums, a document-checker. In return, he received an excellent salary at an age when many of his contemporaries were miserably touring the world in the company of their gaudily bedecked wives. Die Greisen reisen! Herr Tiedemann thought of the vulgar brochures that came through the door and shuddered. He had no intention of joining the band of cheerful, geriatric wanderers; that was as odious to him as the prospect of empty days at home with his quiet spouse. He could not risk any loss of dignity by ever complaining of his lot and thus it was only his wife who was obliged to hear his daily account of petty humiliation. In company he played his part well, every centimetre the venerable partner, and Lotte watched and nodded and dreaded his eventual retirement day far, far more than he could begin to imagine.

Upstairs Victor, half-wondering whether he had not over-reacted to a trifling event, was passing a half-hour in recalling one episode of his life; that brief and unfruitful romance with Johanna Rommer. He had not given her a thought for many months. He was skilled at the game of selective memory, for he had the ability to apply himself fully to the matter in hand and exclude irrelevancies. Victor had rigorously suppressed all the men he might have been, eradicating weaknesses and irrelevancies in order to create the perfect version: an artful, clever assemblage of the attributes which assured success in business and worldly terms. He could not understand contemporaries who let their failures rule their lives, who sat in the box created by a series of poor decisions and allowed the lid to close over their heads.

Victor was his own life's work, the most perfect figure that could be made from his chunk of marble. He had cut out the flaws, rubbed away the dark streaks, honed the whole to perfection and polished it up with years of study and application. Victor had learnt to please when it was necessary; to be ruthless, albeit charmingly so, when it was not. He was not cold-hearted, though some women accused him of that. Simply, he had never found pleasure or satisfaction in the abandonment of self, the morass of self-pitying emotions which they called love. His experiences had taught him that these raw emotions brought nothing but grief and he had suppressed them, alongside such unproductive feelings as envy and malice, and knew that he was now immune. He could not imagine why a sane man would want to place his happiness so entirely in another's hands.

Thus, when he had contemplated marriage, it was for logical and sensible reasons. He had decided to secure a young wife who could be moulded, who neatly rounded off his assets, who could bear him heirs. Johanna Rommer had possessed, in addition to an ingénue's charm, the advantage of one day inheriting the family fortune. He considered it his own long before he took the steps to secure it.

Victor flattered himself that he could have wooed her successfully had she been indifferent, but that was far from being the case. Her liking for him had been a deciding factor; she had long had a schoolgirl crush and nothing could have been easier than gratifying it. She was too young for his tastes, but he saw the importance of securing his due before some chance intervened. The arrangement had been as neat and orderly as he could have hoped for, in the circumstances. He had been obliged to use caution, for he knew Frau Rommer well enough to be sure that she would take a little persuading. It was to have been a fait accompli.

He remembered Johanna, not so much with regret, as with faint pride. In his dealings with her he had exhibited exceptional selflessness. He had put her interests before his: that was the precise phrase he had used, some time after his first declaration, to Frau Rommer during their first and only discussion of the event.

For Johanna, clearly out of her depth, had expected from him – well, he didn't quite know what; a schoolboy's feelings perhaps. He had soon discovered that it was more than a crush. She had a genuine passion for him. How she used to hang on his every word; how quietly she would sit with his friends to please him. It had been touching to watch her look round with those soft brown eyes and listen and learn and copy. It had been flattering and a little alarming to observe her quick intelligence as she perfected her language skills and used that immense, that endless adaptability of hers. Watching her, he had grown wary. She wasn't interested in possessions or clothes like normal girls. She wanted something more. She wanted to own and be owned by him and to get inside his head. That of course had been out of the question.

Observing this, he had withdrawn little by little and found her puzzled naïvety a little painful. Her anxiety had made him nervous, for there had been no way to explain to her that he neither wanted, nor was able to offer, the sort of intimacy she aspired to. He was not capable of such loss of control. Even physical intimacy had become a problem. He had forborne taking her to bed, a piece of self-denial altogether necessary, for if she felt these things about him now, what would happen then? No, there had been no risking it, and that had made matters worse. He had found her troubled, pale face beginning to disturb him. He had discovered in himself a little worm of affection, a desire to spare her a painful awakening. A pity, but he was in any case already rich enough for most men. And so, with some regrets for himself, he had done the unselfish, the honourable thing and cut short an idyll which was destined to be messy. He thought it a pity that Johanna had never understood the rules.

All of Victor's successful amours had been conducted along better-regulated principles, clearly understood by both parties. He prided himself on being scrupulously fair with the women of his choice, selecting independently-minded and soignée ladies who knew how to appreciate all the luxuries of such a liaison. Never promising love, he had waltzed them happily along the little milestones of romance. He never forgot a birthday or anniversary, as husbands did, never failed to produce charming gifts and trinkets on the slightest pretence. His accounts with the discreet jeweller on the Jungfernstieg, with Parfümerie Douglas and the Atlantic Hotel flower shop bore witness to a reckless generosity.

Victor's lovers enjoyed memorable weekends in magnificent luxury in Europe's cultured capitals (it was his rule that his elegant flat was never to be violated by a woman's messy accoutrements). He enjoyed particularly the dual pleasure of

taking a pretty woman to La Scala or the Opéra, Glynde-
bourne or Bayreuth, for the bourgeois arts had become his
sole enduring love. This connoisseur's passion was all the
more precious for having been laboured at, for Victor had
forced himself to listen to scratchy records in his bachelor's
garret and had peered at the mysteries of modern dance from
the cheapest seat in the gods. It was his stated opinion that the
finest pleasures in life, whether gourmet feasts or an evening
with a Diva, not omitting athletic pursuits both amatory and
sporting, were to be bought. The auditors of this revelation,
old pals whose smart dark blue Yacht Club blazers could not
conceal bulging beer bellies, who couldn't even go out with
the lads and get pissed without getting hell for it in the
morning, were frankly, openly envious.

Victor held these truths with all the more certainty for
having made mistakes: mistakes which had female names.
Cherchez la femme, he thought ruefully; surely Ludwig could
not possibly know of Johanna?

He was uneasy with good reason, for there had been a time
when he would have sworn that Ludwig could not possibly
know of Charlotte Bamberg. The first of his mistakes. Eyes
closed, searching in the blackness of an image of her, he found
that he could not, after all, remember her face. Yet she was an
error for which he might be called to pay a price, though what
price remained to be seen.

He recalled instead, vividly, the velvet texture of her pliant
white thights against a brown over-stuffed sofa. The butcher's
daughter. He conjured up the cold white shop with its stone
flagged floor and saw again the red butcher hands wielding
Krupp steel, eternally raised in a gesture of denial against
hungry faces while fat pigs' carcasses lay piled in the cellar. He
saw the white enamel scales which Herr Bamberg daily
balanced minutely in his favour and the pale stains on his
floor-length apron which no amount of bleach would remove.
It was strange, this selective memory of Victor's which had
blotted out his beloved's face. It was lost in a welter of bright
blood.

Victor had been in love. He had known that Ludwig would
have raged, that it would have seemed to him a strange and

abhorrent aberration in his fourteen-year-old self, a bizarre and unhealthy association with plump flesh. For Victor had been so very ready to deny that part of himself, had been almost touchingly eager to remake himself in his master's image. Orphaned, abandoned child, he had cast off his past as his childish revenge upon his parents for deserting him. Asked about them he used to reply, quite simply, 'A bomb,' and would shrug his shoulders, alarmingly composed. He had followed Ludwig as a clever mongrel dog clung to the master who rescued it, who fed it and gave it shelter. And Ludwig had loved him, the brightest, most promising child. He had been Lucifer, the shining angel, the one who had farthest to fall.

There had been no sign in the eleven-year-old of a possible betrayal to come. At twelve he had used his quick intelligence to learn scraps of Russian, of English, of French and, winsome child, to smile at a soldier for chocolate or cigarettes. He brought Ludwig his gifts as a dog would carry a bone and wag its tail. His small body could creep unnoticed through the ruins. He had learnt how to locate scarce goods; by judicious eavesdropping to plot the movements of lorry-loads of valuables. Eggs, boots, cigarettes for the illicit army to plunder.

With the onset of puberty he shot up suddenly and grew too tall for a child's role. At fourteen he had the height of a man; old enough to want a woman, the butcher's daughter with her butter-blonde hair, her soft palpitating bosom under the dark dress and cotton apron, the white cotton stockings rolled up over plump knees. She had smiled at him, cut an extra hundred grams of horseflesh and not charged. She was fifteen and already experienced in taking advantage of the lunchtime break when, stuffed with pork crackling, the butcher lay with his wife, animal grunts turning to regular snores.

Young, precocious Victor had not felt he was taking advantage of her when he felt the exquisite pleasure of resting his head against the round, white body. Their couplings took place on the horse-hair sofa in the parlour, which the parents only entered on Sundays, its dim light filtered through white lace curtains and a green, thorny hedge of Mother-in-law's Tongue. He had become a lunchtime absentee for the forty

87

minutes of Herr Bamberg's nap, his loud rhythmic noises guaranteeing safety and covering theirs. Charlotte: a soft, giving blonde. A type that could only be described as maternal. He, who loved her, knew enough to conceal the liaison from Ludwig. Blue eyes, long plaits curled over her ears which she could sometimes be persuaded to undo, even though this greatly increased the danger, for it took Charlotte at least ten minutes to recreate her prim, matutinal self. He remembered, but still could not see her face. Her image was overlaid with one of Ludwig's creating, with his words spoken nearly twenty-five years ago. A china doll, he had said, with round blue eyes that shut and legs that open when she lies down. A toy.

Victor had thought the liaison perfectly concealed. Certainly the butcher had no time to notice anything. He had tramped home from the war, footsore and ragged, and had fallen onto his great creaking knees and blessed the good lord when he saw his shop intact, his womenfolk spared the Russian atrocities. He had had the further good fortune of discovering a distant American cousin among the GIs based in Dahlem; his brother in the distant countryside was raising chickens. He rapidly set about becoming a rich man, a process which drew from the man of peace feats of cunning and bravery the former soldier would never have contemplated. Herr Bamberg's daring, night-time expeditions in defiance of the curfew made his fat legs tremble; his daytime negotiations with the less favoured sharpened his wits. The effort of putting an expression of sympathetic, albeit unyielding commiseration over his big bleary face gave the soft-hearted butcher nervous headaches and stomach pains.

Nobody saw the thin boy creeping along the back alley, knocking softly at the back door. Sometimes Charlotte gave him chitterlings, which he carried away in damp, soft parcels. Because he loved her, because he feared discovery, he would press these love tokens into the hands of the nearest urchin, the beatings of his tender heart stronger than the rumblings of his stomach. He had feared that Ludwig, unnaturally sharp-eyed, would read a message in the blood stains in his pocket, not realising that Ludwig had already decoded the oracle. For months in that balmy summer, Ludwig had chosen to ignore this aberration in his golden boy, waiting for it to pass.

For Ludwig too was preoccupied; everyone was bustling, hustling, scraping and, thanks to the black market, surviving. The shrewd, the lucky and the well-connected did rather better than that. The Allies with their punitive rationing and their bursting depots provided the defeated nation with the fundamental requirements of entrepreneurship: plentiful supply, separated by a hazardous, lucrative obstacle course from desperate demand. The grey acres of rubble proved to be a fertile training ground for Ludwig's private army. They had survived; now they were determined to flourish. Victor knew just where he had acquired his nose for a bargain, his gift for smelling out a deal; he knew the source of his remarkable single-mindedness in achieving his aims. He had learnt these things, not just from his mentor, but from the heroic conquerors, those masters of the expedient, who trafficked in the streets under the signboards forbidding fraternisation. Victor had learnt their particular brand of callousness, which talked portentously about punishing the guilty nation even while setting about making a handsome profit out of their sufferings.

He used to push his way through the mob in the Tiergarten, threading a route past the Allied uniforms and the clusters of Berliners, each with their pitiful bundle. Victor was pitiless. What did he care, if this object was the last family heirloom? He could not take into account the painful thinness of the old man here, the gnarled, arthritic hands of that one, or let the cry of a child affect his calculations, any more than the Amis did. If he began to waver, the sight of a GI would sustain him, reminding him that only a few years back he'd been ready to risk his pitiful life for a half-smoked butt thrown from a lorry by one of these gods. He and four other kids had been happy to throw themselves under the wheels if there was a chance of getting it. No, there was no going back to that.

Ludwig's boys all despised the workers, who laboured for a day for less than a cigarette would bring and thought themselves lucky to get a hot meal. They thought men stupid, to queue all day for a job with a 'future'. They knew the future was something that had to be manufactured, not in some factory but piece by piece, with cigarettes and pieces of soap. They used to sneer at the gaunt, middle-aged men who stood with cardboard notices round their necks: 'Ich suche Arbeit. Ich nehme jede Arbeit an.' Victor had known that they were defeated, finished, the abandoned relics of a collapsed empire. The future belonged to him and to the others riding out of town on the Silk Stocking Express, taking their flimsy valuables to the country folk in the fertile paradise outside. For stockings, chocolate, cigarettes, anything could be bought. Bartering could give a man a new Persil Certificate identity, whiter than white, or a fine set of professional qualifications. Sometimes, if he had a seat on the train, out of a mad, uncaring bravado Victor would light up a cigarette and consume the whole thing, that unheard-of luxury earning him the open-mouthed respect of all around.

That bright summer was darkened by a new fear, that was lay behind the propaganda front, the cultural competition and the Allies' failure to agree on anything. In London, they had failed to secure a joint German settlement and the city was nervous, electric with rumours. Half the country was still on the move, the displaced with their cardboard suitcases, the scavengers and barterers going about their business. Allegiances shifted; people were afraid. It was a strange time of unholy alliances, of profiteers and black-marketeers and men who said they were idealists and yet were all three. Even Ludwig was nervous, amassing property and at the same time fearful that an eventual return to pre-war stability, which none of them remembered too clearly, would throw up lures to seduce his boys away. Ludwig, by then, had bartered his way to a whole house and lived, as his status demanded, in the whole of the first floor. His rambling flat lay behind a grey façade with tall windows looking onto the flattened remains of a once-elegant boulevard. Miraculously, the house was virtually untouched. Ludwig had seen a new opportunity in it and, in an attempt at respectability, had let a few rooms to lodgers. These were young men with an apprenticeship or some other form of steady work, priggish young men, whom the others avoided.

It was a beautiful day, a brilliantly hot day. Victor had gone to the station early through the summery haze and had heard the rare and precious warbling of a bird singing, somewhere in the rubble. He had passed the walls plastered with hand-lettered posters: 'Looking for Brandt, Heinrich, reward', or 'Schmidt, Alfried, missing Dresden 1940' or 'Flat Wanted'. In that morning clarity he saw them, not as messages of despair, but proclamations of the inextinguishable optimism of the ordinary man. It was too early for the good-time girls, who asked a packet of Lucky Strike for their favours, and who were already plump and affluent in short fox capes and American nylons. The women at the station were those who never gave up, who wore round their necks placards with the name of a missing husband or lover above a tiny passport picture or blurred holiday snap. Rocking on their wooden wedge heels, they used to stare into all the faces that passed, awaiting their personal miracle. It was a good day, a special day. Victor found a seat on the train and by midday he was back, his knapsack bulging, one pocket still stuffed with Allied currency. Running to Dahlem, to his love, he felt the heavy weight of good fortune knocking against his thin shoulder-blades.

There was a crowd outside the shop. People were milling about, ducking, snatching and two policemen tried ineffectually to move them on. Pushing through with violent, desperate motions, Victor saw blood, everywhere, shocking him who had seen so much already without being moved or angered. The fat carcass lay across the door of the cold room, blue eyes gazing at the ceiling in perpetual surprise, the little pink mouth open in an O of shock. The stains on the apron seemed so innocent; pig's blood or human, they both looked the same. And now, horribly, the body began to move, to twitch, as the door was pushed open, as though the creatures inside were coming out, at last, to see the act committed in their name, to avenge their slaughter. Blubbering, her thin body shaking uncontrollably from cold, shock or both, Frau Bamberg pointed towards the parlour. Charlotte lay on the couch, face-down, and could have been asleep, but for the hand, the twisted hand pointing the wrong way, the white

91

skin still gripping the chop with a frenzy that even death had not diminished.

'They said it was a Polish refugee, a madman. That he shot the butcher dead when he refused him meat and then went after – her.' Victor, who had run across the city howling, now sat perfectly motionless in Ludwig's apartment, his hair metallic in the brilliant light.

A long moment passed and then he had held up his hands to Ludwig, showing him the rust-red dried streaks.

'Why should he shoot her?' he had asked, stupidly. 'She gave the meat away.'

Ludwig had stood at the elegant windows, casting his shade over the deep red Persian carpet, which he had bought for 100 pounds of potatoes.

'A casualty. People get killed all the time,' and he had shrugged his shoulders. That was their attitude; that others suffered but it did not matter, as long as the 'family' was all right. Victor would not retreat into this callous safety; like a dog sniffing at its master's clothes for the sausage hidden in a pocket, he whined and pawed.

'He followed her into the parlour to shoot her,' he said and drew from a pocket the Russian army-issue gun. 'The mother said a second man was there who watched and smiled and didn't see her, hiding in the cold room. Dark and thin, your height, Ludwig. In a black shirt like yours.'

He waited for a reply.

'Who doesn't have a shirt like this? Look at yours? And who's fat in these lean times, apart from your butcher friend?' and it was said softly, as though Ludwig had sympathy for his boy, for his adult body which had outstripped the soft mind. 'There was nothing you could do,' he said. 'These things happen every day. Forget her. What was she, a china doll with round blue eyes that shut and legs that open when she lies down. Don't you think you can do better than that?' And Victor saw that Ludwig had given himself away; the older man nevertheless still smiled at him, as though he were offering forgiveness. He had a particularly attractive smile; he had a way of carrying his smallness as though it were an asset. It took Victor a moment to comprehend that Ludwig thought this crime a just punishment for his betrayal; that he expected everything to carry on as before.

It had been a weakness in Victor, one that he had always regretted, that he did not shoot then. He remembered his arm lifting the gun, deciding instead to arch forwards, and the jarring hammer-hit of the blow that knocked his master down.

'You smiled,' he had said at the figure lying stunned, and heard the sound, like china smashing, his front teeth made, audible even through Ludwig's piercing, bubbling cry as the handle came down again, this time rupturing soft lips. He had lifted the gun again, but it was aimed, not at Ludwig, but at the young scared face that appeared at the doorway and was blasted backwards into red, howling pulp. Victor had never known what his name was; he had been new, a worker, an unknown.

It had been clear to Victor, scrambling his way through the American sector to safety, that to love meant to lose. His short life had punched home that lesson, if no other. He had made a consequent and more catastrophic error; he had left behind a mutilated and vengeful Ludwig instead of a corpse. At first he had shivered at every step behind him in a dark street. In mortal terror of his bogeyman, he had not felt safe in Germany and did not experience security until he was on a ship, where every face soon became hatefully familiar. In a world of hard men and hardships and humiliations, Victor became a man. He had learnt that he was more intelligent than the others; he had determined to remake himself, to succeed. In Hamburg he cultivated the hard northern accent, succeeding only in losing his Berliner's twang. He had chosen Rommer's because he knew about ships; had not Ludwig taught him to be adaptable, to please, to listen and to learn? These skills flowered in the fertile ground he had picked out for himself.

As time went by he decided that Ludwig must, surely, be dead. He forgot about him; forgot that he had killed a man and blacked out the unhappy years. He became all that he pretended to be. Herr Genscher's name commanded respect. Wealthy, astute and generous, he belonged to the best clubs, gave to charities supporting orphans and waifs, appeared at his box at the opera on all opening nights and never failed to celebrate each new, dividend-rich year with a magnificent party at the Vier Jahreszeiten. He sat now in his immaculate eyrie and formed the sudden notion that a temporary abandonment of power or his demise, either improbability, would hoist old Otto into the nub of a business empire he barely comprehended. This notion made him laugh out loud.

Frau Meier, hard at work swabbing the top stairs, parted newly-painted lips in a broad smile to rival Ludwig's for sheer pleasure at the sound of lieber Herr Genscher's happiness, so well deserved.

Descending the back stairs in good time for his lunch appointment, Victor noticed a letter in his postbox which must just have been delivered. It had no Absender, but he did not need that detail to identify its provenance. It was a typed single sheet of foolscap with a large margin, double spaced, which had at first glance the look of a legal document. He stood in the entrance hall, turned at a slight angle, and read it. Fräulein Schmidt, passing with a cheerful greeting on the way to rummage through the Alsterhaus's pre-Christmas bargains, was obliged to repeat it twice before she elicited an automatic response.

' . . . with some of the loose girls of the neighbourhood. I was to discover this later from talking to some of the other boys. I believed that he threatened them, to ensure their silent complicity.

'Victor had survived through petty thievery; now, as he grew, this activity became his small piece of self-assertiveness, his form of independence. It was his way of mocking the system. He was clever in his methods and I would not have discovered them, were it not for the complaint of a small boy whose watch, a much-coveted item, disappeared. He returned it with a good grace and accepted his punishment. This incident taught him to conceal his activities, which were of increasing scope.

'He has, indubitably, the soul and spirit of an entrepreneur, quick to see ways to turn events to his own advantage. It was and is the spirit of our times. There was no disgrace in buying and selling on the black market, but rather the notion that anyone who failed to take advantage of it was a fool. Circumstances had obliged us all to trade, in one manner or another. Victor's intelligence, his adaptability, made him an expert and laid the foundations for his current prosperity. The amassing of property and wealth, the manipulation of money, the quick taking of profit are construed, not just as enviable, but as positive virtues in a society where to be poor implies not just material, but spiritual and mental poverty.

'In our simple lessons, we discussed the concepts of real, spiritual wealth, and I would speak of poverty and humility as virtues, rather than disgraces. I remember the charming smile this graceful boy gave me, his reminder that without more material sustenance, however obtained, the hostel could not continue its mission. I made every allowance for his youth, the circumstances we could not control. Young myself, I was a worse teacher then.

'A serious incident at this time gave me pause. I caught Victor attempting to sodomise one of the younger children with whom he shared a room. I fear this incident was but one of many and the child had been bought with the promise of a reward. I could not decide what to do with him. To set him loose would have been an abandonment of all that we stood for and I still believed that he could be saved. He was severely chastised and given a room of his own, a considerable privilege in our cramped quarters. I myself was obliged to share with several young boys. I spoke with him at some length and tried to explain the difference between right and wrong. The moral teachings of a more ordered age were rendered so unassimilable by the facts of his life, by his evident need for love and human warmth. I believed that his amorality was not intrinsic but a condition of his circumstances and knew that I had failed him.'

Victor's impulse was to crumple this piece of hypocritical fantasy. Reflecting, then, he smoothed it out and again climbed the stairs. He locked it in the safe in his flat.

Ludwig had pawed at him; even in public he had been unable to resist touching his hair or straightening his jacket. He had given Victor a room of his own to facilitate his nightly visits; refusal had been the only way for Victor to exercise any power over him. He had known how to make him miserable, if he chose. After sex, embracing him on the narrow bed, Ludwig always used to talk and talk. He would say that it was not wrong, meaning that he knew it was. He would say that their love was something beautiful and glorious and pure. There were days when, catching him alone in a corridor, he would plead for a kiss. That was the price Victor chose to pay for privilege. Once he had embraced one of the smaller boys, seeking his own comfort and love. He remembered the terror he had felt when discovered by Ludwig and the vicious, jealous beating that had followed. He had learnt caution by the time the miraculous affair with Charlotte happened the following year. She, poor innocent, redeeming him from degradation, had usurped Ludwig in body and soul.

He locked his door; he ran down the stairs. He realised that he would have to kill Ludwig. He was a good twenty minutes late at the restaurant, painted dark green with white shutters keeping the muted interior in pleasantly dim, dappled light on bright days. The Kommissar had made himself comfortable while awaiting his host.

Das Fischerhaus, named in that archly rustic style appreciated by Pöseldorf sophisticates, was a fish restaurant of the type that offered carp and caviar, rather than salt herrings, though the proprietor was happy to cater to any fishy whim given a little notice. Victor often lunched there, finding that even jaded bankers and over-worked newspaper magnates could enjoy a dozen oysters or a fragrant mussel soup. Peter Schwantz had not been immune, nor Herr Kortner. Even the Kommissar was almost rubbing his hands at the prospect of a little pot of Beluga caviar to accompany that second glass of aquavit.

Herr Siemens was an old yachting pal. He knew without ever having put it into words that the pleasures of the *Rommery*, all twenty metres of shining beauty, and those of the table, so happily unlike the police canteen's, could be paid for by the reciprocal compliment of a little harmless information of the type businessmen often sought. Nothing illegal, just a little ferreting around and perhaps a call to an old friend growing fat in charge of an army of files. Everybody in the department did it. Herr Siemens suffered terribly from the fact that he, who took, did not give.

His obligations were all the greater, for he was an epicurean who could not afford to lay down wines; a sailor who would never own a boat. He ate his lunch knowing that he would always refuse to overstep the thin line that differentiated everyday helpfulness from minor, understandable corruption, even though a price had to be paid for such pleasures. This unspoken refusal in turn put him further into his host's obligation; he would then compound his misery by agreeing to a weekend trip on the boat or a splendid dinner. The conflict of puritanical beliefs and sensual appetites had etched melancholy ridges down his narrow face. He longed to be offered a fortune, so that he could give up and luxuriate in the comfort of betrayal. How simple it was to be a rich, bent cop. Known to be incorruptible, he was never approached. Instead he accepted minor, temporal pleasures which paid no bills, he obliged nobody and made himself thoroughly miserable. It was a torment that Herr Genscher never asked for anything; he did not even have the glum satisfaction of turning him down.

'Prost!' Victor said and the fiery liquor dispersed some of the chill he felt. 'So,' he said, grimacing at his poor wit, 'how's a life of crime?'

'Fragen Sie bloss nicht,' said the Kommissar moodily. He had recently been seconded to the police officers' training department. Desk work was inevitable, at his age, but training was both tedious and politically sensitive; there was at the time a witch-hunt in progress for left-wingers and subversives. 'I miss the old days. I spent four years in St Pauli picking up drunks, stopping sailors breaking up bars, finding under-age kids on the streets. Can you believe anybody would miss that? I used to end every shift depressed, feeling dirty. Now I'm nostalgic, even for the cells full of vomiting old men. It was a simple job, the dirt was clean,' and he took a delicate teaspoonful of the caviar and smiled in his melancholy, self-deprecating way.

'You were at least a man of action,' said Victor briskly. 'Now look at us both, handcuffed to bureaucracy. The older I get, the more I think we're trapped in the system. We're not capable of doing things any more.' He thought that this applied, certainly, to the Kommissar, a man who had evidently given up.

The Kommissar nodded agreement at the still-youthful face and thought of his ailing wife, who would be waiting anxiously in bed for him, the pain lines on her face temporarily erased by her welcoming smile. Hating himself for it, he went home later and later; he could not bear to watch her suffer. He never told her about pleasant events, such as today's lunch, not since she had become completely bed-ridden. Instead, he exaggerated all the worst aspects of his life in small, bureaucratic echoing of her greater suffering. She thought him dreadfully over-worked and sympathised; if she complained at all, it was on his behalf. He envied Victor profoundly for his complete freedom from responsibilities, from the rigours of sickness, for having the money to do anything he wanted. A happy man, he thought, who lived in no one's debt.

'You're not trapped,' he said. 'You can do anything you want. I can't even resign, I have to think about my pension rights. Still,' he said with an attempt at good cheer, 'it's not so bad, we do a good job. If I didn't train new officers, who'd catch our thieves and murderers, who'd sort out the traffic jams? We keep the wheels turning.' One of the mottoes of the training school, which he particularly disliked, was 'Keeping society safe'.

'Do you catch them all?' Victor said ruminatively. He was referring, of course, to a current scandal, a series of inexplicable attacks on old women living alone, found beaten or clubbed to death for their meagre pensions. The Kommissar, who had installed two new sets of locks on his shabby front door, grimaced.

'Oh, we do pretty well on the percentage of unsolved crimes, considering the sort of city this is.' He had all the figure off pat; it was part of the pep talk he gave at the start of the course. It was important to motivate the new inspectors against the dull grind of paperwork, the average pay, the long and irregular hours. He saw Victor's quizzical face. 'Oh, I know what you're thinking, but we catch a lot of murderers. Some are simple cases, people don't even try to run away.

There are plenty of unpremeditated ones, you know, people who kill out of rage, jealousy, when they're drunk. It's not hard to find the husband who knifes the wife's boyfriend.' He was talking easily, rapidly. A lot of people seemed fascinated by police work, saw it as glamour, all crime and sex. He always tried to recall the details of juicy cases; it was something to offer. The small coin of repayment.

'They always used to teach that there was a pattern to everything; that criminals made mistakes.' The Kommissar smiled at such innocence. 'We still find some arsonists standing around the fire to watch. Firemen are still told to look at the crowd as part of the job. But we live in a different age now, murderers aren't stupid enough to hang around the scene of the crime. Now we get drugs killings, kids who think they're being attacked and defend themselves. People like the "pensions fiend",' and he twisted his mouth over the stupid name, for every policeman in Hamburg was sensitive about it, 'they're hard to find. Psychopaths who do it for fun, who move over a wide area, they're difficult to find. We know what he's looking for, but there are so many possible victims, all living alone. We should have fingerprints of every citizen, but they won't have it, abuse of civil rights. It'll come, though, eventually and the system being what it is, then we'll fail to match them.'

'But there are clever murderers.'

'I wouldn't call them clever,' the Kommissar said. 'People get away with terrible things, yes. By luck perhaps. Sometimes by good planning. A buddy to invent an alibi that stands up in court. I wonder what those pals think afterwards, as the years pass. I wonder what the criminal thinks. Sometimes I feel they probably just feel simple pleasure at having got away with it. No remorse at all.'

The Kommissar, who had experienced all the torments of remorse without ever committing the crime, could envy such simple souls. Victor, who had set up this meeting with a motive beyond the normal routine of keeping in contact during the dry-dock season, was looking at him closely. He had invited him the previous day with the notion of delivering his problem into the hands of the law, or rather these

99

particular, delicate fingers which had often held a fork or pulled a rope at his expense. He had never asked, nor expected any favours. He thought that he could, at the least, expect a sympathetic hearing. He had picked at this idea over the mussels, rolled it round over the unseasonal, unnaturally bright strawberries. He saw that it would never do. He had nothing to incriminate Ludwig, no pasted-up note demanding money with menaces in the bold capitals of the *Bildzeitung*; he had a document which could not be shown to anyone.

'Of course they feel remorse,' Victor said, 'of course they feel guilt, it must eat away at them,' voicing the commonly-held truth to the morose and cynical face. He thought, but could not say, that fear of being caught abated. It gave way to calm. In time a man just forgot about it, as he forgot other incidents in a crowded life. The Kommissar would never understand and Victor knew he could not talk to this man; indeed he could not talk to anyone. He had lacked a person in whom he could confide for so many years that he would have found it distasteful at least, positively embarrassing, to try to talk of himself. He was at ease only when safely locked inside his own head. He would solve his problems by himself, as he always did, and the notion was gone, swallowed as swiftly and irreversibly as a second snifter of cognac down the oesophagus of the melancholy Kommissar. It brought a small measure of warmth to his sad brown eyes.

# Chapter 8

Monday, December 15, 1971

A dozen red roses, the long-stemmed kind, are standing on my desk. They arrived this morning stapled into one of those expensive boxes that attack fingernails. The card inside said 'Dein Sigi'. This courtship of his is the oddest thing, with no expense spared, and yet he doesn't even have a job. On Saturday he bought a single rose in the restaurant, the kind with a rubbery stalk that's dead within half an hour and costs a fortune and he insisted on getting a photograph of us from one of those bright-faced pushy women who come around. The still-damp result was all too revealing, me a smirk of sheer embarrassment, him a practised film-star show of white teeth. He saw my face.

'You think that's common, don't you?' he said. 'I suppose it's not done in Blankenese,' and then, studying it, 'The camera never lies,' and he shoved it in his pocket. He made me feel ungracious; but he was being rude, not me.

Sigi orders the most expensive things, commands absolute service from the head waiter and rewards him accordingly; God forbid that anyone should question his status. It's embarrassing and all the more so for being done in my honour. I bet East End villains are like that when on the spree; throwing money around, enjoying themselves doing corny things and touchy where their pride is concerned.

Linda, advancing with her plate of bacon and eggs, sniffed at the dark perfect blooms, but they are the hot-house kind with no scent. My perfidious Victor used to send me roses; they never smelt real either. These are already wilting under the powerful blast of Frau Beckmann's radiators, formidable, cast iron specimens which, typical of their generation, know no moderation: it's either gurgle, hiss and boiling heat or silence and cold.

'They won't last of course,' Linda said gloomily. 'Just like men.' Hers don't last because she picks them in bunches. I developed this entrancing theory for her benefit: too many alien flora jammed into one receptacle, I said, but she merely severed her bacon rind with precision in order to enjoy it more fully. Far from being offended, I think she's flattered.

Linda is resilient. I would be prostrate after her evening with the Turk, but her appetites are undiminished. He invited us both to dinner, cringing and wheedling, but I cried off to finish my essay on precursors of national socialism in Hugo von Hoffmannsthal, a piece of nonsense for which total abdication of self is required. Then Sigi rang, so I have the awful thing still in front of me.

The wretched Turk didn't take Linda out at all. He cooked himself in a kitchen which she says concentrated the dirt of ages, the nasty fatty mutton bones being assaulted in a black iron pot bearing witness to half a dozen previous culinary attempts. No wonder she couldn't stomach it and became light-headed instead from throwing down several smeary glasses of Turkish fire-water.

The lunge, when it inevitably came, had a certain awful novelty to it. He told her that he actually preferred boys, doing her the honour of considering her voluptuous female bum almost as good. He would accept it, in the circumstances, which were as squalid as they come. He was amazed, baffled, that she shouldn't be flattered, didn't simper and oblige, and he tried to overcome her English reserve with a garlic-flavoured rough and ready attack. She beat him off, of course, after a moment of stunned, alcohol-befuddled bewilderment, delivering what she hopes was an extremely painful kick in the goolies.

What a scene it must have been; the exchange in their garbled German as sole lingua franca and the full horror of his offer not immediately apparent. 'Wie bitte?' she kept saying, politely. Ah, but you could speak in the language of love, I said nastily and, to do her credit, she laughed. She left him writhing on a dirty couch amid a welter of filthy dishes. She's crazy; she must have known what was coming, but she's fatally, insatiably curious. It's extraordinary how Linda exudes and attracts sexual urges, forever getting into dubious situations entirely of her own making. They'll find you in a gutter one day, I told her lugubriously. With your throat cut.

(Now the above, my dear Ingrid, should you chance to rifle through my diaries while innocently looking for a comb, is called BUGGERY. I don't expect you've heard of it.)

The ladies are coming for lunch on Thursday. There was no gainsaying the urge to report to Oma on the state of my living conditions. I am sure that Ingrid's long thin nose will soon detect anything that is not quite ladylike, Linda's lingerie, for example, which I must remember to conceal. I shall indulge in a morning's truancy to make the flat respectable; Linda is to be coached in acceptable small-talk and encouraged not to wear that rather fetching new dress in purple satin which finishes a good ten inches above the knee and is indecent when she sits down. I did think the dress was a trifle provocative for a nation which dresses its women in black floor-length sheets.

She had to be toned down for our afternoon in Aumühle, a select suburb a long way out and not as chic as Blankenese though expensive enough. We were early, for there aren't many trains on a Sunday. The Tiedemanns' house is nearly in the countryside at the end of a long, ill-maintained private road rutted by the frosts, a constant source of rage to Otto, whose perfectly maintained and painted house shames the neighbours, or rather, fails to.

Oma used to take me there on courtesy calls as seldom as was decently possible, for each call entailed a dreaded return visit. They would arrive at the flat; later at the hotel, punctual to the minute, laden with flowers and chocolates, theatre guides and silk scarves, expensive presents which obliged Oma to reciprocate in kind, ever deepening a friendship which must have seemed to them to be beyond price.

True to protocol, they gave me two pearls for a first birthday present. Each year more would arrive with Victor to be viewed with bored incomprehension by my small ungrateful self, always wondering why it couldn't have been a dolly. Last Christmas they were ceremonially returned by Oma for the addition of the final pair, the stringing, the careful choosing of the diamond-set clasp. Herr Tiedemann handed over the long black suede box this summer at my 21st birthday party, thus culminating the ritual which is traditional for godparents. They aren't though, my wayward parents having failed me in that respect; the act of presentation was another of Herr Tiedemann's mutely eloquent reproaches. I should of course be grateful for such an expensive gift, so carefully assembled; just a small token, he said in an interminable speech, of the great affection he has had for me over the years. But I don't like pearls and nobody wears them. They're so old-fashioned. It was deadening, having to express my gratitude, as if I hadn't long known about and dreaded the event. I expect he bought the pearl earrings which are the wedding present; I am sure he is secretly pleased that it hasn't come off. He made another of his long, carefully prepared speeches when our engagement was announced and joked with hollow wit about having held me on his knee first. He expressed his rapture at this union between the two halves of the firm with such wooden enthusiasm that it was only then, watching him mouth his platitudes, that I realised how much he disliked Victor. There he was, once more usurping him, unfairly achieving in one step a closeness to the family which years of flowers and little Andenken and remembering wedding anniversaries haven't brought him. I can't help feeling rather sorry for him. If he only realised how irritating it is to have to feel grateful; the hardening of the heart at another thoughtful little gesture. It's so easy to admire people who are difficult, who must be wooed, whose respect seems unattainable. Any normal person is bound to despise somebody they please without effort. Ergo, my love for unattainable Victor; his rejection of me. Nobody wants the apple that falls at their feet, over-ripe and wormy; everybody wants to have to climb the tree, select and pick for themselves.

However, because I'm such a hypocrite, I wore the pearls to give him pleasure. Lotte got into her usual tizz over us. She's one of those highly nervous, faded thin blondes, carefully manicured to the utmost ridge of her thin and brittle nails. She wears a blue stone signet with the family crest and can't leave it alone, twisting it round and round as though she couldn't get the position quite right. The soft gold has worn, it slips more and more and she adjusts it endlessly. Old Otto stares at her in silent reproof, making her all the more nervous. I bet he puts her through gruesome post mortems on her inadequacies.

Everything came on special doilies, little crocheted ones to anchor the coffee cups, a larger one for the china cake-stand full of home-baked cakes. It's rather an empty house with shiny, polished surfaces with those spiky plants on every window-sill. They have all the fashionable things, English dining-room furniture, modern upholstered sofas, the china sea-captain's dogs, but it's too empty, it's sterile. Of course they never had children to mess things up and make it homely; no grandchildren for Otto to spoil and terrify.

I longed for a cigarette the moment we set foot inside. Linda's bored sighs verged on the audible and after a minute I just had to have one. Lotte darted back and forth emptying each inch of ash and bringing a new ashtray like a manic jack-in-the-box, still maintaining her rigid smile. Otto's welcome wore thinner in the noxious blue haze. Linda, almost totally silent, scoffed and scoffed; poor Lotte couldn't take her eyes off her, gripped by the endless mastication and her hair which is naturally streaky and looks as if somebody has doused it with peroxide. Then there is her make-up, which is evidently excessive for a nice young lady. God knows, Lotte's face has never been polluted with such filth and her crowning glory is lacquered into that awful, straight-back slightly bouffant style, which should make her look younger but just succeeds in emphasising its general sparseness. You can see right through it if there's a light behind.

After the third cup of coffee, Linda's fifth bit of cake, Lotte offered to show Linda round and she, obligingly, stood up at once, scattering a fine shower of crumbs all over the floor, and they left us to our tête à tête. Otto hummed and ha'ed in that way he has, fiddling with his collar. He has to be correct at all times. He'd stoop to tie a shoelace in a fire. He set off in a typical pleasantry about how nice it was to have me there, how he'd like Oma to be there too, what a deep respect he had for her and how she, of course, remembered the old days and so on; what a shame I hadn't seen the office in those days and what good times he and Opa used to have. He calls me Du of course, having known me since I was tiny. When I was seventeen he made a big thing out of my being a young lady now and having to say Sie, obliging me to insist upon Du. He'd have loved to 'duzen' my grandparents, but the offer was never made; a permanent chagrin. I wasn't listening very hard, just nodding sympathetically now and then, when it emerged that he was leading up to something. What it boiled down to from a thousand circumlocutions was that things were not like the good old days, in one particular respect: that Herr Genscher had seen fit to exclude him from his confidence. In other words, Victor was up to something and he wanted to know what it was and, more to the point, he thought that I could help him. Why I can't imagine, for he's been the door-keeper who's made sure I never get near. 'I never see him,' I said unhelpfully and baldly. I had another cigarette then, when matters were getting interesting, and it was a study to see him control himself and even look around for an ashtray in a helpful manner, no doubt gritting his yellow old teeth.

'Ja, ja,' he said, 'die liebe Frau Rommer hat es wie immer gut gemeint, aber die Zeiten ändern sich, nicht wahr?' And he said, smiling ingratiatingly, that he wants me to meet Victor in a sort of semi-official capacity as the other half of the firm and find out what he's doing. And then he added that in these special circumstances he felt it would be quite correct – and he was thinking of my dear grandmother – if he accompanied me to such a meeting. As though I'd want him there, big ears flapping; as though I needed protection from Victor, who is hardly likely to rape me on the carpet. He, who guards Victor as though I had the plague, offers him up now, just because it suits him.

Of course I was furious, but I could hear Lotte's voice dithering on outside about how they'd be redoing the hallway and apologising for its shabbiness, which might be apparent if the wall were examined with a x50 glass. So I said very primly that my grandmother would not approve at all and he winced a little. I even did my best to evoke Oma's robust presence; seeing Linda appear in the doorway with a pleading look, I reminded him that 'ein junges Mädchen geht nie mit leeren Händen aus dem Zimmer', and collected up a heap of china to take out, signalling departure. It reminded me of how I used to tease Oma by carrying quite essential objects, such as her reading glasses, out of the room. I cleared the table, banging Lotte's delicate porcelain down on the shiny draining board where three dirty ashtrays winked reproof. She fluttered about me like a crazed butterfly, nipping at my arm and saying it wasn't necessary, no really not, her anxiety exacerbated by the high probability that I would smash a piece of her irreplaceable set and by Otto's scowling at her as though, as usual, everything was her fault. How can she bear him?

So I have wilfully thrown away an opportunity for an official summit conference with Herr Genscher. We left; Otto was anxious to fumigate me away.

'Herzlichste Grüsse an meine liebe Frau Rommer,' he said. 'Ganz herzliche Grüsse sollst Du von uns bestellen,' as though I didn't know he writes regularly. He couldn't quite bring himself to kiss my nicotine-polluted hand, as he sometimes does, giving me instead his firm Prussian grip while his wife smiled and waved and uttered little choked-off politenesses in between her seigneur's farewells.

I interrupted Linda's description of the antiseptic perfection of the Tiedemann bathrooms with their scrubbed grouting; her little pitcher of scorn lavished on the nattily embroidered guest towels and flower-shaped soap, both of which her own dear mother affects. Lotte showed her everything: the leather volumes in Otto's study alongside the row of pipes, identical to Opa's, which he never smokes, and even the symmetrical pyramids of cans and boxes in the Vorratskeller.

'You know, he may have a point,' she said, and then, 'Oh I see. You only want to see him on your own. Well for God's sake do it, sneak into his flat or something.'

Linda does not appreciate the subtleties of the situation. Even I know that old Otto thinks he is trying to help, in his accursed, nosy way. He always says things like 'I'm ready to serve' or 'I know my duty' with a vaguely military air, though everybody knows he was too young for the first war and evaded the second by staying in the Far East. He thinks girls need protection, as though the one thing a young virgin dreams of in her maidenly bliss is stalwart Otto's crooked arm to lean on. I can't help resenting his assumptions about my purity, even though they're perfectly correct. Does he even know, I wonder, that to be a virgin at my age is an aberration, a shameful anachronism? Sometimes I think there's only me left, and Ingrid naturally.

I think we were the last year at school to leave virgins, with certain exceptions including my precocious friend. The last pure A-level year: another damning epitaph. I have been thinking of it, now that Linda's here, for we were so close then.

That summer was bright and brilliant as exam times always are. We lay in the orchard under snowdrifts of notes until the backs of our legs and forearms were brown, wasps buzzing around the crabapples. The murmur of our strange incantations, German, Spanish and French quotes chanted in unison, rose to the fourth form classrooms where the juniors, poor innocents, hung out enviously and thought us lucky to be outside. Overwrought and slightly hysterical, we played infantile jokes on our mistresses, such as hiding in the locker rooms. We were permanently tired from late-night revision; Linda from her evenings with a student who, more grandly, was to fail his finals for her sake. The night before each exam I sat up until three coaching her, a parade of my knowledge and her abysses of ignorance. I admired her calm, unruffled manner as she sauntered into the sunshine and down to the pub to meet Bobby while we were still scribbling at question two.

We were coldly scornful of the swots who left each exam in tears, swearing they couldn't do a thing, when we'd seen them raise a hand for paper three times. Joyce Highley's pink, mottled face blanched white in horror when the customary cacophonous post mortem on the English Lit paper revealed that she had answered all the questions in one section, throwing away two thirds of the marks; she threw a heel-drumming tantrum and had to be collected by her mother. Joyce it was who went on to find that fairground novelty, a bearded woman, concealed in her French translation. 'Et it entrait une personne barbue, bossue, basanée, qui avançait peu a peu, qui badaudait, qui vacillait . . . ' In came a woman with a beard and hump, wrote Joyce robustly. She mangled that so thoroughly that the ignominy of January re-sits and another term at school became inevitable: Joyce, whose reluctant companion was to be Linda, for this time Mr Davenport put his foot down when three O-level passes joined the eight she already had. It was during the blazing fortnight of our A-levels that we became a little estranged. I found her irresponsible in the face of coming disgrace; she disliked my self-righteous pompousness and we parted a little coolly.

I travelled with two vast trunks full of books and photographs, my sentimental baggage strapped up tight. The night before the ship sailed, I confessed to Oma, who had not failed to notice Victor's characteristic downhill scrawl on Hamburg letters, that a little romance was in progress.

'I know,' she said and shook her head sadly. She spoke of the city's delights and all the young people I would meet and how hard I had to work and how busy I would be; that I should enjoy myself with more of those young people and, on the other hand, not let myself be distracted. She told me the details of Herr Tiedemann funding me and said how pleased she was that I was going out into the world and not a word against Victor. I didn't mention marriage, knowing exactly what her views were; I let her believe it was not serious and callously suppressed the knowledge that she would be lonely without me and worried.

'I am glad that you decided to tell me,' she said and made me feel even more of a heel.

Oma was practical and kind, carefully packing my case, folding layers of tissue paper round dresses and sneaking in bars of chocolate double-wrapped in tin foil and, as her parting gift, a shiny black briefcase. I was in tears, but not she, erect and indomitable on the dusty streets of Harwich. But Oma is nobody's fool and she knows me too well.

'Sei vorsichtig,' she said, at the most vulnerable, parting moment, speaking in her penetrating voice the language that, surely, half the other passengers could understand. 'Enjoy yourself, but do not let Victor take an advantage of you; he is a gentleman and I trust you, but nimm Dich in Acht.'

It cost her an effort to say this and I flushed beetroot at this first-ever mention of sex and gave my word, ambiguously, not to do anything foolish. A promise howling to be broken.

She needn't have worried. Victor behaved impeccably. He was a perfect gentleman, as though he subscribed to the same dated etiquette book as Oma. He installed me in a comfortable, well-guarded hotel near Dammtor station, a place where the chambermaids were motherly types and the manager a personal acquaintance of his. It was full of families of German tourists with scarcely a soul between the ages of twelve and thirty and a wholesome set menu with four kinds of potatoes, to be eaten in a large, immaculately clean dining room where half the tables were always empty. If a bottle of wine was ordered it was a small occasion, the bottle carefully recorked and brought out with a label on it at the next meal. In the evenings, a few old couples would watch television in the faded sitting room where the empty chairs were arranged in neat, sociable circles and nobody under the age of sixty ever intruded. You had to ask for a key if, outrageously, you contemplated a late return.

Victor took me out to dinner a lot, to elegant places where he talked wittily in just the tone he used with my grandparents. At the opera I listened with the right expression, staying awake for love. We frequented smart cafés around the Alster on Sunday afternoons, and a dozen women smiled and waved and weren't always introduced and other tables seemed much jollier than ours. We passed crowded student places and Victor would cock an interrogative eyebrow, as though I was really dying to be there, with the amused look of a parent observing the younger generation at play. We sat once or twice in his flat, chastely apart, with the huge bed throbbing away next door. I never quite knew what to talk about and was silent for long spells, tongue-tied and anxious, my occasional pearls of wisdom coming out as hollow and juvenile as a plastic bead.

Victor's life is studded with formal occasions: black-tie dinners, gala balls, intimate evenings with dressy friends carefully planned around the lobster and asparagus seasons. He sailed away one weekend with his yachting cronies and the water widows invited me to their ladies' evening. Terribly informal, don't dress, they said, so I squirmed in jeans, gauche beside their nautical silk evening sweaters. They jabbered on about their children, who were practically my age, and about the difficulties of looking after parents who were younger than Oma. They ate, drank and laughed a little too much, complimenting me on my cleverness in a way that demonstrated that universities were for ugly blue-stockings and their clever boys. I sat stumm with no meeting ground but Victor, whom they all seemed to know far better than I did; as tense and bored as is mutually compatible. I envied them their womanly elegance, which didn't suit me, while they eyed me over long cigarette holders, clearly wondering what, apart from the Rommer fortune, he saw in me. It was a question I was asking myself.

'Doch keine Schönheit,' I heard one whisper, 'aber sehr liebenswürdig.' An annihilating verdict: sweet, amiable.

These women without a serious idea in their glossy heads, who never read anything more demanding under the hair-dryer than the latest blockbuster by Johannes Mario Simmel, observed, smiled and found me lacking. There was more to Victor, more to me than these brittle ladies thought, but he hid from me behind these ghastly friends, their exquisite flower arrangements and lobster bibs, their pastel tennis skirts and matching balls, their bottles of Sekt and good works.

Meanwhile, as though everything was hunkydory, Victor went on making the right gestures. The roses were delivered each Friday night with a card saying 'See you tonight, greetings Victor', or 'Till Sunday, your Victor' but he never said that he was mine, he never told me that he loved me. He behaved as though everything was arranged.

The engagement was announced privately, to Oma's sad disappointment. There was a half-hearted evening which Otto insisted upon and nobody enjoyed. Oma came for the weekend, looked at me unhappily and insisted on knowing whether I was happy and of course I insisted that I was. We went to an intimidating jeweller's to choose a large sapphire, which he decided should be set with diamonds in an art deco design which I knew was too grand and too adult for my bony fingers. All the time he was watching me, faintly amused, ever charming but remote, kissing me goodnight with respect, without passion. Weak-kneed with silent lust, I told myself that he respected me, unlike my predecessors. His affairs were legion; it could hardly be possible that he didn't believe in sex before marriage. I couldn't bring myself to mention it. I couldn't break through his poised aloofness, the appalling way he kept treating me as though I was an adult and knew the rules. I think he exposed me to the stuffiest of evenings and stiffest business friends in the hope that I would revolt, but I was too biddable, too anxious to please at all costs.

We talked about the future. He said, for example, that he wanted children. I asked myself furiously if it was to be an immaculate conception. I worked very hard at convincing myself that he was truly in love and therefore did not want to take advantage of me. I had all I had dreamed of and felt blank despair. If he loved anything, it was surely our firm and I saw all too clearly how neatly I was an extension of his career, a thought which in England had never entered my head. An ugly suspicion, which nevertheless didn't stop me loving him. As long as he wanted to buy, I was selling, at any price.

That summer I was alone for the first time in my life. I bought a huge lexicon and spent hours looking up words I found in long, solemn books to improve my German; as though the language were at fault; as though in English there would have been no silences. It was a test and I was revising in the only way I knew. I wrote to Oma daily, giving long and, alas, accurate reports on Victor's gentlemanly ways, feeling horribly young, unprepared for everything and out of my depth. He was the same Victor and yet everything was subtly different. In Hamburg he had reverted from lover to uncle, behaving as though they were the same thing. After a while I began to write to Linda, telling her the truth. She was marvellous, encouraging, packing the pages with terse descriptions of her romantic jugglings, so many balls up in the air at once, as it were. She never once said she'd told me so. Go on, seduce him, she said.

I bought new dresses and carefully applied make-up to look older, invested in scent and lace knickers to no effect and made myself sound cheerful and unconcerned while whimpering inside. That Sunday in August I broke the unwritten rules, running to his flat with my A-level results, the telegram stuffed into my pocket. I wanted him to be the first to know how well I'd done.

He was caught unawares in a bathrobe; in a slight, uncharacteristic disorder of Brötchen crumbs and Sunday papers. The rush, the heat, the momentousness of the occasion, my own daring, the aroma of coffee and five flights of hurdled stairs all made my head swim and he looked at me without the mask and with an unfamiliar expression.

Action replay: Victor amorous. The big scene, the one I have watched and criticised hundreds of times. I held out the telegram, but he wasn't looking. He took hold of me (slow motion, first kiss) and he kissed me properly, tasting faintly, deliciously of apricot jam. Heroine, stupid girl, can barely stand. We tumbled onto the sofa in a heap. The cotton dress I wore had at least twenty buttons down the front and he undid every one with care, in between kisses. (Shouldn't he have ripped the dress? Touch of brutality surely de rigueur?) I thought my heartbeat was louder than the Mahler; it should, of course, have been violins. He is beautiful naked, my Victor. He is brown and polished, tiny neat white bum a delicious contrast. Apart from Opa I'd never seen a grown man naked, never realised how huge an erect prick is. Heroine isn't, of course, supposed to look. But then, though I hadn't heard it, somebody shouted, 'Cut!' Inexplicably, without a word, he just got up and put his bathrobe and his face back on and said quite formally I'm sorry, please forgive me. We had all the ingredients for romance: the music, the place, everything, it

113

seemed, but sufficient desire. He had his armour back on but I was half-naked in a crude crumple of clothes and I shut my eyes for a moment and opened them again, as though the scene would change and revert, and had that strange sensation of everything receding you get sometimes when falling asleep. Victor and the room diminished away into the far distance. (Was that the mistake, not keeping my eyes shut the whole time? Would that have helped?) Miles away on the other side of the room he poured a cup of coffee and came back life-size and offered it to me, the cup jangling on the saucer in my shaking hand. Poor heroine, who needed a double brandy at least.

It was bitter. A profound, bitter humiliation. I wanted to vanish or to scream. There was nothing either one of us could find to say. Was that pity in his eyes? I don't know, the camera hasn't recorded it. Suddenly intensely embarrassed, I got up to find one arm was numb and did the buttons up all wrong in my fumbling, shamed haste. I ran away without a word, a blind march back past Sunday strollers, singing the sad Mahler in my head so the thoughts would be driven out until I was safe in my room. I remember thinking, but I have three As, as though they were a talisman to protect me. I didn't realise, until the receptionist handing over the weighty key stared just so, that my dress was all askew.

An hour later the letter came, the first of Victor's special, hand-delivered notes. It was a kind, affectionate letter full of crap, saying how very fond he was of me and how he had realised that I was after all too young and he was taking advantage of my inexperience, though the fact was that he had cruelly quite failed to do that. He regretted, he said, to cause me pain, but I would soon see that he was right. I deserved a far better, younger man than he. It was a horrible letter, the only one of his which I destroyed.

I think I knew the first day in Hamburg that it was already over; knew when he put his bathrobe on that it was hopeless. I knew as I sat in that horrible hotel in the pale green room with its over-stuffed clashing green armchairs with spidery anti-macassars, holding myself together until something happened, until the letter delivered the coup de grâce, that I had failed the test. No amount of revision would have helped. He had found me physically distasteful. Men could screw anybody, I knew, the worst, gaudiest, over-the-hill prostitute, but not Victor, not me. I was helplessly, insuperably inferior.

Poor abject worm that I was, I wanted to see him one more time. Another Victor, yet more remote but politely attentive over lunch in an expensive restaurant with a waiter hovering always too near for intimacy, a place he probably chose for that reason. The smell of fish made me feel sick. My throat ached with keeping back the tears; I couldn't eat. He said all the same meaningless lies again about being too old in a gentle, final voice. We didn't mention Sunday. Too proud to cry there, I listened and tried to make my face look normal, to school my nervous eyelid. Yes, I said, I understand, as though I meant it. We sat on and the coffee came and got cold and we were the very last to leave, because while I stayed there I could still look at him.

I told Oma on the telephone, very carefully, repeating over and over again that I was absolutely fine. Such calls are a mistake. The line magnifies the quavers, accentuates the pauses, conveys a hundred secrets when none is mentioned. She rushed for the next plane and, childish with relief, I sobbed for days and she stroked my hair and soothed me and listened to me insist how kind and considerate Victor had been throughout. A gentleman. She went out one morning to see him and returned without a word.

The next day she took me to a crowded resort in Italy, where from the back every other man had a look of him and where I lay inert, blasted immobile by the sun, feeling my heart thump painfully against sand crests I had no energy to smooth away. Oma told me old family stories to make me smile; she hinted by reference to her first husband that first love was not always the last. One day we got sloshed on schnapps and I told her everything, exactly what had happened and what it felt like. When I had finished and we had bawled our eyes out, she said with restraint that it was all to the good. She said, dear Oma, that she blamed herself for allowing the relationship to develop; she said that she should have known. Much as she liked Victor, he was not suitable husband material for anyone and certainly not for me.

There was something I didn't tell her, could never tell anybody. I had the feeling that I was disfigured, and he knew it; he had seen through the young, unblemished skin to something bad inside. I knew it had nothing to do with age or inexperience. It's almost as though I had always known there was something like that; always expected to be found out one day. The real explanation is hidden behind his courteous, polite phrases and I want that truth, however bad, for my peace of mind. Inscrutable, deceiving Victor: a wicked uncle indeed, not to have told me the truth.

I took my turmoil back to Hamburg and started my course as though nothing had happened. I couldn't face the English university which Oma recommended. It was more alien by far, stuffed with horrible, raucous English youth, with one or two of my immeasurably distant schoolpals from another age. To go back would have been a total defeat; I needed to find myself here and persuaded Oma that I could be safely left alone, putting on a great show of bravado and confidence. Darling Oma; she did her best. If you must stay, she said delicately, it will be less painful if you don't see him at all. I can arrange for Herr Tiedemann to handle all your affairs; nothing would please him more. Selfish in misery, walking wounded with Oma as my crutch, it never occurred to me that I could be putting her in an embarrassing position.

Braves Kind, I agreed to everything. Fine, I wouldn't see Victor; I didn't want to anyway. I needed all my strength to conceal and carry my unhappiness, like a belt of smuggled gold that mustn't be seen to weigh. Oma searched for flats and babied me. She told Opa's best jokes, which she always starts with the punch line. His ghost sauntered around the city. She saw it everywhere, an elegant lounging figure trailing a fragrant plume of smoke from its pipe, while I, heart in my mouth, saw only a blond metallic head: a poltergeist Victor at every street corner. She found the flat, awing Frau Beckmann with the thoroughness of her inspection, and the day I moved in I saw a picture of Victor in the paper. He was at a charity do with a blonde on his arm. I cut it out and later burnt it. How quick he was to console himself.

When Oma left, I determined not to be lonely. I met a few kindred souls in the unlikely environment of Aula II; a few bored window-watchers among the bowed heads. There is a group of Hamburg daughters, smart gossipy young ladies who live at home and snarl the traffic with their little sports cars and summer racing bicycles, whom I avoid. There are dozens of men, hordes of foreign students, glistening-browed giggling Nigerians, young Turks in every sense, bearded radicals plotting in safety at their Stammtisch. There are graduate students with their universal metal-rimmed spectacles and neatly annotated folders; there are the so-called Anglophiles, who dress in Scottish lambswool and tartan scarves, who smoke pipes, drink ice-cold beer at the Queen's Pub in the Gänsemarkt and would love to hone their accents on me. I've tried, but I can't work up the slightest interest in any of them, even those who laugh at my bad puns, tell me I'm pretty and lunge quite effectively – for they all lunge, sooner or later. My type is quite different; regrettably specific, just as Linda is Victor's type. The archetypal female companion: vivacious, a little plump and outrageously blonde.

And now it seems that I am Sigi's type, and yet he's just the sort to go for something flashy. Here is a thought more interesting to consider than my essay, that overdue piece of sleuthing into Prof. Burger's devious little brain cells.

Points about Sigismund Schmidt: No visible means of support, as the bishop said to the actress. No job and yet he spends money lavishly and is carefully put together. His jeans are pressed, shoes polished, and as well as the baubles round the neck there's a thick gold ring. In fact, in a suit he'd look like a ponce. He took us to a dockside Kneipe on Wednesday; we were slumming, but he was clearly in his natural habitat. There was a row of women perched on high stools, exceedingly exposed when it came to cleavage and length of skirt, on the other hand perfectly concealed behind the lavish colouring on the face. Looking at the flounces, sparkly danglers and heels, I thought they might be whores. I realised my mistake when he took us to see the real thing standing next to anchor chains in the docks, bulging bottoms in minis, white plastic boots and black fishnet stockings and surely freezing despite the twee little boleros that never got near covering the upthrust bosoms. They didn't like seeing women in the car one pointedly turned her back. Linda, gripped, asked thousands of questions and Sigi knew a lot of the answers. He is familiar with their world, though highly disapproving. He was scathing about those girls and when I said I felt sorry for them he laughed and said I was mistaken; a lot of them though it easy money. They could get waitressing jobs, if they were less greedy, he said, and that in Hamburg prostitution i strictly regulated by the police with compulsory medica check-ups by doctors who issue certificates to show they are free of disease. A cold business indeed. There was no nonsense in him about sympathising with the oppressed exploited proletariat, none of the generosity of feeling you get from student radicals. As far as Sigi was concerned they were slags and deserved what they got. Some were schoolgirls, he said, run away from home to go on the game and enjoy some freedom. He'd have put them all in a strict reformatory.

There is no question of Herr Schmidt being an Autostrich client. I saw them, fat middle-aged men in big cars who drive slowly past with their ugly heads hanging out of the windows. Greedy-eyed men, who park at the end where the street lamps peter out and screw the girls in the back of their cars. Sigi is much too handsome to ever have to pay.

His car: a bright red baby Alfa which he drives much too fast. Expensive, like the rest of his tastes.

Sigi and women: his attitude to 'decent' women is very protective, downright old-fashioned. He wants to pay for every drink, was offended that I insisted and certainly wouldn't let me collect a round from the bar, that haunt of vice. A drunken old man reeled by and made some stupid remark about him being with two girls and one to spare, eh? and Sigi was beside himself, He got up, took off his jacket and was ready to fight him, sleeves rolled up and fists clenched. The old guy got quite a shock and slunk away, saying no offence, mein Jung. We went on to a transvestites' cabaret, at Linda's request, and he loathed it. I can't say I liked it much myself, as the audience sits jammed together inches from a small central space where the 'girls' sing and prance, staring offensively at any woman in the audience and making rude comments, meanwhile showing off their silicon bosoms. Linda, who didn't understand half of what they said, was smiling, but Sigi wouldn't stay; it was an affront and he shooed us out, though not before making a few cracks of his own in incomprehensible Platt.

That protectiveness does not, however, exclude the arm around the shoulders. He wasn't pushy; no lunge, though that wretch Linda zapped out of the car into the flat like a rocket, leaving us idling at the kerb. He gave me a small ironic smile, which recognised that he wasn't going to be invited in, said might he see me alone some time? and held out his hand, for heaven's sake.

Saturday night was a demonstration that he knows how to live; that he can crack a crab and not drink the water in the finger-bowl. His treat and it cost a bomb; after the way he'd outfaced the waiter I didn't dare offer to pay. I have the usual middle-class guilt about upsetting the servants and always smarmy up to waiters and over-tip if they show the slightest willingness to serve. Not Sigi. 'You think I'm bad-mannered,' he said. 'But they're paid to serve. They laugh at you behind your back for paying so much, they outstare you at the end for a big tip and in the meanwhile they'd spit on your food if they could. Me they understand; they respect me. You watch,' and he was right, 'we'll get the best service in the place.'

It was easier to talk without Linda there, leaning back as if to say go on, enjoy yourselves, don't mind me. He questioned me all about family and friends; even suggested that I had relations I wasn't admitting to as though I hadn't got enough. There was, of course, always Ingrid so I treated him to a few episodes of her unblemished career, and then he started an interrogation about boyfriends. Fine, he said, when I was starting to get cross, now I'll tell you about myself. Fair's fair.

He told me the facts without, somehow, conveying at all what it felt like being him. Widowed, hard-working mother; one brother, a childhood in Altona. He was clever enough to have done his Abitur, but refused to change school and leave his friends. There are some fierce, misplaced loyalties in there. He's sporty and goes to a gym, even thought at one time of becoming a boxer, but decided not to spoil his pretty face, and raised his eyebrows when he said that in self-mockery.

In fact I don't think he's vain. Like pretty girls who stamp their feet and insist it's brains that count, he cares not about looks but status, or presence. What matters to him is being treated with respect. Nobody's going to push Sigi around. He may be, mortifyingly, prettier than me, but educationally he's got pimples. Lots of break-outs. He went to a technical school to be a draughtsman and left because it was boring; started an apprenticeship as a mechanic but hated being bound in that way and the pay was lousy, so left that too. He shrugged his shoulders. Good at drawing, at machines, a man of all parts but no stamina.

Swot Rommer immediately said he could go back to school, get an Abitur, start again, etc., and offended him. In Altona we don't go to University and become doctors and professors and then, disconcertingly, no, don't get me wrong, I don't usually talk to girls like this, I'm not used to it. But don't get me wrong, I think I'm as good as you are, but I do things my way. I sat there thinking what am I doing with this failed mechanic bully-boy and he smiled then (he has a very sweet smile) and said okay, now we're going to the Dom. I'm a hell of a shot, you'll see.

He must have won every prize in the fair ground and hit every bull's eye. He made the coconut man's night a misery. I was laden with blue nylon teddy bears and stale gingerbread hearts and sticky with candy floss. It's terrific at night, icy and brilliantly lit, and we went on every ride and he was admired by every girl who passed and I felt rather proud of him. He cracked jokes with the stallkeepers and bought me junk until I hadn't a spare finger left for another thing.

On the way home we talked about England. It's a mystery to him, a mythical land of pop singers and mini-skirts, tea-drinking and Carnaby Street and an anachronistic Queen, for he is a Republican naturally. We have serious faults, such as warm beer and driving on the wrong side of the road, but much can be forgiven a nation which has given the world the E-Type Jaguar and the Mini-Cooper. Why Hamburg? he said, so I told him about Rommer's and was ashamed of having lied;

and, to expiate, told him about my sort of uncle who wasn't a real relative and that I'd come here to be near him and he said Aha, as if he'd known all along there must have been a romance in it somewhere. I was shrieking over the roar of the nearly exhaustless car; the speed must have loosened my tongue. In the sudden silence outside my front door, quite unnerved, I heard myself asking him in for coffee.

Linda hadn't yet returned from skirmishing with her Gastarbeiter. He wandered around looking at things while I put coffee on and he didn't make a single move. We lay companionably on the fur rug and ate nuts. He said, predictably, have you actually read all those books? and I lied, to impress him. He rolled over then in a nonchalant sort of way to kiss me and instead of leaping to my feet to get more milk I sort of leant towards him and at that precise instant we heard the key in the door and leapt apart like criminals; that fact not unnoticed by Linda, even in her disarray. He didn't stay; he went off saying I'll call you in a casual tone but instead, today, the roses came.

Tuesday, December 16, 1971

I can't believe this. I went to the post office to despatch my long-overdue letter to Oma and when I got back Linda let me ramble on for twenty minutes before throwing in Guess who phoned? in far too mysterious a tone. Victor has asked her out to dinner. I loathed her for an instant and she saw it. For Christ's sake, Johanna, he's probably being polite. Look, I don't have to go. She shook me rather hard. Look, goddamit, have I ever done anything to hurt you.

She's going. I want her to. I have to have confidence in her. We spent the evening avoiding the subject, since it was settled after all, drinking a lot of wine and chattering as though it hadn't happened. I kept waking up in the night and thinking about it, about how neatly she corresponds to his feminine ideal, and then hating myself. Wisely, she's gone out and left me to my own devices. That bloody essay sits here and mocks me with two paragraphs written, both of them lousy. She's seeing him on Thursday. I feel slightly sick all the time, guts churning away. The head sends out messages saying don't be so stupid, but the stomach is deaf.

I want so badly to see him. There are a hundred scenarios: the street-corner encounter, the knock at the door of the flat, the accidental meeting in the great glass foyer of the opera.

'Who is that beautiful girl in the blue dress, Herr Genscher?'

'Why it's little Johanna, grown up at last.'

Surge of violins as hands touch; soft-focus as eyes sink deeply into another pair. But then I remember that Sunday and my courage fails me. What could be more pitiful than raking over the ashes of an old affair, than being seen to care? It's Anne Elliot, I think, who says that women have the dubious privilege of loving longest, when hope is lost. But the tone in which she says it gives the Captain hope. These things happen only in books.

Linda, naturally, subscribes to the realist school, the kitchen-sink drama. She believes in pleasure, not romance. Men are 'tasty' or 'delicious', to be gobbled up; she'd make an excellent female spider, the predatory kind who make love and then crunch up the male, discarding the husk. She, too, had a few night thoughts. Her little pressure-cooker of a head finally blew this morning, venting a lot of hot air. Linda's advice: see him, demystify him, there's nothing more off-putting than an old flame in the flesh. You'll look at him and think how could I, she said, with a wry grimace, that awful retrospective self-disgust. Lay the ghost. Dear Linda, it is not the ghost I want to lay.

The sight of my misery decided her to give me some advice for once and she settled herself in the way people do when preparing to say something unpleasant; arranging her feet, smoothing her skirt, looking me in the eye with friendly concern.

'Now I expect you don't want to hear this,' she said by way of a preamble and I steeled myself, lit a cigarette and said, 'No I don't,' but she carried on as people always do when the proselytising urge overcomes common sense. I have an obsession. An unhealthy fixation; it's awful for a friend to watch me suffer, and so on. Earnest and unstoppable, she zapped me with her nasty mixed metaphors.

'Thank God he doesn't want to know, because you'd run off to be his doormat at the drop of a hat, he only has to raise his little finger.' Or something in that style.

People who pride themselves on never meddling think that when they do, for once, open their mouths, what comes out is Gospel truth. The more unpleasant the revelations, the more honestly and frankly they are delivered.

'This whole business of being in love is a fallacy,' she says. 'All that passion goes away and you'll be stranded in some house with dishes and screaming brats. You don't want that, do you? It's never going to happen to me.' I have got to rely on myself and not the props of romance or the myth of the perfect marriage; unhappiness ever after.

She made out quite a convincing case against Victor. She remembers all the bad things I've ever, stupidly, told her and even my old letters became evidence for the prosecution's accusing finger. I was unhappy when I was with him, I felt completely alone and abandoned, did I remember that? I am, in short, ruining my life and making a mockery of my independence, wasting my time on a shit. This is called being cruel to be kind. She generated as much heat and rage as if she'd been the offended party. I could feel myself harden, not against Victor, but against Linda. For offending the basic rules of friendship.

There is never any defence against this sort of thing. The accused, poor deranged soul, can only plead temporary (or in my case permanent) insanity and hope for leniency. She sailed on to her grand finale, while I muttered, 'I know,' every now and then, ending with her pious hope that I would come to my senses. She tailed off then and became faintly apologetic in a slightly defiant, you'll thank me one day, manner. 'Oh Christ,' she said as I sat mute, 'shall I pack my bags?'

How could I say yes? We made a truce, peace of a sort. I said she was right, as I suppose she is, to console her; I saw her off with a smile. Why do people always need comforting when they've been horrible? The most irritating thing about people meaning well is that you're not allowed to hold their home truths against them; you are expected to be grateful. There seemed no point in explaining that the thing is unfinished; that I mean to let go of Victor the instant I have explained the whole thing to my satisfaction. I can't just proceed with my life as though it hadn't all been turned topsy-turvy.

I must stop and do this essay, I'm supposed to give it in tomorrow. I'm almost relieved at something to fill the great void. I've skipped four lectures since last week, one supposedly obligatory, and must atone. The ladies are coming the day after tomorrow; Ingrid seems a suitably thorny stick to beat myself with.

# Chapter 9

Victor was dismissing Heinz Bruch. For nearly two weeks he had trailed Fräulein Rommer and found it dull work. On the day of composing his little signe de vie to Johanna, Victor had recruited the ex-steward, a dapper little man who had slithered expertly and silently out of upper and lower deck cabins for so long that his whole demeanour was that of a servant: unobtrusive, unnoticeable, laconic and sly. Bruch, infinitely purchaseable, had seemed an excellent choice. His merchant navy career having long since come to a dishonourable end, his happy spell on luxury liners having been abridged by a congenital weakness for gambling which had obliged him to dip without prior permission into the purser's pockets, he had settled happily for lucrative employment with Victor. The windfall had discharged a small, necessary number of debts and enabled him to swagger into the tailor's of his choice with a fistful of the ready. Now, after a fortnight of assiduous work and a good many evenings spent shivering at street corners, he found himself turned off. This was merely, it seemed, because he had not seen any hooligans menacing the young lady. Looking sullenly at his employer, he wished him ill.

Victor paid him no attention at all; Bruch left his mind as abruptly as he left the room. He felt only relief at one thing less to concern him.

Another letter had found its way into Herr Genscher's postbox. Herr Frisch could consider his honour intact; this letter was delivered quite unremarkably by the normal agency of the Bundespost. And yet, if the yellow hunting horn that adorned that worthy system had let out a blast, he could not have received a greater tremor upon discovering it that morning.

This second, anonymous yet perfectly identifiable document was more difficult to decipher than the first. It was not typed but hand-written in a female script. The tone, in other circumstances, would have made Victor laugh.

'My son, Wilfried Ferdinand Meyer, was a handsome, upright young fellow, the pride of my heart. He was struck down, cruelly, before his prime by a wicked murderer who has never been brought to justice. He was seventeen and had just left home. We didn't want him to go, but boys will be boys and he wanted to go into the world. He had been offered a job training as a machine-tool maker, a skilled trade, for Wilfried was always good with his hands. There were few such opportunities in 1947. The factory was on the outskirts of Berlin so he had to travel a great distance every day, for we lived at the other end of the city. It seemed only sensible for the boy to live nearer his workplace and so he found himself a place in a hostel run by a young man looking after boys who had no homes. It was central and clean and decent. We packed up his things and off he went and I remember my dear boy shed a few tears in his mother's arms, old as he was, and my eyes were not dry.

'My poor Wilfried was an industrious and hard-working lad who never got into any trouble. He was gentle and easily influenced. He had sometimes become involved in the sort of childish pranks high-spirited boys think up. In this place, he came under an evil influence. There was a boy there called Victor Genscher, a rough street boy who envied him his earnings and his place. A trouble-maker and violent too. I believe he had run away from home and later I heard that he terrorised some of the small boys in that place. I often think that if only my brave boy had come home, this terrible tragedy would never have happened, but he – '

126

There it stopped; there Victor stopped, staring out over the quiet street. The boy was at his usual place on the street corner opposite. Victor's alter ego, his blond youthful counterpart, lounged under the street lamp and stared blankly into the thin, cold air, unnerving him with the meaninglessness of his vigil. Was Ludwig expecting him to run away?

For Ludwig had issued a challenge, in his own sly way. The second post had brought a note, quite innocuous to other eyes, informing Herr Genscher that his private tuition with Meister Judo was to commence the following week on Monday at 8 p.m. An invoice enclosed demanded the sum of DM200.– for eight lessons, payable upon receipt. There were several typographical errors on these pieces of paper; they would never have been permitted to depart from Herr Tiedemann's august out-tray.

Victor had re-read the letter several times, for there was a wealth of instructions xeroxed onto the rear; to the effect that a traditional Judo suit must be worn (available on a rental basis), that a doctor's check-up was advisable if the pupil had ever experienced back or knee problems; that children under the age of seven could not be admitted; that finger and toe nails should be cut short and rings or other metallic objects should not be worn; that pupils starting a course of instruction did so entirely at their own risk and the school could not be responsible for any injuries sustained. Meister Judo, the bottom line proclaimed, was affiliated to the International Judo Federation. This was, though Victor could not know it, no longer the case. The association with authority had long since lapsed, Ludwig's premises having been rejected on the grounds of insufficient hygiene and notably the absence of the foot baths recommended to practitioners of the sport.

Victor scanned the letter again, seeking the code that made sense of such trivia. He read the documents alternately until he knew them by heart, meanwhile pacing backwards and forwards past the elegant coffee table in a circuit that just stopped short of the windows. Earlier in the day, two little lads with satchels, whom Victor could not acquit of complicity, had amused themselves by drawing faces in the frosty glass of the tradesman's entrance until Herr Frisch shooed them away. No innocent, playful children these: he had seen a certain ancient watchfulness in their eyes. The boy had been there from early that morning. Victor had seen him when he drew back the sitting-room curtains and had suppressed the unreasonable urge to flatten himself against the wall. Didn't he go to school? When did he eat, piss, sleep? These questions revolved tiresomely in Victor's head. He suppressed an urge to go up to him and say something; that would certainly be a defeat of some kind.

He noticed them and gave no sign of so doing. He counted the days. He believed that in another few weeks, when he had the newspaper, he would be invincible. After a while he searched for a match and watched the Meyer paper blacken in his kitchen sink.

Four floors below, Herr Tiedemann worked in utter silence. He had rung Lotte at seven to inform her, with a great degree of satisfaction, that once more he would not be home for dinner; that he would be very late indeed and she was not to wait up for him. With a little smile trembling on her lips she put down the telephone carefully and gathered the artifacts for a minor crime. Carefully, she placed not a doily, but a plate of crackers and cheese, a tumbler and, from the back of the freezer, a bottle of vodka on a little tray. Vodka, she knew, could not be smelt on the breath. The whole was to be consumed with hedonistic abandon in front of the television set, but not before she had carefully set the breakfast table for tomorrow.

The office was dark, apart from the lamp on Herr Tiedemann's desk. Everything was left properly, the typewriters covered, each chair pushed under its desk and the waste paper baskets neatly lined up to make life easier for Frau Meier. Once or twice the telex machine broke into startling, chattering life and the long curl of paper it was pushing out grew by ten or twenty centimetres. Herr Tiedemann's slim gold pen, a gift from Herr Genscher to mark his seventieth birthday, scarcely paused in its task. He was preparing a methodical transcription, line after line, of all of Herr Genscher's assets: the current value of Rommer shares, estimates of profits to be made from transactions in hand, not forgetting current liabilities, the interest on outstanding loans, bad debts and outstanding credits. Nothing was to be omitted. He had before him in a neat pile Herr Genscher's bank statements, his private portfolio of investments, current valuations for the property and, even, for the car. He noted that a great many shares had been sold recently to raise cash.

Herr Tiedemann was in seventh heaven. He quite forgave dem Chef for neglecting to inform him about the land purchase in Bayern made some years ago, for the forthcoming Olympics had sent prices rocketing. He examined with care the risky, speculative stock dealings of five years ago and noted the gains, nodding his head as the figures were totted up. A tribute indeed to his boss's acumen, as was this hush-hush special job: a laborious and exact piece of work which only you, my dear Herr Tiedemann, always so efficient, can be entrusted with. He had devoted a separate sheet, with double underlinings, to Rommer's current and largest yet venture, a risky, difficult undertaking which had elicited a great number of head-shakings and tuts from the old man.

Herr Tiedemann was the first to know about these secret negotiations. Foolhardy, frightening and yet, Otto thought, an interesting proposition: *Der Abend*, no less. The city's ailing evening paper, in constant and unsuccessful competition with the flourishing *Abendblatt*, was known to be a bed of radicals, peepers and priers who feathered their nest while they raked over the doings of Hamburg's eminent citizens, pretending sanctimonious shock. A paper known to be a mere scandal sheet, which had never passed through Aumühle's shiny front door. A fat manila folder at Otto's elbow contained a jumbled set of documents that had occupied him for an evening: the balance sheet of the flagging concern, whose proprietor was eager to unload to the right party; photocopies of an article in an equally scurrilous, satirical weekly listing the prospective purchasers. These ranged, incredibly enough, from Axel Springer (an asterisk pointed to a footnote: unlikely) down to a half-forgotten 60s radical student turned lawyer who had formed a consortium with a group of left-wing friends (yet more dubious, the footnote said: journalists reject overt political inteference). Herr Genscher was not mentioned. He was a surprise candidate and likely, it seemed, to be favoured, for the publishers wanted a non-political proprietor, the sort of respectable money-man who could put the paper back in the black while honouring the views of an independent editorial board.

Herr Tiedemann had read through a document produced by the circulation department which purported to prove that although three hundred thousand people bought the paper each day, it was actually read by a further 4.8 persons per copy. There was a 'readership profile' listing the assets of these supposed readers, each with their Eigentumswohnung and Opel Kadett, their annual holiday in Gran Canaria with 1.8 children and subscriptions to 1.4 weekly magazines, their Krankenkasse contributions and passion for football. There was, it seemed, an identikit *Abend* man, an imaginary low-to-middle grade manager, small garage owner or lesser official, whose every thought and expense were known.

There was, too, an analysis of advertising, explaining the downward curve in evasive terms and always in reference to such factors as 'across-the-board agency cuts', to socio-economic trends and, above all, to other newspapers which were doing even less well.

Herr Tiedemann had turned almost with relief to a separate, crisper document outlining plans for improving all these figures in a hundred different ways: reader competitions with holiday prizes, Lotto, advertising supplements, special feature issues, sporting spin-offs and television personality columns. Every idea, it seemed, had been rejected by the editorial policy committee. *Der Abend* regularly offended its major advertisers by publishing articles finding fault with their products, their sales methods or the private lives of their directors, articles 'without fear or favour'. Herr Tiedemann had smiled at the suggestions from the journalists on how to improve their paper. More money for them, new management, more money for contacts, budgets for 'feature exclusives', for travel, for research, for exclusive photographs of film stars and royalty; a special fund for paying the wives and girlfriends of murderers, rapists and bank robbers for their exclusive stories. They wanted a tabloid format, more staff, a weekly magazine in colour. He had glanced with distaste at a piece of paper setting out the current annual wage claim of these excitable, opinionated journalists: more money, shorter hours, paternity and maternity leave, time off for educational activities, more staff and fewer duties. He had turned with relative relief to a list of printing costs; appended to it were lists of printing firms and estimates from all over Europe and even from Singapore and Hong Kong for printing the *Abend*'s projected magazine.

Amongst all these papers, Herr Tiedemann had come across a small set of clippings: references to Rommer's. There was a photograph of Herr Genscher with a beauty queen at a charity ball, a three-line reference to his winning a yacht race five years previously and one to Rommer's undertaking a large lease-back venture with a major Reederei; nothing, naturally of a more scurrilous nature. He had been pleased to note that his firm offered little of interest to *Abend* readers. From the half a dozen copies of the paper attached, he had learnt that the Opel Kadett driver enjoyed shocking revelations about the private lives of Hamburg's worthies; their messy divorces; 'The night I had to say no'; the secret life of the 'Beast of Binnefeld'; the police officers' porno party; the local councillors' hidden SS past. All was revealed under the banner of truth and decency. SPD or CDU, FDP or NPD, none was exempt; it was noticeable, however, that the paper, broadly speaking, backed the SPD on major policy issues and took particular pleasure in mocking the activities of the CSU and Herr Franz Josef Strauss, a man whom Otto Tiedemann held in the highest esteem, even though he was a Bavarian.

And, right at the bottom, lay a letter from the editor-in-chief, Herr Franz Walther, a confidential letter advising Herr Genscher that his offer was being favourably received and that, in view of his unblemished standing, impeccable credentials and non-political stance, it was likely that he would prove more acceptable to the staff than a proprietor 'of the old school'. Herr Tiedemann had sighed over this letter. 'We all believe that the time is right for a liberal proprietor, a man of sound standing, who can finance the *Abend* towards a healthy future, providing new confidence and a vigorous outlook, while wisely leaving the editorial policy to those old hands who understand it best.'

He had no idea why Herr Genscher wanted this newspaper. He could not believe that he would wish to stand back from his ailing, expensive toy and feed these rapacious people. He smiled at the erroneous notion that Herr Genscher would leave matters in wise old hands. Then Otto reflected that the bank would not advance such a large sum if they did not have good cause to believe a success could be made of it and look, he thought, at the profits being mopped up in Bayern. A newspaper, he mused, would occupy Herr Genscher a great deal; he would barely have time for the day to day affairs of Rommer's. This thought had prompted a small pencil note in the margin, a cheery little 'Sehr interessant! Hals und Bein-bruch Herr Genscher!', an expression he considered suitably sporting. He wrote this a couple of centimetres from the bottom line figure: a projected loss, for the next half-year, of at least three quarters of a million, conservatively speaking.

Tonight, the fourth night of Lotte's liberty, Otto began listing Herr Genscher's personal assets. A prudent man, Victor had recently chosen to triple his life-insurance, the premium tax-deductible. Otto made a faint pencil asterisk beside the sum which estimated annual maintenance and running costs for that expensive boat. Such pale stars represented Herr Tiedemann's humble personal contribution to his master's affairs, for he meant to repay this exceptional expression of confidence with one or two astute suggestions. These were modest enough but, he liked to think, nevertheless rewarding. The *Rommery*, for instance, which ate up so much money, should be sold to the firm and run as a chargeable business expense for official entertaining.

Drifting in and out of Herr Tiedemann's mind was the notion that Herr Genscher could again be contemplating matrimony. What other reason could there be for a man in the prime of life wanting to draw up a balance sheet of everything that he possessed? A trifle old-fashioned, perhaps, but that was a virtue in Otto's eyes. There were one or two ladies he could think of, charming young ladies of good family and well-connected. Herr Genscher of course, ever the individualist, would find someone a little unusual. He hoped that the lady would be a worthier – no, a more suitable choice than dear little Johanna. He respected the young lady's modern, independent mind but then there were her odd friends and her, well there was no other word for it, her ingratitude. A small scenario formed quietly at the back of his mind in which he and Lotte befriended an older, a charming and yet modest Frau Genscher, a girl who appreciated the finer things in life. There would be Sunday afternoon trips to Aumühle and, yes, small blond children tottering on the lawn with genial Uncle Otto to lend a hand with their first steps. It had not escaped his notice that there was no beneficiary named in Herr Genscher's will, a document still unsigned that lay near the bottom of the pile.

Marriage was a stable, a sensible choice. He kept returning to this notion as an escape from the sea of paper. It was curious: much as he had wanted to know, much as he had ferreted and probed and worried about being left out, knowledge did not really satisfy Herr Tiedemann. These undertakings fell outside his normal orbit and he foresaw dangers and difficulties in these supposed opportunities. Herr Tiedemann tended to worry about things. He needed to have all his problems solved, to have everything neatly docketed as Disposed Of. He hated things that ran away with him, hated the unpredictable, the unsafe. For all his new self-importance and the not by any means negligible pleasure of letting Lotte know how indispensable he had become, a little bit of him kept thinking that he had been easier in his mind when he had had only his own position to worry about. Now he was worrying about Herr Genscher's as well. Now he had real issues to think about and they upset him.

One floor below, in the caretaker's flat, Herr Frisch delicately inserted his fleshy tongue into Frau Meier's mouth, avoiding the gleaming new bridge at the front which so remarkably altered her face, making it, as he had assured her, positively youthful and plump. He tasted of the Römertopf she'd brought, carefully wedged with towels into her shopping bag. Now it lay nearly empty on the table. She, relaxing in this long-awaited embrace, uncomfortably aware however of the grinding against her narrow pelvis of the hard buckle of his leather belt, a truss to support his overhanging, well-nourished belly, resolved inwardly that when they were married he would be put on a diet. One eye half-open, she again examined the furnishings. They would have to be replaced. The caretaker, lost in the rapturous enjoyment of sensual pleasures, all unaware of her busy little notions, wouldn't have changed places with anybody in the world. Not even with rich Herr Genscher who, for all his wealth, sat alone, again, tonight.

Something was going on. Even Frau Meier sniffed it through the carbolic. Herr Genscher had cancelled his week-end at La Scala, pleading overwork, but his desk was empty. He had put off seeing Heidi, as rosy and flaxen-haired as her name suggested, for the fourth time and she, offended, was turning a little snappish. It would take more than the sapphire pendant to placate her; that she considered her due and already overdue. His mind was not on her and that had been noted with a certain degree of sharpness, of disappointed sulking. The flesh did not fail him, it never did, but the spirit had been absent and Heidi had sat up with a flounce, saying that she could be a puppet for all he cared. He had marvelled at this, her first perceptive remark, happening just at the moment when he had mentally abandoned her. He would, as his florist suggested, 'Sag'es mit Blumen!', a most apologetic and florid arrangement with a small farewell card, a 'Leb wohl' tucked into the fragile, hypocritical blossoms.

Victor had lost his sense of well-being. That ease of his, an invisible but vital garment, had slithered from his shoulders; now his skin felt as though it no longer fitted. Other people, behaving as though everything was normal, seemed to him shockingly callous. He could hardly bring himself to thank Fräulein Schmidt when she placed that first, best cup of coffee of the day on its little place mat. He touched the pile of papers on his desk as gingerly and reluctantly as though they had been metamorphosed into cuneiform slabs. To append his signature to a letter or memo had become so meaningless that he felt a weight of gravity he could not begin to combat sticking the pen fast to its tray.

He had been happy without knowing it. He dwelt with

unbearable poignancy upon the young man who, in a fervour of desire, had planned the takeover of Rommer's in a shabby furnished room; who had read balance sheets with the trembling amorousness more appropriate to a billet-doux. He had recreated that desire in recent months, reading issue after issue of *Der Abend* with premature paternal pride. How tame Rommer's seemed by comparison; he had outgrown it by virtue of becoming the new Herr Rommer, a position that could never be sufficient because he had achieved it with such ease, and because, now, he would never own the entire firm as his predecessor had.

Victor had toured the newspaper's premises which he already thought of as his, mentally refurbishing his office and shaking the somnolent room of sub-editors into life. He had practised the negligent, familiar tone of address used to the burly line of men operating linotype machines in his head. Following Herr Walther's rotund form through the news room, he had found the cynical glee with which the news editor greeted a news-wire catastrophe as intoxicating as the acid inky smell of newsprint and the thundering of the presses. He was an ardent suitor, forcing the pace for a speedy union. He had cajoled the dour bankers into acquiescence, if not enthusiasm; he held Herr Walther in the palm of his hand. This was a romance which had to be consummated; he had only to stave off Ludwig for a matter of days.

Victor knew that his story would make excellent copy. It was precisely the sort of horrific, murky-past revelation the *Abend* liked to splash on its cover in lip-smacking, alliterative capitals. When news was thin, they exhumed the corpses of old atrocities. The human fodder was plentiful: there was always some old SS man, a pitiful white-haired blur hiding his just-recognisable face behind a shielding arm, fool enough to seek an official post in the quiet town of his birth; there was always some ex-convict holding a position of trust in a school or Kindergarten. If Victor became grist for that mill he would lose everything and he had more to lose than any dim-wit official.

He had consoled himself, hitherto, with the lack of evidence: what was Ludwig's word against his? He could already hear himself saying that these were the fabrications of a deranged person, saying it moreover in a kindly, pitying tone. He had thought, too, that Ludwig, himself guilty, would not slay his fatted calf. But now a grim purpose was emerging as this evidence, so spuriously manufactured, rose to mock him. The mother of Wilfried Ferdinand Meyer: a harridan shaking bleached old bones.

Victor sat down at his elegant escritoire and for half an hour scribbled away at his own account of the affair before tearing the useless pages into thin, angry strips. His notes could not begin to equal his enemy's in their complexity. He knew what kind of labour Ludwig had undergone in his maniacal, vengeful zeal. Ludwig had typed a portrait in o's and x's, an uncanny portrayal of the shades and hollows of a face, a demonic and yet still recognisable Victor. He would not demean himself by playing this game; it was better to eliminate the writer and his works with him. He was, after all, a man of action and not a man of words. That facility was one the future newspaper proprietor would develop when it became necessary.

He did have one regret: that he had not already accomplished the deed. How could he kill a man who was having him followed by this nightmare of youth, these parodies of innocence? Even at night they were there, sharp-beaked owls who fixed their vast glittering eyes upon him. It was absurd, a black joke. He thought that he was for the time being in a state of – call it grace. On Monday, Ludwig would advance some proposition, would ask for money. Of course he would not pay; such an admission of guilt would bind them together forever. Today was Tuesday.

Like many householders struck by the sharp rise in crime statistics, Victor possessed a small hand-gun of the type a man might reasonably use to defend himself against intruders. The cold greasy metal soon warmed in his hand. He thought that he could not use it, its number being filed with his licence application, but that a gun could be used as a club. He held it as he read the document again and imagined the further accumulation of detail that must exist elsewhere. It struck him with unpleasant force that nobody in the world knew so much

136

about him or would have taken such trouble over him as Ludwig. It was a compliment of the most threatening kind.

Across town, Ludwig soothed himself smoothing out the soil around his rare Australian orchids. The sharp, peremptory rapping at the door was unwelcome and unusual.

'I know, I know,' Frau Liebmann said, hunched and sharp in the doorway, her sallow face poking through with an annoyed look. 'I know you don't want to be disturbed, but he insisted. Wouldn't take no for an answer, the young –'

She disliked them all, resented their importunate knockings and ringings which obliged her to trudge down two flights of stairs as though she was at their beck and call, and the light bulb so weak that she knew one day she'd fall and hurt herself, not that they'd care. The wall was marked in a hundred places where Frau Liebmann, nervous in her shuffling decline, had reached out a hand to steady herself. She disliked this one particularly, for he did not even contribute to her income. He came and went as though he owned the place. Ludwig went to the wash basin and let the cold water run over his hands. He was wearing a long, ragged grey T-shirt over underpants. Sigi knew that this was not unusual, despite the bitter cold. Like quite a few former and present pupils, he knew about the glass house; Ludwig was, he thought, far less concealed than he believed. Once he had smashed a pane of glass by lobbing a brick from the street side over the high wall when, a wilful sixteen-year-old, acting on an impulse, he had needed to announce to himself that he would never go back.

'How's the heiress?' Ludwig said, turning and wiping his hands, 'What news of Herr Genscher?' That same ironic, smug tone; he spoke to him with the familiarity due an accomplice. Looking at the ugly face which his laughter contorted into a monkey's wrinkled skull, Sigi gave his usual, non-committal reply.

'She's very well. Thriving you might say,' and he curved up the corners of his mouth in a knowing smile. He gave up his scraps of information with some reluctance, which was firstly, simply, because he disliked this bitter man. He thought him a kind of bum, who gave away food to down and outs and thought that made him a saint; who was a sucker for certain boys and by no means the man of iron he made himself out to be. Sigi had seen through him long ago; he had realised that he had, fundamentally, no self-respect. Because he was working for him, all the same, if it could be called work, because he was obliged to deliver something, if he was going to get his money, he found himself picking through the ragbag of tittle-tattle, selecting with care the items which would please and always holding something back. It was a purely instinctive decision.

'I've got something that might surprise you,' he now said.

'My dear boy I wonder if I have that facility,' and Ludwig's face wore its usual, mocking expression, as though he could expect nothing of any interest, yet he always listened with the most extreme care and attention, for all his relaxed poses. Sigi had seen through him all right, but it bothered him, that extreme interest.

'A love story, a tragic little romance,' he said, hearing in himself the faint echo of Ludwig's jeering manner. He watched the little man all but smack his lips over the story of Fräulein Rommer's pitiful romance, he lapped it up and he smiled in a knowing way. He was as eager as an old woman oohing over her neighbours' transgressions; his pleasure was disproportionate and Sigi, finishing, felt a slightly queasy sensation in his stomach.

'Run through it again, dear boy. And you didn't say what year this was,' and, while he listened, he cleaned his black-rimmed nails on the edge of a business card. Fastidious Sigi watched the round worms of dirt coil onto the card and drop to the floor; observed with repelled fascination that he dropped the card back into the drawer when he had completed his toilette.

He had already decided that he wasn't going to tell Ludwig that she never saw Genscher now; that seemed tantamount to wringing the neck of this particular golden goose. Now aggrieved, somehow, at Ludwig's sly pleasure, he began to reckon up the other facts he had suppressed: his credit at the bank. He hadn't yet described her flat, nor mentioned the English friend. There was another fact he had decided need not concern this man, that he liked the girl. There was something

138

endearing about her, the careful way she picked the right word, the little jokes. Yet she was a serious girl, with more on her mind than the next new dress. He would never have described her as pretty. Her features were not regular enough and she was almost alarmingly thin, but she had a beautiful, pale, clear skin. What he thought of as an English complexion, and in contrast to it a great mane of dark curly hair. Her hands were particularly fine. He gazed at Ludwig's bony specimens and thought of her white, tapering fingers with their clean oval nails. She wore no make-up at all and while he approved of this, he imagined she would look dashing with it on. Mentally he applied colour and smoothed the hair.

Ludwig, who had no idea of what was being omitted, seemed to find his remarks a good return on his investment. He shook his head disbelievingly at the restaurant bill, but he didn't quibble, he paid up at once.

'It's good,' he said, 'it's very good, they are close. A first confidence, my dear Sigi, should lead to others,' and Sigi said nothing to disillusion him. The judo master said he had an errand to run and they went out together; in one of those gestures Sigi had grown to loathe, Ludwig clapped his back as they parted in the deserted street.

Sigi walked slowly down the Beckerstrasse in a strange mixture of emotions, for his dislike of the man was transforming itself into a revulsion that he felt more and more strongly. The old Geizkragen had money to burn and he, who had taken it, nevertheless did not care to think of himself as somebody who could be bought. This now seemed to matter more than his long overdue rent. And there was Johanna. What would she think of him, if she knew?

He sat back in the cold bucket seat of the little car, reviewing all that he had said. He had remarked, with some bravado, I've not had her yet, but I will. It was a coarse thing to say, to please Ludwig and he'd said it as men did when talking to each other even though he knew that Ludwig was not, precisely a man; even though he was not that sort himself. Put into a false situation, he was acting the part too well for his own liking. Sigi, who was cocky and streetwise, had nevertheless a certain delicacy. He knew a lady when he saw one.

He turned the key and the motor complained; at the third attempt it sputtered into feeble life. Of course he needed the money badly; he always did. Despite this urgency, he wasn't even looking for a job. He revved up; it took a long time for the heat to begin to penetrate through. At the third intersection he realised where he was going. He was doing what came naturally to him, even at his age. He was going to see his mother.

Vera Schmidt was leaning against the bar, bending down to rub one aching foot with tired fingers. Years of working on her feet had swollen her ankles, pushed out bunions and built corns. Now though she had long abandoned the sharp stilettos of her youth and wore only comfortable shoes, her feet still hurt. On Sundays she would sit for hours with her feet resting on a red Moroccan leather pouffe he'd bought her, but after twenty minutes in the restaurant they would be throbbing as painfully as ever.

Sigi pushed through the door; through the glass he had watched her with the usual mixture of affection and gentle exasperation, the faint twinge of annoyance that she, so expert on what was best for him, wouldn't do what was best for her. She had been offered the easier job of cashier but after a week perched on the high stool had asked to waitress again. She was bored, she missed the tips and she couldn't stand watching the girl who'd replaced her mix the orders up and flirt with her regulars.

'Du bist es,' she said and smiled and poured him a glass of beer. 'It's terrible tonight, Lili's off again, another row with him,' she jerked her head in the direction of the far corner, 'so I'm cooking and serving. Come on, you can stir the pot.'

So Sigi stood in the little kitchen and stirred the huge pot of goulash and watched her wrestle ready-prepared platefuls of frozen snails out of their wrappings and shove them into the tiny oven.

'Twenty minutes at least,' she said. 'Yesterday a regular got them still frozen inside,' and she went out, straightening in the doorway and putting on a smile, a last quick smear of lipstick at the mirror there, a jaunty air.

The Kneipe was almost empty. It was the dead time

between nine thirty when the first wave went home and eleven thirty when the television people up the road came off work and would eat and drink until one in the morning. This lucky chance had kept the place in business, for the proprietor was generally absent, the cook involved in an agonised romance with a Gastarbeiter forever threatening to bring his real family over. They lived upstairs and the man came down for his dinner every night; he glowered in the corner and waited for his beloved, fifteen years older than him. Lili was a fat, good-tempered blonde who was crazily in love. Nobody seeing her in the street with her shopping bags full of onions would have believed that a short time ago it had taken four customers to drag her off her lover, whom she was threatening to eviscerate. He looked moody sitting there, but then his dark face was always closed up and incomprehensible.

'She's sobbing her heart out up there,' whispered Sigi's mother. 'It's the change that does it,' and she made a little moue of distaste, for it would happen to her eventually, though she fought it off, sucked in her tummy and wiggled her hips a bit as she walked. The Yugoslav had made advances to her once, but she'd laughed him away. She'd never get mixed up with a foreigner; she knew trouble when she saw it.

The customers came pouring in in one swift wave that filled all the tables. In and out Vera came, laughing, busy, hands quickly scraping off leavings into the pig bin, dumping dishes in the sink, grabbing a fresh tray and off. She knew she was a marvel, irreplaceable, that they wouldn't manage without her. She'd been there for eight years and knew every regular's name. The place was her life, the goings on better than the movies.

Sigi filled the bread baskets, turned down the bubbling vat to simmer and unwrapped the cling-film from a new dish of potato salad, putting it on the side so it wouldn't be too cold. They sold half a dozen dishes, all simple but good, and the place was friendly and even its shabbiness pleasant. He'd always said his mother could make a fortune running it for herself, but she said he was crazy. She had no aspirations, unlike her big-shot son whom she loved and scolded and sometimes, late at night, cried over, blaming herself because he didn't have a decent job, nor any prospects to speak of. She loved him; he loved her; she couldn't in the end think she'd done such a bad job when there were so many kids around who wouldn't even speak to their parents, and vice versa.

By one fifteen the closed sign was on the door and there were only two men left, quiet ones who liked to play a game of cards and drink a few beers after the late shift. Their glasses were full, everything was back in the fridge, big Hans behind the bar polishing the glasses dry and treating himself to a whisky; she sat down with Sigi at the table in the corner, sighed at the relief and eased off the shoes. Pushing a cup of coffee across the table at him, she gave him a quick kiss.

'Thanks. You're a great kid Sigi. How's the flat looking?' He had left home only two months previously, having pulled strings and got himself a cheap but nice place in a big new housing block. He'd bought a lot of stuff she knew he couldn't afford; she put that out of her mind.

'Nice, very nice. You're tiring yourself out here, Mutti,' and his brow was wrinkled up, just like when he was a little boy, and she wanted to smooth it out.

'I'll take you home.'

'Let me sit a bit. I like it when it's nearly empty. I like to sit for a bit, I don't come on again until three.'

Her blue eye shadow was too bright; it had spread into the laughter lines around her eyes, just as the lipstick edged into the little creases round her mouth. He looked at her rough hands with love and anxiety.

'You need money, don't you?' she said. 'Hans will give you thirty, for tonight,' but he wouldn't let her get up.

'Look,' he said, 'I met a girl. A nice girl. Very clever, English, a student. Rich,' and he smiled winningly. 'Didn't you always say I should go for a rich one?'

'Oh Sigi,' she said, helplessly, shading her eyes. He was tender-hearted and very proud; she knew he could be hurt very easily for all his toughness. She and Wolfgang were different, stronger in many ways, they didn't take life so seriously. Sigi took after his father.

The look on her face pierced Sigi with sudden truth; this tenderness, the unspoken misgivings, the anticipation of a rivalry which hadn't yet occurred. His confused general thoughts suddenly clarified under the beam of maternal jealousy. Of course, he thought, now I understand.

'The thing is,' he said. 'I borrowed money from Levison to take her out. I want to pay him back, I don't like to owe him anything, you know what he's like.'

She crinkled up her face at this. She didn't like the man, but he was good to Wolfgang who had nowhere to go after school and who seemed to enjoy the lessons there. She hadn't liked his influence over Sigi and was relieved when he took up the gym instead. She had no choice. She'd have to take a different kind of job altogether to be there for the afternoons, and she looked down at her hands. The hard nails were cracking a little from too many immersions in harsh detergents. She knew she wouldn't give it up.

'You have to pay him back,' she said after a while. 'How much?' and she fished out a bag from under the seat and started to rummage in it. It was more than she'd hoped; it always was. 'Expensive places,' she said, not able to stop herself. 'Look, Sigi, take it, I don't want it back, but you've got to find a job. Any job. You'll get into trouble, you know you will. Please.' He watched her count out the battered notes, lit a cigarette and remembered how he'd always promised her, when he was a kid, that she'd never have to work again when he grew up.

'I'll pay you back,' he said. She looked older every time, particularly when she didn't smile, when she lost her bounce. He wanted to give her something, to make it up to her somehow. 'I've tried, with jobs,' he said. 'They're never the right ones. No, I know what you think,' he waved her silent, 'it's not that I have to start at the top, it's just that they're wrong. I'm not made to work as a mechanic, with my hands, and I'm not trained for anything else.'

Hans, disliking the silence, put on another tape, her favourite old one, 'Ännchen von Tharau bittet zum Tanz', and the bouncy melodies made her tap her feet, in spite of herself.

'I sometimes think that I should get a proper education,' Sigi said. 'Night school or technical school or something. Get out of that circle. You always said you didn't like my friends.'

She smiled at him, weakly. She could hear the girl speaking

143

already; she could see how she might ruin him. He'd just be a temporary thrill for a girl like that, something different. With his expensive tastes, that instinctive liking for fine things, things he couldn't afford, Sigi would be ruined. And she'd drop him soon enough. There he sat, so good-looking that she wanted to weep, his gentle hands playing with that lighter, another expensive toy. Vera knew that she couldn't say a word against the girl. He looked up now, for encouragement, for hadn't she always told him to try and better himself? One word from some upper-class girl and he's interested, she thought bitterly.

'Come on, you can take me home now,' and the bunion throbbed, even in the sloppy shoes, and she made an effort, straightened up and patted her hair and smiled at big, silent Hans, who winked. Sigi wasn't tired; he loped easily to the door, swinging her bag of groceries, held it open for her. He had good manners that came naturally to him and a good heart. He was good enough for anybody, just as he was.

'Would you like to meet her?' he said, and her heart sank.

'Of course,' she said and, because a sacrifice deserved some return, 'Sigi, will you do something for me? Spend a bit of time with Wolfgang? He hangs around that judo school all the time in his holidays and I don't like some of those boys. That Bernd Aubrecht, you remember him? His mother's worried, he's only fifteen but he's sly and secretive and always out. You could take him out, go to a picture with him. He looks up to you,' and Sigi, driving at exciting speeds through the empty streets, smiled at her and said of course he would, laying his hand on her arm.

'Don't worry so much,' he said, knowing she would. She loved her boys but couldn't control them; either of them could persuade her into almost anything. She wanted to be a good mother but had always left them alone a lot; she fretted about them, blamed herself and atoned with expensive presents she couldn't afford.

'Please,' he said, 'I'll keep an eye on Wolfgang.' He wasn't really thinking about Wolf at all. He was seeing Johanna in his mind's eye. She had leapt unexpectedly into that tight, protective cordon he held around the few people he loved. He thought how odd it was that he had had to see his mother to realise that.

Sigi's matchmaker, meanwhile, being a thrifty fellow, had taken the last S-Bahn to the Hauptbahnhof and made his way through the near-deserted streets of the city centre. Around two o'clock in the morning, he stepped lightly through the back door of Rommer's, treading with extreme care on his crepe-soled shoes across Frau Meier's polished floor. In his pocket lay a set of locksmith's tools, wrapped carefully in a soft cloth so they would not jingle. He was sufficiently practised in the art to be confident that he could open any of these doors, but it was a nerve-racking business all the same and his hands were moist inside the thin gloves, a film of sweat on his brow. He moved his body with the utmost care, with all the trained, cautious discipline of the master, sliding step by step along the long hallway. A strange noise echoed through its empty spaces. He stood stock-still.

He waited, frozen, and there it was, repeated in heavy rhythm. It became clear that this was the sound of a man snoring. It came from the room that opened onto the stairwell; the caretaker's flat. A fat old fool, slow on his feet; his snore that of a man who wouldn't wake in a hurry.

The dark figure passed slowly through the hallway, hugging the wall in case a passing policeman should think to shine his flashlight through the glass door at the front. There, the office door. The glass looked wired, but wasn't. The alarm box proud on the outside of the building was a sham. Herr Genscher's flat, full of valuables, was wired; the rest was not. The building had only adequate locks and the inadequate caretaker to protect its complement of office furniture, regulation chairs and battleship-grey filing cabinets and the instruments of torture belonging to the dentists who rented rooms upstairs. Indeed there was nothing here any self-respecting thief would bother with.

He was inside. He took the tiny flashlight from his pocket and looked around. There was a heart-stopping moment when his foot grazed a metal waste-paper basket placed immediately beside the entrance. He proceeded in complete silence through the empty desks, tried a filing cabinet and found it locked and wasted not a few moments in flicking through a set of dull papers containing various cargo and salvage fees before once more clicking it shut. A large wooden cupboard set into the corner which looked as though it might house a safe turned out to contain a set of coffee mugs neatly up-ended on a piece of paper and tins of coffee and sugar labelled Goldberg, Brinckmann, Schmidt, the latter one ringed by a crudely drawn chain of flowers. The large pictures, poor-quality reproductions of tea clippers, hid nothing and he went on to a smaller row of brownish colour plates depicting quaintly attired tradesmen from long-gone days. Their ugly, finely cross-hatched faces scowled down at Ludwig as the small spotlight passed over them and on in search of richer booty. Nothing there. He was careful, despite a growing feeling that he had to hurry, not to become hasty in his movements.

Very quietly, he opened the door beside the pretentious glass partition that separated a large, old-fashioned desk from the humbler variety. A pile of folders lay on top of it. Herr Tiedemann had even provided an inventory of contents, a slip of a list neatly written in an old-fashioned hand which was taped to the top of the first dossier.

Worthy Herr Tiedemann had departed for Aumühle on the very last train at much the time Ludwig pulled in on his. He had, for once, permitted himself the luxury of not clearing his desk in his anxiety to proceed with the work in hand first thing the next morning. The old gentleman, who prided himself on his discretion, would never have left any important document where Fräulein Schmidt's unworthy gaze might alight upon it, were he not secure in the knowledge that he would be the first person in.

He could not have forseen Frau Meier's unusual decision to run her vacuum cleaner across the carpet first thing; her work revolutionised by an early start made possible by her having spent the night so comfortably on the premises. She had no interest in papers; her ambitions were centred elsewhere and she was in a particularly good mood at getting the office done an hour early. She did notice one small detail, however, as she leant to plug in her machine at the accustomed spot. Most unusually, that stupid Fräulein Schmidt had left the photocopier on all night and with a tut she pulled out the plug and, her labours completed, decided, not without a touch of malice, to replace it as before.

This was the first thing Herr Tiedemann noticed upon his majestic entrance. No little matter ever escaped him and this was puzzling, for he had not seen the glow of the machine in the darkened office of last night. He was obliged to conclude that he himself had committed the grievous fault and, because his obsessional nature was made that way, he found himself dwelling upon it. He was half-inclined to think that Herr Genscher had been in the office overnight and had half a mind to tax him upon it. But in case he had indeed perpetrated that small bureaucratic crime known as over-heating the machine (a fault for which he would have had the secretary in tears) he decided to refrain. He would not expose himself to the censure of Herr Genscher at this propitious moment.

Herr Tiedemann felt positively unhappy if he could not consider himself blameless at every second of his day. He didn't feel right at all today; he was uneasy. He told himself that he had plenty to be glad about. Happy, he thought, be happy. He tried to feel happy. The unthinkable happened; a smile of solitary happiness creased his leathery cheeks and he did not realise it until he looked up and met the astonished gaze of Fräulein Schmidt, busy little fingers for once stilled by the extraordinary event. It felt peculiar; he didn't like it and, while she watched, the corners of his mouth turned down into their heavy, habitual ridges.

By the time the afternoon came, Sigi was flush with borrowed cash; his small store of credit totally used up, he headed for the Beckerstrasse. A generous fraternal impulse took him first into the dingy building, which reeked of cabbage. The small cramped flat smelt of dust and, faintly, of the acrid ozone the fan heaters gave off. The living room had the bleakness and stale chill of a place where curtains had been left drawn all day; where daytime light and fresh air had been ignored. The sofa bore the impress of a lounging, idle body. There was no beer in the fridge. An overflowing bin sat inches from a pile of laundry; there was a pathetic little bottle of corn remover, half-full, sticking to the glass of his mother's bedside table. Wolfgang's room was a litter of clothes and yellow fag-ends. The bed looked as though it smelt.

He took off his watch and rolled up his shirt sleeves, plunging his hands with distaste into the greasy grey water in the sink, finding the slimy blockage and, throat working in faint nausea, soaking the pile of crusty plates. Vera Schmidt, who polished the Kneipe's steel draining board until it shone, had no energy at home.

Sigi was sitting at the kitchen table when the latchkey clinked in the door and, a second later, the telephone rang in the hallway.

'Yeah, I just got back.' His brother. 'Ach du grosse Scheisse. Look I did it, I'll get the money. What's the problem then, I've done it before, haven't I?'

Sigi, sitting quite still, listened.

'Your old man's an arsehole. Yes, yes, I know, reg' dich nicht auf. Me and Heini will do it, on Friday.' A pause. 'What's the big deal about it? Don't worry, you're like an old woman. We'll watch him, we're not going to lose him, I've done it before, haven't – hang on, just a minute.'

The kitchen door opened.

'Oh it's you,' he said in quite a different tone and returned to the telephone. 'Okay, bye, talk to you tonight.'

He gave Sigi a spiteful, malicious look.

'Don't tell me, Mutti asked you to keep an eye on her little boy.'

'What've you done this time?' Sigi sat back, lit a cigarette and watched Wolf's face turn wary.

'Been listening at the keyhole, have you? I've been having fun. I've been a naughty boy, haven't I. Don't beat me, Papa,' and he pretended to cringe away, folding up his lean body into a protective huddle on the wooden chair.

Sigi, who often felt like smashing his brother's head against something very hard, said, 'What now?'

'A little accident.' Wolfgang smiled. 'No wheels now, I smashed up Bernd's bike and no insurance. Got any spare cash? No, never mind, good old Mutti will pay.'

Slowly, Sigi peeled off a couple of notes from his roll; he

148

pushed them across the table.

'Now don't tell Mutti,' Wolf said in an admonitory tone, wagging a finger. 'You know how upset she gets with naughty little Wolfie,' and then, looking down, 'It's not enough.'

Sigi shrugged. Wolfgang's stacked heels found a perch on the table; the body stretched out its over-long legs and yellow-stained, gnawed fingers helped themselves to a cigarette which he smoked in silence, throwing back his head to exhale streams of smoke in the direction of the ceiling. When it was finished, he got up and minced across the kitchen with swaying hips.

'Your old friend Ludwig is getting to like me. I hope I'm going to be one of his favourite boys.' Glass after glass of water was thrown down his long throat; the Adam's apple bobbed up and down.

'Course it keeps me up to all hours. But I don't mind. I just want to be appreciated,' and his voice attempted a Berlin accent.

'You're stupid, Wolf,' Sigi said calmly. 'You don't know what you're getting into half the time. You just follow Bernd around and copy him.'

'Ooh, jealous,' he said, falsetto. 'Course I can't expect to be a real favourite like you. Haven't got the body, have I? But I do my very best to copy you, Sigi, ooh, yes, I do, even when it's very very difficult,' and pleased with his wit, he wandered out of the kitchen.

As soon as he was gone, Sigi reached across for Wolf's jacket and rifled through the pockets. A packet of cigarettes his brother had not thought to offer; a dirty comb and a couple of crumpled Tempo handkerchiefs. He felt inside the zip pocket: a small card. One of Herr Judo Meister's. He flipped it over and read on the reverse, in tiny capitals, the name VICTOR GENSCHER and ROMMER IMPORT-EXPORT HANDELSGESELLSCHAFT with the address, a telephone number, a crude sketch map and up one side the pencil scrawl, unmistakably his brother's: Never out before 9 a.m. Now he heard his brother's clippety-clop down the lino floor of the hall and stuffed it back.

149

Wolfgang was holding a tarnished gold medallion and chain of the cheapest kind; he rubbed at it with the kitchen towel before handing it over; the thing dangled in grotesque mockery in his hands.

'What do you think?' he said. 'Only DM12.–, it looks exactly the same though,' and he bared his teeth in satisfaction. 'Got it in the market. Here, let's see yours.' Sigi looked at the tawdry little fake, which he would have liked to rip apart and hammer.

'Nice,' he said, with an effort. 'Listen, Wolf, you leave Levison alone. And tell Bernd to keep away from him. You know, he's using you. Don't be an arsehole, Wolf, you always get into trouble on other people's account. Be clever, for once.'

Wolf wasn't even listening; humming, he was fastening the chain around his neck, bent in front of the tiny mirror propped on the window sill to admire himself.

'Naughty Sigismund,' he said, archly. 'Selfish boy. Wanting to keep the best all to yourself. Now you know Mutti always said we boys should share,' and he pranced about, admiring himself, with the medallion swinging on his pigeon chest.


The door, unusually, was unlocked, so Sigi let himself in and closed it very quietly behind him, crossing the great, gloomy room at the edge of the mat. He stood for a moment in the stairwell and heard the sound of the old woman's television above; cautiously, he pushed the office door an inch. Ludwig was not there.

Quickly he knelt at the filing cabinet, flicking through the dusty pieces of paper. All his documents were there. If there was anything to be found, this was the place, he knew his man, and meanwhile he listened acutely, for Ludwig moved like a cat. There was no discernible order. An anarchic sea of paper was stuffed into a couple of files, the remaining blue-black folders hanging limp and rusty, marked in homage to more ordered times with the names of pupils long gone. A yellowing roll of paper set out the oath sworn by newcomers, the 'Gokajo no seimon'; against it lay a thick wodge of xeroxed sheets, all bent at one corner, detailing the timetable of the school. He shoved all this aside and pulled out various documents which he glanced at and discarded: a map of West Berlin in a shiny plastic cover; a pile of electricity bills stapled together; two curling photographs of Professor Jigoro Kano. The white-haired old man stared coldly out of the picture from drooping eyelids with pouches below, hair flattened neatly across the top of his head from a low side parting. This small piece of vanity unreasonably made him seem less, rather than more, human.

He pricked his finger on an unseen drawing pin and swallowed a curse. The bottom of the cabinet was full of old pins and rusting cartridges of staples, rubber bands holding thick, felted balls of dust and the odd hair, pencil stubs and old keys. A thick packet at the bottom seemed more promising and he pulled it out, blowing away the dust. He glanced inside and then stuffed it quickly into the inside pocket of his jacket. He remained for two long minutes on his knees, breathing in the dust and faintly fungal smell of rotting paper that emanated from a pile of Japanese martial arts magazines jammed into the heavy bottom drawer. He lifted them up. There was nothing underneath. He let the wrinkled pile drop back with a thud; a puff of dirt, a mushroom cloud, rose from below and settled on his shoes. By the time Ludwig appeared, he was leaning back on the chair, steadying it by holding his feet flat against the desk. The rackety contrivance was kept in exact balance only by the interplay of thigh muscles and rigidly braced knees.

'Ja, die Liebe ist so schön,' Ludwig sang, in a cracked voice. He took in the rigid pose, the jutting chin. 'Well, what have you got for me?'

Sigi nodded at the envelope lying on the table; there were banknotes inside.

'What's this?'

'It's finished, you've got plenty of boys for your games. I don't want to play any more. Go on, count it, it's all there.'

Slowly, Ludwig pushed it back towards him. 'Oh no,' he said, 'It's not as easy as that. You're involved. You're bought and paid for.' It was rich. He despised Sigi as much for his attempt to get out of his obligations as for his weakness in agreeing in the first place.

'I won't take it,' Sigi said. 'I'm out and you can count my brother out too.'

'Your brother? What has he to do with me? He's your worry, my dear Sigi, not mine. So you're out, are you? You find you don't like the work after all? You don't like my money any more?' His tone was soft and infinitely malicious. 'More fool you, my dear boy, for after all it can hardly make any difference, can it? What you've done, is done.' He gazed at the closed, sullen face.

'Pretty girl, Johanna? Thinking of seeing her on your own account? My poor Sigi, I wonder what she is going to think of you when she finds out how – purchasable you are.' Now his smile was broad; it encompassed a huge scorn of weakness, of failure. Sigi could not even console himself with the thought that he had acted in a just cause; he had no consolation at all.

'You leave her alone,' he said and, jerking himself to his feet, towered over Ludwig, fists clenching and unclenching, 'I want your word, that you won't interfere with her life, do you understand?'

'My dear Sigi, how very ridiculous you are being. Do you want to fight me? With pleasure, but you know you will most certainly be defeated. What do you want me to say, that I promise not to see her, or that I shall never speak to her? My poor Sigi, try to be a realist, as I am. I don't make promises, which I later regret. I don't know what will happen, tomorrow, to make me change my mind. Try to be accountable to yourself and not to others, there is a piece of advice for you.' The boy looked, at this moment, as though he would have liked to kill him; Ludwig tilted up his head and gazed, blandly, at the mottled ceiling.

'Understand this,' he said. 'That nothing is going to interfere with my plans. Not even you, with your newly-active conscience. Do you know, Sigi, I almost find it in me to feel sorry for you? Do what you want, whatever makes you happy, my dear boy. I bought you, and you were very cheap. You're very weak, very soft. A little man, yes, even smaller than I am. No, I don't think I need you, after all,' and he yawned ostentatiously and the lad, standing there with a stupid, bemused expression on his face, a look which recognised the impossibility of his doing anything at all, now turned sharply on his heel and left the room, slamming the door with all his force, so that the walls hummed with the shock and a calendar, hanging next to the door, slipped an inch on its frayed thread.

Ludwig forgot him at once. For, in truth, Sigi was redundant. Ludwig had found Victor's true love and she was a whore. It had taken him most of the night to absorb the information on the photocopied pages. In the early morning he had gone out and found a copy of yesterday's paper. It was a dirty thing, which left grubby marks on the mind akin to the film of black it smeared on the fingers. *Der Abend* set out to titillate, disguising its revelations with the name of decency. He hated its tone of lubricious shock. And Victor wanted to possess this whore; without understanding that, he felt a certain pride in such an overweening ambition, as a parent, punishing a wilful child, could still appreciate its exceptional strength of will. The man gave in to his worst impulses; he courted them with intensity. To redirect such impulses was, to use the *Abend*'s favourite editorialising phrase, a moral imperative. He smiled; it was a piece of poetic perfection, for nothing could have suited his purpose better than this. The pieces of the puzzle were coming together, arranging themselves into a whole with a precision and inevitability that even he, the master, could not have bettered.

Sigi did not have time to examine his prize; the thick packet was jammed against his rapidly beating heart. He couldn't be late. He gunned at the engine in a fury and the little car belched out its fumes with a roar of protest, stopping jerkily not far from a street lamp. The concert was at seven thirty. Twenty yards down the street stood a small familiar figure: Heini, at a shop window, staring unconvincingly at a pyramid of books. The rapid pulsating of Sigi's blood, which beat fast with loathing, above all with self-disgust, slowed to a normal rhythm. Three minutes before he had to leave, a man came through the glass doors of the old building and Heini followed him up the street. The target. Herr Genscher. Tall, good-looking, blond. About forty. With the most extreme and careful interest, Sigi watched his rival out of sight.

# Chapter 10

Thursday, December 18, 1971

It's only six thirty, but I can hear bath water running; Linda always empties Frau Beckmann's great old-fashioned hot water cauldron for the duration. She may scorn Victor utterly, but she would never miss her ritual immersion, Venus in Badedas. I'm pretending to work on my essay, but I can't stop myself listening for her movements. Just now I heard the door creak and found myself spreading out my notes in a horrible, furtive way to cover this up.

I have been on the verge of telling her a hundred times and I don't know why I don't. What can I say? Victor is a scoundrel, you were right. And I don't put it past her to accost him about his dealings and I shan't be there to hear his answers. She would commiserate with me first: equally unbearable. Fraudulent Victor, it's a topic too new, too painful, I can't begin to broach it. The proposition is not yet proven; my eager-beaver brain keeps turning it over and seeking explanations, reasons, for he must have his reasons. He has been out the whole afternoon; Fräulein Schmidt does not expect him back. Please do not trouble yourself to call again, she said with patronising insolence. I can assure you he will get your message as soon as he returns to the office. If he returns. I have called the flat a dozen times and listened to the long dull buzzing tone for minutes at a time, willing him to answer. He's not trying the effect of this tie or that; he's not lathering himself and humming. There is something about the way Linda prepares for the evening with her usual thoroughness which makes me feel slightly sick. She just buzzed in to borrow my silver necklace and pretended not to notice my guilty start. She is making every kind allowance for my vulnerable state. 'How does it look with the purple dress?' 'Terrific. Lovely.' She's even got new make-up to match. God, I must stick to neutral topics. I have an endless evening, hours of privacy to come. Now she's splashing and singing, a warbling mermaid.

A neutral topic. I don't seem to own that rare commodity. My overdue essay, perhaps. Would that be finished, if we'd not gone to the John Mayall concert? Linda's idea, so can I blame her for it? I must stop this. This senseless jealousy is wicked.

The concert. Last night Linda, a veteran of such occasions, dressed appropriately in long Indian silk scarves and an ethnic skirt in heavy felt with little mirrors sewn onto it and gaudy ric-rac. It was at the Kongresshalle and the soberly-clad middle-aged attendants were shaken rigid by the look of the audience. Hamburg's freaks, still clinging to their hippie uniform of stiff sheepskin waistcoats and faded denims, do not often grace those plush seats. Europeans, so good at romantic ballads and folk, don't seem to manufacture rock or pop stars with the same international status. Rock's always English or American, imported, an instant sell-out. When a German group actually manages a Schlager, it's always sung in English. With an American accent, naturally. She durn seema know/Har murch ah lurve her. Germans make the best hippies though, for they alone have the necessary seriousness, that Teutonic devotion to the cause. Students who neglect their work do so with great thoroughness. The Mensa is always full of long-haired types in greatcoats cutting lectures but making sure they get full value out of their subsidised lunch tickets. They support each other in studied indolence, majoring in drugs, sex and politics. They are so desperately earnest about all three that it's alarming. English laissez-faire liberalism, our celebrated understatement and self-deprecatory jokes, are all lost on them.

German nature abhors a vacuum. Our worthy professors are always talking about die Gliederung of works, allocating them to their correct place, picking and worrying away at books until they've minced up the meat on them and can form them into the right shape. I can quite see how *Werther* must have shocked the burgers in its day, how Sturm and Drang freaked them out. Now it's safe, just another category. Then, though, the sober citizens smelt a whiff of the French Revolution in *Die Räuber* and how they shuddered in their feather beds. Today's revolutionaries don't, of course, go in for lyrical expression of their case. They get together in organised cells. The Marxist groups study the great man's works one line at a time, taking a whole evening to tease out the meaning. Who but a German could stomach the notion of devoting years to one book? But they get double pleasure out of it, the pedantic study they do so well enhanced and made piquant by its anti-establishmentarianism.

No, it's not true, for there are lots of new plays. Europe is full of earnest young playwrights carefully selecting a grim and static 'situation' to unravel their theories on. There is no humour in this; it's all tension, aggression and betrayal. The emptiness of self: no wit, but heavy irony. In case we've missed the point, which is all too easy when what's unsaid is what matters, they publish their 'discussions'. Spontaneous theatre may seem formless, anarchic, avant-garde, but really it's just the modern expression of that essential seriousness.

The bare-boards, no-scenery school is the one that depresses me most. Static drama: anguished figure centre stage broods in silence; broken soliloquy by tormented outcast, etc. Of course they're saying something, it's 'valid', but oh, the boredom. They're not always young either, for look at Beckett, the worst of the lot, an éminence very grise. How can an Irishman write like that? Easy, he does it in French, he distances himself. The English language simply won't let itself be reduced in that way, unless it has the barrenness of a translation. Its richness subverts.

The new films are to the same formula: jerky, hand-held camera stares coldly at haggard, un-made-up actor staring coldly back. This is best of all in black and white. Spontaneous non-dialogue, meaningful irrelevancies, bodily obsessions. Careful excision of wit, humour, warmth, humanity in favour of bleak inner monologue. Here we go again: more stress and betrayal, touch of the surreal, youthful alienation, bleakness of age, collapse of values and so on. And these intellectual bourgeois European audiences love it, they pay fortunes to sit in their silks and watch it all. I always have the same reaction as the ignorant, observing the flat panels of colour smoothed out in the name of modern art. Give me a box of paints, or rather, give me the minimalist vocabulary, and I'd do you one of those on the cheap.

Now the Germans adopt all this no-nonsense stuff with particular enthusiasm. That's something to do with their taking their pleasures so very seriously. I met a student recently who told us the story of a friend of his who pays rent to his divorcee landlady in an unconventional manner. Every second night there is a knock on his door and off he goes to her room to pleasure her. Never impromptu, never uninvited, never on a different night: it's a business arrangement, there must be Ordnung. As Oma always says, Ordnung ist das halbe Leben. And his friend made the appropriately ponderous joke about this guy being worried about the forthcoming rent increases and we all laughed with the right measure of broad-minded malice.

I laughed too, naturally. In the human Gliederung, I fear I count as honorary German. Worse, German by choice. What do I do, but sieve and collage my miserable little history into more acceptable form, a retrospective Buchhälterin seeking form among the mass. Ordnung, in my case, being always leaving exactly the same margin, always insisting on the same size of book, so they will look neat lined up on my shelf. Sometimes I have the impression that it's my English persona that makes all the mistakes; the German one coldly makes notes and criticises.

Neither of them enjoyed the concert. There was a sudden high-pitched throbbing whine and then a great blast of sound, the muezzin to summon the faithful and off went the freaks in uniform abandonment to jump about at the front. Music to pulsate to, dancing being almost impossible. Half the seats were suddenly empty. Linda went too, that's how we lost her. Sigi was stiff with dislike. Partly, I think, a certain fastidiousness about the musky smells, the drugs, which he doesn't approve of, the trendy rags; partly the feeling I also had of being a spectator when only participants are welcome.

I can't let myself go like that. Too stiff, too bourgeois, uncomfortable without disapproving, yet likely, if alone, to conform and hop about with the rest. We watched and, after a moment, exchanged a speaking look. Then we distinguished ourselves by leaving early. We pushed our way through the thick metal doors past an usher leaning weakly against the cold wall and mopping his head in sheer disbelief at such anarchy. Sigi, who had gone to tell Linda we were going, had spotted her through the mêlée dancing with a group of girls all wearing those semi-transparent Indian maxi dresses and waved, but she didn't see him.

'She'll be all right,' he said, 'She knows how to look after herself,' whereas I, it seemed, didn't.

We went back to his place; it was, as he said, nearer. The moment had clearly come for a proper lunge on his part; by his reckoning probably overdue. And I, understanding this unspoken etiquette, was perfectly ready to give him the opportunity in order then to repulse him. So there was a half-look and a general understanding between us when we went to get the car; a complicity in the attempt, if not the outcome.

His flat is a small, modern one in a faceless but as yet undefaced block in a new housing development behind the Holstenstrasse where two big roads cross noisily. It looks down on a church and beyond the converging mass of Holstenstr. Station. Thin walls and children's crying echoing out into the concrete corridors, but his flat is quiet, sound-proofed, anonymous. Every stick of furniture was brand new, bland and modern like a KEPA sitting room. Space-saving units with sliding glass doors; smoked glass coffee table, fitted carpets, large rubber plants. Not a single old thing, nothing from the Sperrmüll, no clutter. It smelt of Pledge and plywood. Lucky you, I said, to get it with all the furniture new, but he'd gone out and bought it all himself on the never-never.

There's one bedroom, a temple to love, with a vast bed on a dais which probably has black satin sheets. Net curtains, even though he's on the twelfth floor and can't be overlooked and other curtains on top. Three books next to the bed: *Und ruhig fliesst die Donau*, a Van der Valk detective story and *Kodokan Judo*. How can I go out with somebody like that? He caught me looking at them. I haven't unpacked my personal stuff yet, he said.

We sat down awkwardly and had tea with condensed milk and brittle biscuits and I was quite rigid thinking oh no, don't lunge, for I couldn't bear it. It was the model cars that settled it: two of them sat on the glass shelves, not even coloured and realistic, but silvery, moulded and totally fake. His lack of a single item I could value and my total physical inexperience. A combination too dreadful to contemplate. The horror of it, to be found lacking by a man who's never read a classic book or for that matter even heard of Proust or James Joyce or anyone that matters. A man who knows the names of football players.

So I sat stiffly and gulped the nasty tea too fast, burning my mouth, and he turned off the main light, plunging us into romantic gloom, and put on 'A Man and a Woman', which is one of my favourites. I heard myself twitter on about how I'd have left home for Jean-Louis Trintignant when I was fourteen and impressionable and he said, but I thought it was Victor you had on your mind and I felt a hot flush of shame for having told him so much; the sensation of being paid back fully for my own stupidity.

Victor Genscher, he said, ruminating, and I sat quite still. I am sure I never mentioned his surname and I have an excellent memory. 'He isn't a bit like Trintignant,' he said. 'Same sort of age but bigger and much more dangerous-looking.' I wish I'd had the dignity to refrain from replying, but, as usual, I was bristling defensively. He said something very odd. 'This man is not reliable, he's not trustworthy. He uses people, he'll use you. You keep away from him.' It was, in the circumstances, a joke, for he doesn't really know him at all. Victor is to him that mythical beast, a friend of a friend. He was inventing it to make himself interesting, as Oma would say, out of some silly jealousy, and I thought that were they ever to meet, which is unlikely, I'd be ashamed of Sigi, of having chosen mediocrity, with the same sort of embarrassment I used to feel when introducing Oma to school friends I suddenly realised were shallow and stupid. Today, remembering what he'd said, I found it uncanny, but I was very angry with him then, I was furious and when he got up I was ready to hit at him. My heart was thudding away with some kind of dread, but he was merely fetching whisky and two glasses. Cut-glass; in a cocktail bar unit. Prost! and I needed the drink, for Dutch courage.

Neither of us spoke for a while. His face was half-lit by the lamp, the eyelashes casting huge shadows down the smooth planes of his face when he drank. We watched each other, mesmerised and immobile, and I felt a little afraid of him but also conscious of how sexy he is, with that face and powerful body and every time he reached for the glass I caught myself holding my breath in anticipation. When he slithered, at last, across the sofa, it was as the snake approaches the mongoose.

'Do you know why I wanted to see him? Because I find it incredible that any man wouldn't want you, do you understand?' and he said it with enormous anger, but very quietly. We stared at each other. Part of me hated him, then, and part was aching for him to touch me, but he didn't, he stopped six inches away.

'I would like to go to bed with you, Johanna. You are a most – exceptional girl. But now would be the wrong time, not now, not today,' and he still was angry, but his face was giving out a different message altogether. I must have had the silliest look on my face; positively piqued, at being denied my refusal, and not knowing what to say, for I was ready to argue, to be cross, and he had just cut the ground away, leaving me both relieved and disappointed. So we just looked at each other and suddenly both began to laugh, and couldn't stop. I must have shrieked for ten minutes. I had tears streaming down my face; every time I looked at him it bubbled up again.

After that we became natural again and pleasant, and it was very innocent. He curled up like a puppy on the sofa and grinning, daring me to say no, put his head on my lap and closed his eyes and promptly fell asleep. I can't decide whether he is very clever or stupid. I must have sat there for an hour, with one leg going numb, and stroked his hair which smelt deliciously of shampoo and he smiled in his sleep.

I didn't get home until very late. I woke him in the end and we drove home without saying much, each of us in our different ways thinking that something was settled. I was ready to assert myself, to say I wouldn't see him again, but he took me so much for granted that he didn't even try to fix a date. Where can it lead to, after all? Sigi the cul-de-sac; Victor the highway to perdition. A Department of Works melodrama.

This morning Linda, the very picture of virtue, gave me a most old-fashioned look. I don't suppose you'll be telling Ingrid and your auntie about last night, she said, miffed at having to clear up; put out by my unusual, early-morning assault with the duster. She wouldn't stay for them. I'll go to town, she said, I'll amuse myself; I got in early, unlike some and, in the same breath, well did you or didn't you?

She's gone. She went five minutes ago in the purple dress with my necklace and black silk stockings, worn for her own pleasure naturally. And shoes he is certainly not fit to lick, black patent leather ones with four-inch heels. For God's sake don't worry, she said with emphasis as she left. This is beginning to be a phrase people throw at me. 'Don't worry', like 'Don't get excited', expressions guaranteed to work anyone up into a frenzy.

I have simply got to see Victor. I want to be a fly on the wall; at the same time I want to be Linda, just for tonight. He gives me the creeps, she said, just you remember that. I'm glad I didn't tell her. It's my job, not hers, to protect the family interests. I have wasted hours of my life dreaming up excuses to see him, compelling reasons to meet, and now that I've got one I feel sick.

I knew something was up as soon as they arrived. Tante Mausi was particularly twitchy. She was laden with cakes and a weighty parcel containing the Bock family's newest tribute to German womanhood's dewy beauty, a range of creams and skin tonics called 'Frühlingsfrische'. She rushed around, still clutching her parcels admiring everything with effusive kindness. Her faded friendly eyes, rimmed with startling turquoise, zig-zagged around madly to take in every detail and praise. She is always nice, the nicest person I know, but so nervous and all the more so in the presence of the ice maiden. Without uttering a word, Ingrid manages to put her mother in the wrong.

Ingrid's pallor had a certain glow, which couldn't just be the bracing effect of the stair temperature between limo and flat. She was all lit up with news of some kind. I can always tell when Ingrid's got something on me from her way of tilting her nose up a fraction higher in order to stare down it more effectively. She had a good look round my bedroom while I hung up Tante Mausi's coat, preferring to spread her own couture offering on my fur bedcover rather than risk it next to the downmarket rags in my wardrobe. Ingrid suffers slightly from the knowledge that Rommer's is both bigger and wealthier than Bock's, a chagrin she has always managed to overcome by a great deal of spending. 'You look well,' she said, computing the small cost of my plain, neat sweater and skirt against her cream pleated affair. She had ribbed cream tights on, a perfect match of course, for Ingrid's neat muscular legs are her best feature, and one of those crocodile bags on a long chain and matching shoes, the sort with Gucci links across them that are de rigueur in her set. I feel less sorry for the crocodiles knowing they've found a home from home.

So I opened the first bottle of Sekt and we had soup with Knödel, the cunning deceptive combination of one of Oma's glass jars and a packet, which I remembered to hide. Ingrid sipped at it delicately, spreading her napkin with care to avoid sullying her perfection. Tante Mausi praised the soup and started admiring the gold-rimmed crockery, which is Frau Beckmann's third best set, and would perhaps have gone on to the cutlery, but Ingrid broke in and said Mama, don't you think we ought to tell Johanna what we have heard, for she is not one to shrink from an unpleasant duty. She didn't mince her words. Victor is in trouble. The bank is refusing him a large loan he must have to buy, of all things, *Der Abend*. She pursed her lips up at such a sensational choice. The bank was reluctant but willing, she said, according to Peter Prick, but now they have changed their minds. It's the putative best man who's in on the deal. He told Peter that Victor has already bought a considerable block of shares in the open market, not only using his money but the liquid float: that means Oma's money. You see, she said, in a patient way as if talking to a child, if the deal doesn't go through, and it won't, without the bank, Peter says it's unlikely the paper will find another buyer. He says prospective buyers have lost interest because it's losing so much money, only a very rich man could afford it. He says they're likely to close and if they do all the money is lost. I had to warn you, she said, for Oma's sake and yours, but Peter doesn't know I'm telling you. It's very unethical to break a confidence, you must never tell anyone I told you. Ingrid had clearly tussled with her ethical conundrum and altruism won the day. It may have been without a selfish thought in her head that she spilled the beans, but I just wonder if she was thinking about her eventual small share. She added a rider: her clever, knowing Peter had said that nobody in his right mind would buy shares in it now. So that is Victor disposed of.

Tante Mausi, though, had tears in her eyes. 'Of course Peter knew you would tell Johanna,' she said, and Ingrid snapped no, certainly not. Poor Tante Mausi rallied. 'Of course it will be all right, don't worry,' she said, and then 'I am so unhappy for Mutti,' and she quite broke down and it took several more glasses of Sekt to restore her. Money is always a serious matter to Ingrid; the prospect of losing some of her own knitted up those finely plucked brows. She kept insisting that Peter and Uwe can't tell Oma to sell the shares, that it's a breach of confidence and we had to be discreet, whatever we did. I admired my own calmness; that's another of Ingrid's salutory effects upon me. I couldn't break down with her watching.

We sat after that in silence for a while and then, over more drinks, started on old family history. We went through all the ritualised history, that honoured way of facing disaster, as though we were already at Rommer's wake. Ingrid suffered this nonsense with a patient, pitying smile. She never urges her mother to greater feats of memory, as I do. For her the past is dead: a sentimental appendage other people have.

It's nine thirty. I keep picking up the phone to call Oma

and putting it down again. I think the telegram was a mistake: it will frighten her, which worries me, but what is the use of calling when I have nothing to add? I have an unparalleled ability to make things sound wrong. I am clock-watching as avidly as Uwe Schenck. How slowly the hands move; no doubt he thought the same. His inscrutability, his manic hilarity were a deciding factor in the telegram. A panic decision, from the need to do something at once. I should never have wasted my time with him; I should have gone straight to Victor.

He is smiling at Linda now, waiting for the main course. She'll have downed her aperitif and munched a handful of peanuts. Victor will have advised with his usual savoir-faire what's best to eat. He will have selected something both choice and appropriate from the wine list. I know the restaurant well: a smart one, his favourite, with peach upholstery and intimate little alcoves to hold hands in.

I have thought it out very carefully; it's easy, knowing the timing so well. I know exactly what he will do. At eleven thirty he will glance at his gold watch, ruefully, with his charming little grimace – how time flies when you're enjoying yourself – and he will run Linda home in his great car, speeding just a little on the straight stretches of the Elbchaussee. Meanwhile I shall be on my way to his flat and when he gets back I shall be waiting for him.

Nine forty-three; how can it go so slowly?

The afternoon shot by. The instant they left I was on the phone to Schenck, whose snooty secretary hummed and ha'ed and then grudgingly said all right, if you come straight away. I rushed, burningly hot from the over-heated train and in the next moment cold with fear. I should have known.

'My dear Fräulein Rommer, there is absolutely nothing for you to worry about,' he said in reassuring, false joviality. His is a name for a footballer, not a banker. Clearly his parents hoped for better things. We had the most evasive and odd conversation, exacerbated by his wanting to talk about nothing at all and by my difficulty in saying everything while giving nothing away.

What a pleasant surprise to see me, he said, coming right out of the office and past Fräulein Wichtigkeit to greet me like a long-lost pal and he busied himself getting her to scurry around for English tea, that delicate compliment, for an ashtray, then for a lighter, and so on. There were copies of *Horse and Hound* and *Country Life* on his desk. Now wasn't the Ratsweinkeller an excellent restaurant? and he settled back, ready to give up his valuable time in gastronomic mouthings. He's one of those people who smile and chuckle a lot when they don't have anything much to say, filling the void with good cheer, so you have to smile back as though they'd been tremendously witty. No doubt he has an excellent reputation as a good chap down at the club. He had written all over him the knowledge that he knew that I knew that he knew and nothing was going to induce him to admit to a thing. He is taller than I'd remembered and has the onset of a banker's belly under his blue and white stripe shirt, though he can't be much over thirty. He smells strongly of soap and has round pink cheeks and round blue eyes and the effect is of a hugely elongated baby.

We discussed the weather and Ingrid's wedding plans and he seemed quite ready to discourse on the choice of hymns, or, if I preferred, the furbelows of her pure white dress if that would consume his twenty minutes. He kept gazing at the absurd international clock on his wall; a huge plaque with a metal map of the world, the seas done in shiny copper, with a digital clock at the side and chrome name places sticking out in relief and all the international times ever-moving down the side. It's the German banker's equivalent of the sunburst clock, a large executive rattle, and he looked as though he wished he could shake it and magically whisk ahead to Bangkok or Peking time.

'Are you going to Ascot this summer?' he said, just like that, a propos no doubt of ritual clothing, and said, 'I don't like flat racing much myself,' chortling away at his wit and saying that Schockemöhle was his hero, and I had a vision of that belly resting on a saddle, bouncing up and down clippety-clop and the blue eyes staring out from under a hard black cap. He'd been to marvellous point-to-pointing in Gloucestershire, he said, with a little smirk to underpin his savoir-faire in not saying Glow-cester-shire, and I tried to think of something obliging to say back. The only horsy memory I could summon up was the televised Horse of the Year Show with all those identikit men in black jackets jumping Humpty-Dumpty cardboard walls and going round and round a sawdust ring with the Queen watching, and how we used to stampede to the box to switch it off.

He was a brick wall of indifferent good humour; to humour him was pointless, so I said I wanted to concern myself with the firm's affairs since I was now of age and had to be briefed on current activities. Of course, he would be delighted, he said smiling hugely and benevolently, and perhaps he and Victor could take me out to lunch one of these days? I was not – yet – a partner, he said with a little laugh, and it was for Herr Genscher to divulge such information. Victor was not a topic any more; there were no compliments about his superb intellect and no jolly laughs over his brilliance, which perhaps has faded a little. Well, could I have information just on the current major acquisition? and he chuckled at this good joke and denied me in the politest possible way. Really, he said, there was nothing for me to be worrying about and soon enough I would be an active partner, nicht wahr? And then, and I can hardly believe it happened, he said with a sentimental sigh that he envied Peter his bride and how much he wanted to settle down and marry the right girl and he gave me a great, glassy wink and burst into peals of aw-aw guffaws like some loony old delinquent. A moment later his secretary was simpering firmly in the doorway with the next client in tow and, this time, a great sheaf of files under one arm. See you at the wedding! he called out merrily as I went.

It was a farce. I decided on the way home to send the telegram and just made it to the post office in time. I wish I knew what time she'll get it. I was the last to be served and afterwards soothed my nerves with a small, burningly hot and bitter cup of coffee and the necessary cigarette in the stand-up Tchibo opposite.

It is still only ten fifteen. Linda has been persuaded into a pudding. Afterwards she is always on the look-out for the goodies, petits fours and chocolates. In middle age she will be one of those stout, highly finished madams with an enormous pneumatic bosom and there will be a streak or two of peroxide by then on those curls. She'll probably be running a casino in

Rio or on a yacht on the Mediterranean. She'll be terrifically popular and people will say she's a 'character'.

It is not exactly that I don't trust Linda. I simply don't know what goes on in her head half the time. I don't know where she went today and whom she met for lunch. A man, of course, but she was evasive. She does things without worrying, she lives for present pleasures. Enviable, like a child's life, every moment counting. Not for Linda the if only ifs. Perhaps she's right. The rest of us are so frozen in our time warps, Ingrid ever waiting, me picking over my unresolved past. Perhaps that is why I don't, quite, trust Linda not to do some impulsive thing. That is why I am so reluctant to tell her about the shares. She'll know she was right about Victor all along. And since she dislikes him so much, why am I worrying? If only she weren't so very precisely Victor's type, a walking cliché of everything I know he likes in a woman.

I should be thinking about my grandmother. Tomorrow we'll talk; I hope that Victor is going to be very convincing. For all her robustness, she is not strong. She is an old lady after all and how she hates to worry about anything, and money in particular. She has such utter trust in the firm, in the dividends arriving as surely as the sun rises and sets. Her eyes light up when the envelope arrives with 'die Ausschüttung', she saves the opening, a ritual pleasure, for special delectation alongside a good cup of coffee and a tiny, medicinal brandy. Opa never breathed a syllable if he was even contemplating a slightly risky proposition as it gave her stomach upsets. Her generation remembers going shopping with a suitcase full of money; she has a horror of inflation and of debts and studies the exchange rate in the paper daily to reassure herself that she profits by it.

Oma rushes off to the gas board the moment the bill hits the mat, as though to keep it in the house for five minutes would stain her reputation. The word overdraft is as appalling to her as the wickedest vice. She trusts Victor absolutely, that is as far as his business sense is concerned. Our interests are the same, she always says. Herr Tiedemann has standing instructions to invest from her large liquid float in the stock Victor recommends with no need to consult her and she has always been pleasantly surprised by the results.

Oma is a thrifty soul. We have a cupboard full of neatly folded sheets of slightly used brown paper and huge balls of different bits of string, carefully knotted. Her pencils survive to their last inch; she writes shopping lists on bus tickets and marches off with her huge basket in strawberry or peach season to make sure of great mounds of these expensive fruits, at the best price, for her to preserve. The larder is full of her huge glass jars with rubber seals: pickles and jam, apricots in brandy, Sauerkraut, apple and pear mousse and tiny baby carrots with sliced-up beans. It is akin to a scandal in our house to open a tin of 'expensive rubbish'.

On the rare occasions when Oma spends money on herself, it is always foundations. Corsets and girdles, items of lasting value. She is proud of her figure and for years has been having these garments made for her in the latest colours and designs. Twice annually she visits a lady corsetière for a series of fittings; each year both discover with pleasure that she has not gained an inch. For the winter she has long bras that reach to the waist with dozens of hooks and eyes behind; in the summer she wears an outrageously skimpy version of the same. The summer bras, which Linda and I used to call Brunnhildes, have giant sturdy spans of elastic supplemented by cotton panels in lilac and coffee, pale pink and delicate grey. Once, flushed at her daring, giggling like a girl at the wicked extravagance of it, she showed me a garment hidden under a dozen layers of tissue paper in sinful, Folies Bergère black; a set of underclothes which Oma considered the height of decadence and which encased her solidly from the armpits to just above the knees. She budgets, carefully, for these follies. They are, she says, not a luxury but an investment. There is not a day of her life when Oma hasn't known exactly how much money she has in each of her various bank accounts, to the very last penny. Thank God, it's eleven o'clock at last. They will be drinking coffee; Linda will have some liqueur to sip at; she's regaling him with some of her stories and he'll be watching her as he does, smiling courteously but inside sitting in judgment.

I shan't change for him, I'm going just as I am. No perfume, no high heels. I would like myself better if that had happened naturally, if it hadn't been such a conscious decision.

168

# Chapter 11

As he crossed the road, Victor could feel that their heads were swivelling to watch him. He had grown sensors, which told him that they had moved off, that they followed a dozen paces behind, silent, soft-soled. Sometimes, in the evenings, he would think them gone and then the hairs would rise on the back of his neck and somewhere among the shadows a small, dark mass turned itself into the outline of a boy. There were half a dozen of them, in all, and though he never looked directly he knew them. A series of impressions, of outlines, was stamped into the cortex of his brain. Now, as he walked, he felt them slouching behind, felt the eyes on his back and one hand clenched in the pocket of the navy cashmere coat.

He had a vivid mental image of scything them down; saw the sharp blade whistling towards the thin, animal legs. He had been seeing, in short, bright flashes, a revolver butt beating on a bleeding mouth. The image, in continual action replays, had become imbued with a kind of tender nostalgia. The swift brutality of these fantasies corresponded to his needs.

It was Friday and as the moment grew nearer when he would see Ludwig again, he imagined crushing him, as a foot might stamp down on a beetle and crack it, like a nut. He felt surges of anger that this excrescence should have survived.

The shadows were drawing in, they seemed to him to come ever nearer, and behind their menace lay the broken mouth twisted into a hideous grimace of pleasure. In his mind, he likened Ludwig to a loathsome, flat grey thing found under a stone that remains still for a second as the light hits it and then scuds blindly away, thin veins pulsating on its slimy skin. His sensible, rational mind was full of such images; there had come a moment the previous day when they had ceased to be voluntary and he had felt invaded by them. Standing in the bright bathroom, propped against the bath, he had shaken his head to clear them away and seen a strange, wild face in the mirror, an old man's face. The brilliant light made it look bleak, it etched new furrows in his cheeks. Staring into the shaving mirror he had looked for minutes at the giant pores and traced the cruel lines. Now, as he walked, his tongue like a furtive night animal would dart out and press newly formed ulcers in painful, continuous confirmation of their presence.

He had made the error, then, of calling Heidi; had spent the afternoon in her soft bed chasing away the demons with love-making that had left him satisfactorily blank for an hour. His ardour had awakened new expectations that he would not fulfil. Having set himself to charm her out of her pouting sulks, he found he disliked her more than ever for her feigned coolness, her too-eager subsequent acquiescence.

The bank had called and requested an appointment. He carried a sheaf of papers in his case, which swung at his side with a rhythm of its own, syncopated to each steady beat of his right foot against the pavement. The movement soothed his restlessness. Herr Kortner, like Heidi, wanted to be wooed and comforted, soothed against the risk of his own under-taking. And yet the banker had found the project fascinating. How like a woman it was, to say yes and afterwards seek justification.

As he passed through the revolving doors and placed himself in the custody of the blue-uniformed official who would conduct him up to the sixth floor, Victor was thinking about Linda Davenport. She had a vitality that was infectious; she ate with real appetite like a healthy, exuberant animal; her skin and hair had a sheen that made other women look tired.

She had the directness, almost brusqueness, he associated with the English.

'Well,' she'd said, even in the act of sitting down, 'I'm sure you want to see me for a reason. What is it?'

To be that young had seemed, at that moment, infinitely desirable.

'So, you want to talk about Jo,' she said, and for an instant he'd not understood the soft English dz. 'Good, so do I.' Her fluent, mangled German started each phrase confidently and sidestepped such awkward issues as genders and declensions; her verbs were conjugated with anarchic facility. 'Let's talk in English,' she said, 'I want to be absolutely clear.'

Victor, who had thought to approach the subject with delicacy, had been astonished by her forthrightness; their sudden intimacy. He didn't know any women who spoke like this. She breached the verbal stockade that he took for granted in the male-female war, that barricade behind which each party concealed their evident, but unspoken ambitions, each protagonist considering it a success if he or she nudged the fortifications a centimetre closer to the other side.

'She's mad about you, you must know that,' she had said, and, 'It's time something was done to sort it out once and for all.' He could not understand why she chose to tell him this and to expose her friend so cruelly; he would never have asked that question, but she divined it from his face and answered it directly.

'You know,' she had said, 'I've never liked you very much, I mean, I'm enjoying this evening (here Victor had raised his glass in salute) but I don't approve of you, not for Jo. But you're like me, a doer, not a talker, not a romantic. I care about her, I want her to be happy. And she's, somehow, stuck, she needs to get you out of her mind. I give you due warning, I shan't help you one bit to get near to her. I'm on the other side. But I want something to happen all the same, do you understand?'

'Of course I understand,' he had said and they had both laughed, hers a bubbly giggle, and she had sat back then, with the air of one who had done her duty, and carried on talking, a warm lively girl, silky and perfumed. She had insulted him quite in the English style, without rancour, and even while he absorbed this news, knowing how to turn it to his advantage, he felt a small pang of regret that it couldn't have been her. A part of his mind quite automatically calculated his chances with her and concluded that he had none; this made her all the more desirable. He thought that Linda would not achieve what she wanted, nor as it happened would he.

He had prolonged the evening beyond its usual course with more coffee, another brandy; she had regaled him with stories about a Hamburg he barely recognised, with an amusing series of encounters with types he knew existed, but would never meet. She was perfectly conscious of her own sexuality; feminine to the extreme, but without employing the usual artifices. Yes, she would flirt with him, and enjoy it, but she warned him that there was nothing doing, not with the half-gestures he knew so well how to overcome, but with direct words. Come back to my flat, he had said, I want to talk about Johanna, and she had given him an acute, penetrating look and said, fine, why not, but don't think you're getting anything else. And, unlike most women, she meant it. They had gone, had talked of Johanna, that necessity his excuse, with Linda trying in her inimitable way now to put him off. He had teased her with his sudden interest. He had shown her around, for the pleasure of trying her out in his setting; he compared her with Heidi, with past amours whom he had never brought there. For Linda, he would have been happy to make an exception. She had a brightness that filled a room, that made the chilling, silent wakefulness of the night to come the lonelier.

Victor advanced to greet little Herr Kortner with a smile compounded of all these ironies. In the junior boardroom portraits of long-gone worthies hung on thick ropes and gazed calmly down at their successors. These reinforcements did not today suffice Herr Kortner, who had waxed enthusiastic over the project often enough in convivial tête à têtes with Herr Genscher. My two assistants, he said, and Victor shook hands with the swarthy Herr Holm, pressed the pink palm of Herr Schenck, and turned a mildly surprised eye upon his backer.

Herr Kortner sat stiffly in the uncomfortable, brass-studded chair, removing and replacing the blotting paper in its leather holder, each clumsy movement the signal of an acutely embarrassed man. He opened his mouth, then thought better of it. Pressing his full red lips together he glanced at a document. His face took on an unfamiliar, formal expression.

'I am sorry to have to tell you, Herr Genscher, that the Bank has decided it is unable to proceed with the loan.' His voice, over-confident and too loud in the hush, was obliged to proceed at the same excessive volume and seemed to Victor to boom into his skull.

Silence. The young men stared at the floor, the three of them exaggeratedly still. Victor waited. Herr Kortner, perforce, carried on.

'We have given your application a great deal of consideration,' he said. 'We value our long relationship with Rommer's as you know. But this is a, um, a particularly risky field.' Now his voice was taking on a more confiding and apologetic tone, the wooden phrases modulated as though they were saying something quite different.

Silence; the young men looked expectantly at Victor, who had not moved. He had the impression that they were acting a play for his benefit; that in a moment the curtain would fall and they would become normal again. He waited, now, for Herr Kortner to talk himself out. Kortner licked his lips. He had said to Victor, 'I can't see any reason why it shouldn't sail through,' and, 'Of course you're the sort of client the Bank likes best. Old firm, good name, fine business.' The room was very hot. A ray of sunshine miraculously penetrated the grey clouds and blocked out a bright rectangle on the table; now a million tiny motes of dust pulsated in its path. Victor's eyes rested on this brightness and absorbed the infinite detail of the fine grain; his tongue, tracing the line where two leaves of the table met, pushed hard and deliberate against the inflamed skin of his palate.

Kortner could not bear the silence.

'Our directors have of course the final veto,' he said and, growing voluble, 'Please understand me Herr Genscher, when I say this in no manner reflects upon your own creditworthiness or standing at the Bank. It is the nature of the business which concerns us. We do not see, um, how it can be made to pay.' Again, he licked dry lips. 'We have certainly studied your, ah, documentation very thoroughly, extremely carefully indeed. It is what you might call a leap into the unknown. Frankly, Herr Genscher, *Der Abend* is a very difficult, a very troubled concern and the Bank does not feel prepared to take the risk.' In the deep hush, the sound of Herr Kortner swallowing was perfectly audible, the tiny gulping noise of a frog. 'Personally, I ah, sincerely regret this whole unhappy business. I am sure it will make no difference to the, um, excellent relationship we have always enjoyed.'

At last he was winding up. His colleagues, as though released from imprisonment, were shuffling, crossing legs. Uwe Schenck leant forwards and pushed the folder he held five centimetres towards the centre of the table, as if to say, here, we wash our hands of it, and earned a black look from his superior for his pains. And still Victor did not speak; the two younger men exchanged expressive looks. Both anticipated that in their usual, short unofficial conference some moments hence they would exhibit immature glee at having been in on such an unusual event; at having caught old Kortner with egg on his face. This anticipatory Schadenfreude was restrained by the difficulty of departing; they couldn't just leave him there, like a statue.

'Rommer's has a credit balance. The firm has banked with you for twenty-five years; you may recall a lunch to celebrate that event last year.' Victor spoke so quietly that they had to lean forwards to hear him. Herr Kortner, who knew these facts perfectly well, stammered a little.

'Yes, w-well, naturally we –'

'I myself have introduced a number of new clients.' Smoothly, Victor proceeded. 'You, Herr Kortner, have financed several ventures for us, all highly profitable.' Turning his head now, he fixed him with a look so violent that Kortner involuntarily recoiled.

'Yes, yes –'

'You've had your say,' he said unpleasantly. 'I shall spare your embarrassment by reminding you of your own statements about this project. Your, shall we call it, boyish enthusiasm. Your opinion clearly doesn't count. So one conclusion only remains, which is that something or some-body has interfered. I want to know who. You, Kortner, tell me who.'

Herr Kortner has profoundly shocked, as much by the reference which he took to denigrate his 1.65 metres as by such insolence in his own building. Conscious, moreover, that there was an element of truth in what Genscher said, he was for a moment unable to reply. Looking to his colleagues for help, he noticed with dismay that that fool Schenck was blushing. A wave of pink colour rose from the starched white collar encircling his soft throat and even touched his ears. 'The decision was made by the board of directors,' he said, staring at Schenck, who had taken out a handkerchief as though to mop his glowing face and, thinking better of it, began instead to crease one side into tiny pleats. 'Do you wish to add something, Herr Schenck?' he addressed his junior with heavy irony.

'May I have a word in private?' the unfortunate young man said and let out a trilling, inappropriate laugh.

Victor, left alone, relaxed his face for a moment in a sudden manic grimace. The air seemed thick, a stuffiness of heat and dust and what he thought was the smell of money. His veins throbbed with it, and with an angry rage.

Outside the gentlemen conferred in whispers. Herr Kort-ner, who wanted nothing more than to be shot of the whole business as soon as possible, vented his spleen upon the idiot Schenck. For once, dedicated career-man that he was, Kortner had actually made a small fuss about this decision; he had been put in his place in a way that rankled. He, as usual, was left with the unpleasant job of telling the client, without being able to tell the truth. The bank knew that this deal would never come off. An in-house rescue operation was in progress and would shortly be announced, pre-empting any outside buyers. They might have said yes to the loan, knowing it would never go through, but that was not how they did things. He could not even give his client the small consolation of knowing that this refusal made no difference to his chances. No outsider would ever get the *Abend*; he had heard it himself from the lips of the editor-in-chief.

They re-entered the room and Kortner tried to smile. 'I must apologise for my colleague,' he said with polite acidity. 'A misunderstanding. Fräulein Rommer visited him yesterday. She was interested in details of the loan, but naturally he told her nothing. He suggested, quite properly, that you, my dear Herr Genscher, were better placed to impart any information, if you so desired. That is all.' He was using the tone of patronising condescension a superior could adopt to rebuke his junior in public; implicit was the understanding that he and Herr Genscher were allied in superiority to the junior men; that they could part on this tone. But Herr Genscher, staring at the light as though transfixed by it, refused to let him off.

'Fräulein Rommer has nothing to do with it,' he said in a quiet, caressing tone. He was even smiling. 'I know who's behind it, I'm not a fool.' The sharp salty pain in his mouth as he spoke was almost pleasurable. 'I've worked for this, I've always made everything for myself.' He leant back, but two hands rested lightly on the table-top. His voice was pitched so low that the three men again craned to hear. 'I'm not dependent on a fat-arsed banker behind a desk. I'll get the money elsewhere. But you're finished, Kortner, I'll make sure of that, and you can forget the special relationship with Rommer's.' The voice sank to a whisper, yet it measured out each word with slow intensity. Herr Kortner sat like a man in a trance.

'Your career's over, Kortner – not mine. You're finished.' He said this with the quietest, surest finality, with his charming, urbane smile, and Herr Kortner could not suppress a shudder. 'Dead and buried, mein lieber Herr Kortner.' They were perfectly still, watching him, as he sauntered from the room; they remained so for a further minute.

Only then did Herr Holm and Herr Schenck dare to glance at one another. Herr Kortner, whose eyes remained fixed on the now-empty chair, on the neat set of fingerprints left on the shining mahogany, finally rose.

'Such language,' Schenck said in his archest, high-comedy voice. Herr Kortner gave him a look of the purest dislike.

'Would you come along to my office, Schenck, right away,'

he said. He had, at least, the comfort of releasing his anxieties in the traditional manner: by creating an equal or preferably greater stress in the mind of his junior.

The chill air, coming from a sky now slate-coloured and threatening snow, was pleasant on Victor's face and he opened his mouth to let it flow in. How simple it had all become. He had to eliminate Ludwig and then find a new backer. No. First Johanna, who could not be allowed to meddle. He had the timetable for action, at last. He quickened his pace, weaving through the crowd of Christmas shoppers, and inhaled great gulps of the delicious, icy air, which seemed to mount into his head with cold, cleansing effect.

It was this rapid progress which drew the eye of Herr Tiedemann. Planted outside the glass doors of the Rommer building, he was scanning the street through the jammed traffic. Fräulein Schmidt, at the office window above, had a far superior view of events. Her mug of coffee rested on the window sill. She was spooning in sugar, her slightly humped back in its bright emerald sweater blocking what little light could penetrate on such a dark day.

She watched Herr Genscher approach with the usual thrill of pleasure, as though he hurried for her benefit. Anna Schmidt was in the habit of embellishing her account of office doings to her married friend, fabricating a romance ever trembling on the brink of accomplishment. Though she always listened avidly, Jutta, looking pityingly at the hump, could not believe that Herr Genscher was as handsome and, well, as interested as Anna said. Fräulein Schmidt looked forward to astonishing Jutta with his magnificence, one day soon.

She confined these elaborate daydreams to her leisure hours and prided herself on her efficiency in office time. She would never have been found gawping out of the window in that vulgar way, were it not for Herr Tiedemann's extraordinary behaviour. He had been taking a long-distance call from England for the past fifteen minutes. She knew it was, most unusually, Frau Rommer, for she had put her through herself. Working her way busily through a stack of invoices, tearing them off at the perforations with a satisfying rip, she had become aware of unusual motion behind the glass partition. Herr Tiedemann's large fleshy hand gestured in the air. He had noticed her looking and then actually turned his back to carry on the conversation. Of course nothing could be heard through the glass wall and for half a minute she had been tempted to pick up the receiver, very gently. She didn't, of course. He had snapped the receiver down so hard she almost thought she heard it; his face had turned that dull brick colour it sometimes did. He had marched straight out without even putting on his coat.

Fräulein Schmidt had listened to the click of his metal-tipped soles on the stairs, an agitated, hurrying click, before rising and going to the tea and coffee cupboard conveniently near the window. He was just standing there. He was waiting for Herr Genscher, something he'd never done before. She stared down at the foreshortened figure leaning forwards, now raising an arm to wave an urgent summons.

Herr Genscher was drawing level. Fräulein Schmidt could see two youths behind him, so close they almost grazed his heels. She saw one nod to the other; they sprang forwards and now walked one on either side of him; she stared in amazement as one darted out a hand towards his briefcase. Horrified, she rapped smartly on the window.

'Aufpassen!'

Behind her, Herr Goldberg rose. He almost had to shoulder her out of the way to see.

Herr Genscher pulled the briefcase tight against his chest; hugging it, he ran straight over the road towards Herr Tiedemann; those hooligans were right behind him and, with the lights about to change to green, all three just leapt onto the pavement in time. They swayed, all four figures in a confused cluster dominated by the blond head; Fräulein Schmidt pressed her bony nose against the pane to see better and another spoonful of sugar slid, half into the mug, half onto the sill. My God, in broad daylight, my God, and she saw a tangle of arms, reaching, and held her breath in alarm and excitement. Now the blond head stepped back; one arm swung the case round aiming for a youth, who side-stepped nimbly. A shriek leapt out of Fräulein Schmidt and condensed on the

178

window. The cluster suddenly separated out; Herr Tiedemann's mighty bulk was toppling, right into the road and he crashed, unable to save himself, right into the path of the huge van and the sudden squeal of brakes penetrated right into the office.

Fräulein's Schmidt's eyes were squeezed shut. Tentatively, after a moment, she opened them. Now the scene was confused, for a crowd was gathering and in it she could see Herr Genscher, just, but there was no sign of the youths. Automatically, she raised her hand and sipped the coffee, which tasted cloyingly sweet. Bewildered, she put it down and, collecting herself, pushed past Herr Goldberg and ran across to telephone for an ambulance. She flung her coat across her narrow shoulders before running downstairs to become another figure on the pavement in a confused jumble of people, a babble of voices saying move him to the side, no don't, give him a coat for a pillow, cover him up, while in a background rumble the van driver could be heard explaining to anyone who would listen that it wasn't his fault and irritated drivers behind, who could not see the reason for the hold-up, overlaid the whole with a cacophony of blaring horns.

An ambulance eventually inched its way in and took the immobile figure off in a blaze of headlights and sirens and Herr Genscher with it. Fräulein Schmidt took it upon herself to telephone Frau Tiedemann and tell the poor woman that there had been a terrible accident, but she was not to worry and, assuming another small piece of responsibility, that she was sending a taxi to take her to the hospital right away.

Lotte immediately assumed that her Otto was dead, or as good as. She put on her coat and sat waiting for the cab which, delayed by the heavy traffic, took nearly an hour to make its way out of the congested centre. By this time she had drunk three quarters of a bottle of vodka straight from the bottle and had to be helped, giggling helplessly, onto the back seat where she lay in a state of collapse. There was no question of her being allowed to see her husband, not in that state. The nurse, a stout Berliner, jabbed her stubby hand into the small of Frau Tiedemann's back, propelling her with perhaps unnecessary force into the small waiting room. The doctors were still with

Herr Tiedemann; she could not in any case have seen him, but the nurse with her cynical view of mankind preferred to let the little woman contemplate her own shortcomings during the long wait.

It was very quiet in the office until Herr Genscher returned. Fräulein Schmidt, solemn with self-importance, began to give him her account of the whole incident and was dismissed with a wave as he proceeded on into his office. She followed, after a moment's panicky reflection, and he, lifting the receiver from the phone, gazed at her coldly as she asked after dear Herr Tiedemann. 'It's concussion,' he said, 'he'll be fine,' and dialled. Fräulein Schmidt, who knew her duty, told him that it was a telephone call from Frau Rommer which had agitated dear Herr Tiedemann to such an extent, uttering these words very slowly and deliberately, with a strong note of disapproval.

'Hello, Johanna?' he said and, covering the receiver, motioned her away. As she backed slowly from the room, Fräulein Schmidt heard him say that he would like to go and see that girl. Intent on his conversation, he did not even look up, did not even see her angry moue of distaste. She, who had been heroic, who would appear more so in her account to Jutta that evening, hurried out into the hallway. Safe on the cold lavatory seat, she burst into a passion of angry, frustrated tears.

He was looking at his watch when the phone buzzed; one fifteen precisely. Four hours had gone by. Bloody Wolfgang. His truculence transmuted Sigi's sharp disappointment into acute irritation and he interrupted, brusquely.

'You're a big boy, you're so proud of yourself, you sort out your own bloody problems.'

Wolf's voice turned sly. 'Well I'll have to call Mutti then. It'll upset her. But she won't leave her little boy stranded in town. Heini buggered off with all my cash.'

Sigi exhaled his annoyance.

'Come on Sigi,' the voice said, wheedling. 'Look you can't

just leave me here in the shit can you? What'm I going to do?'

'You fucking arsehole,' and Sigi looked again at his splendid watch. 'I'll come. This is the last time I'm ever going to do anything for you. Where are you?'

Wolf was not one to show gratitude or pleasure, but, getting into the Alfa, he let out a sigh of relief.

'You took your time,' he said. There was a trickle of blood around one nail where he had gnawed at the cuticles down to the quick and ripped away a raw red segment; he had sucked his thumb until he was a good ten years old. The traffic was so slow that they made virtually no headway and Sigi tapped his fingers impatiently on the wheel. The pretty girl in the Volkswagen alongside looked at his handsome profile and smiled winningly, but he didn't look her way. There was a kid in the car, talking with violent gestures into the air. She shrugged her shoulders, she fiddled with the dial of the radio.

Sigi could not find it in himself to offer his brother the slightest crumb of comfort; he wanted him to suffer. He was babbling about it being an accident, but nothing Wolfgang did was accidental. Sigi wanted him to weep and howl. He executed a U-turn outside the shabby building which made the wheels spin, and saw the gangling dolt in his idiot shoes trip on the low step. His head was pounding with anxiety. She called the old man Uncle, and now he was dead or maimed. Jesus, what would she think? He tried to formulate excuses, which even in his head sounded inadequate. He knew that he should have done something to prevent it; with grim satisfaction, he pictured Wolfgang incarcerated, for years.

The telephone stopped ringing when he was one pace away and he cursed, fluently. He had been gone nearly an hour; she might not try again. In the whole bloody sequence of events, this one circumstance emerged as the most important. Sigi's long and successful career with women was notable in one respect: he had never been the pursuer. Girls were attracted to him to the extent of giggling, forward little tarts at discos pushing each other forwards to ask him to dance. She, who had promised to call him, might not want to see him again; she might hate him for giving her the papers. She didn't even know the half of what he'd done to wreck her life. It was five hours since she'd left. Why didn't she call?

Sigi had had dozens of girls, the sort who considered themselves good in bed and liked to squirm and shriek and act, the whole event a performance that they asked to be rated on afterwards. Girls who faked shuddering, dramatic orgasms or cried; girls who would insist on talking when he wanted to sleep; who asked him, off-puttingly, the second before he came whether he loved them. Girls with tricks and techniques and sharp perfumes that smelt as though they must be burning their flesh; who wanted to sleep with him and didn't always expect a meal first.

He'd always been glad to be rid of them, even the ones with model-girl looks who were the envy of his friends. They were the worst. They cried over a spot, asked a hundred times if they hadn't put on a little weight and jumped out of bed in the morning with little cries of horror, rushing to slap make-up on in case, God forbid, he saw them as they really were. He'd never had to try to please any of them. Johanna was so different that she could have belonged to a different species. She had turned up on his doorstep at two thirty that morning, desperately pale, and without a word she had walked straight through into the bedroom. 'I've come to seduce you,' she'd said. Dumbfounded, he had stared at her, seen the smile tremble a little. 'Is it – inconvenient, right now?'

How cold she'd been, like a statue in ice; not just chilled, but frozen in her determination. Something had happened, but she wasn't going to tell him what it was. He thought that he would have refused, had he realised beforehand that this was her act of revenge; for she had used him, blatantly, outrageously; it was a kind of rape of the mind. Moodily, he watered the rubber plants, for the leaves were already turning yellow. No, he would not have refused. He loved her anyway, he simply couldn't help himself. He spent all his time thinking about her. The brandy had warmed her; relaxed her a little. She had peeped at him mockingly over the blankets. It's now or never, Sigi, she said. I'm beginning to think that you've changed your mind. As though he was the reluctant virgin.

He stood up, rubbing his eyes, dragged in the cardboard box of books and started to arrange them on the empty shelves. With grim determination, she had suffered his embraces. He, who had never told a girl that he loved her, who would never have allowed that word to be dragged out of him, had told her over and over again. You really don't have to say that, she'd said, it's awfully nice of you, but you don't have to, you know. I don't mind. As though the word was common currency on his lips; as though that was his stock in trade. He almost felt shocked, at such cynicism and disbelief.

There had been no lovers' breakfast in the morning; no coffee and kisses. He was the one to urge her to stay, uncharacteristically even to plead a little. How anxious she'd been to be gone, efficient and cool, rushing to shower, to dress. And distant, alarmingly so, as though it had all been a dream, making no concession just because they had spent the night in each other's arms. The attitude of a man, he thought, with a small, sour smile. Saying, off-hand, that she'd call him, with that tone in her voice that implied the urgency was all his. There was no reason in the world for her to care about him; five years of eager female flesh were annulled in one night by this cold English girl. She wasn't even beautiful; the whole thing was a joke, and yet he suffered, he sat and waited for the telephone to ring and catalogued, over and over, the list of his misdeeds.

Johanna, who did not care for him, could not be told the story of their introduction; not yet. He shuddered at that idea. He had lain awake in the night, as she slept, one thin arm clutching the pillow tight, and had known that he had to give her Levison's papers. For she had told him, calmly, after they had made love, that her friend Linda was with Genscher. That fact alone had brought her to him; she did not say it so directly, but it was understood. The man's spectre stalked them; it had to be exorcised. He would not have her by default.

While she showered, he had wrapped the papers with care in brown paper the packers had left. He had given her the unwieldy parcel with no explanation. Lying on the sofa, watching smoke rings curl up to the white ceiling, he imagined her opening it. He saw her reading, with that slight frown of concentration, at her desk. He wished upon Wolfgang the torments of hell. He said in his head, please God, please let the telephone ring and listened to the utter blank silence.

A boy was running down the Beckerstrasse at full pelt. His outline, passing the Judo Master's windows, was perceived by Frau Liebmann as a series of black flashes through the stripes in the glass. There was a hammering at the door and she, hunched over her bucket and mop, straightened up laboriously.

'Let me in. I have to see Herr Levison.'

A pink nose; one eye, projected themselves through the letter box.

'Go away. He's busy.'

'Let me in, let me in, it's urgent,' and two fists pummelled at the door, making the panels groan under the assault.

'Wait,' she said, and made her way with deliberate slowness to the office. Herr Levison sat at his desk; he was looking at a picture he kept in it, his head bent low over it. When she clicked on the light, brightening the gloomy room, he gave a start.

'It's a boy,' she said, 'I told him to go away, but he says he has to see you. I don't know who. I can't remember their names,' and she shrugged her shoulders in unvarying indifference.

'Let him in.'

Her progress across the mat was very slow; she kicked off her shoes, bent with a grunt to carry them to the other side, held herself carefully upright on the door at the far end to replace them, oblivious to the hammering on the door and irritating, bleating cries through the letterbox. The lad practically fell on top of her when she opened it, and she pushed him away, clutching at her heart, and he sprinted past. Shaking her head and muttering to herself, she closed the door and drew the large bolt.

Heini looked very peculiar indeed; he was flushed and strangely rigid looking.

'What is it?'

'He's dead, he's dead,' the boy gasped, with his mouth all askew, and collapsed suddenly into the chair which tilted back and back and with the ludicrous comedy of a slow-motion farce deposited him with a crack onto the floor. Ludwig, who had felt a sharp shudder of fear, jumped up and went towards him; his shadow fell across the boy's face, which was now, suddenly, perfectly white and he saw with a certain horror that Heini was flinching away, as though he expected to be hit.

Victor, progressing smoothly along the Elbchaussee, glimpsed through a set of gates a woman on the lawn in front of large white-shuttered house. She was sawing at the branches of a small fir tree while a child capered behind, swinging a basket of fir cones. He was rehearsing his little speech to Johanna; it occurred to him now that he would be obliged to spend Christmas with her. For the first time in years, he had failed to make arrangements for skiing.

Curiously, he had forgotten about it completely; had seen the glittering façade of trees on the Alsterhaus without making the connection. And yet everywhere glossy-leaved garlands with bright ribbons hung on doors. The Christmas trees were set out in serried ranks outside the ugly face of the Petrikirche, where the Christmas fair had spread its colourful manifestations and stallholders offered wooden decorations, Lebkuchen and almonds. For some years now he had avoided the family celebrations of friends, those gatherings to celebrate the season of goodwill when even the greasy goose, the roast carp and exchange of costly gifts did not obliterate the faint animosity garnered during the year. He hated these occasions; too much Sekt, a present for him in the bright pile and a pitying glance when the children came in to see the tree, as though he had the slightest desire to duplicate the event on his own behalf. It was a hangover which perpetuated itself, faintly, for a week, until the bright hilarity of Sylvester, the streamers and din and wet, drunken kisses put paid to the whole business for another year. He wondered what he and Johanna would do; he thought with distaste of the extraordinary vulgarity of the English counterpart and remembered how shopkeepers covered their plate glass windows with black tape and sprayed fake snow into the corners. A nation which ate dry turkey and wet vegetables and listened to its monarch; there, even the Rommers hung lights on the great grim fir outside the house in twinkling homage to their neighbours' brightly bedecked windows. The weight of these future occasions oppressed him. Feeling in his pocket for the ring in its little case, he allowed himself a last, ironic smile. He would make the pretty speeches. He closed his fingers tight around the gun; transferred it to the glove compartment. He thought that, after all, he had his Christmas present to look forward to. First Johanna, then Ludwig, then the great glittering packed parcel, that most expensive of indulgences, *Der Abend*. He would have it, whatever it cost.

The telephone rang and rang. Finally it was picked up. Silence.

'Are you all right?' he said. Her voice was small and hollow; he could barely make it out.

'All right? No. No. I'm not. What do you think I am?'

'You've read it.'

'I thought it was a present, isn't that funny. I thought you'd given me a gift, a souvenir, well I suppose that's what you might call it. Very memorable, your souvenir. I only opened it an hour ago, I forgot about it.'

'I see.' She sounded very peculiar indeed; now he could hear her yawning into the telephone.

'I'm tired,' she said, 'but Victor's coming over. He wants to see me, he said, about business and other matters. So I'll just have to stay awake.'

'You let him come? You said he could come?'

'Oh, don't get excited about it. I hadn't opened it then, I didn't know. And I have to get it over with some time, don't I? I wish Linda was here. We had an awful row and she's gone out.'

'Jesus bloody Christ,' he said. 'Look, I'm coming. I'm coming over right now,' he paused; she didn't say no. That

186

was something. 'Johanna, would you have rung me? Tell me. Quick.' Very faintly, he could hear the tiny, tinny ring of animated voices talking on the line, as though on another planet.

'No. Probably not.' A faint sigh whispered down the line. 'I'm sorry Sigi, but no.' It was a ghostly little voice, the English accent very pronounced. Click. He dialled again in a fever of anxiety.

'Don't tell him about it, do you hear? Don't do anything about it, just pretend, right? He's dangerous,' and he slammed down the phone before she could reply and ran down the stairs; he cursed the little car when it wouldn't start first time. Herr Victor Genscher, he thought, must have a good half-hour's start on him, maybe more. Embroiled in the rush hour traffic, realising that he had left his cigarettes at home, he beat his hand upon the wheel in disproportionate thumping rage.

# Chapter 12

Half a dozen typed pieces of paper had carefully been placed edge to edge, as though for purposes of comparison; as a scholar might examine a manuscript. The remainder were heaped in an untidy pile, any old how; a long green ribbon snaked carelessly across it. The desk was littered. Barely a square inch of its mahogany surface peeped out. A bundle of pencils jostled an ash tray; a vase of brackish water containing flowers which were shedding their brown, furling petals over the whole overhung a coffee cup in which pollen floated.

The diary lay open on the top right-hand corner of the desk, its edges exactly aligned with it in neurotic pedantry. It was a hard-cover exercise bok, not a printed diary at all. It was the sort of handsome book, neatly bound, which would command a good price in a stationer's shop, but which would always prove disappointing, later. Once opened, there was nothing to distinguish it from the cheapest kind of exercise book: the same green lines ruled across slightly too-thin, yellowy paper and the same double, wavy red line across the top of the page. The date was hand-written, neatly, above every entry and the margins, not ruled but nevertheless straight and identical, controlled by that same exacting eye. A shelf full of identical volumes bore witness to past industry, no doubt subject to the same format.

No formality constrained the content of this book, however. ' . . . had all the intellectual bite and subtlety of the playground,' the page began.

'Did/Didn't, but with adult venom and bile. She accuses me of obsessional paranoia; wide-eyed innocence and reproach is something she does rather well. "Of course I was there; we were talking about you, and that's the Gospel truth." A consummate performance and that bit cleverest of all, for it hurts. She's gone out to get her ticket home. "You're completely wrong," she said. "I'm not going because of anything I did, but because if you can't trust me there's not much of a relationship left, is there?" Why does she pretend? I even saw the bedroom light go on: as though they were having coffee in there, it's a farce. She denies and denies: guilty as hell, can't admit she's choking on a great slab of it, remorse with Schlag. She thought I'd never find out.

'It's a bit of fun for Linda, that's why she did it. She doesn't need to like a man to sleep with him: proven fact. It's just a mechanical response to a situation. Fuck her, and he did. She wasn't to know I was lurking around outside. I thought I'd been too clever, for the windows were dark and I wasn't going to wake him, so I hung around in hope and dread, with my entire attention fixed upon the watch: another minute and I'll go, and another. It's a phobia, the timing thing, like rearranging the letters of signs in alphabetical order, over and over. I do that, too. Then they arrived. Pretty, the two blond heads, standing at the balcony windows. The first glimpse I've had in two and a half years. A nightcap, what could be more pleasant? Except that he never took me home at night: inviolable territory. Not for Linda, though. I knew through every bone and fibre of flesh that he had taken her home to make love to her. It was quarter to one in the morning by then, and bitterly cold. I gave them another minute, then another, sixty revolutions of the hand went by and I knew, then, that she wasn't coming out. It was as though my whole insides were filled with hot sourness, like that Chinese soup. It was unthinkable, to just go home and wait. I wanted to punish them, to spite Victor. Like a tart, needing a man, any man, but of course there was Sigi. And I thought that I could have described myself as fortunate, if that is the – '

No hand moved to turn the page. The typed documents were not in fact consecutive, though at first glance they gave that impression.

'I, Ludwig Jakob Levison, born 1928, by profession teacher of Judo, self-employed of 48 Beckerstrasse, 2-Hamburg Altona, am writing this testimony after long and careful thought. This document is a record of events that happened nearly twenty-five years ago and some might say that old history is better left alone: let the dead bury the dead. But I feel that it is my duty to tell the truth. No one, apart from myself, knows exactly what happened all those years ago.

'My position is an unusual one, perhaps. For I am guilty, by association; not guilty of any crime, no, but blameable in a moral sense. In these pages, I believe I have made that much apparent. This is a document devised to trace that borderline between remorse, of the type we all suffer, and real culpability. There is a difference between what I term "physical" and "moral" outrages. I must, perhaps, first explain that these are issues which concern me, closely, every day. I teach the young. I uphold, in so doing, the old-fashioned virtues of discipline, of pride and integrity in honest labour, of humility in victory and of continual striving for self-improvement. Our sport contains all these lessons and many more beside. I try to lead my life along these lines, which nowadays some people would call unfashionable, or no longer justifiable.

'I have reached a point in my life when I can no longer justify silence. I see a man walking through the streets of my adopted city, not just living, where I thought him dead, but flourishing where he had no right to prosper. A man who has committed the worst of crimes, murder, and never been brought to justice.

'What kind of justice am I talking about? This is not a letter to the police; this is not the dry language of official documents or of legal testimony. This piece of paper is a mirror, in which a man, this man, should see himself, should recognise what he was and what he has become. And there shall be justice, real justice, the sort which does not merely punish, but remakes the world as it should have been. Perhaps I should call that my notion of justice. I am writing this without the aid of a lawyer and entirely of my own volition. It is a true story, it is also my story, and I must tell it in my own way. I have had to overcome something in myself before writing this down.'


'This man was once my protégé. I raised him, if anyone could be said to do that, from the age of ten years old. At that time I was known by a different name, Levi, that of my birth. If that seems an admission of guilt, then I must admit it. For I say that he is guilty, and he is, but I am not blameless. His faults are mine. His problems are also of my doing. I admit that freely. It is one of the ironies of maturity that it is possible to look back and see how acts of stupidity can pervert the course of simple, straightforward things. Many bad, even wicked things, are brought about, not by wicked men, but by a combination of errors that, in happier circumstances, might only have produced a small mishap. But I am anticipating my story.

'I was, at the time of the events I mean to describe, in charge of a hostel for the homeless in Berlin. War orphans, misfits, the children nobody wanted, all made their way to me. It was not an official place. I ran it myself, to give these children shelter. Nobody cared, in wartime, what became of them, particularly those who could be described as simple. Many children, indeed, were simple: children abandoned by parents who were relieved, perhaps, to be rid of them.

'I had seen many such children rounded up and taken away; their destinations unknown. Those who had eluded the dragnet lived in terror, lived a half-life sheltering by day in the basement which also served us as a bomb shelter. We know, today, the deadly nature of the buses which took them away, and which brutal sanatoria took them in for the last moments of their short, unhappy lives. One of the consequences of the events I describe was that I, too, was forced to abandon them; I do not know if any of them were able to make any sort of life for themselves. Unable, as they were, to distinguish right from wrong, innocents who nevertheless were living proof of their parents' afflictions and wrong-doing, I fear our society, which had elevated the crude basics of survival and, later, the more luxurious artifacts of living into its tribal totems, would consider them the disposable rubbish of the new affluence. I had enjoyed a measure of success with these simple souls, succeeding often in training them in basic skills where others had failed. I take no credit for it; fear had sharpened even dull wits and the most backward of them could understand a simple ritual, performance of which ensured a piece of bread and a bowl of soup. Today, such methods sound harsh, perhaps. I do not apologise for them. In those dark days, an existence could rest upon the satisfactory performance of a simple greeting – '

' . . . the community was divided, accordingly, and those who had some form of work had special status. They, who contributed a part of their income, had better rooms and food. Their presence gave the hostel a semi-legitimate status; visiting relatives were kept away from the crowded attics and back-rooms where the children slept.

'Among these "normal" children, whom I can term such only by virtue of the fact that they suffered from no obvious disability, Victor was exceptional. He was so very different from the rest; intelligent and alive, quick-witted. A child who had all the virtues, all the possibilities within him. It was not surprising that I soon discovered that I loved him more than the rest; an affection which made me uncritical, which overlooked faults. This was my fault, my error, which, although I did not see it at the time, was to exacerbate his problem, for it blinded me. Growing fond of him, I excluded him from the continual search for foster-parents, which was one of the main purposes of the mission. It was not, at first, a conscious decision; later, realising that I did not wish to be parted from him, I considered it and decided that he could benefit more from the care of a just, but loving parent, a father, for I saw myself in that role, than by living with a family. It was true, that I cared for him more than strangers ever could, but the decision was nevertheless wrong. I believe that Victor has suffered all his life, continues to suffer, from the lack of the parental bond, from the need for close ties to a loving family. It is a measure of my grave fault in this that he, forced by circumstances into early independence, has grown a shell so thick that he does not even recognise that lack. My decision, however wrong, was soon justified by events, for it soon became clear that no family would wish to take this boy.

'For Victor was a thief and worse; he used his acquisitions to buy himself special status and to dominate others, not just exacting obedience, but sexual submission. This did not immediately become apparent; for it was the sickness of the age. He was roaming the streets, sheltering where he could when I took him in. By eleven years old, he already seemed mature for his age. He was quiet and did not speak much of his past. That he had survived by stealing was evident; there was no other way to live on the streets. He carried on taking things, for the old habits died hard, but he committed the sin of taking from the hostel. We had practised, through the war years, a moral code which some might term hypocritical, but which conditions made necessary: it was one thing to find or barter outside, and quite another to take from fellow-sufferers. Inside our shabby little house, there was order and discipline. This phenomenon was by no means unusual; I believed that the atmosphere of our house would influence him, in time, and so for a while let him be. This boy had the face of an angel. It was hard to believe that he was intrinsically capable of wrong.

'By the age of fourteen Victor was very tall and strong and precocious for his age. He was already having sexual relation-ships – '

'It was a time of change. I had succeeded in moving our family to a house which could accommodate all of us. Emerging from the cramped, cold basement in which we had huddled, learning by rote, into a bright classroom was at first disorienting and strange. Like moles emerging from their burrows, the children congregated in the familiar safety of the corridors. The city was not safe and I imposed a curfew; one from which our three new lodgers, among them Wilfried Meyer, were exempt. Nevertheless there was an excitement, a new optimism, a sense of change. It is hard to believe how little things could delight us then, what certainty I had that a better future had already started to happen. To walk upon a carpet was a luxury few of my poor orphans had known, but soon there were books, too, and I even began to fear that a return to prosperity would undermine our simple, pure regime. Many people believed that a new world could be built upon the ruins of the old, as though overthrowing one tyranny would obliterate the beast forever. The survivors, the widows and children of the millions who had died for ideologies, could find comfort in that belief, could see a virtue in the senseless slaughter. It was a beast of a different sort which killed Meyer; a wild thing hitting out at anything which stood in its path. The wilfulness, the abstract evil of that murder haunts me; it is not too extreme to say that it has destroyed my life. I was the keeper of the beast; I was the one who failed to train it and it hit at me. I bear the scars today and I accept them, my punishment for a failure. My misdeeds made evident upon my face, and they are ugly things which make people avert their gaze. Just as there is no justice, no consolation for Frau Meyer, there is no justice in a world that allows Victor to walk abroad, unblemished, a personification of handsome health, of the new order, of esteemed, respectable sobriety. He knows, as I know, that it is a sham, that I am his dark shade, the true delineation of his deformity. I cry justice, not revenge, that is the prerogative of the innocent. Let the beast show itself, let it atone for evil by doing good, let it acknowledge and expiate its sins. I do not believe in the possibility of redress in another world, I cannot abdicate responsibility so easily.

'For I failed him in so many ways. He broke the curfew; knowing that, unable to exact obedience, I set a child to follow him. He was eluding me in every sense, straying into a world of corruption, of flesh. Victor chose as his object a young girl who could satisfy his carnal desires and, daughter of a butcher, could contribute to his black-market profiteering. Perhaps I should have informed the parents of this girl, I no longer know. I had a reluctance to become involved with the father, whose greed was known, who refused sustenance to the starving. . . '

'By holding aloof, by permitting Victor to corrupt the girl, I let him slip into a world which was profoundly tainted. He was only fourteen. For all his strength and precocity, he had not the inner resources to face evil, when it surely came, and I, his teacher, had let him slip too far. I know, now, that a good father must be stern, must root out corruption and inculcate strength with a disciplined regime, must face unpleasant tasks. My love for him made me weak.

'There were riots in the city and a crude mob, demanding justice in their own fashion, stormed shops and looted. This poor girl, her name was Charlotte Bamberg, paid a penalty for her father's greed. A man asked for meat and, refused, killed the butcher, killed the girl. Victor came upon the scene and my young boy, following him, terrified, ran to tell me the story. I remember waiting for him to return, uncertain what course to take, walking up and down. With my grief on his behalf was mingled the knowledge that the time had come for him to face his life and what he had become. Too late, I decided to play the role of the stern father, to upbraid him, but gently, with a father's love. To make him strong. He came carrying a gun and accused me of her murder, not understanding that in reality he accused me of failing him. I remember his young face staring at me, the piercing gaze of his eyes which could not cry, which had outgrown childish sorrows, and indeed his sorrow was that of a man. I remember telling him that, that he had to be a man. How he punished me for that, for his boyhood, my failure to raise him to the stature of an adult.

'He broke my jaw, using the gun, and smashed my teeth. I was good-looking once, as a young man. He turned his gun upon Wilfried and shot him through the skull. He died within minutes. I held him in my arms, blood streaming from my face onto his, unable to speak as I was for months to come. His eyes were terrible, frantic and uncomprehending, and I had not the ability to offer a word of comfort. His was a cruel, a pointless death. It is the weak, the vulnerable who suffer in this world for the transgressions of others and my children paid a heavy price for Victor's. He vanished; I believed, later, that he must have killed himself. I cannot live so lightly with my guilt, but Victor, if he has a conscience, does not display it. He gives money to orphans now. I wonder if he thinks of mine, whom he rendered homeless, for Meyer's mother, hysterical with grief, instigated an investigation into the death which brought severe penalties. My premises were closed, the children dispersed, taken away from me, and I was not told where. Too ill to fight my case, found guilty in absentia, as was Victor, we were both made outcasts, condemned to wander. A strange chance has brought us both to this city, and allowed our lives to link once more. Our story is not ended yet. I believe that I have been given the opportunity to remake history and this time I shall not permit any weaknesses to hinder me – '

'Today he is thirty-nine years old, a respectable business man. Victor is the managing director of the old-established firm of Rommer Import-Export Handelsgesellschaft, of which he owns a fifty percent share. He has been working for this company for over twenty years and is now a prominent citizen in Hamburg's small, well-to-do business community. He belongs to a number of clubs and associations, including some formed for charitable purposes, and it is known that he gives generously in support of waifs, orphans, refugees, the homeless and abandoned.

'That he is an orphan himself is known; the remainder of his life cannot be common knowledge. I venture here into the realms of conjecture, for it is impossible for me to know how much Victor confides in his close friends. I believe, however, that he does not in truth possess a close friend. I believe that he has told no one of his early life; that he lives a lie and shuns situations so intimate that confidences could not be avoided.

'Victor is not married; his predilections may be unchanged. Hamburg is a city in which many encounters of a louche type can easily be arranged. Many men in his situation marry; he has chosen not to. He is often seen with women, pretty women of a certain type. Women who dress expensively, who are perhaps married to particularly complaisant husbands or separated; who enjoy a social life, furs, jewels and fine clothes in return for their favours. This sort of cold-blooded arrangement, whereby each partner receives precisely what he bargains for and expects no more, is the basis upon which his network of relationships has been constructed. In short, if he were to lose his position, all would be lost. If this man could not buy a friend or lover, he would have none. He is incapable of a relationship of any other sort. Even as a boy he was skilled at using possessions or threats as a means of obtaining sexual compliance.'

A sheet torn from a student block, one covered in tiny squares, partly obliterated this last page. The writing on it, identical to that of the diary, had set out a series of short, cryptic statements down the left hand side of the page, each one neatly separated by four spaces from the next:

L Levison/Sigi/phone boxes
Possessions or threats = sexual compliance
*Homosexual*
Buying women/cold-blooded arrangement
Proof (1) Frau Meyer (2) Levison

The note-taker had laid the pen upon this piece of paper; it was held in position by the further, substantial weight of an unused round glass ashtray. Under its round base, the words 'proof' and 'sexual', hugely distorted, curved in upon themselves, but there was no eye looking to appreciate the phenomenon. The room was empty; it was also extremely cold. A window near the desk had been opened and a half-drawn curtain now flapped into the room, the bitter northern wind lifting up a billowing fold of the net curtain snatched at the papers and sent them sliding among a flurry of brown petals and rippled the black liquid in the cup. The door slammed to.

# Chapter 13

Frau Beckmann, twitching at the lace curtains, saw a white Mercedes draw up and park grandiosely and illegally on the narrow pavement directly under her gaze. A good-looking man emerged from the car and locked it. She watched from her perch as he walked to her front door and just made out the bell shrilling in the flat above. She strained to hear the sound of footsteps ascending the stairs. This was, as far as she knew, the first male visitor Fräulein Rommer had ever received. Her curiosity was perfectly natural. Undecided whether to remain sitting at the window or to station herself nearer to the door, she wandered about the room in vague, circular movements. Even turning up the sound level of the small hearing aid to full; even listening as hard as she could, she could make out nothing. There was complete silence.

Above her, Johanna stared at the desk, at the papers so carefully laid out which rippled in the stiff breeze with small sinister flappings, like an animal trying to crawl. Two polite rings at the bell were succeeded, now, by one more urgent tone. Suddenly she stooped, gathered together the whole in an unwieldy mass and stuffed the bundle into a drawer that, for an agonising moment, refused to close. She jammed it shut; banging down the window she could see the car that must be his and ran, frightened that he might go away, to let him in.

He carried his smile before him up the two flights of stairs until his dark bulk dwarfed her and they shook hands awkwardly. They stared at each other for a moment and then both looked away. He had made a small motion, as though to kiss her cheek and she, recoiling slightly, found herself awkward, gauche.

'I'll make coffee,' she said, 'please sit down,' politely and was startled when he laughed.

'Marvellous,' he said. 'It's incredible. I do believe you've got a Hamburg accent. Say something else.'

'You make me sound like a talking monkey. I'm not going to gratify you, you're the one who's come to talk. Milk, no sugar, is that right?' and she thought that's it, that's the right tone, and came in and out with coffee cups. He was examining the room, scrutinising her. Shrugging off his coat, he lounged, now, at his ease.

'I like it here. It's charming. Peaceful. What a long time it's been, Johanna. I must have startled you when I called,' and he crinkled up his eyes ruefully and, with that familiar boyish gesture, ran a hand through his hair.

'No,' she said and, 'I was expecting it,' and without a tremor filled their cups. The reality was never as bad as the anticipation of it. They both knew how to behave; there would be no histrionics. And yet part of her felt almost paralysed by the shocking fact of his presence. He had aged. His hair was beginning to grey at the sides, the white so close to the gold that, as yet, it barely showed. More apparent were the furrows on the forehead and deep creases round the eyes. Veins stood out on the back of his hands.

Victor, as though unconscious of these changes, curled up the corners of his mouth in the old, self-deprecatory, charming smile. The Victor of old was still there, the one who had had the ability to make her heart lurch so violently and unfairly. As the room began to warm up, she detected the faint smell of lemons.

'You're going to explain, aren't you, but really it should be to Oma. The deal's going to fail, isn't it?' and, because this was so bald, she added, 'Of course you had to get in touch, sooner or later,' giving him a thin smile and then, regretting this,

200

'You're not going to let her lose all that money, are you?' And Oma's investment was minor, compared to that she had made in Victor. Was that a flicker of irritation in his face? He sighed a little and leant forwards.

'I should have spoken to your grandmother, I fear you've alarmed her unnecessarily. There are two issues here. Firstly, as far as consultation is concerned, I'm sure you know that I am empowered to invest as I see fit, a system which has often allowed us to act swiftly and reap high profits. But you couldn't know what was going on, I do see that. If you'd come to me, I could have explained everything, and that's the issue, that we have had no – lines of communication. My fault,' and he clasped his hands on his knees and watched her as he talked, full of sincerity. 'I can't reproach you for not coming to me, can I? What reason could you have for trusting me, after all? I can't tell you how happy I am to see you today, oh not just because of this silly misunderstanding with the shares. Because we've opened communications, haven't we? Now we can speak honestly to each other, we can put everything right. It's a new beginning, don't you feel that too?'

Johanna sat perfectly still, staring at him. While her ears absorbed this message, an unmistakable churning of the guts warned her of what was coming; she understood perfectly the nature of the bargain he was expecting to strike with her. And yet this was so unlikely that it couldn't be true; she must be misunderstanding him, and for a moment she faltered and didn't know what to say. She clattered at the coffee cups with sudden, manic abruptness and looked up to see him smiling intimately at her, at his eyes watching her eyes with a sort of satisfaction. They were so very blue.

'Honesty, that's right, that is what matters, isn't it Victor? To tell the truth? That's why you came here, isn't it,' and because she was willing him to tell her everything, because she couldn't help wanting the truth to be the real one, she added, quickly. 'I ought to tell you Victor, perhaps you don't know this, but I told her she should sell those shares straight away. We can't afford to be involved with this – newspaper of yours, can we, we can still pull out.'

'You think I've let your grandmother down, I know. Tell

me, Johanna, who has told you about this deal? What is it that makes you so certain that it is going to fail?'

'I, um, met Uwe Schenck,' she said, after a slight hesitation. 'From the bank. At a party.'

Victor nodded, with a kind of amused contempt.

'I fear he has been remarkably indiscreet. But, Johanna, I don't think he told you that the deal would fail, merely that it is not going through his bank. The young man has jumped to conclusions. And I believe he, quite properly, then referred you to me.'

'But it is going to fail.'

'Why? I have backers, the deal is virtually accomplished. You can discount Herr Schenck, he's a petty official. You know, I have a great deal of money riding on this purchase and I don't intend to lose a Pfennig of it. If your grandmother wants to pull out, she can. She has already spoken to Herr Tiedemann about it, didn't you know? She will do what she wants, of course, but I can tell you that if she sells now, it will be at a loss. On the other hand, she stands to make a considerable profit when the purchase goes through. Do you think I would involve her if I wasn't certain? It's a marvellous project, Johanna, it will put Rommer's on the map and I'm very excited about it, very confident,' and now he was animated, smiling, his hands gesturing. 'But I don't want to persuade you into something you don't like. Your grandmother has the matter in hand, we don't need to discuss it, or rather Herr Tiedemann has everything organised, as always, you know he always does what Frau Rommer wants. You can take my word for it. This time. Is that what you've been thinking, that you've not always been able to take my word? No – don't look away – didn't we agree that today we could be honest, at last, that we could be open with each other?'

For she was blushing and, made miserably self-conscious, could not look at him. Against that frankness, that open, confiding air, she felt horribly duplicitous. She, who was ready to accuse, was being made to feel that her lack of confidence was something discreditable, that she was letting him down.

'You should be talking to Oma, it's her decision,' she said.

'Oh no, for you both must decide. And I like to talk to you, I prefer that by far,' he said caressingly. 'I've missed you, Johanna. Very much. Seeing you now has made me realise how much. Do you know what I feel? It is the chagrin of the collector, who has held a rare and beautiful piece without recognising its worth, who has let it leave his hands and never ceases regretting his mistake. We can all make mistakes, my dear girl, even banks can,' and he smiled wryly. 'I don't believe in dwelling on past mistakes. Regret, self-blame, those are pernicious, destructive emotions, they weaken us and sap our strength. I believe that we have to live in the present, to have confidence in our actions, to choose our course and follow it.' She was watching him now, as though mesmerised; he broke off and, rising suddenly, paced across the room. 'I'm not, quite, coming to the point, am I, dear girl? Do you know why? I shall be frank with you, it's because I am a little scared. I am afraid of failure. How many years have we known each other? Fifteen, sixteen years? And yet I can't at all guess what you are thinking now, what's behind those big brown eyes of yours,' and he gave her a particularly sweet smile. 'You are an honest person, Johanna, you have a certain integrity. I admire that. And I know too that you no longer feel that you can trust me and I have only myself to blame for that. Once I told you that you were too young and the truth of it is that I was an old fool, and a dishonest one. I lied to you. But you know that already, don't you?'

The big brown eyes were fixed on him, sharpened by an extreme attentiveness. He was speaking hesitantly, picking his words with care, talking in a way that was completely unprecedented. He was opening himself to her; she had not expected it and felt as though they were on the brink of the revelation she had long ceased expecting. Speaking like this, he surely could not be lying, not now. In the drawer of her desk, somewhere among the papers, lay the accusation that Victor was a compulsive, congenital liar. 'He lied easily and fluently and had an unusual ability to convince himself and other people that he spoke the truth.' She believed that document, she had accepted it, all its shocking entirety. She had read it twice with the utmost care. On the second reading, she had realised with a sad, sinking, sick feeling that it was not just an accusation but a love letter. Why should the words of a man she didn't know be so very believable? But she knew that man was telling the truth, or thought he was.

Did she trust Victor? A small, incredulous voice in her head said I think he's a murderer, but I'm going to hear him out. I believe him, too. What's wrong with me? She had a sudden, vivid knowledge of herself as a creature so weak that it did not have the power to distinguish the truth. The material was so anarchic, that she could not form it into any kind of order inside her head. She found herself wishing that she could write down what he was saying; that she could analyse and annotate on paper, in a way that was impossible in her head. In a sudden anguish, she realised that she was going to be forced to make a decision.

Victor was leaning back against the window. He looked tired, his face intent with effort.

'I understand a lot of things now,' he said. 'That summer – in '68 – I suddenly realised that I would have to change. I wasn't prepared for that. I was, how can I put it, naïve in my expectations. When you came to Hamburg I realised at once that I wouldn't be able to continue leading the same sort of life, that I couldn't after all change you, make you more like me. Oh, it sounds cold-blooded, I know,' and he screwed up his face in a grimace. 'The truth isn't always pleasant. I wanted your love, I enjoyed your youth, your energy, but I didn't think I'd have to work at deserving it. I felt – exposed, suddenly. I didn't like it. That was what finished it, Johanna, and when I said you were too young I was really saying that I was too old and selfish for you.'

He looked at her and Johanna, who could not yet trust herself to speak, nodded, twice.

'It was despicable, wasn't it? But I don't need to tell you that. I couldn't find the words to explain to you exactly what I felt, I didn't even try. I don't think I even understood it properly myself. So many things have changed since then. I have had occasion to examine my life, to decide for myself what I want. I surprised myself, Johanna, by finding you were there, on the top of the list. I miss you, you know, and more than that, I need you. I respect you, I think I understand your independence, your way of seeing the world. I wouldn't try to change that. The need is quite the reverse, you know, I want you to change me, I want you to teach me how to live a better life. No, wait – ' for she had made a motion, as though to speak. 'This is the old selfish Victor speaking, who wants to be heard out. I have an opportunity to do great things, with this newspaper. I believe in that, I know I can make it work, that we can make it work and enjoy it together. To create something fine, oh, I suppose a kind of memorial, something that will last. You know, Johanna, I believe there's nothing I can't do with your confidence, your trust in me. I – lay myself open to you. Believe me, I have never spoken to another person like this.' He moved slowly across to where she still sat, perfectly motionless, and stood looking down at her.

'There's something else, isn't there? Yes, I know there is. I spoke of honesty, didn't I? Well I mean to be perfectly and absolutely honest to you.'

The world had condensed down to his face, the mobile mouth and the soft, persuasive voice. Her legs were trembling; she could not have moved an inch. In her head, a little voice was whispering this is real, this is it, this is the truth.

'There is a word missing, I know. I haven't spoken to you of love. I haven't told you that I love you. You're thinking, what kind of man is this, to ask so much and promise so little? Well, I can't say that I love you, in the conventional sense. Oh, it would be easy enough to do, but you mean too much to me for me to lie to you. I feel for you – the most tender friendship and affection, the most urgent need. I don't believe I have ever used that word and meant it, I don't know exactly what it means. But I am certain, Johanna that we can, we will love each other, that what we have is so very precious, that from it love will grow. You will teach me how to love.' Now she was ready to speak, but once again he forestalled her. 'Wait,' he said. 'Don't speak for a moment, reflect. I want you to marry me, Johanna. I want you to do so with conviction, with certainty. I think, well, I have an idea what you are feeling. I must be honest about that, too. I know by now you must have spoken to your friend and she will have told you how much we talked about you. You know she acted with the best, her uttermost convictions in telling me as much as she did. I'm glad she's not here today, I know she doesn't approve of me, she told me so quite frankly. Wait, what is it? – no you mustn't be embarrassed – she said nothing you wouldn't be pleased to hear – ' he broke off. Johanna, conscious of the blood draining from her face and thinking for a moment that she might faint, got up. With a quick, fluttering gesture of one hand, motioning him away, she walked jerkily out of the room. Behind the locked door of the bathroom, grateful for its icy cold, she laid her burning head on the tiled wall which seemed to throb in time with her pulse.

Victor could hear the sound of running water in the bathroom. She had been in there for an inordinate length of time. He walked about the room, studied the photograph of Frau Rommer on the desk and noted the family resemblance, which was increasing as time passed. Johanna was prettier than he had remembered. Her pallor had something distinguished about it, something fine. He was beginning to imagine what it would be like to lead a life together. It was imaginable, it was possible. He could make it work. She had changed; she was of course older and less ingenuous. Grown more mature, wary of him and less trusting. That was perhaps inevitable, though he regretted it. He had a nostalgic image of the little girl with thick pigtails and solemn brown eyes who had sat upon his knee and listened while he told her a story. An age of innocence had passed.

Restless, he paced up and down. What was she doing in there? He kept looking at his watch, conscious that so much had to be accomplished in so short a time. In mentioning Linda, he had made a mistake, he had embarrassed her deeply. Unused to so many naked emotions, he had forgotten the profound vulnerability of a young girl.

This was the marriage that was always meant for him, that had always been inevitable, and he delivered himself up to it with good grace; better, with a genuine willingness to please. When had he talked so frankly or for so long about himself? He had offered more of himself than he had ever given anyone. He did not love her, that was true, but then perhaps he was no longer capable of loving anybody. Theirs would be an honest, an open relationship; he would profit immeasurably from that kind of intimacy with another human being and he saw now that he needed it. He had been alone too long. A bright bubble of optimism was kindling itself in him: perhaps he would grow to love her after all. It would help to have children. He could not help wishing just a little that she was prettier, more obviously attractive, more suited to being the wife of a newspaper magnate, a public man. It was an ignoble thought and he suppressed it. What was she doing in there? He began to calculate the time it would take to drive back to Altona.

He thought he heard a noise, a gentle swish of short skirts against the doorway, and he turned. A gaudy woman stood at the entrance to the sitting room, cheeks brightly rouged. Her lips, outlined in cerise, were smiling brilliantly at him. She was so altered that for a moment he stared without recognition and with a kind of sudden horror. He could not help himself; she looked extremely ugly.

It had taken some time for Johanna to compose herself. She gave the obligatory second's pause before making an impressive entrance and in that instant, when he thought he was unobserved, she saw him looking at his watch, wearing a frown of impatience. He looked up and it smoothed itself at once, to be succeeded by something far worse, a look of the purest, nastiest, sheerest dislike. The lines on his advancing face were a web of deceit she hadn't seen before and he pulled her close to him and the real Johanna, who was not the one he wanted or thought he needed, looked with the most damningly exact eye upon the folds of his face, the open pores, the little lines around the mouth, and shuddered. Misinterpreting that little quake, he bent down to kiss her and she allowed it to happen. Frozen, she waited for some surge of emotion to blank out her brain. Dry lips on hers, a hot breath through his nostrils, his tongue in her mouth and she nearly gagged and pushed him away, suddenly, with a rude strength that made him stagger.

'No,' she heard herself say it loudly and then, stupidly, 'Sorry.' She sat down abruptly and looked up the grey perspective of his elegant waistcoat. 'I can't, I mean the answer is no.'

Frau Beckmann, dozing in the comfortable chair, was jerked awake by the loud roaring of a car screaming round the corner, brakes squealing even over the roar of the throaty exhaust. A little red car shrieked to a halt behind the white Mercedes. Bang. The door slammed behind another young man, one with dark hair. She barely got a decent look at him as he hurtled to the house. She heard the thundering of his footsteps as he scaled the risers and then silence. A noise had to be very loud or very near to penetrate the old lady's auditory passages.

She waited for several minutes before arming herself with a duster and issuing forth, a fine flowered apron tied around her ample bulk. She made much of dusting the banisters and then the small vase of dried flowers and grasses near her door. With enormous stealth, she crept up the stairs to Fräulein Rommer's door, a few steps at a time. Still, and another shake of the head did nothing to help, she couldn't hear a thing. She advanced. Another step saw her with her good ear pressed to the door, the duster still in her hand as she steadied herself against the genteel striped wallpaper, her matronly heart beating away at a slightly higher than usual rate inches from the wooden panels.

Sigi stormed into the room, stopping short when he saw Victor standing there. His fierce look, his clenched fists were comical and inappropriate. 'Sigi Schmidt – Victor Genscher,' Johanna said in a weary voice; they made no motion to shake hands.

'This, I suppose, is the boyfriend,' Victor said, eyebrows raised, in a tone that implied that this explained everything. Calmly, he went to pick up his coat, put it on gracefully, wrapping a silk scarf around his throat and, offering her a hand, bowed his head slightly with a formality she had seen Herr Tiedemann use. He was encased and distant; the mental retreat was effected and swiftly succeeded by the actual one.

'Thank you for seeing me. Good-bye Johanna,' and his eyes were looking somewhere over her head and he did not smile, though he spoke with his automatic, impersonal courtesy. She was already obliterated; the last hour might not have happened. Mutely she watched the elegant back retreat. The door met a large, soft obstruction. There was a faint shriek, a vision of Frau Beckmann clinging desperately to the banister. Victor passed by her and was gone. Johanna watched without understanding as the old woman scrabbled herself back into an upright position and retreated down the stairs. She closed the door and there, with a hangdog face, was Sigi.

'You – bloody idiot.'

'I'm sorry, I came as quickly as I could. Have you got a cigarette?'

'Go away and you can take your – horrible papers with you,' and she tore them from the desk and threw them at him, and they fell heavily around his feet. 'You've spoiled everything, why did you have to give me those? You knew all about him, didn't you, you and your clever phone boxes, you bloody liar,' and she was forcing her arms into a coat, throwing a scarf around her neck with a violent gesture. 'What right have you got to come in here? You get out, I'm going out, you can just bugger off.'

The process of explanation and expiation went on all the way up the steep hill, along the wooded seclusion of the Bismarckstein, that destination, never attained, of Bismarck's imposing memorial. He tried to kiss her in the dark seclusion of the little tower – which, far from being rural and gothic, smelt unpleasantly of urine – and was savagely rebuffed. He told her about Levison; she hardly protested at the manner of their introduction, staring at him in dislike, her sufferance suggesting not so much that his explanation was adequate, as that she didn't care about him and so it didn't matter. The street-lamps, flickering on, revealed their faces; she pushed him away at the moment when a white Mercedes passed them. It wasn't him; a pretty woman with a dark curly mop of hair smiled at the lovers' tiff, parked in front of the old patrician villa at the end of the row. Johanna talked and talked and he had the impression that she was talking to herself; certainly she treated all his remarks with scorn. 'I could have been happy with him, not knowing,' she said, and, 'I would have made myself believe in him, I'm good at that, at projecting the attributes that are lacking. J. Rommer the projectionist, sending out pretty pictures of what she wants to see, seeing them reflected on his face. But the power's been shut off, no beam. The screen's empty. A tabula rasa. Do you know what I mean? No, I suppose you don't.' He told her that she was too complicated. She said something else: 'When I sensed a deficiency in myself, perhaps it was just a rip in the screen, a hole showing the void, the blackness. Perhaps all I'm doing now is projecting another version and making it believable, perhaps this is false too. The reality could be quite different again. We're all just blank human beings, when you take away the reflections of other people's needs and desires, that's what colours us up. We're just mounds of flesh, cold and uncaring, that's what real is. The rest is imagination.' He, who had such simple, such very understandable needs, attempted to expound them without success. It was a cold tramp back, the steps were slippery. It wasn't until they were the length of the beach from her flat that he told her about how it was an accident with Wolf and old man Tiedemann, and then she broke away from him and started to run. He sat, silent and useless, while she telephoned her grandmother in England. He poured her a brandy and she took it. 'Your brother's a thug, like you,' she said, 'an interfering bully,' but her heart wasn't in it; she was still talking about Genscher. 'He lied to me, right here, he didn't even tell me about poor old Otto, but it's part of the con, do you see? All he wants is his bloody deal. Not me. I still believe that he told me the truth. Some of the truth. Perhaps he doesn't know it himself. Perhaps that is asking too much,' and she sat for a long time staring into space as though he wasn't there. When he took her hand, she smiled sardonically. 'I suppose you think you've got me now, well you haven't, you're going when Linda comes home,' but she didn't take her hand away. For a long time they sat in the darkness like exhausted combatants in the sudden silence that follows a battle; who know that the war must rage elsewhere, but have no stomach to seek it out.

# Chapter 14

The white Mercedes executed an illegal U-turn and headed
back into town, escaping by one minute the return visit of a
policeman who affixed a ticket to the windscreen of the red
car, such being the unfairness of life in general and of traffic
policemen in particular. Frau Beckmann, twitching at her net
curtain, did not fail to notice the misdemeanour.

Victor drove with great care, to avoid attracting any
attention. He was fully occupied in reckoning the advantages
and possible disadvantages of his position; he did not have it in
his character to view events in terms of defeat, or failure; he
saw them rather as episodes which presented further choices,
further decisions. Thus Johanna's refusal, her strange behaviour, had positive consequences. He was now certain that
she knew nothing of Ludwig; he was free of any commitment
to her. He knew that in Herr Tiedemann's absence, the shares
could not be sold by anyone but himself; days would pass in
which nothing would be done, and in that time he would
secure his deal. The old man was old, tired, he might not
recover. Victor thought that a lengthy convalescence and an
honourable retirement were now in store for Rommer's oldest
and most faithful servant. A new clarity and order was
manifesting itself, to which the only obstacle remaining was
Ludwig. He had no plan, other than to confront him; he did

not waste his time in imagining what difficulties there might be. He was perfectly collected, prepared for an ugly scene, for the necessary violence. And yet his hands, gripping the wheel, were shaking slightly.

He observed them with a certain dismay. Upon the face reflected in the broad-angled driving mirror, he noted new and unpleasant manifestations of the passage of time. His flesh was sagging, decaying inside his mouth, gums lifting from the teeth. The surface was beginning the inexorable process of moving away from the bone beneath, the sack of skin loosening in anticipation of its fall. The years had barely touched him until the observers came, to witness his dissolution. His youth, his strength, had stolen away and turned tail and they mocked him in the shape of a boy in a blue anorak. He understood that he would age at this accelerated, unnatural rate until the watching stopped, until Ludwig was destroyed.

Ludwig was sitting cross-legged upon the mat in the quiet house. Upstairs, Frau Liebmann would be sleeping, refilling her small reservoir of patience for the evening class. The weekends released her to practise a form of semi-hibernation. She spent the hours cat-napping in her small, dark room, waking to stare at the screen with a concentration which left her heavy-lidded on Mondays.

Frau Liebmann was as inaccessible to Ludwig as the most perfect stranger. He knew nothing at all about her; he had never asked her a single question. This arrangement, so admirably discreet, suddenly seemed impossibly bleak. Had she ever, perhaps, wanted to talk to him, needed a human contact? It was too late now; it was unthinkable that he should, for example, knock on her door, for a purpose as minimal as seeing another human face. He would pass the next days like a man on a desert island. He, who didn't care for company or for idle talk, felt with a pang that after this class there would be nothing, nothing until Monday. Tiedemann was dead. There would be no Bernd, this Sunday, to make his tea. There would be no glass house; he had no better way to punish himself than to deprive himself of that. He already lived in solitary confinement, in prison conditions. No vengeful agency could starve or beat him with greater vindictiveness than that he exercised against himself. Punishment, for him, took on a more refined, more elegant form. He was tied to an acute consciousness of self, a thinking mind which revolved endlessly on its arid circuit, denied release.

He thought that the worst suffering he could inflict upon himself would be to abandon the Victor project, condemning that mind to ceaseless re-enactments of the same, sterile speculations and regrets. Against this he balanced the fact that its continuance was a duty, his way of benefiting others. Thus, to punish himself would be selfish, if it deprived them. He took this casuistry a step further. His mission was a form of charity, which others might construe as being devised for his greater glorification. Yet he could not remove himself from the equation; he was the linch-pin upon which it all turned. The mission was the object he most ardently desired; it was also his opportunity to do good and the latter must always outweigh the former. There were good precedents to support this view; he thought, with irony, that the Church in its wisdom knew to take an expedient view of charity, whatever its motivations.

Ludwig was a man who manufactured his own doctrines. He examined the succession of past events with a pragmatic eye. Where did this train of events start? A minor occurrence, an accident with a motorbike, which had hurt nobody. Two boys larking around on a slippery back-street had found nothing better to do with themselves than to smash up a machine they particularly prized for giving them mobility. Bernd's father had confined him to his room for this; so Wolf had taken his place and precipitated the 'accident' that was no accident at all. Blame Proto-Neolithic man, who first saw the virtues of the wheel; blame the internal combustion engine; blame the ice upon the street. Ludwig would not take a simplistic view; his dark eye, inward-looking perceived more.

There was another interpretation: that this was a piece of summary justice which, in striking down Tiedemann, was punishing him in a particularly apposite way. An innocent suffered in his place: that was a torment chosen very particularly for him. Was that insufferable vanity, to believe that there might be some destiny at work, rather than a succession

213

of trivial incidents? He contemplated the chain of events and saw in it an emotional house of cards that had toppled flat. Ludwig's coldness to Bernd, that unavoidable necessity, had made him set his friends on to snatch the briefcase. That fitted too, for it was a worthless object, a symbol of a businessman's prestige, nothing more. They had ascribed to it a different value: they had seen it as a bribe. Bernd would have brought him this empty, shiny thing and expected caresses in return. Ludwig saw that, since he had never admitted anyone into his confidence, they could never have known that it held no value for him; he could not deny that he coveted Victor's wealth, in a manner of speaking. Their actions, grotesquely, mirrored his; he could not blame his boys. It did not even end there; there was a further causality, another link in the chain. Their stupid, juvenile amorality, their mindless brutality, seemed justifiable to them, indeed they did not even question the nature of the activities he had asked them to perform. They did everything for his benefit. The judo teacher could not complain, because his class had learnt its lessons too well. Force used against itself. He looked into the darkness and saw the emptiness of the skills he taught, unless a thinking, warm humanity controlled them. He, who had given them the opportunity for evil, could not marvel at the consequences.

Another illumination came: that the boys had not the capacity to learn, to profit from their mistakes. That was one of Ludwig's redeeming graces: why had he not taught it to them? For he had seen on Heini's face, not just fear, the dread of punishment for pushing a man who now was dead, but something greater. Ludwig had seen that the boy's strongest emotion was, quite simply a naked terror of him. Not the pangs of remorse, not the anguish of guilt, but fear of his teacher. It could not be possible, surely, that that was all he had taught them?

There was a thick, sour taste in Ludwig's mouth. He would not drink, to wash it away. He would not drink or eat at all that day. History was repeating itself and it was a frightening thing, to see how each event engendered another so uncontrollably. What historical inevitability had brought Bernd to him, with that poignant resemblance? What had made him

214

decide to force himself upon Ludwig? The judo master knew that he had fought against the likeness and, in so doing, he had repeated his mistake, albeit in a new variant. In guarding against loving too much, he had loved too little. The irony of such determinism did not escape him.

Ludwig had forged these chains which bound him so securely. He could not have been more safely imprisoned. And now he smiled to himself and showed the darkness his deformities. There were no choices left. No, he would not abandon Victor, for that meant that he was abandoning himself to all the consequences of his errors. He would not condemn himself to suffer with no hope of redress. He thought that while he retained some ability to think and to reason, he was obliged to use those powers as best he could. From the back of his mind the phrase 'moral imperative', as though it had been lying in wait, now drifted up to mock him. How neatly he had seized the expression from the inky pages of the *Abend* to justify his aims; now he saw what poor shelter the ambiguous phrase gave.

An elegantly dressed man was not, after all, such a novelty for the Beckerstrasse, where the bourgeoisie rubbed shoulders with the working class in common pursuit of a skill which each thought would help to defend them against the other. It was already dark and no light shone through the legend on Meister Judo's window. The man stopped, looked through the thin transparent stripes in the glass and then, stepping boldly up to the door, rang the bell. It jangled in the distant office. His dark grey suit blended against the doorway; over one arm he was carrying a coat. Now the door opened and swallowed him up into the blackness beyond so swiftly that his mass seemed to absorb itself, as though the façade had assimilated him.

They faced each other, standing on the mat. Reflecting the sudden brightness of the lights above, its whiteness made their outlines sharp and threw a pallor onto their faces. 'So you're alone,' Victor said softly. 'That surprises me. Where are your watchers? They didn't follow me here.'

Ludwig, curiously, was smiling. Twenty years had taught him to use that gesture, not to signify friendship or pleasure, but as a means of exercising control. He was small, thin and ugly. He was looking at his physical opposite, a man who all his life had rejoiced in possession of the visible indicators of what was considered desirable and good; to this formidable armoury, he had added the accoutrements and powers of a powerful elite. Knowing that the splendid edifice was a sham did not make it less attractive or less deceptive; Ludwig looked through the blue holes in the face and thought, for an instant, that he glimpsed the creature scuttling inside the hollow chamber; thought that he had provided it with a grievance, a cause. Instinctively, he adopted the classic, loose-limbed position for combat. The elegant man in front of him laughed.

'Oh, have they deserted you?' the soft voice said.

'I am alone, apart from the old housekeeper. Nobody can hear us, if that is your concern. I didn't expect you, and yet I should have known that you would come. Action, reaction, nothing alters under the sun.' The harsh lights gave Victor's hair an almost unbearable brilliance. Ludwig turned and beckoned him towards the office.

'Come, we'll talk in here,' he said and turned his back upon him. The time of manoeuvring for position, of taunts, of veiled threats was gone and now the moment for openness had come and he glanced back over his shoulder and said, with almost tenderness in his voice, 'The end of the game, isn't it?' and saw a strange, a haunting smile upon his adversary's face.

Ludwig did not see that the coat, negligently flung over one arm, had now slid back to reveal the muzzle of a gun. Coyly, it peeped out. He did not see it until they were in the office and he was sitting behind his desk and had placed that barrier between himself and Victor. This mistake, indeed Ludwig's absurd simplicity, his error in walking away as he did, his subsequent, ludicrous look of surprise, so akin to the tragi-comic grimace of a clown, milking a situation for all the cheap laughs he could force, all these things made Victor, who now held the balance of power, laugh out loud.

'Yes,' he said, with an effort, for the impulse to mirth was almost insuperable, 'All over,' and, 'The end,' and then, pulling himself together in an instant, 'Give me the papers, hurry. Your delightful autobiography or whatever you call it, where is it?'

'So Tiedemann's dead, I see. I wasn't sure.' Ludwig made no effort to move. He stared at Victor's face and then at the gun and back at his face with a flickering movement of the eyes which made Victor wary and cold.

Victor was not going to enlighten him.

'Shut up,' he said. 'The papers.' And slowly he cocked the gun, letting the coat fall to the floor, and now held the weapon with both hands; it was aimed at Ludwig's mouth. The man just sat there, looking at him, as though he didn't even know what a gun was. It was very difficult to control the urge to pull the trigger, it was such a very small movement, such a very fine thing. Victor was aware that it could go off in his hand, right now, and that he would not have pulled the trigger; it would have been an accident, a slip of the finger. With slight regret he concentrated on controlling the small tremor; he thought that the noise would bring the old woman down. It was like trying to operate somebody else's hands.

'Hurry,' he said and Ludwig rose slowly. He walked over to the filing cabinet and knelt in front of it. The drawer scraped and creaked in protest as its weight was pulled forward and the whole cabinet swayed for an instant, as though it might topple on the small man. With maddening slowness, he began to pull out a stack of magazines, one by one.

And Ludwig started to talk now, glancing back over his shoulder. 'You understand, my dear Victor, that the story is exactly the same. Do you see that, how curious it is that history should repeat itself so neatly and offer us the same set of choices. You see that, don't you, that I have made choices?'

Victor, watching his hands, did not reply.

'I am not a vindictive man,' the voice said, 'I have never thought, for example, that you should be made to suffer physically, that you should taste blood. I wonder if you know that feeling, to gag on warm blood running down your throat, your own blood that you can't stop.' The pile was growing, there were barely half a dozen issues left in the cabinet which now settled back upon itself in a little jolting movement, achieving a new balance. 'No, probably not,' Ludwig said and now the thin fingers were feeling through a maze of rusty folders. 'Do you see how redundant that thing in your hand is? How can that be a solution, to permit violence to engender more violence? The preferred solution of the morally and mentally deficient. Is that what you want to demonstrate, Victor, that you still have a capacity for violence? I think not, for we all have it. Our strength, our goodness, lies in overcoming it.'

Now the cabinet was half-empty and he leant forwards and began with scooping movements to bring out handfuls of things; the debris and odd items that lay there, dirty, dusty paraphernalia which stuck to his fingers. His movements seemed to Victor to be growing increasingly frenetic, but the voice continued in its calm, its insufferably arrogant manner. Craning forwards, looking into the blackness of the empty drawer to reassure himself that Ludwig was not concealing anything, Victor sat back again and watched Ludwig repeat the process with the drawer above.

'I believe in intelligence, in a moral intelligence, that gives us the capacity for choice,' and the thin arms reached with nervous energy, pulling out folders and dropping them around his sides, so that he soon sat in the centre of circles of objects, which grew out concentrically from his bent back. 'What difference is there, between Meyer and Charlotte Bamberg, or in Tiedemann's death? Sudden death, in the midst of life, shocking and needless, but even that can be a catalyst for change.' Now he turned and looked at Victor with his cunning, inscrutable eye. 'We're the same, you and I, now more than ever. Meyer's death taught me something, I learnt what my responsibilities were. I was made to see what I owed to others, not just to myself. And you're going to learn that now, do you see it? The old man's dead, but there is a – legacy he leaves.' He stretched himself now and turned back and pulled out the topmost drawer.

It was only at this point that Victor realised that of course Ludwig wasn't going to find the papers; that the occasion suited him, gave him the chance to produce his complex little pieces of self-justification, so neatly woven around a travesty of the truth. At the same moment, Ludwig feigned a weary sigh; he rubbed a dirty hand across his brow.

'They've gone, I don't understand it, I don't know who – ' and he made as though to walk across to the desk.

'Stay where you are,' and Victor almost wanted to applaud; it was the performance of a life-time. In the Schauspielhaus he would certainly have stood to salute a performer of this quality. 'Would you like to know what I've learnt – the, as you term it, legacy of the old man? I don't have your sophistry, Ludwig, your cunning to twist the facts. It's a little simpler where I stand. You've brought violence with you, and death, you're an agent of destruction, I see that quite, quite clearly. I think you also like playing the fool with me, Ludwig,' and as he spoke he kicked open the drawers of the desk and glanced at the miserable contents, finding nothing of interest. 'A cautious man like you makes a copy of his documents, puts it in a safe place, isn't that what blackmailers do? "To be opened in the event of my sudden demise",' and he smiled at him with a gloating feeling of his power. 'Well, Ludwig? Where is the copy of your masterpiece?' and now he was feeling his way round the room, never turning his back for an instant, flicking over the calendars, looking behind the chair, even, with a grimace of distaste, flicking back the shabby strip of carpet and looking underneath it. 'Are you going to make me search the whole miserable place? No, I think you will search for me, I shall merely keep this – redundant thing in my hand. Where shall we start?'

'There's a copy at my lawyer's,' Ludwig said, simply. 'He's probably left for the weekend, I shouldn't think it possible to obtain now,' and he said it with such a tone of regret, such quiet sincerity, that Victor rapped the knuckles of one hand sharply on the desk in the traditional, student salute.

'Bravo, bravo!' He gestured with the gun towards the telephone. 'But shall we try, however? I had forgotten what you are, Ludwig, I've wronged you. You have the cunning soul of a Jesuit, the tone of a holy man, I do believe you were born out of your time. Come, hurry,' he said, and now he banged the gun against the desk, one, two, three, in a gesture of impatience, suddenly bad-tempered at the way it was stretching out, for they could be interrupted at any time. He was standing around where he should be acting; he had been too easily taken in by the amusement value of Ludwig trying to evade responsibility for Tiedemann's supposed death and it now occurred to him that they could be surrounded, that the boys could be standing all around the house and he hurried to the window, wrenched it open, and looked outside.

It was almost a shock to see nothing but darkness where he expected a circle of eyes and, staring into the gloom, he saw that there was a high brick wall at the back and that there could be no way out there.

'There is nobody here, is there?' and for a moment Ludwig looked steadily at him and did not reply.

'No, we're alone,' he said, looking up from the finger dialling and giving him that vulpine smile. 'I could say yes, couldn't I? A small choice. I am not going to lie any more, that is over. The enemy lies within, my dear Victor, that is the one to vanquish, not me, for I am not your enemy, nor those poor children even if they make mistakes, as we have.' He had a power to do good, to change everything; he felt it surging through him.

The telephone rang four, five times. It was ten minutes past five, a Friday afternoon; people went home early.

'Ja?' A man's voice, irritated. The tony of somebody with his coat on, with a briefcase hanging heavy in the other hand. He was annoyed, he demurred; it was the weekend, couldn't it wait until Monday? Staring sardonically into the muzzle of the gun, noting that it was trembling just a little, Ludwig said no. Grudgingly, the lawyer said he would have it dropped round. He would call up a motorbike messenger, a good firm, the one they used for genuinely urgent matters, and the angry voice stressed the last three words with heavy irony, that tone of voice which clients foolish enough to evoke paid for dearly.

They waited, Victor sitting behind the desk, resting his arm on it, which enabled him to point the gun without any strain; Ludwig sat cross-legged on the floor and watched him. 'When you've read it,' he said, 'I think you will understand what I planned for you, you will see what our aims should be. You will understand yourself better. You have no idea how active your shadows have been, what a lot they have learnt about you.' He watched him very carefully, for there was something

220

strange about the way Victor was staring into space, for seconds at a time, and then his eyes would focus again upon Ludwig and he was taking aim at different parts of his body, first the face, then the knees, then the groin.

'Force always turns upon itself,' Ludwig said. 'Don't play these games.' He saw that the face, under the naked bulb, was harrowed and he spoke very gently. 'There was no other way, do you understand? You see how entrenched in your life you are, how cold? I can help you, I can build a new life, we can start again. It's not too late for that, to remake the past. Put down the gun, Victor, that is not a solution. There shall be no more killing. You are the product of false values, do you hear me, of empty materialism, of meaningless acquisitions. So many good impulses gone wrong, perverted, that can be put right. Open up your mind, think of all your wealth can do, think of yourself as a force for good. It's not too grandiose a word, I can show you – ' he flinched as the gun crashed down onto the metal table. The noise was very loud; it did not, however, go off.

'Spare me your fine moral judgments,' Victor said. 'You make me vomit, with your clever justifications, with your talk of virtues. You've not changed, you were always the same, using power to pervert, adept at finding excuses for yourself, for your perverted lust. Fine words to excuse blackmail and murder, but you forget, I'm not a boy any more,' and his voice was a slow and deliberate, rhythmical tone. 'You couldn't bear it, could you, that I should succeed where you failed? You're still a little man, in every sense, a hypocrite, who talks about morality and finds excuses to put his arms around little boys.' Pausing, he lifted an interrogative eyebrow. 'You don't deny it? How can you,' and his voice became quieter, until it was almost a whisper, a flat trickle of venom. 'You forgot something, Ludwig. I'm a man, I know your kind and I've dealt with them before. Anarchists, wreckers, who talk like you of materialism, of false values, who hide their aims behind big words, but who don't shrink from violence and terror, from blackmail, anything goes, doesn't it, you justify any act to advance your cause. But you don't have a cause, Ludwig, what's your excuse? Is this the new world, the new order,' and he swept a hand around and smiled. 'We're the new order, we're stability and prosperity. I've built an empire, you know that don't you, and you think you want a share in it. You actually thought I would help you finance your dirty games,' and now he laughed, throwing his head back.

'You don't understand,' Ludwig said, and spoke louder. 'Listen to me, Victor, you don't understand, there is a new order, we can change everything,' and he was shouting now, over the terrible noise that came out of Victor's throat, 'I am talking about a mission –'

The noise of the motorbike outside was loud; they both hushed. A moment later a peremptory rapping on the door was heard. 'Open up,' Victor said calmly. 'I'm right behind you.'

Ludwig had become aware, as the minutes passed, of the hard floor under his coccyx; the small deadening of nerve ends. That was life, that was what living came down to; small, definite sensations and their absence. The brown paper parcel was nearly empty. Victor had rifled through its contents, glancing at and abandoning the worthless documents that made up Ludwig's life: the deeds to his house, his will, his passport. He was now engaged upon burning the testimony of Frau Meyer, page by page. He did not read it.

'You're a fool,' he'd said, picking up the first page and looking at Ludwig over the room, and he had giggled. 'What made you think I'd want to read it?'

The pages blackened, curled, fell in plumes of grey ash to the floor. Victor's face was beaded with sweat, his shirt stained with it, but he was perfectly concentrated. The gun lay on the desk. Whenever Ludwig made the slightest movement, Victor reached for it. Ludwig sat very still and imperceptibly tensed one muscle after another. A match hissed and flared in the violent silence; the piece of paper curled in the white hand, which allowed the flame to lick almost to the fingers before letting it drop.

'Who told you about the newspaper?' Victor asked; Ludwig did not reply.

'Have you given this to anybody else?' and, when he said nothing, added, 'Where's your openness now? You're a kind of devil, there's something uncanny, evil about you,' and then he stopped, abruptly.

Watching him, alert to his slightest motion, to each flickering muscle on his face, Ludwig thought that Victor was quite eaten away inside. Behind the façade of this man there was, after all, perhaps nothing left of the boy and he said to himself that he had made a mistake, but that he could not regret it and he thought that Victor, whose hands trembled uncontrollably, could not sustain his effort for much longer.

'You'll never know what I've said, will you? You will lie awake worrying about that, my dear Victor,' and Ludwig laughed. He knew so much better than Victor how to control a fight. 'My poor Victor,' he said, goading. 'How are you ever going to find out? What if there are another five copies? What if there are ten?'

In an odd way, Ludwig pitied him then, as much for his brutal indifference to everything that mattered as for any other reason. He would survive even this; yet, as a private joke with the God he knew didn't exist, he recited the Sh'ma in his head and with equal irreverence the Credo. He felt preternaturally alert; he was trusting in his training, his own religion, to perform the work of personal salvation. 'Will you finish off the old lady, upstairs?' he now said. 'She's deaf, she might not hear a shot. But I wouldn't let that influence you, if you want to be secure. An important man like you needs security.'

'I should have killed you in Berlin,' Victor said in a conversational tone. 'I had too many scruples. I still couldn't hurt a woman, I'm not like you. Remember Charlotte? I should have finished you then, I could have spared you the trouble of being alive so long. Your life for other, more valuable ones, doesn't that make sense on your moral balance sheet?'

Ludwig sprang to his feet and in the same instant threw himself to one side. He rolled, came up again, cracking his head against the desk and, hearing the loud report of the gun being fired, thought for an instant that he must have been hit. He seized the weapon, which Victor held limply as though he couldn't believe that his shot could possibly have missed. With all his strength, Ludwig hurled it backwards out of the open

223

window; it hit against the top pane which smashed under the assault.

He lunged across the desk for Victor who ducked and aimed a clumsy punch. He had him by the shirt front and one arm, but could not get at him from this position; he kicked and shoved at the desk to get it out of the way and Victor, suddenly nimble, darted around the other side of it and made, not for the judo room, but up the stairs with Ludwig just behind him, their feet hammering against the wooden risers. He caught up with him in his bedroom, as Victor thrust his head through the window. Ludwig knew there was no way out from there; he pulled him back roughly. Staring up at him in the instant before he closed in, the thought formed clearly that it was a waste, a tragic waste of a man, of the time and love and effort he had put into this human being. They wrestled, in silent, blind, tussling fury at the open window.

The room was dark, the only illumination the orange street lamp outside which shimmered around two unequal silhouettes, one so much larger than the other; it lit up a profile for a split second and glinted on pale hair on a head that bobbed and wavered. It showed a small black arm, reaching forwards. The dark man, springing back, had the agility and sure-footedness of a monkey. Ludwig gained, in that instant, the space he needed for a backwards throw. He grasped tight, but the big man took hold of him, lifted his slight body into the air and with a grunt propelled him into the void. A confused shape hung at the window, a two-headed monster with flailing arms and legs; and then there was nothing there at all but the misty night and its artificial, orange moon. For Ludwig, with his trained, rigid grip, did not let go. Even in the act of falling, even in the free, cold air, he twisted his body to take Victor with him, toppled the other man backwards, falling down. Unlucky Victor, not to have reckoned with this; unlucky Ludwig, who had not the time to say as he badly wanted, despite everything, to do, that he had had nothing to do with Charlotte Bamberg. That some crazed Pole or Hungarian had killed her and, yes, he had not regretted it, insane with jealousy as he then was, but God knew he was not a murderer.

An explosion woke Frau Liebmann; a few minutes later

there came a tremendous crash of breaking glass. She crept downstairs in trepidation and looked through the ground floor for signs of breakage. There. The window of Herr Levison's office was indeed broken and the room now chill as the cold wind swept the warmth away. Walking closer to inspect the damage, Frau Liebmann could not understand how such a small window could have made such a noise.

It was only when she went upstairs looking for Herr Levison, who must, surely, be in the house somewhere, that she understood. His window was open, as it always was, but through it her eye caught a flash of colour. The whole grey expanse of glass below was smashed, its jagged edges revealing a brilliant patch of green, in stark contrast to the concrete and brickwork all around. In this riot of foliage, there among the bright blossoms, her weak eyes just made out two figures. One lay in the centre, on a bed of plants, and was, she thought, moving. The other lay quite still on the hard stone floor. Tutting with excitement and distress, Frau Liebmann hurried up the stairs to get her glasses before she did anything else.

# Chapter 15

Rain dripped through the dark laurel leaves, soaked into the small card fixed onto them and obliterated the spidery script. The men carrying the coffin had turned up their coat collars against the drizzle. Persistent, the water found its way through thick leather gloves, infiltrated their shoes, beat in treacherous gusts against their raw-chapped faces. Rivulets ran across the shiny pale wood of the coffin and found their way down to the freshly-turned earth, which glinted yellow where the spade had struck patches of clay. Clods of it clung heavily to shoes. Surreptitiously, one of the men tried to scrape it off against the neighbouring gravestone, a marble slab, marring its rain-washed pallor with an ugly crust.

The principal mourner, dressed in black, her head perfectly concealed under a scarf, observed this process with a cold eye. She stepped forwards and dropped a flower onto the coffin, from which the wreath had been removed. This gesture released the bearers, who now hurried to the gravel path, stamping feet against the cold, before proceeding in a more measured way back to the relative warmth of the chapel, where the next funeral party waited. But the woman remained there, quite alone, as though unconscious of the cold, her head bent down. She might have been crying, but at this distance it was impossible to tell.

When every figure had disappeared from the landscape and she stood, the only living, breathing creature among the cold stones, she began to speak. This was not the eulogy that had been lacking in the short and badly-attended funeral service, but a hopeless, angry interrogation of the dead man.

'Well, is this it? Are you really there, in that box? Over, finished, all gone? And what am I to do without you? What becomes of me?'

A day or two later on the other side of town, the neurosurgeon charged with the delicate and probably impossible task of reassembling the broken pieces of a badly injured man, was interrupted in the very task of scrubbing up. With the patient weariness of a busy man with not an instant to spare, he addressed his laconic persecutor. 'This really won't do, there is nothing I can tell you now.'

'One question.' The Kommissar's ears stuck out behind the mask; he looked for all the world like a bloodhound, subjected to the ignominy of a bath and now wrapped up in a sheet

'Just give me an idea of when I can speak to him.'

Backing away from possible contamination, his gloved hands raised protectively, the surgeon began to utter the ambiguous and vaguely soothing phrases he more usually employed with anxious relatives. 'Always hope . . . too early to tell . . . have known remarkable improvements to occur . . . understand your concern . . . assure you we are doing our utmost . . . ' and he disappeared smartly behind a door marked 'Strictly No Entrance Except For Authorised Personnel'.

For a long time the patient seemed perfectly unaware of the regular visitor seated at his bedside. His physical condition, which the surgeons spoke of amongst themselves as a triumph of their delicate skills, seemed to the policeman quite hopeless. He lay perfectly immobile and never spoke, staring vacantly at the white wall or the shiny door for hours at a time. He showed no sign of responding to, let alone hearing, the questions thrown at him.

At last the spring came, the season of growth bringing its familiar rituals. Two weddings took place on the same day in the Hansastadt, two ceremonies of very different types. There

227

was a grand affair in the Michaeliskirche; the wedding party, substantial as it was, still dwarfed by its massive vaulting arches. No bride could compete with the splendour of the massive altar with its pink marble columns, nor with the brightness of the fresh gilding on pilasters and above doorways.

Across town, Herr Frisch and Frau Meier tied the knot in a purely civil ceremony. The bride, bony hips and well-muscled, scrawny arms veiled in cream chiffon, bore a smile of genuine pleasure. Herr Frisch seemed less delighted, which was no doubt due to the tight new shoes he wore, so uncomfortable that he longed to sit down. The bride carried a small posy of artificial silk flowers and took care to toss these in the direction of Fräulein Schmidt, who showed unexpected agility in scrambling after them.

At the reception, the Fräulein was seen to annex a bottle of Schnapps, which she used to keep her glass perpetually full. The groom, whose round face was flushed with heat and excitement, was about to refill his own glass for perhaps the third time, when he felt a sudden sharp pinch in the fleshy part of his upper arm. Turning his head to discover the cause of this odd manifestation, he was astonished to see his charming new wife looking at him with an unfamiliar expression. Her look was so hard and penetrating and so completely novel, that his jaw sagged.

'Nein, nein, nein, das kommt nicht in Frage. Das muss sofort aufhören,' said the new Frau Frisch adding, sotto voce, out of delicacy, 'Enlarged liver,' and two fingers closed like pincers over the neck of the bottle and removed it from his slackened grasp.

Perhaps the consequent increase in liquor supply for the remaining small circle of well-wishers was not altogether desirable. Fräulein Schmidt was to be observed, an hour or two later, hiccuping tearfully into her glass. She sat next to a stranger, introduced to her as Frau Frisch's former brother-in-law, who started at this point to stroke her knee under the table. This sensation was so novel to her that it took her some time to realise precisely what was happening and a further age passed before she decided to register a protest. By then this quiet, middle-aged man had somehow worked his way up to her thigh and had the good spinster in such a state that she had neither the strength nor the desire to resist and simply stared at him in amazement at his audacity, in pleasure and in fear that he might desist.

The other, grander, wedding was characterised by that particular, faintly sexual and hilarious atmosphere always present when a young couple is solemnly and ritually adjured to go forth and copulate. The reception offered that classic and curious mixture of envy, innuendo, a consciousness of money spent and the onset of headaches from too much alcohol, from smiling and talking too much; the guests, having gossiped and drunk to excess, drove home in silence, wondering whether they would be held to the invitations issued in rash bonhomie to other couples they only ever met at weddings.

In short, a memorable affair, complete with top hats and tails, dear Ingrid so marvellously calm and composed, so suitable, so worthy of her happiness. Indeed the new Frau Schwantz was perfection itself, splendid in a frothy white confection; so wonderfully controlled that on this, the happiest day of her life, she didn't once avail herself of the bride's traditional privilege of being unpleasant to her mother. Mausi Bock was nevertheless overwrought. She wept during the ceremony and was ecstatic and unintelligible afterwards, irritating the waiters by wandering about and attempting to serve the guests herself. Her husband, who shrank from any public exhibition of his country accent, relegated his honours to Herr Tiedemann. The latter spent much of his time furtively examining the notes in his pocket for the speech he had in any case been determined to make and which proved as long-winded as those who knew him had feared.

This was, naturally, the perfect occasion at which to discuss the affairs of the house of Rommer and ogle the participants in the drama. Jovial Uncle Otto could be persuaded to give his version of events, one which proved disappointing as it concentrated interminably on the details of his concussion, his convalescence and the lucky escape he had had. Fortunately the 'shocking tragedy' of Herr Genscher had not set him back too much; he had found the strength to shoulder his new and important responsibilities. Not for anything in the world would he have let dear Frau Rommer down in her hour of need.

Frau Rommer, seemingly unconscious of any special interest, chatted amiably with everyone and was overheard in deep discussion about foundation wear with that funny, timid little Frau Tiedemann. Nearly everyone noticed the pretty English girl, who laughed so much and danced so well and was followed wherever she went by a young American in an ill-fitting suit with the shortest of crewcuts. Somebody said she was studying drama, in London, and certainly that seemed to suit her; somebody else said the American had been a monk, but of course nobody believed it.

Dear Ingrid's quiet little cousin, that studious, rather odd girl, also had an admirer, good-looking but dreadfully common, and it was said that the family did not approve. Some people whispered something about an involvement with Herr Genscher, for they all remembered the broken engagement a few years back, but that was generally held to be mere speculation and unkind too, given the circumstances. Dear Ingrid took special care to throw her pretty bouquet for her cousin to catch, but she turned her back quite rudely and it was the lively Linda who caught it. That witty young man, the banker, Herr Schenck, who had made such an amusing speech describing Ingrid as a pretty filly brought to bridle, watched this little scene with a most sentimental look and was heard to utter a deep sigh.

The following day at nine o'clock sharp, when the bridal party were engaged in the appropriately self-congratulatory post mortem, a woman carrying a bunch of spring flowers walked briskly through the gates of the cemetery and made purposefully for the distant corner. Something untoward made her pause for a moment and then accelerated the rhythmic crunching of stout shoes against gravel; she was straining forwards to see what it was. A dark silhouette was hovering over the grave, still and ethereal, an angel cut out of black marble.

Frau Liebmann blinked. At a distance of ten metres the divine became mortal, a lanky boy who started into life, darting, veering, then turning suddenly and racing past her with an averted face, a blur. A shorn head, the tip of a nose. It was a blind, instinctive retreat, the panicked rush of the young animal confronted by a predator. Guilty, thought Frau Liebmann grimly; carefully she examined the newly-planted shrubs for signs of any disturbance. Shaking her head, she drew a small mat from her large shopping bag and knelt clumsily, leaning forwards to poke inexpertly at the earth with her trowel. Everything seemed to be in order. With satisfaction she contemplated her handiwork, tweaking with motherly solicitude at the leaves of the puny-looking winter flowering jasmine. Staring sightlessly at the fine new marble slab, she knew that she knew that boy. There was something distinctive, memorable about the vulnerable nape of the adolescent neck. The hair, the long hair, that was it. It hadn't fooled her. Now she remembered how he had hidden behind it, in the chapel, concealing a tear-stained face. She sat back on her haunches, slowly she rolled open the paper cone of flowers. His grief had astonished her; he had left the service before the end with his head hanging low. She looked down at the bright tulips and thought he'd got his come-uppance then, hadn't he. Without knowing exactly what she meant by that, she began to clip the stems, her face a frown of concentration. Against such single-mindedness, the boy's face, so formless and innocuous, was soon to fade.

Frau Liebmann had found the will herself, lying in a pile of dirt and ash on the office floor; she had been going about the work of clearing up in a dreary and half-hearted way and had picked the papers up before she realised what they were. Hurriedly glancing through, she had finally made out her own name in the blurred print and had fallen to her knees in gratitude. The house was not worth a fortune, but it had bought her a place in a decent old people's home and a colour television and she was deeply grateful.

In due course the plants she had selected with such care put out tender new shoots. Their roots groped down for nourishment. They fastened upon the lid of the cheap wooden box and prised it open, inching down to the rotting matter underneath. Their forked tangles, always reaching out and intertwining in the small space, finally achieved a rearrangement of matter which would have pleased Ludwig, had he known of it.

With reluctance, the Kommissar closed the case. For a long time the file on Victor Genscher hung around in his office, the neat manila folder growing grubby around the edges, the few papers inside leafed through so often that they became quite ragged. The file remained prominent, becoming at first the mat on which his coffee was placed and then a perpetual reproach in the pending tray. At last it disappeared in a stout bundle of folders, tied with twine, down to the permanent files in the basement where so many unfinished stories were left to moulder.

There were no witnesses and no proof; there was not sufficient evidence to bring a charge. The Rommer family maintained its obdurate, albeit charming silence, maintaining to the end that it knew and understood nothing. The firm's employees seemed equally ignorant of their boss's affairs. The whole issue of the newspaper, which had seemed so promising a lead, dwindled to nothing. *Der Abend* was the subject of an internal take-over and later the shares in it were sold by the family at a small profit. The Kommissar had never managed to establish Levison's authorship of the strange document found in Herr Genscher's safe, a piece of blackmail if ever he'd seen one, with its explicit references to theft and sodomy, its lamentable absence of detail on the date and place. The Kommissar had taken the unprecedented step of pulling strings and using influence to get this job, as eloquent in its pursuit as another man might have been in his manoeuvrings for promotion. Now he feared that the Genscher business had left a small black mark on his blameless career. He would, unsolicited, have done his utmost to save the man, to find mitigating circumstances, once he knew the truth, but he was denied the facts, denied an opportunity to render service. He felt outmanoeuvred, excluded and bitter; more than any single fact in the unsubstantial mess of half-evidence, this feeling of being cheated convinced him of the man's guilt.

And then there was the man himself, victim or aggressor, the powerful Herr Genscher. He lay day after day in his silent room, beneficiary of the best possible medical care. The doctors described his recovery as remarkable: he was, it seemed, fortunate in terms of paraplegics in being able to move one arm and his head; matters could have been so much worse. He broke his silence: he talked about the weather. Daily the Kommissar had taken his melancholy face to the invalid's bedside where he would sit with his notebook open on his lap, observing with a jaundiced eye the efficient and protective ministrations of the well-paid staff. The room became as familiar to him as his own sitting room. Patiently, he questioned the stricken man. And Herr Genscher would reply, turning his placid face towards his questioner, perfectly lucid. 'Altona?' he would muse in his pleasant voice. 'I don't make a habit of going there. It's not a good district and I always remember to lock the car doors when I drive through,' and he would smile with faint irony, with the slight puzzlement of a man who was too polite to inquire why he was being asked such things. The name Levison was completely new to him; the word blackmail provoked his melodious laugh. Occasionally the Kommissar, growing irritable, would shout and accuse, and then Herr Genscher would retreat into a faintly wounded silence, waiting for the display of bad manners to cease. Nothing moved him. Nothing provoked any kind of defence or explanation. As far as he was concerned, nothing whatsoever had occurred; he did not even seem to wonder what he was doing there, in the crisp white bed. Scrutinising him carefully, the policeman could not detect any hint of conscious deception. He had gone away each time with his notebook empty, a frustrated man.

June 11, 1972

Victor is going away, to live in Switzerland. Oma has worked out a deal with the bank to buy him out of the company. She is jubilant, for that means she can go home at last. She is taking all Levison's documents with her; for months she has carried them around with her in her great, unwieldly ostrich-skin bag, afraid to leave them anywhere. She calls them our insurance policy, though nobody thinks Victor will ever be active again. He is imprisoned in that immobile body; a sufficient punishment. Switzerland, as a solution, pleases everyone. Victor will be well looked-after and able to afford a complete entourage of servants; with care, they say he should live for many years.

He is very strange now. He sent Oma a formal letter of resignation, thanking her for past kindnesses and saying that he intended to pursue a different path, but would always wish her well. She has been to see him several times and has tried to wring the truth out of him, but he gives nothing away. He actually laughed, when she asked him about the judo school; he said skiing was his sport.

For some strange reason, I suppose for old times' sake I went to visit him today. He gave me an odd look but was as courteous and polite as ever. He waved his good hand towards the seat at his bedside and I could see that in his mind's eye he was standing, that he pulled the chair forwards and helped me to sit, as he always has.

# Meta-Analysis
# of Controlled Clinical Trials

# Statistics in Practice

*Advisory Editor*

**Stephen Senn**
University College London, UK

*Founding Editor*

**Vic Barnett**
Nottingham Trent University, UK

*Statistics in Practice* is an important international series of texts which provide detailed coverage of statistical concepts, methods and worked case studies in specific fields of investigation and study.

With sound motivation and many worked practical examples, the books show in down-to-earth terms how to select and use an appropriate range of statistical techniques in a particular practical field within each title's special topic area.

The books provide statistical support for professionals and research workers across a range of employment fields and research environments. Subject areas covered include medicine and pharmaceutics; industry, finance and commerce; public services; the earth and environmental sciences, and so on.

The books also provide support to students studying statistical courses applied to the above area. The demand for graduates to be equipped for the work environment has led to such courses becoming increasingly prevalent at universities and colleges.

It is our aim to present judiciously chosen and well-written workbooks to meet everyday practical needs. Feedback of views from readers will be most valuable to monitor the success of this aim.

A complete list of titles in this series appears at the end of the volume.

# Meta-Analysis
# of Controlled Clinical Trials

**Anne Whitehead**

*Medical and Pharmaceutical Statistics Research Unit,*

*The University of Reading, UK*

JOHN WILEY & SONS, LTD

**Other Wiley Editorial Offices**

John Wiley & Sons Inc., 111 River Street, Hoboken, NJ 07030, USA

Jossey-Bass, 989 Market Street, San Francisco, CA 94103-1741, USA

Wiley-VCH Verlag GmbH, Boschstr. 12, D-69469 Weinheim, Germany

John Wiley & Sons Australia Ltd, 33 Park Road, Milton, Queensland 4064, Australia

John Wiley & Sons (Asia) Pte Ltd, 2 Clementi Loop #02-01, Jin Xing Distripark, Singapore
129809

John Wiley & Sons Canada Ltd, 22 Worcester Road, Etobicoke, Ontario, Canada M9W 1L1

**British Library Cataloguing in Publication Data**

A catalogue record for this book is available from the British Library

ISBN 0-471-98370-5

Typeset in 10/12pt Photina by Laserwords Private Limited, Chennai, India
Printed and bound in Great Britain by Biddles Ltd, Guildford, Surrey
This book is printed on acid-free paper responsibly manufactured from sustainable forestry
in which at least two trees are planted for each one used for paper production.

*To John*

# *Contents*

## 4 Combining estimates of a treatment difference across trials   **57**

## 5 Meta-analysis using individual patient data   **99**

# Preface

Since the 1980s there has been an upsurge in the application of meta-analysis to medical research. Over the same period there have been great strides in the development and refinement of the associated statistical methodology. These developments have mainly been due to greater emphasis on evidence-based medicine and the need for reliable summaries of the vast and expanding volume of clinical research. Most meta-analyses within the field of clinical research have been conducted on randomized controlled trials, and the focus of this book is on the planning, conduct and reporting of a meta-analysis as applied to a series of randomized controlled trials.

There is wide variation in the amount and form of data which might be available for a meta-analysis. At one extreme lie individual patient data and at the other just a $p$-value associated with each test of the treatment difference. Consequently, a number of different approaches to the conduct of a meta-analysis have been developed, and this has given the impression that the methodology is a collection of distinct techniques. My objective has been to present the various approaches within a general framework, enabling the similarities and differences between the available techniques to be demonstrated more easily. In addition, I have attempted to place this general framework within mainstream statistical methodology, and to show how meta-analysis methods can be implemented using general statistical packages. Most of the analyses presented in this book were conducted using the standard statistical procedures in SAS. Other statistical packages, namely MLn, BUGS and PEST, were used for the implementation of some of the more advanced techniques.

In this book, the meta-analysis techniques are described in detail, from their theoretical development through to practical implementation. Emphasis is placed on the consequences of choosing a particular approach and the interpretation of the results. Each topic discussed is supported by detailed worked examples. The example data sets and the program code may be downloaded from either the Wiley website or my own (for details, see Section 1.6).

Meta-analyses have often been performed retrospectively using summary statistics from reports of individual clinical trials. However, the advantages of prospectively planning a meta-analysis are now being recognized. The advantages of using individual patient data are also well accepted. The techniques covered in the book include those for conducting prospectively planned meta-analyses as well as retrospective meta-analyses. Methods based on individual patient data are included, as well as those based on study summary statistics. This book will be of relevance to those working in the public sector and in the pharmaceutical industry.

This book is based on a short course which has been presented numerous times to practicing medical statisticians over the last ten years and has also been influenced by my involvement in several large meta-analyses. I am grateful to colleagues with whom I have undertaken collaborative research, in particular, Andrea Bailey, Jacqueline Birks, Nicola Bright, Diana Elbourne, Julian Higgins, Rumana Omar, Rebecca Turner, Elly Savaluny, Simon Thompson and John Whitehead.

I am grateful to John Lewis, Stephen Senn, Sue Todd, John Whitehead and Paula Williamson for providing helpful comments and suggestions on earlier drafts of the book.

*Anne Whitehead*
*Reading*
2002

# 1

# *Introduction*

## 1.1 THE ROLE OF META-ANALYSIS

*Meta-analysis* was defined by Glass (1976) to be 'the statistical analysis of a large collection of analysis results from individual studies for the purpose of integrating the findings'. Although Glass was involved in social science research, the term 'meta-analysis' has been adopted within other disciplines and has proved particularly popular in clinical research. Some of the techniques of meta-analysis have been in use for far longer. Pearson (1904) applied a method for summarizing correlation coefficients from studies of typhoid vaccination, Tippet (1931) and Fisher (1932) presented methods for combining *p*-values, and Yates and Cochran (1938) considered the combination of estimates from different agricultural experiments. However, the introduction of a name for this collection of techniques appears to have led to an upsurge in development and application.

In the medical world, the upsurge began in the 1980s. Some of the key medical questions answered by meta-analyses at this time concerned the treatment of heart disease and cancer. For example, Yusuf *et al.* (1985) concluded that long-term beta blockade following discharge from the coronary care unit after a myocardial infarction reduced mortality, and the Early Breast Cancer Trialists' Collaborative Group (1988) showed that tamoxifen reduced mortality in women over 50 with early breast cancer. By the 1990s published meta-analyses were ubiquitous. Chalmers and Lau (1993) claimed: 'It is obvious that the new scientific discipline of meta-analysis is here to stay'. They reported a rise in the number of publications of meta-analyses of medical studies from 18 in the 1970s to 406 in the 1980s. Altman (2000) noted that Medline contained 589 such publications from 1997 alone.

The rapid increase in the number of meta-analyses being conducted during the last decade is mainly due to a greater emphasis on evidence-based medicine and the need for reliable summaries of the vast and expanding volume of clinical research. Evidence-based medicine has been defined as 'integrating individual clinical expertise with the best available external clinical evidence from systematic research' (Sackett *et al.*, 1997). A systematic review of the relevant external evidence provides a framework for the integration of the research, and meta-analysis offers a quantitative summary of the results. In many cases a systematic review will include a meta-analysis, although there are some situations when

1

this will be impossible due to lack of data or inadvisable due to unexplained inconsistencies between studies.

The Cochrane Collaboration, launched in 1993, has been influential in the promotion of evidence-based medicine. This international network of individuals is committed to preparing, maintaining and disseminating systematic reviews of research on the effects of health care. Their reviews are made available electronically in the Cochrane Database of Systematic Reviews, part of the Cochrane Library (http://www.update-software.com/cochrane).

Within the pharmaceutical industry, meta-analysis can be used to summarize the results of a drug development programme, and this is recognized in the International Conference on Harmonization (ICH) E9 guidelines (ICH, 1998). In accordance with ICH E9, meta-analysis is understood to be a formal evaluation of the quantitative evidence from two or more trials bearing on the same question. The guidelines indicate that meta-analysis techniques provide a useful means of summarizing overall efficacy results of a drug application and of analysing less frequent outcomes in the overall safety evaluation. However, there is a warning that confirmation of efficacy from a meta-analysis only will not usually be accepted as a substitute for confirmation of efficacy from individual trials. Certainly the magnitude of the treatment effect is likely to be an important factor in regulatory decision-making. If the treatment effect is smaller than anticipated, then statistical significance may not be reached in the individual trials. Even if statistical significance is reached in the meta-analysis, the magnitude of the treatment effect may not be *clinically* significant, and thus be considered insufficient for approval.

Fisher (1999) considered the two conditions under which one large trial might substitute for the two controlled trials usually required by the Food and Drug Administration (FDA) in the USA. The first relates to the strength of evidence for demonstrating efficacy. He showed that if the evidence required from the two controlled trials is that they should each be statistically significant at the two-sided 5% significance level, then the same strength of evidence is obtained from one large trial if it is statistically significant at the two-sided 0.125% level. The same type of argument could be applied to combining trials in a meta-analysis. It would seem reasonable to set a more stringent level of statistical significance corresponding to proof of efficacy in a meta-analysis than in the individual trials.

The second condition discussed by Fisher relates to evidence of replicability, and he proposes criteria which need to be met by the one large trial. A meta-analysis will always involve at least two trials, and it will be important to assess the consistency of the results from the individual trials. The extent of any inconsistencies amongst the trials will be influential in the choice of model for the meta-analysis and in the decision whether to present an overall estimate. These issues are discussed in detail in Chapter 6 of this book.

A recent 'Points to Consider' document (Committee for Proprietary Medicinal Products, 2001) has provided guidance on when meta-analyses might usefully be undertaken. Reasons include the following:

- To provide a more precise estimate of the overall treatment effects.
- To evaluate whether overall positive results are also seen in pre-specified subgroups of patients.
- To evaluate an additional efficacy outcome that requires more power than the individual trials can provide.
- To evaluate safety in a subgroup of patients, or a rare adverse event in all patients.
- To improve the estimation of the dose-response relationship.
- To evaluate apparently conflicting study results.

There is much to be gained by undertaking a meta-analysis of relevant studies before starting a new clinical trial. As Chalmers and Lau (1993) note, this allows investigators to ascertain what data are needed to answer the important questions, how many patients should be recruited, and even whether a new study is unnecessary because the questions may have already been answered. Meta-analysis also has a useful role to play in the generation of hypotheses for future studies.

The conduct of a meta-analysis requires a team, which should include both statisticians and knowledgeable medical experts. Whilst the statistician is equipped with the technical knowledge, the medical expert has an important role to play in such activities as identifying the trials, defining the eligibility criteria for trials to be included, defining potential sources of heterogeneity and interpreting the results.

Most meta-analyses within the field of medical research have been conducted on randomized controlled trials, and this is the focus of this book. Other application areas include epidemiological studies and diagnostic studies. The special problems associated with observational studies are outside the scope of this book, and the interested reader is referred to Chapter 16 of Sutton *et al.* (2000) and Chapters 12–14 of Egger *et al.* (2001).

Over the last twenty years there have been great strides in the development and refinement of statistical methods for the conduct of meta-analyses, as illustrated in the books by Sutton *et al.* (2000) and Stangl and Berry (2000). A number of different approaches have been taken, giving the impression that the methodology is a collection of distinct techniques. The present book is self-contained and describes the planning, conduct and reporting of a meta-analysis as applied to a series of randomized controlled trials. It attempts to present the various approaches within a general unified framework, and to place this framework within mainstream statistical methodology.

## 1.2 RETROSPECTIVE AND PROSPECTIVE META-ANALYSES

Meta-analyses are often performed retrospectively on studies which have not been planned with this in mind. In addition, many are based on summary statistics which have been extracted from published papers. Consequently, there are a number of potential problems which can affect the validity of such meta-analyses.

A major limitation is that a meta-analysis can include only studies for which relevant data are retrievable. If only published studies are included, this raises concern about publication bias, whereby the probability of a study being published depends on the statistical significance of the results. Even if a study is published, there may be selective reporting of results, so that only the outcomes showing a statistically significant treatment difference are chosen from amongst the many analysed. If the outcomes of interest have not been defined or recorded in the same way in each trial, it may not be appropriate or possible to combine them. Even if identical outcomes have been recorded in each trial, the way in which the summary statistics have been calculated and reported may differ, particularly with regard to the choice of the subjects included and the mechanism of dealing with missing values. Matters can be improved if time and effort are devoted to obtaining data from all (or nearly all) of the randomized trials undertaken, irrespective of their publication status. Retrieving individual patient data from trial investigators is especially advantageous.

Typically, the objective of a meta-analysis is to estimate and make inferences about the difference between the effects of two treatments. This involves choosing an appropriate measure of the treatment difference, for example the log-odds ratio for binary data or the difference in means for normally distributed data, and calculating individual study estimates and an overall estimate of this difference. In a retrospective meta-analysis the available studies may vary in design, patient population, treatment regimen, primary outcome measure and quality. Therefore, it is reasonable to suppose that the true treatment difference will not be exactly the same in all trials: that is, there will be heterogeneity between trials. The effect of this heterogeneity on the overall results needs to be considered carefully, as discussed by Thompson (1994). Great care is needed in the selection of the trials to be included in the meta-analysis and in the interpretation of the results.

Prospectively planning a series of studies with a view to combining the results in a meta-analysis has distinct advantages, as many of the problems associated with retrospective meta-analyses then disappear. The individual trial protocols can be designed to be identical with regard to the collection of data to be included in the meta-analysis, and individual patient data can be made available.

In drug development, a co-ordinated approach to the trial programme, in which meta-analyses are preplanned, would seem to be a natural way to proceed. The results of a meta-analysis will be more convincing if it is specified prior to the results of any of the individual trials being known, is well conducted and demonstrates a clinically relevant effect.

Within the public sector, collaborative groups are beginning to form in order to conduct prospective meta-analyses. For example, the Cholesterol Treatment Trialists' Collaboration (1995) reported on their protocol for conducting an overview of all the current and planned randomized trials of cholesterol treatment regimens. In such cases it is unlikely that the meta-analysis can be planned before the start of any of the trials, but certainly the preparation of a protocol prior to the analysis of any of them offers considerable advantages.

The conduct of both retrospective and prospective meta-analyses will be discussed in this book. Many of the analysis methods are common to both, although methodological difficulties tend to be fewer and more manageable for the prospective meta-analysis.

## 1.3   FIXED EFFECTS VERSUS RANDOM EFFECTS

One of the controversies relating to meta-analysis has concerned the choice between the fixed effects model and the random effects model for providing an overall estimate of the treatment difference. The topic has usually been discussed in the context of a meta-analysis in which the data consist of trial estimates of the treatment difference together with their standard errors. In the fixed effects model, the true treatment difference is considered to be the same for all trials. The standard error of each trial estimate is based on sampling variation within the trial. In the random effects model, the true treatment difference in each trial is itself assumed to be a realization of a random variable, which is usually assumed to be normally distributed. As a consequence, the standard error of each trial estimate is increased due to the addition of this between-trial variation.

The overall estimate of treatment difference and its confidence interval based on a fixed effects model provide a useful summary of the results. However, they are specific to the particular trials included in the meta-analysis. One problem is that they do not necessarily provide the best information for determining the difference in effect that can be expected for patients in general. The random effects model allows the between-trial variability to be accounted for in the overall estimate and, more particularly, its standard error. Therefore, it can be argued that it produces results which can be considered to be more generalizable. In principle, it would seem that the random effects model is a more appropriate choice for attempting to answer this question. However, there are some concerns regarding the use of the random effects model in practice. First, the random effects model assumes that the results from the trials included in the meta-analysis are representative of the results which would be obtained from the total population of treatment centres. In reality, centres which take part in clinical trials are not chosen at random. Second, when there are only a few trials for inclusion in the meta-analysis, it may be inappropriate to try to fit a random effects model as any calculated estimate of the between-study variance will be unreliable. When there is only one available trial, its analysis can only be based on a fixed effects model.

When there is no heterogeneity between trials both models lead to the same overall estimate and standard error. As the heterogeneity increases the standard error of the overall estimate from the random effects model increases relative to that from the fixed effects model. The difference between the overall estimates from the two approaches depends to a large extent on the magnitude of the estimates from the large informative trials in relation to the others. For example, if a meta-analysis is based on one large study with a small positive estimate and several small studies with large positive estimates, the overall estimate from the random effects model will be larger than that from the fixed effects model, the difference increasing with increasing heterogeneity. The more conservative approach of the random effects model will in general lead to larger numbers of patients being required to demonstrate a significant treatment difference than the fixed effects approach.

It may be useful in many cases to consider the results from both a fixed effects model and a random effects model. If they lead to important differences in conclusion, then this highlights the need for further investigation. For example, this could be due to variability in study quality, differences in study protocols, or differences in the study populations.

When individual patient data are available the models can be extended to include the trial effect. As the trial effect may also be included as a fixed or random effect, this leads to an increased choice of models, as discussed by Senn (2000). These models are presented in detail in Chapter 5 of this book, and comparisons made between them.

## 1.4    INDIVIDUAL PATIENT DATA VERSUS SUMMARY STATISTICS

There is wide variation in the amount and form of data which might be available for a meta-analysis. At one extreme a common outcome measure may have been used in all studies, with individual data available for all patients. At the other extreme the only available data may be the $p$-value from each study associated with the test of a treatment difference, or, even worse, a statement in a published paper to the effect that the $p$-value was or was not smaller than 0.05. In between, we may be confronted with summary statistics from published papers, individual patient data based on similar but not identically defined outcome measures, or a mixture of individual patient data and summary statistics.

A meta-analysis using individual patient data is likely to prove more comprehensive and reliable than one based on summary statistics obtained from publications and reports. Such an analysis will benefit from a standardized approach being taken to the extraction of relevant data and to the handling of missing data. In addition, if data at a patient level, such as age, gender or disease severity, are available, the relationship between these and the treatment difference can be explored. To be successful, such a meta-analysis will usually involve a considerable amount of time devoted to the planning, data collection and analysis stages. The advantages of a prospectively planned meta-analysis now become apparent.

Pharmaceutical statisticians are often in a good position to perform a meta-analysis on individual patient data, as they will usually have access to all original data from trials on the company's own as yet unlicensed product. Even if the meta-analysis is retrospective, data from the various trials will often have been stored electronically in similarly structured databases. Outside the pharmaceutical industry, the task is more daunting. Details of the practical issues involved in such an undertaking can be found in Stewart and Clarke (1995), a paper resulting from a workshop held by the Cochrane working group on meta-analysis using individual patient data.

Meta-analyses based on individual patient data have clear advantages over those based on extracted summary statistics. However, they are time-consuming and costly, and the situation may arise in which the additional resources needed to obtain individual patient data are not available or cannot be justified. Even if it is planned to obtain individual patient data, it may not be possible to obtain these from all relevant studies. Therefore, many meta-analyses are conducted using summary statistics collected from each trial.

If the purpose of the meta-analysis is to provide an overall estimate of treatment difference, an individual trial can only be included if there is sufficient information from that trial to calculate an estimate of the treatment difference and its standard error. In some cases the summary statistics which are available from a trial enable the same calculations to be performed as if individual patient data were available. For example, for a binary outcome knowledge of the number of successes and failures in each treatment group is sufficient.

Because of the variety of ways in which data are made available for meta-analyses, a number of different techniques for conducting meta-analyses have been developed. This book attempts to present the various approaches within a general framework, highlighting the similarities and differences.

## 1.5 MULTICENTRE TRIALS AND META-ANALYSIS

Multicentre trials are usually conducted to enable the required number of patients to be recruited within an acceptable period of time and to provide a wider representation of the patient population than would be found at a single centre. A multicentre trial will have been designed prospectively with a combined analysis of the data from all centres as its main objective. Individual centres are expected to follow a common protocol, at least with respect to collection of the main efficacy data. When a meta-analysis is to be undertaken on a series of clinical trials, in which a common outcome measure has been recorded and individual patient data are available, it could be analysed using the same linear modelling techniques as are applied to the analysis of a multicentre trial. Here 'trial' would play the role of 'centre'. On the other hand the analysis of a multicentre trial could be conducted using traditional meta-analysis methods, in which 'centre' plays the role of 'trial'.

There is a continuum from the true multicentre trial, in which all centres follow an identical protocol, to a collection of trials addressing the same general therapeutic question but with different protocols. The same statistical methods can be applied across the continuum, but the choice of the most appropriate method and the validity of the results may vary. There are differences between the approaches *traditionally* applied to the analysis of multicentre trials and those applied in meta-analysis, as discussed by Senn (2000). This is perhaps because most of the meta-analyses which appear in the medical literature are retrospective and based on summary data from published papers. The differences relate to the way in which the trial estimates of treatment difference are combined and the choice between random and fixed effects models. These issues will be covered in Chapter 5.

## 1.6    THE STRUCTURE OF THIS BOOK

The focus of this book is on the planning, conduct and reporting of a meta-analysis as applied to a series of randomized controlled trials. It covers the approaches required for retrospective and prospective meta-analyses, as well as for those based on either summary statistics or individual patient data.

The meta-analysis techniques are described in detail, from their theoretical development through to practical implementation. The intention is to present the various statistical methods which are available within a general unified framework, so that the similarities and differences between them become apparent. This is done at a level that can be understood by medical statisticians and statistically minded clinicians and health research professionals. Emphasis is placed on the consequences of choosing a particular approach, the implementation of the chosen method and the interpretation of the results. For interested readers, the mathematical theory underlying the methods is summarized in the Appendix.

The methodology throughout this book is illustrated by examples. All of the methods presented can be implemented using mainstream statistical packages. Most of the analyses presented in the book were conducted using the standard statistical procedures in SAS (Version 8.0: website at http://www.sas.com). At appropriate places in the text, SAS code relating to the specification of the model is provided. For fitting random effects models when individual patient data are available and the response type is binary or ordinal, the program MLn (Version 1.0A) or its interactive Windows version MLwiN (Version 1.10: website at http://multilevel.ioe.ac.uk) was utilized. The interactive Windows version of BUGS, WinBUGS (Version 1.3: website at http://www.mrc-bsu.cam.ac.uk/bugs) was used for the Bayesian analyses and PEST 4 (website at http://www.rdg.ac.uk/mps/mps_home/software/software.htm) was used for the cumulative meta-analyses. For these other packages, the details of their implementation are discussed in the text. The example data sets and the program code for the analyses may be obtained electronically from the Wiley ftp site at ftp://ftp.wiley.co.uk/pub/books/whitehead and also from the author at http://www.rdg.ac.uk/mps/mps_home/misc/publications.htm.

There is now a wide range of software available specifically for performing a meta-analysis. These include both specialist packages and general statistical packages with meta-analysis routines. They have not been used for the implementation of the methods presented in this book because they have a limited range of options and lack the flexibility to accommodate the more advanced statistical modelling techniques. A recent review of meta-analysis software has been undertaken by Sterne *et al.* (2001b) and the reader is referred to this for further details. This review updates a previous one by Egger *et al.* (1998).

The preparation of a protocol is an important first stage in the conduct of a meta-analysis, and the items which need to be considered for inclusion in the protocol are discussed in Chapter 2.

The main statistical methods used in performing a meta-analysis are described in Chapters 3–5. The methodology is presented in detail for the situation in which each trial has a parallel group design, and a comparison is to be made between two treatments each of which are studied in each trial. This is the most straightforward application and the most common in practice. Usually one treatment will be the newly developed treatment of interest and the other a placebo or standard treatment. The main emphasis is on estimating and making inferences about the difference between the effects of the two treatments.

Meta-analyses are being conducted for an increasing diversity of diseases and conditions, involving a variety of outcome measures. In this book five different types of outcome are discussed in detail, namely binary, survival, interval-censored survival, ordinal and normally distributed. Chapter 3 is divided into sections, each of which considers one particular type of data. For each data type, the choice of an appropriate measure of treatment difference is addressed, together with the methods of estimation which are traditionally used within the context of an individual clinical trial.

Chapter 4 presents a methodology for combining the trial estimates of a treatment difference, based on Whitehead and Whitehead (1991). This approach is of use primarily when data available for the meta-analysis consist of summary statistics from each trial. It may also be used when individual patient data are available, but in this case the more advanced statistical modelling techniques of Chapter 5 may be preferred. In Chapter 4, meta-analyses based on the fixed effects model are illustrated for the different data types. The extension to the random effects model is also presented.

Chapter 5 considers various models which can be fitted making full use of individual patient data. These models include terms for the trial effect, which can be assumed to be a fixed effect or a random effect. The pros and cons of each model are discussed, and comparisons made with models used for multicentre trials.

It is important to assess the consistency between the individual trial estimates of treatment difference. Chapter 6 discusses the issues involved in this assessment, and how the amount of heterogeneity might affect the choice of model for the meta-analysis or even whether to present an overall estimate at all. In some situations the treatment difference may be expected to vary from one level of a factor to another. Regression techniques can be used to explore this if additional data at the trial level or at the patient level are available. Such techniques are described in this chapter. Finally, a strategy for dealing with heterogeneity is proposed.

The presentation and interpretation of results is addressed in Chapter 7. The QUOROM statement (Moher *et al.*, 1999) which provides guidance on the reporting of meta-analyses of clinical trials is used as a basis for the discussion of the structure of a report. Graphical displays, which have an important role to play, are described.

When judging the reliability of the results of a meta-analysis, attention should focus on factors which might systematically influence the overall estimate of the treatment difference. One important factor is the selection of studies for inclusion in the meta-analysis. Chapter 8 considers the possible reasons why some trials may be excluded from a meta-analysis and how the problems might be addressed, focusing particularly on publication bias.

Chapter 9 deals with some of the issues arising from non-standard data sets. These include the problems of having no events in one or more of the treatment arms of individual trials and the use of different rating scales or different times of assessment across trials. Ways of combining trials which report different summary statistics and of combining *p*-values when it is impossible to estimate the treatment difference are also discussed.

Although the main focus of the book is on parallel group studies comparing two treatments, it is often desirable to consider the inclusion of other types of study in the meta-analysis. Chapter 10 considers the incorporation of data from multi-centre trials, cross-over trials and sequential trials. Also, the handling of multiple treatment comparisons and the investigation of dose – response relationships are discussed.

Most of the statistical methods presented in this book have been derived from a classical (frequentist) approach. Chapter 11 presents a Bayesian approach to meta-analysis. Comparisons are made with the results from the frequentist analyses.

A cumulative meta-analysis involves repeated meta-analyses following completion of a further one or more studies addressing the same question. Repeated meta-analyses are becoming more common, and are encouraged within the Cochrane Collaboration so that the information in the Cochrane Library can be kept up to date. An analogy can be made with the conduct of a sequential clinical trial, in which information about the treatment difference is updated by conducting interim analyses. Chapter 12 considers the role that sequential methods may play in the conduct of a cumulative meta-analysis. Application to prospectively planned meta-analyses is discussed.

# 2

# *Protocol Development*

## 2.1  INTRODUCTION

Before starting a clinical trial it is standard practice to prepare a study protocol, specifying in detail the procedures to be followed. Likewise, it should be standard practice to prepare a protocol for conducting a meta-analysis, particularly as this is often a complex process. As is the case for an individual study, it may be necessary to make changes to the meta-analysis protocol due to unforeseen circumstances. Protocol amendments can be made for a meta-analysis, in the same way as they can for an individual trial. Such changes should be documented and their impact on the results discussed. In a meta-analysis protocol it will be necessary to state the key hypotheses of interest. This should not prevent the conduct of exploratory analyses, undertaken to explain the findings and to suggest hypotheses for future studies. However, when the results are reported it is important to make a clear distinction between the preplanned analyses and the exploratory analyses.

In the development of a new drug or medical intervention there is an obvious advantage in designing the clinical trial programme to take account of the need for a meta-analysis. Individual trial protocols can include common elements, such as identically defined outcome measures. Preparation of the protocol for a meta-analysis before the start of any of the trials is the ideal situation. Certainly the existence of a meta-analysis protocol is a reminder that the impact of changes to a study protocol needs to be considered on a global scale rather than on an individual trial basis. There will, of course, be times when the need for a meta-analysis will not be identified until after some or all of the trials have started. Provided that the meta-analysis protocol is prepared before results from any of the trials are available, this is unlikely to compromise the integrity of the meta-analysis in any important way.

The preparation of a protocol is perhaps even more crucial for a retrospective meta-analysis, or for one planned following the disclosure of the results from one or more trials. For such meta-analyses there is the possibility of bias being introduced due to study selection. In many cases it may only be possible to perform the meta-analysis on a subset of the studies because of inconsistency in the recording and/or reporting of outcome measures or incompatible trial designs. Further, if the meta-analysis is restricted to data obtained from published papers, the overall treatment difference may be overestimated because studies with statistically significant results are more likely to be published than those without. If the meta-analysis is undertaken because of the announcement of some very positive results, this may lead to an overestimation of the treatment difference. As a consequence, more attention will need to be given in the protocol to addressing the implications of these potential biases for the meta-analysis.

This chapter is concerned with the content of a meta-analysis protocol. Many of the items discussed will be common to both prospective and retrospective meta-analyses, although for a retrospective analysis the investigation of selection bias will require specific attention. Comprehensive guidelines for undertaking systematic reviews have been produced (see, for example, Cook et al., 1995; Deeks et al., 1996; Clarke and Oxman, 2001). Their focus is on retrospective reviews and meta-analyses, usually undertaken on summary statistics extracted from published papers. In this chapter, the list of topics covered is similar to those which appear in these guidelines. However, the topics are discussed in the context of a prospective as well as a retrospective meta-analysis, and also for individual patient data as well as summary statistics.

## 2.2   BACKGROUND

Background information helps to set the scene for the meta-analysis. Topics which might be included are a definition of the disease or condition in question, its incidence, prognosis, public health importance and alternative available treatments. General information on the treatment being evaluated will relate to its mechanism of action, results from its use in other indications and the rationale for its use in the disease or condition in question. The results of earlier meta-analyses could be discussed. The reasons for undertaking the current meta-analysis should be provided.

## 2.3   OBJECTIVES

The main objectives of the meta-analysis should be stated. For example, in the case of a new treatment for Alzheimer's disease, the objective might be to evaluate the efficacy and safety of the new treatment, when administered for up to six months according to a particular dosing regimen to patients with mild to moderate Alzheimer's disease, where efficacy is assessed in terms of cognitive performance and clinical global impression, and safety is assessed in terms of the occurrence of adverse events. A brief description should be provided of the types of study which will be examined.

## 2.4   OUTCOME MEASURES AND BASELINE INFORMATION

A list of all of the outcome measures to be analysed, with definitions where appropriate, should be given. As in the case of an individual trial, it is advisable to specify which of the efficacy measures is the primary one, so that the problem associated with multiple testing – that is, too many false positives – can be minimized. Often assessments are repeated at various timepoints during the trial, and how these are to be dealt with should be mentioned. If the assessment at one particular timepoint is of primary interest this should be stated. For example, the primary efficacy measure in the Alzheimer's disease meta-analysis might be the change in the cognitive subscale of the Alzheimer's Disease Assessment Scale between baseline and the six-month assessment.

It will often be important to obtain data on baseline variables such as demographic characteristics, prognostic factors and baseline assessments of efficacy and safety measures. There are several ways in which such data may be useful. First, they can be used to check the comparability of patients allocated to each of the treatment arms in each study, enabling within-study and between-study comparisons to be made. Second, if individual patient data are available, an analysis of covariance may be performed in which adjustment is made for one or more baseline variables considered likely to have an important affect on the outcome measure. Such variables would be prespecified. Third, baseline variables may be used to investigate heterogeneity in the treatment difference across studies or subgroups.

## 2.5   SOURCES OF DATA

In order to minimize problems associated with selection bias, it is important to identify all trials which could potentially contribute to the meta-analysis. This part of the protocol should provide details of the search strategy to be employed. When the meta-analysis is preplanned no search strategy is required because the relevant trials are identified before they are undertaken. A pharmaceutical company undertaking a retrospective meta-analysis on one of its own unlicensed drugs is likely to know about all trials which have been undertaken with the drug. In this case the search strategy will be reasonably straightforward, and a list of the company data sources can be provided. However, in all other cases careful thought needs to be given to the search strategy. Possible information sources include online bibliographic databases of published and unpublished research, trial registries, expert informants and the pharmaceutical industry. The restrictions to be applied, such as, publication status, language of publication and the time-frame concerning the year of publication should be specified. For example, in a meta-analysis conducted to examine the benefits of adding salmeterol as opposed to increasing the dose of inhaled steroid in subjects with symptomatic asthma, the EMBASE, Medline and GlaxoWellcome databases were searched for all relevant publications and abstracts from 1985 until 1998 in any language (Shrewsbury *et al.*, 2000). For further information about searching strategies, the reader is referred to Chapters 4–7 of Cooper and Hedges (1994) and Clarke and Oxman (2001).

## 2.6   STUDY SELECTION

The selection criteria for studies in the meta-analysis should be specified. If there is more than one hypothesis to be tested it may be necessary to define separate selection criteria for each one. In addition, for each hypothesis of interest, it may be desirable to create two groups of studies. The first group would consist of the primary studies on which the formal meta-analysis would be undertaken. The second group would consist of additional studies whose results may be included in a sensitivity analysis, or in a graphical presentation of individual study results. Such studies may involve different patient populations or treatment comparisons from the primary studies, or may have less appropriate designs. However, their results may still be informative.

Careful thought needs to be given to the selection criteria for the primary studies. If they are very strict, the results of the meta-analysis may only be applicable to a small subset of the patient population or to a very specific treatment regimen, whereas if they are too liberal, it may not be possible to combine the individual trial results in an informative way.

Typically, the selection criteria will define the treatment of interest and the relevant subject population. This should follow logically from the statement of the objectives of the meta-analysis. In addition, they may relate to the type of study design used. For example, the selection criteria used in the salmeterol meta-analysis mentioned in Section 2.5 were stated as follows: a randomized controlled trial; direct comparison between adding salmeterol to the current dose of inhaled steroid and increasing (at least doubling) the dose of the current inhaled steroid; study duration of 12 weeks or longer; subjects aged 12 years or older with symptomatic asthma on the current dose of inhaled steroids.

The assessment of the methodological quality of a trial may also be used to determine its eligibility for inclusion in the group of primary studies. The most important aspect of this assessment concerns the avoidance of bias in the estimation of the treatment difference of interest. Therefore, design issues, such as the method of randomizing subjects to treatment group, blinding, method of assessing patient outcome, follow-up of patients, and handling of protocol deviations and patient withdrawals from the trial, are likely to feature prominently. It may be appropriate to categorize studies according to how well they adhere to important methodological standards. For further discussion on the types of scoring systems which have been devised, the reader is referred to Moher *et al.* (1995).

In the report of a meta-analysis it will be necessary to include a list of studies which were excluded as well as a list of studies which were included. The reason for exclusion should be provided for each excluded study. It may be advantageous to have more than one assessor decide independently which studies to include or exclude, together with a well-defined checklist and a procedure which will be followed when they disagree.

In some cases, new information may surface during the reading of the study reports which indicate a need to modify the study selection criteria.

## 2.7   DATA EXTRACTION

A specification of the data items to be extracted should be provided. It may be useful to produce an additional document which details the desired format for the data, the recommended coding and the data checking procedures.

A meta-analysis based on individual patient data is likely to provide the most reliable information, as it will not depend on the way in which individual trial results are reported. For such a meta-analysis the aim should be to obtain individual patient data from all randomized subjects in all relevant trials. This will enable a consistent approach to be taken towards the coding of data and the handling of missing data across all trials. If there is a common database structure for all trials, this will facilitate the integration of their data. However, for many retrospective meta-analyses the data are not centrally located, and considerable time and effort are required to collect all of the necessary items together. Stewart and Clarke (1995) discuss the practical aspects of data collection and data checking when data are being supplied by individual trialists.

In many cases meta-analyses are conducted using summary information from published papers or trial reports. Even if the plan is to collect individual patient data from all trials, there may be some trials for which this is not possible. Also, as part of a sensitivity analysis it may be desirable to include results from additional studies from which only summary information is available. In these situations, consideration needs to be given to the type of information which will be required. Take, for example, the case of a dichotomous outcome, in which the patient response is either 'success' or 'failure'. To use the meta-analysis methodology described in Chapter 4, a measure of treatment difference must be chosen. Suppose that the chosen measure is the log-odds ratio of success on the new treatment relative to placebo. A trial can only be included in the meta-analysis if the available data from the trial enable an estimate of the log-odds ratio and its variance to be calculated. Knowledge of the number of successes and failures in each treatment group in each trial is sufficient. However, if the only available data from a trial is the estimate of the difference in the success probabilities between the two treatment groups, the trial cannot be included. Further details about what constitutes sufficient information are provided in Chapter 3. In addition, Section 9.5 considers ways of combining trials which report different summary statistics and Section 9.6 ways of imputing estimates of the treatment difference and its variance.

If the data available for the meta-analysis are mainly summary statistics from trial reports and publications, then it may be possible to extract some useful additional information from the trialists. For example, the trialist may be able to clarify whether the reported analysis of a binary response was based on all randomized patients or on a selected subset. If the latter, the trialist may be able to provide the numbers of 'successes' and 'failures' amongst the excluded patients. A data collection form, detailing the information required, can be distributed to the trialists. The process of extracting additional information from trialists is facilitated by having as part of the meta-analysis team clinical experts who know the field and the trialists.

## 2.8   STATISTICAL ANALYSIS

The principal features of the statistical analysis should be included in the main protocol, although it may also be useful to produce separately a detailed statistical analysis plan. For each outcome variable to be analysed the following items should be considered.

### 2.8.1   Analysis population

The set of subjects who are to be included in the meta-analysis should be defined. This will usually be based on the intention-to-treat principle, which in respect of an individual trial specifies that all randomized patients should be included in the analysis as members of the treatment group to which they were randomized. This principle is important in preventing bias and providing an objective basis for statistical analysis.

In the ideal situation in which all randomized subjects satisfy all of the trial selection criteria, comply with all of the trial procedures and provide complete data, the intention-to-treat analysis is straightforward to implement. However, this ideal situation is unlikely to be achieved in practice. Provided that there is proper justification and that bias is unlikely to be introduced, it may be considered appropriate to exclude certain randomized subjects from the analysis set. In the ICH E9 (ICH, 1998) guidelines the term 'full analysis' set is used to describe the analysis set which is as complete as possible and as close as possible to the intention-to-treat ideal of including all randomized subjects.

Reports of clinical trials often include analyses undertaken on a second set of subjects, referred to as the 'per protocol' set. The 'per protocol' set is a subset of patients who are more compliant with the protocol. For example, they are not classified as major protocol violators, they complete a minimum period on study treatment and provide data for the primary efficacy analysis. Sometimes an analysis is undertaken on all subjects who complete the study period and provide data on the primary efficacy variable, referred to as a 'completers' analysis. This is an example of a 'per protocol' analysis. Because adherence to the study protocol may be related to the treatment and to the outcome, analyses based on the 'per protocol' set may be biased. For example, in a comparison of a new treatment with placebo, if patients who cannot tolerate the new treatment withdraw early from the trial, the analysis based on the 'per protocol' set may produce a larger estimate of the treatment difference than that based on the 'full analysis' set. Therefore, whilst a meta-analysis based on a 'per protocol' set may be undertaken as part of a sensitivity analysis, the evidence from an analysis based on the 'full analysis' set will usually be more convincing.

Whilst it is envisaged that most meta-analyses will be undertaken to determine if one treatment is superior to another, some will be undertaken to determine if two treatments are equivalent. In the latter case, the conservative nature of the intention-to-treat approach may be inappropriate and the meta-analysis based on a 'per protocol' set should be looked at on a more equal footing with that based on the 'full analysis' set.

When the meta-analysis is to be conducted using individual patient data, it is desirable to obtain data from all randomized patients, so that the most appropriate analysis can be undertaken. Difficulties may arise when a meta-analysis is based on summary information from published papers or trial reports in which the various authors have chosen different criteria for their main analysis set. In particular, some papers may only provide results from a 'full analysis' set, whereas others may only provide results from a 'per protocol' set. In such situations it may be advisable to separate the studies using 'full analysis' sets from those using 'per protocol' sets, before ascertaining whether or not it would be appropriate to combine them.

The set of subjects to be included in the assessment of safety and tolerability is often defined as those subjects who received at least one dose of the study medication, and is sometimes referred to as the 'safety analysis' set. The 'safety analysis' set would seem to be an appropriate choice for a meta-analysis of safety and tolerability data.

## 2.8.2 Missing data at the subject level

Difficulties arise in the analysis of a clinical trial when data are missing from some subjects. The intention-to-treat principle defines the set of subjects to be included in the analysis, but does not specify how to deal with missing data. As for an individual trial, the effect of data missing at the subject level on the overall results from a meta-analysis will need to be addressed.

Some subjects who meet the criteria for the 'full analysis' set may not provide data on some of the outcomes of interest, including the primary efficacy variable. This could occur if a subject withdraws from treatment part-way through the study and provides no further data after this point or if the subject is lost to follow-up. One option is to perform the analysis of each outcome variable using only those subjects who provide data on that particular variable. This means that the set of subjects contributing to each analysis may vary. More importantly, this approach relies on the assumption that data are missing at random, that is, the absence of a recorded value is not dependent on its actual value (see, for example, Little and Rubin, 1987). In particular, if the mechanisms for data being missing differs between the study treatments, then the exclusion of the subject from the analysis may introduce bias into the estimate of the treatment difference.

An alternative strategy is to substitute values for the missing data. If the outcome of interest is measured at various timepoints during the study, values from early timepoints can be used to impute data for the later missing values. Imputation techniques range from carrying forward the last observation to the use of complex mathematical models (see, for example, Rubin, 1987; Little, 1995). However, caution is required as imputation techniques may themselves lead to biased estimates of the treatment difference. In some trials data continue to be collected according to the intended schedule on patients who withdraw early from study treatment. Such data may be used in the analysis, although careful thought needs to be given to this as such patients may have received alternative medication.

If there is a substantial amount of missing data, the reliability of the analysis may be questioned. In this case it may be useful to undertake sensitivity analyses in which the effects of different imputation schemes are compared.

When the meta-analysis is to be performed using individual patient data, the planned method for dealing with missing data should be described. If no imputation is to be undertaken, then this should be stated.

When meta-analyses are based on summary information from published papers, the amount of missing data and the way in which they have been handled by the author may be factors for consideration in the assessment of the methodological quality of a trial.

### 2.8.3   Analysis of individual trials

It is important to present the results from the individual trials as well as the results from the meta-analysis. Individual trial summaries may not be the same as those presented in earlier trial reports and publications because it is desirable to take the same approach to the analysis of each of the trials and to make this consistent with the meta-analysis. When individual patient data are available a reanalysis using a common approach will often be possible. However, this is unlikely to be the case for meta-analyses based on summary information. In this situation one hopes that the summary information will permit the use of the same measure of treatment difference in all studies.

The chosen measure of treatment difference should be specified. For example, for binary data this might be the log-odds ratio or for continuous data it might be the absolute difference in means. Details of the various measures of treatment difference which can be used for commonly occurring types of data are presented in Chapter 3.

## 2.8.4 Meta-analysis model

The proposed meta-analysis model should be specified, including which terms are to be treated as fixed effects and which random effects. Models which can be used for the combination of trial estimates of treatment difference are discussed in Chapter 4. A model which assumes that the parameter measuring treatment difference is the same across all trials is typically referred to as a 'fixed effects' model. A model which allows this parameter to act as a random variable taking different values from one trial to the next is typically referred to as a 'random effects' model. Issues relating to the choice of a fixed or random effects model are discussed in Chapter 6. When individual patient data are available the statistical modelling approach of Chapter 5 may be used. Within this framework it is straightforward to include additional covariates in the model, to enable adjustment for prognostic factors which are considered likely to affect the outcome data.

## 2.8.5 Estimation and hypothesis testing

The main hypotheses to be tested should be specified. For example, in the comparison of a new treatment against the standard treatment the null hypothesis of no treatment difference might be tested against the two-sided alternative of some difference between the two treatments. If the new treatment has been tested at more than one dose level, it may not be appropriate to combine the data from all doses together. There may be one dose level of prime interest. Alternatively, or additionally, it may be of interest to investigate the dose-response relationship.

## 2.8.6 Testing for heterogeneity

Meta-analyses are often performed retrospectively on studies which were not planned with this in mind. In many situations it might be expected that differences in the study protocols will produce heterogeneity. Also, even if the same protocols are used for all studies, variability in study quality, possibly due to mistakes in implementing the protocol, may give rise to heterogeneity. Therefore, it is common to include a test for heterogeneity in the treatment difference parameter across studies. A test for heterogeneity when trial estimates are being combined is presented in Chapter 4, and analogous tests based on individual patient data are presented in Chapter 5.

The test for heterogeneity is sometimes used to decide whether to present an overall fixed effects or an overall random effects estimate of the treatment difference. For example, if the $p$-value is less than or equal to 0.05 then the random effects estimate may be calculated, and otherwise the fixed effects estimate. Although the result of a statistical test for heterogeneity provides some useful descriptive information about the variability between trials, a decision based purely on the $p$-value, as described above, is not to be recommended. Further discussion of this point is provided in Chapter 6.

### 2.8.7   Exploration of heterogeneity

Potential sources of heterogeneity can be identified in advance, and methods for their investigation described. Their investigation can be undertaken via the inclusion of covariate by treatment interaction terms in the meta-analysis model. Further details are given in Chapter 6. If an interaction reaches statistical and clinical significance, then it will be appropriate to present the relationship between the magnitude of the treatment difference and the covariate. For a continuous variable, such as age, a graphical display of its effect on the magnitude of the treatment difference may be informative. When the covariate term represents a factor with a small number of levels, the treatment difference can be presented for each level of the factor. This is often referred to as a subgroup analysis. A test of the hypothesis of a common treatment difference across all subgroups is the same as a test of the hypothesis that a covariate by treatment interaction term is zero. To avoid too many false positive results, it is desirable to limit the number of covariates investigated in this way.

## 2.9   SENSITIVITY ANALYSES

Consideration should be given to performing sensitivity analyses to test the key assumptions made. In particular, meta-analyses may be repeated with some trials excluded. Alternatively, or in addition, the results from studies not classified as primary studies can be considered. One option is to display their results alongside the primary studies in a graphical display. Also, the meta-analysis can be repeated with these results included.

Potential sources of systematic bias in the overall estimate of treatment difference need to be addressed. In the case of a retrospective meta-analysis, or a meta-analysis conducted after some of the individual trial results are available, the selection of studies for inclusion in the meta-analysis may introduce a systematic bias. The possible impact that this may have on the results of the meta-analysis needs to be addressed. Selection bias is discussed in detail in Chapter 8.

## 2.10 PRESENTATION OF RESULTS

Thought should be given to the way in which the results are to be reported. For example, individual study estimates of treatment difference and their confidence intervals can be presented and displayed graphically together with those from the meta-analysis. Further discussion of this topic is deferred to Chapter 7.

# 3

# *Estimating the Treatment Difference in an Individual Trial*

## 3.1  INTRODUCTION

Many meta-analyses concern the comparison of two treatments in terms of a selected set of outcome measures. For each chosen outcome measure, the aim is usually to estimate and make inferences about the difference between the effects of the two treatments. This involves choosing an appropriate measure (parameterization) of the treatment difference, and calculating individual study estimates and an overall estimate of this difference. A traditional meta-analysis is one in which the overall estimate of treatment difference is calculated from a weighted average of the individual study estimates.

Meta-analyses may be performed on studies for which the available data are in the form of summary information from trial reports or publications, or on studies for which individual patient data are available. The form of the data available from each study has implications for the meta-analysis, and here three forms which are commonly encountered are considered.

The first consists of an estimate of the treatment difference and its variance or standard error – the minimum amount of information needed. If a study provides an estimate of treatment difference which is not an estimate of the chosen parameterization it may not be possible to include it. For example, in the context of binary data, we may wish to estimate the log-odds ratio, and so a study for which only an estimate of the probability difference is available cannot be used.

The second form of data is slightly more detailed, consisting of summary statistics for each treatment group, enabling a choice to be made between several different parameterizations of the treatment difference. For example, in the context of normally distributed data, knowing the sample size, mean and standard deviation for each treatment group allows estimation of the absolute mean difference or the standardized mean difference.

The third form, individual patient data, allows the most flexibility. In this case it is possible to choose any sensible parameterization of the treatment difference and method of estimation. In addition, if all the studies provide individual patient data, a more thorough analysis can be undertaken by employing a statistical modelling approach.

The traditional meta-analysis approach can be used when the available data are in the form of study estimates, study summary statistics, individual patient data or a combination of the different forms of data. This chapter focuses on the estimation of the treatment difference from an individual study, and Chapter 4 presents a methodology for combining such study estimates.

In this chapter five different types of outcome data are discussed in detail, namely binary, survival, interval-censored survival, ordinal and normally distributed. The chapter is divided into sections, each of which addresses one particular data type. At the start of each section an example data set is introduced for illustrative purposes. Then, within the context of a parallel group study comparing a treated group with a control group, there is discussion of the various parameterizations of the treatment difference and methods of estimation which are commonly used. Methods of estimation based on individual patient data are presented. The reasons for this are twofold. First, these methods could be used to calculate study estimates when individual patient data are indeed available. Second, these methods are likely to be the ones used to calculate study estimates which are presented in trial reports or publications.

In an individual clinical trial the likelihood ratio test is frequently used to test the hypothesis concerning the treatment difference. The maximum likelihood (ML) estimate of the treatment difference is then typically presented with a standard error or confidence interval. ML estimation has the advantages of asymptotic optimality and general availability in statistical packages. This is the principal method of estimation which is presented in this book. As ML estimation involves iterative procedures and is usually performed via a statistical package, a specification of the methodology is presented together with a SAS procedure which could be utilized. The likelihood approach to a single clinical trial can be extended to the meta-analysis of all of the trials when individual patient data are available. This likelihood approach to meta-analysis is described in Chapter 5, and the mathematical formulation of the underlying statistical models is deferred to that chapter.

A simpler approach to estimation, based on the efficient score and Fisher's information statistics, has been widely used for meta-analysis, and so will also be presented in this chapter and discussed in some of the later chapters. This approach, on which a number of commonly used statistical tests are based, produces approximate ML estimates. Explicit formulae are available, which are straightforward to use.

Notation is now introduced that will be used in this and later chapters. The parameter $\theta$ will denote the measure of treatment difference. Usually, $\theta$ will be defined to take the value 0 when the two treatments are equivalent. The estimate of $\theta$ will be represented by $\hat{\theta}$, the estimated variance of $\hat{\theta}$ by $\text{var}(\hat{\theta})$ and its standard error by $\text{se}(\hat{\theta})$. The efficient score for $\theta$ evaluated under the null hypothesis that $\theta = 0$ is denoted by $Z$, and the observed Fisher's information also evaluated at $\theta = 0$ by $V$. When $\theta$ is small, the approximate distributional result $Z \sim N(\theta V, V)$ can be used. The estimate $\hat{\theta} = Z/V$ is an approximate ML estimate, with corresponding standard error $1/\sqrt{V}$ and variance $= 1/V$. The score test statistic $Z^2/V$ can be referred to the chi-squared distribution on one degree of freedom in an approximate likelihood ratio test.

The technical detail showing the relationship between the ML approach and that based on efficient score and Fisher's information is presented in Section A.5 of the Appendix. The estimate of $\theta$ given by $Z/V$ is sometimes referred to as the 'one-step estimate' because it is obtained on the first step of a Newton–Raphson procedure to maximize the log-likelihood function when the starting value for $\theta$ is 0. Although this estimate is asymptotically unbiased under the null hypothesis that $\theta = 0$, it becomes increasingly biased the further $\theta$ moves from 0. This has been discussed in the context of the log-odds ratio parameter for binary data by Greenland and Salvan (1990). The usual concerns about the accuracy of the asymptotic theory underlying the properties of both the ML and the score approaches are less pertinent in meta-analysis, where total sample sizes are almost always large.

## 3.2 BINARY DATA

### 3.2.1 Example: Stroke in hypertensive patients

Collins *et al.* (1990) presented a meta-analysis of the results from 14 randomized trials of antihypertensive drugs, which were chiefly diuretics or beta-blockers. These trials were conducted in patients with hypertension in which comparison was made between antihypertensive treatment and either placebo or 'usual care'. The trials were grouped according to the level of hypertension of the patients. Four trials included only people with mild hypertension (diastolic blood pressure (DBP) < 110 mmHg) at entry, and a further three included only people with mild to moderate hypertension (DBP ≤ 115 mmHg). One of the trials, the Hypertension Detection and Follow-up Program (HDFP) study, was reported in such a way that people with DBP < 110 mmHg and 110–115 mmHg could be examined separately from those with DBP > 115 mmHg and therefore the results from each stratum were presented separately. Here, as in Collins *et al.*, each stratum will be considered as a separate study. The response of interest will be taken to be the effects of antihypertensive treatment on stroke. Table 3.1 shows the number of patients who suffered a stroke in each treatment group in each study. Patients had been followed up for an average of 5 years.

### 3.2.2 Measurement of treatment difference

A binary variable takes one of two possible values, commonly referred to as 'success' and 'failure'. A binary outcome is recorded for each patient. The

**Table 3.1**    The number of hypertensive patients experiencing a stroke

| Study | Treated group | | Control group | | Treated group % strokes | Control group % strokes |
|---|---|---|---|---|---|---|
| | Number of strokes | Total number | Number of strokes | Total number | | |
| Trials in which all patients had entry DBP < 110 mmHg | | | | | | |
| 1  VA-NHLB1 | 0 | 508 | 0 | 504 | 0.0 | 0.0 |
| 2  HDFP (Stratum I) | 59 | 3 903 | 88 | 3 922 | 1.5 | 2.2 |
| 3  Oslo | 0 | 406 | 5 | 379 | 0.0 | 1.3 |
| 4  ANBPS | 13 | 1 721 | 22 | 1 706 | 0.8 | 1.3 |
| 5  MRC | 60 | 8 700 | 109 | 8 654 | 0.7 | 1.3 |
| Trials in which all patients had entry DBP ⩽ 115 mmHg | | | | | | |
| 6  VAII | 5 | 186 | 20 | 194 | 2.7 | 10.3 |
| 7  USPHS | 1 | 193 | 6 | 196 | 0.5 | 3.1 |
| 8  HDFP (Stratum II) | 25 | 1 048 | 36 | 1 004 | 2.4 | 3.6 |
| 9  HSCSG | 43 | 233 | 52 | 219 | 18.5 | 23.7 |
| Trials in which some or all patients had entry DBP > 115 mmHg | | | | | | |
| 10  VAI | 1 | 68 | 3 | 63 | 1.5 | 4.8 |
| 11  WOLFF | 2 | 45 | 1 | 42 | 4.4 | 2.4 |
| 12  Barraclough | 0 | 58 | 0 | 58 | 0.0 | 0.0 |
| 13  Carter | 10 | 49 | 21 | 48 | 20.4 | 43.8 |
| 14  HDFP (Stratum III) | 18 | 534 | 34 | 529 | 3.4 | 6.4 |
| 15  EWPHE | 32 | 416 | 48 | 424 | 7.7 | 11.3 |
| 16  Coope | 20 | 419 | 39 | 465 | 4.8 | 8.4 |
| Total | 289 | 18 487 | 484 | 18 407 | 1.6 | 2.6 |

underlying model for the data recorded from one study is that patients in the treated group succeed with probability $p_T$ and patients in the control group succeed with probability $p_C$. Suppose that outcome data are available on $n_T$ patients in the treated group and $n_C$ patients in the control group. The numbers of successes and failures in the treated group are given by $s_T$ and $f_T$ respectively, and in the control group by $s_C$ and $f_C$ respectively. The data can be presented in the form of a 2 × 2 table as shown in Table 3.2. When the response is a binary variable, knowledge of the individual patient data adds nothing to the summary shown in this table for the purpose of estimating the treatment difference. The summary statistics presented in a trial report or publication usually enable this table to be constructed, so that an identical estimate to that based on individual patient data can be calculated.

In the example of stroke in hypertensive patients, interest lies in modelling the probability of a stroke. In this application the occurrence of a stroke will play the role that a 'success' plays in the generic description above. Naturally, in this application it is desirable for the probability of a stroke to be lower on the treatment than on the control. Table 3.3 presents the data for study 2 in the format of Table 3.2.

**Table 3.2** Data for a parallel group study with a binary outcome

| Outcome | Treated group | Control group | Total |
|---------|---------------|---------------|-------|
| Success | $s_T$ | $s_C$ | $s$ |
| Failure | $f_T$ | $f_C$ | $f$ |
| Total | $n_T$ | $n_C$ | $n$ |

**Table 3.3** Occurrence of a stroke in hypertensive patients in study 2

| Outcome | Treated group | Control group | Total |
|---------|---------------|---------------|-------|
| Success (stroke) | 59 | 88 | 147 |
| Failure (no stroke) | 3844 | 3834 | 7678 |
| Total | 3903 | 3922 | 7825 |

For binary data, there are several measures of treatment difference which could be used. One is the probability difference, $p_T - p_C$. If the event of interest being modelled is undesirable, for example the occurrence of a stroke, $p_T - p_C$ may be referred to as the risk difference. A second is the log-odds ratio, $\log[p_T(1 - p_C)/\{p_C(1 - p_T)\}]$. A third is the log-relative risk, $\log(p_T/p_C)$, although this name makes sense only when an undesirable event is being modelled. Of these, the log-odds ratio is to be preferred, because the adherence of corresponding test statistics to their asymptotic normal or chi-squared distributions is closest (Sprott, 1973). Problems can arise with the use of the probability difference, as it is restricted to values between $-1$ and $+1$, yet confidence intervals based on asymptotic theory can include points outside these limits. An additional advantage of the log-odds ratio over the log-relative risk is that if the probability of failure is put in place of the probability of success, the resulting log-odds ratio will be of opposite sign and equal magnitude, whereas the log-relative risk will be of opposite sign but not of equal magnitude. The main reason for using the log-odds ratio as opposed to the odds ratio is that the latter has only a finite interval from 0 to 1 to represent values corresponding to a lower relative success probability in the treated group, but an infinite interval from 1 upwards for a higher relative success probability.

It should be noted that the weight of one study relative to another will differ from one parameterization of the treatment difference to another. This has implications for the meta-analysis and is discussed further in Section 4.2.5.

### *Log-odds ratio*

Consider the log-odds ratio

$$\theta = \log\left\{\frac{p_T(1 - p_C)}{p_C(1 - p_T)}\right\},$$

where the logarithm is to base e, as is the case for all logarithms in this book. This is the log-odds of success on treatment relative to control.

Methods for analysing binary data using the full likelihood consider an unconditional distribution of the data based on the binomial distribution, in which $s_T$ and $s_C$ are treated as observations from random variables. The ML estimate of the log-odds ratio can be found by fitting a linear logistic regression model, using for example SAS PROC GENMOD. For the GENMOD procedure, the data for each patient can be entered separately. Suppose that the binary response (resp) is coded '1' for a success and '0' for a failure, and the explanatory variable (treat) is an indicator variable, which takes the value 0 for the control group and 1 for the treated group. The treatment indicator variable is coded in this way and considered as a continuous covariate in all of the models presented in this chapter. The following statement defines the model:

```
MODEL resp = treat / dist = bin link = logit;
```

The 'dist' option specifies the distribution of the observations which in this case is binomial, and the 'link' option specifies the link function (see Section 5.3). The estimate of $\theta$ appears in the SAS output as the 'treat' parameter estimate.

For a more efficient way of running the program, the data can be entered in binomial form. In this case the number of successes (succ) out of the total number of patients (tot) are provided for each treatment group, resulting in just two lines of data in this case. The MODEL statement now changes to

```
MODEL succ/tot = treat / dist = bin link = logit;
```

The ML estimate of the log-odds ratio can also be calculated from an explicit formula: it is the sample log-odds ratio, given by

$$\hat{\theta} = \log\left(\frac{s_T f_C}{s_C f_T}\right). \tag{3.1}$$

The asymptotic estimate of variance derived by the delta method (see, for example, Azzalini, 1996) and used in the Wald test is

$$\text{var}(\hat{\theta}) = \frac{1}{s_T} + \frac{1}{s_C} + \frac{1}{f_T} + \frac{1}{f_C}. \tag{3.2}$$

Using formulae (3.1) and (3.2) for study 2 in the stroke example gives

$$\hat{\theta} = \log\left(\frac{59 \times 3834}{88 \times 3844}\right) = -0.402$$

and

$$\text{var}(\hat{\theta}) = \frac{1}{59} + \frac{1}{88} + \frac{1}{3844} + \frac{1}{3834} = 0.029.$$

The corresponding efficient score and Fisher's information statistics are given by

$$Z = s_T - \frac{n_T s}{n} \tag{3.3}$$

and

$$V = \frac{n_T n_C s f}{n^3}. \tag{3.4}$$

The score test statistic $Z^2/V$ is that used in Pearson's chi-squared test and usually denoted by

$$\frac{\sum_{k=1}^{4}(O_k - E_k)^2}{E_k},$$

where the summation is over the four cells in the $2 \times 2$ table, and $O_k$ and $E_k$ are the observed and expected number of counts in the $k$th cell. Using formulae (3.3) and (3.4) for study 2 gives

$$Z = 59 - \frac{3903 \times 147}{7825} = -14.322,$$

$$V = \frac{3903 \times 3922 \times 147 \times 7678}{7825^3} = 36.059,$$

$$\hat{\theta} = \frac{Z}{V} = -0.397$$

and

$$\mathrm{var}(\hat{\theta}) = \frac{1}{V} = 0.028.$$

Binary data can also be analyzed using a likelihood which conditions on the total number of successes in the study. Under the null hypothesis, the number of successes in the treated group then follows the hypergeometric distribution. The ML estimate of the log-odds ratio can be found by fitting a conditional linear logistic regression model, using for example SAS PROC PHREG. If the binary outcome (resp2) is coded '1' for a success and '2' for a failure, then it can be analysed as a survival time with a failure considered to be a censored observation. To use PROC PHREG the binary outcomes must be presented as separate records for each patient, and the adjustment for ties based on the Cox approach should be used by setting ties = discrete. The MODEL statement is

```
MODEL resp2*cens(0) = treat / ties = discrete;
```

where cens is the censoring variable, taking the value 0 if resp2 = 2 and 1 otherwise. The estimate of $\theta$ appears as the 'treat' parameter estimate. This approach is analogous to that for grouped survival data, and is considered in more detail in Section 3.3.2.

Estimates for study 2 in the stroke example computed using PROC PHREG are given by

$$\hat{\theta} = -0.402$$

and

$$\mathrm{var}(\hat{\theta}) = 0.029.$$

The corresponding efficient score and Fisher's information statistics are given by

$$Z = s_T - \frac{n_T s}{n} \tag{3.5}$$

and

$$V = \frac{n_T n_C s f}{n^2 (n-1)}. \tag{3.6}$$

It can be seen from formulae (3.3) and (3.5) that the same $Z$ is obtained from both the unconditional and conditional approaches. The $V$ from the conditional approach (3.6) is $n/(n-1)$ times the $V$ from the unconditional approach (3.4). For study 2 of the stroke example, the $V$ for the conditional approach is given by 36.064. Because of the large number of subjects in study 2, it can be seen that this value is very close to that based on the unconditional approach. This will be true for large sample sizes.

The Peto method used for the meta-analysis of binary data, described in Yusuf *et al.* (1985), is based on formulae (3.5) and (3.6). Notice that $Z$ can be expressed as $O - E$, where $O$ and $E$ are the observed and expected number of successes in the treated group under the null hypothesis of no treatment difference. The $Z$ and $V$ statistics for the conditional approach can alternatively be obtained from a statistical package which calculates the log-rank statistic and its null variance for survival data, such as SAS PROC LIFETEST. To use PROC LIFETEST the data should be available in the same form as for PROC PHREG described above. The treatment groups would form the strata and the test is conducted using a STRATA statement. This method uses the adjustment for ties based on the Cox approach. PROC LIFETEST does not have a MODEL statement. Instead the following lines of code are required:

```
TIME resp2*cens(0);
STRATA treat;
```

In the SAS output, the value of $Z$ appears under the heading 'Rank Statistics' under the column headed 'Log-Rank' in the row associated with $treat = 1$. The value of $V$ appears on the diagonal of the 'Covariance Matrix for the Log-Rank Statistics'.

## Probability difference

Consider setting the parameter $\theta$ equal to the probability difference

$$\theta = p_T - p_C.$$

The unconditional ML estimate of the probability difference is given by the difference in the observed success probabilities

$$\hat{\theta} = \frac{s_T}{n_T} - \frac{s_C}{n_C}. \tag{3.7}$$

The asymptotic estimate of variance derived by the delta method is

$$\text{var}(\hat{\theta}) = \frac{s_T f_T}{n_T^3} + \frac{s_C f_C}{n_C^3}. \tag{3.8}$$

The estimate and variance for the difference in the probability of a stoke on antihypertensive treatment and on control in study 2 would be given by

$$\hat{\theta} = \frac{59}{3903} - \frac{88}{3922} = -0.007\,32$$

and

$$\text{var}(\hat{\theta}) = \frac{59 \times 3844}{3903^3} + \frac{88 \times 3834}{3922^3} = 0.000\,009\,4.$$

## *Log-relative risk*

Consider setting the parameter $\theta$ equal to the log-relative risk

$$\theta = \log\left(\frac{p_T}{p_C}\right).$$

The unconditional ML estimate of the log-relative risk is given by the sample log-relative risk,

$$\hat{\theta} = \log\left(\frac{s_T/n_T}{s_C/n_C}\right). \tag{3.9}$$

The asymptotic estimate of variance derived by the delta method is

$$\text{var}(\hat{\theta}) = \frac{f_T}{s_T n_T} + \frac{f_C}{s_C n_C}. \tag{3.10}$$

The estimate and variance for the log-relative risk of a stoke on antihypertensive treatment compared with control in study 2 would be given by

$$\hat{\theta} = \log\left(\frac{59/3903}{88/3922}\right) = -0.395$$

and

$$\text{var}(\hat{\theta}) = \frac{3844}{59 \times 3903} + \frac{3834}{88 \times 3922} = 0.028.$$

## 3.3   SURVIVAL DATA

### 3.3.1   Example: Mortality following myocardial infarction

The Multicenter Diltiazem Postinfarction Trial (MDPIT) was designed to determine whether long-term therapy with diltiazem in patients with a previous myocardial infarction would reduce rates of mortality and infarction (Multicenter Diltiazem Postinfarction Trial Research Group, 1988). A total of 2466 patients from 38 hospitals in the United States and Canada were randomized to either diltiazem or placebo and followed up for between 12 and 52 months. Here the mortality data will be considered. Mortality rates were found to be almost identical in the two treatment groups. The analyses as described in the paper provide the definitive results. For the purpose of illustrating meta-analysis methodology for survival data, the data arising from each of seven geographical regions will be treated as if from a separate study. Table 3.4 shows the number of deaths in each treatment group from each region. The 2-year mortality rates obtained from Kaplan–Meier estimation of the survival curves are also presented.

The survival times were recorded to the nearest day, and analyses based on these data will be presented. However, this level of detail is unlikely to be available from published papers. Therefore, additional analyses based on grouped data, which might be reported or which might be read off survival curves, will be presented. Table 3.5 shows the survival times grouped into yearly intervals. Patients whose survival time is known to be 1 year or more count towards the number of survivors of the interval 0−1, those whose survival time is known to be 2 years or more contribute to the number of survivors of the interval 1−2, and so on. Patients who have a censored survival time during a particular time interval count as a

**Table 3.4**   Mortality data from the MDPIT study

| Region | Diltiazem | | Placebo | | Diltiazem 2-year Mortality (%)* | Placebo 2-year Mortality (%)* |
|---|---|---|---|---|---|---|
| | Deaths | Total number | Deaths | Total number | | |
| New York City (US) | 33 | 262 | 25 | 256 | 11.5 | 8.4 |
| Northeast (US) | 46 | 305 | 39 | 298 | 12.2 | 9.9 |
| Mideast (US) | 4 | 72 | 13 | 71 | 4.2 | 14.4 |
| Midwest (US) | 24 | 127 | 19 | 125 | 16.4 | 12.6 |
| Southwest (US) | 23 | 169 | 28 | 184 | 11.9 | 11.8 |
| Ontario (Canada) | 21 | 121 | 27 | 122 | 19.3 | 22.0 |
| Quebec (Canada) | 15 | 176 | 16 | 178 | 8.7 | 8.3 |

*Kaplan–Meier estimation.

**Table 3.5** Survival times from the MDPIT study grouped into yearly intervals

| Region | Interval (years) | Diltiazem | | | Placebo | | |
|---|---|---|---|---|---|---|---|
| | | Survival | Death | Withdrawal | Survival | Death | Withdrawal |
| New York City (US) | 0–1 | 229 | 23 | 10 | 234 | 17 | 5 |
| | 1–2 | 175 | 6 | 48 | 182 | 4 | 48 |
| | 2–3 | 103 | 3 | 69 | 107 | 3 | 72 |
| | 3–4 | 19 | 1 | 83 | 21 | 1 | 85 |
| Northeast (US) | 0–1 | 281 | 24 | 0 | 276 | 21 | 1 |
| | 1–2 | 189 | 11 | 81 | 191 | 7 | 78 |
| | 2–3 | 104 | 7 | 78 | 106 | 10 | 75 |
| | 3–4 | 21 | 4 | 79 | 22 | 1 | 83 |
| Mideast (US) | 0–1 | 68 | 3 | 1 | 58 | 10 | 3 |
| | 1–2 | 49 | 0 | 19 | 44 | 0 | 14 |
| | 2–3 | 24 | 1 | 24 | 21 | 2 | 21 |
| | 3–4 | 3 | 0 | 21 | 1 | 1 | 19 |
| Midwest (US) | 0–1 | 110 | 12 | 5 | 110 | 11 | 4 |
| | 1–2 | 75 | 7 | 28 | 83 | 4 | 23 |
| | 2–3 | 41 | 5 | 29 | 49 | 4 | 30 |
| | 3–4 | 16 | 0 | 25 | 12 | 0 | 37 |
| Southwest (US) | 0–1 | 151 | 14 | 4 | 171 | 12 | 1 |
| | 1–2 | 117 | 5 | 29 | 122 | 8 | 41 |
| | 2–3 | 70 | 4 | 43 | 71 | 6 | 45 |
| | 3–4 | 23 | 0 | 47 | 19 | 2 | 50 |
| Ontario (Canada) | 0–1 | 102 | 15 | 4 | 101 | 16 | 5 |
| | 1–2 | 50 | 6 | 46 | 49 | 8 | 44 |
| | 2–3 | 6 | 0 | 44 | 10 | 3 | 36 |
| | 3–4 | 0 | 0 | 6 | 0 | 0 | 10 |
| Quebec (Canada) | 0–1 | 162 | 9 | 5 | 164 | 10 | 4 |
| | 1–2 | 69 | 5 | 88 | 63 | 4 | 97 |
| | 2–3 | 0 | 1 | 68 | 0 | 2 | 61 |
| | 3–4 | 0 | 0 | 0 | 0 | 0 | 0 |

withdrawal during that time interval. Patients who have a censored survival time at the upper limit of a time interval are considered to be a withdrawal during the following time interval.

### 3.3.2 Measurement of treatment difference

A survival analysis uses the time from randomization until the time of the event of interest. This might, for example, be the time until death or the time until recurrence of a tumour. This time is referred to as a 'survival time'. The mathematical model is expressed in terms of the hazard function or the survivor function. The hazard function is the limiting probability that the event occurs at time $t$, conditional on it not occurring before $t$. The survivor function is the probability that the event occurs after time $t$. Let $h_T(t)$ and $h_C(t)$ represent the hazard functions for the treated and control groups and $S_T(t)$ and $S_C(t)$ their respective survivor functions.

The survival time will be known for each patient observed to have had the event. Patients who have not had the event during the follow-up time or who are lost to follow-up before the event occurred have unknown survival times. These patients have a right-censored survival time, calculated from the date of randomization to the last date seen. The actual survival time is known to be larger than this value. It is assumed that non-informative censoring occurs, that is, that censoring occurs independently of the survival time.

At the time of analysis, the data available can be tabulated as in Table 3.6. If survival times are recorded exactly, then the ordered survival times $t_1, \ldots, t_d$ of the $d$ patients experiencing the event will be distinct. Each of $o_1, \ldots, o_d$ will be equal to 1, and the $o_{kT}$ and $o_{kC}$ will be equal to 0 or 1. The $r_k$-values represent the 'at risk' group of patients at time $t_k$, that is, those patients who are event-free and uncensored at a time just prior to $t_k$.

Consider the log-hazard ratio as a measure of treatment difference

$$\theta = \log \left\{ \frac{h_T(t)}{h_C(t)} \right\}.$$

The proportional hazards model under which $h_T(t) = \exp(\theta)h_C(t)$ for all $t$ is being assumed. As a positive effect of treatment would be to reduce the hazard, $\theta$ will be negative when the treated group is better than the control group. An alternative and equivalent form for $\theta$ available in terms of the survivor functions is given by

$$\theta = \log[-\log\{S_T(t)\}] - \log[-\log\{S_C(t)\}].$$

**Table 3.6**  Data for a parallel group study with a survival outcome

|  | Treated group | Control group | Total |
|---|---|---|---|
| Number of events | $O_T$ | $O_C$ | $O$ |
| Number of survival times equal to |  |  |  |
| $t_1$ | $o_{1T}$ | $o_{1C}$ | $o_1$ |
| $\vdots$ | $\vdots$ | $\vdots$ | $\vdots$ |
| $t_d$ | $o_{dT}$ | $o_{dC}$ | $o_d$ |
| Number of survival times greater than or equal to |  |  |  |
| $t_1$ | $r_{1T}$ | $r_{1C}$ | $r_1$ |
| $\vdots$ | $\vdots$ | $\vdots$ | $\vdots$ |
| $t_d$ | $r_{dT}$ | $r_{dC}$ | $r_d$ |

Cox (1972) proposed a method for analysing survival data, based on a partial likelihood function. The ML estimate of the log-hazard ratio can be found by fitting the Cox proportional hazards model, using for example SAS PROC PHREG. If the survival time (time) is recorded for each patient, and the censoring variable (cens) takes the value 0 if the survival time is censored and 1 otherwise, the following MODEL statement can be used:

```
MODEL time*cens(0) = treat;
```

In the SAS output, the estimate of $\theta$ appears as the 'treat' parameter estimate.

Efficient score and Fisher's information statistics based on the same likelihood function are given by

$$Z = O_{\mathrm{T}} - \sum_{k=1}^{d} \frac{o_k r_{k\mathrm{T}}}{r_k} \tag{3.11}$$

and

$$V = \sum_{k=1}^{d} \frac{o_k(r_k - o_k) r_{k\mathrm{T}} r_{k\mathrm{C}}}{(r_k - 1) r_k^2}. \tag{3.12}$$

As all of the $o_k$ are in fact equal to one, the above formulae can be simplified. The forms above are presented for later generalization.

An alternative and equivalent expression for Z is

$$Z = \sum_{k=1}^{d} \frac{r_{k\mathrm{C}} o_{k\mathrm{T}} - r_{k\mathrm{T}} o_{k\mathrm{C}}}{r_k}.$$

The statistic Z is the log-rank statistic and the associated score test is the log-rank test. Values of Z and V can be obtained from any statistical package which calculates the log-rank statistic and its null variance for survival data, such as SAS PROC LIFETEST. Instead of a MODEL statement, the following lines of code are required:

```
TIME   time*cens(0);
STRATA treat;
```

In the SAS output, the value of Z appears under the heading 'Rank Statistics' under the column headed 'Log-Rank' in the row associated with treat $= 1$. The value of V appears on the diagonal of the 'Covariance Matrix for the Log-Rank Statistics'.

For some meta-analyses, we may only have access to grouped data as illustrated in Table 3.5. The data now take the general form presented in Table 3.7, where $u_1, \ldots, u_m$ represent the upper limits of the time intervals.

One way of approaching such data is to treat them as if each event occurred at the upper limit of the time interval in which it lies. In this case the likelihood

**Table 3.7**  Data for a parallel group study with grouped survival data

|  | Treated group | Control group | Total |
|---|---|---|---|
| Number of events | $O_T$ | $O_C$ | $O$ |
| Number of events in the interval |  |  |  |
| $\quad (0, u_1]$ | $o_{1T}$ | $o_{1C}$ | $o_1$ |
| $\quad \vdots$ | $\vdots$ | $\vdots$ | $\vdots$ |
| $\quad (u_{m-1}, u_m]$ | $o_{mT}$ | $o_{mC}$ | $o_m$ |
| Number of patients recruited at least time $t$ ago, and still being followed up, for $t$ equal to |  |  |  |
| $\quad u_1$ | $r_{1T}$ | $r_{1C}$ | $r_1$ |
| $\quad \vdots$ | $\vdots$ | $\vdots$ | $\vdots$ |
| $\quad u_m$ | $r_{mT}$ | $r_{mC}$ | $r_m$ |

function has to be modified to allow for the resulting tied observations. This is done in Cox (1972), resulting in a form of likelihood similar to that based on distinct survival times, deduced from a discrete survival model. The measure of treatment difference is the log-odds ratio

$$\theta = \log \left\{ \frac{\pi_{kT}(1 - \pi_{kC})}{\pi_{kC}(1 - \pi_{kT})} \right\}, \qquad \text{for } k = 1, \ldots, m,$$

where $\pi_{kT}$ is the probability of an event in the interval $(u_{k-1}, u_k]$, conditional on survival to time $u_{k-1}$, and $\pi_{kC}$ is similarly defined. The first interval is defined by setting $u_0 = 0$. In the limit as the width of the discrete time intervals becomes zero, the log-odds ratio tends to the log-hazard ratio. In practice this distinction is often blurred. In general, survival times will be recorded to the nearest day, month or year and so in a typical survival analysis some survival times will share the same value. The approach described for grouped data can also be applied to ungrouped data with ties, letting the $u_k$ represent each distinct event time. This is the more conventional use of the methodology.

In order to apply the Cox approach for ties the observed survival times have been chosen to equal the upper limit of the interval in which they occur, that is, $u_1, \ldots, u_m$. In addition, censored survival times will be set to the lower limit of the interval during which they occur. This means that patients with a censored survival time in a particular interval do not count in the risk set for events in that interval. In particular, patients withdrawn during the first interval are right-censored at 0 and do not influence the analysis at all.

The ML estimate of the parameter $\theta$ can be found by fitting the Cox proportional hazards model, using for example SAS PROC PHREG. To use PROC PHREG the survival time (timegp) must be presented as a separate record for each patient, and the adjustment for ties based on the Cox approach can be made by setting ties = discrete. The MODEL statement presented earlier in this section needs to be changed to

```
MODEL timegp*cens(0) = treat / ties = discrete;
```

Using the individual survival times recorded to the nearest day, the estimate and variance for the log-hazard ratio for New York City are

$$\hat{\theta} = 0.282, \qquad \text{var}(\hat{\theta}) = 0.070.$$

The grouped survival data for New York City, shown in Table 3.8, provide the estimates

$$\hat{\theta} = 0.305, \qquad \text{var}(\hat{\theta}) = 0.075,$$

where $\theta$ now represents the log-odds ratio defined above.

When ties are present the formulae for $Z$ and $V$ follow from the discrete form of Cox's likelihood. The formulae are similar to (3.11) and (3.12), except that the summation takes place over the $m$ time intervals instead of the $d$ distinct survival times. The values of $o_k$, $o_{kT}$ and $o_{kC}$ now relate to the number of events within the $k$th time interval and, therefore, may be greater than one.

Values of $Z$ and $V$ can be obtained from any statistical package which calculates the log-rank statistic and its null variance for survival data, such as SAS PROC LIFETEST. To use PROC LIFETEST the survival time must be presented as a separate record for each patient. The following statements would be used:

```
TIME timegp*cens(0);
STRATA treat;
```

The values of $Z$ and $V$ for New York City using individual survival times recorded to the nearest day from formulae (3.11) and (3.12) give

$$Z = 4.064,$$

$$V = 14.496,$$

$$\hat{\theta} = \frac{Z}{V} = 0.280$$

**Table 3.8**  Grouped survival data for New York City

| Interval (years) | Diltiazem | | | Placebo | | |
|---|---|---|---|---|---|---|
| | Survival | Death | At risk | Survival | Death | At risk |
| (0, 1] | 229 | 23 | 252 | 234 | 17 | 251 |
| (1, 2] | 175 | 6 | 181 | 182 | 4 | 186 |
| (2, 3] | 103 | 3 | 106 | 107 | 3 | 110 |
| (3, 4] | 19 | 1 | 20 | 21 | 1 | 22 |

and

$$\mathrm{var}(\hat\theta) = \frac{1}{V} = 0.069.$$

The values of $Z$ and $V$ for New York City using the grouped survival times from formulae (3.11) and (3.12) give

$$Z = 4.132,$$

$$V = 13.613,$$

$$\hat\theta = \frac{Z}{V} = 0.304$$

and

$$\mathrm{var}(\hat\theta) = \frac{1}{V} = 0.073.$$

For grouped survival data decisions are required regarding the choice of the timepoint to represent the event time in each time interval, how censored times will be handled, and the method for dealing with tied observations. Alternative methods of adjustment for ties are given by Breslow (1974) and Efron (1977) and are discussed by Collett (1994). The Cox approach to ties used in this chapter has assumed that all events within the same time interval occur simultaneously. If the time intervals are large, a more appropriate approach is one based on interval-censored survival data, described in Section 3.4.2.

## 3.4   INTERVAL-CENSORED SURVIVAL DATA

### 3.4.1   Example: Ulcer recurrence

To illustrate the meta-analysis of interval-censored survival data, the data reported in Whitehead (1989) are considered. They are from a double-blind clinical trial of a new drug intended to inhibit relapse after primary therapy has successfully healed an endoscopically proven ulcer. A total of 337 patients were randomized between the new drug (treatment 2) and a control (treatment 1). Regular and frequent visits to doctors' surgeries were arranged for all patients, but endoscopies were planned routinely only for the visits at 6 and 12 months. Between the scheduled endoscopies patients could experience symptoms of relapse, visit the doctor and be diagnosed, perhaps by an unscheduled endoscopy. Such relapses are referred to as interval-detected relapses. The data for analysis are therefore drawn from a mixture of asymptomatic relapses diagnosed at scheduled times and symptomatic interval-detected relapses, and consist of the time of diagnosis of each relapse. Interest centres on the difference in times to relapse between the two treatments.

To avoid being misled by treatment effects on suppression of symptoms, the actual time to relapse is not analysed. Instead the time to relapse is allocated to one of two intervals, the first being before or at the 6-month scheduled visit and the second being after the 6-month but before or at the 12-month scheduled visit. Patients who have a negative endoscopy at their final visit are given a censored time of 12 months, if the final visit is at 12 months, and a censored time of 6 months if the final visit is at or after 6 months but before 12 months. The 36 patients who dropped out without having any of the scheduled endoscopies are given a censored time of 0 and therefore have no influence in the analysis. The study took place in five countries, and for the purpose of illustrating meta-analysis methodology the data from each country are considered as comprising a separate study. It should be noted that here patient 182 has been included as ulcer-free at 12 months and consequently ulcer-free at 6 months, whereas in the original paper he was omitted from the 6-month analysis. The data are presented in Table 3.9.

### 3.4.2   Measurement of treatment difference

Situations can arise where the event is known to have occurred during a particular interval of time but the exact time cannot be ascertained, as illustrated in the ulcer recurrence example. The data are in the form of interval-censored survival data. In the example recurrences are known to have occurred in the interval (0, 6] or (6, 12], or are right-censored at 0, 6 or 12 months. If it is assumed that all events occurring within the same time interval occur at the same time, then the

**Table 3.9**   The number of patients experiencing a recurrence of their ulcer

| Country | Interval (months) | Treatment 2 | | | Treatment 1 | | |
|---------|-------------------|-------------------|-----------------|-----------------|-------------------|-----------------|-----------------|
| | | No recurrence | Recur- rence | With- drawal | No recurrence | Recur- rence | With- drawal |
| Austria | (0, 6] | 40 | 12 | 3 | 38 | 15 | 6 |
| | (6, 12] | 34 | 3 | 3 | 27 | 4 | 7 |
| Belgium | (0, 6] | 22 | 2 | 5 | 16 | 3 | 4 |
| | (6, 12] | 17 | 5 | 0 | 12 | 1 | 3 |
| France | (0, 6] | 15 | 4 | 3 | 15 | 5 | 5 |
| | (6, 12] | 10 | 1 | 4 | 12 | 1 | 2 |
| Holland | (0, 6] | 55 | 0 | 7 | 46 | 6 | 3 |
| | (6, 12] | 47 | 5 | 3 | 38 | 3 | 5 |
| Norway | (0, 6] | 3 | 0 | 0 | 4 | 0 | 0 |
| | (6, 12] | 3 | 0 | 0 | 3 | 0 | 1 |

Cox approach for ties could be used, as described in the previous section. A more appropriate approach which does not make this assumption is described here.

In general, consider that data are collected at scheduled visits by the patient to the doctor at times $u_1, u_2, \ldots, u_m$ after randomization. At each visit information about whether the event has occurred since the last visit will be recorded. At the time of analysis the data can be tabulated as in Table 3.7. Knowledge of the individual patient data adds nothing to the summary shown in this table for the purpose of estimating the treatment difference. Provided it is possible to extract the necessary summary statistics to create such a table, then the estimate obtained will be identical to that calculated using individual patient data.

Consider the measure of treatment difference to be the log-hazard ratio

$$\theta = \log \left\{ \frac{h_T(t)}{h_C(t)} \right\}.$$

Each patient contributes multiple binary records, equal to the number of intervals of observation, that is, the number of intervals during which they belong to the 'at risk' set. Occurrence of the event during an interval constitutes a 'success'; otherwise the binary outcome is recorded as a 'failure'. The likelihood can be presented in terms of the conditional probabilities $\pi_{kT}$ and $\pi_{kC}$, for $k = 1, \ldots, m$, defined in Section 3.3.2. The method of analysis described in Whitehead (1989) – see also Chapter 8 of Collett (1994) – is based on a full likelihood. Assuming that the proportional hazards model holds, the data are related to the log-hazard ratio, $\theta$, through a binary model with the complementary log-log link function. This is given by

$$\log\{-\log(1 - \pi_{kT})\} = \alpha_k + \theta$$

and

$$\log\{-\log(1 - \pi_{kC})\} = \alpha_k,$$

where $\alpha_k$ is the parameter associated with the $k$th interval.

The ML estimate of the log-hazard ratio can be found using a logistic regression procedure such as SAS PROC GENMOD with the CLOGLOG link. For the GENMOD procedure, the data can be entered separately for each time interval of observation for each patient. The binary outcome (resp) is coded '1' if the event occurs in that particular interval for that patient and '0' if the patient is event-free during that particular interval. In addition to the treatment indicator variable, it is necessary to include a factor which associates each binary observation with its time interval (int). The following SAS statements can be used:

```
CLASS int;
MODEL resp = int treat / dist = bin link = cloglog;
```

**Table 3.10** Interval-censored survival data from Austria

| Interval (months) | Treatment 2 | | | Treatment 1 | | |
|---|---|---|---|---|---|---|
| | No recurrence | Recurrence | At risk | No recurrence | Recurrence | At risk |
| (0, 6] | 40 | 12 | 52 | 38 | 15 | 53 |
| (6, 12] | 34 | 3 | 37 | 27 | 4 | 31 |

The link function selected is the complementary log-log link function (see Section 5.6). The estimate of $\theta$ appears in the SAS output as the 'treat' parameter estimate.

Alternatively, the data can be entered in binomial form. For each time interval for each treatment group the number of patients experiencing the event (succ) out of the total number of patients being observed during that time interval (tot) can be provided. The MODEL statement now changes to

```
MODEL succ/tot = int treat / dist = bin link = cloglog;
```

Consider the data from Austria which are extracted into Table 3.10. The ML estimate for the log-hazard ratio of a recurrence on treatment 2 relative to treatment 1 and its variance are given by

$$\hat{\theta} = -0.290, \qquad \text{var}(\hat{\theta}) = 0.120.$$

The corresponding efficient score and Fisher's information statistics are given by

$$Z = \sum_{k=1}^{m} \frac{q_k}{o_k} (r_{kC} o_{kT} - r_{kT} o_{kC}) \tag{3.13}$$

and

$$V = \sum_{k=1}^{m} \frac{q_k^2 (r_k - o_k) r_{kT} r_{kC}}{o_k r_k}, \tag{3.14}$$

where

$$q_k = -\log\left(1 - \frac{o_k}{r_k}\right), \qquad k = 1, \ldots, m.$$

When few events have occurred in each interval, so that the $o_k$ are small relative to the $r_k$, $q_k \approx o_k/r_k$. Making this substitution in $Z$ gives the log-rank statistic. Substituting in $V$ gives the null variance of the log-rank statistic apart from a factor of $r_k/(r_k - 1)$. Therefore, when the intervals form a fine grid, the method of this section reduces to the method of the previous section.

The estimates based on the $Z$ and $V$ formulae (3.13) and (3.14) for the Austrian data are

$$Z = -2.439, \qquad V = 8.435,$$

$$\hat{\theta} = \frac{Z}{V} = -0.289, \qquad \text{var}(\hat{\theta}) = \frac{1}{V} = 0.119.$$

This approach can also be applied to the MDPIT data set from Section 3.3 as grouped by year in Table 3.5. For New York City the ML estimate and its variance are

$$\hat{\theta} = 0.297, \qquad \text{var}(\hat{\theta}) = 0.070.$$

Estimates based on $Z$ and $V$ from formulae (3.13) and (3.14) are

$$Z = 4.273, \qquad V = 14.492,$$

$$\hat{\theta} = \frac{Z}{V} = 0.295, \qquad \text{var}(\hat{\theta}) = \frac{1}{V} = 0.069.$$

## 3.5   ORDINAL DATA

### 3.5.1   Example: Global impression of change in Alzheimer's disease

The Clinical Global Impression of Change (CGIC) scale is used to provide an overview by the clinician of whether a patient with Alzheimer's disease is getting better or worse. It is a seven-point scale that is intended to assess change from baseline, where scores 1, 2 and 3 represent 'very much improved', 'much improved' and minimally improved', 4 indicates 'no change', and 5, 6 and 7 represent 'minimally worse', 'much worse' and 'very much worse'. Table 3.11 shows the results from five trials comparing tacrine with placebo, in which the CGIC scale was used. A meta-analysis of these data has been reported by Qizilbash *et al.* (1998). As can be seen from the table, the majority of patients were placed in the middle three categories, with hardly any in the two extreme categories. For the meta-analysis presented in this book, categories 1 and 2 will be combined, as will categories 6 and 7, to give a five-category response.

### 3.5.2   Measurement of treatment difference

Patient responses fall into one of $m$ categories $C_1, \ldots, C_m$ which are ordered in terms of desirability: $C_1$ is the best and $C_m$ the worst. The mathematical model is expressed in terms of the probability of falling into category $k$ given by $p_{kT}, k = 1, \ldots, m$ for the treated group and $p_{kC}, k = 1, \ldots, m$ for the control group. Cumulative probabilities of falling into category $C_k$ or better for the treated

**Table 3.11**   Number of patients in each category of the CGIC scale in the tacrine studies

| Study | Treatment | 1 | 2 | 3 | 4 | 5 | 6 | 7 | Total |
|-------|-----------|---|---|---|---|---|---|---|-------|
| | | | | | CGIC scale | | | | Total |
| 1 | Tacrine | 2 | 2 | 23 | 45 | 22 | 2 | 0 | 96 |
| | Placebo | 0 | 2 | 22 | 54 | 29 | 3 | 0 | 110 |
| 2 | Tacrine | 0 | 14 | 119 | 180 | 54 | 6 | 0 | 373 |
| | Placebo | 0 | 1 | 22 | 35 | 11 | 3 | 0 | 72 |
| 3 | Tacrine | 1 | 12 | 20 | 24 | 10 | 1 | 0 | 68 |
| | Placebo | 0 | 7 | 16 | 17 | 10 | 3 | 0 | 53 |
| 4 | Tacrine | 3 | 18 | 106 | 175 | 62 | 15 | 2 | 381 |
| | Placebo | 0 | 8 | 24 | 73 | 52 | 13 | 0 | 170 |
| 5 | Tacrine | 0 | 3 | 14 | 19 | 3 | 0 | 0 | 39 |
| | Placebo | 0 | 2 | 13 | 18 | 7 | 1 | 0 | 41 |

and control groups are denoted by $Q_{kT}$ and $Q_{kC}$, respectively:

$$Q_{kT} = p_{1T} + \cdots + p_{kT}, \quad Q_{kC} = p_{1C} + \cdots + p_{kC}, \quad k = 1, \ldots, m.$$

The data can be presented in the form of an $m \times 2$ table as shown in Table 3.12. The summary data shown in this table are sufficient for estimating the treatment difference. Provided that it is possible to extract the necessary information to create such a table, the estimate will be identical to that based on individual patient data.

Two measures of treatment difference will be considered for ordinal data. The first is a log-odds ratio based on the proportional odds model, and the second is a log-odds ratio based on the continuation ratio model. The latter is analogous to the log-odds ratio for the discrete survival model as described in Section 3.3.2.

## Log-odds ratio (proportional odds model)

Consider the log-odds ratio

$$\theta = \log \left\{ \frac{Q_{kT} (1 - Q_{kC})}{Q_{kC} (1 - Q_{kT})} \right\}.$$

**Table 3.12**   Data for a parallel group study with an ordinal outcome

| Number of patients in category | Treated group | Control group | Total |
|-------------------------------|---------------|---------------|-------|
| $C_1$ | $n_{1T}$ | $n_{1C}$ | $n_1$ |
| $\vdots$ | $\vdots$ | $\vdots$ | $\vdots$ |
| $C_m$ | $n_{mT}$ | $n_{mC}$ | $n_m$ |
| Total | $n_T$ | $n_C$ | $n$ |

It is assumed that $\theta$ is constant over all values of $k$. The parameter $\theta$ can be viewed in the same way as the log-odds ratio for binary data: it is the log-odds of being better off on treatment relative to control. Suppose that the ordinal scale is reduced to a success/failure outcome, with categories $C_1, \ldots, C_k$ representing success and $C_{k+1}, \ldots, C_m$ representing failure. Then $Q_{kT}$ and $1 - Q_{kT}$ are the respective probabilities of success and failure for the treated group; $Q_{kC}$ and $1 - Q_{kC}$ are defined similarly for the control group. There are $m - 1$ possible binary splits of the $m$ categories. The proportional odds assumption is equivalent to supposing that all $m - 1$ binary analyses refer to the same log-odds ratio $\theta$. When there are only two response categories the proportional odds model is equivalent to the usual linear logistic model for binary data.

McCullagh (1980) proposed a method for fitting the proportional odds model using the full likelihood function based on a multinomial distribution. The ML estimate of the log-odds ratio can be found using for example SAS PROC GENMOD. For PROC GENMOD the data can be entered for each patient individually. The response variable (resp) would take the value $k$ if the patient had a response in category $k$. The MODEL statement is as follows:

```
MODEL resp = treat/ dist = multinomial link = cumlogit;
```

The link function selected is the cumulative logit link function (see Section 5.4). PROC GENMOD does not require the data from each patient to be presented as a separate record, as the $n_{kT}$ and $n_{kC}$ can be entered via a weighting variable. In this case, the data consist of three items for each category in each treatment group, namely the category (cat), the treatment group (treat) and the number of patient responses (num). The MODEL statement above is replaced by

```
FREQ num;
MODEL cat = treat/ dist = multinomial link = cumlogit;
```

Consider the $5 \times 2$ table (Table 3.13) created for study 1. The ML estimate for study 1 and its variance are given by

$$\hat{\theta} = 0.284, \qquad \text{var}(\hat{\theta}) = 0.068.$$

**Table 3.13**   CGIC data from tacrine study 1

| Treatment | Category | | | | | Total |
|---|---|---|---|---|---|---|
| | C1 | C2 | C3 | C4 | C5 | |
| Tacrine | 4 | 23 | 45 | 22 | 2 | 96 |
| Placebo | 2 | 22 | 54 | 29 | 3 | 110 |

Using a marginal likelihood based on the ranks, with allowance for ties (Jones and Whitehead, 1979), the test statistics Z and V for this case are given by

$$Z = \frac{1}{n+1} \sum_{k=1}^{m} n_{kC}(L_{kT} - U_{kT}) \tag{3.15}$$

and

$$V = \frac{Z^2}{n+2} + \frac{B}{(n+1)(n+2)}, \tag{3.16}$$

where

$$L_{kT} = n_{1T} + \cdots + n_{(k-1)T}, \qquad k = 2, \ldots, m,$$

$$U_{kT} = n_{(k+1)T} + \cdots + n_{mT}, \qquad k = 1, \ldots, m-1,$$

$$L_{1T} = U_{mT} = 0,$$

with similar expressions defining $L_{kC}$ and $U_{kC}$, and

$$B = \sum_{k=1}^{m} \{ n_{kT}(n_C - n_{kC}) + n_{kT}n_{kC}(n - n_k) + 2n_{kT}L_{kC}U_{kC} + 2n_{kC}L_{kT}U_{kT} \}.$$

An approximate large-sample formula for $V$ is

$$V' = \frac{n_T n_C n}{3(n+1)^2} \left\{ 1 - \sum_{k=1}^{m} \left( \frac{n_k}{n} \right)^3 \right\}. \tag{3.17}$$

Comparison of $Z^2/V'$ with the chi-squared distribution on one degree of freedom amounts to performing the Mann–Whitney U test (Mann and Whitney, 1947).

Using the data from Table 3.13 estimates are calculated as follows:

$$Z = 4.155, \qquad V = 14.668,$$

$$\hat{\theta} = \frac{Z}{V} = 0.283, \qquad \text{var}(\hat{\theta}) = \frac{1}{V} = 0.068.$$

Formula (3.17) gives $V' = 14.611$, which is close to V.

A further interpretation of $\theta$ can be made when the categories are a result of grouping originally continuous data. A continuous response $Y$ is observed on each patient, and then the patient is designated as category $C_k$ if $Y$ lies between $\alpha_{k-1}$ and $\alpha_k$ for some increasing sequence of numbers $\alpha_0, \ldots, \alpha_m$. If the response of a subject in the treated group is denoted by $Y_T$ and that in the control group $Y_C$, then the probability that the person in the treated group does better is

$$P(Y_T > Y_C) = \frac{1 - e^{-\theta} - \theta e^{-\theta}}{\left(1 - e^{-\theta}\right)^2}.$$

### Log-odds ratio (continuation ratio model)

Consider the probability of being in a particular category conditional on being in that category or a worse one. This is a sort of 'discrete hazard', but it is of a desirable outcome. The approach to the analysis is similar to that described for grouped survival data in Section 3.3.2. Here we define $h_{kT}$ as

$$h_{kT} = \frac{p_{kT}}{1 - Q_{(k-1)T}},$$

where $Q_{0T} = 0$. The term $h_{kC}$ is defined similarly.

Consider the log-odds ratio

$$\theta = \log\left\{\frac{h_{kT}(1 - h_{kC})}{h_{kC}(1 - h_{kT})}\right\}, \qquad \text{for } k = 1, \ldots, m - 1.$$

Because the hazard is of a desirable event, $\theta$ will be positive if the treated group is better than the control group.

It can be seen that for $k = 1$, the log-odds ratio based on the proportional odds model is the same as the log-odds ratio based on the continuation ratio model. Therefore, estimates from the two approaches are likely to be of the same order of magnitude. McCullagh (1978) has called the proportional odds model 'palindromic invariant', meaning that modelling cumulative probabilities starting with the best category and moving towards the worst will only change the sign and not the magnitude of the parameter estimates which would be obtained by starting with the worst category and moving towards the best. However, the continuation ratio model is not palindromic invariant. For the continuation ratio model it is important to decide whether to model the hazard of a desirable event or of an undesirable event. Reversing the order of the categories and modelling the hazard of an undesirable event would make the analogy with grouped survival data more obvious.

If the continuation ratio model is chosen, the estimation of the corresponding log-odds ratio proceeds as follows. Table 3.14 shows how the data can be presented in a way analogous to grouped survival data shown in Table 3.7. Here

$$R_{kT} = n_{kT} + U_{kT}, \qquad k = 1, \ldots, m - 1,$$

and $R_{kC}$ is similarly defined.

**Table 3.14**  Data for a parallel group study with ordinal data, presented in the form of survival data

|  | Treated group | Control group | Total |
|---|---|---|---|
| Number of patients in categories $C_1$ to $C_{m-1}$ | $L_{(m-1)T}$ | $L_{(m-1)C}$ | $L_{(m-1)}$ |
| Number of patients in category | | | |
| $C_1$ | $n_{1T}$ | $n_{1C}$ | $n_1$ |
| $\vdots$ | $\vdots$ | $\vdots$ | $\vdots$ |
| $C_{m-1}$ | $n_{(m-1)T}$ | $n_{(m-1)C}$ | $n_{(m-1)}$ |
| Number of patients in the same or a worse (higher) category than | | | |
| $C_1$ | $R_{1T}$ | $R_{1C}$ | $R_1$ |
| $\vdots$ | $\vdots$ | $\vdots$ | $\vdots$ |
| $C_{m-1}$ | $R_{(m-1)T}$ | $R_{(m-1)C}$ | $R_{(m-1)}$ |

The likelihood which conditions on the $R_k$, $k = 1, \ldots, m - 1$, is equivalent to the discrete form of the partial likelihood under the Cox proportional hazards model. It is therefore possible to calculate the ML estimate for the log-odds ratio from any package which fits the Cox proportional hazards model. To carry out the analysis, a response variable (cat) would be calculated to take the value $k$ if the patient had a response in category $k$. This response variable would then be treated as a survival time, with values in the highest category considered as censored observations with value $m$. To use SAS PROC PHREG the response variable from each patient must be presented as a separate record, and the adjustment for ties based on the Cox approach should be used by setting ties = discrete. The MODEL statement would be

```
MODEL cat*cens(0) = treat / ties = discrete;
```

where cens is the censoring variable, taking the value 0 if the patient's response is in category $m$ and 1 otherwise.

Table 3.15 shows the data from tacrine study 1, already shown in Table 3.13, in the form of survival data. The ML estimate and its variance are given by

$$\hat{\theta} = 0.227, \qquad \mathrm{var}(\hat{\theta}) = 0.050.$$

The corresponding values of $Z$ and $V$ can be calculated as follows. Substitute $L_{(m-1)T}$, $n_{kT}$, $n_{kC}$, $n_k$, $R_{kT}$, $R_{kC}$ and $R_k$ for $O_T$, $o_{kT}$, $o_{kC}$, $o_k$, $r_{kT}$, $r_{kC}$ and $r_k$ in formulae (3.11) and (3.12), and sum over $k$ from 1 to $m - 1$ to calculate $Z$ and $V$ as for the log-rank statistic and its null variance:

$$Z = L_{(m-1)T} - \sum_{k=1}^{m-1} \left( \frac{n_k R_{kT}}{R_k} \right) \tag{3.18}$$

**Table 3.15**   Data from tacrine study 1 in the form of survival data

| Category | Tacrine | | | Placebo | | |
|---|---|---|---|---|---|---|
| | Number in worse category | Number in category | Number in this or worse category | Number in worse category | Number in category | Number in this or worse category |
| 1 | 92 | 4 | 96 | 108 | 2 | 110 |
| 2 | 69 | 23 | 92 | 86 | 22 | 108 |
| 3 | 24 | 45 | 69 | 32 | 54 | 86 |
| 4 | 2 | 22 | 24 | 3 | 29 | 32 |

and

$$V = \sum_{k=1}^{m-1} \left\{ \frac{n_k(R_k - n_k)R_{kT}R_{kC}}{(R_k - 1)R_k^2} \right\}. \tag{3.19}$$

For study 1 this gives

$$Z = 4.576, \qquad V = 20.190,$$

$$\hat{\theta} = \frac{Z}{V} = 0.227, \qquad \text{var}(\hat{\theta}) = \frac{1}{V} = 0.050.$$

The values of $Z$ and $V$ may also be obtained from PROC LIFETEST, using the following statements:

```
TIME cat*cens(0);
STRATA treat;
```

As an alternative to the conditional likelihood approach described above, a full likelihood based on the multinomial distribution can be utilized. In this approach each patient contributes multiple recordings of binary data, dependent on the category into which their response falls. If the response falls into category $k$ the patient contributes a 'success' to category $k$ and a 'failure' to each of categories 1 to $k - 1$. No contribution is made to categories with index larger than $k$. The likelihood can be presented in terms of the conditional probabilities $h_{kT}$ and $h_{kC}$, for $k = 1, \ldots, m - 1$. These binary data are related to the log-odds ratio, $\theta$, through a binary model with the logit link function. This is given by

$$\log \left\{ \frac{h_{kT}}{(1 - h_{kT})} \right\} = \alpha_k + \theta$$

and

$$\log \left\{ \frac{h_{kC}}{(1 - h_{kC})} \right\} = \alpha_k,$$

where $\alpha_k$ is the parameter associated with the $k$th category.

The ML estimate of the log-odds ratio can therefore be found, using for example SAS PROC GENMOD with the LOGIT link. A patient with a response in category $k$ provides a binary outcome (resp) for categories $1, \ldots, k$. For categories $1, \ldots, k - 1$, resp $= 0$, and for category $k$, resp $= 1$. The data can be entered as a separate record for each category for each patient. In addition to the treatment indicator variable, it is necessary to include a factor which associates each binary observation with the appropriate category (level). The following SAS statements can be used:

```
CLASS level;
MODEL resp = level treat / dist = bin link = logit;
```

Once again, the estimate of $\theta$ appears in the SAS output as the 'treat' parameter estimate. The data could alternatively be entered in binomial form in a similar way to that indicated in Section 3.4.2.

The estimate for tacrine study 1 and its variance are

$$\hat{\theta} = 0.228, \qquad \text{var}(\hat{\theta}) = 0.050.$$

If there are a large number of categories this approach is unsatisfactory and the model cannot be fitted. In particular, if there are zero cells in the $m \times 2$ table, this may result in non-convergence. In such cases the approach based on the conditional likelihood is to be preferred.

The $Z$ and $V$ statistics based on the full likelihood are given by

$$Z = L_{(m-1)\text{T}} - \sum_{k=1}^{m-1} \left( \frac{n_k R_{k\text{T}}}{R_k} \right) \tag{3.20}$$

and

$$V = \sum_{k=1}^{m-1} \left\{ \frac{n_k(R_k - n_k)R_{k\text{T}}R_{k\text{C}}}{R_k^3} \right\}. \tag{3.21}$$

It can be seen that the $V$ from the conditional approach (3.19) differs from the $V$ from the unconditional approach (3.21) by a factor $(R_k - 1)/R_k$ in the denominator of each summand. The value of $V$ for study 1 from formula (3.21) is 20.062. As can be seen from formulae (3.18) and (3.20), the same $Z$ is obtained from both the unconditional and conditional approaches.

## 3.6 NORMALLY DISTRIBUTED DATA

### 3.6.1 Example: Recovery time after anaesthesia

A multicentre study was undertaken to compare two anaesthetic agents (A and B) in patients undergoing short surgical procedures, where rapid recovery

**Table 3.16**    Recovery time (log-transformed) after anaesthesia

| Centre | Treatment A | | | Treatment B | | |
|---|---|---|---|---|---|---|
| | Number of patients | Mean | Standard deviation | Number of patients | Mean | Standard deviation |
| 1 | 4 | 1.141 | 0.967 | 5 | 0.277 | 0.620 |
| 2 | 10 | 2.165 | 0.269 | 10 | 1.519 | 0.913 |
| 3 | 17 | 1.790 | 0.795 | 17 | 1.518 | 0.849 |
| 4 | 8 | 2.105 | 0.387 | 9 | 1.189 | 1.061 |
| 5 | 7 | 1.324 | 0.470 | 10 | 0.456 | 0.619 |
| 6 | 11 | 2.369 | 0.401 | 10 | 1.550 | 0.558 |
| 7 | 10 | 1.074 | 0.670 | 12 | 0.265 | 0.502 |
| 8 | 5 | 2.583 | 0.409 | 4 | 1.370 | 0.934 |
| 9 | 14 | 1.844 | 0.848 | 19 | 2.118 | 0.749 |

is important. Here data from nine of the centres are considered as being from separate studies, for inclusion in a meta-analysis. The response of interest is the recovery time (time from when the anaesthetic gases are turned off until the patient opens their eyes (minutes)). Following a logarithmic transformation of the data, they are treated as being normally distributed. Means and standard deviations for each treatment group within each centre are shown in Table 3.16.

### 3.6.2    Measurement of treatment difference

A quantitative measurement on a continuous scale can often be treated as following a normal distribution. Even if this is not the case, a transformation applied to the values may produce normally distributed data. Data from subjects in the treated group are modelled as being normally distributed with mean $\mu_T$ and standard deviation $\sigma$. For subjects in the control group the mean is $\mu_C$ and the standard deviation $\sigma$. Here a common between-patient standard deviation within each treatment group is being assumed. Suppose that there are $n_T$ subjects in the treated group with responses $y_{jT}, j = 1, \ldots, n_T$, and $n_C$ subjects in the control group with responses $y_{jC}, j = 1, \ldots, n_C$. For the treated group the sample mean ($\bar{y}_T$), sample standard deviation ($s_T$), sum of the observations ($A_T$) and sum of squares of the observations ($B_T$) are defined as follows:

$$\bar{y}_T = \frac{1}{n_T} \sum_{j=1}^{n_T} y_{jT},$$

$$s_T^2 = \frac{\left(\sum_{j=1}^{n_T} y_{jT}^2\right) - n_T \bar{y}_T^2}{n_T - 1},$$

$$A_T = \sum_{j=1}^{n_T} y_{jT},$$

$$B_T = \sum_{j=1}^{n_T} y_{jT}^2.$$

$\bar{y}_C$, $s_C^2$, $A_C$ and $B_C$ are similarly defined for the control group, and $A = A_T + A_C$, and $B = B_T + B_C$. The data are summarized in Table 3.17.

Often published reports present the number of patients, sample mean and sample standard deviation for each treatment group, and this is all that is needed to estimate the treatment difference. The values of $A_T$ and $B_T$ can be calculated from the sample mean and sample standard deviation as follows:

$$A_T = n_T \bar{y}_T$$

and

$$B_T = (n_T - 1)s_T^2 + n_T \bar{y}_T^2.$$

Table 3.18 shows the data from centre 1 of the anaesthetic study presented in the form of Table 3.17.

For normally distributed data two parameters of treatment difference will be considered. They are the absolute difference between means, $\mu_T - \mu_C$, and the standardized difference between means, $(\mu_T - \mu_C)/\sigma$. The absolute difference is

**Table 3.17**    Data for a parallel group study with normally distributed outcomes

| Data | Treated group | Control group | Total |
|------|---------------|---------------|-------|
| Number of patients | $n_T$ | $n_C$ | $n$ |
| Mean | $\bar{y}_T$ | $\bar{y}_C$ | |
| Standard deviation | $s_T$ | $s_C$ | |
| Sum of observations | $A_T$ | $A_C$ | $A$ |
| Sum of squares of observations | $B_T$ | $B_C$ | $B$ |

**Table 3.18**    Recovery time (log-transformed) from centre 1 of the anaesthetic study

| Data | Treated group | Control group | Total |
|------|---------------|---------------|-------|
| Number of patients | 4 | 5 | 9 |
| Mean | 1.141 | 0.277 | |
| Standard deviation | 0.967 | 0.620 | |
| Sum of observations | 4.564 | 1.385 | 5.949 |
| Sum of squares of observations | 8.013 | 1.921 | 9.934 |

easier to interpret and is appropriate if the same measurement has been used in all studies. However, because the standardized difference is dimensionless, it can be used when different units or scales are to be combined. In addition, it is possible to calculate the probability that a patient in the treated group will do better than a patient in the control group in terms of the standardized difference.

For $\theta = (\mu_T - \mu_C)/\sigma$, $P(Y_T > Y_C) = \Phi(\theta/\sqrt{2})$, where $\Phi$ is the standard normal distribution function.

## Absolute difference between means

Using the full likelihood, the ML estimate of the absolute difference between means is the difference between the sample means,

$$\hat{\theta} = \bar{y}_T - \bar{y}_C. \tag{3.22}$$

The variance is given by

$$\text{var}(\hat{\theta}) = \sigma^2 \left( \frac{1}{n_T} + \frac{1}{n_C} \right). \tag{3.23}$$

In order to calculate the variance of $\hat{\theta}$, it is necessary to choose an appropriate estimate for the variance component, $\sigma^2$. One choice is the ML estimate $\hat{\sigma}^2_M$, where

$$\hat{\sigma}^2_M = \frac{B_T - A_T^2/n_T + B_C - A_C^2/n_C}{n}. \tag{3.24}$$

However, as this estimate is known to be biased, it is more common to use the usual pooled sample standard deviation $s^2$, an unbiased estimate obtained by replacing the denominator in formula (3.24) by $n - 2$. This estimate is known as the (residual) restricted maximum likelihood estimate (see, for example, Searle et al., 1992). Thus,

$$s^2 = \frac{B_T - A_T^2/n_T + B_C - A_C^2/n_C}{n - 2}. \tag{3.25}$$

The ML estimate $\hat{\theta}$ and its variance based on $s^2$ can be found from fitting a general linear model, using for example SAS PROC GLM. For the GLM procedure the data from each patient are entered as a separate record. If the response variable is denoted by $y$, the following MODEL statement can be used:

```
MODEL y = treat;
```

In the SAS output the estimate of $\theta$ appears as the 'treat' parameter estimate and $s^2$ appears as the error mean square in the analysis of variance table.

For centre 1 of the anaesthetic study,

$$\hat{\theta} = 0.864,$$

$$s^2 = 0.621$$

and

$$\text{var}(\hat{\theta}) = 0.279.$$

The efficient score and Fisher's information could be obtained for this parameterization of the treatment difference, but this approach is not very accurate and is little used in practice. Consequently, further details are not presented here.

### Standardized difference between means

The ML estimate of the standardized difference between means is

$$\hat{\theta} = \frac{\bar{y}_T - \bar{y}_C}{\hat{\sigma}_M}. \tag{3.26}$$

More often the unbiased estimate of $\sigma^2$ is used, giving

$$\hat{\theta} = \frac{\bar{y}_T - \bar{y}_C}{s}. \tag{3.27}$$

In either case the approximate variance of $\hat{\theta}$ is given by

$$\text{var}(\hat{\theta}) = \frac{n}{n_T n_C}. \tag{3.28}$$

Estimates for centre 1 of the anaesthetic study based on formulae (3.27) and (3.28) are

$$\hat{\theta} = \frac{0.864}{0.788} = 1.097, \qquad \text{var}(\hat{\theta}) = 0.450.$$

Glass (1976) proposed an estimate of $\sigma$ obtained only from the control group, because otherwise, if several treatments were compared with control in a study, the pairwise comparisons of each treated group with control could lead to different standardized values of identical mean differences. Although the sample standard deviations will generally differ amongst the treatment groups, in many cases the assumption of a common variance is reasonable. In Chapter 5 of Hedges and Olkin

(1985) it is shown that the estimate $\hat{\theta}$ given in (3.27) is biased in small samples. They define a new estimate to remove this bias:

$$\hat{\theta} = \frac{J(n-2)(\bar{y}_T - \bar{y}_C)}{s}, \qquad (3.29)$$

with variance estimate

$$\text{var}(\hat{\theta}) = \frac{n}{n_T n_C} + \frac{\hat{\theta}^2}{2n}, \qquad (3.30)$$

where values of the function $J(m)$ are listed in Table 3.19, and for large $m$ can be found from

$$J(m) \approx 1 - \frac{3}{4m-1}.$$

As $m$ gets large $J(m)$ approaches unity, so that the distributions of the estimates defined in (3.27) and (3.29) tend to a normal distribution with identical means and variances.

Estimates for centre 1 of the anaesthetic study from formulae (3.29) and (3.30) are

$$\hat{\theta} = 0.973, \qquad \text{var}(\hat{\theta}) = 0.503.$$

The efficient score and Fisher's information for the standardized mean difference are

$$Z = \frac{n_T n_C (\bar{y}_T - \bar{y}_C)}{ns^*} \qquad (3.31)$$

**Table 3.19** Exact values of the bias correction factor $J(m)$

| $m$ | $J(m)$ | $m$ | $J(m)$ | $m$ | $J(m)$ | $m$ | $J(m)$ |
|---|---|---|---|---|---|---|---|
| 2 | 0.5642 | 15 | 0.9490 | 27 | 0.9719 | 39 | 0.9806 |
| 3 | 0.7236 | 16 | 0.9523 | 28 | 0.9729 | 40 | 0.9811 |
| 4 | 0.7979 | 17 | 0.9551 | 29 | 0.9739 | 41 | 0.9816 |
| 5 | 0.8408 | 18 | 0.9577 | 30 | 0.9748 | 42 | 0.9820 |
| 6 | 0.8686 | 19 | 0.9599 | 31 | 0.9756 | 43 | 0.9824 |
| 7 | 0.8882 | 20 | 0.9619 | 32 | 0.9764 | 44 | 0.9828 |
| 8 | 0.9027 | 21 | 0.9638 | 33 | 0.9771 | 45 | 0.9832 |
| 9 | 0.9139 | 22 | 0.9655 | 34 | 0.9778 | 46 | 0.9836 |
| 10 | 0.9228 | 23 | 0.9670 | 35 | 0.9784 | 47 | 0.9839 |
| 11 | 0.9300 | 24 | 0.9684 | 36 | 0.9790 | 48 | 0.9843 |
| 12 | 0.9359 | 25 | 0.9699 | 37 | 0.9796 | 49 | 0.9846 |
| 13 | 0.9410 | 26 | 0.9708 | 38 | 0.9801 | 50 | 0.9849 |
| 14 | 0.9453 | | | | | | |

and

$$V = \frac{n_T n_C}{n} - \frac{Z^2}{2n},$$ (3.32)

where

$$s^* = \sqrt{\left[\left\{\frac{B}{n} - \left(\frac{A}{n}\right)^2\right\}\right]}.$$

The estimate $s^*$ is the ML estimate of $\sigma$ under the assumption that $\mu_T = \mu_C$.

When $\theta$ is small and $n$ large then $Z/V$ and $\hat{\theta}$ from (3.29) are approximately equal, and $V \approx 1/\mathrm{var}(\hat{\theta})$ from (3.30) because

$$\left(\frac{n}{n_T n_C} + \frac{\hat{\theta}^2}{2n}\right)^{-1} = \frac{n_T n_C}{n}\left(1 - \frac{\hat{\theta}^2 n_T n_C}{2n^2}\right) \approx \frac{n_T n_C}{n} - \left(\frac{Z}{V}\right)^2 \frac{V^2}{2n} = V.$$

Estimates for centre 1 of the anaesthetic study from equations (3.31) and (3.32) are

$$\hat{\theta} = 1.227, \qquad \mathrm{var}(\hat{\theta}) = 0.522.$$

# 4

# Combining Estimates
# of a Treatment Difference
# Across Trials

## 4.1 INTRODUCTION

This chapter presents a methodology for combining the study estimates of a treatment difference, as described in Whitehead and Whitehead (1991). The methodology is for use primarily when the data available from each study consist solely of estimates of treatment difference (with their standard errors) or of summary statistics. It can also be used when individual patient data are available. However, in the latter case, it may be advantageous to exploit the more advanced statistical modelling techniques discussed in Chapter 5. The methodology presented in this chapter can also be used for combining studies some of which provide individual patient data and others only estimates of treatment difference or summary statistics. For example, even if the primary meta-analysis is based on individual patient data, it may be desirable as part of a sensitivity analysis to include additional studies for which only summary data are available.

As in Chapter 3, it is assumed that each study has a parallel group design comparing a treated group with a control group. It is also assumed that the meta-analysis is to be conducted on an outcome measure which has been recorded in the same way in each trial, and that the same parameterization of the treatment difference and method of estimation is used for each trial. A general fixed effects parametric approach, which is applicable to many different data types, is presented in Section 4.2. This includes the calculation of an overall estimate of treatment difference and a statistic for testing the null hypothesis that there is no difference between the two treatments. In addition, a statistic for testing for heterogeneity between the study parameters of treatment difference is presented. This approach is then illustrated using the five examples introduced in Chapter 3.

When meta-analyses are performed retrospectively there are likely to be differences in the study protocols. These differences might be expected to lead to heterogeneity. In other situations there may be strong evidence of heterogeneity from the study estimates. If heterogeneity is believed to exist, then the reasons for its presence should be explored, and this is discussed in detail in Chapter 6. In cases where no reason is found to explain heterogeneity or if no further data are available to explore heterogeneity it is still possible to allow for the parameter measuring treatment difference to vary from study to study by considering a random effects model. In Section 4.3 a general random effects parametric approach is presented, and illustrated using some of the examples from Chapter 3.

## 4.2   A GENERAL FIXED EFFECTS PARAMETRIC APPROACH

### 4.2.1   A fixed effects meta-analysis model

Suppose that there are $r$ independent studies each comparing the treated group with the control group. There is a common outcome measure reported for each patient. The parameter representing the measure of treatment difference is denoted by $\theta$. This may, for example, be the difference between treatment means for normally distributed data or the log-odds ratio for binary data. It is assumed here that $\theta$ equals 0 when the two treatments have equal effect. Denote by $\hat{\theta}_i$ an estimate of $\theta$ from the $i$th study. The general fixed effects model is given by

$$\hat{\theta}_i = \theta + \varepsilon_i, \tag{4.1}$$

for $i = 1, \ldots, r$, where the $\varepsilon_i$ are error terms and are realizations of normally distributed random variables with expected value 0 and variance denoted by $\xi_i^2$. It follows that

$$\hat{\theta}_i \sim N(\theta, \xi_i^2).$$

### 4.2.2   Estimation and hypothesis testing of the treatment difference

Usually, the estimated variance of $\hat{\theta}_i$, $\text{var}(\hat{\theta}_i)$, is treated as if it were the true variance $\xi_i^2$, that is, no allowance is made for error in the calculated term $\text{var}(\hat{\theta}_i)$. Let $w_i$ be the estimated inverse variance of $\hat{\theta}_i$, that is, $w_i = 1/\text{var}(\hat{\theta}_i)$. The distributional assumption that is made is that

$$\hat{\theta}_i \sim N(\theta, w_i^{-1}),$$

for $i = 1, \ldots, r$. Under the null hypothesis that the treatment difference in each study is equal to 0,

$$\hat{\theta}_i w_i \sim N(0, w_i),$$

for $i = 1, \ldots, r$, and, as the study estimates are independent,

$$\sum_{i=1}^{r} \hat{\theta}_i w_i \sim N\left(0, \sum_{i=1}^{r} w_i\right).$$

The global null hypothesis that the treatment difference in all studies is equal to 0 is tested by comparing the statistic

$$U = \frac{\left(\sum_{i=1}^{r} \hat{\theta}_i w_i\right)^2}{\sum_{i=1}^{r} w_i}$$

with the chi-squared distribution with one degree of freedom. Assuming that there is a common treatment difference in all studies,

$$\sum_{i=1}^{r} \hat{\theta}_i w_i \sim N\left(\theta \sum_{i=1}^{r} w_i, \sum_{i=1}^{r} w_i\right)$$

and the overall fixed effect $\theta$ can be estimated by $\hat{\theta}$, where

$$\hat{\theta} = \frac{\sum_{i=1}^{r} \hat{\theta}_i w_i}{\sum_{i=1}^{r} w_i}.$$

If $w_i$ were the true inverse variance of $\hat{\theta}_i$, rather than being an estimate, then $\hat{\theta}$ would be the maximum likelihood estimate of $\theta$. The standard error of $\hat{\theta}$ is given by

$$\text{se}(\hat{\theta}) = \sqrt{\frac{1}{\sum_{i=1}^{r} w_i}},$$

and an approximate 95% confidence interval (CI) for $\theta$ is given by

$$\hat{\theta} \pm 1.96 \sqrt{\frac{1}{\sum_{i=1}^{r} w_i}}.$$

The calculations require an estimate of the treatment difference and its variance from each study. Usually a trial report will quote the standard error, and then $w_i$ can be calculated as $1/\{\text{se}(\hat{\theta}_i)\}^2$. If using efficient score and Fisher's information statistics, $\hat{\theta}_i = Z_i/V_i$. For this choice of $\hat{\theta}_i$ it follows that $w_i = V_i$. Also $\hat{\theta}_i w_i = Z_i$ and $\hat{\theta}_i^2 w_i = Z_i^2/V_i$. Thus

$$\hat{\theta} = \frac{\sum_{i=1}^{r} Z_i}{\sum_{i=1}^{r} V_i}$$

and

$$U = \frac{\left(\sum_{i=1}^{r} Z_i\right)^2}{\sum_{i=1}^{r} V_i}.$$

The fixed effects approach is sometimes referred to as an 'assumption-free' approach (see, for example, Early Breast Cancer Trialists' Collaborative Group, 1990) because it is argued that the fixed effects estimate does not rely on the assumption of a common treatment difference parameter across all studies. Suppose that the assumption of a common treatment difference in all studies is relaxed and that the distributional assumption for the individual study estimates becomes

$$\hat{\theta}_i \sim N(\theta_i, w_i^{-1}),$$

where $\theta_i$ is the treatment difference parameter in study $i$. The overall fixed effect estimate $\hat{\theta}$ can now be viewed as an estimate of

$$\frac{\sum_{i=1}^{r} \theta_i w_i}{\sum_{i=1}^{r} w_i},$$

the weighted mean of the study treatment difference parameters. Whilst this is an acceptable interpretation of $\hat{\theta}$, it would not appear to go far enough. Once variation between studies is conceded it would seem natural to investigate the amount of heterogeneity and to allow for it when making inferences about the difference between the two treatments.

### 4.2.3   Testing for heterogeneity across studies

To test for heterogeneity in the treatment difference parameter across the studies, a large-sample test is used. This is based on the statistic

$$Q = \sum_{i=1}^{r} w_i(\hat{\theta}_i - \hat{\theta})^2,$$

which is a weighted sum of squares of the deviations of individual study estimates from the overall estimate (Cochran, 1954). When treatment difference parameters are homogeneous, $Q$ follows a chi-squared distribution with $r - 1$ degrees of freedom. An easier and equivalent formula for calculation is given by

$$Q = \sum_{i=1}^{r} \hat{\theta}_i^2 w_i - U.$$

When using efficient score and Fisher's information statistics, $Q$ can be written as

$$Q = \sum_{i=1}^{r} V_i \left( \frac{Z_i}{V_i} - \frac{\sum_{i=1}^{r} Z_i}{\sum_{i=1}^{r} V_i} \right)^2 = \sum_{i=1}^{r} \left( \frac{Z_i^2}{V_i} \right) - \frac{\left( \sum_{i=1}^{r} Z_i \right)^2}{\sum_{i=1}^{r} V_i}.$$

### 4.2.4 Obtaining the statistics via weighted least-squares regression

The test statistics $U$ and $Q$ and the estimate $\hat{\theta}$ and its standard error can be obtained by performing a weighted least-squares regression, in which the observed responses ($y$) are the study estimates of treatment difference, $\hat{\theta}_i$, and there are no explanatory variables, only a constant term. The weights ($w$) are the values $w_i$. Further details about the method of weighted least squares can be found in Section A.3 of the Appendix. This method is available in many statistical packages, for example PROC GLM in SAS. Within PROC GLM the following statements can be used:

```
MODEL  y = / inverse;
WEIGHT w;
```

There are no explanatory variables on the right-hand side of the MODEL statement, and in the SAS output the value for $\hat{\theta}$ appears as the estimate for the 'intercept' parameter. The option 'inverse' in the MODEL statement requests the matrix $(X'WX)^{-1}$ to be printed, where $X$ is the matrix of explanatory variables which in this case is a vector of length $r$ with components equal to 1, and $W$ is a $r \times r$ diagonal matrix with the $i$th diagonal element equal to $w_i$. In this case $(X'WX)^{-1}$ consists of one element, which is associated with the 'intercept' parameter and equal to $\left( \sum_{i=1}^{r} w_i \right)^{-1}$, the variance of $\hat{\theta}$. It should be noted that the standard error and test statistics displayed for the intercept parameter are incorrect for the required model, because they assume that $\text{var}(\varepsilon_i) = \sigma^2 / w_i$, where $\sigma^2$ is to be estimated from the data, instead of equal to 1. This will also be the case for other statistical packages.

The $U$ statistic will appear as the model sum of squares and the $Q$ statistic as the error sum of squares in the analysis of variance table. Again, the test statistics in this table are incorrect for the required model.

### 4.2.5 Example: Stroke in hypertensive patients

Consider the stroke example described in Section 3.2.1. From Table 3.1 it can be seen that two of the studies (1 and 12) have no occurrence of stroke in either treatment group and one study (3) has no occurrence of stroke in the treated group. These three studies are omitted from the meta-analyses presented in this chapter because for some of the estimation methods described in Section 3.2.2 a study estimate of the treatment difference cannot be calculated. This issue will be addressed in Section 9.2.

Table 4.1 shows the study estimates of the log-odds ratio of a stroke on antihypertensive treatment relative to control treatment (placebo or 'usual care'). Calculations in the table are based on formulae (3.1) and (3.2), the unconditional ML approach. A negative estimate indicates that antihypertensive treatment has a beneficial effect in preventing strokes. All of the individual study estimates, with the exception of study 11, are negative. Six of the studies show a statistically significant benefit of the treatment; the other seven are equivocal. A CI plot is presented in Figure 4.1.

Table 4.2 shows the results of the fixed effects meta-analysis based on the study estimates from Table 4.1. The $Q$ statistic is not statistically significant ($p = 0.65$), indicating that there is no strong evidence of heterogeneity amongst the studies. The overall estimate of treatment difference shows a beneficial effect of antihypertensive treatment ($\hat{\theta} = -0.535$), and the $U$ statistic is statistically significant ($p < 0.001$), providing strong evidence of an effect.

In Section 3.2.2, four approaches to the estimation of the individual study log-odds ratios were presented. The results of a fixed effects meta-analysis based on each approach are presented in Table 4.3 for comparison. It can be seen that there is good agreement between all of the approaches. The performance of a meta-analysis on trials which were not originally planned with that in mind is not going to be an exact science. It is likely that the decision about which method of estimation to use will be relatively unimportant compared with the decision about which studies to include in the meta-analysis. However, there are a few points to note. First, the study estimates based on the efficient score

**Table 4.1**  Study estimates of the log-odds ratio of a stroke on antihypertensive treatment relative to control treatment, based on the unconditional maximum likelihood approach (formulae (3.1) and (3.2))

| Study | $\hat{\theta}_i$ | se($\hat{\theta}_i$) | 95% CI |
|---|---|---|---|
| 2 HDFP (Stratum I) | −0.402 | 0.170 | (−0.735, −0.070) |
| 4 ANBPS | −0.540 | 0.352 | (−1.229,  0.149) |
| 5 MRC | −0.608 | 0.161 | (−0.925, −0.292) |
| 6 VAII | −1.426 | 0.511 | (−2.428, −0.424) |
| 7 USPHS | −1.802 | 1.085 | (−3.929,  0.324) |
| 8 HDFP (Stratum II) | −0.420 | 0.264 | (−0.938,  0.098) |
| 9 HSCSG | −0.319 | 0.232 | (−0.773,  0.135) |
| 10 VAI | −1.209 | 1.168 | (−3.499,  1.081) |
| 11 WOLFF | 0.646 | 1.244 | (−1.793,  3.084) |
| 13 Carter | −1.110 | 0.459 | (−2.008, −0.211) |
| 14 HDFP (Stratum III) | −0.678 | 0.298 | (−1.262, −0.093) |
| 15 EWPHE | −0.427 | 0.239 | (−0.896,  0.043) |
| 16 Coope | −0.602 | 0.284 | (−1.158, −0.046) |

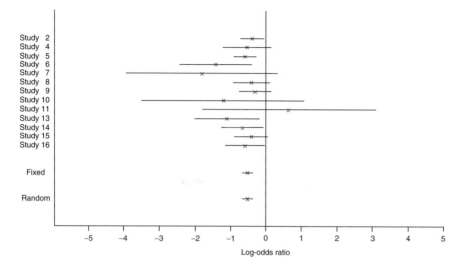

**Figure 4.1** The log-odds ratio of a stroke on antihypertensive treatment relative to control. Individual study estimates and overall fixed and random effects estimates are presented, with 95% CIs. Individual study calculations are based on formulae (3.1) and (3.2). The method of moments estimate of $\tau^2$ is used.

and Fisher's information statistics are reasonably good approximations to the ML estimates when the values are small, that is, between $-1$ and $1$. For more extreme values, the approximation is less good (Greenland and Salvan, 1990). Typically, the estimates based on the efficient score and Fisher's information statistics are underestimates (closer to 0), as are the associated standard errors.

Consider now the parameterization of the treatment difference in terms of the probability difference. In the stroke example, this could be presented as the difference in the risk of a stroke between patients on antihypertensive treatment and those on control. A negative value indicates a beneficial effect of the treatment. Table 4.4 shows the study estimates for this risk differ-ence, and Figure 4.2 the corresponding CI plot. Calculations in the table are based on (3.7) and (3.8), the unconditional ML approach. As for the log-odds ratio estimates, a negative estimate indicates that antihypertensive treatment has a beneficial effect in preventing strokes. All estimates, with the excep-tion of study 11, are negative, and the same six studies show a statistically significant benefit of the treatment as was the case with the log-odds ratio parameterization. However, the CI plots for the two parameterizations look quite different. The log-odds ratio estimates in Figure 4.1 appear to be reasonably homogeneous, whereas the probability difference estimates indicate some het-erogeneity. In particular, study 13 shows a much larger effect than the other studies.

**Table 4.2** Fixed effects meta-analysis of the log-odds ratio of a stroke on antihypertensive treatment relative to control treatment, based on the study estimates from Table 4.1

| Study | Treated group | | Control group | | $\hat{\theta}_i$ | $w_i$ | $\hat{\theta}_i w_i$ | $\hat{\theta}_i^2 w_i$ |
|---|---|---|---|---|---|---|---|---|
| | Success (stroke) | Failure | Success (stroke) | Failure | | | | |
| 2 HDFP (Stratum I) | 59 | 3 844 | 88 | 3 834 | −0.402 | 34.68 | −13.96 | 5.62 |
| 4 ANBPS | 13 | 1 708 | 22 | 1 684 | −0.540 | 8.09 | −4.37 | 2.36 |
| 5 MRC | 60 | 8 640 | 109 | 8 545 | −0.608 | 38.35 | −23.32 | 14.18 |
| 6 VAII | 5 | 181 | 20 | 174 | −1.426 | 3.83 | −5.46 | 7.78 |
| 7 USPHS | 1 | 192 | 6 | 190 | −1.802 | 0.85 | −1.53 | 2.76 |
| 8 HDFP (Stratum II) | 25 | 1 023 | 36 | 968 | −0.420 | 14.33 | −6.02 | 2.53 |
| 9 HSCSG | 43 | 190 | 52 | 167 | −0.319 | 18.61 | −5.94 | 1.89 |
| 10 VAI | 1 | 67 | 3 | 60 | −1.209 | 0.73 | −0.89 | 1.07 |
| 11 WOLFF | 2 | 43 | 1 | 41 | 0.646 | 0.65 | 0.42 | 0.27 |
| 13 Carter | 10 | 39 | 21 | 27 | −1.110 | 4.76 | −5.28 | 5.86 |
| 14 HDFP (Stratum III) | 18 | 516 | 34 | 495 | −0.678 | 11.25 | −7.62 | 5.16 |
| 15 EWPHE | 32 | 384 | 48 | 376 | −0.427 | 17.44 | −7.44 | 3.17 |
| 16 Coope | 20 | 399 | 39 | 426 | −0.602 | 12.42 | −7.48 | 4.51 |
| Total | | | | | | 165.98 | −88.88 | 57.16 |

$U = (-88.88)^2/165.98 = 47.59;$ (1 df) $p < 0.001$

$Q = 57.16 - 47.59 = 9.57;$ (12 df) $p = 0.65$

$\hat{\theta} = -88.88/165.98 = -0.535;$ $\mathrm{se}(\hat{\theta}) = 1/\sqrt{165.98} = 0.078$

95% CI $= (-0.535 \pm 1.96/\sqrt{165.98}) = (-0.688, -0.383)$

**Table 4.3** Fixed effects meta-analysis of the log-odds ratio of a stroke on antihypertensive treatment relative to control treatment: comparison of four methods of calculating study estimates. Estimates are shown with standard error in square brackets

| Study | Estimation method | | | |
|---|---|---|---|---|
| | Unconditional ML: (3.1), (3.2) | Unconditional Z and V: (3.3), (3.4) | Conditional ML: | Conditional Z and V: (3.5), (3.6) |
| 2 HDFP (Stratum I) | −0.402 [0.170] | −0.397 [0.167] | −0.402 [0.170] | −0.397 [0.167] |
| 4 ANBPS | −0.540 [0.352] | −0.528 [0.340] | −0.540 [0.351] | −0.528 [0.340] |
| 5 MRC | −0.608 [0.161] | −0.591 [0.155] | −0.608 [0.161] | −0.591 [0.155] |
| 6 VAII | −1.426 [0.511] | −1.240 [0.414] | −1.422 [0.511] | −1.237 [0.413] |
| 7 USPHS | −1.802 [1.085] | −1.439 [0.763] | −1.798 [1.084] | −1.435 [0.762] |
| 8 HDFP (Stratum II) | −0.420 [0.264] | −0.416 [0.260] | −0.420 [0.264] | −0.416 [0.260] |
| 9 HSCSG | −0.319 [0.232] | −0.319 [0.231] | −0.318 [0.232] | −0.318 [0.231] |
| 10 VAI | −1.209 [1.168] | −1.112 [1.016] | −1.200 [1.165] | −1.103 [1.012] |
| 11 WOLFF | 0.646 [1.244] | 0.620 [1.176] | 0.638 [1.238] | 0.613 [1.169] |
| 13 Carter | −1.110 [0.459] | −1.073 [0.435] | −1.098 [0.456] | −1.062 [0.433] |
| 14 HDFP (Stratum III) | −0.678 [0.298] | −0.657 [0.284] | −0.677 [0.298] | −0.656 [0.284] |
| 15 EWPHE | −0.427 [0.239] | −0.421 [0.235] | −0.426 [0.239] | −0.421 [0.235] |
| 16 Coope | −0.602 [0.284] | −0.580 [0.270] | −0.602 [0.284] | −0.580 [0.270] |
| $U$ (1 df) | 47.59; $p < 0.001$ | 50.96; $p < 0.001$ | 47.53; $p < 0.001$ | 50.90; $p < 0.001$ |
| $Q$ (12 df) | 9.57; $p = 0.65$ | 9.47; $p = 0.66$ | 9.49; $p = 0.66$ | 9.40; $p = 0.67$ |
| $\hat{\theta}$ [se($\hat{\theta}$)] | −0.535 [0.078] | −0.534 [0.075] | −0.535 [0.078] | −0.533 [0.075] |
| 95% CI | (−0.688, −0.383) | (−0.680, −0.387) | (−0.687, −0.383) | (−0.680, −0.387) |

**Table 4.4**   Study estimates of the difference in the probability of a stroke between antihypertensive treatment and control treatment, based on the unconditional maximum likelihood approach (formulae (3.7) and (3.8))

| Study | $\hat{\theta}_i$ | $\text{se}(\hat{\theta}_i)$ | 95% CI |
|---|---|---|---|
| 2 HDFP (Stratum I) | −0.0073 | 0.0031 | (−0.0133, −0.0013) |
| 4 ANBPS | −0.0053 | 0.0034 | (−0.0121, 0.0014) |
| 5 MRC | −0.0057 | 0.0015 | (−0.0086, −0.0028) |
| 6 VAII | −0.0762 | 0.0248 | (−0.1249, −0.0275) |
| 7 USPHS | −0.0254 | 0.0133 | (−0.0516, 0.0007) |
| 8 HDFP (Stratum II) | −0.0120 | 0.0075 | (−0.0268, 0.0028) |
| 9 HSCSG | −0.0529 | 0.0384 | (−0.1281, 0.0223) |
| 10 VAI | −0.0329 | 0.0305 | (−0.0928, 0.0270) |
| 11 WOLFF | 0.0206 | 0.0387 | (−0.0552, 0.0965) |
| 13 Carter | −0.2334 | 0.0919 | (−0.4135, −0.0533) |
| 14 HDFP (Stratum III) | −0.0306 | 0.0132 | (−0.0565, −0.0047) |
| 15 EWPHE | −0.0363 | 0.0202 | (−0.0758, 0.0033) |
| 16 Coope | −0.0361 | 0.0165 | (−0.0686, −0.0037) |

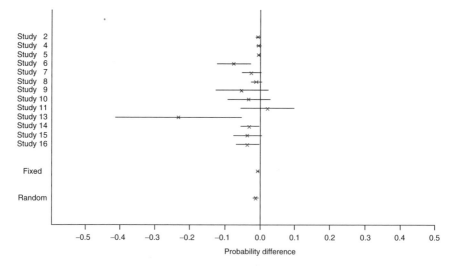

**Figure 4.2**   The difference in the probability of a stroke between antihypertensive treatment and control. Individual study estimates and overall fixed and random effects estimates are presented, with 95% CIs. Individual study calculations are based on formulae (3.7) and (3.8). The method of moments estimate of $\tau^2$ is used.

Table 4.5 shows the results of the fixed effects meta-analysis based on the study estimates from Table 4.4. Compared with Table 4.2, the study estimates, $\hat{\theta}_i$, and weights, $w_i$, are of completely different orders of magnitude, because of the change in the parameterization of the treatment difference. It can also be seen that

**Table 4.5** Fixed effects meta-analysis of the difference in the probability of a stroke between antihypertensive treatment and control treatment, based on the study estimates from Table 4.4

| Study | Treated group | | Control group | | $\hat{\theta}_i$ | $w_i$ | $\hat{\theta}_i w_i$ | $\hat{\theta}_i^2 w_i$ |
|---|---|---|---|---|---|---|---|---|
| | Success (stroke) | Failure | Success (stroke) | Failure | | | | |
| 2 HDFP (Stratum I) | 59 | 3 844 | 88 | 3 834 | −0.0073 | 106 303 | −778 | 5.70 |
| 4 ANBPS | 13 | 1 708 | 22 | 1 684 | −0.0053 | 84 620 | −452 | 2.41 |
| 5 MRC | 60 | 8 640 | 109 | 8 545 | −0.0057 | 449 571 | −2 562 | 14.60 |
| 6 VAII | 5 | 181 | 20 | 174 | −0.0762 | 1 620 | −123 | 9.41 |
| 7 USPHS | 1 | 192 | 6 | 190 | −0.0254 | 5 614 | −143 | 3.63 |
| 8 HDFP (Stratum II) | 25 | 1 023 | 36 | 968 | −0.0120 | 17 651 | −212 | 2.54 |
| 9 HSCSG | 43 | 190 | 52 | 167 | −0.0529 | 679 | −36 | 1.90 |
| 10 VAI | 1 | 67 | 3 | 60 | −0.0329 | 1 072 | −35 | 1.16 |
| 11 WOLFF | 2 | 43 | 1 | 41 | 0.0206 | 668 | 14 | 0.28 |
| 13 Carter | 10 | 39 | 21 | 27 | −0.2334 | 118 | −28 | 6.45 |
| 14 HDFP (Stratum III) | 18 | 516 | 34 | 495 | −0.0306 | 5 725 | −175 | 5.35 |
| 15 EWPHE | 32 | 384 | 48 | 376 | −0.0363 | 2 454 | −89 | 3.23 |
| 16 Coope | 20 | 399 | 39 | 426 | −0.0361 | 3 653 | −132 | 4.77 |
| Total | | | | | | 679 749 | −4 751 | 61.44 |

$U = (-4751)^2 / 679\,749 = 33.21; (1\ \text{df})\ p < 0.001$

$Q = 61.44 - 33.21 = 28.23; (12\ \text{df})\ p = 0.005$

$\hat{\theta} = -4751/679\,749 = -0.0070;\ \text{se}(\hat{\theta}) = 1/\sqrt{679\,749} = 0.0012$

$95\%\ \text{CI} = (-0.0070 \pm 1.96/\sqrt{679\,749}) = (-0.0094, -0.0046)$

the weight of one study relative to another changes from one parameterization to the other. For example, study 9 has a much larger weight than study 11 for the log-odds ratio parameterization, but they have almost the same weight for the probability difference parameterization. The weight for the log-odds ratio parameterization calculated from (3.2) will be small if the number of successes or failures in either treatment group is close to 0. For a given sample size, the closer the proportion of successes in each treatment group is to 0.5 the higher the weight. The reverse is true for the weight calculated from (3.8) for the probability difference parameterization. In fact, if there are either no successes or no failures in both treatment groups the weight is equal to infinity. This means that small studies will be given a large weight when they have no or very few successes (failures).

For the probability difference parameterization, the $Q$ statistic is highly significant ($p = 0.005$), indicating that there is strong evidence of heterogeneity amongst the studies. It can be seen from Table 3.1 that amongst these 13 studies the percentage of patients in the control group who suffered a stroke varied considerably (from 1.3% to 43.8%), and the absolute risk difference has a positive relationship with risk in the control group. The overall estimate of treatment difference shows a beneficial effect of antihypertensive treatment ($\hat{\theta} = -0.0070$), and the $U$ statistic is significant ($p < 0.001$). However, because of the evident heterogeneity of the study estimates, it would be unwise to make inferences from such results. The log-odds ratio parameterization seems more reasonable for this data set.

The third parameterization of the treatment difference considered in Section 3.2.2 was the log-relative risk. In the stroke example, this would be the log-relative risk of a stroke on antihypertensive treatment relative to the control. A negative value indicates a beneficial effect of the treatment. Table 4.6 shows the study estimates for the log-relative risk. Calculations in the table are based on (3.9) and (3.10), the unconditional ML approach. Comparing Tables 4.1 and 4.6, it can be seen that for many of the studies the estimate of the log-relative risk is similar to the estimate of the log-odds ratio. This is generally the case when the event of interest, in this case a stroke, is an infrequent occurrence – that is, when $(1 - p_C)/(1 - p_T)$ is close to 1. However, when this is not the case there can be substantial differences; see, for example, studies 9 and 13. It is important, therefore, to be clear about which parameterization is being used. There can be a problem when study estimates are extracted from published papers, as an odds ratio is sometimes referred to as a relative risk.

The weight for the log-relative risk parameterization calculated from (3.10) will be small if the number of successes in either treatment group is close to 0, but will be large if the number of failures in both treatment groups is close to 0. If there are no failures in both treatment groups the weight is equal to infinity. This means that small studies will be given a large weight when they have no or very few failures. When the event of interest occurs infrequently, the weights will be

**Table 4.6**   Study estimates of the log-relative risk of a stroke on antihypertensive treatment compared with control treatment, based on the unconditional maximum likelihood approach (formulae (3.9) and (3.10))

| Study | $\hat{\theta}_i$ | $\text{se}(\hat{\theta}_i)$ | 95% CI |
|---|---|---|---|
| 2 HDFP (Stratum I) | −0.395 | 0.167 | (−0.722, −0.068) |
| 4 ANBPS | −0.535 | 0.348 | (−1.217,   0.148) |
| 5 MRC | −0.602 | 0.160 | (−0.916, −0.289) |
| 6 VAII | −1.344 | 0.489 | (−2.303, −0.385) |
| 7 USPHS | −1.776 | 1.075 | (−3.884,   0.331) |
| 8 HDFP (Stratum II) | −0.408 | 0.257 | (−0.910,   0.095) |
| 9 HSCSG | −0.252 | 0.183 | (−0.611,   0.107) |
| 10 VAI | −1.175 | 1.141 | (−3.412,   1.062) |
| 11 WOLFF | 0.624 | 1.206 | (−1.739,   2.988) |
| 13 Carter | −0.763 | 0.326 | (−1.402, −0.123) |
| 14 HDFP (Stratum III) | −0.645 | 0.285 | (−1.204, −0.087) |
| 15 EWPHE | −0.386 | 0.218 | (−0.813,   0.040) |
| 16 Coope | −0.564 | 0.267 | (−1.086, −0.041) |

similar to those for the log-odds ratio parameterization. However, as the rate of occurrence increases the difference between the two weights becomes larger.

Table 4.7 shows the results of the fixed effects meta-analysis based on the study estimates from Table 4.6. They are very similar to those in Table 4.2. The $Q$ statistic is not significant ($p = 0.65$), indicating that there is no strong evidence of heterogeneity amongst the studies. The overall estimate of treatment difference shows a beneficial effect of antihypertensive treatment ($\hat{\theta} = -0.494$), and the $U$ statistic is significant ($p < 0.001$), providing strong evidence of an effect.

If it were decided to model the probability of not having a stroke instead of the probability of having a stroke, then the parameter for the meta-analysis would be the log-relative 'risk' of not having a stroke on antihypertensive treatment relative to the control. In addition to the changes to the study estimates, there would be substantial changes to the weights. For example, the weight for study 9 would change from 29.74 to 417.86, and the weight for study 11 would change from 0.69 to 619.46. The test for heterogeneity now becomes statistically significant ($Q = 27.51$, 12 df, $p = 0.007$). In general, the results of the meta-analysis based on the probability of not having the event will be different from those based on the probability of having the event. This is not the case for the other two parameterizations discussed.

### 4.2.6   Example: Mortality following myocardial infarction

For the MDPIT study described in Section 3.3.1, interest lies in estimating the log-hazard ratio for mortality on diltiazem relative to placebo. Table 4.8 shows the estimates from each region, and Figure 4.3 the corresponding CI plot. These

**Table 4.7** Fixed effects meta-analysis of the log-relative risk of a stroke on antihypertensive treatment compared with control treatment, based on the study estimates from Table 4.6

| Study | Treated group | | Control group | | $\hat{\theta}_i$ | $w_i$ | $\hat{\theta}_i w_i$ | $\hat{\theta}_i^2 w_i$ |
|---|---|---|---|---|---|---|---|---|
| | Success (stroke) | Failure | Success (stroke) | Failure | | | | |
| 2 HDFP (Stratum I) | 59 | 3 844 | 88 | 3 834 | −0.395 | 35.97 | −14.21 | 5.61 |
| 4 ANBPS | 13 | 1 708 | 22 | 1 684 | −0.535 | 8.25 | −4.41 | 2.36 |
| 5 MRC | 60 | 8 640 | 109 | 8 545 | −0.602 | 39.05 | −23.52 | 14.16 |
| 6 VAII | 5 | 181 | 20 | 174 | −1.344 | 4.18 | −5.61 | 7.55 |
| 7 USPHS | 1 | 192 | 6 | 190 | −1.776 | 0.86 | −1.54 | 2.73 |
| 8 HDFP (Stratum II) | 25 | 1 023 | 36 | 968 | −0.408 | 15.19 | −6.19 | 2.52 |
| 9 HSCSG | 43 | 190 | 52 | 167 | −0.252 | 29.74 | −7.49 | 1.89 |
| 10 VAI | 1 | 67 | 3 | 60 | −1.175 | 0.77 | −0.90 | 1.06 |
| 11 WOLFF | 2 | 43 | 1 | 41 | 0.624 | 0.69 | 0.43 | 0.27 |
| 13 Carter | 10 | 39 | 21 | 27 | −0.763 | 9.40 | −7.17 | 5.47 |
| 14 HDFP (Stratum III) | 18 | 516 | 34 | 495 | −0.645 | 12.31 | −7.95 | 5.13 |
| 15 EWPHE | 32 | 384 | 48 | 376 | −0.386 | 21.13 | −8.17 | 3.16 |
| 16 Coope | 20 | 399 | 39 | 426 | −0.564 | 14.06 | −7.93 | 4.47 |
| Total | | | | | | 191.60 | −94.65 | 56.37 |

$U = (-94.65)^2 / 191.60 = 46.76; (1\,\text{df})\, p < 0.001$

$Q = 56.37 - 46.76 = 9.61; (12\,\text{df})\, p = 0.65$

$\hat{\theta} = -94.65/191.60 = -0.494$: $\text{se}(\hat{\theta}) = 1/\sqrt{191.60} = 0.072$

$95\% \text{ CI} = (-0.494 \pm 1.96/\sqrt{191.60}) = (-0.636, -0.352)$

are ML estimates based on the individual survival times recorded to the nearest day. A negative estimate indicates that diltiazem reduces mortality relative to placebo, and a positive estimate that it increases mortality. There is no statistically significant difference between the treatments in any of the regions with the exception of the Mideast, in which diltiazem is shown to reduce mortality significantly.

Table 4.9 shows the results of the fixed effects meta-analysis based on the study estimates from Table 4.8. The $Q$ statistic is not significant ($p = 0.22$), indicating that there is no strong evidence of heterogeneity amongst the different regions.

**Table 4.8**  Estimates of the log-hazard ratio for mortality in each region of the MDPIT study based on individual survival times recorded to the nearest day and using a maximum likelihood approach

| Region | $\hat{\theta}_i$ | $se(\hat{\theta}_i)$ | 95% CI |
|---|---|---|---|
| New York City (US) | 0.282 | 0.265 | (−0.238,  0.802) |
| Northeast (US) | 0.145 | 0.218 | (−0.282,  0.571) |
| Mideast (US) | −1.244 | 0.572 | (−2.365, −0.123) |
| Midwest (US) | 0.258 | 0.307 | (−0.345,  0.860) |
| Southwest (US) | −0.122 | 0.282 | (−0.674,  0.429) |
| Ontario (Canada) | −0.293 | 0.291 | (−0.864,  0.278) |
| Quebec (Canada) | −0.071 | 0.359 | (−0.776,  0.634) |

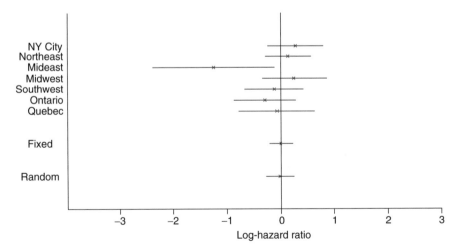

**Figure 4.3**  The log-hazard ratio for mortality on diltiazem relative to placebo. Individual region estimates and overall fixed and random effects estimates are presented, with 95% CIs. Individual region calculations are based on maximum likelihood estimates from individual survival times recorded to the nearest day. The method of moments estimate of $\tau^2$ is used.

**Table 4.9** Fixed effects meta-analysis of the log-hazard ratio for mortality on diltiazem relative to placebo for the MDPIT study, based on the region estimates from Table 4.8

| Region | Diltiazem | | Placebo | | $\hat{\theta}_i$ | $w_i$ | $\hat{\theta}_i w_i$ | $\hat{\theta}_i^2 w_i$ |
|---|---|---|---|---|---|---|---|---|
| | Number of deaths | Total number of patients | Number of deaths | Total number of patients | | | | |
| New York City (US) | 33 | 262 | 25 | 256 | 0.282 | 14.22 | 4.01 | 1.13 |
| Northeast (US) | 46 | 305 | 39 | 298 | 0.145 | 21.10 | 3.05 | 0.44 |
| Mideast (US) | 4 | 72 | 13 | 71 | −1.244 | 3.06 | −3.80 | 4.73 |
| Midwest (US) | 24 | 127 | 19 | 125 | 0.258 | 10.59 | 2.73 | 0.70 |
| Southwest (US) | 23 | 169 | 28 | 184 | −0.122 | 12.61 | −1.54 | 0.19 |
| Ontario (Canada) | 21 | 121 | 27 | 122 | −0.293 | 11.79 | −3.45 | 1.01 |
| Quebec (Canada) | 15 | 176 | 16 | 178 | −0.071 | 7.74 | −0.55 | 0.04 |
| Total | | | | | | 81.11 | 0.44 | 8.24 |

$U = (0.44)^2/81.11 < 0.01;\ (1\,\mathrm{df})\ p = 0.96$

$Q = 8.24 - 0.00 = 8.24;\ (6\,\mathrm{df})\ p = 0.22$

$\hat{\theta} = 0.44/81.11 = 0.005;\ \mathrm{se}(\hat{\theta}) = 1/\sqrt{81.11} = 0.111$

$95\%\ \mathrm{CI} = (0.005 \pm 1.96/\sqrt{81.11}) = (-0.212, 0.223)$

There is no evidence of a treatment difference ($\hat{\theta} = 0.005$), in fact there seems to be quite strong evidence that diltiazem has no effect on mortality. The estimate from the Mideast has the smallest weight as it is based on the smallest number of deaths.

In Section 3.3.2, four approaches to the estimation of the treatment difference in the individual regions were described. The results of a fixed effects meta-analysis based on each approach are presented in Table 4.10 for comparison. In the first two approaches the study estimates are calculated from individual survival times recorded to the nearest day, and the treatment difference is the log-hazard ratio for diltiazem relative to placebo. In the last two the survival times are grouped into yearly intervals, and the treatment difference is the log-odds ratio for an earlier death on diltiazem relative to placebo. As was the case for the log-odds ratios for binary data, the estimates based on the efficient score and Fisher's information statistics are reasonably good approximations to the ML estimates, although they tend to be smaller and have smaller standard errors. There is a larger difference between the estimates based on the aggregated survival times and those based on the survival times recorded to the nearest day. The way in which the survival times are aggregated and the way in which censored observations are treated will affect the estimates. Nevertheless, the overall conclusion from all four approaches is very similar.

## 4.2.7  Example: Ulcer recurrence

The ulcer recurrence study was described in detail in Section 3.4.1, and the data displayed in Table 3.9. From that table it can be seen that there are very few patients in Norway, and none of these have suffered a relapse. Because an estimate of the treatment difference using the methods presented in Section 3.4.2 cannot be calculated in this situation, the data from Norway have been pooled with the data from Holland for the meta-analyses presented in this chapter. The issue of pooling data across subsets of studies will be addressed in Section 9.2.

Table 4.11 shows the study estimates of the log-hazard ratio of ulcer recurrence on treatment 2 relative to treatment 1, and Figure 4.4 the corresponding CI plot. Calculations in the table are based on ML estimation. A negative estimate indicates that treatment 2 has a more beneficial effect in preventing ulcer recurrence than treatment 1. In Belgium treatment 2 seems to be worse than treatment 1, but in the other three countries treatment 2 seems to be better. However, there is no statistically significant difference between treatments in any country.

Table 4.12 shows the results of the fixed effects meta-analysis based on the country estimates from Table 4.11. The $Q$ statistic is not significant ($p = 0.72$), indicating that there is no strong evidence of heterogeneity amongst the studies. The overall estimate of treatment difference indicates a beneficial effect of treatment 2 ($\hat{\theta} = -0.278$), but this is not statistically significant ($p = 0.25$).

**Table 4.10**  Fixed effects meta-analysis of the treatment difference for the MDPIT study: comparison of four methods. The treatment difference is expressed as the log-hazard ratio for mortality on diltiazem relative to placebo in the first two pairs of columns and as the log-odds ratio for earlier death in the third and fourth pairs of columns. Estimates with standard error in square brackets

| Region | Estimation method | | | |
|---|---|---|---|---|
| | Survival times (recorded to nearest day) ML | Survival times (recorded to nearest day) $Z$ and $V$: (3.11), (3.12) | Survival times (yearly aggregates) ML | Survival times (yearly aggregates) $Z$ and $V$: (3.11), (3.12) |
| New York City (US) | 0.282 [0.265] | 0.280 [0.263] | 0.305 [0.273] | 0.304 [0.271] |
| Northeast (US) | 0.145 [0.218] | 0.145 [0.217] | 0.163 [0.225] | 0.163 [0.225] |
| Mideast (US) | −1.244 [0.572] | −1.125 [0.486] | −1.341 [0.588] | −1.224 [0.505] |
| Midwest (US) | 0.258 [0.307] | 0.257 [0.305] | 0.298 [0.320] | 0.297 [0.318] |
| Southwest (US) | −0.122 [0.282] | −0.122 [0.280] | −0.132 [0.290] | −0.131 [0.289] |
| Ontario (Canada) | −0.293 [0.291] | −0.292 [0.289] | −0.230 [0.312] | −0.229 [0.310] |
| Quebec (Canada) | −0.071 [0.359] | −0.071 [0.359] | −0.021 [0.389] | −0.021 [0.389] |
| $U$ (1 df) | <0.01; $p = 0.96$ | <0.01; $p = 0.96$ | 0.07; $p = 0.79$ | 0.03; $p = 0.87$ |
| $Q$ (6 df) | 8.24; $p = 0.22$ | 8.91; $p = 0.18$ | 8.53; $p = 0.20$ | 9.26; $p = 0.16$ |
| $\hat{\theta}$ [se($\hat{\theta}$)] | 0.005 [0.111] | −0.006 [0.110] | 0.030 [0.116] | 0.018 [0.115] |
| 95% CI | (−0.212, 0.223) | (−0.221, 0.209) | (−0.197, 0.257) | (−0.206, 0.243) |

**Table 4.11**    Estimates of the log-hazard ratio for ulcer recurrence on treatment 2 relative to treatment 1 from each country, based on a maximum likelihood approach

| Country | $\hat{\theta}_i$ | $se(\hat{\theta}_i)$ | 95% CI |
|---|---|---|---|
| Austria | −0.290 | 0.347 | (−0.970, 0.389) |
| Belgium | 0.195 | 0.628 | (−1.035, 1.426) |
| France | −0.129 | 0.607 | (−1.319, 1.062) |
| Holland and Norway | −0.748 | 0.558 | (−1.842, 0.346) |

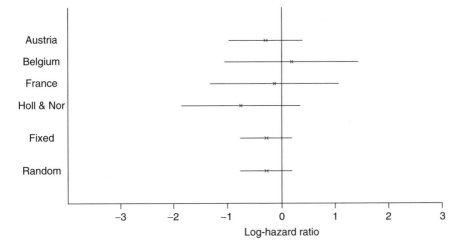

**Figure 4.4**    The log-hazard ratio of ulcer recurrence on treatment 2 relative to treatment 1. Individual country estimates and overall fixed and random effects estimates are presented, with 95% CIs. Individual country calculations are based on maximum likelihood estimation. The method of moments estimate of $\tau^2$ is used.

Comparison of the fixed effects meta-analyses based on the two methods of estimation described in Section 3.4.2 indicates close agreement (Table 4.13). As found with the other example data sets, the individual country estimates based on the efficient score and Fisher's information statistics are underestimates, as are the associated standard errors. However, this has not led to a smaller overall estimate of treatment difference than that based on ML estimation.

Revisiting the MDPIT study described in Section 3.3.1, it can be seen that the survival times when grouped into yearly intervals can be considered as interval-censored survival data. Table 4.14 shows the results of two fixed effects meta-analyses of the log-hazard ratio as calculated using the interval-censored survival approach, one based on ML estimates and the other on the efficient score

**Table 4.12** Fixed effects meta-analysis of the log-hazard ratio for ulcer recurrence on treatment 2 relative to treatment 1, based on the country estimates from Table 4.11

| Country | Treatment 2 | | Treatment 1 | | $\hat{\theta}_i$ | $w_i$ | $\hat{\theta}_i w_i$ | $\hat{\theta}_i^2 w_i$ |
|---|---|---|---|---|---|---|---|---|
| | Number with ulcer recurrence | Total number of patients | Number with ulcer recurrence | Total number of patients | | | | |
| Austria | 15 | 55 | 19 | 59 | −0.290 | 8.32 | −2.41 | 0.70 |
| Belgium | 7 | 29 | 4 | 23 | 0.195 | 2.54 | 0.50 | 0.10 |
| France | 5 | 22 | 6 | 25 | −0.129 | 2.71 | −0.35 | 0.04 |
| Holland and Norway | 5 | 65 | 9 | 59 | −0.748 | 3.21 | −2.40 | 1.80 |
| Total | | | | | | 16.78 | −4.67 | 2.64 |

$U = (-4.67)^2/16.78 = 1.30$; (1 df) $p = 0.25$

$Q = 2.64 - 1.30 = 1.34$; (3 df) $p = 0.72$

$\hat{\theta} = -4.67/16.78 = -0.278$; $\text{se}(\hat{\theta}) = 1/\sqrt{16.78} = 0.244$

95% CI $= (-0.278 \pm 1.96/\sqrt{16.78}) = (-0.757, 0.200)$

**Table 4.13**    Fixed effects meta-analysis of the log-hazard ratio for ulcer recurrence on treatment 2 relative to treatment 1: comparison of two methods of calculating country estimates. Estimates with standard error in square brackets

| Country | Estimation method | |
|---|---|---|
| | ML | Z and V: (3.13), (3.14) |
| Austria | −0.290 [0.347] | −0.289 [0.344] |
| Belgium | 0.195 [0.628] | 0.193 [0.617] |
| France | −0.129 [0.607] | −0.128 [0.605] |
| Holland and Norway | −0.748 [0.558] | −0.736 [0.537] |
| $U$ (1 df) | 1.30; $p = 0.25$ | 1.36; $p = 0.24$ |
| $Q$ (3 df) | 1.34; $p = 0.72$ | 1.37; $p = 0.71$ |
| $\hat{\theta}$ [se($\hat{\theta}$)] | −0.278 [0.244] | −0.280 [0.241] |
| 95% CI | (−0.757, 0.200) | (−0.752, 0.191) |

**Table 4.14**    Fixed effects meta-analysis of the log-hazard ratio for mortality on diltiazem relative to placebo for the MDPIT study, based on an interval-censored survival approach: comparison of two methods of calculating region estimates. Estimates with standard error in square brackets

| Region | Estimation method | |
|---|---|---|
| | ML | Z and V: (3.13), (3.14) |
| New York City (US) | 0.297 [0.265] | 0.295 [0.263] |
| Northeast (US) | 0.158 [0.218] | 0.158 [0.217] |
| Mideast (US) | −1.322 [0.573] | −1.198 [0.486] |
| Midwest (US) | 0.286 [0.307] | 0.285 [0.305] |
| Southwest (US) | −0.126 [0.282] | −0.125 [0.280] |
| Ontario (Canada) | −0.217 [0.292] | −0.216 [0.290] |
| Quebec (Canada) | −0.021 [0.378] | −0.021 [0.378] |
| $U$ (1 df) | 0.07; $p = 0.80$ | 0.02; $p = 0.89$ |
| $Q$ (6 df) | 8.64; $p = 0.19$ | 9.47; $p = 0.15$ |
| $\hat{\theta}$ [se($\hat{\theta}$)] | 0.029 [0.112] | 0.016 [0.110] |
| 95% CI | (−0.190, 0.247) | (−0.200, 0.232) |

and Fisher's information statistics. The results are in good agreement with those in the last two columns of Table 4.10.

### 4.2.8   Example: Global impression of change in Alzheimer's disease

Consider the example of global impression of change in Alzheimer's disease described in Section 3.5.1, for the situation in which the chosen parameterization of the treatment difference is the log-odds ratio from the proportional odds model. Table 4.15 shows the estimates of the log-odds ratio for being in a better category on tacrine than on placebo, and the corresponding CI plot is shown in Figure 4.5. These are ML estimates, for which a positive value indicates that tacrine is better than placebo. All five studies indicate a beneficial effect of tacrine, but only study 4 demonstrates a statistically significant effect, the estimate from this study being considerably larger than the other four estimates.

Table 4.16 shows the results of the fixed effects meta-analysis based on the study estimates from Table 4.15. The $Q$ statistic is not significant ($p = 0.30$), indicating that there is no strong evidence of heterogeneity amongst the studies. There is evidence of a treatment difference. The overall estimate shows a beneficial effect of tacrine ($\hat{\theta} = 0.503$), and the $U$ statistic is significant ($p < 0.001$). Comparison with the results based on the efficient score and Fisher's information (Table 4.17) shows good agreement.

The second parameterization of the treatment difference considered in Section 3.5.2 was the log-odds ratio from the continuation ratio model. This parameterization is the same as the log-odds ratio from the discrete survival model, but in the CGIC example it is concerned with a hazard of a desirable outcome. A positive value for the log-odds ratio indicates a beneficial effect of tacrine. Table 4.18 shows the conditional ML estimates of this log-odds ratio for the five studies.

As expected, the estimates from the continuation ratio model (Table 4.18) are of a similar magnitude to the estimates from the proportional odds model

**Table 4.15**   Study estimates of the log-odds ratio from the proportional odds model for the tacrine studies, based on the maximum likelihood approach

| Study | $\hat{\theta}_i$ | se($\hat{\theta}_i$) | 95% CI |
|-------|------|--------|----------|
| 1 | 0.284 | 0.261 | (−0.228, 0.797) |
| 2 | 0.224 | 0.242 | (−0.251, 0.699) |
| 3 | 0.360 | 0.332 | (−0.290, 1.011) |
| 4 | 0.785 | 0.174 | ( 0.444, 1.126) |
| 5 | 0.492 | 0.421 | (−0.334, 1.318) |

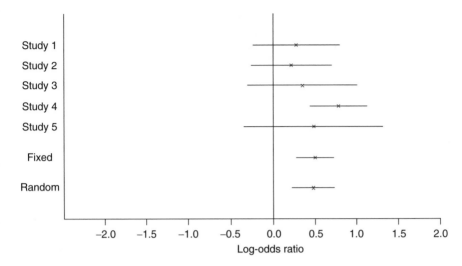

**Figure 4.5** The log-odds ratio for being in a better CGIC category on tacrine than on placebo. Individual study estimates and overall fixed and random effects estimates are presented, with 95% CIs. Individual study calculations are based on maximum likelihood estimation for the proportional odds model. The method of moments estimate of $\tau^2$ is used.

**Table 4.16** Fixed effects meta-analysis of the log-odds ratio from the proportional odds model for the tacrine studies, based on the study estimates from Table 4.15

| Study | Treatment | Category | | | | | $\hat{\theta}_i$ | $w_i$ | $\hat{\theta}_i w_i$ | $\hat{\theta}_i^2 w_i$ |
|---|---|---|---|---|---|---|---|---|---|---|
| | | C1 | C2 | C3 | C4 | C5 | | | | |
| 1 | Tacrine | 4 | 23 | 45 | 22 | 2 | 0.284 | 14.63 | 4.16 | 1.18 |
| | Placebo | 2 | 22 | 54 | 29 | 3 | | | | |
| 2 | Tacrine | 14 | 119 | 180 | 54 | 6 | 0.224 | 17.02 | 3.81 | 0.85 |
| | Placebo | 1 | 22 | 35 | 11 | 3 | | | | |
| 3 | Tacrine | 13 | 20 | 24 | 10 | 1 | 0.360 | 9.08 | 3.27 | 1.18 |
| | Placebo | 7 | 16 | 17 | 10 | 3 | | | | |
| 4 | Tacrine | 21 | 106 | 175 | 62 | 17 | 0.785 | 33.03 | 25.92 | 20.34 |
| | Placebo | 8 | 24 | 73 | 52 | 13 | | | | |
| 5 | Tacrine | 3 | 14 | 19 | 3 | 0 | 0.492 | 5.63 | 2.77 | 1.36 |
| | Placebo | 2 | 13 | 18 | 7 | 1 | | | | |
| Total | | | | | | | | 79.41 | 39.94 | 24.92 |

$U = (39.94)^2/79.41 = 20.09; (1\,\mathrm{df})\, p < 0.001$

$Q = 24.92 - 20.09 = 4.83; (4\,\mathrm{df})\, p = 0.30$

$\hat{\theta} = 39.94/79.41 = 0.503; \mathrm{se}(\hat{\theta}) = 1/\sqrt{79.41} = 0.112$

$95\%\ \mathrm{CI} = (0.503 \pm 1.96/\sqrt{79.41}) = (0.283, 0.723)$

**Table 4.17**   Fixed effects meta-analysis of the log-odds ratio from the proportional odds model for the tacrine studies: comparison of two methods of calculating study estimates. Estimates with standard error in square brackets

| Study | Estimation method | |
|---|---|---|
| | ML | Z and $V$: (3.15), (3.16) |
| 1 | 0.284 [0.261] | 0.283 [0.261] |
| 2 | 0.224 [0.242] | 0.224 [0.242] |
| 3 | 0.360 [0.332] | 0.358 [0.331] |
| 4 | 0.785 [0.174] | 0.778 [0.172] |
| 5 | 0.492 [0.421] | 0.487 [0.420] |
| $U$ (1 df) | 20.09; $p < 0.001$ | 20.30; $p < 0.001$ |
| $Q$ (4 df) | 4.83; $p = 0.30$ | 4.80; $p = 0.31$ |
| $\hat{\theta}$ [se($\hat{\theta}$)] | 0.503 [0.112] | 0.502 [0.112] |
| 95% CI | (0.283, 0.723) | (0.284, 0.721) |

**Table 4.18**   Study estimates of the log-odds ratio from the continuation ratio model for the tacrine studies, based on the conditional maximum likelihood approach

| Study | $\hat{\theta}_i$ | se($\hat{\theta}_i$) | 95% CI |
|---|---|---|---|
| 1 | 0.227 | 0.223 | (−0.210, 0.664) |
| 2 | 0.228 | 0.205 | (−0.174, 0.631) |
| 3 | 0.339 | 0.264 | (−0.179, 0.857) |
| 4 | 0.600 | 0.142 | ( 0.321, 0.879) |
| 5 | 0.502 | 0.362 | (−0.208, 1.211) |

(Table 4.15). The results of the fixed effects meta-analysis (Table 4.19) are similar in interpretation to those in Table 4.16.

Comparison of the four approaches to the estimation of the log-odds ratio from the continuation ratio model shows very similar results in all cases (Table 4.20).

For completeness, the fixed effects meta-analyses for the MDPIT study described in Section 3.3.1, in which survival times are grouped into yearly intervals, are shown for the unconditional likelihood approach to the continuation ratio model. The aggregated survival times correspond to the ordered categories, and it is the hazard of dying which is being modelled. Table 4.21 shows the results of a fixed effects meta-analysis based on ML estimates and on the efficient score and Fisher's information statistics from this approach. The results are in good agreement with those in the last two columns of Table 4.10.

**Table 4.19** Fixed effects meta-analysis of the log-odds ratio from the continuation ratio model for the tacrine studies, based on the study estimates from Table 4.18

| Study | Treatment | C1 | C2 | C3 | C4 | C5 | $\hat{\theta}_i$ | $w_i$ | $\hat{\theta}_i w_i$ | $\hat{\theta}_i^2 w_i$ |
|---|---|---|---|---|---|---|---|---|---|---|
| 1 | Tacrine | 4 | 23 | 45 | 22 | 2 | 0.227 | 20.09 | 4.56 | 1.03 |
|   | Placebo | 2 | 22 | 54 | 29 | 3 | | | | |
| 2 | Tacrine | 14 | 119 | 180 | 54 | 6 | 0.228 | 23.69 | 5.41 | 1.24 |
|   | Placebo | 1 | 22 | 35 | 11 | 3 | | | | |
| 3 | Tacrine | 13 | 20 | 24 | 10 | 1 | 0.339 | 14.30 | 4.85 | 1.64 |
|   | Placebo | 7 | 16 | 17 | 10 | 3 | | | | |
| 4 | Tacrine | 21 | 106 | 175 | 62 | 17 | 0.600 | 49.35 | 29.62 | 17.78 |
|   | Placebo | 8 | 24 | 73 | 52 | 13 | | | | |
| 5 | Tacrine | 3 | 14 | 19 | 3 | 0 | 0.502 | 7.63 | 3.83 | 1.92 |
|   | Placebo | 2 | 13 | 18 | 7 | 1 | | | | |
| Total | | | | | | | | 115.07 | 48.27 | 23.62 |

$U = (48.27)^2/115.07 = 20.25;$ (1 df) $p < 0.001$
$Q = 23.62 - 20.25 = 3.37;$ (4 df) $p = 0.50$
$\hat{\theta} = 48.27/115.07 = 0.419;$ $se(\hat{\theta}) = 1/\sqrt{115.07} = 0.093$
95% CI $= (0.419 \pm 1.96/\sqrt{115.07}) = (0.237, 0.602)$

**Table 4.20** Fixed effects meta-analysis of the log-odds ratio from the continuation ratio model for the tacrine studies: comparison of four methods of calculating study estimates. Estimates with standard error in square brackets

| Study | Conditional ML | Conditional Z and V: (3.18), (3.19) | Unconditional ML | Unconditional Z and V: (3.20), (3.21) |
|---|---|---|---|---|
| 1 | 0.227 [0.223] | 0.227 [0.223] | 0.228 [0.224] | 0.228 [0.223] |
| 2 | 0.228 [0.205] | 0.227 [0.204] | 0.229 [0.206] | 0.228 [0.204] |
| 3 | 0.339 [0.264] | 0.336 [0.261] | 0.343 [0.266] | 0.340 [0.263] |
| 4 | 0.600 [0.142] | 0.580 [0.137] | 0.602 [0.143] | 0.581 [0.137] |
| 5 | 0.502 [0.362] | 0.495 [0.356] | 0.510 [0.365] | 0.504 [0.359] |
| $U$ (1 df) | 20.25; $p < 0.001$ | 20.71; $p < 0.001$ | 20.37; $p < 0.001$ | 20.82; $p < 0.001$ |
| $Q$ (4 df) | 3.37; $p = 0.50$ | 3.17; $p = 0.53$ | 3.36; $p = 0.50$ | 3.17; $p = 0.53$ |
| $\hat{\theta}$ [$se(\hat{\theta})$] | 0.419 [0.093] | 0.415 [0.091] | 0.422 [0.093] | 0.417 [0.091] |
| 95% CI | (0.237, 0.602) | (0.236, 0.593) | (0.239, 0.605) | (0.238, 0.596) |

**Table 4.21**   Fixed effects meta-analysis of the log-odds ratio for earlier death on diltiazem relative to placebo for the MDPIT study, based on the continuation ratio model: comparison of two methods of calculating region estimates from an unconditional likelihood approach. Estimates with standard error in square brackets

| Region | Estimation method | |
|--------|--------|--------|
| | ML | Z and V: (3.20), (3.21) |
| New York City (US) | 0.306 [0.274] | 0.304 [0.271] |
| Northeast (US) | 0.164 [0.226] | 0.164 [0.225] |
| Mideast (US) | −1.374 [0.595] | −1.251 [0.510] |
| Midwest (US) | 0.300 [0.321] | 0.299 [0.319] |
| Southwest (US) | −0.132 [0.291] | −0.132 [0.290] |
| Ontario (Canada) | −0.232 [0.313] | −0.231 [0.311] |
| Quebec (Canada) | −0.021 [0.390] | −0.021 [0.390] |
| $U$ (1 df) | 0.07; $p = 0.79$ | 0.03; $p = 0.87$ |
| $Q$ (6 df) | 8.67; $p = 0.19$ | 9.41; $p = 0.15$ |
| $\hat{\theta}$ [se($\hat{\theta}$)] | 0.031 [0.116] | 0.019 [0.115] |
| 95% CI | (−0.197, 0.258) | (−0.207, 0.244) |

## 4.2.9   Example: Recovery time after anaesthesia

Table 4.22 shows the individual centre estimates of the absolute mean difference (treatment A − treatment B) in recovery time (log-transformed) from the anaesthetic study described in Section 3.6.1. For each centre, the usual pooled sample variance, $s_i^2$, is calculated from (3.25). The standard error and 95% CI for the estimate of treatment difference are based on $s_i$. The CI plot is shown in Figure 4.6 In centres 1−8 the recovery time is longer on anaesthetic A than on anaesthetic B, significantly so in six of the centres. However, in centre 9 the effect is reversed, although the treatment difference does not reach statistical significance.

Consider the first parameterization of the treatment difference described in Section 3.6.2, that is the absolute mean difference. The fixed effects meta-analysis based on the estimates of absolute mean difference could proceed in one of two ways. The first depends on the assumption of a common within-treatment group variance across all centres, $\sigma^2$. This common variance is estimated by $s_p^2$, where

$$s_p^2 = \frac{\sum_{i=1}^{r} (n_i - 2)s_i^2}{\sum_{i=1}^{r} (n_i - 2)},$$

and $n_i$ is the total number of patients from centre $i$. For the recovery time example $s_p^2 = 0.506$, with corresponding standard deviation 0.711. Table 4.23 presents the fixed effects meta-analysis results based on (3.22) and (3.23), in which $\sigma^2$

**Table 4.22**  Estimates of the absolute mean difference (treatment A − treatment B) in log-recovery time for each centre in the anaesthetic study (formulae (3.22) and (3.23))

| Centre | Pooled sample variance ($s_i^2$) | Pooled standard deviation ($s_i$) | $\hat{\theta}_i$ | se($\hat{\theta}_i$) | 95% CI |
|---|---|---|---|---|---|
| 1 | 0.621 | 0.788 | 0.864 | 0.528 | (−0.172, 1.900) |
| 2 | 0.453 | 0.673 | 0.646 | 0.301 | ( 0.056, 1.235) |
| 3 | 0.676 | 0.822 | 0.272 | 0.282 | (−0.281, 0.825) |
| 4 | 0.670 | 0.819 | 0.916 | 0.398 | ( 0.136, 1.696) |
| 5 | 0.318 | 0.564 | 0.867 | 0.278 | ( 0.322, 1.412) |
| 6 | 0.232 | 0.482 | 0.819 | 0.210 | ( 0.407, 1.232) |
| 7 | 0.341 | 0.584 | 0.809 | 0.250 | ( 0.319, 1.299) |
| 8 | 0.469 | 0.685 | 1.212 | 0.459 | ( 0.312, 2.113) |
| 9 | 0.627 | 0.792 | −0.273 | 0.279 | (−0.820, 0.274) |

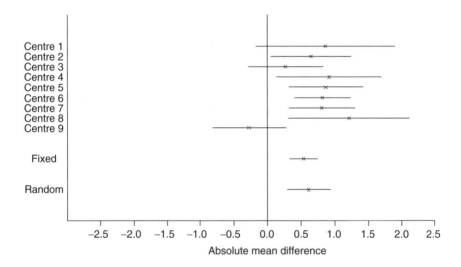

**Figure 4.6**  Difference in mean log-recovery time between treatment A and treatment B. Individual centre estimates and overall fixed and random effects estimates are presented, with 95% CIs. The calculations for each centre are based on formulae (3.22) and (3.23), with the pooled sample variance from that centre. The overall fixed and random effects calculations use the pooled sample variance from all centres. The method of moments estimate of $\tau^2$ is used.

is replaced by $s_p^2$. The $Q$ statistic is significant ($p = 0.02$), indicating evidence of heterogeneity amongst the centres. Although the overall estimate of treatment difference demonstrates a longer recovery time with anaesthetic A ($\hat{\theta} = 0.535$), and the $U$ statistic is significant ($p < 0.001$), centre 9 indicates the reverse effect

**Table 4.23**  Fixed effects meta-analysis of the absolute mean difference (treatment A − treatment B) in log-recovery time, assuming a common variance across all centres

| Centre | Treatment A | | Treatment B | | $\hat{\theta}_i$ | $w_i$ | $\hat{\theta}_i w_i$ | $\hat{\theta}_i^2 w_i$ |
|---|---|---|---|---|---|---|---|---|
| | $n$ | Mean | $n$ | Mean | | | | |
| 1 | 4 | 1.141 | 5 | 0.277 | 0.864 | 4.40 | 3.80 | 3.28 |
| 2 | 10 | 2.165 | 10 | 1.519 | 0.646 | 9.89 | 6.39 | 4.12 |
| 3 | 17 | 1.790 | 17 | 1.518 | 0.272 | 16.81 | 4.58 | 1.25 |
| 4 | 8 | 2.105 | 9 | 1.189 | 0.916 | 8.38 | 7.68 | 7.03 |
| 5 | 7 | 1.324 | 10 | 0.456 | 0.867 | 8.15 | 7.07 | 6.13 |
| 6 | 11 | 2.369 | 10 | 1.550 | 0.819 | 10.36 | 8.49 | 6.95 |
| 7 | 10 | 1.074 | 12 | 0.265 | 0.809 | 10.79 | 8.73 | 7.06 |
| 8 | 5 | 2.583 | 4 | 1.370 | 1.212 | 4.40 | 5.33 | 6.46 |
| 9 | 14 | 1.844 | 19 | 2.118 | −0.273 | 15.95 | −4.35 | 1.19 |
| Total | | | | | | 89.12 | 47.69 | 43.48 |

$U = (47.69)^2/89.12 = 25.52;\ (1\ \mathrm{df})\ p < 0.001$
$Q = 43.48 − 25.52 = 17.95;\ (8\ \mathrm{df})\ p = 0.02$
$\hat{\theta} = 47.69/89.12 = 0.535;\ \mathrm{se}(\hat{\theta}) = 1/\sqrt{89.12} = 0.106$
$95\%\ \mathrm{CI} = (0.535 \pm 1.96/\sqrt{89.12}) = (0.328, 0.743)$

and is the centre with the second highest weight. Further investigation is required, and this is discussed in detail in Chapter 6.

The second approach to the fixed effects meta-analysis does not make the assumption of a common within-treatment group variance across all centres. Instead centre $i$ has its own variance term, $\sigma_i^2$, which is estimated by $s_i^2$. Table 4.24 provides a comparison of the two sets of calculations. The change in the weights due to the use of individual centre variance estimates has led to an increase in the overall fixed effect estimate of treatment difference. However, the $Q$ statistic is still significant ($p = 0.04$), and the overall picture is not changed substantially.

The assumption of a common variance parameter across all centres can be investigated using Bartlett's test (Bartlett, 1937). The test statistic is given by

$$\frac{1}{c}\left\{(n - 2r)\log s_{\mathrm{p}}^2 - \sum_{i=1}^{r}(n_i - 2)\log s_i^2\right\},$$

where

$$c = 1 + \frac{1}{3(r - 1)}\left\{\left(\sum_{i=1}^{r}\frac{1}{n_i - 2}\right) - \frac{1}{n - 2r}\right\}.$$

When variances are homogeneous, the test statistic follows a chi-squared distribution with $r - 1$ degrees of freedom. For the anaesthetic study, the test statistic is equal to 10.21, and compared with the chi-squared distribution on 8 degrees of

**Table 4.24**  Fixed effects meta-analysis of the absolute mean difference (treatment A − treatment B) in log-recovery time: comparison of two methods. In the first pair of columns, a common variance parameter across all centres is estimated by $s_p^2$. In the second pair of columns a different variance parameter is estimated for each centre. Estimates with standard error in square brackets

| Centre | Absolute mean difference | |
|---|---|---|
| | Common variance $(s_p^2)$ | Different variances $(s_i^2)$ |
| 1 | 0.864 [0.477] | 0.864 [0.528] |
| 2 | 0.646 [0.318] | 0.646 [0.301] |
| 3 | 0.272 [0.244] | 0.272 [0.282] |
| 4 | 0.916 [0.345] | 0.916 [0.398] |
| 5 | 0.867 [0.350] | 0.867 [0.278] |
| 6 | 0.819 [0.311] | 0.819 [0.210] |
| 7 | 0.809 [0.304] | 0.809 [0.250] |
| 8 | 1.212 [0.477] | 1.212 [0.459] |
| 9 | −0.273 [0.250] | −0.273 [0.279] |
| $U$ (1 df) | 25.52; $p < 0.001$ | 40.33; $p < 0.001$ |
| $Q$ (8 df) | 17.95; $p = 0.02$ | 16.46; $p = 0.04$ |
| $\hat{\theta}$ [se($\hat{\theta}$)] | 0.535 [0.106] | 0.627 [0.099] |
| 95% CI | (0.328, 0.743) | (0.433, 0.820) |

freedom is not significant ($p = 0.25$). Therefore, there is insufficient evidence to challenge the assumption of a common variance.

The decision to assume a common variance could be taken if the test does not provide significant evidence (for example, $p > 0.05$) of heterogeneity amongst the individual centre variance estimates. However, strict adherence to a specific significance level for this test is inadvisable. It suffers from the same problem as the test for heterogeneity of treatment difference estimates, in that for small sample sizes large variation may not reach statistical significance, whereas for large sample sizes small variation may reach statistical significance (see Section 6.2). Also, Scheffé (1959) notes that Bartlett's test is extremely sensitive to non-normality of the data. For the anaesthetic study the ratios of the individual centre estimates of standard deviation do not vary by more than a factor of 2, and so the assumption of a common variance is not unreasonable. Under the assumption of a common variance, the overall pooled estimate is considered to be a better estimate for use with each centre.

The second parameterization of treatment difference considered in Section 3.6.2 was the standardized mean difference. Table 4.25 shows the individual centre estimates based on (3.27) and (3.28), and Figure 4.7 the corresponding CI plot.

**Table 4.25**   Study estimates of the standardized mean difference (treatment A − treatment B) in log-recovery time, based on formulae (3.27) and (3.28)

| Centre | $\hat{\theta}_i$ | Pooled standard deviation ($s_i$) | $\text{se}(\hat{\theta}_i)$ | 95% CI |
|---|---|---|---|---|
| 1 | 1.097 | 0.788 | 0.671 | (−0.218,  2.411) |
| 2 | 0.959 | 0.673 | 0.447 | ( 0.083,  1.836) |
| 3 | 0.331 | 0.822 | 0.343 | (−0.341,  1.003) |
| 4 | 1.119 | 0.819 | 0.486 | ( 0.167,  2.072) |
| 5 | 1.537 | 0.564 | 0.493 | ( 0.571,  2.503) |
| 6 | 1.701 | 0.482 | 0.437 | ( 0.844,  2.557) |
| 7 | 1.386 | 0.584 | 0.428 | ( 0.547,  2.225) |
| 8 | 1.770 | 0.685 | 0.671 | ( 0.455,  3.085) |
| 9 | −0.345 | 0.792 | 0.352 | (−1.035,  0.346) |

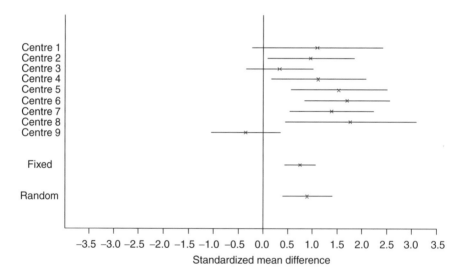

**Figure 4.7**   The standardized mean difference in log-recovery time between treatment A and treatment B. Individual centre estimates and overall fixed and random effects estimates are presented, with 95% CIs. The calculations for each centre are based on formulae (3.27) and (3.28), with the pooled sample variance from that centre. The overall fixed and random effects calculations use formulae (3.29) and (3.30), with the individual centre pooled sample variances. The method of moments estimate of $\tau^2$ is used.

For each centre, the usual pooled sample variance, $s_i^2$, is calculated using (3.25). The estimate of the standardized mean difference for centre $i$ can be seen to be equal to the estimate of the absolute mean difference for centre $i$ (Table 4.22) divided by $s_i$.

Table 4.26 shows the results of the fixed effects meta-analysis based on the Hedges and Olkin approach (formulae (3.29) and (3.30)), in which the estimate of the standardized mean difference is adjusted to remove the sample bias in the estimate $s_i$. The results are similar to those based on the absolute mean difference, in that the $Q$ statistic is significant ($p = 0.02$), indicating evidence of heterogeneity amongst the centres.

The overall fixed effects estimate of the standardized mean difference is 0.749. This is on a dimensionless scale and cannot be compared directly with the estimate of 0.535 from Table 4.23, which has the same units as the observations. It can be seen that multiplication of 0.749 by the overall pooled estimate of standard deviation, 0.711, results in a value of 0.533, which is close to the fixed effects estimate of the absolute difference. The question of how to present results from the analysis based on the standardized difference is considered in more detail in Chapter 7.

In Section 3.6.2 three approaches to the estimation of the standardized mean difference were presented. The results of the fixed effects meta-analysis based on each approach are presented in Table 4.27. The overall picture from the three methods is similar. In all cases there is evidence of heterogeneity between the centres. As expected, the individual centre estimates are smaller for the Hedges and Olkin method than for the other methods, resulting in a smaller overall fixed effects estimate.

**Table 4.26** Fixed effects meta-analysis of the standardized mean difference (treatment A − treatment B) for log-recovery time, based on the Hedges and Olkin approach, with $\sigma_i^2$ estimated by $s_i^2$

| Centre | Treatment A | | Treatment B | | $\hat{\theta}_i$ | $w_i$ | $\hat{\theta}_i w_i$ | $\hat{\theta}_i^2 w_i$ |
|--------|-----|-------|-----|-------|--------|-------|---------|---------|
|        | $n$ | Mean  | $n$ | Mean  |        |       |         |         |
| 1  | 4  | 1.141 | 5  | 0.277 | 0.974  | 1.99  | 1.94  | 1.89  |
| 2  | 10 | 2.165 | 10 | 1.519 | 0.919  | 4.52  | 4.16  | 3.82  |
| 3  | 17 | 1.790 | 17 | 1.518 | 0.323  | 8.39  | 2.71  | 0.88  |
| 4  | 8  | 2.105 | 9  | 1.189 | 1.062  | 3.71  | 3.94  | 4.19  |
| 5  | 7  | 1.324 | 10 | 0.456 | 1.459  | 3.27  | 4.78  | 6.97  |
| 6  | 11 | 2.369 | 10 | 1.550 | 1.633  | 3.93  | 6.42  | 10.48 |
| 7  | 10 | 1.074 | 12 | 0.265 | 1.333  | 4.47  | 5.96  | 7.95  |
| 8  | 5  | 2.583 | 4  | 1.370 | 1.572  | 1.70  | 2.68  | 4.21  |
| 9  | 14 | 1.844 | 19 | 2.118 | −0.336 | 7.95  | −2.67 | 0.90  |
| Total |  |  |  |  |  | 39.94 | 29.91 | 41.27 |

$U = (29.91)^2/39.94 = 22.39$; (1 df) $p < 0.001$
$Q = 41.27 - 22.39 = 18.88$; (8 df) $p = 0.02$
$\hat{\theta} = 29.91/39.94 = 0.749$; se$(\hat{\theta}) = 1/\sqrt{39.94} = 0.158$
95% CI $= (0.749 \pm 1.96/\sqrt{39.94}) = (0.439, 1.059)$

**Table 4.27**   Fixed effects meta-analysis of the standardized mean difference (treatment A − treatment B) for log-recovery time: comparison of three approaches. Estimates with standard error in square brackets

| Centre | Estimation method | | |
|---|---|---|---|
| | Hedges and Olkin bias correction: (3.29), (3.30) | Modified ML: (3.27), (3.28) | Z and V: (3.31), (3.32) |
| 1 | 0.974 [0.709] | 1.097 [0.671] | 1.227 [0.726] |
| 2 | 0.919 [0.470] | 0.959 [0.447] | 1.005 [0.472] |
| 3 | 0.323 [0.345] | 0.331 [0.343] | 0.341 [0.345] |
| 4 | 1.062 [0.519] | 1.119 [0.486] | 1.178 [0.521] |
| 5 | 1.459 [0.553] | 1.537 [0.493] | 1.587 [0.550] |
| 6 | 1.632 [0.504] | 1.701 [0.437] | 1.714 [0.495] |
| 7 | 1.333 [0.473] | 1.386 [0.428] | 1.422 [0.471] |
| 8 | 1.572 [0.766] | 1.770 [0.671] | 1.893 [0.774] |
| 9 | −0.336 [0.355] | −0.345 [0.352] | −0.356 [0.355] |
| $U$ (1 df) | $22.39; p < 0.001$ | $33.32; p < 0.001$ | $27.32; p < 0.001$ |
| $Q$ (8 df) | $18.88; p = 0.02$ | $23.48; p = 0.003$ | $22.60; p = 0.004$ |
| $\hat{\theta}$ [se($\hat{\theta}$)] | 0.749 [0.158] | 0.860 [0.149] | 0.827 [0.158] |
| 95% CI | (0.439, 1.059) | (0.568, 1.152) | (0.517, 1.137) |

## 4.3   A GENERAL RANDOM EFFECTS PARAMETRIC APPROACH

### 4.3.1   A random effects meta-analysis model

In a random effects model it is assumed that the treatment difference parameters in the $r$ studies $(\theta_1, \ldots, \theta_r)$ are a sample of independent observations from $N(\theta, \tau^2)$. The general random effects model is given by

$$\hat{\theta}_i = \theta + \nu_i + \varepsilon_i, \tag{4.2}$$

for $i = 1, \ldots, r$, where the $\nu_i$ are normally distributed random effects with mean 0 and variance $\tau^2$. The terms $\nu_i$ and $\varepsilon_i$ are assumed to be independently distributed. It follows that

$$\hat{\theta}_i \sim N(\theta, \xi_i^2 + \tau^2).$$

### 4.3.2   Estimation and hypothesis testing of the treatment difference

Usually $\tau^2$ is unknown and must be estimated from the data. Therefore, the distributional assumption that is made is that

$$\hat{\theta}_i \sim N(\theta, w_i^{-1} + \hat{\tau}^2),$$

where $\hat{\tau}^2$ is an estimate of $\tau^2$. By setting

$$w_i^* = (w_i^{-1} + \hat{\tau}^2)^{-1},$$

it follows that

$$\hat{\theta}_i \sim N(\theta, (w_i^*)^{-1}).$$

Treating the term $(w_i^*)^{-1}$ as if it were the true variance of $\hat{\theta}_i$ provides the test statistic

$$U^* = \frac{\left(\sum_{i=1}^r \hat{\theta}_i w_i^*\right)^2}{\sum_{i=1}^r w_i^*},$$

which follows a chi-squared distribution with one degree of freedom under the null hypothesis of no treatment difference ($\theta = 0$). If $(w_i^*)^{-1}$ is the true variance of $\hat{\theta}_i$, then the ML estimate of $\theta$ is given by $\hat{\theta}^*$, where

$$\hat{\theta}^* = \frac{\sum_{i=1}^r \hat{\theta}_i w_i^*}{\sum_{i=1}^r w_i^*}.$$

Now $\hat{\theta}^*$ is asymptotically unbiased for $\theta$, with variance approximately equal to $1/\sum_{i=1}^r w_i^*$. The standard error is given by

$$\text{se}(\hat{\theta}^*) = \sqrt{\frac{1}{\sum_{i=1}^r w_i^*}},$$

and an approximate 95% CI for $\theta$ is given by

$$\hat{\theta}^* \pm 1.96 \sqrt{\frac{1}{\sum_{i=1}^r w_i^*}}.$$

If $\hat{\tau}^2$ is small then the modified weights $w_i^*$ will be close to the original weights $w_i$. In this case the standard error and CI obtained from the random effects model will be similar to those from the fixed effects model. Also the overall estimate of treatment difference from both models will be similar. If $\hat{\tau}^2$ is large then the standard error and CI will be much larger for the random effects model. The random effects estimate of treatment difference will move closer towards the arithmetic mean of the individual study estimates. How much this estimate differs from the fixed effects estimate will depend on the extent to which the studies with the largest original weights $w_i$ are associated with the extreme estimates of treatment difference.

### 4.3.3   Estimation of $\tau^2$ using the method of moments

The approach to the estimation of $\tau^2$ considered here is that based on the method of moments. This estimate can be readily calculated without the need for a statistical software package. Discussion of the approach based on likelihood methods is considered in Section 4.3.8.

The following considerations provide the method of moments estimate for $\tau^2$. Under the random effects model, the fixed effects estimate of $\theta$,

$$\hat{\theta} = \frac{\sum_{i=1}^{r} \hat{\theta}_i w_i}{\sum_{i=1}^{r} w_i},$$

still has mean $\theta$, but its variance is now given by

$$\mathrm{var}(\hat{\theta}) = \frac{\sum_{i=1}^{r} w_i^2 \mathrm{var}(\hat{\theta}_i)}{\left(\sum_{i=1}^{r} w_i\right)^2} = \frac{\sum_{i=1}^{r} w_i^2 (w_i^{-1} + \tau^2)}{\sum_{i=1}^{r} w_i^2}$$

$$= \frac{1}{\sum_{i=1}^{r} w_i} + \frac{\tau^2 \sum_{i=1}^{r} w_i^2}{\left(\sum_{i=1}^{r} w_i\right)^2}.$$

The statistic $Q$ used for testing heterogeneity is

$$Q = \sum_{i=1}^{r} w_i(\hat{\theta}_i - \hat{\theta})^2 = \sum_{i=1}^{r} w_i(\hat{\theta}_i - \theta)^2 - \left(\sum_{i=1}^{r} w_i\right)(\hat{\theta} - \theta)^2,$$

so that the expected value of $Q$, $E(Q)$, is given by

$$E(Q) = \sum_{i=1}^{r} w_i \mathrm{var}(\hat{\theta}_i) - \left(\sum_{i=1}^{r} w_i\right) \mathrm{var}(\hat{\theta})$$

$$= \sum_{i=1}^{r} w_i(w_i^{-1} + \tau^2) - \left(\sum_{i=1}^{r} w_i\right) \left\{ \frac{1}{\sum_{i=1}^{r} w_i} + \frac{\tau^2 \sum_{i=1}^{r} w_i^2}{\left(\sum_{i=1}^{r} w_i\right)^2} \right\}$$

$$= (r - 1) + \tau^2 \left( \sum_{i=1}^{r} w_i - \frac{\sum_{i=1}^{r} w_i^2}{\sum_{i=1}^{r} w_i} \right).$$

This motivates use of the method of moments estimate $\hat{\tau}^2$ for $\tau^2$, where

$$\hat{\tau}^2 = \frac{Q - (r - 1)}{\sum_{i=1}^{r} w_i - \sum_{i=1}^{r} w_i^2 / \sum_{i=1}^{r} w_i},$$

as described by DerSimonian and Laird (1986).

Because of the possibility of a negative method of moments estimate, in practice the estimate used is the maximum of the values 0 and $\hat{\tau}^2$. This means that when $Q$ is smaller than its degrees of freedom the method of moments estimate will be set equal to 0. Examples of this situation can be seen in Tables 4.2 and 4.12.

The test for heterogeneity, using $Q$, is a test of $H_0 \colon \tau^2 = 0$. Should $\hat{\tau}^2 \leqslant 0$, a fixed effects analysis is more appropriate, because this happens when $Q < E(Q; \tau^2 = 0) = r - 1$. It can be seen that setting $\tau^2 = 0$ in the random effects model leads to the fixed effects model. If $\hat{\tau}^2 > 0$ the following approximate result may be used:

$$\hat{\theta}_i \sim N(\theta, w_i^{-1} + \hat{\tau}^2) \equiv N(\theta, (w_i^*)^{-1}).$$

### 4.3.4 Obtaining the statistics via weighted least-squares regression

In a similar way to that described in Section 4.2.4, the test statistic $U^*$ and the estimate $\hat{\theta}^*$ and its standard error can be obtained by performing a weighted least-squares regression. The only difference is that for the random effects analysis the weights are the values $w_i^*$ instead of $w_i$.

In some packages, for example PROC GLM, it is possible to store the residuals from a fitted model and then add them to the original data set. The residuals from the model presented in Section 4.2.4 are the values $\hat{\theta}_i - \hat{\theta}$, from which the statistic $Q$ can be calculated. Therefore, by fitting the model in Section 4.2.4. and adding the residuals to the original data set, it is possible to calculate the method of moments estimate of $\tau^2$ and the values $w_i^*$ for use in the weighted least-squares regression needed for the random effects model.

### 4.3.5 Example: Mortality following myocardial infarction

In this subsection a random effects model is fitted to the log-hazard ratios presented in Table 4.9. The test for heterogeneity was not statistically significant ($p = 0.22$). However, as the $Q$ statistic is larger than its associated degrees of freedom, it is possible to calculate a method of moments estimate of $\tau^2$. The estimated value was 0.033 (Table 4.28). Comparison of the modified weights $w_i^*$ with the original weights $w_i$ shows a moderate decrease in magnitude. The random effects estimate $\hat{\theta}^*$ is $-0.016$, a small change from the fixed effects estimate of 0.005, with an increase in the standard error from 0.111 to 0.134. Although the width of the CI based on the random effects model has increased relative to that based on the fixed effects model, the overall conclusion has not changed much. As there seems to be little evidence of a treatment difference, this increase will be important only if the limits of the CI from the random effects model extend beyond the limits of a clinically important difference, whereas for the fixed effects model they did not.

**Table 4.28** Random effects meta-analysis of the log-hazard ratio for mortality on diltiazem relative to placebo for the MDPIT study, based on region estimates from Table 4.9

| Study | Diltiazem | | Placebo | | $\hat{\theta}_i$ | $w_i$ | $w_i^2$ | $w_i^*$ | $\hat{\theta}_i w_i^*$ |
|---|---|---|---|---|---|---|---|---|---|
| | Number of deaths | Total number of patients | Number of deaths | Total number of patients | | | | | |
| New York City (US) | 33 | 262 | 25 | 256 | 0.282 | 14.22 | 202.2 | 9.64 | 2.72 |
| Northeast (US) | 46 | 305 | 39 | 298 | 0.145 | 21.10 | 445.2 | 12.38 | 1.79 |
| Mideast (US) | 4 | 72 | 13 | 71 | −1.244 | 3.06 | 9.3 | 2.77 | −3.45 |
| Midwest (US) | 24 | 127 | 19 | 125 | 0.258 | 10.59 | 112.1 | 7.83 | 2.02 |
| Southwest (US) | 23 | 169 | 28 | 184 | −0.122 | 12.61 | 159.1 | 8.88 | −1.09 |
| Ontario (Canada) | 21 | 121 | 27 | 122 | −0.293 | 11.79 | 139.0 | 8.46 | −2.48 |
| Quebec (Canada) | 15 | 176 | 16 | 178 | −0.071 | 7.74 | 59.9 | 6.15 | −0.44 |
| Total | | | | | | 81.11 | 1126.8 | 56.11 | −0.92 |

$Q = 8.24; k - 1 = 6$

$\hat{\tau}^2 = (8.24 - 6)/(81.11 - 1126.8/81.11) = 0.033$

$U^* = (-0.92)^2/56.11 = 0.02$; (1 df) $p = 0.90$

$\hat{\theta}^* = -0.92/56.11 = -0.016$; $se(\hat{\theta}^*) = 1/\sqrt{56.11} = 0.133$

$95\%\ CI = (-0.016 \pm 1.96/\sqrt{56.11}) = (-0.278, 0.245)$

### 4.3.6 Example: Global impression of change in Alzheimer's disease

The random effects model is fitted to the log-odds ratios presented in Table 4.16. As was the case for the MDPIT study, the test for heterogeneity was not statistically significant ($p = 0.30$). As the $Q$ statistic was slightly larger than its associated degrees of freedom, a method of moments estimate of $\tau^2$ can be calculated, and is found to be 0.014 (Table 4.29). Because the estimate of $\tau^2$ is small the modified weights $w_i^*$ are not substantially different from the $w_i$. The random effects estimate of the log-odds ratio, calculated to be 0.481, is similar to that of 0.503 calculated from the fixed effects model. The standard error and CI have increased slightly (Figure 4.5).

### 4.3.7 Example: Recovery time after anaesthesia

The test for heterogeneity based on the estimates of absolute mean difference from Table 4.23 was statistically significant ($p = 0.02$). In this case the method of moments estimate of $\tau^2$, 0.128, is large enough to have a substantial impact on the weights (Table 4.30). It can be seen that the modified weights $w_i^*$ are

**Table 4.29** Random effects meta-analysis of the log-odds ratio from the proportional odds model for the tacrine studies, based on study estimates from Table 4.16

| Study | Treatment | Category | | | | | $\hat{\theta}_i$ | $w_i$ | $w_i^2$ | $w_i^*$ | $\hat{\theta}_i w_i^*$ |
|---|---|---|---|---|---|---|---|---|---|---|---|
| | | C1 | C2 | C3 | C4 | C5 | | | | | |
| 1 | Tacrine | 4 | 23 | 45 | 22 | 2 | 0.284 | 14.63 | 214.1 | 12.09 | 3.44 |
| | Placebo | 2 | 22 | 54 | 29 | 3 | | | | | |
| 2 | Tacrine | 14 | 119 | 180 | 54 | 6 | 0.224 | 17.02 | 289.9 | 13.67 | 3.06 |
| | Placebo | 1 | 22 | 35 | 11 | 3 | | | | | |
| 3 | Tacrine | 13 | 20 | 24 | 10 | 1 | 0.360 | 9.08 | 82.5 | 8.03 | 2.89 |
| | Placebo | 7 | 16 | 17 | 10 | 3 | | | | | |
| 4 | Tacrine | 21 | 106 | 175 | 62 | 17 | 0.785 | 33.03 | 1091.2 | 22.39 | 17.57 |
| | Placebo | 8 | 24 | 73 | 52 | 13 | | | | | |
| 5 | Tacrine | 3 | 14 | 19 | 3 | 0 | 0.492 | 5.63 | 31.7 | 5.21 | 2.56 |
| | Placebo | 2 | 13 | 18 | 7 | 1 | | | | | |
| Total | | | | | | | | 79.41 | 1709.4 | 61.39 | 29.53 |

$Q = 4.83; k - 1 = 4$
$\hat{\tau}^2 = (4.83 - 4)/(79.41 - 1709.4/79.41) = 0.014$
$U^* = (29.53)^2/61.39 = 14.20; (1\,\mathrm{df})\,p < 0.001$
$\hat{\theta}^* = 29.53/61.39 = 0.481; \mathrm{se}(\hat{\theta}^*) = 1/\sqrt{61.39} = 0.128$
$95\%\ \mathrm{CI} = (0.481 \pm 1.96/\sqrt{61.39}) = (0.231, 0.731)$

**Table 4.30**   Random effects meta-analysis of the absolute mean difference (treatment A − treatment B), based on centre estimates from Table 4.23

| Centre | Treatment A | | Treatment B | | $\hat{\theta}_i$ | $w_i$ | $w_i^2$ | $w_i^*$ | $\hat{\theta}_i w_i^*$ |
|---|---|---|---|---|---|---|---|---|---|
| | $n$ | Mean | $n$ | Mean | | | | | |
| 1 | 4 | 1.141 | 5 | 0.277 | 0.864 | 4.40 | 19.3 | 2.81 | 2.43 |
| 2 | 10 | 2.165 | 10 | 1.519 | 0.646 | 9.89 | 97.8 | 4.36 | 2.81 |
| 3 | 17 | 1.790 | 17 | 1.518 | 0.272 | 16.81 | 282.7 | 5.32 | 1.45 |
| 4 | 8 | 2.105 | 9 | 1.189 | 0.916 | 8.38 | 70.2 | 4.04 | 3.70 |
| 5 | 7 | 1.324 | 10 | 0.456 | 0.867 | 8.15 | 66.3 | 3.98 | 3.45 |
| 6 | 11 | 2.369 | 10 | 1.550 | 0.819 | 10.36 | 107.4 | 4.45 | 3.64 |
| 7 | 10 | 1.074 | 12 | 0.265 | 0.809 | 10.79 | 116.4 | 4.52 | 3.66 |
| 8 | 5 | 2.583 | 4 | 1.370 | 1.212 | 4.40 | 19.3 | 2.81 | 3.41 |
| 9 | 14 | 1.844 | 19 | 2.118 | −0.273 | 15.95 | 254.3 | 5.23 | −1.43 |
| Total | | | | | | 89.12 | 1 033.8 | 37.52 | 23.12 |

$Q = 17.95; k - 1 = 8$
$\hat{\tau}^2 = (17.95 - 8)/(89.12 - 1\,033.8/89.12) = 0.128$
$U^* = (23.12)^2/37.52 = 14.25; (1\,\text{df})\,p < 0.001$
$\hat{\theta}^* = 23.12/37.52 = 0.616; \text{se}(\hat{\theta}^*) = 1/\sqrt{37.52} = 0.163$
$95\%\,\text{CI} = (0.616 \pm 1.96/\sqrt{37.52}) = (0.296, 0.936)$

substantially smaller than the original weights $w_i$. This has the effect of increasing the standard error and the width of the CI for the overall estimate of treatment difference. The random effects estimate of $\theta$ is 0.616, which is also different from the fixed effects estimate of 0.535. The two centres with the highest weights in the fixed effects model also had the lowest estimates of treatment difference. In the random effects model the weights move closer together and as a result the weighted average moves towards the other higher centre estimates (Figure 4.6).

### 4.3.8   A likelihood approach to the estimation of $\tau^2$

The random effects model has the distributional assumption

$$\hat{\theta}_i \sim N(\theta, \xi_i^2 + \tau^2).$$

In the likelihood approach to the estimation of $\tau^2$ described here, $w_i^{-1}$ is treated as if it were known and equal to $\xi_i^2$. The contribution to the likelihood function from study $i$ is

$$L(\theta, \tau^2; \hat{\theta}_i) = \frac{1}{\sqrt{2\pi(w_i^{-1} + \tau^2)}} \exp\left\{\frac{-(\hat{\theta}_i - \theta)^2}{2(w_i^{-1} + \tau^2)}\right\}.$$

For a meta-analysis which involves $r$ independent studies the likelihood function is given by the product of the individual study likelihood functions, and the log-likelihood function by

$$\ell(\theta, \tau^2; \hat{\theta}_i, i = 1, \ldots, r) = \text{constant} - \frac{1}{2} \sum_{i=1}^{r} \log(w_i^{-1} + \tau^2) - \frac{1}{2} \sum_{i=1}^{r} \frac{(\hat{\theta}_i - \theta)^2}{(w_i^{-1} + \tau^2)}.$$

ML estimates of $\tau^2$ and $\theta$ can be found through an iterative scheme, in which each iteration involves two steps. First, the variance parameter $\tau^2$ is treated as fixed and the value of $\theta$ which maximizes the log-likelihood is calculated. Then $\theta$ is treated as fixed and the value of $\tau^2$ which maximizes the log-likelihood is calculated. Thus the estimate of $\theta$ at the $(t + 1)$th cycle of the iteration is given by

$$\hat{\theta}^*_{t+1} = \frac{\sum_{i=1}^{r} \hat{\theta}_i w^*_{it}}{\sum_{i=1}^{r} w^*_{it}}, \tag{4.3}$$

for $t = 0, 1, \ldots$, where $w^*_{it} = (w_i^{-1} + \hat{\tau}^2_{M,t})^{-1}$ and $\hat{\tau}^2_{M,t}$ is the ML estimate of $\tau^2$ at the $t$th cycle of the iteration. The ML estimate of $\tau^2$ at the $(t + 1)$th cycle of the iteration can be found using the Newton–Raphson procedure. Alternatively, as it needs to satisfy the equation

$$\sum_{i=1}^{r} w^*_{i,t+1} = \sum_{i=1}^{r} (w^*_{i,t+1})^2 (\hat{\theta}_i - \hat{\theta}^*_{t+1})^2,$$

an approximate estimate is given by

$$\hat{\tau}^2_{M,t+1} = \frac{\sum_{i=1}^{r} (w^*_{it})^2 \{(\hat{\theta}_i - \hat{\theta}^*_{t+1})^2 - w_i^{-1}\}}{\sum_{i=1}^{r} w^{*2}_{it}}. \tag{4.4}$$

To start the iterative process the method of moments estimate of $\tau^2$ could be used as the initial value $\hat{\tau}^2_{M,0}$.

The maximum likelihood estimate of $\tau^2$ will usually be an underestimate because the method takes no account of the information used in estimating $\theta$. Residual (or restricted) maximum likelihood (REML) takes account of this loss of information by modifying the likelihood equation to eliminate the parameter $\theta$ (see Section A.7 in the Appendix, or Chapter 2 of Brown and Prescott, 1999). The REML log-likelihood function is based on the residual terms, $(\hat{\theta}_i - \hat{\theta}^*_{t+1})$, instead of the observations $\hat{\theta}_i$, and is given by

$$\ell_R\{\tau^2; (\hat{\theta}_i - \hat{\theta}^*_{t+1})i = 1, \ldots r\} = \text{constant} - \frac{1}{2} \sum_{i=1}^{r} \log(w_i^{-1} + \tau^2)$$

$$- \frac{1}{2} \sum_{i=1}^{r} \frac{(\hat{\theta}_i - \hat{\theta}^*_{t+1})^2}{(w_i^{-1} + \tau^2)} - \frac{1}{2} \log \left\{ \sum_{i=1}^{r} \frac{1}{(w_i^{-1} + \tau^2)} \right\}.$$

REML estimates are found via a similar iterative scheme to that described above, where now $w_{it}^* = (w_i^{-1} + \hat{\tau}_{R,t}^2)^{-1}$. At the $(t+1)$th cycle of the iteration, (4.3) is used to calculate an updated estimate of $\theta$. The REML estimate of $\tau^2$ at the $(t+1)$th cycle of the iteration can be found using the Newton–Raphson procedure. Alternatively, as it needs to satisfy the equation

$$\sum_{i=1}^{r} w_{i,t+1}^* = \sum_{i=1}^{r} (w_{i,t+1}^*)^2 (\hat{\theta}_i - \hat{\theta}_{t+1}^*)^2 + \frac{\sum_{i=1}^{r} (w_{i,t+1}^*)^2}{\sum_{i=1}^{r} w_{i,t+1}^*},$$

an approximate estimate is given by

$$\hat{\tau}_{R,t+1}^2 = \frac{\sum_{i=1}^{r} (w_{it}^*)^2 \{r(\hat{\theta}_i - \hat{\theta}_{t+1}^*)^2 / (r-1) - w_i^{-1}\}}{\sum_{i=1}^{r} (w_{it}^*)^2}. \tag{4.5}$$

Programs can be written to calculate the ML and REML estimates based on (4.3)–(4.5). Alternatively, ML and REML estimates can be found from statistical packages which fit multilevel models such as MLn and SAS PROC MIXED. This is achieved in SAS PROC MIXED by reversing the roles of the within-study and between-study variance components to enable the within-study variance components $w_i^{-1}$ to be treated as known without error and the between-study variance component $\tau^2$ to be estimated.

REML estimates can be obtained from PROC MIXED in the following way. Suppose that the values of $i$, $\hat{\theta}_i$ and $w_i$ have been entered into the data set 'meta' under the variable names 'study', 'y' and 'w' respectively. It is necessary to create a diagonal variance matrix with the estimated within-study variance components as the diagonal elements. The following code can be used for this purpose:

```
DATA remlma;
SET meta;
var = 1/w;
col = _n_;
row = _n_;
value = var;
```

Then the following PROC MIXED statements are required:

```
PROC MIXED data = remlma method = reml order = data;
CLASS study;
MODEL y = / solution;
RANDOM study / gdata = remlma;
REPEATED diag;
```

In the SAS output, the REML estimate of $\tau^2$ appears as a covariance parameter estimate for 'diag' and the REML estimate of $\theta$ appears as the estimate of the fixed effect 'intercept', together with its standard error. Further details may be found in Normand (1999). Maximum likelihood estimates may be obtained by replacing 'method = reml' with 'method = ml' in the PROC MIXED line.

Comparison of the three methods of estimation of $\tau^2$ can be made for the three example data sets presented in Sections 4.3.5–4.3.7. Table 4.31 shows that for the MDPIT study both ML and REML estimates are set to 0. It should be noted that for this example SAS PROC MIXED produces estimates which are greater than 0, but these are incorrect. On looking at the log file, the message 'Estimated G matrix is not positive definite' appears, indicating a problem. This will occur if the unconstrained estimate of $\tau^2$ is less than 0.

For the tacrine studies (Table 4.32) the ML and method of moments estimates are similar, and for the anaesthetic study (Table 4.33) the REML and the method of moments estimates are similar.

## 4.3.9    Allowing for the estimation of $\tau^2$

In the above approaches to fitting the random effects meta-analysis model, the estimated variance of $\hat{\theta}^*$ is treated as if it were the true variance, with no allowance

**Table 4.31**    Comparison of estimation methods for $\tau^2$ for the MDPIT study based on region estimates from Table 4.9

| Estimation method | $\hat{\tau}^2$ | $\hat{\theta}^*$ | $se(\hat{\theta}^*)$ |
|---|---|---|---|
| Method of moments | 0.033 | −0.016 | 0.133 |
| ML | 0 | 0.006 | 0.111 |
| REML | 0 | 0.006 | 0.111 |

**Table 4.32**    Comparison of estimation methods for $\tau^2$ for the tacrine studies based on study estimates from Table 4.16

| Estimation method | $\hat{\tau}^2$ | $\hat{\theta}^*$ | $se(\hat{\theta}^*)$ |
|---|---|---|---|
| Method of moments | 0.014 | 0.481 | 0.128 |
| ML | 0.017 | 0.478 | 0.130 |
| REML | 0.031 | 0.467 | 0.143 |

**Table 4.33**    Comparison of estimation methods for $\tau^2$ for the anaesthetic study based on centre estimates from Table 4.23

| Estimation method | $\hat{\tau}^2$ | $\hat{\theta}^*$ | $se(\hat{\theta}^*)$ |
|---|---|---|---|
| Method of moments | 0.128 | 0.616 | 0.163 |
| ML | 0.102 | 0.608 | 0.154 |
| REML | 0.124 | 0.615 | 0.162 |

made for error in the calculated terms $w_i$ and $\hat{\tau}^2$. Therefore, the CI obtained for $\theta$ will be too small.

Hardy and Thompson (1996) consider a likelihood approach using profile log-likelihoods to construct likelihood based CIs for $\theta$ and $\tau^2$. They obtain maximum likelihood estimates of $\theta$ and $\tau^2$ as determined from (4.3) and (4.4), although REML estimates could be used instead. When there are only a small number of studies the CI for $\tau^2$ will necessarily be wide, and this will impact on the CI for $\theta$. However, Hardy and Thompson showed that the increased width of the CI for $\theta$ depends more on the strength of the relationship between $\hat{\tau}^2$ and $\hat{\theta}^*$ than simply on the number of trials and the precision of $\hat{\tau}^2$.

Hartung (1999) proposes an alternative test statistic for testing the null hypothesis that $\theta = 0$. This test statistic,

$$\frac{\hat{\theta}^*}{\sqrt{\left\{\sum_{i=1}^{r} w_i^*(\hat{\theta}_i - \hat{\theta}^*)^2\right\} \Big/ \left\{(r-1)\sum_{i=1}^{r} w_i^*\right\}}},$$

approximately follows the $t$ distribution with $r - 1$ degrees of freedom under the null hypothesis. Estimates of $\theta$ and $\tau^2$ are required to evaluate the test statistic. These could be based on the method of moments, maximum likelihood or REML approaches.

So far no allowance has been made for imprecision in the calculated $w_i$-values. This can be addressed by using exact methods based on the full likelihood. Hardy and Thompson argue that the use of exact methods is unnecessarily sophisticated for most practical purposes. The within-study variances are most imprecisely estimated when the sample size is small. Such studies have least weight in the meta-analysis, and also their relative weight is determined more by the value of $\hat{\tau}^2$ than by $w_i$.

# 5

# Meta-Analysis Using Individual Patient Data

## 5.1 INTRODUCTION

When individual patient data are available, individual study estimates of treatment difference can be calculated and combined using the methods of Chapter 4. However, dealing with the outcome measurement on a patient basis instead of a study basis allows for a more extensive exploration of the data, particularly when individual patient data on demographic and prognostic variables are available. In this chapter attention is focused on a statistical modelling approach based on likelihood theory. When individual patient data are available, the meta-analysis model can be viewed as a natural extension of the linear model for a single study, and can often be fitted using the same statistical software. In particular, a meta-analysis can be undertaken in precisely the same way as the analysis of a multicentre study.

The meta-analysis models are considered within a general framework which encompasses the traditional meta-analysis approach presented in Chapter 4, as well as meta-regression and investigation of patient-level covariates which are discussed in Chapter 6. It is assumed that the same outcome measure has been recorded in the same way in each trial. Fixed effects models which are analogous to the general fixed effects parametric approach of Section 4.2 are presented first. For each response type one specific parameter measuring treatment difference will be considered in detail, each being in some sense a natural model parameter. The models and parameter estimation for normally distributed data are discussed first, because the methodology is more straightforward in this case and forms a basis for extension to other data types. The inclusion of the treatment difference as a random instead of a fixed effect is then addressed within the framework of a mixed model. This is analogous to the general random effects parametric approach of Section 4.3. Finally, the meta-analysis model is extended to include random study effects.

In the final section of this chapter, a comparison is made between the various meta-analysis models and the differences between them are highlighted. The *traditional* approach to meta-analysis, as described in Chapter 4, is different from that typically taken towards the analysis of a multicentre trial. This issue is also discussed.

## 5.2 FIXED EFFECTS MODELS FOR NORMALLY DISTRIBUTED DATA

### 5.2.1 A fixed effects meta-analysis model

Let $y_{ij}$ denote the response from patient $j$ in study $i$, where $j = 1, \ldots, n_i$, for $i = 1, \ldots, r$, and let $n = \sum_{i=1}^{r} n_i$ be the total number of patients in all of the studies combined. The observation $y_{ij}$ is assumed to be a realization of a random variable $Y_{ij}$, which is normally distributed with expected value $\mu_{ij}$ and variance $\sigma^2$. The general linear model can be written as

$$y_{ij} = \mu_{ij} + \varepsilon_{ij},$$

where the $\varepsilon_{ij}$ are error terms and are realizations of normally distributed random variables with expected value 0 and variance $\sigma^2$. Initially it is assumed that the error terms are uncorrelated and homogeneous.

The systematic part of the model may be written as

$$\mu_{ij} = \alpha + \eta_{ij},$$

where $\alpha$ is the intercept and $\eta_{ij} = \beta_1 x_{1ij} + \beta_2 x_{2ij} + \cdots + \beta_q x_{qij}$ is a linear combination of explanatory variables. Explanatory variables can be quantitative, such as age or number of years since diagnosis. Alternatively, they can correspond to qualitative variables referred to as factors, which take a limited number of values, known as the levels of the factor. An example of a factor is study. A factor is handled by including it in the model as a linear combination of indicator variables, which take the value 0 or 1. For example, the study effect, denoted by $\beta_{0i}$, could be expressed as

$$\beta_{0i} = \beta_{01} x_{01ij} + \beta_{02} x_{02ij} + \cdots + \beta_{0(r-1)} x_{0(r-1)ij},$$

where $x_{0hij} = 1$ if the patient is in study $h$ and 0 otherwise. This results in the parameter $\beta_{0r}$ being constrained to equal 0. Many statistical modelling packages generate indicator variables automatically when a term in the model has been specified as a factor. However, as there are a number of ways in which this can be done, it is essential to know which one has been used in any implementation, so that the parameter estimates can be interpreted correctly.

In many of the SAS procedures, a variable is identified as a factor by its inclusion in the CLASS statement. If the coding of the levels of a factor is numerical, then SAS lists the factor levels in ascending numerical order. Other orderings of the factor levels are possible, such as alphabetical. Whichever ordering is chosen, SAS generates the indicator variables in the same way. This is illustrated here for the study effect. The variable $x_{0hij} = 1$ if the patient is in the $h$th study in the list and $0$ otherwise, for $h = 1, \ldots, r - 1$. The parameter $\beta_{0h}$, $h = 1, \ldots, r - 1$, represents the difference in effect between the $h$th study in the list and the $r$th (last) study in the list.

In this book, the term 'covariate' will be used to include both quantitative variables and indicator variables. The values of the covariates are assumed to be fixed and known without error. Unless otherwise stated, the following coding of the study and treatment covariates is adopted. Studies are ordered as study 1, study 2, etc., and the study covariates, $x_{0hij}$, $h = 1, \ldots, r - 1$, are defined as above. When the comparison is between a treated group and a control group, the treatment covariate, $x_{1ij}$, is coded '1' for the treated group and '0' for the control group.

The model which will provide an overall fixed effects estimate of the absolute mean difference between the two treatments, analogous to that in Chapter 4, includes study and treatment as covariates. It is given by

$$\mu_{ij} = \alpha + \beta_{0i} + \beta_1 x_{1ij}. \tag{5.1}$$

For the adopted coding of the treatment and study covariates, the term $\alpha + \beta_{0i}$ represents the effect in the control group in study $i$, and $\alpha$ represents the effect in the control group in study $r$. The parameter $\beta_1$ represents the absolute mean difference between the treated and control groups, which is common across all studies. To obtain the fixed effects model of Section 4.2.1, put $\beta_1 = \theta$.

## 5.2.2 Estimation and hypothesis testing

Estimates of the fixed effect parameters and the variance component, $\sigma^2$, are obtained using the method of least squares. A covariance matrix is obtained for the estimates of the fixed effect parameters, from which the standard error of a single parameter estimate or a linear combination of the parameter estimates can be calculated. Confidence intervals are based on the $t$ distribution. Hypothesis tests for the fixed effect parameters are based on changes in the residual sum of squares between two models, of which one contains the parameter(s) of interest and the other is identical except that it does not contain the parameter(s) of interest. The resulting test statistic is compared with the $F$ distribution. Further details are provided in Section A.2 of the Appendix. Many statistical packages can fit a general linear model. For example, the procedure PROC GLM in SAS can be used.

To test the null hypothesis that the treatment difference in all studies is equal to 0, model (5.1) is compared with a model which only contains the study effects, namely

$$\mu_{ij} = \alpha + \beta_{0i}. \tag{5.2}$$

Model (5.2) has $r$ degrees of freedom associated with the model terms and model (5.1) has $r + 1$, so that the numerator of the $F$ statistic is associated with one degree of freedom. The estimate of $\sigma^2$ from model (5.1), which forms the denominator of the $F$ statistic, is associated with $n - r - 1$ degrees of freedom. The resulting $F$ statistic is compared with the $F$ distribution with 1 and $n - r - 1$ degrees of freedom.

The following SAS statements may be used to fit model (5.1) and to obtain the results of the $F$ test mentioned above:

```
PROC GLM;
CLASS study;
MODEL  y = study treat / ss1 solution;
```

Here 'y' contains the values of $y_{ij}$, 'study' the code for the study and 'treat' the values of $x_{1ij}$. The variable 'study' is defined as a factor via the CLASS statement. The option 'ss1' refers to the type I sum of squares, as defined by SAS. This option gives the effect of each explanatory variable in the model adjusted only for those that come before it in the MODEL statement. Changing the order of variables in the MODEL statement will change the type I sum of squares. In the SAS output, the required $F$ statistic is that associated with the term 'treat'. The option 'solution' provides a printout of the parameter estimates, standard errors and associated statistics, in which the estimate of $\beta_1$ appears as the 'treat' parameter estimate.

As an alternative, the following set of SAS statements, which include 'treat' as a factor via the CLASS statement, may be used:

```
PROC GLM;
CLASS study treat;
MODEL  y = study treat / ss1 solution;
LSMEANS  treat / pdiff cl;
```

However, in order to obtain the estimate of $\beta_1$ instead of $-\beta_1$, it is necessary to ensure that the control treatment appears as the last level of the factor. The LSMEANS statement requests that the least-squares mean estimates of the treatment effects be printed. The least-squares mean estimate of the new treatment minus the least-squares mean estimate of the control provides an estimate of $\beta_1$. The 'pdiff' option requests that the $p$-value for the difference between treatments be printed, and 'cl' requests that the confidence intervals for the treatment means and difference be presented.

For the fixed effects analyses with two treatment groups it makes no difference whether 'treat' is handled as a continuous covariate or a factor. However, when random effects are introduced into the model in Section 5.8, it will be seen that whilst the two approaches lead to an identical parameterization of the treatment difference, they will lead to different parameterizations of some of the variance components. In order to maintain comparability with the random effects model of Chapter 4, 'treat' should be considered as a continuous covariate, enabling the model to be expressed within a multilevel framework.

When 'treat' is considered as a factor, the model is expressed as a traditional mixed linear model. The latter framework is particularly useful when there are more than two treatment groups. The connection between the multilevel model and the traditional mixed linear model is considered in detail in Section 5.8.4. Unless specified otherwise, the SAS code presented in this book will include 'treat' as a continuous covariate when there are only two treatment groups.

### 5.2.3 Testing for heterogeneity in the absolute mean difference across studies

In order to perform a test for heterogeneity of the treatment difference parameter across all studies, it is necessary to fit the model which includes the study by treatment interaction term. This is given by

$$\mu_{ij} = \alpha + \beta_{0i} + \beta_{1i}x_{1ij}, \tag{5.3}$$

where the $\beta_{1i}$ may now differ from study to study. This has $2r$ degrees of freedom associated with the model terms and $n - 2r$ degrees of freedom associated with the estimate of $\sigma^2$. The test for heterogeneity is a test of the study by treatment interaction term and involves the comparison of models (5.1) and (5.3). The resulting $F$ statistic is compared with the $F$ distribution on $r - 1$ and $n - 2r$ degrees of freedom.

Model (5.3) may be fitted and the test for heterogeneity conducted by changing the MODEL statement in Section 5.2.2 as follows:

```
MODEL y = study treat study*treat / ss1 solution;
```

The appropriate $F$ statistic is that associated with the 'study*treat' term. When 'treat' is entered as a continuous covariate, the estimate which appears alongside 'treat' is an estimate of the absolute mean difference between the treated and control groups in study $r(\beta_{1r})$. The estimate which appears alongside the parameter 'study $i$ * treat', for $i = 1, \ldots, r - 1$, is the estimate of the mean difference between the treated and control groups in study $i$ minus the estimate of the mean difference between the treated and control groups in study $r$ – that is, it is an estimate of $\beta_{1i} - \beta_{1r}$.

### 5.2.4   Example: Recovery time after anaesthesia

Consider the anaesthetic study described in Section 3.6.1. Results of the hypothesis tests in connection with the overall treatment difference and the centre by treatment interaction are presented in Table 5.1. The $F$ statistic for testing the centre by treatment interaction term is significant ($p = 0.03$), indicating evidence of heterogeneity in the treatment difference between centres.

**Table 5.1**    Recovery time after anaesthesia: comparison of models

| Model comparisons | Effect tested | Change in residual sums of squares | Change in degrees of freedom | Estimate of $\sigma^2$ | Degrees of freedom | $F$ statistic | $p$-value |
|---|---|---|---|---|---|---|---|
| (5.1) vs (5.2) | Treat | 12.90 | 1 | 0.535 | 172 | 24.13 | <0.001 |
| (5.3) vs (5.1) | Centre by Treat | 9.07 | 8 | 0.506 | 164 | 2.24 | 0.03 |

**Table 5.2**    Fixed effects meta-analysis of the absolute mean difference (treatment A − treatment B) in log-recovery time, assuming a common variance across all centres

| Centre | Treatment A | | Treatment B | | $\hat{\theta}_i$ | $\text{se}(\hat{\theta}_i)$ (based on $s_i^2$) |
|---|---|---|---|---|---|---|
| | $n$ | Mean | $n$ | Mean | | |
| 1 | 4 | 1.141 | 5 | 0.277 | 0.864 | 0.528 |
| 2 | 10 | 2.165 | 10 | 1.519 | 0.646 | 0.301 |
| 3 | 17 | 1.790 | 17 | 1.518 | 0.272 | 0.282 |
| 4 | 8 | 2.105 | 9 | 1.189 | 0.916 | 0.398 |
| 5 | 7 | 1.324 | 10 | 0.456 | 0.867 | 0.278 |
| 6 | 11 | 2.369 | 10 | 1.550 | 0.819 | 0.210 |
| 7 | 10 | 1.074 | 12 | 0.265 | 0.809 | 0.250 |
| 8 | 5 | 2.583 | 4 | 1.370 | 1.212 | 0.459 |
| 9 | 14 | 1.844 | 19 | 2.118 | −0.273 | 0.279 |

Test of treatment difference, $F = 24.13$; $(1, 172 \text{ df})$, $p < 0.001$
Test for heterogeneity, $F = 2.24$; $(8, 164 \text{ df})$, $p = 0.03$
Estimate of treatment difference $(\hat{\beta}_1) = 0.535$; $\text{se}(\hat{\beta}_1) = 0.109$
95% CI $= (0.535 \pm 1.974 \times 0.109) = (0.320, 0.750)$

Table 5.2 shows the results of the fixed effects meta-analysis. Each individual centre estimate of the absolute mean difference (treatment A − treatment B), $\hat{\theta}_i$, and its standard error have been calculated as in Table 4.22. Each standard error is based on the individual centre pooled sample variance $s_i^2$. The standard error for the fixed effects estimate of treatment difference, $\hat{\beta}_1$, is calculated from the estimate of $\sigma^2$, denoted by $s_f^2$, from fitting model (5.1). The value of $s_f^2$ for the anaesthetic study is 0.535. This is also used in the $F$ test for the overall treatment difference. The $F$ test for the centre by treatment interaction uses the overall pooled sample variance, $s_p^2$, which for the anaesthetic study is equal to 0.506. Details of the calculation of $s_f^2$ and $s_p^2$ can be found in Section 4.2.9.

### 5.2.5 Modelling of individual patient data versus combining study estimates

The meta-analysis based on the modelling of individual patient data has similarities with and differences from that based on combining study estimates as presented in Table 4.23. In both cases a common variance parameter, $\sigma^2$, is assumed, although estimates of $\sigma^2$ may differ. For models (5.1)–(5.3), the estimate of $\sigma^2$ is dependent on the fixed effect parameters present in the model. As a result, the estimate of $\sigma^2$ obtained from model (5.1), $s_f^2$, will usually be different from the overall pooled sample variance, $s_p^2$, obtained from model (5.3). The fixed effect estimates, $\hat{\beta}_1$ and $\hat{\theta}$ are the same. It can be seen from Tables 4.23 and 5.2 that $\hat{\theta}$ and $\hat{\beta}_1$ are both equal to 0.535. It is the standard error of $\hat{\beta}_1$ computed from individual patient data which will be different from the standard error of $\hat{\theta}$, as these depend on the estimate of $\sigma^2$ used. For the former, the estimate $s_f^2$ is used, which is obtained from the model without interaction terms. For the latter, the estimate $s_p^2$ is used, which is obtained from the model with interaction terms, even though a fixed effects meta-analysis is being performed. If the study by treatment interaction effect is small the two estimates of $\sigma^2$ will be close. For the anaesthetic study $s_f^2 = 0.535$ and $s_p^2 = 0.506$, resulting in similar standard errors of 0.109 and 0.106 respectively for the fixed effects estimate.

When the $U$ and $Q$ statistics, described in Chapter 4, are based on (3.22) and (3.23) and use $s_p^2$ they have close connections with the $F$ statistics introduced in this chapter. To test the null hypothesis of no treatment difference, model (5.1) would be compared with model (5.2), using the $F$ test with 1 and $n - r - 1$ degrees of freedom. The $F$ statistic used is equal to $Us_p^2/s_f^2$. To test the null hypothesis of no study by treatment interaction, model (5.3) would be compared with model (5.1), using the $F$ test with $r - 1$ and $n - 2r$ degrees of freedom. The $F$ statistic used is equal to $Q/(r - 1)$, as both test statistics would be calculated using $s_p^2$. For the test for heterogeneity of the treatment difference across trials, comparison with the $F_{(r-1,n-2r)}$ distribution is to be preferred to comparison with the $\chi_{r-1}^2$ distribution, as it takes account of the estimation of $\sigma^2$. These two distributions become the same when $n - 2r$ approaches $\infty$, so that $\sigma^2$ is effectively known. The same argument applies to the test of the treatment difference.

### 5.2.6 Heterogeneity in the variance parameter across studies

The assumption of a common variance parameter, $\sigma^2$, across all of the studies can be investigated by using Bartlett's test (Bartlett, 1937). Details of its application are given in Section 4.2.9. For the anaesthetic study, Bartlett's test for heterogeneity in the variance parameter across the centres was not statistically significant ($p = 0.25$). Therefore, the assumption of a common variance is not contradicted. However, as discussed in Section 4.2.9, the decision to assume or not assume a common variance should not depend solely on the

$p$-value from Bartlett's test. Scheffé (1959) notes that the test is extremely sensitive to non-normality of the data and does not recommend its routine use. Another justification for proceeding with the methods described above is that they are reasonably robust, even if the variances are unequal, as long as there are approximately equal numbers of patients in each treatment arm per trial. In situations where the assumption of a common variance is not acceptable, there are alternative ways to proceed, two of which are described here.

The first approach is of use if the same outcome measure has been recorded in each trial and interest lies in estimating the absolute mean difference. In this case, the analysis proceeds as above, except that a separate variance parameter is specified for each trial. Now $\varepsilon_{ij}$ are realizations of normally distributed random variables with expected value 0 and variance $\sigma_i^2$, resulting in the need to estimate $r$ variance parameters. Estimation and hypothesis testing proceed as for the general linear mixed model, details of which are provided in Section A.7 of the Appendix. The approach based on residual (restricted) maximum likelihood is generally preferred to that based on maximum likelihood as it avoids the downward bias of ML estimates of the variance parameters. The procedure PROC MIXED in SAS can be utilized for this purpose. The following statements may be used to fit model (5.1):

```
PROC MIXED method = reml;
CLASS study;
MODEL  y = study treat / htype = 1 ddfm = kenwardroger solution;
REPEATED / group = study;
```

In general, all of the fixed effect parameters should appear in the MODEL statement and there is no RANDOM statement, because in this case there are no random effects in the model. The 'htype = 1' option plays a similar role to the 'ss1' option in PROC GLM. The 'group' option within the REPEATED statement introduces different variance parameters for each study. Both ML and REML approaches are available with PROC MIXED. As the default option is REML, the option 'method = reml' may be omitted. Wald test statistics, produced by PROC MIXED, can be used for inferences concerning the fixed effect parameters. The Wald test statistic approximately follows an $F$ distribution, but it is necessary to estimate the denominator degrees of freedom instead of using the default produced by the program. The option 'ddfm = kenwardroger' is used to inflate the estimated variance matrix of the fixed and random effects to allow for estimation of the variance components and to estimate the denominator degrees of freedom using Satterthwaite's procedure (Satterthwaite, 1941; Kenward and Roger, 1997). Alternative methods for testing the fixed effect parameters are discussed in Section A.7 of the Appendix. In the case of the anaesthetic study, the results from such an analysis (Table 5.3) differ a little from those in Table 5.2.

There is a connection between this meta-analysis based on the modelling of individual patient data and that based on combining study estimates. For model (5.3), the estimate of $\sigma_i^2$ is $s_i^2$, which is the same as that used in the

**Table 5.3**   Fixed effects meta-analysis of the absolute mean difference (treatment A − treatment B) in log-recovery time, allowing different variance estimates from each centre

| Centre | Treatment A | | Treatment B | | $\hat{\theta}_i$ | $se(\hat{\theta}_i)$ |
| --- | --- | --- | --- | --- | --- | --- |
| | | | | | | (based on $s_i^2$) |
| | $n$ | Mean | $n$ | Mean | | |
| 1 | 4 | 1.141 | 5 | 0.277 | 0.864 | 0.528 |
| 2 | 10 | 2.165 | 10 | 1.519 | 0.646 | 0.301 |
| 3 | 17 | 1.790 | 17 | 1.518 | 0.272 | 0.282 |
| 4 | 8 | 2.105 | 9 | 1.189 | 0.916 | 0.398 |
| 5 | 7 | 1.324 | 10 | 0.456 | 0.867 | 0.278 |
| 6 | 11 | 2.369 | 10 | 1.550 | 0.819 | 0.210 |
| 7 | 10 | 1.074 | 12 | 0.265 | 0.809 | 0.250 |
| 8 | 5 | 2.583 | 4 | 1.370 | 1.212 | 0.459 |
| 9 | 14 | 1.844 | 19 | 2.118 | −0.273 | 0.279 |

Test of treatment difference, $F = 33.49$; $(1, 140\,\text{df})$, $p < 0.001$
Test for heterogeneity, $F = 1.87$; $(8, 44.1\,\text{df})$, $p = 0.09$
Estimate of treatment difference $(\hat{\beta}_1) = 0.658$; $se(\hat{\beta}_1) = 0.109$
95% CI $= (0.658 \pm 1.977 \times 0.109) = (0.443, 0.873)$

calculations for the meta-analysis presented in the 'different variances' columns of Table 4.24. If the $F$ statistic calculated for the test for heterogeneity is not adjusted to account for estimation of the variance components it would be equal to $Q/(r - 1)$. For model (5.1), the estimates of $\sigma_i^2$ will usually be different from $s_i^2$, and therefore even the unadjusted $F$ statistic for testing the treatment difference will not be equal to $U$. The fixed effect estimates, $\hat{\beta}_1$ and $\hat{\theta}$, will usually be different. Although both estimates are calculated as a weighted average of study estimates, the weight attached to study $i$ is a function of the estimate of $\sigma_i^2$, which is different in the two cases. For the recovery time example $\hat{\beta}_1$ and $\hat{\theta}$ are given by 0.658 and 0.627, respectively.

The second approach to heterogeneity of variance is to consider the standardized treatment difference as the parameter of interest and to proceed using the methods described in Section 4.2.9.

## 5.3   FIXED EFFECTS MODELS FOR BINARY DATA

### 5.3.1   A fixed effects meta-analysis model

The observation $y_{ij}$ is assumed to be a realization of a random variable $Y_{ij}$, which has a binomial distribution with parameter $p_{ij}$ and denominator $n_{ij} = 1$. If $p_{ij}$ represents the probability of success for patient $j$ in trial $i$, then $y_{ij} = 1$ if the patient response is a 'success' and 0 if the response is a 'failure'. The expected value of $Y_{ij}$ is $p_{ij}$ and the variance $p_{ij}(1 - p_{ij})$.

In order to model the dependence of $p_{ij}$ on the explanatory variables $x_1, x_2, \ldots, x_q$, a transformation which maps the unit interval $(0, 1)$ onto the real line $(-\infty, \infty)$ is used. This transformation is known as the link function. The natural choice for estimating odds ratios is the logit link function, given by

$$\log\left(\frac{p_{ij}}{1 - p_{ij}}\right).$$

The logit link function leads to the linear logistic model

$$\log\left(\frac{p_{ij}}{1 - p_{ij}}\right) = \alpha + \eta_{ij},$$

where $\alpha$ is the intercept and $\eta_{ij}$ is a linear combination of explanatory variables. This model is an example of a generalized linear model, details of which can be found in Section A.6 of the Appendix. An analogy with the general linear model can be seen with $\log\{p_{ij}/(1 - p_{ij})\}$ replacing $\mu_{ij}$.

The model which will provide an overall fixed effects estimate of treatment difference, analogous to that in Chapter 4, includes study and treatment as covariates. It is given by

$$\log\left(\frac{p_{ij}}{1 - p_{ij}}\right) = \alpha + \beta_{0i} + \beta_1 x_{1ij}. \tag{5.4}$$

The parameter $\beta_1$ represents the common log-odds ratio of success on treatment relative to control.

Discussion about other link functions, which can be used with binary data, can be found in Collett (1991) and McCullagh and Nelder (1989). One of these, the complementary log-log function, will be considered in Section 5.6 for interval-censored survival data.

### 5.3.2 Estimation and hypothesis testing

Parameter estimates are obtained using the method of maximum likelihood, as described in Sections A.4 and A.6 of the Appendix. The standard error for a single parameter or a linear combination of the parameters can be calculated from the observed or expected Fisher's information matrix. Confidence intervals are based on asymptotic normality. Models are compared by means of the likelihood ratio test statistic, that is, the change in deviance ($-2$ times the log-likelihood) between two models, one of which contains the parameter(s) of interest while the other is identical except that it does not contain the parameter(s) of interest. This test statistic is compared with the chi-squared distribution. Further details are provided in Section A.4 of the Appendix. Any package which fits a linear logistic regression model can be utilized, for example PROC GENMOD in SAS.

To test the null hypothesis that the treatment difference in all studies is equal to 0, model (5.4) is compared with a model which only contains the study effects, namely

$$\log\left(\frac{p_{ij}}{1 - p_{ij}}\right) = \alpha + \beta_{0i}. \tag{5.5}$$

Model (5.4) has $r + 1$ degrees of freedom associated with the model terms and model (5.5) has $r$. The likelihood ratio statistic, equal to the change in deviance between the two models, is compared with the chi-squared distribution with one degree of freedom, in the same way as the $U$ statistic described in Chapter 4.

The following SAS statements may be used to fit model (5.4) and to obtain the results of the likelihood ratio test mentioned above:

```
PROC GENMOD;
CLASS study;
MODEL  y = study treat / type1 dist = bin link = logit waldci;
```

The option 'type 1' plays the role of 'ss1' in PROC GLM (see Section 5.2.2), the 'dist' option specifies the distribution of the observations $y_{ij}$ which in this case is binomial, and the 'link' option specifies the link function. In the SAS output $\beta_1$ is associated with the parameter 'treat'. Wald CIs for the parameter estimates can be obtained via the 'waldci' option. Alternatively, the option 'lrci' can be used to obtain CIs based on the profile likelihood. In PROC GENMOD, the default option is to use the observed Fisher's information matrix in the computation of parameter estimates, variances and associated statistics. The 'scoring' option can be inserted in the MODEL statement to request that the expected Fisher's information matrix be used instead.

For a more efficient way of running the program, the data can be entered in binomial form, in which for each treatment group in each study the number of patients ($n$) and the sum of the $y_{ij}(s)$ are provided. The analysis proceeds with the MODEL statement above replaced by

```
MODEL s/n = study treat / type1 dist = bin link = logit waldci;
```

The GENMOD procedure also allows inclusion of 'treat' as a factor via the CLASS statement.

### 5.3.3 Testing for heterogeneity in the log-odds ratio across studies

In order to perform a test for heterogeneity of the treatment difference parameter across studies it is necessary to fit the model which includes the study by treatment interaction term. This is given by

$$\log\left(\frac{p_{ij}}{1 - p_{ij}}\right) = \alpha + \beta_{0i} + \beta_{1i}x_{1ij}, \tag{5.6}$$

which has $2r$ degrees of freedom associated with the model terms. The test for heterogeneity is a test of the study by treatment interaction term and involves the comparison of models (5.4) and (5.6). The change in deviance between these two models is compared with the chi-squared distribution on $r - 1$ degrees of freedom, in the same way as the $Q$ statistic described in Chapter 4.

Model (5.6) may be fitted and the test for heterogeneity conducted by changing the MODEL statement in Section 5.3.2 as follows:

```
MODEL y = study treat study*treat / type1 dist = bin link = logit;
```

In the SAS output, the appropriate chi-squared statistic is that associated with the 'study*treat' term. As noted in Section 5.2.3, the parameter associated with 'treat' is $\beta_{1r}$ and the parameter associated with 'study $i$ * treat' is $\beta_{1i} - \beta_{1r}$.

### 5.3.4   Example: Stroke in hypertensive patients

Results of the hypothesis tests in connection with the overall treatment difference and the study by treatment interaction are presented in Table 5.4 for the stroke example described in Section 3.2.1. The chi-squared statistic for testing the study by treatment interaction term is not significant ($p = 0.56$), providing no evidence for heterogeneity in the log-odds ratio between studies. There is a statistically significant difference between treatments ($p < 0.001$).

Table 5.5 shows the results of the fixed effects meta-analysis. Each individual study estimate of the log-odds ratio and its standard error have been calculated as in Table 4.1. The fixed effects estimate of the log-odds ratio is $-0.545$, with standard error $0.077$.

### 5.3.5   Modelling of individual patient data versus combining study estimates

The meta-analysis based on modelling individual patient data is similar but not identical to that based on combining study estimates using (3.1) and (3.2) and presented in Table 4.2. The tests of treatment difference and heterogeneity in the log-odds ratios, described in Sections 5.3.2 and 5.3.3, are based on likelihood ratio

**Table 5.4**   Stroke in hypertensive patients: comparison of models

| Model comparisons | Effect tested | Change in deviance | Change in degrees of freedom | $p$-value |
|---|---|---|---|---|
| (5.4) vs (5.5) | Treat | 51.48 | 1 | <0.001 |
| (5.6) vs (5.4) | Study by Treat | 10.60 | 12 | 0.56 |

**Table 5.5**    Fixed effects meta-analysis of the log-odds ratio of a stroke on antihypertensive treatment relative to control

| Study | Treated group | | Control group | | $\hat{\theta}_i$ | $se(\hat{\theta}_i)$ |
|---|---|---|---|---|---|---|
| | Success (stroke) | Failure | Success (stroke) | Failure | | |
| 2 HDFP (Stratum I) | 59 | 3844 | 88 | 3834 | −0.402 | 0.170 |
| 4 ANBPS | 13 | 1708 | 22 | 1684 | −0.540 | 0.352 |
| 5 MRC | 60 | 8640 | 109 | 8545 | −0.608 | 0.161 |
| 6 VAII | 5 | 181 | 20 | 174 | −1.426 | 0.511 |
| 7 USPHS | 1 | 192 | 6 | 190 | −1.802 | 1.085 |
| 8 HDFP (Stratum II) | 25 | 1023 | 36 | 968 | −0.420 | 0.264 |
| 9 HSCSG | 43 | 190 | 52 | 167 | −0.319 | 0.232 |
| 10 VAI | 1 | 67 | 3 | 60 | −1.209 | 1.168 |
| 11 WOLFF | 2 | 43 | 1 | 41 | 0.646 | 1.244 |
| 13 Carter | 10 | 39 | 21 | 27 | −1.110 | 0.459 |
| 14 HDFP (Stratum III) | 18 | 516 | 34 | 495 | −0.678 | 0.298 |
| 15 EWPHE | 32 | 384 | 48 | 376 | −0.427 | 0.239 |
| 16 Coope | 20 | 399 | 39 | 426 | −0.602 | 0.284 |

Test of treatment difference, $\chi^2 = 51.48$; (1 df), $p < 0.001$
Test for heterogeneity, $\chi^2 = 10.60$; (12 df), $p = 0.56$
Estimate of treatment difference $(\hat{\beta}_1) = -0.545$; $se(\hat{\beta}_1) = 0.077$
95% CI = $(-0.696, -0.394)$

test statistics, whereas the $U$ and $Q$ statistics in Table 4.2 use the assumption of normality for the log-odds ratio in each individual study as used by the Wald test. The reader is referred to Section A.5 of the Appendix for further details. The fixed effects estimate of the log-odds ratio and its standard error will also be slightly different for the two approaches. From Table 4.2 the log-odds ratio estimate is −0.535 with standard error 0.078, whereas from Table 5.5 they are −0.545 and 0.077, respectively. The overall conclusions from the two approaches will usually be the same.

The $U$ statistic calculated using (3.3) and (3.4) is the score test statistic, analogous to the likelihood ratio test statistic for testing the treatment difference as described in Section 5.3.2.

## 5.4    FIXED EFFECTS MODELS FOR ORDINAL DATA

### 5.4.1    A fixed effects meta-analysis model

Suppose that each patient has a response which falls into one of $m$ categories, $C_1, \ldots, C_m$, which are ordered in terms of desirability: $C_1$ is the best and $C_m$ the worst. The patient observation $y_{ij}$ is assumed to be a realization of a random variable $Y_{ij}$, which has a multinomial distribution with parameters $p_{ijk}$, where $k = 1, \ldots, m$, and denominator $n_{ij} = 1$. The observation $y_{ij}$ takes the value $k$ if the $j$th subject in study $i$ has a response in the $k$th category. The parameter $p_{ijk}$ is the probability that the $j$th subject in study $i$ has a response in the $k$th category. Let $Q_{ijk}$ be the associated probability of a response in category $k$ or better, so that $Q_{ijk} = p_{ij1} + \cdots + p_{ijk}$ and $Q_{ijm} = 1$.

The modelling approach taken here is based on the proportional odds model, and is described in detail in Whitehead *et al.* (2001). This model has the advantage that it is consistent with the existence of a 'latent' continuous variable for the response of each patient, a property which proves useful when different cut-points are used amongst studies. When there are only two response categories it is equivalent to the usual linear logistic model for binary data.

The proportional odds model is defined by

$$\log\left(\frac{Q_{ijk}}{1 - Q_{ijk}}\right) = \alpha_k + \eta_{ij}, \qquad k = 1, \ldots, m - 1,$$

where $\alpha_k$ is referred to as the $k$th intercept and $\eta_{ij}$ is a linear combination of explanatory variables. The model assumes 'proportional odds' in that the log-odds ratio $\beta_p$, associated with a unit increase in the $p$th explanatory variable, does not depend on the intercept $k$.

The model can be considered as arising from a 'latent' continuous variable. Assume that the response of the $j$th subject in study $i$ is truly equal to $G_{ij}$, although this 'latent' response will never be observed. Suppose that $G_{ij}$ has a logistic distribution with parameters $-\eta_{ij}$ and 1, that is,

$$P(G_{ij} \leqslant x) = \frac{1}{1 + e^{-(x - \mu_{ij})/\sigma_{ij}}},$$

where $\mu_{ij} = -\eta_{ij}$ and $\sigma_{ij} = 1$.

If $\alpha_1, \ldots, \alpha_{m-1}$, are the cut-points for determining the response category, then putting

$$Q_{ijk} = P(G_{ij} \leqslant \alpha_k) = \frac{1}{1 + e^{-(\alpha_k + \eta_{ij})}}$$

results in the proportional odds model defined above.

Consider the proportional odds model in which the explanatory variables are study and treatment. Here

$$\log\left(\frac{Q_{ijk}}{1 - Q_{ijk}}\right) = \alpha_k + \beta_{0i} + \beta_1 x_{1ij}. \tag{5.7}$$

The parameter $\beta_1$ represents the log-odds ratio of having a better response on the experimental treatment than on the control, which is assumed common across all intercepts and studies.

In model (5.7) there is an assumption of proportional odds across all covariates, implying a shift in the distribution of the underlying latent variable according to study and treatment group but not a change of shape. This means that within each study there is a common log-odds ratio, $\beta_1$, for the treated group relative to control for each value of $k$, $k = 1, \ldots, m - 1$. It also means that within each treatment group there is a common log-odds ratio, $\beta_{0i} - \beta_{0i'}$, for any study $i$ relative to a different study $i'$ for each value of $k$. This second assumption in relation to the studies seems to be rather restrictive and perhaps unlikely to be true in practice. It can be relaxed by considering a stratified model, in which the covariates representing the study effects are allowed to vary with the level of $k$. Such a model assumes proportional odds between treatments, but stratifies by study. This means that the cutpoints associated with the distribution of the underlying latent variable for determining the response category are allowed to vary from study to study but are the same for both treatment groups within a study. The model is given by

$$\log\left(\frac{Q_{ijk}}{1 - Q_{ijk}}\right) = \alpha_{ik} + \beta_1 x_{1ij}. \tag{5.8}$$

The term $\alpha_{ik}$ represents the $k$th intercept for the $i$th study. It is model (5.8) which is analogous to that used in Chapter 4, as in both cases there is stratification by study. Attention will be focused on models stratified by study, although in Section 5.4.7 there is a discussion of the approach based on the meta-analysis model (5.7).

## 5.4.2 Estimation and hypothesis testing

Maximum likelihood estimation of the parameters can be based on the full likelihood for the multinomial distribution. The standard error for a single parameter or a linear combination of the parameters can be calculated from the observed or expected Fisher's information matrix. Confidence intervals are based on asymptotic normality. Models are compared by means of the likelihood ratio test statistic, that is, the change in deviance ($-2$ times the log-likelihood) between two models, one of which contains the parameter(s) of interest while the other is identical except that it does not contain the parameter(s) of interest. This test statistic is compared with the chi-squared distribution. Further details can be found in Section A.4 of the Appendix.

The stratified proportional odds models can be fitted using PROC NLMIXED in SAS. Although its main purpose is to fit non-linear mixed models, PROC NLMIXED can also be used to obtain ML estimates for fixed effects models. In the case of the stratified proportional odds models, this is achieved by constructing the log-likelihood function using SAS programming statements. Each subject's contribution to the log-likelihood function is specified in terms of the model parameters. The contribution from the $j$th subject in study $i$ is

$$\sum_{k=1}^{m} \delta_{ijk} \log(p_{ijk}),$$

where $\delta_{ijk}$ is 1 if the subject has a response in category $k$ and 0 otherwise. The terms $p_{ijk}$ are expressed as functions of the $Q_{ijk}$, that is $p_{ijk} = Q_{ijk} - Q_{ij,k-1}$, $k = 2, \ldots, m$ and $p_{ij1} = Q_{ij1}$.

As an example, the following code could be used to fit model (5.8) with two studies and an ordinal response with three categories:

```
PROC NLMIXED data = one;
PARMS  a11 a12 a21 a22 =1, beta1 =0;
BOUNDS a12 a22 > 0;

eta = beta1*treat;

if study = 1 and y = 1 then do;
qk = 1/(1+exp(-a11-eta));
qk_1 = 0;
end;
if study = 1 and y = 2 then do;
qk = 1/(1+exp(-(a11 + a12)-eta));
qk_1 = 1/(1+exp(-a11-eta));
end;
if study = 1 and y = 3 then do;
qk = 1;
qk_1 = 1/(1+exp(-(a11 + a12)-eta));
end;
if study = 2 and y = 1 then do;
qk = 1/(1+exp(-a21-eta));
qk_1 = 0;
end;
if study = 2 and y = 2 then do;
qk = 1/(1+exp(-(a21 + a22)-eta));
qk_1 = 1/(1+exp(-a21-eta));
end;
if study = 2 and y = 3 then do;
qk = 1;
qk_1 = 1/(1+exp(-(a21 + a22)-eta));
end;

p =qk-qk_1;
if p>1e-8 then ll =log(p);
else ll =-1e100;

MODEL y ~ general(ll);
```

The data set 'one' contains the variables 'study', 'treat' and 'y'. In order to preserve the ordering of the intercept terms, $\alpha_{ik}$, they are expressed in terms of the parameters $a_{ik}$, where

$$\alpha_{ik} = \sum_{h=1}^{k} a_{ih},$$

and the $a_{ik}$ are restricted to being greater than 0 for $k = 2, \ldots, m - 1$. The model parameters and their initial values are specified in the PARMS statement, and the bounds for the $a_{ik}$ parameters are specified in the BOUNDS statement. The rest of the program is devoted to calculating the log-likelihood function. An error trap is included in case the likelihood becomes too small.

The SAS output includes the $(-2\times)$ log-likelihood value and parameter estimates and associated statistics. PROC NLMIXED uses the observed Fisher's information matrix. The estimate of $\beta_1$ appears as the 'beta1' parameter estimate.

PROC NLMIXED does not require the data from each patient to be presented as a separate record. The data set 'one' may consist of four items for each category in each treatment group in each study, namely the category (cat), the treatment group (treat), the study (study) and the number of patient responses (num). The variable 'cat' replaces 'y' in the above SAS statements, and the following additional statement appears after the MODEL statement.

```
REPLICATE num;
```

To test the null hypothesis that the treatment difference in all studies is equal to 0, model (5.8) is compared with a model which only contains the study effects, namely

$$\log\left(\frac{Q_{ijk}}{1 - Q_{ijk}}\right) = \alpha_{ik}. \tag{5.9}$$

Model (5.8) has $(m - 1)r + 1$ degrees of freedom associated with the model terms and model (5.9) has $(m - 1)r$. The change in deviance between these two models is compared with the chi-squared distribution with one degree of freedom. This is analogous to the $U$ statistic described in Chapter 4. Model (5.9) may be fitted by removing the 'beta1' and 'eta' terms in the PROC NLMIXED statements above.

### 5.4.3   Testing for heterogeneity in the log-odds ratio across studies

Heterogeneity can be tested by including a study by treatment interaction term in the model. A model which includes the study by treatment interaction would be given by

$$\log \left( \frac{Q_{ijk}}{1 - Q_{ijk}} \right) = \alpha_{ik} + \beta_{1i} x_{1ij}, \tag{5.10}$$

which has $mr$ degrees of freedom associated with the model terms. The test for heterogeneity is a test of the study by treatment interaction term and involves the comparison of models (5.8) and (5.10). The change in deviance between these two models is compared with the chi-squared distribution on $r - 1$ degrees of freedom. Such a test is analogous to the test for heterogeneity based on the $Q$ statistic described in Chapter 4.

Model (5.10) may be fitted by replacing lines 2 and 4 in the PROC NLMIXED program in Section 5.4.2 by

```
PARMS  a11 a12 a21 a22 =1, beta11 beta12 = 0;

eta = beta11*treat*study1 + beta12*treat*study2;
```

where 'study1' takes the value 1 for patients in study 1 and 0 otherwise, and 'study2' takes the value 1 for patients in study 2 and 0 otherwise. The parameters $\beta_{11}$ and $\beta_{12}$ are associated with 'beta11' and 'beta12' respectively in the SAS output.

### 5.4.4 Example: Global impression of change in Alzheimer's disease

Table 5.6 shows the results of hypothesis tests for the tacrine studies described in Section 3.5.1. The chi-squared statistic for testing the study by treatment interaction term is not significant ($p = 0.30$), providing no evidence of heterogeneity in the log-odds ratio across studies. There is a statistically significant difference between treatments ($p < 0.001$).

Table 5.7 shows the results of the fixed effects meta-analysis. Each individual study estimate of the log-odds ratio and its standard error have been calculated as in Table 4.15. The fixed effects estimate of the log-odds ratio is 0.505, with standard error 0.112.

**Table 5.6** Global impression of change in Alzheimer's disease: comparison of models

| Model comparisons | Effect tested | Change in deviance | Change in degrees of freedom | $p$-value |
|---|---|---|---|---|
| (5.8) vs (5.9) | Treat | 20.43 | 1 | <0.001 |
| (5.10) vs (5.8) | Study by Treat | 4.84 | 4 | 0.30 |

**Table 5.7** Fixed effects meta-analysis of the log-odds ratio from a stratified proportional odds model for the tacrine studies

| Study | Treatment | Category | | | | | $\hat{\theta}_i$ | $se(\hat{\theta}_i)$ |
|---|---|---|---|---|---|---|---|---|
| | | C1 | C2 | C3 | C4 | C5 | | |
| 1 | Tacrine | 4 | 23 | 45 | 22 | 2 | 0.284 | 0.261 |
| | Placebo | 2 | 22 | 54 | 29 | 3 | | |
| 2 | Tacrine | 14 | 119 | 180 | 54 | 6 | 0.224 | 0.242 |
| | Placebo | 1 | 22 | 35 | 11 | 3 | | |
| 3 | Tacrine | 13 | 20 | 24 | 10 | 1 | 0.360 | 0.332 |
| | Placebo | 7 | 16 | 17 | 10 | 3 | | |
| 4 | Tacrine | 21 | 106 | 175 | 62 | 17 | 0.785 | 0.174 |
| | Placebo | 8 | 24 | 73 | 52 | 13 | | |
| 5 | Tacrine | 3 | 14 | 19 | 3 | 0 | 0.492 | 0.421 |
| | Placebo | 2 | 13 | 18 | 7 | 1 | | |

Test of treatment difference, $\chi^2 = 20.43$; (1 df), $p < 0.001$
Test for heterogeneity, $\chi^2 = 4.84$; (4 df), $p = 0.30$
Estimate of treatment difference $(\hat{\beta}_1) = 0.505$; $se(\hat{\beta}_1) = 0.112$
95% CI $= (0.285, 0.725)$

### 5.4.5 Modelling of individual patient data versus combining study estimates

The meta-analysis based on modelling individual patient data is similar but not identical to that based on combining study estimates presented in Table 4.16. The reasons for this are the same as those outlined in Section 5.3.5 for binary data. From Table 4.16 the log-odds ratio estimate is 0.503 with standard error 0.112, and from Table 5.7 they are 0.505 and 0.112 respectively. For this example, there is very good agreement between the two approaches. In general, the overall conclusions from the two approaches will be the same.

### 5.4.6 Testing the assumption of proportional odds between treatments

The assumption of proportional odds between treatments can be tested separately for each study, for example by using the score test in PROC LOGISTIC in SAS. A global test of this assumption, however, involving all studies will be more powerful and is presented here.

The assumption of proportional odds between treatments across intercepts can be investigated by fitting the model

$$\log \left( \frac{Q_{ijk}}{1 - Q_{ijk}} \right) = \alpha_{ik} + \beta_{2k} x_{1ij}. \qquad (5.11)$$

This model, which has $(m-1)(r+1)$ degrees of freedom associated with the model terms, is compared with model (5.8). The change in deviance between these two models is compared with the chi-squared distribution with $m-2$ degrees of freedom.

To fit model (5.11) the PROC NLMIXED program in Section 5.4.2. should be modified as follows:

```
PARMS   a11 a12 a21 a22 =1, beta21 beta22 =0;
BOUNDS a12 a22 > 0;


if study = 1 and y = 1 then do;
qk = 1/(1+exp(-a11-beta21));
qk_1 = 0;
end;
if study = 1 and y = 2 then do;
qk = 1/(1+exp(-(a11 + a12)-beta22));
qk_1 = 1/(1+exp(-a11-beta21));
end;
if study = 1 and y = 3 then do;
qk = 1;
qk_1 = 1/(1+exp(-(a11 + a12)-beta22));
end;
if study = 2 and y = 1 then do;
qk = 1/(1+exp(-a21-beta21));
qk_1 = 0;
end;
if study = 2 and y = 2 then do;
qk = 1/(1+exp(-(a21 + a22)-beta22));
qk_1 = 1/(1+exp(-a21-beta21));
end;
if study = 2 and y = 3 then do;
qk = 1;
qk_1 = 1/(1+exp(-(a21 + a22)-beta22));
end;
```

For the tacrine studies, the change in deviance was calculated to be 0.91, which compared with the chi-squared distribution on three degrees of freedom is not statistically significant ($p = 0.82$). This indicated that the assumption of proportional odds between treatments was satisfactory.

### 5.4.7  A proportional odds model for studies and treatments

A test of the assumption of proportional odds between studies would involve a comparison between model (5.7), which has $m + r - 1$ degrees of freedom associated with the model terms, and model (5.8). The change in deviance between the two models is compared with the chi-squared distribution on $(m - 2)(r - 1)$ degrees of freedom.

The proportional odds models, of which model (5.7) is an example, can be fitted using PROC NLMIXED. However, such models can be fitted more easily using PROC GENMOD. The SAS statements are similar to those presented in Section 5.3.2 for binary data, and the following can be used to fit model (5.7):

```
PROC GENMOD;
CLASS study;
MODEL y = study treat/ type1 dist = multinomial link = cumlogit
        waldci;
```

In the SAS output $\beta_1$ is associated with the parameter 'treat'.

As was the case with binary data, PROC GENMOD does not require the category from each patient to be presented as a separate record. Instead the number of patient responses (num) in each category (cat) in each treatment group in each study can be provided. The MODEL statement above is replaced by

```
FREQ num;
MODEL cat = study treat/ type1 dist = multinomial link = cumlogit
        waldci;
```

For the tacrine studies, the change in deviance between models (5.7) and (5.8) was calculated to be 29.93, which compared with the chi-squared distribution on 12 degrees of freedom is statistically significant ($p = 0.003$). This indicated that the assumption of proportional odds between studies was not appropriate.

When the assumption of proportional odds across all covariates is appropriate, the meta-analysis model (5.7) can be used, and the test for heterogeneity in the log-odds ratios across studies can be tested by fitting a model which extends model (5.7) to include a study by treatment interaction term. This interaction term can be fitted and tested by changing the MODEL statement to

```
MODEL y = study treat study*treat/ type1 dist = multinomial
        link = cumlogit;
```

Table 5.8 shows the meta-analysis results under the proportional odds assumption for the tacrine studies. It can be seen that, even though the assumption of proportional odds between studies was not considered appropriate, making this assumption has had little effect on the estimate of the treatment difference.

**Table 5.8**  Fixed effects meta-analysis of the log-odds ratio from a proportional odds model for the tacrine studies

| Study | Treatment | Category | | | | | $\hat{\theta}_i$ | $se(\hat{\theta}_i)$ |
|---|---|---|---|---|---|---|---|---|
| | | C1 | C2 | C3 | C4 | C5 | | |
| 1 | Tacrine | 4 | 23 | 45 | 22 | 2 | 0.284 | 0.261 |
| | Placebo | 2 | 22 | 54 | 29 | 3 | | |
| 2 | Tacrine | 14 | 119 | 180 | 54 | 6 | 0.224 | 0.242 |
| | Placebo | 1 | 22 | 35 | 11 | 3 | | |
| 3 | Tacrine | 13 | 20 | 24 | 10 | 1 | 0.360 | 0.332 |
| | Placebo | 7 | 16 | 17 | 10 | 3 | | |
| 4 | Tacrine | 21 | 106 | 175 | 62 | 17 | 0.785 | 0.174 |
| | Placebo | 8 | 24 | 73 | 52 | 13 | | |
| 5 | Tacrine | 3 | 14 | 19 | 3 | 0 | 0.492 | 0.421 |
| | Placebo | 2 | 13 | 18 | 7 | 1 | | |

Test of treat difference, $\chi^2 = 21.23$; (1 df), $p < 0.001$
Test for heterogeneity, $\chi^2 = 5.93$; (4 df), $p = 0.20$
Estimate of treatment difference $(\hat{\beta}_1) = 0.517$; $se(\hat{\beta}_1) = 0.113$
95% CI $= (0.296, 0.737)$

Comparison with Table 5.7 shows a change in the estimate of the log-odds ratio from 0.505 to 0.517, and a change in the standard error from 0.112 to 0.113.

## 5.5   FIXED EFFECTS MODELS FOR SURVIVAL DATA

### 5.5.1   A fixed effects meta-analysis model

Suppose that the response variable $y_{ij}$ is the time from randomization until the event of interest occurs, referred to as the 'survival time'. A patient who has been observed to have the event of interest will have a known survival time. A patient who has not will have a right-censored survival time, censored at the date they were last seen. The actual survival time is to be used in the analysis. Let $h_{ij}(t)$ be the hazard function and $S_{ij}(t)$ the survivor function for patient $j$ in study $i$.

The modelling approach taken here is based on the proportional hazards model (Cox, 1972). This model is referred to as a semi-parametric model as no distributional assumption is made for the survival times. The proportional hazards model is defined by

$$\log\left(\frac{h_{ij}(t)}{h_0(t)}\right) = \eta_{ij}, \qquad t > 0,$$

where $\eta_{ij}$ is a linear combination of explanatory variables, and $h_0(t)$ is the hazard function relating to a patient for whom all values of the explanatory variables are set to 0. The function $h_0(t)$ is known as the *baseline hazard function*. No assumption is made about its actual form.

Consider the proportional hazards model in which the explanatory variables are study and treatment:

$$\log\left(\frac{h_{ij}(t)}{h_0(t)}\right) = \beta_{0i} + \beta_1 x_{1ij}. \tag{5.12}$$

The parameter $\beta_1$ represents the log-hazard ratio for treatment relative to control, which is assumed common across all studies and for all $t > 0$.

In model (5.12) there is an assumption of a common baseline hazard function for all patients. However, the assumption of a common baseline hazard function across all studies seems to be rather restrictive. This assumption can be relaxed by allowing a different baseline hazard function for each study. This results in a stratified model, similar to that discussed in Section 5.4.1 in connection with ordinal data. The stratified model is given by

$$\log\left(\frac{h_{ij}(t)}{h_{0i}(t)}\right) = \beta_1 x_{1ij}, \tag{5.13}$$

where $h_{0i}$ represents the baseline hazard function for patients in study $i$ (in this case patients in the control group). It is model (5.13) which is analogous to that used in Chapter 4, as in both cases there is stratification by study. Attention will be focused on the models stratified by study, although in Section 5.5.7 there is discussion of the approach based on the meta-analysis model (5.12).

## 5.5.2 Estimation and hypothesis testing

Maximum likelihood estimation of the parameters for both the Cox proportional hazards model and the stratified models can be obtained, for example using SAS PROC PHREG. This procedure uses the observed Fisher's information matrix.

Models are compared by means of the likelihood ratio statistic, that is, the change in deviance ($-2$ times the log-likelihood) between two models, one of which contains the parameter(s) of interest while the other is identical except that it does not contain the parameter(s) of interest. The resulting test statistic is compared with the chi-squared distribution. Further details are provided in Section A.4 of the Appendix.

To fit model (5.13), the following SAS statements can be used:

```
PROC PHREG;
MODEL  y * cens(0) = treat / ties = discrete;
STRATA study;
```

where 'cens' is the censoring variable which takes the value 0 if the survival time is censored and 1 otherwise. The option 'ties $=$ discrete' requests that the Cox approach to the adjustment for tied survival times is used. In the SAS output, the parameter $\beta_1$ is associated with the parameter 'treat'.

To test the null hypothesis that the treatment difference in all studies is equal to 0, model (5.13) is compared with a model in which there are no terms,

$$\log \left( \frac{h_{ij}(t)}{h_{0i}(t)} \right) = 0. \tag{5.14}$$

The change in deviance between models (5.13) and (5.14) is compared with the chi-squared distribution with one degree of freedom. This test statistic is produced in the SAS output from fitting model (5.13), and is analogous to the $U$ statistic described in Chapter 4.

### 5.5.3   Testing for heterogeneity in the log-hazard ratio across studies

Heterogeneity can be tested by fitting a model which includes a study by treatment interaction term. A model which assumes a common baseline hazard function for all patients in the same study and includes the study by treatment interaction would be given by

$$\log \left( \frac{h_{ij}(t)}{h_{0i}(t)} \right) = \beta_{1i} x_{1ij}. \tag{5.15}$$

The test for heterogeneity would involve a comparison between model (5.13) and model (5.15). The change in deviance between the two models is compared with the chi-squared distribution on $r - 1$ degrees of freedom. Such a test is analogous to the test for heterogeneity based on the $Q$ statistic described in Chapter 4.

As an example, the following code could be used to fit model (5.15) with four studies:

```
PROC PHREG;
MODEL  y * cens(0) = treat1 treat2 treat3 treat4 / ties =discrete;
STRATA study;
```

where 'treat1' takes the value 1 for a subject in the treated group in study 1 and 0 otherwise, 'treat2' takes the value 1 for a subject in the treated group in study 2 and 0 otherwise, and so on.

### 5.5.4   Example: Mortality following myocardial infarction

Consider the MDPIT study described in Section 3.3.1. The survival times recorded to the nearest day are used in the analyses presented in this chapter. Results of the hypothesis tests in connection with the overall treatment difference and the region by treatment interaction are presented in Table 5.9. The chi-squared statistic for testing the region by treatment interaction term is not significant

**Table 5.9**    Mortality following myocardial infarction: comparison of models

| Model comparisons | Effect tested | Change in deviance | Change in degrees of freedom | p-value |
|---|---|---|---|---|
| (5.13) vs (5.14) | Treat | 0.003 | 1 | 0.96 |
| (5.15) vs (5.13) | Region by Treat | 9.16 | 6 | 0.16 |

**Table 5.10**    Fixed effects meta-analysis of the log-hazard ratio for mortality on diltiazem relative to placebo for the MDPIT study, based on a stratified proportional hazards model

| Region | Diltiazem | | Placebo | | $\hat{\theta}_i$ | se($\hat{\theta}_i$) |
|---|---|---|---|---|---|---|
| | Number of deaths | Total number of patients | Number of deaths | Total number of patients | | |
| New York City (US) | 33 | 262 | 25 | 256 | 0.282 | 0.265 |
| Northeast (US) | 46 | 305 | 39 | 298 | 0.145 | 0.218 |
| Mideast (US) | 4 | 72 | 13 | 71 | −1.244 | 0.572 |
| Midwest (US) | 24 | 127 | 19 | 125 | 0.258 | 0.307 |
| Southwest (US) | 23 | 169 | 28 | 184 | −0.123 | 0.282 |
| Ontario (Canada) | 21 | 121 | 27 | 122 | −0.293 | 0.291 |
| Quebec (Canada) | 15 | 176 | 16 | 178 | −0.071 | 0.359 |

Test of treatment difference, $\chi^2 = 0.003$; (1 df), $p = 0.96$
Test for heterogeneity, $\chi^2 = 9.16$; (6 df), $p = 0.16$
Estimate of treatment difference $(\hat{\beta}_1) = -0.006$; se$(\hat{\beta}_1) = 0.110$
95% CI $= (-0.221, 0.209)$

($p = 0.16$), providing no evidence of heterogeneity in the log-hazard ratio across regions. There is no evidence either of a treatment difference ($p = 0.96$).

Table 5.10 shows the results of the fixed effects meta-analysis. Each individual region estimate of the log-hazard ratio and its standard error have been calculated as in Table 4.8. The fixed effects estimate of the log-hazard ratio is −0.006, with standard error 0.110.

### 5.5.5    Modelling of individual patient data versus combining study estimates

For the reasons detailed in Section 5.3.5, the meta-analysis based on modelling individual patient data is similar but not identical to that based on combining study estimates presented in Table 4.9. From Table 4.9 the log-hazard ratio estimate is 0.005 with standard error 0.111, and from Table 5.10 they are −0.006 and 0.110 respectively. For this example, there is good agreement between the two approaches, both indicating very little difference between the treatments. In general, the overall conclusions from the two approaches will be the same.

### 5.5.6   Testing the assumption of proportional hazards between treatments

The assumption of proportional hazards between treatments can be investigated by fitting a piecewise Cox model. Suppose that the time period for patient follow-up is divided into $m$ intervals $(0, u_1], (u_1, u_2], \ldots, (u_{m-1}, \infty]$. Within each of these intervals it is assumed that the hazards are proportional. The piecewise Cox model is given by

$$\log \left( \frac{h_{ij}(t)}{h_{0i}(t)} \right) = \beta_1 x_{1ij} + \sum_{k=2}^{m} \beta_{2k} x_{2kij}(t) x_{1ij}, \tag{5.16}$$

where $x_{2kij}(t)$ is equal to 1 if $u_{k-1} < t \leqslant u_k$, and 0 otherwise, for $k = 2, \ldots, m$ and $u_m = \infty$. The terms $x_{2kij}(t) x_{1ij}$ are known as *time-dependent variables*. The log-hazard ratio for the treatment relative to the control changes from one time interval to the next. For the first time interval it is equal to $\beta_1$, for the second interval it is equal to $\beta_1 + \beta_{22}$, and so on. To test the assumption of proportional hazards between treatments model (5.16), with $m$ degrees of freedom associated with the model terms, is compared with model (5.13). The change in deviance between the two models is compared with the chi-squared distribution with $m - 1$ degrees of freedom.

As an example, the following SAS statements may be used to fit model (5.16) for the four time intervals $(0, 365], (365, 731], (731, 1096], (1096, \infty]$:

```
PROC PHREG;
MODEL y*cens(0) = treat piece2 piece3 piece4 / ties = discrete;
piece2 = ((y gt 365) - (y gt 731))*treat;
piece3 = ((y gt 731) - (y gt 1096))*treat;
piece4 = (y gt 1096)*treat;
STRATA study;
```

In the MODEL statement, programming statements have been included to create the time-dependent explanatory variables.

For the MDPIT study, the follow-up time was divided into seven intervals. These consisted of 6-monthly intervals for the first 3 years plus a last category of more than 3 years. The change in deviance between the two models was calculated to be 4.58 which, compared with the chi-squared distribution with six degrees of freedom, was not significant ($p = 0.60$). This indicated that the assumption of proportional hazards between treatments was satisfactory.

### 5.5.7   A proportional hazards model for studies and treatments

When the assumption of a common baseline hazard function across all studies is appropriate, the meta-analysis model (5.12) can be used and the test for heterogeneity in the log-hazard ratio across studies can be tested by fitting a model which extends model (5.12) to include a study by treatment interaction term.

As an example, the following SAS statements can be used to fit model (5.12) to data from four studies:

```
PROC PHREG;
MODEL y*cens(0) = study1 study2 study3 treat / ties = discrete;
```

Unfortunately PROC PHREG does not contain a CLASS statement, so that factors must be entered into the MODEL statement as a set of indicator variables. The term 'study1' takes the value 1 for a patient in study 1 and 0 otherwise, 'study2' takes the value 1 for a patient in study 2 and 0 otherwise, and so on. In the SAS output $\beta_1$ is associated with the parameter 'treat'.

To test for heterogeneity in the log-hazard ratios across studies, a study by treatment interaction term can be included in the MODEL statement as follows:

```
MODEL y*cens(0) = study1 study2 study3 treat s1trt s2trt s3trt/
                  ties = discrete;
```

where 's1trt' takes the value 1 for patients in the treated group in study 1 and 0 otherwise, 's2trt' takes the value 1 for patients in the treated group in study 2 and 0 otherwise, and so on.

Table 5.11 shows the meta-analysis results under the proportional hazards assumption for studies and treatments. The results are very similar to those in Table 5.10.

**Table 5.11** Fixed effects meta-analysis of the log-hazard ratio for mortality on diltiazem relative to placebo for the MDPIT study, based on a proportional hazards model

| Region | Diltiazem | | Placebo | | $\hat{\theta}_i$ | se($\hat{\theta}_i$) |
|---|---|---|---|---|---|---|
| | Number of deaths | Total number of patients | Number of deaths | Total number of patients | | |
| New York City (US) | 33 | 262 | 25 | 256 | 0.282 | 0.265 |
| Northeast (US) | 46 | 305 | 39 | 298 | 0.145 | 0.218 |
| Mideast (US) | 4 | 72 | 13 | 71 | −1.244 | 0.572 |
| Midwest (US) | 24 | 127 | 19 | 125 | 0.258 | 0.307 |
| Southwest (US) | 23 | 169 | 28 | 184 | −0.123 | 0.282 |
| Ontario (Canada) | 21 | 121 | 27 | 122 | −0.293 | 0.291 |
| Quebec (Canada) | 15 | 176 | 16 | 178 | −0.071 | 0.359 |

Test of treatment difference, $\chi^2 = 0.005$; (1 df), $p = 0.94$
Test for heterogeneity, $\chi^2 = 9.41$; (6 df), $p = 0.15$
Estimate of treatment difference ($\hat{\beta}_1$) = −0.008, se($\hat{\beta}_1$) = 0.110
95% CI = (−0.223, 0.207)

## 5.6    FIXED EFFECTS MODELS FOR INTERVAL-CENSORED SURVIVAL DATA

### 5.6.1    A fixed effects meta-analysis model

Consider the situation in which the response variable is a survival time, but the exact time of the event is unknown. Instead, it is known that the event occurred during a particular interval of time. The time intervals are defined by $(0, u_1], (u_1, u_2], \ldots, (u_m, \infty]$. Let $S_{ij}(t)$ be the survivor function for patient $j$ in study $i$. Let $\pi_{ijk}$ be the probability that patient $j$ from study $i$ has an event in the interval $(u_{k-1}, u_k]$ given that they have not had an event in a previous interval, where $k = 1, \ldots, m$, and $u_0 = 0$.

The modelling approach taken is to assume a proportional hazards model which can be shown (Whitehead, 1989; Collett, 1994) to be equivalent to the model

$$\log\{-\log(1 - \pi_{ijk})\} = \alpha_k + \eta_{ij}, \qquad k = 1, \ldots, m,$$

where the intercept $\alpha_k$ is equal to $\log[-\log\{S_0(u_k)/S_0(u_{k-1})\}]$, $\eta_{ij}$ is a linear combination of explanatory variables, and $S_0(t)$ is the survivor function of a patient for whom all values of the explanatory variables are set to 0. No assumption is made about the actual form of the baseline survivor function. The model is a linear model for the complementary log-log transformation of $\pi_{ijk}$, and can be fitted using standard methods for modelling binary data.

Consider the proportional hazards model

$$\log\{-\log(1 - \pi_{ijk})\} = \alpha_k + \beta_{0i} + \beta_1 x_{1ij}, \tag{5.17}$$

in which the explanatory variables are study and treatment. The parameter $\beta_1$ represents the log-hazard ratio which is assumed common across all intercepts and studies. In this model there is an assumption of proportional hazards across all studies, so that the survival distributions for the individual studies share common features, as defined by the $\alpha_k$. It can be seen that model (5.17) is similar to model (5.7), and that the assumption with regard to studies can be relaxed by fitting a model which is similar to model (5.8), namely

$$\log\{-\log(1 - \pi_{ijk})\} = \alpha_{ik} + \beta_1 x_{1ij}. \tag{5.18}$$

It is model (5.18) which is analogous to that used in Chapter 4, as in both cases there is stratification by study. Attention will be focused on models stratified by study, although in Section 5.6.7 there is discussion of the approach based on the meta-analysis model (5.17).

## 5.6.2 Estimation and hypothesis testing

Parameter estimates are obtained using the method of maximum likelihood. The approach is similar to that for the linear logistic regression model, as described in Section 5.3.2. However, in this case, each patient contributes multiple recordings of binary data, equal to the number of time intervals of observation, that is, the number of intervals during which they belong to the 'at risk' set. Occurrence of the event during an interval constitutes a 'success'; otherwise the binary outcome is recorded as a 'failure'. As the underlying binary variables are independent, estimation and hypothesis testing proceed as for logistic regression analysis as described in Section 5.3.2, with the exception that the complementary log-log function is used instead of the logit function as the link function.

To test the null hypothesis that the treatment difference in all studies is equal to 0, model (5.18) is compared with a model which only contains the study effects, namely

$$\log\{-\log(1 - \pi_{ijk})\} = \alpha_{ik}. \tag{5.19}$$

Model (5.18) has $mr + 1$ degrees of freedom associated with the model terms, and model (5.19) has mr. The change in deviance between these two models is compared with the chi-squared distribution with one degree of freedom. This is analogous to the $U$ statistic described in Chapter 4.

To fit model (5.18) and to obtain the results of the likelihood ratio test mentioned above, the following SAS statements can be used:

```
PROC GENMOD;
CLASS int study;
MODEL  y = int study int*study treat / type1 dist = bin
        link = cloglog waldci;
```

where 'y' takes the value 1 if the event occurs in that particular time interval for that patient and 0 otherwise, and 'int' is a factor which associates each binary observation with the corresponding time interval. The estimate of $\beta_1$ is associated with the parameter 'treat' in the SAS output. As discussed in Section 5.3.2, the data may alternatively be entered in binomial form, and the MODEL statement modified accordingly.

## 5.6.3 Testing for heterogeneity in the log-hazard ratio across studies

Heterogeneity in the log-hazard ratio across studies can be tested by including a study by treatment interaction term in the model. A model which includes the study by treatment interaction would be given by

$$\log\{-\log(1 - \pi_{ijk})\} = \alpha_{ik} + \beta_{1i}x_{1ij}, \tag{5.20}$$

which has $(m + 1)r$ degrees of freedom associated with the model terms. The test for heterogeneity is a test of the study by treatment interaction term and involves the comparison of models (5.18) and (5.20). The change in deviance between these two models is compared with the chi-squared distribution on $r - 1$ degrees of freedom. Such a test is analogous to the test for heterogeneity based on the $Q$ statistic described in Chapter 4.

Model (5.20) may be fitted and the test for heterogeneity conducted by changing the MODEL statement in Section 5.6.2 as follows:

```
MODEL y = int study int*study treat study*treat / type1 dist = bin
          link = cloglog;
```

In the SAS output, the appropriate chi-squared statistic is that associated with the 'study*treat' term. As noted in Section 5.2.3, the parameter associated with 'treat' is $\beta_{1r}$ and the parameter associated with 'study $i$ * treat' is $(\beta_{1i} - \beta_{1r})$.

### 5.6.4    Example: Ulcer recurrence

For the ulcer recurrence example described in Section 3.4.1, the chi-squared statistic for testing the country by treatment interaction term is not significant $(p = 0.71)$, providing no evidence of heterogeneity in the log-hazard ratio across countries (Table 5.12). The treatment difference is also not statistically significant $(p = 0.24)$.

Table 5.13 shows the results of the fixed effects meta-analysis. Each individual country estimate of the log-hazard ratio and its standard error have been calculated as in Table 4.11. The fixed effects estimate of the log-odds ratio is $-0.280$, with standard error $0.241$.

### 5.6.5    Modelling of individual patient data versus combining study estimates

As is the case for binary data (see Section 5.3.5), the meta-analysis of interval-censored survival data based on modelling individual patient data is similar but not identical to that based on combining study estimates presented in Table 4.12.

**Table 5.12**   Ulcer recurrence: comparison of models

| Model comparisons | Effect | Change in deviance | Change in degrees of freedom | $p$-value |
|---|---|---|---|---|
| (5.18) vs (5.19) | Treat | 1.35 | 1 | 0.24 |
| (5.20) vs (5.18) | Country by Treat | 1.39 | 3 | 0.71 |

**Table 5.13**   Fixed effects meta-analysis of the log-hazard ratio for ulcer recurrence on treatment 2 relative to treatment 1, based on a stratified proportional hazards model

| Country | Treatment 2 | | Treatment 1 | | $\hat{\theta}_i$ | $se(\hat{\theta}_i)$ |
|---|---|---|---|---|---|---|
| | Number with ulcer recurrence | Total number patients | Number with ulcer recurrence | Total number patients | | |
| Austria | 15 | 55 | 19 | 59 | −0.290 | 0.347 |
| Belgium | 7 | 29 | 4 | 23 | 0.195 | 0.630 |
| France | 5 | 22 | 6 | 25 | −0.129 | 0.607 |
| Holland and Norway | 5 | 65 | 9 | 59 | −0.748 | 0.558 |

Test of treatment difference, $\chi^2 = 1.35$; (1 df), $p = 0.24$
Test for heterogeneity, $\chi^2 = 1.39$; (3 df), $p = 0.71$
Estimate of treatment difference $(\hat{\beta}_1) = -0.280$; $se(\hat{\beta}_1) = 0.241$
95% CI $= (-0.752, 0.193)$

From Table 4.12 the log-hazard ratio estimate is $-0.278$ with standard error $0.244$, and from Table 5.13 they are $-0.280$ and $0.241$ respectively. For this example, there is good agreement between the two approaches. In general, the overall conclusions from the two approaches will be the same.

## 5.6.6   Testing the assumption of proportional hazards between treatments across timepoints

The assumption of proportional hazards for treatments across timepoints can be investigated by fitting the model

$$\log\{-\log(1 - \pi_{ijk})\} = \alpha_{ik} + \beta_{2k}x_{1ij}. \qquad (5.21)$$

This model, which has $m(r + 1)$ degrees of freedom associated with the model terms, is compared with model (5.18). The change in deviance between the two models is compared with the chi-squared distribution with $m - 1$ degrees of freedom.

Model (5.21) may be fitted and the test for proportional hazards conducted by changing the MODEL statement in Section 5.6.2 as follows:

```
MODEL y = int study int*study treat int*treat / type1 dist = bin
        link = cloglog;
```

In the SAS output, the appropriate chi-squared statistic is that associated with the 'int*treat' term. The parameter associated with 'treat' is $\beta_{2m}$ and the parameter associated with 'int $k$ * treat' is $\beta_{2k} - \beta_{2m}$.

For the ulcer recurrence example, the change in deviance was calculated to be 2.00, which compared with the chi-squared statistic with 1 degree of freedom was not statistically significant ($p = 0.16$). This indicated that the assumption of proportional hazards between treatments across timepoints was satisfactory.

### 5.6.7   A proportional hazards model for studies and treatments

A test of the assumption of proportional hazards between studies would involve a comparison between model (5.17) and model (5.18), which have respectively $m + r$ and $mr + 1$ degrees of freedom associated with the model terms.

Model (5.17) may be fitted by changing the MODEL statement in Section 5.6.2 as follows:

```
MODEL y = int study treat / type1 dist = bin link = cloglog waldci;
```

For the ulcer recurrence example, the change in deviance between models (5.17) and (5.18) was calculated to be 7.52, which compared with the chi-squared distribution on three degrees of freedom just failed to reach statistical significance ($p = 0.06$). This indicated that the assumption of proportional hazards between studies might not be satisfactory.

When the proportional hazards assumption across studies and treatments is considered appropriate, the meta-analysis model (5.17) can be used and the test for heterogeneity in the log-hazard ratio across studies can be tested by fitting a model which extends model (5.17) to include a study by treatment interaction term. In order to include and test the interaction term, the MODEL statement is modified as follows:

**Table 5.14**   Fixed effects meta-analysis of the log-hazard ratio for ulcer recurrence on treatment 2 relative to treatment 1, based on a proportional hazards model

| Country | Treatment 2 | | Treatment 1 | | $\hat{\theta}_i$ | $se(\hat{\theta}_i)$ |
|---|---|---|---|---|---|---|
| | Number with ulcer recurrence | Total number patients | Number with ulcer recurrence | Total number patients | | |
| Austria | 15 | 55 | 19 | 59 | −0.290 | 0.347 |
| Belgium | 7 | 29 | 4 | 23 | 0.195 | 0.630 |
| France | 5 | 22 | 6 | 25 | −0.129 | 0.607 |
| Holland and Norway | 5 | 65 | 9 | 59 | −0.748 | 0.558 |

Test of treatment difference, $\chi^2 = 1.32$; (1 df), $p = 0.25$
Test for heterogeneity, $\chi^2 = 1.42$; (3 df), $p = 0.70$
Estimate of treatment difference $(\hat{\beta}_1) = -0.276$, $se(\hat{\beta}_1) = 0.241$
95% CI = $(-0.748, 0.196)$

```
MODEL y = int study treat study*treat/ type1 dist = bin
      link = cloglog;
```

Table 5.14 shows the meta-analysis results under the proportional hazards assumption for studies and treatments. The results are very similar to those in Table 5.13.

## 5.7 THE TREATMENT DIFFERENCE AS A RANDOM EFFECT

Random effects can be introduced into a meta-analysis model within the framework of a hierarchical (multilevel) model. The usual approach is to include the random effects as part of the term $\eta_{ij}$, which represents the linear combination of explanatory variables, and assume that they have a multivariate normal distribution, the variance components of which are to be estimated from the data. In this case there are two levels: patient at the lower level (level 1) nested within study at the higher level (level 2).

Consider the fixed effects model (5.3), which contains the study by treatment interaction term. Here $\eta_{ij}$ is defined as

$$\eta_{ij} = \beta_{0i} + \beta_{1i}x_{1ij}.$$

As an alternative to defining the study by treatment interaction terms as fixed effects, they can be defined as level 2 random effects as follows:

$$\eta_{ij} = \beta_{0i} + \gamma_{1i}x_{1ij}, \tag{5.22}$$

where $\gamma_{1i} = \beta_1 + \nu_{1i}$, and the $\nu_{1i}$ are normally distributed random effects with mean 0 and variance $\tau^2$. Rewriting this, grouping separately the fixed and random effects, yields

$$\eta_{ij} = \beta_{0i} + \beta_1 x_{1ij} + \nu_{1i}x_{1ij}. \tag{5.23}$$

The meta-analysis model (5.23) is an example of a mixed model, because it contains both fixed and random effects. The analogy with the random effects model presented in Section 4.3.1 as (4.2) can be seen, as $\beta_1$ is equal to $\theta$ and $\nu_{1i}$ is equal to $\nu_i$.

## 5.8 RANDOM EFFECTS MODELS FOR NORMALLY DISTRIBUTED DATA

### 5.8.1 A random effects meta-analysis model

The random effects meta-analysis model for the normally distributed responses $y_{ij}$ is given by

$$y_{ij} = \alpha + \beta_{0i} + \beta_1 x_{1ij} + \nu_{1i}x_{1ij} + \varepsilon_{ij}. \tag{5.24}$$

This model contains two random terms, namely $\nu_{1i}$ and $\varepsilon_{ij}$, and is an example of a general linear mixed model. It fits into a general framework for meta-analysis models, as discussed by Higgins *et al.* (2001). The $\varepsilon_{ij}$, which are the level 1 terms, are assumed to be uncorrelated with the level 2 terms, $\nu_{1i}$.

### 5.8.2 Estimation and hypothesis testing

Estimates will be required for the fixed effect parameters $\alpha$, $\beta_{0i}$ and $\beta_1$ and the variance components $\sigma^2$ (or $\sigma_i^2$) and $\tau^2$. These can be calculated using a maximum likelihood approach. However, the alternative residual (restricted) maximum likelihood approach is generally preferred, as it avoids the downward bias of ML estimates of the variance parameters. The ML and REML approaches are analogous to those described in Section 4.3.8, although when individual patient data are available the full likelihood for the data can be utilized, instead of the likelihood based on study estimates of the treatment difference. For the fixed effects model (5.1), in which there is only the one variance component $\sigma^2$, at level 1, REML is equivalent to the method of least squares.

The random effects $\nu_{1i}$ can be estimated using shrinkage estimates. Shrinkage estimates of $\gamma_{1i} = \beta_1 + \nu_{1i}$ can also be obtained. The shrinkage estimate of $\gamma_{1i}$ is a prediction of the location within the normal distribution from which the estimate of treatment difference from study $i$ has arisen. It is an optimally weighted linear combination of the estimated overall treatment difference, $\hat{\beta}_1$, and the estimated treatment difference from study $i$. The degree of shrinkage depends on the magnitude of the variation in the study estimates of treatment difference and the number of patients in study $i$, $n_i$. When $n_i$ is small, the shrinkage estimate for the treatment difference in study $i$ will be close to the overall estimate $\hat{\beta}_1$, but as $n_i$ increases it moves closer to the estimated difference from study $i$.

Some details of the methods mentioned above can be found in Section A.7 of the Appendix, but for a comprehensive coverage the reader is referred to Brown and Prescott (1999), which also discusses their implementation in SAS PROC MIXED. The next two paragraphs present a brief summary of the procedures which can be used for hypothesis testing.

Wald tests can be used for inferences concerning the variance components. Although valid for large samples, the Wald test can be unreliable due to the skewed and bounded nature of the sampling distribution for a variance component. Likelihood ratio tests based on the REML likelihood are preferable, although the results should be interpreted with caution when estimates of the variance components are close to 0. For the likelihood ratio test the change in deviance ($-2$ times the REML log-likelihood) between models with and without the terms of interest is compared with the chi-squared distribution with degrees of freedom equal to the difference in the number of variance components between the two models (Morrell, 1998). Alternatively, parametric bootstrapping can be utilized (Efron and Tibshirani, 1993).

Wald tests can be used for inferences concerning the fixed effect parameters. The Wald test statistic has a chi-squared distribution under the null hypothesis when the variance components are known. However, when the variance components are estimated, the estimated standard errors of the fixed effect parameters will tend to be downwardly biased. One option is to compare the Wald test statistic with the *F* distribution. Usually this statistic only approximately follows the *F* distribution and the denominator degrees of freedom must be estimated. Kenward and Roger (1997) consider a scaled Wald statistic together with an *F* approximation to its sampling distribution, and estimate the denominator degrees of freedom using Satterthwaite's (1941) procedure. Likelihood ratio tests may be performed for the fixed effect parameters. However, the $(-2\times)$ log-likelihood values used in the comparison should be obtained from the ML procedure as the penalty term associated with REML depends on the fixed effect terms in the model. Welham and Thompson (1997) consider a likelihood ratio statistic based on modified REML log-likelihoods. Alternatively, parametric bootstrapping may be utilized.

REML procedures are now available in a number of statistical packages. SAS PROC MIXED implements both the ML and REML methods, the default option being REML. The package MLn uses an iterative generalized least-squares estimation procedure (IGLS) which has been shown to be equivalent to ML (Goldstein, 1986) and a restricted iterative generalized least-squares estimation procedure (RIGLS) which has been shown to be equivalent to REML (Goldstein, 1989). Details of the approach adopted by MLn can be found in Section A.8 of the Appendix. Wald statistics for the variance components are produced by both packages. The preferable REML likelihood ratio test statistics are available with SAS, and the parametric bootstrap may be performed using MLn. For the fixed effect parameters, SAS PROC MIXED produces Wald *F* and *t* statistics with the option of using the Kenward and Roger approach, amongst others. Within MLn parametric bootstrapping may be used.

The following PROC MIXED program may be used to fit model (5.24):

```
PROC MIXED;
CLASS study;
MODEL y = study treat/ htype = 1 ddfm = kenwardroger solution;
RANDOM treat/ subject = study;
```

The fixed effect terms appear in the MODEL statement and the random effect terms in the RANDOM statement. The 'subject = study' option declares that the random effect 'treat' varies from study to study. The 'htype = 1' option plays a similar role to the 'ss1' option in PROC GLM (see Section 5.2.2).

### 5.8.3   Example: Recovery time after anaesthesia

Table 5.15 shows the results of the random effects meta-analysis based on individual patient data for the anaesthetic study, in which a common variance parameter $\sigma^2$ has been assumed across all centres. The estimate of $\sigma^2$ is 0.503,

**Table 5.15** Random effects meta-analysis of the absolute mean difference (treatment A − treatment B) in log-recovery time, assuming a common $\sigma^2$ across all centres

|  | Random effects (individual patient data) REML | Random effects (combining centre estimates) REML |
|---|---|---|
| Test of $\beta_1 = 0$ | 14.29 (cf. $F_{1,9.26}$) | 14.48 (cf. $\chi_1^2$) |
|  | $p = 0.004$ | $p < 0.001$ |
| $\hat{\beta}_1$ [se($\hat{\beta}_1$)] | 0.615 [0.163] | 0.615 [0.162] |
| 95% CI | (0.249, 0.982) | (0.298, 0.932) |
| $\hat{\sigma}^2$ | 0.503 | 0.506 |
| $\hat{\tau}^2$ | 0.124 | 0.124 |

which is very close to 0.506, the estimated pooled variance $s_p^2$ from Section 4.2.9. For comparison, the results of the random effects analysis using REML estimation in conjunction with the centre estimates of the treatment difference (Table 4.33) are also shown in Table 5.15. Comparison of the two columns shows identical estimates (to three decimal places) of the treatment difference, $\hat{\beta}_1 = \hat{\theta}^* = 0.615$, with corresponding standard errors of 0.163 and 0.162. The REML estimates of the heterogeneity parameter are also identical (to three decimal places), $\hat{\tau}^2 = 0.124$. The confidence interval for the treatment difference in the first column is wider than that in the second, as it makes an allowance for the estimation of the variance components. The former is based on the $t$ distribution with degrees of freedom estimated to be 9.26 using Satterthwaite's procedure, as opposed to the normal distribution. This results in multiplication of the standard error by 2.253 instead of 1.96.

### 5.8.4   The connection between the multilevel model and the traditional mixed effects linear model

This subsection shows the connection, as described by Higgins *et al.* (2001), between the multilevel model (model 5.24) and the traditional mixed effects linear model, described in Searle (1971). The latter has a longer history than the multilevel model, and provides a useful framework when there are more than two treatment groups.

Within the traditional mixed effects linear model, let $y_{ihj}$ be the response from patient $j$ in treatment group $h$ in study $i$. The model which includes the study, treatment and study by treatment interaction terms is given by

$$y_{ihj} = \mu + s_i + t_h + (st)_{ih} + \varepsilon_{ihj}, \tag{5.25}$$

where $\mu$ is a constant, $s_i$ is the effect of being in study $i$, for $i = 1, \ldots, r$, $t_h$ the effect of being on treatment $h$, for $h = $ T, C, $(st)_{ih}$ the study by treatment interaction term, and $\varepsilon_{ihj}$ the residual error terms, for $j = 1, \ldots, n_{hi}$. In the case of homogeneous error terms, $\varepsilon_{ihj}$ are uncorrelated normally distributed random effects with expected value 0 and variance $\sigma^2$. The random effects meta-analysis model (5.24) corresponds to model (5.25) in which the study and treatment effects are fixed and the study by treatment interaction term is random. In the traditional mixed effects linear model, the treatment effects are fixed and the study and study by treatment interaction terms are random. Model (5.25) can be viewed as a three-level model with study at the highest level, treatment at the middle level and patient at the lowest level.

In order to facilitate the comparison with the multilevel model (24), the subscript $h$ can be removed and indicator variables used to code the treatment effects in model (5.25). Let $x_{1Tij}$ and $x_{1Cij}$ be the treatment indicator variables such that $x_{1Tij}$ takes the value 1 for a patient in the treated group and 0 otherwise and $x_{1Cij}$ takes the value 1 for a patient in the control group and 0 otherwise. The comparison with the random effects meta-analysis model can be made by expressing model (5.25) as

$$y_{ij} = \mu + s_i + \beta_{1T}x_{1Tij} + \beta_{1C}x_{1Cij} + v_{1Ti}x_{1Tij} + v_{1Ci}x_{1Cij} + \varepsilon_{ij}, \qquad (5.26)$$

where $j = 1, \ldots, n_i, n_i = n_{Ti} + n_{Ci}, s_i$ is the fixed study effect, $\beta_{1T} = t_T$ and $\beta_{1C} = t_C$ are the fixed treatment effects, $v_{1Ti} = (st)_{iT}$ and $v_{1Ci} = (st)_{iC}$ are the random study by treatment interaction effects and the $\varepsilon_{ij}$ are uncorrelated normally distributed random effects with expected value 0 and variance $\sigma^2$. The correlations between all of the random effects are assumed to be zero.

In model (5.26) constraints are required on $\beta_{1T}, \beta_{1C}, v_{1Ti}$ and $v_{1Ci}$ in order to make all parameters identifiable. Particular choices of constraints lead to the random effects meta-analysis model (5.24) with differing codings of the treatment covariate, $x_{1ij}$. For example, setting $v_{1Ci} = 0$, for $i = 1, \ldots, r, \beta_{1C} = 0$ and $v_{1Ti}$ to be normally distributed with mean 0 and variance $\sigma_\tau^2$ leads to $x_{1ij}$ being coded 1 for the treated group and 0 for the control group. In this case, $\beta_{1T} = \beta_1, v_{1Ti} = v_{1i}$ and $\sigma_\tau^2 = \tau^2$. Alternatively, setting $v_{1Ti} + v_{1Ci} = 0$, for $i = 1, \ldots, r, \beta_{1T} + \beta_{1C} = 0$ and $v_{1Ti}$ to be normally distributed with mean 0 and variance $\sigma_\tau^2$ leads to $x_{1ij}$ being coded $+\frac{1}{2}$ for the treated group and $-\frac{1}{2}$ for the control group. In this case, $\beta_{1T} = \beta_1/2, v_{1Ti} = v_{1i}/2$ and $\sigma_\tau^2 = \tau^2/2$.

In order to fit the mixed effects linear model, in which the study and treatment effects are fixed and the study by treatment interaction is random, the following set of SAS statements may be used:

```
PROC MIXED;
CLASS   study treat;
MODEL   y = study treat / htype = 1 ddfm = kenwardroger;
RANDOM  study*treat;
LSMEANS   treat / pdiff cl;
```

Provided that the control group appears as the last level of the factor 'treat', the output produced is that from fitting model (5.26), in which $\beta_{1C} = 0, v_{1Ci} = -v_{1Ti}$, for $i = 1, \ldots, r$, and $\nu_{1Ti}$ is normally distributed with mean 0 and variance $\sigma_\tau^2$. This is equivalent to a random effects meta-analysis model given by

$$y_{ij} = \alpha + \beta_{0i} + \beta_1 x_{1ij} + \nu_{1i} x_{2ij} + \varepsilon_{ij},$$

where $x_{1ij}$ takes the value 1 for the treated group and 0 for the control group and $x_{2ij}$ takes the value $+\frac{1}{2}$ for the treated group and $-\frac{1}{2}$ for the control group. In this case $\beta_{1T} = \beta_1$, $\nu_{1Ti} = \nu_{1i}/2$ and $\sigma_\tau^2 = \tau^2/2$. In the SAS output the difference between the treatment least-squares means provides an estimate of $\beta_1$, and the estimate alongside the covariance parameter 'study*treat' is an estimate of $\tau^2/2$.

## 5.9 RANDOM EFFECTS MODELS FOR BINARY DATA

### 5.9.1 A random effects meta-analysis model

The random effects meta-analysis model for the binary response in which the logit link function is to be used is given by

$$\log\left(\frac{p_{ij}}{1 - p_{ij}}\right) = \alpha + \beta_{0i} + \beta_1 x_{1ij} + \nu_{1i} x_{1ij}, \tag{5.27}$$

and has been discussed by Turner *et al.* (2000). This model is an example of a generalized linear mixed model.

### 5.9.2 Estimation and hypothesis testing

The methodology and the software for fitting generalized linear mixed models has recently been and still is undergoing development. For a full maximum likelihood analysis based on the joint marginal distribution, numerical integration techniques are required for calculation of the log-likelihood, score equations and Fisher's information matrix. As one of its options, the SAS procedure PROC NLMIXED directly maximizes an approximate integrated likelihood, using a numerical quadrature approach (see, for example, Hedeker and Gibbons, 1994; or Diggle *et al.*, 1994). Maximum likelihood estimates of the parameters are produced in this case.

Approximate inference, which is available with the MLn program, involves the use of either marginal quasi-likelihood (MQL) or penalized quasi-likelihood (PQL), and either first-order or second-order Taylor expansion approximations for the logit link function. Approximate ML and REML estimates are found via the IGLS and RIGLS procedures. PQL produces improved estimates of variance components in mixed models, in general, whilst model convergence is more easily achieved with MQL. The second-order Taylor expansion provides greater accuracy than the first-order expansion. Some details of this approach can be found in Section A.9 of the Appendix. For further details about generalized linear mixed models, the reader is referred to Brown and Prescott (1999).

Wald tests can be used for inferences concerning the variance components. However, for the reasons given in Section 5.8.2, likelihood ratio tests based on the REML are preferable. Wald tests can be used for inferences concerning the fixed effect parameters. However, the calculated standard errors of the parameter estimates and the corresponding CIs are usually too narrow, because no allowance is made for the estimation of the variance components. Within MLn parametric bootstrapping may be used.

For the examples in Sections 5.9.3 and 5.10.2, the package MLn or its interactive Windows version MLwiN was utilized. MLn is a command-driven program, and the commands for fitting model (5.27) are as follows:

```
DINPUT c1-c7
meta.dat
NAME c1 'subject' c2 'study' c3 'treat' c4 'y' c5 'cons' c6 'bcons'
c7 'denom'
RESP 'y'
IDEN 1 'subject' 2 'study'
EXPL 'treat' 'cons' 'bcons'
FPAR 'bcons'
SETV 2 'treat'
LINK 'bcons' G9
SETV 1 'bcons'
DUMM 'study' c8-c15
EXPL c8-c15
FPAT c:\mln\discrete
PREF pre
POST post
SET   b10   0
SET   b11   1
SET   b12   1
SET   b13   0
SET   b14   0
SET   b15   1
SET   b16   0
METH  0
```

The data set 'meta.dat' is a rectangular file containing seven variables. When the data are entered individually for each subject, the variable 'subject' contains a unique value for each subject, 'study' contains the study number, 'treat' the value of $x_{1ij}$, and 'y' the $y$-values. The data must be ordered according to the hierarchical structure of the model, with the values of the lowest level changing the most often. The variable 'denom' is the number of subjects contributing to the line of data, which in this case is 1. The variables 'cons' and 'bcons' take the value 1 everywhere. The variable 'cons' is used to define the intercept term in the model. The variable 'bcons' is needed to model the level 1 variance. If 'bcons' is set to 1, then the variation is purely binomial. The commands 'DINPUT' and 'NAME' read the data from 'meta.dat' into MLn. The data are held by MLn in the columns of a worksheet, referred to as c1, c2, and so on. The command 'RESP' defines the binary response variable. The command 'IDEN' defines the hierarchical structure of the data, that is, 'subject' is at level 1 and 'study' at level 2. The 'EXPL' command declares all variables which are involved in the model, including those connected with the variance terms. The 'FPAR' command acts as a toggle between adding and removing variables from the fixed effects part of the model. As 'bcons' is included in the 'EXPL' command, it is automatically included in the fixed effects part of the model unless removed by means of the 'FPAR' command. The first 'SETV' command requests that the treatment difference be random across studies. The 'LINK' and second 'SETV' commands set up the binomial errors. The command 'DUMM' creates a set of indicator variables for the study effect. In this example, there are nine studies, so that eight indicator variables are created. The subsequent 'EXPL' command declares these as fixed terms in the model.

MLn macros are used to fit non-linear models (Yang *et al.*, 1996), and it is assumed that these are located in the subdirectory called 'discrete'. The non-linear models are implemented by having two sets of macro instructions: the option 'PREF' makes the necessary data transformations to run a non-linear model and the option 'POST' transforms the data back to their original state. The settings for the non-linear macros are specified by the values in boxes B10–B16. B10 specifies the distribution of the data, which is set to 0 for the binomial distribution. B11 specifies whether a first- or second-order Taylor expansion is to be used, coded as 1 and 2 respectively. B12 specifies whether MQL or PQL is to be used, coded as 0 or 1 respectively. B13 specifies the link function, which in this case is 0 for the logit link function. B14 controls the estimation of the level 1 variance. If it is set to 0 then the variance is constrained to be binomial. B15 is set to 1 for a univariate model, and B16 set to 0 because it is not a mixed response model. The command 'METH' acts as a toggle between the use of IGLS and RIGLS. The default option is IGLS. The 'METH' command then switches the method to RIGLS.

It is possible to obtain approximate REML estimates based on a first-order PQL from SAS, although not via an established SAS procedure. Instead, a SAS macro known as GLIMMIX may be utilized. This macro, which can be used to fit all types of generalized linear mixed models, was written by Russ Wolfinger (from SAS) and is available from the SAS website at http://www.sas.com. The macro iteratively computes a pseudo-variable based on a first-order Taylor expansion of the link function and fits a weighted mixed model using PROC MIXED. It is based on the approach described in Wolfinger and O'Connell (1993). The following SAS code may be used for fitting model (5.27):

```
%inc 'c:\glimmix.sas';

%GLIMMIX( stmts = %str(
   CLASS study;
   MODEL y = study treat/ htype = 1 solution;
   RANDOM treat/ subject = study;
   ),
   error = binomial,
   link = logit
   )
RUN;
```

It can be seen that the SAS code includes a mixture of PROC MIXED and PROC GENMOD statements. The 'stmts' parameter includes the PROC MIXED statements which are similar to the PROC MIXED program in Section 5.8.2. However, 'y' now contains the binary observations. The 'error' option specifies the error distribution, which in this case is binomial. It plays the role of 'dist' in PROC GENMOD. The 'link' option specifies the link function as in PROC GENMOD.

### 5.9.3   Example: Pre-eclampsia

To illustrate the methodology a second example concerning binary data is introduced in which there is heterogeneity between the study estimates. This example, which involves nine clinical trials examining the effect of taking diuretics during pregnancy on the risk of pre-eclampsia, has been discussed by Brown and Prescott (1999) and Turner *et al.* (2000). The data, together with the individual study estimates of the log-odds ratio of pre-eclampsia on diuretic treatment relative to control, are presented in Table 5.16. Each study estimate and its standard error

**Table 5.16**   Trial estimates of the log-odds ratio of pre-eclampsia on diuretic treatment versus control during pregnancy, based on formulae (3.1) and (3.2)

| Trial | Treated group | | Control group | | $\hat{\theta}_i$ | $se(\hat{\theta}_i)$ |
|---|---|---|---|---|---|---|
| | Cases of pre-eclampsia | Total | Cases of pre-eclampsia | Total | | |
| 1 | 14 | 131 | 14 | 136 | 0.042 | 0.400 |
| 2 | 21 | 385 | 17 | 134 | −0.924 | 0.343 |
| 3 | 14 | 57 | 24 | 48 | −1.122 | 0.422 |
| 4 | 6 | 38 | 18 | 40 | −1.473 | 0.547 |
| 5 | 12 | 1011 | 35 | 760 | −1.391 | 0.338 |
| 6 | 138 | 1370 | 175 | 1336 | −0.297 | 0.121 |
| 7 | 15 | 506 | 20 | 524 | −0.262 | 0.347 |
| 8 | 6 | 108 | 2 | 103 | 1.089 | 0.828 |
| 9 | 65 | 153 | 40 | 102 | 0.135 | 0.261 |

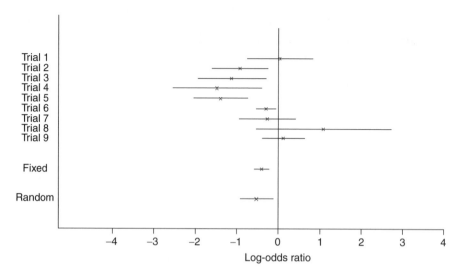

**Figure 5.1**   The log-odds ratio of pre-eclampsia on diuretic treatment relative to control. Individual study estimates and overall fixed and random effects estimates are presented, with 95% confidence intervals. Individual study calculations are based on formulae (3.1) and (3.2). The fixed and random effects estimates are calculated using the methods of Chapter 4 with the method of moments estimate of $\tau^2$.

are calculated using the unconditional maximum likelihood approach (3.1) and (3.2). A CI plot is shown in Figure 5.1.

The results of various meta-analyses of this dataset are presented in Table 5.17. In the first column are the results from a fixed effects meta-analysis of the study estimates from Table 5.16, based on the general fixed effects parametric approach described in Chapter 4. The fixed effects estimate from this analysis is the one presented in Figure 5.1. The fixed effects analysis based on individual patient data, as described in Section 5.3, is presented in the second column. These two sets of results are very similar. In the third and fourth columns are the results from random effects analyses using the general random effects parametric approach of Chapter 4. In the first case the estimation of the heterogeneity parameter $\tau^2$ is based on the method of moments (Figure 5.1) and in the second case on REML. Although the overall estimate of the log-odds ratio is similar in both cases, the larger estimate of $\tau^2$ from REML produces a wider CI. The last column shows the results of a random effects analysis using individual patient data. In this analysis, first-order PQL estimates under RIGLS were derived using MLn. The Wald test statistic is presented in the table for testing the treatment effect. The estimate of the log-odds ratio from this approach is similar to those obtained in the third and fourth column. Further analyses of this data set, including the use of bootstrapping to obtain a more accurate CI for the log-odds ratio, can be found in Turner *et al.* (2000). Brown and Prescott (1999) do not fit model (5.27), but

**Table 5.17** Meta-analysis of the log-odds ratio of pre-eclampsia on diuretic treatment versus control

| | Fixed effects (combining study estimates) | Fixed effects (individual patient data) | Random effects (combining study estimates) Method of moments | Random effects (combining study estimates) REML | Random effects (individual patient data) REML |
|---|---|---|---|---|---|
| Test of $\beta_1 = 0$ | 19.85 (cf. $\chi_1^2$) $p < 0.001$ | 21.65 (cf. $\chi_1^2$) $p < 0.001$ | 6.44 (cf. $\chi_1^2$) $p = 0.01$ | 5.37 (cf. $\chi_1^2$) $p = 0.02$ | 5.09 (cf. $\chi_1^2$) $p = 0.02$ |
| $\hat{\beta}_1$ [se($\hat{\beta}_1$)] | $-0.398$ [0.089] | $-0.410$ [0.089] | $-0.517$ [0.204] | $-0.518$ [0.224] | $-0.512$ [0.227] |
| 95% CI | $(-0.573, -0.223)$ | $(-0.584, -0.237)$ | $(-0.916, -0.118)$ | $(-0.956, -0.080)$ | $(-0.956, -0.068)$ |
| $\hat{\tau}^2$ | — | — | 0.230 | 0.300 | 0.321 |

instead consider the model in which both the study effects and the treatment differences are random. Such models are considered in Section 5.11.

## 5.10    RANDOM EFFECTS MODELS FOR OTHER DATA TYPES

Multilevel models for ordinal responses and for survival and interval-censored survival data are discussed by Goldstein (1995) and may be fitted using MLn via macros (Yang *et al.*, 1996). However, methods for inference are more complicated than for normally distributed and binary data, and are currently restricted to the use of Wald test statistics. In this section we consider application to ordinal responses, using the tacrine data set described in Section 3.5.1 as an illustration.

### 5.10.1    A random effects meta-analysis model for ordinal data

The random effects meta-analysis model for the ordinal response, stratified by study, is given by

$$\log \left( \frac{Q_{ijk}}{1 - Q_{ijk}} \right) = \alpha_{ik} + \beta_1 x_{1ij} + \nu_{1i} x_{1ij}, \qquad (5.28)$$

and has been discussed by Whitehead *et al.* (2001). To fit model (5.28) using MLn, the ordinal response for patient $j$ in study $i$ is considered as a correlated set of $m - 1$ binary response variables $Y_{ij1}, \ldots, Y_{ij,m-1}$, where the observed values are denoted by $y_{ij1}, \ldots, y_{ij,m-1}$. Let $y_{ijk}$ equal 1 if patient $j$ in study $i$ has a response in a category less than or equal to $k$, and 0 otherwise. This means that if the patient has a response in category 1 then $y_{ij1} = y_{ij2} = \ldots = y_{ij,m-1} = 1$, if the patient has a response in category 2 then $y_{ij1} = 0$ and $y_{ij2} = \ldots = y_{ij,m-1} = 1$, and so on. For a response in category $m$, $y_{ij1} = y_{ij2} = \ldots = y_{ij,m-1} = 0$. The random variable $Y_{ijk}$ has expected value $Q_{ijk}$. The $(h, k)$th element of the covariance matrix associated with the binary responses for patient $j$ in study $i$ is given by $Q_{ijh}(1 - Q_{ijk})$, for $h \leqslant k$, and $Q_{ijk}(1 - Q_{ijh})$ for $h > k$, $k = 1, \ldots, m - 1$. The model is then considered to have three levels, namely category (level 1), patient (level 2) and study (level 3), where category refers to the $m - 1$ correlated binary responses.

The following MLn commands may be used to fit model (5.28) with two studies and an ordinal response with three categories:

```
DINPUT c1-c12
meta.dat
NAME c1 'binm' c2 'subject' c3 'study' c4 'treat'
NAME c5 'alpha11' c6 'alpha12' c7 'alpha21' c8 'alpha22'
NAME c9 'y' c10 'cons' c11 'bcons' c12 'denom'
RESP 'y'
```

```
IDEN 1 'binm' 2 'subject' 3 'study'
EXPL 'cons' 'bcons' 'alpha11' 'alpha12' 'alpha21' 'alpha22'
EXPL 'treat'
FPAR 'bcons' 'cons'
SETV 3 'treat'
LINK 'bcons' G9
SETV 1 'bcons'
FPAT c:\mln\multicat
PREF pre
POST post

SET b10 1
SET b11 1
SET b12 1
SET b13 0
SET b14 0
SET b16 0
METH 0
```

The data set 'meta.dat' is a rectangular file containing 12 variables. Each patient contributes $m - 1$ lines of data. For patient $j$ in study $i$ the $m - 1$ values of 'y' are $y_{ij1}, \ldots, y_{ij,m-1}$. The variable 'binm' takes the value $k$ when the value in 'y' is $y_{ijk}$. The variable 'alphaik' for $i = 1, \ldots, r$ and $k = 1, \ldots, m - 1$ takes the value 1 when the patient is in study $i$ and the value in 'y' is $y_{ijk}$, and 0 otherwise. The data must be ordered according to the hierarchical structure – that is, by study, subject and binary response variable – with the lowest level changing the most quickly. It is assumed that the MLn macros used to fit the non-linear model are located in the subdirectory called 'multicat'. The settings for the non-linear macros are specified by the values in boxes B10–B16. B10 specifies the distribution of the data, which is set to 1 for an ordered multinomial distribution. B14 controls the estimation of the level 1 variance; if it is set to 0 then the variance is constrained to be multinomial. The other boxes serve the same purpose as described for the program presented in Section 5.9.2.

## 5.10.2   Example: Global impression of change in Alzheimer's disease

Table 5.18 shows the results of fitting model (5.28) to the tacrine studies described in Section 3.5.1. using individual patient data. In the analysis first-order PQL estimates under RIGLS were derived using MLn. The estimate of the overall log-odds ratio and its standard error, based on individual patient data, are identical (to three decimal places) to those based on combining study estimates using the REML approach (Table 4.32). Estimates of the heterogeneity parameter are in close agreement.

**Table 5.18**  Random effects meta-analysis of the log-odds ratio from a stratified proportional odds model for the tacrine studies

| | Random effects (individual patient data) REML |
|---|---|
| Test of $\beta_1 = 0$ | 10.67 (cf. $\chi_1^2$) |
| | $p = 0.001$ |
| $\hat{\beta}_1 [\mathrm{se}(\hat{\beta}_1)]$ | 0.467 [0.143] |
| 95% CI | (0.187, 0.747) |
| $\hat{\tau}^2$ | 0.032 |

## 5.11  RANDOM STUDY EFFECTS

In the two-level hierarchical model it perhaps seems logical also to include the study effects as random effects rather than fixed effects. In this case patient groups recruited into different studies are considered to be a random sample from a wider collection of patient populations. Treating the study effects as random parameters is controversial in the field of meta-analysis. The issue is analogous to that for multicentre trials, about which there has been considerable debate. The implications of fitting the study effects as fixed or random is discussed further in Section 5.12. The present section presents the models and discusses their implementation.

Random study effects can be introduced as additional level 2 random effects, so that model (5.22) becomes

$$\eta_{ij} = \gamma_{0i} + \gamma_{1i}x_{1ij}, \tag{5.29}$$

where $\gamma_{0i} = \beta_0 + \nu_{0i}$, and $\nu_{0i}$ are normally distributed random effects with mean 0 and variance $\zeta^2$. Rewriting this, grouping separately the fixed and random effects, yields

$$\eta_{ij} = \beta_0 + \beta_1 x_{1ij} + \nu_{0i} + \nu_{1i}x_{1ij}. \tag{5.30}$$

Because model (5.30) now contains two level 2 random effects terms, it is necessary to consider the correlation between them. The covariance matrix for $\eta_{ij}$ is given by

$$\mathrm{cov}(\eta_{ih}, \eta_{ij}) = \zeta^2 + \tau^2 x_{1ih}x_{1ij} + \rho\zeta\tau(x_{1ih} + x_{1ij}),$$

$$\mathrm{cov}(\eta_{ih}, \eta_{i'j}) = 0, \qquad \text{for } i \neq i',$$

where $\rho$ is the correlation between $\nu_{0i}$ and $\nu_{1i}$.

There are now three variance components to be estimated. In the case of a meta-analysis based on a small number of studies, when estimation of the correlation coefficient is problematic or impossible, it may be necessary to make the assumption of zero correlation. If $\rho$ is required to be 0, then care will be needed regarding the coding of the treatment covariate. In order to produce a common variance for $\eta_{ij}$ for each treatment group, $x_{1ij}$ will need to take the value $-\frac{1}{2}$ for the control group and $+\frac{1}{2}$ for the treated group.

Including the study effects as random effects allows recovery of any between-study treatment information which will be present when the relative sizes of the treatment groups differ between studies.

### 5.11.1 Random study and study by treatment effects: normally distributed data

The model for the $y_{ij}$ based on (5.30) is given by

$$y_{ij} = \beta_0 + \beta_1 x_{1ij} + \nu_{0i} + \nu_{1i} x_{1ij} + \varepsilon_{ij}. \tag{5.31}$$

This now contains three random effects terms. The level 1 and level 2 random effects are assumed to be uncorrelated, but it is necessary to consider the correlation between the two level 2 random effects $\nu_{0i}$ and $\nu_{1i}$, as described a few paragraphs ago. Also note that the term $\alpha + \beta_{0i}$ in model (5.24) has now been replaced by the term $\beta_0 + \nu_{0i}$. In model (5.31), the term $\beta_0$ represents the mean effect in the control group across the whole population of studies.

To fit model (5.31) in which $\rho = 0$, the following SAS statements can be used:

```
PROC MIXED;
CLASS study;
MODEL y = treat/ htype = 1 ddfm = kenwardroger solution;
RANDOM int treat/ subject = study;
```

Note that 'treat' will need to take the value $-\frac{1}{2}$ for the control group and $+\frac{1}{2}$ for the treated group.

To fit Model (5.31) in which $\rho$ is estimated, the 'RANDOM' statement needs to be changed as follows:

```
RANDOM int treat/ type = un subject = study;
```

The 'type' option specifies the structure of the covariance matrix for the two level 2 random effects within each study. The default is that there is no correlation, and the choice of 'type = un' specfies an unstructured covariance matrix, to allow $\rho$ to be estimated.

Model (5.31) can also be expressed as a traditional mixed effects linear model, in which the treatment effects are fixed and the study and study by treatment interaction terms are random. Suppose that in model (5.25) the study effects, $s_i$, are normally distributed random effects with mean 0 and variance $\sigma_s^2$. When using the traditional mixed effects linear model it is common to assume that all random effects are uncorrelated, which is equivalent to model (5.31) in which $\rho = 0$. This model can be fitted by using the SAS statements presented in Section 5.8.4, but in which the MODEL and RANDOM statements are altered as follows:

```
MODEL  y = treat / htype = 1 ddfm = kenwardroger;
RANDOM study study*treat;
```

In the SAS output, the estimate of $\sigma_s^2$ is printed alongside the covariance parameter 'study'. The constraints used by PROC MIXED lead to the connections $\beta_{1T} = \beta_1$, $\sigma_\tau^2 = \tau^2/2$ and $\sigma_s^2 = \zeta^2 - \tau^2/4$.

## 5.11.2   Example: Recovery time after anaesthesia

Table 5.19 shows the results of the meta-analysis of the anaesthetic study, in which there are two level 2 random effects, for centre and treatment difference within centre. In the first column the correlation between the two level 2 random effects is assumed to be 0. In the second column the correlation between the two random effects is estimated. The results with respect to the treatment difference are very similar for both analyses.

Comparison of the two sets of results with the first column of Table 5.15 indicates little difference in the estimate of the treatment difference and its standard error between the three analyses. For this data set there is no gain in information by including centre as a random effect.

**Table 5.19**   A mixed model for the absolute mean difference (treatment A − treatment B) in log-recovery time, assuming a common $\sigma^2$ across all centres. The two level 2 random effects are for centre and the treatment difference in each centre

|  | $\rho = 0$ | $\rho$ is estimated |
|---|---|---|
| Test of $\beta_1 = 0$ | 14.29 (cf. $F_{1,9.21}$) | 14.50 (cf. $F_{1,9.29}$) |
|  | $p = 0.004$ | $p = 0.004$ |
| $\hat{\beta}_1 [\text{se}(\hat{\beta}_1)]$ | 0.623 [0.165] | 0.623 [0.164] |
| 95% CI | (0.252, 0.995) | (0.255, 0.992) |
| $\hat{\sigma}^2$ | 0.502 | 0.504 |
| $\hat{\zeta}^2$ | 0.287 | 0.279 |
| $\hat{\rho}\zeta\tau$ | − | −0.103 |
| $\hat{\tau}^2$ | 0.130 | 0.125 |

### 5.11.3 Random study and study by treatment effects: other data types

Other data types can be handled in a similar fashion to that illustrated for normally distributed data. However, for ordinal, survival and interval-censored survival data, where the stratified models are considered to be the more appropriate, some thought needs to be given to the inclusion of random study effects. It is difficult to envisage incorporating a random effect for the $\alpha_{ik}$ terms in the stratified model as this could lead to intercept terms which do not follow the natural ordering. Using the ordinal model as an example, a random study effect could be incorporated, as follows:

$$\log\left(\frac{Q_{ijk}}{1 - Q_{ijk}}\right) = \alpha_k + \gamma_{0i} + \gamma_{1i}x_{1ij}.$$

Rewriting this, grouping separately the fixed and random effects, yields

$$\log\left(\frac{Q_{ijk}}{1 - Q_{ijk}}\right) = \alpha_k + \beta_0 + \beta_1 x_{1ij} + \nu_{0i} + \nu_{1i}x_{1ij}.$$

Models which include the two level 2 random effects can be fitted using MLn.

## 5.12 COMPARISONS BETWEEN THE VARIOUS MODELS

Three types of meta-analysis model have been presented in this chapter. In the first case, study effects were treated as fixed and the treatment difference parameter as fixed and common across all studies. In the second case the treatment difference parameter was allowed to vary randomly across studies, and in the third case study effects were additionally allowed to vary randomly. In this section we look at the implications of using the different models.

When individual patient data are available, a meta-analysis can be undertaken in the same way as the analysis of a multicentre trial. Therefore, the issues involved in the choice of the model might be expected to be the same for both situations. Brown and Prescott (1999) present the same models for both a meta-analysis and the analysis of a multicentre trial. However, as discussed by Senn (2000), there are differences between the approaches *traditionally* applied to each. These differences are highlighted in the discussion of the various models.

The various models are presented within the context of normally distributed data, although the same issues apply to other data types. Table 5.20 presents the three meta-analysis models (5.1), (5.24) and (5.31) together with three additional ones, (5.3), (5.32) and (5.33). Model (5.3) is a fixed effects model, which is similar to model (5.1) except that it includes study by treatment interaction terms.

**Table 5.20**    Models for meta-analysis and multi-centre trials

| Model | Fixed effects | Random effects |
|---|---|---|
| (5.32) | $\alpha + \beta_1 x_{1ij}$ | – |
| (5.1) | $\alpha + \beta_{0i} + \beta_1 x_{1ij}$ | – |
| (5.3) | $\alpha + \beta_{0i} + \beta_{1i} x_{1ij}$ | – |
| (5.33) | $\beta_0 + \beta_1 x_{1ij}$ | $v_{0i}$ |
| (5.24) | $\alpha + \beta_{0i} + \beta_1 x_{1ij}$ | $v_{1i} x_{1ij}$ |
| (5.31) | $\beta_0 + \beta_1 x_{1ij}$ | $v_{0i} + v_{1i} x_{1ij}$ |

Model (5.32) only includes one fixed effect term, the treatment difference, and model (5.33) extends this model to include random study effects. These six models are based on those presented by Senn. He also considers Bayesian approaches, but in this section we focus on the frequentist approaches. A Bayesian approach to meta-analysis is presented in Chapter 11.

Model (5.32), which contains only the treatment effect, is the simplest model for the analysis of an individual trial. It is the model underlying the calculation of study estimates of treatment difference as presented in Chapter 3. When data from a number of studies are said to be 'pooled', for example in the case of safety data, it is likely to be this model which is used. Model (5.32) is not used for meta-analysis because no allowance is being made for any differences between the patients recruited to the different studies. Neither is the model used for the analysis of a multicentre trial, unless there are a large number of centres and the number of patients per centre is very small. In such situations, however, centres may be pooled together in homogeneous groups to form larger units.

Model (5.1) is commonly used for the analysis of multicentre trials, and is the model analogous to the 'traditional' fixed effects meta-analysis model of Section 4.2. The overall estimate of treatment difference from this model is a weighted average of the individual centre (trial) estimates of treatment difference, where the weight is the inverse variance of the estimate. When the residual error terms have a common variance, $\sigma^2$, each patient is given equal weight. If this model is used, then the overall estimate of treatment difference is specific to those centres (trials) included in the analysis. If the results from the individual centres (trials) appear to be reasonably consistent then it may be reasonable to conclude that the treatment difference does not depend on the centre (trial).

In Model (5.3) the centre (trial) by treatment interaction terms are included as fixed effects. The overall estimate of treatment difference from this model is obtained by giving equal weight to each centre (trial) estimate. This corresponds to using the type III sums of squares for the treatment effect, as defined by SAS. This model has been used for the analysis of multicentre trials, but it is controversial (Senn, 1997). If there are large differences in the number of patients in each centre, then the results can be quite different from those obtained from model (5.1). Another potential problem is that the overall estimate of treatment difference cannot be estimated unless there are results from both treatments in each centre. Model (5.3) is not used for estimating the treatment difference in a meta-analysis, but can be used for testing heterogeneity in the study estimates of treatment difference, as discussed in Section 5.2.3. In addition, if the estimate of $\sigma^2$ from this model is used as opposed to that from model (5.1), then the meta-analysis based on model (5.1) is identical to the 'traditional' fixed effects meta-analysis model of Section 4.2 (see Section 5.2.5). This latter approach has also been recommended for the analysis of a multicentre trial (Kallen, 1997).

Model (5.33) includes the centre (trial) as a random effect and the treatment difference as a fixed effect. This approach is rarely used. Taking the trial effect as random would allow recovery of any between-trial treatment information which will be present when the relative sizes of the treatment groups differ between trials. This may lead to smaller standard errors for the treatment difference than would be obtained from model (5.1). In many cases there will be little between-study information to recover, because the degree of imbalance is small. However, the recovery of extra information gains in importance when there are more than two treatments to compare and not all of the treatments are included in every trial. In a meta-analysis the recovery of between-trial treatment information involves comparing patients across trials, which may be undesirable. This may not be as much of a problem for a multicentre trial.

The random effects meta-analysis model is described by model (5.24). In this case the trial effects are fixed and the treatment difference varies randomly across trials. This model is analogous to model (4.2), which is applied to trial estimates of treatment difference. Because these trial estimates eliminate the trial effects, there is no possibility of recovering between-trial treatment information. The random effects model is commonly used in meta-analysis, probably because meta-analyses are often performed retrospectively on studies which have not been planned with this in mind. In such cases it is believable that differences in study design and inclusion criteria will lead to some heterogeneity in the treatment difference across studies. The random effects analysis allows the between-trial variability in the estimates of treatment difference to be accounted for in the overall estimate and its standard error. It is argued that it produces results which are more generalizable than those from model (5.1). However, this assumes that the results from the included trials are representative of what one would see from the total population of treatment centres, even though centres taking part in clinical trials are not chosen at random. In the case of a meta-analysis with a small number of studies, the variance term associated with the heterogeneity parameter, $\tau^2$, will be poorly estimated. Random effects models are rarely used for the analysis of multicentre trials. Given that such trials are designed prospectively with a combined analysis of the data in mind, there may be less reason to suspect heterogeneity than for the retrospective meta-analysis. This may also be the case for a prospectively planned meta-analysis.

Model (5.31) contains random effects for both study and treatment difference. As with model (5.33), this allows recovery of any between-study treatment information which will be present when the relative sizes of the treatment groups differ between studies. The amount of extra information will depend on the degree of the treatment imbalance across studies and the ratio of the between-study variance component, $\zeta^2$, and the heterogeneity parameter associated with the treatment difference, $\tau^2$. The issues involved in the recovery of between-study information are the same as for model (5.33). In model (5.31) there are now two or possibly three variance components at the study level. When there are only a small number of studies in the meta-analysis, this may be problematic. Model (5.31) is rarely used for meta-analysis or for the analysis of a multicentre trial.

# 6

# *Dealing with Heterogeneity*

## 6.1  INTRODUCTION

Meta-analyses are often undertaken retrospectively, so that results are combined from studies which have not followed a common protocol. In a prospectively planned multicentre study, on the other hand, it is usual for all centres to follow a common protocol for the collection of key data. There is a continuum from the prospectively planned multicentre study to the retrospectively conducted meta-analysis in terms of the validity of combining results. There would generally be less concern in presenting combined results from a multicentre study than from a meta-analysis in which different patient selection criteria, treatment regimens and definitions of the response measure may have been used. As discussed in Chapter 5, the same statistical methods can be used for a meta-analysis as for the analysis of a multicentre trial. The studies in a meta-analysis are considered in the same way as centres in a multicentre trial. However, the validity of the assumptions made in order to conduct the analysis may be different in the two cases.

Any mathematical model chosen for a meta-analysis is only an approximation to the truth. It is important to choose models which aid the interpretation of the results. Often there are a large number of analyses which might be undertaken. Therefore, in order to provide a focus, it is necessary to define the main analysis strategy *a priori*. Once the main analyses have been completed, then additional exploratory analyses may be undertaken to aid interpretation of the results or to address secondary issues.

A number of the issues which need to be addressed in the specification and/or conduct of the main analysis concern heterogeneity in the treatment difference across trials. Deciding whether or not the amount of heterogeneity is of concern and, if it is, how to deal with it is not straightforward. This task is made easier if certain issues are addressed at the protocol design stage, as discussed in Chapter 2. In this chapter these issues are discussed in detail.

In Section 6.2 the use of a formal test for heterogeneity is discussed. Factors affecting the choice between a fixed effects and a random effects model and the situations in which it is inappropriate to present any overall estimate of treatment difference are considered in Sections 6.3 and 6.4, respectively. The choice of an appropriate measure of treatment difference is addressed in Section 6.5.

In some situations the treatment difference may be expected to vary from one level of a factor to another. For example, a larger difference might be expected in patients with a severe form of the disease than a mild form. Such factors are sometimes referred to as potential effect modifiers. Specification *a priori* of a small number of factors as potential sources of heterogeneity is useful. If the size of the treatment difference is affected by the level of one of these factors – for example, if there is indeed a larger effect in patients with the severe form of the disease than the mild form – then the treatment difference can be presented for each of the subgroups separately. The additional data which are available for investigation of heterogeneity might be at the study level or the patient level. When individual patient data are available, there is also the possibility of adjusting for prognostic factors which are considered likely to affect the outcome data. This is commonly undertaken in the analysis of individual trials. For example, in trials of an antihypertensive agent blood pressure may be adjusted for the age of the patient, and in trials in Alzheimer's disease cognitive impairment may be adjusted for baseline disease severity. If the randomization scheme has produced important differences in the distributions of these prognostic factors for the two treatment groups, then the calculated treatment difference needs to be adjusted to account for this. The use of study-level covariate information is addressed in Section 6.6 and patient-level covariate information in Section 6.7.

A case study which illustrates the types of investigations which might be undertaken in order to explore heterogeneity is presented in Section 6.8. This is followed in Section 6.9 by a suggested strategy for dealing with heterogeneity.

## 6.2  THE USE OF A FORMAL TEST FOR HETEROGENEITY

A formal statistical test for heterogeneity across trials, of the parameter measuring treatment difference, can be performed. Appropriate test statistics were described in Chapter 4 for the case in which study estimates of the treatment difference are to be combined, and in Chapter 5 for the case in which individual patient data are available. In the latter situation heterogeneity was tested via a likelihood ratio test. Such a test is sometimes used to decide whether to present an overall fixed effects or an overall random effects estimate of the treatment difference. For example, if the $p$-value is less than or equal to 0.05 then the random effects estimate may be calculated, and otherwise the fixed effects estimate.

Although the result of a statistical test for heterogeneity provides some useful descriptive information about the variability between trials, a decision based purely on the $p$-value is not to be recommended. It is necessary to distinguish between a clinically important difference and a statistically significant difference. Usually a single study is designed with sufficient power to detect a clinically important difference. There is an attempt to match statistical significance with clinical significance. In a retrospective meta-analysis there is usually no control over the sample size, therefore it is helpful to consider the amount of variation in the size of the effect which would be considered clinically important. In large data sets a trivial amount of heterogeneity may be statistically significant, whereas in small data sets a large amount of heterogeneity may not be statistically significant. In the random effects model (4.2), the study treatment difference parameters are assumed to be independent observations from $N(\theta, \tau^2)$. The coefficient of variation, $\tau/\theta$, therefore might be a useful additional measure. It can be estimated by substituting estimates of $\tau$ and $\theta$ into the numerator and denominator, respectively.

Hardy and Thompson (1998) investigated the power of the test for heterogeneity based on the statistic $Q$ (defined in Section 4.2.3) under different scenarios. These included varying the size of the heterogeneity parameter, $\tau^2$, the number of trials included in the meta-analysis $(r)$, and the weight $w_i$ allocated to the $i$th study, for $i = 1, \ldots, r$. They concluded that the power can be low especially in the case of sparse data or when one trial has a much larger weight than the others. They state that the result of the test for heterogeneity for assessing the validity of the fixed effects model is of limited use, particularly when the total information (sum of the weights) is low, or when there is large variability between the weights of the trials.

## 6.3 THE CHOICE BETWEEN A FIXED EFFECTS AND A RANDOM EFFECTS MODEL

The choice between a fixed effects and a random effects model should not be made solely on the statistical significance of the test for heterogeneity. Additional criteria such as the number of trials and the distribution of the study estimates of treatment difference need to be considered. For a meta-analysis based on a small number of studies, the estimate of the heterogeneity parameter from the data is likely to be unreliable. If the results from the trials appear to be reasonably consistent then the fixed effects analysis may be the more appropriate one to present. If there is inconsistency then no overall estimate should be calculated, and further investigation into the cause of the inconsistency needs to be undertaken. For a meta-analysis based on a larger number of trials the random effects analysis may be preferred anyway, for reasons given in the next paragraph. However, if the distribution of the trial estimates is very far from the assumed normal distribution then further investigation needs to be undertaken.

The overall estimate from the fixed effects model provides a summary of the results obtained from the particular sample of patients contributing data. Extrapolation of the results from the fixed effects model to the total population of patients makes the assumption that the characteristics of patients contributing data to the meta-analysis are the same as those in the total patient population. A common argument in favour of the random effects model is that it produces results which can be considered to be more generalizable. However, the underlying assumption of the random effects model is that the results from studies in the meta-analysis are representative of the results which would be obtained from the total population of treatment centres, and study centres are usually not chosen at random. The choice of a normal distribution for modelling the heterogeneity in the treatment difference parameter across trials is made because of its robustness and computational ease, although alternatives could be considered. One advantage of the random effects model is that it allows the between-study variability in the treatment difference estimates to influence the overall estimate and, more particularly, its precision. Therefore, if there is substantial variability this will be reflected in a wide confidence interval. This more conservative approach will in general lead to larger numbers of patients being required to demonstrate a significant treatment benefit than the fixed effects approach. As a result, definitive evidence of treatment efficacy from a random effects model will usually be more convincing.

It may be useful in many cases to consider the results from both a fixed effects model and a random effects model. If there is no heterogeneity, then the random effects analysis will be the same as the fixed effects analysis, because $\tau^2$ will be estimated to be 0. On the other hand, if the two analyses lead to important differences in conclusion, this highlights the need for further investigation. Sections 6.5–6.9 discuss various approaches which might then be taken.

## 6.4   WHEN NOT TO PRESENT AN OVERALL ESTIMATE OF TREATMENT DIFFERENCE

If the study estimates differ substantially then it may be inappropriate to present an overall estimate. Consider the following hypothetical example concerned with three studies comparing a new drug against placebo (Table 6.1). Each study individually shows a statistically significant difference in favour of the new drug, as illustrated by the 95% CIs, all of which lie entirely above 0 (Figure 6.1). Studies 1 and 3 have a similar size of effect, but in study 2 the effect is much larger. Consider a meta-analysis of these studies using the methods for combining study estimates described in Chapter 4. The 95% CI based on a fixed effects model (0.85, 1.33) lies between the two extremes but is not consistent with either: it does not seem an appropriate summary of the results. The test for heterogeneity using the Q statistic is highly significant. The 95% CI based on a random effects model (−0.09, 2.81) is much wider and includes small negative values. Using the random effects model the treatment difference is not significantly different from 0 at the 5% level. It does not seem appropriate to present this CI either. Clearly it would be desirable to investigate the studies further, in particular to investigate why the effect in study 2 is different from the other two.

Even though all three studies show a statistically significant benefit for the new drug, there should be concern about the variation in the size of the effect. If the

**Table 6.1**   Hypothetical example: meta-analysis of three studies comparing a new drug with placebo. The measure of treatment difference is denoted by θ, which is positive when the new drug is beneficial

| Study | $\hat{\theta}_i$ | 95% CI | $w_i$ | $\hat{\theta}_i w_i$ | $\hat{\theta}_i^2 w_i$ |
|---|---|---|---|---|---|
| 1 | 0.6 | (0.2, 1.0) | 22 | 13.2 | 7.9 |
| 2 | 3.0 | (2.5, 3.5) | 15 | 45.0 | 135.0 |
| 3 | 0.5 | (0.1, 0.9) | 30 | 15.0 | 7.5 |
| Total | | | 67 | 73.2 | 150.4 |

$U = (73.2)^2/67 = 80.0;$ (1 df) $p < 0.001$
$\hat{\theta} = 73.2/67 = 1.09;$ se($\hat{\theta}$) $= 1/\sqrt{67} = 0.12;$ 95% CI $= (0.85, 1.33)$
$Q = 150.4 - 80.0 = 70.4;$ (2 df) $p < 0.001$
$\hat{\tau}^2 = (70.4 - 2)/(67 - 1609/67) = 1.59$
$U^* = (2.487)^2/1.831 = 3.37;$ (1 df) $p = 0.07$
$\hat{\theta}^* = 2.487/1.831 = 1.36;$ se($\hat{\theta}^*$) $= 1/\sqrt{1.831} = 0.74;$ 95% CI $= (-0.09, 2.81)$

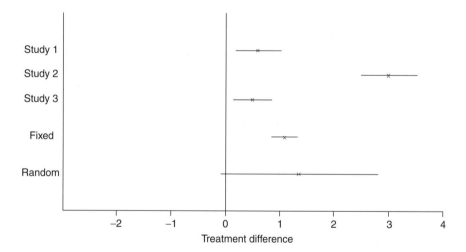

**Figure 6.1**   Hypothetical example: individual study estimates and overall fixed and random effects estimates are presented, with 95% confidence intervals.

random effects model is used to calculate the probability that the new drug is worse than placebo at a fourth centre, which is $1 - \Phi(1.36/\sqrt{1.59})$, where $\Phi$ is the standard normal distribution function, we find that the resulting value of 0.14 is not reassuringly small.

A distinction can be made between quantitative interaction and qualitative interaction. Quantitative interaction is the term applied to heterogeneity between studies, when the effects are either all positive or all negative, whereas qualitative interaction implies that the drug may be beneficial in some cases and harmful in others. More concern is expressed if qualitative interaction occurs. The example described above illustrates quantitative interaction. However, by subtracting 2 from all of the study estimates and CIs, we would have qualitative interaction. In this case studies 1 and 3 would have individually concluded a significant effect in favour of placebo, whilst study 2 would still have shown a significant effect in favour of the new drug. Is it right that more effort should be put into exploring heterogeneity under this latter scenario? Surely, quantitative interaction needs to be understood too.

## 6.5  THE CHOICE OF AN APPROPRIATE MEASURE OF TREATMENT DIFFERENCE

For many of the response variables which are encountered in clinical trials there is more than one measure of treatment difference which could be used. For example, consider the Collins *et al.* (1990) data set from Table 3.1. In Section 4.2.5 three parameterizations of the treatment difference were considered, namely the log-odds ratio, the probability difference and the log-relative risk, and a fixed effects meta-analysis based on study estimates performed for each of them. On choosing the log-odds ratio or the log-relative risk as a measure of treatment difference, it was found that the test for heterogeneity was not significant (Tables 4.2 and 4.7). On the other hand, on choosing the probability difference there was significant heterogeneity (Table 4.5). In this data set it can be seen that the percentage of strokes in the control group varies from 1.3 to 43.8. On the whole the estimates of the log-relative risk and log-odds ratio are similar, but because of the advantages of the log-odds ratio discussed in Section 3.2.2 the latter is to be preferred as the measure of treatment difference for binary data. Because there is not a linear relationship between the log-odds ratio and the probability difference, unless the treatment difference is zero, homogeneity of the treatment effect across all studies in one scale implies heterogeneity in the other. Heterogeneity in the probability difference scale is likely to arise if the control rates take a wide range of values, or if all the rates are close to 0% or close to 100%. If the control rate is 43.8%, a reduction of 0.05 on the probability difference scale leads to a rate in the treated group of 38.8%. If the control rate is 1.3%, a reduction of 0.05 on the probability difference scale leads to a rate of $-3.7$%, which is not possible: the largest possible difference is 0.013. In this example it is perhaps more plausible that the treatment will reduce the rate by a multiplicative factor, for example reduce the rate to 90% of the control rate. The log-odds ratio is a more satisfactory measure in this respect. Unless there are good reasons to choose otherwise, the parameterization which can if necessary be used in a more general regression approach should be chosen. Such parameterizations were discussed in Chapter 5 in connection with meta-analysis models using individual patient data.

## 6.6   META-REGRESSION USING STUDY ESTIMATES OF TREATMENT DIFFERENCE

The dependence of the treatment difference on one or more characteristics of the trials in the meta-analysis can be explored via meta-regression. This corresponds to a regression analysis in which the trial estimates of treatment difference are the observations and trial-level covariates, each of which have a value defined for each trial, are the explanatory variables. Unless there are a large number of studies, however, it may be practicable to investigate only one covariate (or factor) at a time. Therefore the case of one explanatory variable is discussed in detail, although extension to more than one is straightforward.

To incorporate a trial-level covariate within the fixed effects model, equation (4.1) is extended as follows:

$$\hat{\theta}_i = \beta_1 + \eta_i + \varepsilon_i, \tag{6.1}$$

where $\eta_i = \beta_2 x_{2i}$ in the case of a continuous explanatory variable $x_{2i}$, and $\eta_i = \beta_2 x_{2i} + \beta_3 x_{3i} + \cdots + \beta_q x_{qi}$ in the case of a factor with $q$ levels. Here $x_{2i}, \ldots, x_{qi}$ are a set of $q - 1$ indicator variables which take the values 0 or 1 (see Section 5.2.1). The error terms, $\varepsilon_i$, are realizations of normally distributed random variables with expected value 0 and variance $\xi_i^2$. If there were no explanatory variables then $\beta_1$ would be equal to $\theta$.

Maximum likelihood estimates of the $\beta$s can be obtained by performing a weighted least-squares regression of $\hat{\theta}_i$ on the explanatory variables, with weights $w_i$, where $w_i$ is the estimated inverse variance of $\hat{\theta}_i$ (see Section A.3 in the Appendix and Hedges, 1994). This is similar to the approach described in Section 4.2.4 for the calculation of the test statistics $U$ and $Q$. To perform this analysis in PROC GLM in SAS for the case of one explanatory variable 'x2', the MODEL statement used in Section 4.2.4 should be modified as follows:

```
MODEL y = x2 / inverse;
```

As discussed in Section 4.2.4, although the correct estimates of the regression coefficients are presented in the SAS output, the standard errors and test statistics are incorrect for the meta-analysis model. In common with other statistical packages, the assumption that is made is that $\xi_i^2 = \sigma^2/w_i$, where $\sigma^2$ is to be estimated from the data, instead of $\xi_i^2 = 1/w_i$. To obtain the correct standard error for $\hat{\beta}_j$, the standard error for $\hat{\beta}_j$ given by the package should be divided by the square root of the residual (error) mean square. Alternatively, the correct standard errors can be obtained as the square roots of the diagonal elements of the matrix $(X' WX)^{-1}$, where $X$ is the $r \times q$ matrix of explanatory variables associated with the $\beta$s, and $W$ is the $r \times r$ diagonal matrix with $i$th element $w_i$. Many packages will present this matrix as an option. For example, the option 'inverse' in the MODEL statement above requests that this matrix be printed in the SAS output. Confidence intervals for the regression coefficients are based on asymptotic normality.

As discussed in Section 4.2.4, if the model includes only the intercept term $\beta_1$, the estimate of $\beta_1$ is the overall fixed effect estimate $\hat{\theta}$. In addition, the $U$ and $Q$ statistics appear as the model sum of squares and residual (error) sum of squares respectively in the analysis of variance table. When an explanatory variable is fitted, the $Q$ statistic is divided into two components, both of which appear in the analysis of variance table. The first, $Q_B$, is the variation explained by the covariate (or factor), and this appears as the model sum of squares. The second, $Q_W$, is the remaining unexplained variation, which appears as the residual sum of squares.

If the explanatory variable is a factor with $q$ levels, then to test for heterogeneity in the treatment difference parameter between studies which have the same factor level, $Q_W$ is compared with the chi-squared distribution with $r - q$ degrees of freedom. In order to test for heterogeneity between studies due to the different levels of the factor, $Q_B$ is compared with the chi-squared distribution with $q - 1$ degrees of freedom. The statistic $Q_B$ is given by

$$Q_B = \sum_{k=1}^{q} \left\{ \frac{\left( \sum_{i=1}^{n_k} w_{ki} \hat{\theta}_{ki} \right)^2}{\sum_{i=1}^{n_k} w_{ki}} \right\} - \frac{\left( \sum_{k=1}^{q} \sum_{i=1}^{n_k} w_{ki} \hat{\theta}_{ki} \right)^2}{\sum_{k=1}^{q} \sum_{i=1}^{n_k} w_{ki}}, \qquad (6.2)$$

where $\hat{\theta}_{ki}$ is the estimate of treatment difference from the $i$th study at the $k$th level of the factor and $w_{ki}$ its weight, for $i = 1, \ldots, n_k$ and $k = 1, \ldots, q$. When using efficient score and Fisher's information statistics, $Q_B$ can be written as

$$Q_B = \sum_{k=1}^{q} \left\{ \frac{\left( \sum_{i=1}^{n_k} Z_{ki} \right)^2}{\sum_{i=1}^{n_k} V_{ki}} \right\} - \frac{\left( \sum_{k=1}^{q} \sum_{i=1}^{n_k} Z_{ki} \right)^2}{\sum_{k=1}^{q} \sum_{i=1}^{n_k} V_{ki}}, \qquad (6.3)$$

where $Z_{ki}$ and $V_{ki}$ are the efficient score and Fisher's information from the $i$th study at the $k$th level of the factor.

If the additional explanatory variable is a continuous covariate, then $Q_B$ is compared with the chi-squared distribution with one degree of freedom. The statistic $Q_B$ is then given by

$$Q_B = \frac{\left\{ \sum_{i=1}^{r} w_i (x_{2i} - \bar{x}_2) \hat{\theta}_i \right\}^2}{\sum_{i=1}^{r} w_i (x_{2i} - \bar{x}_2)^2}, \qquad (6.4)$$

where

$$\bar{x}_2 = \frac{\sum_{i=1}^{r} w_i x_{2i}}{\sum_{i=1}^{r} w_i}.$$

When using efficient score and Fisher's information statistics, $Q_B$ can be written as

$$Q_B = \frac{\left\{ \left( \sum_{i=1}^{r} x_{2i} Z_i \right) - \bar{x}_2 \sum_{i=1}^{r} Z_i \right\}^2}{\left( \sum_{i=1}^{r} x_{2i}^2 V_i \right) - \bar{x}_2 \sum_{i=1}^{r} x_{2i} V_i}, \tag{6.5}$$

where

$$\bar{x}_2 = \frac{\sum_{i=1}^{r} V_i x_{2i}}{\sum_{i=1}^{r} V_i}.$$

Formula (6.5) is related to the statistic for testing for a linear trend when there is a natural ordering to the levels of a factor (see, for example, Early Breast Cancer Trialists' Collaborative Group, 1990). If the factor levels are ordered and assigned values 1, 2, 3, etc., then $Z$ and $V$ are calculated for each factor level and $x_2$ takes the value 1, 2, 3, etc., depending on the factor level. The summation is over the different levels of the factor.

If models are fitted which include additional explanatory variables, comparisons between models can be made using the residual sum of squares from each model. Suppose that a model with $q$ parameters is to be compared with a model which includes these $q$ parameters and an additional $p$ parameters. If RSS(1) and RSS(2) are the residual sum of squares on fitting these two models, then under the null hypothesis that all of the additional $p$ parameters are equal to 0, RSS(1) $-$ RSS(2) follows a chi-squared distribution with $p$ degrees of freedom.

To allow for the remaining unexplained variation between studies a random effect can be incorporated as follows:

$$\hat{\theta}_i = \beta_1 + \eta_i + v_i + \varepsilon_i, \tag{6.6}$$

where the $v_i$ are normally distributed random effects with mean 0 and variance $\tau^2$ and the $\varepsilon_i$ are realizations of normally distributed random variables with expected value 0 and variance $\xi_i^2$. The terms $v_i$ and $\varepsilon_i$ are assumed to be independently distributed. It can be seen that model (6.6) is an extension of model (4.2). The $v_i$ represents the $i$th trial's deviation from the mean of all trials having the same covariate values specified in $x_{2i}$ (or the $x_{ji}$, $j = 2, \ldots, q$, for a factor).

Maximum likelihood estimates of the $\beta$s and $\tau^2$ can be obtained by an iterative process, similar to that defined by equations (4.3) and (4.4). The estimates of the $\beta$s at the $(t + 1)$th cycle of the iteration are obtained by calculating a weighted least-squares regression of $\hat{\theta}_i$ on the explanatory variables, using weights $w_{it}^*$, and an estimate of $\tau^2$ is then given by

$$\hat{\tau}_{M,t+1}^2 = \frac{\sum_{i=1}^{r} (w_{it}^*)^2 \{ (\hat{\theta}_i - \hat{\beta}_{1,t+1} - \hat{\eta}_{i,t+1})^2 - w_i^{-1} \}}{\sum_{i=1}^{r} (w_{it}^*)^2}, \tag{6.7}$$

for $t = 0, 1, \ldots$, where $w_{it}^* = (w_i^{-1} + \hat{\tau}_{M,t}^2)^{-1}$. To start the iterative process an initial estimate of $\tau^2$ is required, for example $\hat{\tau}_{M,0}^2 = 0$.

Residual (restricted) maximum likelihood estimates can also be calculated. An approximate updated REML estimate of $\tau^2$ can be calculated as follows:

$$\hat{\tau}^2_{R,t+1} = \frac{\sum_{i=1}^{r}(w_{it}^*)^2\{(r/(r-q-1))(\hat{\theta}_i - \hat{\beta}_{1,t+1} - \hat{\eta}_{i,t+1})^2 - w_i^{-1}\}}{\sum_{i=1}^{r}(w_{it}^*)^2}. \quad (6.8)$$

Implementation of these methods is similar to that described in Section 4.3.8. However, for meta-regression the fixed effect part of the regression model is $\beta_1 + \eta_i$ instead of $\beta_1$. For example, to obtain REML estimates using SAS PROC MIXED for the case of one explanatory variable 'x2', the MODEL statement used in Section 4.3.8 should be modified as follows:

```
MODEL y = x2 / solution;
```

Berkey *et al.* (1995) consider a similar approach to that based on the approximate REML estimate given in equation (6.8), by replacing the $(w_{it}^*)^2$ terms by $w_{it}^*$.

The method of moments approach to the estimation of $\tau^2$, as described in Section 4.3.3, can also be extended to the case when there are covariates. However, this extension is neither as accurate or straightforward as those given above, and so it is not presented here. Thompson and Sharp (1999) discuss the method of moments procedure in the case of one covariate.

Although originally applied to the situation in which the observations are the study estimates, this type of analysis can be undertaken with individual patient data. In fact a covariate which takes a common value for all patients in the same study is just a special type of patient-level covariate. Meta-regression when individual patient data are available is considered in Section 6.7.4.

### 6.6.1 Example: Global impression of change in Alzheimer's disease

We return to the data from the tacrine studies, described in Section 3.5.1. The test for heterogeneity across the studies in Table 4.16 was not statistically significant ($p = 0.30$). However, it was of interest to investigate the effect of the dose of tacrine on the treatment difference, the log-odds ratio. The relationship between the log-odds ratio and dose was difficult to assess because in most studies the dose for each patient was titrated to or selected to be the patient's best dose. The average final dose actually received by patients in a trial was considered to be a measure of the intended level of dosing for the trial. These doses were 62, 39, 66, 135 and 65 mg/day for studies 1–5, respectively. Figure 6.2 shows a CI plot of the study estimates from Table 4.15, in which the studies are ordered by increasing dose. This indicates an increase in the treatment effect as the dose increases. Dose was considered as a continuous variable in the meta-regression, and is associated with the parameter $\beta_2$. Table 6.2 shows that the residual sum of squares from fitting the null model, that is, the model with the intercept term only,

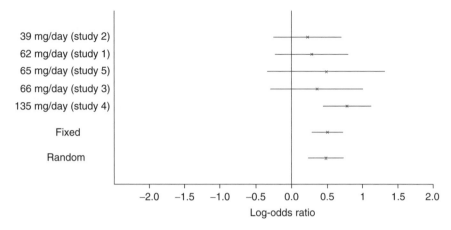

**Figure 6.2**   Global impression of change in Alzheimer's disease: the log-odds ratio for being in a better CGIC category on tacrine than on placebo (Figure 4.5 with studies ordered by dose of tacrine).

**Table 6.2**   Global impression of change in Alzheimer's disease: meta-regression of the log-odds ratio from the proportional odds model on the dose of tacrine

| Model | Residual sum of squares | Degrees of freedom |
|---|---|---|
| Intercept only | 4.83 | 4 |
| Dose | 0.15 | 3 |

is equal to the value for the $Q$ statistic in Table 4.16. Inclusion of the covariate for dose substantially reduces the residual sum of squares from 4.83 to 0.15, that is, by 4.68. Comparing 4.68 with the chi-squared distribution with one degree of freedom gives a $p$-value of 0.03, indicating that the log-odds ratio increases significantly with dose. Estimates of the log-odds ratio from the meta-regression for doses of 65 and 135 (Table 6.3) show good agreement with the individual study estimates. The residual sum of squares after fitting dose is very small. Compared with the chi-squared distribution with three degrees of freedom, the value of 0.15 is not statistically significant, $p = 0.98$. Both ML and REML estimates of the residual variance component after fitting dose were 0.

### 6.6.2   Example: Recovery time after anaesthesia

The anaesthetic study was introduced in Section 3.6.1. From Table 4.23 it can be seen that there is heterogeneity between the individual centre estimates.

**Table 6.3**   Global impression of change in Alzheimer's disease: parameter estimates from the meta-regression of the log-odds ratio from the proportional odds model on the dose of tacrine

| Parameter | Estimate | Standard error | 95% CI |
|---|---|---|---|
| $\beta_1$ | −0.023 | 0.268 | (−0.549, 0.502) |
| $\beta_2$ | 0.005 97 | 0.002 76 | (0.000 56, 0.011 39) |
| Dose 65 mg/day ($\beta_1 + 65\beta_2$) | 0.365 | 0.129 | (0.112, 0.618) |
| Dose 135 mg/day ($\beta_1 + 135\beta_2$) | 0.783 | 0.171 | (0.447, 1.119) |

**Table 6.4**   Recovery time after anaesthesia: meta-regression of the absolute mean difference on premedication

| Model | Residual sum of squares | Degrees of freedom |
|---|---|---|
| Intercept only | 17.95 | 8 |
| Premedication | 5.27 | 7 |

In particular, a negative absolute mean difference in centre 9 indicates that anaesthetic A reduces recovery time relative to anaesthetic B, whereas in the other eight centres the reverse is the case. The test for heterogeneity was statistically significant ($p = 0.02$). Further investigation of the study protocol showed that the centres were able to choose the premedication drug administered, provided that the same drug was used for all patients at that centre. Centre 9 used a different premedication drug from centres 1–8, which had all used the same one. A study-level covariate can, therefore, be created based on the premedication drug used. Let this covariate take the value 0 for premedication 1 used in centres 1–8 and 1 for premedication 2 used in centre 9, and be associated with the parameter $\beta_2$. Table 6.4 shows that the residual sum of squares from fitting the model with the intercept term only is equal to the value for the $Q$ statistic in Table 4.23. Inclusion of the covariate for premedication substantially reduces the residual sum of squares from 17.95 to 5.27, that is, by 12.68. Comparing 12.68 with the chi-squared distribution with one degree of freedom gives a $p$-value less than 0.001, indicating that the type of premedication has a significant effect on the treatment difference. Anaesthetic B significantly reduces recovery time relative to anaesthetic A when premedication 1 is used (Table 6.5). However, for premedication 2 there is some evidence that anaesthetic A is better, although this is not statistically significant. The same estimates of the treatment difference

**Table 6.5** Recovery time after anaesthesia: parameter estimates from the meta-regression of the absolute mean difference on premedication

| Parameter | Estimate | Standard error | 95% CI |
|---|---|---|---|
| $\beta_1$ | 0.711 | 0.117 | (0.482, 0.940) |
| $\beta_2$ | −0.984 | 0.276 | (−1.526, −0.443) |
| Premedication 1 ($\beta_1$) | 0.711 | 0.117 | (0.482, 0.940) |
| Premedication 2 ($\beta_1 + \beta_2$) | −0.273 | 0.250 | (−0.764, 0.218) |

and its standard error for premedication 1 as obtained from the meta-regression could have been calculated from a fixed effects meta-analysis of centres 1–8 only, provided that the same estimate of $\sigma^2$ was used. For example, this might be the pooled variance estimate $s_p^2$ presented in Section 4.2.9, but calculated from centres 1–8 only. More generally, for the situation in which the one explanatory variable is a factor, there are two options. The first is to perform a meta-regression as illustrated. The second is to perform a fixed effects meta-analysis for each level of the factor. Provided that the same weights, $w_i$, are used in both cases, the same estimates and standard errors for each level of the factor will be obtained.

The residual sum of squares after fitting premedication can be compared with the chi-squared distribution with seven degrees of freedom. The value of 5.27 is not statistically significant ($p = 0.63$), indicating that there is no strong evidence of heterogeneity between the first eight studies. Both ML and REML estimates of the residual variance component after fitting premedication were 0. The conclusion that could be drawn from this meta-regression is that the choice of anaesthetic agent might depend on the premedication to be used. For premedication 1 anaesthetic B provides a quicker recovery time. For premedication 2 the result is not clear-cut, but there is some indication that anaesthetic A might be better.

### 6.6.3 Extension to study estimates of treatment difference from subgroups

When study estimates of treatment difference are available for different subgroups of patients, the meta-regression technique may be used to explore the variation in the magnitude of the treatment difference between these subgroups. When the subgroups are represented by a factor with $q$ levels, the fixed effects model (6.1) can be extended as follows:

$$\hat{\theta}_{ki} = \beta_1 + \eta_{ki} + \varepsilon_{ki},$$

where $\hat{\theta}_{ki}$ is the estimate of treatment difference from the $k$th subgroup in the $i$th study, for $k = 1, \ldots, q$ and $i = 1, \ldots r$. The term $\eta_{ki}$ is equal to $\beta_2 x_{2ki} + \beta_3 x_{3ki} +$

$\cdots + \beta_q x_{qki}$, and $x_{2ki}, \ldots, x_{qki}$ are a set of $q - 1$ indicator variables which take the values 0 or 1 (see Section 5.2.1). The error terms, $\varepsilon_{ki}$, are realizations of normally distributed random variables with expected value 0 and variance $\xi_{ki}^2$. It is assumed that $\xi_{ki}^2$ is known and equal to $1/w_{ki}$, where $w_{ki}$ is the estimated inverse variance of $\hat{\theta}_{ki}$.

When a weighted least-squares regression analysis is performed for the $\hat{\theta}_{ki}$ on the explanatory variables in $\eta_{ki}$, using weights $w_{ki}$, the model sum of squares, $Q_B$, is identical to formula (6.2) with the exception that $n_k$ is replaced by $r$. The same is also true in respect of formula (6.3). In order to test for heterogeneity between the different subgroups, $Q_B$ is compared with the chi-squared distribution with $q - 1$ degrees of freedom.

If there is a natural ordering to the factor levels, the factor levels can be ordered and given numerical values, for example, $1, 2, \ldots, q$. Now $\eta_{ki} = \beta_2 x_{2ki}$, where $x_{2ki}$ is a continuous covariate. In this case, the model sum of squares from the weighted least-squares regression analysis will be similar to formula (6.4). The statistic $Q_B$ will be given by

$$Q_B = \frac{\left\{ \sum_{k=1}^q \sum_{i=1}^r w_{ki}(x_{2ki} - \overline{x}_2)\hat{\theta}_{ki} \right\}^2}{\sum_{k=1}^q \sum_{i=1}^r w_{ki}(x_{2ki} - \overline{x}_2)^2},$$

where

$$\overline{x}_2 = \frac{\sum_{k=1}^q \sum_{i=1}^r w_{ki} x_{2ki}}{\sum_{k=1}^q \sum_{i=1}^r w_{ki}}.$$

When using the efficient score and Fisher's information, the formula for $Q_B$ will be similar to formula (6.5), and is given by

$$Q_B = \frac{\left\{ \left( \sum_{k=1}^q \sum_{i=1}^r x_{2ki} Z_{ki} \right) - \overline{x}_2 \sum_{k=1}^q \sum_{i=1}^r Z_{ki} \right\}^2}{\left( \sum_{k=1}^q \sum_{i=1}^r x_{2ki}^2 V_{ki} \right) - \overline{x}_2 \sum_{k=1}^q \sum_{i=1}^r x_{2ki} V_{ki}},$$

where

$$\overline{x}_2 = \frac{\sum_{k=1}^q \sum_{i=1}^r V_{ki} x_{2ki}}{\sum_{k=1}^q \sum_{i=1}^r V_{ki}}.$$

and $Z_{ki}$ and $V_{ki}$ are the efficient score and Fisher's information for the $k$th subgroup in the $i$th study. Under the null hypothesis of no linear trend amongst the subgroups, $Q_B$ follows a chi-squared distribution on one degree of freedom.

The analyses described in this section can be undertaken when individual patient data are available. In fact it is very likely that they will only be undertaken if there is access to individual patient data, because the required summary statistics for the various subgroups are usually not presented in published papers or trial reports. However, if individual patient data are available, it may be advantageous to exploit the more advanced statistical modelling techniques described in Section 6.7.2.

## 6.7    PATIENT-LEVEL COVARIATES

When the meta-analysis is based on individual patient data, covariates measured at the level of the individual patient may be incorporated into the meta-analysis model. The models presented in Chapter 5 can be extended to accommodate these covariates. Several options are available in practice, requiring choices of whether to allow the covariates to be fixed or random effects or to include fixed or random effects for an interaction with treatment. An important consideration is to avoid inappropriate complexity and over-fitting of the data. The various uses to which covariate information may be put are described and illustrated in the rest of this section.

### 6.7.1    Adjustment for imbalance in prognostic factors

If a modelling approach is to be utilized, as described in Chapter 5, it is straightforward to adjust for prognostic factors common to all studies through the inclusion of patient-level covariates. Consider the fixed effects model (5.1) which contains study effects and the treatment difference. Here $\eta_{ij}$, the linear combination of explanatory variables for the regression model, is defined as

$$\eta_{ij} = \beta_{0i} + \beta_1 x_{1ij}.$$

Inclusion of $p$ patient-level covariates leads to the model

$$\eta_{ij} = \beta_{0i} + \beta_1 x_{1ij} + \sum_{a=2}^{p+1} \beta_a x_{aij}. \tag{6.9}$$

In this model, the regression coefficients, $\beta_a$, $a = 2, \ldots, p$, are common across all studies. As an alternative $\beta_a$ could be replaced by $\beta_{ai}$, so that the coefficients vary across studies. This would correspond to adjusting for covariates separately within each trial.

Random effects can be introduced into the model in place of one or more of the $\beta_a$, $a = 1, \ldots, p + 1$. For example $\beta_a$ could be replaced by $\gamma_{ai}$, with

$$\gamma_{ai} = \beta_a + \nu_{ai},$$

where $\nu_{ai}$ is normally distributed with mean 0 and variance $\sigma_a^2$. It should be noted that if there is more than one study level (level 2) random effect term then it will be necessary to consider the correlation between them, as was the case for random study effects and random treatment differences in Section 5.11.

Analyses are still possible if different covariates are available from trial to trial. For each trial the estimate of treatment difference can be adjusted for particular prognostic factors, and the adjusted estimates combined using the methods of Chapter 4.

If a fixed effects meta-analysis is to be conducted using the methods of Chapter 4 with efficient score and Fisher's information statistics, it is possible to adjust for prognostic factors. There are two ways in which this can be accomplished, the first using stratification and the second covariate adjustment. For the stratification method, the patients must be allocated to mutually exclusive subgroups referred to as strata, which can arise from one factor or a combination of two or more factors. The Z and V statistics are calculated for each stratum. Each stratum plays the role of study in the traditional meta-analysis. Typically, study will be included as one of the factors. If, in addition, there is one prognostic factor with $q$ levels, then the fixed effects estimate is given by

$$\hat{\theta} = \frac{\sum_{k=1}^{q} \sum_{i=1}^{r} Z_{ki}}{\sum_{k=1}^{q} \sum_{i=1}^{r} V_{ki}},$$

where $Z_{ki}$ and $V_{ki}$ are the efficient score and Fisher's information for the $k$th stratum in the $i$th study. This is equivalent to a model which adjusts for study, prognostic factor and their interaction. Details of the method using covariate adjustment are not provided here but can be found in Chapter 7 of J. Whitehead (1997).

### 6.7.2  Investigation of potential sources of heterogeneity

Investigation of factors which might affect the magnitude of the treatment difference may be undertaken by adding interaction terms between treatment and patient-level covariates to the model. Model (6.9) could then be extended to

$$\eta_{ij} = \beta_{0i} + \beta_1 x_{1ij} + \sum_{a=2}^{p+1} (\beta_a x_{aij} + \beta_{a+p} x_{aij} x_{1ij}). \tag{6.10}$$

The interaction coefficients, $\beta_{a+p}$, must be interpreted with care. They describe a mixture of between-trial and within-trial relationships. In particular, if the same spread of covariate values appears in every trial then they are based entirely on within-trial relationships, whereas if all covariate values are identical within each trial then they describe between-trial relationships. In most applications the situation will lie between these extremes.

Theoretically, it is possible to replace the fixed effect parameters in model (6.10) by random effects. If $\beta_1$, the treatment difference parameter, is treated as random across studies then it would be logical to treat the interaction terms involving treatment likewise. However, the majority of meta-analyses include rather few trials and it is problematic to estimate more than one or two variance components across a small number of trials. Therefore, it is the fixed effect models that are more likely to be of use in practice.

### 6.7.3   Example: Global impression of change in Alzheimer's disease

Baseline data were collected from individual patients in the tacrine studies. Here we consider one covariate, the assessment of disease severity by the Mini-Mental™ State Examination (MMSE™); see Folstein *et al.* (1975). The MMSE can take values between 0 and 30, where a lower value relates to a higher disease severity. In the following analyses, the MMSE is treated as a continuous covariate. First, we extend model (5.8) to include the MMSE as a covariate. This fixed effects model is given by

$$\log\left(\frac{Q_{ijk}}{1 - Q_{ijk}}\right) = \alpha_{ik} + \beta_1 x_{1ij} + \beta_2 x_{2ij}, \qquad (6.11)$$

where $x_{2ij}$ is the MMSE of the $j$th patient in study $i$.

This model can be fitted using PROC NLMIXED in SAS, by modifying the program in Section 5.4.2 as follows. The number of intercept terms 'aik' is increased to cater for five studies and four cut-points, and one additional parameter 'beta2' is included. The fourth line of code is replaced by

```
eta = beta1*treat + beta2*mmse;
```

As the MMSE was missing for 17 patients, the comparisons made below are based on 1386 patients instead of 1403. The new estimate of the log-odds ratio (tacrine relative to placebo) from model (5.8) is 0.494 with a standard error of 0.113. Adjusting for MMSE (model (6.11)), the estimate of the log-odds ratio changes to 0.478 with a standard error of 0.113. It can be seen that adjustment for MMSE has had little effect on the estimate of treatment difference.

To test whether there is an interaction between MMSE and treatment, the following model can be fitted:

$$\log\left(\frac{Q_{ijk}}{1 - Q_{ijk}}\right) = \alpha_{ik} + \beta_1 x_{1ij} + \beta_2 x_{2ij} + \beta_3 x_{2ij} x_{1ij}. \qquad (6.12)$$

The change in deviance ($-2$ times the log-likelihood) between model (6.11) and model (6.12) is compared with the chi-squared distribution on one degree of freedom.

To fit model (6.12) in PROC NLMIXED, an additional parameter 'beta3' is added, and the fourth line of code is changed to

```
eta = beta1*treat + beta2*mmse + beta3*mmse*treat;
```

The change in deviance is calculated to be 0.12, which is not statistically significant ($p = 0.73$). This indicates that the magnitude of the treatment difference is not affected by disease severity.

## 6.7.4   Meta-regression using individual patient data

The case in which there is a single continuous covariate $x_{2ij}$, taking different values from one trial to the next but the same value for all patients within a trial, leads to a model which is similar to model (6.1). It is referred to here as meta-regression using individual patient data. By writing the covariate as $x_{2i}$ it can be seen that model (6.10) reduces to

$$\eta_{ij} = \beta_{0i} + \beta_1 x_{1ij} + \beta_2 x_{2i} + \beta_3 x_{2i} x_{1ij}. \tag{6.13}$$

Noting that $\beta_{0i}$ and $\beta_2 x_{2i}$ are not separately identifiable and may be written as a single fixed trial effect, $\beta_{0i}$, model (6.13) becomes

$$\eta_{ij} = \beta_{0i} + \beta_1 x_{1ij} + \beta_3 x_{2i} x_{1ij}. \tag{6.14}$$

As in model (6.1), $\beta_1$ is the treatment difference when $x_{2i}$ is 0. The parameter $\beta_3$ is the same as $\beta_2$ in model (6.1). Although the meta-regression based on study estimates of treatment difference and the meta-regression based on model (6.14) are similar, they are not identical. For the latter the hypothesis tests associated with the $\beta$ parameters are based on likelihood ratio test statistics, whereas for the former they are based on the assumption of normality for the study estimates of treatment difference.

Random effects can be introduced into model (6.14), as described in Section 6.7.1.

## 6.7.5   Example: Recovery time after anaesthesia

The meta-regression on the premedication covariate undertaken in Section 6.6.2 is now repeated using individual patient data. To test the effect of premedication on the treatment difference, two models are compared. The first is model (5.1), which includes study and treatment as covariates. The second includes the treatment by premedication interaction term, and is model (6.14) expressed in terms of $\mu_{ij}$, that is,

$$\mu_{ij} = \alpha + \beta_{0i} + \beta_1 x_{1ij} + \beta_3 x_{2i} x_{1ij}. \tag{6.15}$$

The parameter $\beta_1$ from model (6.15) is the same $\beta_1$ as that defined in Section 6.6.2, and $\beta_3$ is the same as $\beta_2$. Model (6.15) was fitted using PROC GLM in SAS with the following statements.

```
CLASS centre;
MODEL y = centre treat premed*treat/ ss1 solution;
```

The results are presented in Tables 6.6 and 6.7. The estimates of treatment difference in Table 6.7 are identical to those presented in Table 6.5. The standard

**Table 6.6** Recovery time after anaesthesia: meta-regression of the absolute mean difference on premedication, using individual patient data

| Model comparisons | Effect tested | Change in residual sums of squares | Change in degrees of freedom | Estimate of $\sigma^2$ | Degrees of freedom | $F$ statistic | $p$-value |
|---|---|---|---|---|---|---|---|
| (6.15) vs (5.1) | Treat by Premed | 6.41 | 1 | 0.500 | 171 | 12.82 | <0.001 |
| (6.16) vs (6.15) | Centre by Treat | 2.66 | 7 | 0.506 | 164 | 0.75 | 0.63 |

**Table 6.7** Recovery time after anaesthesia: parameter estimates from the meta-regression of the absolute mean difference on premedication, using individual patient data

| Parameter | Estimate | Standard error | 95% CI |
|---|---|---|---|
| $\beta_1$ | 0.711 | 0.116 | (0.482, 0.941) |
| $\beta_3$ | −0.984 | 0.275 | (−1.527, −0.442) |
| Premedication 1 ($\beta_1$) | 0.711 | 0.116 | (0.482, 0.941) |
| Premedication 2 ($\beta_1 + \beta_3$) | −0.273 | 0.249 | (−0.765, 0.219) |

errors are slightly smaller because the estimate of $\sigma^2$ is slightly smaller, 0.500 as opposed to 0.506. The CIs in Table 6.7 are based on the $t$ distribution with 171 degrees of freedom, whereas those in Table 6.5 are based on the normal distribution.

To investigate whether the significant centre by treatment interaction has been explained by the premedication by treatment interaction, the following model is fitted and compared with model (6.15):

$$\mu_{ij} = \alpha + \beta_{0i} + \beta_1 x_{1ij} + \beta_3 x_{2i} x_{1ij} + \sum_{s=1}^{7} \beta_{1s} x_{1ij} \delta_{si}, \qquad (6.16)$$

where $\delta_{si}$ is Kronecker delta, taking the value 1 if $s = i$ and 0 otherwise. Model (6.16) was fitted using PROC GLM with the above MODEL statement changed to

```
MODEL y = centre treat premed*treat centre*treat/ ss1
    solution;
```

The $F$ statistic of 0.75, compared with the $F$ distribution on 7 and 164 degrees of freedom, is not significant ($p = 0.63$); see Table 6.6. This is in close agreement with the result from the meta-regression of Section 6.6.2.

## 6.8   AN INVESTIGATION OF HETEROGENEITY: ASPIRIN IN CORONARY HEART DISEASE

This example is taken from Canner (1987). It concerns the overview of six major clinical trials of aspirin compared with placebo in coronary heart disease. The all-cause mortality figures are given in Table 6.8. The meta-analysis is based on the unconditional maximum likelihood estimation of the log-odds ratio for mortality on aspirin relative to placebo (formulae (3.1) and (3.2)). A CI plot (Figure 6.3) shows that the first five trials are in remarkably good agreement. The test of heterogeneity is not significant ($p = 0.96$), and the overall test of a treatment difference is highly significant ($p = 0.001$). However, when study 6 is added the picture is changed dramatically. In study 6 there is higher mortality on aspirin than on placebo. Because this study is much larger than the other studies, its inclusion reduces the positive effect to a level which is not statistically significant ($p = 0.11$). In addition, the test for heterogeneity is pushed towards borderline significance ($p = 0.08$). Canner presents his investigations of this apparent heterogeneity of the findings, focusing on the large difference between study 6 and the others.

The first potential source of heterogeneity explored was that to do with the design and operational features of the six trials. Table 6.9 shows some of the design features of the trials. Study 6 had the smallest mean age, but the range across all trials was very small. Two of the trials included males only, but study 6 was one of the four that included both sexes. The total daily dose of aspirin varied from 300 mg to 1500 mg, but study 6 with a dose of 1000 mg was close to three other studies (2, 4 and 5). The dosage schedule ranged from once to

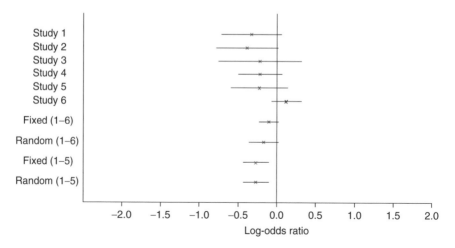

**Figure 6.3**   Aspirin in coronary heart disease: the log-odds ratio of mortality on aspirin relative to placebo. Individual study estimates and overall fixed and random effects estimates are presented, with 95% confidence intervals.

**Table 6.8**   Aspirin in coronary heart disease: log-odds ratio of mortality on aspirin relative to placebo, using formulae (3.1) and (3.2)

| Study | Aspirin | | Placebo | | $\hat{\theta}_i$ | $w_i$ | $\hat{\theta}_i w_i$ | $\hat{\theta}_i^2 w_i$ |
|---|---|---|---|---|---|---|---|---|
| | Number of deaths | Total number patients | Number of deaths | Total number patients | | | | |
| 1 | 49 | 615 | 67 | 624 | −0.329 | 25.7 | −8.46 | 2.78 |
| 2 | 44 | 758 | 64 | 771 | −0.385 | 24.3 | −9.34 | 3.59 |
| 3 | 27 | 317 | 32 | 309 | −0.216 | 13.3 | −2.86 | 0.62 |
| 4 | 102 | 832 | 126 | 850 | −0.220 | 48.8 | −10.71 | 2.35 |
| 5 | 85 | 810 | 52 | 406 | −0.225 | 28.4 | −6.41 | 1.44 |
| Total (1−5) | | | | | | 140.5 | −37.78 | 10.78 |
| 6 | 246 | 2267 | 219 | 2257 | 0.125 | 104.0 | 12.96 | 1.62 |
| Total (1−6) | | | | | | 244.5 | −24.82 | 12.40 |

Studies 1−5
$U = (-37.78)^2/140.5 = 10.16; (1 \text{ df}) p = 0.001$
$Q = 10.78 - 10.16 = 0.63; (4 \text{ df}) p = 0.96$
$\hat{\theta} = -37.78/140.5 = -0.269; \text{se}(\hat{\theta}) = 1/\sqrt{140.5} = 0.084$
$95\% \text{ CI} = (-0.269 \pm 1.96/\sqrt{140.5}) = (-0.434, -0.104)$

Studies 1−6
$U = (-24.82)^2/244.5 = 2.52; (1 \text{ df}) p = 0.11$
$Q = 12.40 - 2.52 = 9.88; (5 \text{ df}) p = 0.08$
$\hat{\theta} = -24.82/244.5 = -0.102; \text{se}(\hat{\theta}) = 1/\sqrt{244.5} = 0.064$
$95\% \text{ CI} = (-0.102 \pm 1.96/\sqrt{244.5}) = (-0.227, 0.024)$

three times daily, although study 6 had a twice daily dosing regimen. The mean time from the qualifying myocardial infarction to entry into the trial ranged from 8 days to 85 months, with study 6 having a mean of 25 months. The mean duration of follow-up varied from study to study from 11.9 to 41.0 months, with studies 5 and 6 having the longest follow-up times. Canner concluded that there was nothing obvious in the design features of the studies that might explain any possible differences in the mortality results.

The next line of investigation undertaken by Canner was to consider adjustment of the individual study estimates for prognostic factors. For each of seven risk factors (history of congestive heart failure, history of angina pectoris, history of ECG-documented arrhythmia, use of digitalis, use of nitroglycerin, use of propranolol or other beta-blockers, and use of other drugs), it was found that the occurrence was significantly higher in the aspirin group than the placebo group in study 6. This might explain the more negative findings of the study. For three of the studies (2, 5 and 6) it was possible to adjust the log-odds ratio estimate for a variety of baseline characteristics. As different baseline variables were collected in each study, the adjustment was undertaken separately for each

**Table 6.9**   Aspirin in coronary disease: design features of the studies

|  | Study 1 | Study 2 | Study 3 | Study 4 | Study 5 | Study 6 |
|---|---|---|---|---|---|---|
| Time period | 1971–73 | 1972–75 | 1970–77 | 1975–79 | 1975–79 | 1975–79 |
| Number of patients | 1126 | 1529 | 626 | 1682 | 1216 | 4524 |
| Mean age | 55.0 | 56.5 | 58.9 | 56.2 | 56.3 | 54.8 |
| Gender | M | M | M, F | M, F | M, F | M, F |
| Total daily dose (mg) | 300 | 972 | 1500 | 900 | 972 | 1000 |
| Dosage schedule | o.d. | t.i.d. | t.i.d. | t.i.d. | t.i.d. | b.i.d. |
| Time from qualifying MI to entry | | | | | | |
| mean | 70 days | 85 mo. | 40 days | 8 days | 20 mo. | 25 mo. |
| range | 0.5–6 mo. | 21 days–22 yr | 28–42 days | days–weeks | 2–60 mo. | 2–60 mo. |
| Duration of patient follow-up (months) | | | | | | |
| mean | 11.9 | 22.0 | 24.0 | 12.0 | 41.0 | 39.6 |
| range | 2–30 | 10–28 | 24–24 | 12–12 | 35–48 | 35–48 |

Notes: MI = myocardial infarction; o.d. = once daily; b.i.d. = twice daily; t.i.d. = three times daily.

study. The estimates of the log-odds ratios presented in the rest of this section are calculated from summary statistics from the Canner paper and so will be approximate. Adjustment in study 6 resulted in a reduction of the log-odds ratio to 0.054, but there was only a minor effect on studies 2 and 5. No adjustment was possible for the other three studies. A repeated fixed effects meta-analysis of the six studies using the three adjusted estimates in place of the unadjusted estimates was undertaken. The $Q$ statistic changed from 9.88 to 7.30, resulting in a $p$-value of 0.20. The fixed effects estimate of the log-odds ratio changed from $-0.102$ to $-0.128$, a statistically significant effect ($p = 0.04$). Thus the baseline imbalance in study 6 may have contributed to the heterogeneity.

Although the data so far have been treated as binary responses, it may be more appropriate to treat them as survival times as this would allow for the differing follow-up times of the patients. In addition, mortality rates over specific time periods, such as one-year mortality rates, could be investigated using survival analysis techniques. In the paper, mortality within each year of follow-up was analysed, using the log-odds ratio approach based on binary data. The results are

**Table 6.10**    Aspirin in coronary heart disease: log-odds ratio of mortality on aspirin relative to placebo by year of follow-up

| Study | 1st year | 2nd year | 3rd and 4th years |
|---|---|---|---|
| 1 | −0.312 | −0.676 | ∞ |
| 2 | −0.200 | −0.842 | 0.938 |
| 3 | −0.245 | −0.146 | − |
| 4 | −0.214 | − | − |
| 5 | −0.063 | −0.673 | −0.059 |
| 6 | −0.178 | 0.214 | 0.260 |
| $\hat{\theta}$ | −0.211 | −0.174 | 0.231 |
| $U$ (1 df) | 6.00; $p = 0.01$ | 1.72; $p = 0.19$ | 3.06; $p = 0.08$ |
| $Q$ | 0.48; (5 df) $p = 0.99$ | 11.52; (4 df) $p = 0.02$ | 2.53; (3 df) $p = 0.47$ |

presented in Table 6.10. For mortality during the first year of follow-up, there is a consistent beneficial effect of aspirin amongst all six trials. The fixed effects estimate of the log-odds ratio was −0.211, a statistically significant effect ($p = 0.01$). The test for heterogeneity was not significant ($Q = 0.48$ (5 df), $p = 0.99$). For the second year of follow-up study 4 is excluded because it only had a 1-year follow-up period. There is evidence of heterogeneity amongst the other five studies ($Q = 11.52$ (4 df), $p = 0.02$). In study 6 there is higher mortality in the aspirin group than in the placebo group, whereas the opposite is true for the other studies. During the third and fourth years of follow-up the four studies contributing data show no effect or an adverse effect of aspirin over placebo. As there were no deaths during this period in the placebo group in study 1, the estimated log-odds ratio is ∞, although this study appears to have been included in the analysis presented in the paper. Heterogeneity is not significant ($Q = 2.53$ (3 df), $p = 0.47$). It appears that after a consistently positive effect of aspirin in the first year, the benefit disappears by the third year. In study 6 the reversal of the effect occurs earlier than in the other studies, causing the apparent heterogeneity.

To see whether or not heterogeneity was confined just to mortality, fixed effects meta-analyses were undertaken on a number of non-fatal outcomes. Data on the occurrence of non-fatal myocardial infarction reported in studies 2−6 provided evidence of a strong beneficial aspirin effect but no significant evidence of heterogeneity. On a number of other cardiovascular and gastrointestinal outcomes reported in studies 2, 5 and 6 there was good agreement between the studies.

Summarizing the results of the investigation into the apparent heterogeneity of the mortality results amongst the studies, the following conclusions were drawn. There was no obvious difference in the design of study 6 to offer an explanation. The heterogeneity was confined to the second year of follow-up, during which a reversal of the beneficial effect of aspirin began for study 6 but not the other studies. This reversal did not begin in the other longer-term studies until later. With respect to a number of other outcomes recorded, there was good agreement between study 6 and the other studies. Adjustment for imbalance in the distribution of risk factors between the two treatment groups in study 6 helped to reduce the amount of heterogeneity. The overall conclusion was that it seemed as if there was no real heterogeneity in mortality findings amongst the six studies, and that the results were consistent with a true aspirin effect that was beneficial in the short term of 1–2 years.

## 6.9   A STRATEGY FOR DEALING WITH HETEROGENEITY

In any meta-analysis it is important to evaluate heterogeneity. Investigation of heterogeneity can be divided into two parts, the first of which is specified *a priori* in the protocol, and the second is an additional exploratory approach which may or may not be required.

Topics that might be addressed in the protocol include:

(a)  the smallest treatment difference which would be considered to be clinically important;

(b)  the statistic which will be used for testing heterogeneity;

(c)  study-level covariates for inclusion in a meta-regression;

(d)  patient-level covariates to adjust for imbalance in the distribution of specific prognostic factors and baseline characteristics across treatment groups;

(e)  patient-level covariates to be evaluated as potential effect modifiers.

If the amount of heterogeneity found is considered to be clinically important and cannot be explained by the potential sources of heterogeneity specified above, then extra exploratory analyses involving other covariates may be needed. In addition, it would be advisable to check that the chosen parameterization of the treatment difference is appropriate. For example, in the case of binary data, should it be the log-odds ratio or the probability difference? Analysis of other related variables will indicate whether or not the heterogeneity is restricted to the primary response variable. If no explanation can be found for the heterogeneity then consideration should be given to fitting a random effects model, which allows for the treatment difference to vary from study to study.

# 7

# *Presentation and Interpretation of Results*

## 7.1 INTRODUCTION

It is important that the report of a meta-analysis provides the reader with the information required to evaluate and interpret its results. The reader needs to know how the meta-analysis was performed in order to be able to judge the reliability of the findings. Of particular concern are factors which might systematically influence the estimates of treatment difference. In 1996 the CONSORT statement (Begg *et al.*, 1996) was published with a view to improving the quality of reporting of randomized controlled trials. This comprised a checklist of key items of information considered necessary for the evaluation of the internal and external validity of the trial, and a flow diagram of the numbers of patients progressing through various stages of the trial. In a similar vein, the QUOROM statement (Moher *et al.*, 1999) was subsequently published in relation to the reporting of meta-analyses of clinical trials. Although the QUOROM statement focuses on the reporting of retrospective meta-analyses, it also provides a useful guideline for the reporting of prospective meta-analyses. It is therefore used as a basis for the discussion of the structure of a report in Section 7.2. Other guidelines for the reporting of a meta-analysis have been presented (see, for example, Deeks *et al.*, 1996; Clarke and Oxman, 2001; and Halvorsen, 1994). They focus on retrospective meta-analyses, based on summary information from published papers, and include more detail than is presented in this chapter.

Graphical displays have an important role to play in a report of a meta-analysis, as they can allow the reader to assimilate key information easily and quickly. When present in a report they are often the main focus of attention for the reader. Such displays are discussed in Section 7.3.

Although in the conduct of a meta-analysis the choice of parameterization of the treatment difference should be based on statistical considerations, it may be desirable to present the results in a way that is more interpretable in a clinical setting. Section 7.4 considers ways in which this might be achieved by transforming the original parameter.

## 7.2    STRUCTURE OF A REPORT

In many respects the report of a meta-analysis is similar to that for a clinical trial, and the main headings for the QUOROM checklist (Table 7.1) are identical to those of the CONSORT checklist. The term 'RCT' used in the checklist stands for randomized controlled trial. For an example of a publication based on the QUOROM statement, see Shrewsbury *et al.* (2000).

There should be a close correspondence between the meta-analysis protocol and the report, and many of the items in the QUOROM checklist were discussed in Chapter 2. The importance of these items in relation to the meta-analysis was considered in detail in that chapter, whereas here the focus is on the reporting aspects. The items which need to be addressed in the report will depend on the specific meta-analysis. For a retrospective meta-analysis based on published papers, it is likely that all items are relevant, whereas for a planned meta-analysis within the drug development process, the items relating to the searching strategy, the selection of studies, the assessment of methodological quality and publication bias will not usually be required.

When reporting the results of a meta-analysis it is useful to include the term 'meta-analysis' in the title, and to include a structured abstract or summary. The QUOROM statement divides the body of the report into four main sections – introduction, methods, results and discussion – each of which is now discussed in turn.

### 7.2.1    Introduction

The introduction will usually be based on the material included in the 'Background' and 'Objectives' section of the protocol (see Sections 2.2 and 2.3). At the end of the introduction section the reader should be told what information they might expect to obtain from reading the report.

### 7.2.2    Methods

A statement can be made regarding the existence of a protocol prior to the conduct of the meta-analysis. The prespecified hypotheses should be stated. Modifications to the protocol during the meta-analysis procedure should be described, with reasons given. A clear distinction between prespecified hypotheses and hypotheses generated after the data have been inspected should be made.

The methods section will include such items as the searching procedure and study selection criteria. These were discussed and illustrated in Sections 2.5 and 2.6. The validity assessment mentioned in the checklist in Table 7.1 relates to the methodological quality of the trials. Shrewsbury *et al.* (2000) provide an example of the reporting of the validity assessment:

**Table 7.1** The QUOROM statement checklist

| Heading | Subheading | Descriptor |
|---|---|---|
| Title | | Identify the report as a meta-analysis (or systematic review) of RCTs. |
| Abstract | | Use a structured format. |
| | Objectives | Describe the clinical question explicitly. |
| | Data sources | Describe the databases (i.e. list) and other information sources. |
| | Review methods | Describe the selection criteria (i.e. population, intervention, outcome, and study design), methods for validity assessment, data abstraction, study characteristics, and quantitative data synthesis in sufficient detail to permit replication. |
| | Results | Describe the characteristics of the RCTs included and excluded, qualitative and quantitative findings (i.e. point estimates and confidence intervals), and subgroup analyses. |
| | Conclusion | Describe the main results. |
| Introduction | | Describe the explicit clinical problem, biological rationale for the intervention, and rationale for the review. |
| Methods | Searching | Describe the information sources in detail (e.g. databases, registers, personal files, expert informants, agencies, hand-searching), and any restrictions (years considered, publication status, language of publication). |
| | Selection | Describe the inclusion and exclusion criteria (defining population, intervention, principal outcomes and study design). |
| | Validity assessment | Describe the criteria and process used (e.g. masked conditions, quality assessment, and their findings). |
| | Data abstraction | Describe the process or processes use (e.g. completed independently, in duplicate). |
| | Study characteristics | Describe the type of study design, participants' characteristics, details of intervention, outcome definitions, and how heterogeneity was assessed. |
| | Quantitative data synthesis | Describe the principal measures of effect (e.g. relative risk), method of combining results (statistical testing and confidence intervals), handling of missing data, how statistical heterogeneity was assessed, a rationale for any *a priori* sensitivity and subgroup analyses, and any assessment of publication bias. |
| Results | Trial flow | Provide a meta-analysis profile summarizing trial flow (see Figure 7.1). |

*(continued overleaf)*

**Table 7.1**     (*continued*)

| Heading | Subheading | Descriptor |
| --- | --- | --- |
| | Study characteristics | Present descriptive data for each trial (e.g. age, sample size, intervention, dose, duration, follow-up period). |
| | Quantitative data synthesis | Report agreement on the selection and validity assessment, present simple summary results (for each treatment group in each trial, for each primary outcome), present data needed to calculate effect sizes and confidence interals in intention-to-treat analyses (e.g. 2 × 2 tables of counts, means and standard deviations, proportions). |
| Discussion | | Summarize key findings, discuss clinical inferences based on internal and external validity, interpret the results in light of the totality of available evidence, describe potential biases in the review process (e.g. publication bias), and suggest a future research agenda. |

> All included studies were sponsored by Glaxo-Wellcome and all met company-wide minimum quality thresholds. All were randomised . . . . In all studies, maintenance of the treatment blind was carefully managed with adherence to in-house standard operating procedures. In all studies, treatment packs were supplied numbered in non-identifiable packaging and were dispensed by investigators to the next sequential patient to be randomised in the trial. All studies were conducted according to good clinical practice, and all had received ethical approval.

The outcome measures and baseline data used (see Section 2.4) and the methods of data extraction (see Section 2.7) should be outlined. Shrewsbury *et al.* (2000) describe the data extraction method as follows:

> Data abstraction was based on reported summary statistics (mean, SD and SE, proportions) for the intention to treat population. Two independent coworkers extracted data from study reports and manuscripts, and their results were compared. Discrepancies were resolved by consensus.

For each hypothesis tested the method used for the statistical analysis (see Section 2.8) should be described. Any sensitivity analyses performed (see Section 2.9) should be described. Finally, an explanation of the summary statistics which will presented in the results section should be given.

## 7.2.3   Results

Careful consideration needs to be given to the tabular and graphical presentation of results.

For retrospective meta-analyses, information on the number of included and excluded studies, from the list of studies which could potentially contribute, should be presented. The excluded studies should be summarized by reason for exclusion. This will also be necessary for prospective meta-analyses if for some reason some studies were excluded. The QUOROM statement flow diagram (Figure 7.1) is a useful way of presenting these data.

Descriptive data showing the main design characteristics of the included studies should be presented. This can usefully be presented in tables. For example, Table 7.2 reproduces Table 2 from Shrewsbury *et al.* (2000). The objective of this

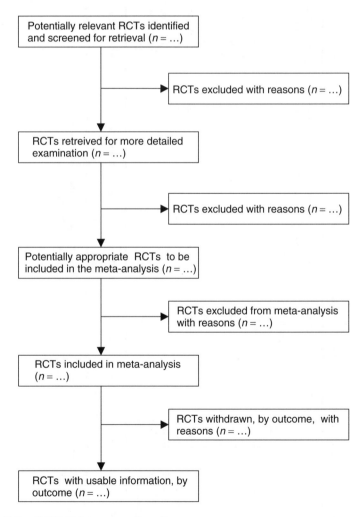

**Figure 7.1**    QUOROM statement flow diagram.

**Table 7.2** Individual study designs for treatment of asthma

| Trial | Country | Number of patients | Run-in period (weeks) | Duration (weeks) | Definition of ITT* | Inhaled steroid** | Baseline dose (µg/day) | Comparison dose (µg/day) |
|---|---|---|---|---|---|---|---|---|
| Greening | UK | 426[†] | 2 | 26 | 1 | BDP | 400 | 1000 |
| Ind | Europe, Canada | 336 | 4 | 24 | 1 | Fluticasone | 500 | 1000 |
| Woolcock | Worldwide | 494 | 1–5 | 24 | 1 | BDP | 1000 | 2000 |
| Kelsen | US | 483 | 2 | 24 | 2 | BDP | 400 (336)[‡] | 800 (672) |
| Murray | US | 514 | 2 | 24 | 2 | BDP | 400 (336)[‡] | 800 (672) |
| Kalberg | US | 488 | 2–4 | 24 | 2 | Fluticasone | 200 (176)[‡] | 500 (440) |
| Condemi | US | 437 | 2–4 | 24 | 2 | Fluticasone | 200 (176)[‡] | 500 (440) |
| Van Noord | Holland | 60 | 4 | 12 | 1 | Fluticasone | 200 (LD) | 400 (LD) |
| Van Noord | Holland | 214 | 4 | 12 | 1 | Fluticasone | 500 (HD) | 1000 (HD) |
| Vermetten | Holland | 233 | 2 | 12 | 1 | BDP | 200–400 | 800 |

*ITT = intention to treat. 1, all patients randomized to treatment; 2, all patients randomized to treatment who took at least a single dose of study medication.

**BDP = beclometasone dipropionate.

[†] 430 patients were randomized, but data for four patients were reported as 'unverifiable' and so these patients were not included in the ITT population.

[‡] UK equivalent dose (dose leaving valve), with US dose (dose leaving mouthpiece) in parentheses.

Reproduced from Shrewsbury *et al.*, 2000 (Table 2) by permission of The British Medical Journal.

meta-analysis was to examine the benefits for patients with symptomatic asthma of adding salmeterol to the current dose of inhaled corticosteroid compared with increasing the dose of the latter. This table provides information about the countries in which each trial was conducted, and the number of patients in and duration of each trial. The last three columns provide details of the inhaled steroid. It should be noted that for the meta-analysis the Van Noord study was split into two, one part comprising patients who at the start of the study were on a low dose of inhaled steroid and the other comprising patients on a high dose.

Each hypothesis of interest, as specified in the protocol, should be addressed in turn. Individual study results should be presented, as well as the overall results from the meta-analysis. Simple summary information for each treatment group within each study should be provided, as well as study estimates of treatment difference and their confidence intervals. For simple meta-analyses using the methods of Chapter 4, it may be possible for the reader to reproduce the results from such summary information. Even though this is unlikely to be the case for the methods described in Chapter 5, the summary information may still provide some useful insight into the data. Table 7.3 demonstrates one option for presenting results for the stroke example introduced in Section 3.2.1. This table includes information extracted from Tables 3.1, 4.1 and 4.2, and presents the treatment difference as a log-odds ratio. If preferred, the exponential of the log-odds ratio estimates and the upper and lower limits of the 95% CIs can be presented instead, providing results in terms of the odds ratio. In this case a standard error cannot be presented.

If it were planned to adjust for covariates in the main meta-analysis, then the adjusted results should be presented instead of the unadjusted ones. The results of prespecified tests of covariate by treatment interactions should be presented. If these interaction terms are statistically and clinically significant, consideration should be given to presenting the results separately for each subgroup. In the case of a continuous covariate the estimate and CI for the regression coefficient representing the relationship between the treatment difference and the covariate can be provided.

Finally, the results of any sensitivity analyses and any exploratory analyses should be discussed.

### 7.2.4   Discussion

The discussion section is for summarizing the key findings and drawing inferences from the results. Methodological limitations of the included studies and the meta-analysis, particularly in relation to the possibility of systematic bias in the estimation of treatment difference, should be addressed. An assessment of the clinical significance of the findings and their interpretation in the context of other available evidence is needed. Clinical recommendations and proposals for future research can be made.

**Table 7.3**    The occurrence of a stroke in hypertensive patients: comparison between antihypertensive treatment and control treatment from 13 studies

| Study | Patients with stroke/Total number (%) | | | | | Log-odds ratio* | Std. error | 95% CI |
|---|---|---|---|---|---|---|---|---|
| | Treated group | | Control group | | | | | |
| 2 HDFP (Stratum I) | 59/3903 | (1.5) | 88/3922 | (2.2) | | −0.40 | 0.17 | (−0.74, −0.07) |
| 4 ANBPS | 13/1721 | (0.8) | 22/1706 | (1.3) | | −0.54 | 0.35 | (−1.23, 0.15) |
| 5 MRC | 60/8700 | (0.7) | 109/8654 | (1.3) | | −0.61 | 0.16 | (−0.93, −0.29) |
| 6 VAII | 5/186 | (2.7) | 20/194 | (10.3) | | −1.43 | 0.51 | (−2.43, −0.42) |
| 7 USPHS | 1/193 | (0.5) | 6/196 | (3.1) | | −1.80 | 1.09 | (−3.93, 0.32) |
| 8 HDFP (Stratum II) | 25/1048 | (2.4) | 36/1004 | (3.6) | | −0.42 | 0.26 | (−0.94, 0.10) |
| 9 HSCSG | 43/233 | (18.5) | 52/219 | (23.7) | | −0.32 | 0.23 | (−0.77, 0.14) |
| 10 VAI | 1/68 | (1.5) | 3/63 | (4.8) | | −1.21 | 1.18 | (−3.50, 1.08) |
| 11 WOLFF | 2/45 | (4.4) | 1/42 | (2.4) | | 0.65 | 1.24 | (−1.79, 3.08) |
| 13 Carter | 10/49 | (20.4) | 21/48 | (43.8) | | −1.11 | 0.46 | (−2.01, −0.21) |
| 14 HDFP (Stratum III) | 18/534 | (3.4) | 34/529 | (6.4) | | −0.68 | 0.30 | (−1.26, −0.09) |
| 15 EWPHE | 32/416 | (7.7) | 48/424 | (11.3) | | −0.43 | 0.24 | (−0.90, 0.04) |
| 16 Coope | 20/419 | (4.8) | 39/465 | (8.4) | | −0.60 | 0.28 | (−1.16, −0.05) |

Meta-analysis

| | |
|---|---|
| Fixed effects estimate | −0.54  0.08  (−0.69, −0.38) |
| Random effects estimate | −0.54  0.08  (−0.69, −0.38) |
| Test for treatment difference ($\chi^2$) (fixed effects model) | 47.59; (1  df) $p < 0.001$ |
| Test for treatment difference ($\chi^2$) (random effects model) | 47.59; (1  df) $p < 0.001$ |
| Test for heterogeneity ($\chi^2$) | 9.57; (12  df) $p = 0.65$ |

*The log-odds ratio of a stroke on antihypertensive treatment relative to control treatment.

## 7.3   GRAPHICAL PRESENTATION

A good graphical display will provide information on the magnitude of the individual study estimates of treatment difference, an indication of the precision of these estimates and a means of assessing consistency amongst the studies. Even if it is not considered appropriate to calculate an overall estimate of the treatment difference, a graphical display of the individual study results can be informative. When an overall estimate has been calculated, this can be included. Two types of graphical display, the CI plot and the radial plot, are considered below.

## 7.3.1 A confidence interval plot

One commonly used graphical display is the CI plot, examples of which have appeared earlier in this book. This is also referred to as a forest plot, although the origin of this name appears to be unknown (Lewis and Clarke, 2001). Consider Figure 4.1, which shows a CI plot for the Collins *et al.* (1990) data set, in which the treatment difference is the log-odds ratio of a stroke on antihypertensive treatment relative to control. Typically, studies are listed down the page. The x-axis represents the treatment difference, θ, and usually a vertical line is drawn at the point which represents no treatment difference. For each study there is a symbol marking the point estimate of treatment difference and a horizontal line joining the lower and upper limits of the 95% CI.

This type of display is good at providing information on the magnitude of each study estimate and its precision. Given a point estimate $\hat{\theta}_i$ and the assumption of asymptotic normality, the 95% CI would be given by $\hat{\theta}_i \pm 1.96\text{se}(\hat{\theta}_i)$, that is, it would have width $3.92\text{se}(\hat{\theta}_i)$. *Precision* is defined as the inverse of variance, $1/[\text{se}(\hat{\theta}_i)]^2$ (or $w_i$), and so the shorter the CI the greater the precision. The relative precision of two study estimates can be seen by comparison of the widths of their CIs.

To provide the reader with a visual assessment of relative precision, it is necessary for the CIs to be symmetrical about their point estimates. This means that the scale for the x-axis must be linear in terms of the parameterization of the treatment difference used in the meta-analysis. For example, when using the log-odds ratio for binary data, then the x-axis scale should be linear on the log-odds ratio scale (Figure 4.1), and not linear on the odds ratio scale (Figure 7.2). Figure 7.3, in which the x-axis represents the odds ratio on a log scale, is equivalent to Figure 4.1, and may be preferred because it provides tick marks and labelling for particular values of the odds ratio. In Figure 7.2 the CIs do not appear to be symmetrical about their point estimates. This is demonstrated clearly for study 10. The reason for this is that the point estimates are given by $\exp(\hat{\theta}_i)$, and the 95% CIs by $\exp[\hat{\theta}_i \pm 1.96\text{se}(\hat{\theta}_i)]$. This also means that the width of the CI depends not only on the standard error but also on the study estimate. For two studies with equal precision, the one having a larger odds ratio will be associated with a wider CI. Whereas in Figure 4.1 studies 7 and 10 had CIs of similar width, in Figure 7.2 the width of the CI for study 10 is more than twice that of study 7. Notice also in Figure 7.2 that the full length of the CI for study 11 cannot be shown, because on this scale it is far too long to present meaningfully with the other ones. An additional problem with Figure 7.2 is in the visual comparison of positive and negative results. The values of an odds ratio and its reciprocal, for example 2 and 0.5, represent treatment differences of the same magnitude but in opposite directions. When these two values are plotted on a linear odds ratio scale they are not equidistant from 1. However, if plotted on a log-odds ratio scale

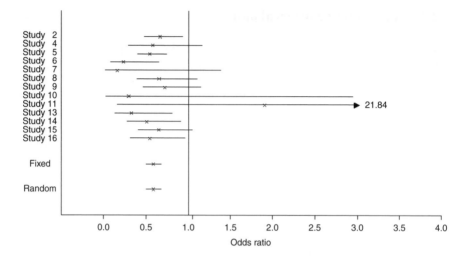

**Figure 7.2** Confidence interval plot on the odds ratio scale. Estimates and 95% confidence intervals of the odds ratio of a stroke on antihypertensive treatment relative to control treatment, calculated from the data in the first column of Table 4.3.

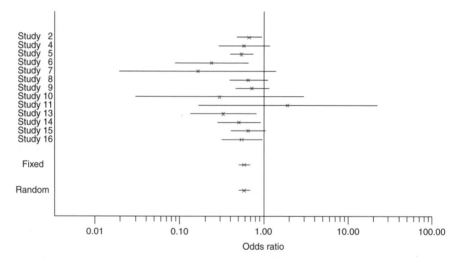

**Figure 7.3** Confidence interval plot of odds ratios on the log scale, using the same data as in Figure 7.2.

they are equidistant from 0, taking the values ±0.693. This is a second reason for keeping the x-axis linear on the log-odds ratio scale.

Although Figure 4.1 provides some information about the precision of study estimates, a better visual impact is obtained by making the size of the symbol representing the study estimate proportional to the precision. This has been

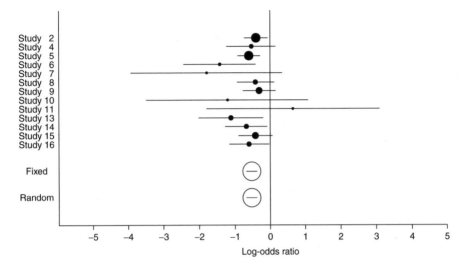

**Figure 7.4**   Confidence interval plot on the log-odds ratio scale, using the same data as in Figure 7.2. The area of the circle is proportional to the inverse variance of the estimate.

achieved in a number of published meta-analyses by presenting a shaded square, with the length of its sides proportional to $1/[\mathrm{se}(\hat{\theta}_i)]$ and centred at the point estimate $\hat{\theta}_i$. Alternatively, as illustrated in Figure 7.4, a shaded circle could be produced, centred at $\hat{\theta}_i$ and with radius proportional to $1/[\mathrm{se}(\hat{\theta}_i)]$. Usually, a different symbol from that used for the individual studies is chosen for the overall estimate. In the examples presented in this chapter, the same constant of proportionality for the area of this symbol has been used for the overall estimates and the individual studies.

For the CI plot there is a choice about the order in which the study estimates appear on the vertical axis. For example, if based on published papers one might chose alphabetical order of the first author, or date of publication. Alternatively, it may be more enlightening to order them according to some aspect of the study design or a study-level covariate. Figure 6.2 illustrates a plot of the tacrine studies by the dose of tacrine used. Another possibility is to order them according to precision. In the absence of any bias in the selection of studies included in the meta-analysis, one would expect to see a higher degree of consistency amongst the estimates from studies with higher precision than those with lower precision. This is shown for the Collins *et al.* data set in Figure 7.5.

Although the CI plot has some useful features and is fairly straightforward to produce, it is often difficult to obtain from it a measure of the amount and importance of heterogeneity between the studies. It is expected that study estimates will differ from one another because of sampling error, but it is not obvious how the plot will change when there are underlying differences between studies.

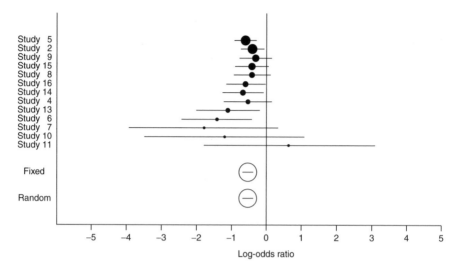

**Figure 7.5**   Confidence interval plot on the log-odds ratio scale, identical to Figure 7.4 with the exception that the studies are ordered by decreasing precision.

## 7.3.2   A radial plot

The radial plot, described by Galbraith (1988), is a bivariate scatter plot $(x, y)$ of the 'standardized estimate' of treatment difference against 'precision' for each study. The 'standardized estimate' is given by $\hat{\theta}_i/\text{se}(\hat{\theta}_i)$ (or $\hat{\theta}_i\sqrt{w_i}$). Galbraith defines 'precision' as $1/[\text{se}(\hat{\theta}_i)]$ (or $\sqrt{w_i}$), which is the square root of the usual definition of precision. Figure 7.6 shows a radial plot for the Collins *et al.* data set. The circular axis represents the treatment difference, $\theta$. The value of an individual study estimate $\hat{\theta}_i$ can be read from the $\theta$ scale by drawing a line from $(0, 0)$ through the point $(x_i, y_i)$. Because a larger $x$-value corresponds to higher precision, small trials correspond to points lying close to the origin whereas large trials provide influential points on the right-hand edge of the plot.

If a linear regression line of the 'standardized estimate' on 'precision' were to be fitted so as to pass through the origin, then the least-squares estimate of the slope would be given by the fixed effects estimate $\hat{\theta} = \sum_{i=1}^{r} \hat{\theta}_i w_i \big/ \sum_{i=1}^{r} w_i$. The line $y = \hat{\theta}x$ is drawn in Figure 7.6 meeting the $\theta$-axis at $\hat{\theta} = -0.535$. Under the fixed effects model (4.1) the 'standardized estimate' will have a variance of 1. The residual from the fitted regression line associated with study $i$ is equal to $(\hat{\theta}_i - \hat{\theta})\sqrt{w_i}$, which has a variance of $1 - w_i\big/\sum_{i=1}^{r} w_i$. Assuming that this variance is approximately equal to 1, a plot of the parallel lines $y = \hat{\theta}x \pm 2$ provides an approximate 95% confidence band for individual study results. If there is a common treatment difference, $\theta$, across all studies, then 95% of study estimates would be expected to lie within this band and 5% outside. Trials which are not consistent with the overall picture are easily identified because they

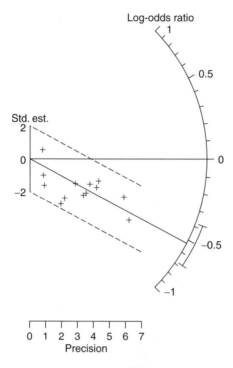

**Figure 7.6**   Radial plot of the study 'standardized estimates' of the log-odds ratio of a stroke on antihypertensive treatment relative to control treatment, against 'precision'. The fitted regression line which passes through the origin and meets the circular axis at the fixed effects estimate is represented by a solid line. The dashed parallel lines provide an approximate 95% confidence band for individual study results. The arc to the right of the circular axis represents the 95% confidence interval for the fixed effects estimate.

correspond to points falling outside this confidence band. This is analogous to identifying outliers from a plot of standardized residuals. All of the studies in Figure 7.6 fall within this confidence band, indicating no obvious problem with heterogeneity, and consistent with the non-significant test for heterogeneity found in Chapter 4. This is to be contrasted with the radial plot based on the probability difference parameterization, in which two studies fall outside of the confidence band (Figure 7.7). For this parameterization the test for heterogeneity was found to be statistically significant.

The way in which study estimates scatter about the regression line can be informative. In the absence of any bias in the selection of studies included in the meta-analysis, one would expect to see a random scatter of study estimates about the fitted regression line, with points above and below the line at all levels of precision. If, on the other hand, there is publication bias, resulting in larger estimates of treatment difference from smaller studies than from larger studies, then points on the left-hand side of the plot will tend to fall on one side of the

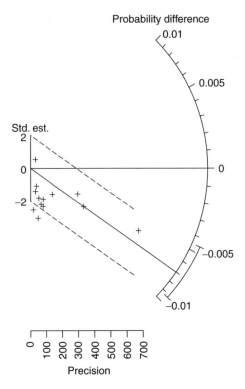

**Figure 7.7**   Radial plot of the study 'standardized estimates' of the difference in the probability of a stroke on antihypertensive treatment relative to control treatment, against 'precision'.

regression line, whereas the points on the right-hand side will tend to fall on the opposite side. There is no obvious pattern to the study estimates shown in Figure 7.6.

Care should be taken in the interpretation of the 95% confidence band. This band does not represent the 95% CI for the fixed effects estimate $\hat{\theta}$. Therefore, to avoid confusion, the lines $y = \hat{\theta}x \pm 2$ should not extend to the θ-axis. A CI for the overall estimate can be presented as an arc close to but to the right of the θ-axis, as illustrated in Figure 7.6.

In summary, the radial plot provides information on the magnitude of the individual study estimates of treatment difference, an indication of the precision of these estimates and a means of assessing consistency amongst the studies. It is this last property which provides its advantage over the CI plot. However, it is more difficult to construct using graphical software, due mainly to the circular axis. Although desirable, it is not essential for this axis to be circular. For example, a vertical axis on the right-hand side of the diagram could be used, as illustrated in Figure 7.8.

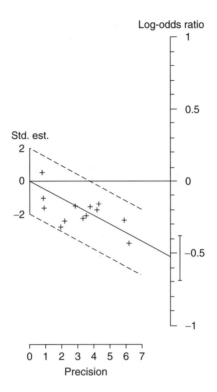

**Figure 7.8**    A radial plot identical to Figure 7.6 with the exception that the log-odds ratio axis is vertical instead of circular.

## 7.4   CLINICALLY USEFUL MEASURES OF TREATMENT DIFFERENCE

The choice of the parameterization of the treatment difference and the method of estimation in both individual studies and the meta-analysis needs to be made on the basis of statistical considerations. For full scientific evaluation, it is important for the results to be available in terms of the chosen parameterization. However, the results of a meta-analysis are likely to be of interest to a wide range of people, including statisticians, clinicians, regulators, health care providers and patients, and consideration needs to be given to appropriate ways of presenting the results to the different audiences.

Sometimes the chosen parameterization itself has a straightforward inter-pretation. In other cases, a simple transformation of the parameter may be helpful. This is illustrated in Section 7.4.1 for some typical parameterizations. In Sections 7.4.2 and 7.4.3, two particular types of transformation are discussed in detail.

## 7.4.1    Simple transformations of the treatment difference parameter

First consider continuous measurements, which are assumed to be normally distributed. The means in the treated and control groups are $\mu_T$ and $\mu_C$ respectively, and the common variance within each treatment group is $\sigma^2$. The interpretation of the absolute mean difference parameter $\theta = \mu_T - \mu_C$ seems to be straightforward. For example, in the case of blood pressure measurements, this represents the mean change in blood pressure between two treatments. When the standardized mean difference, $\theta = (\mu_T - \mu_C)/\sigma$, has been used, the interpretation is more difficult. One option is to select a value for $\sigma$. Multiplying $\theta$ by $\sigma$ will provide a value for the mean difference on the original scale. The calculated mean difference and its 95% CI are obtained by multiplying respectively the estimated treatment difference for $\theta$ and its 95% confidence limits by $\sigma$. The value of $\sigma$ chosen may be a pooled estimate calculated from relevant studies in the meta-analysis, or from a specific population of patients for whom the results are being interpreted.

For binary data, consider the log-odds ratio given by

$$\theta = \log \left\{ \frac{p_T \, (1 - p_C)}{p_C \, (1 - p_T)} \right\},$$

where $p_C$ and $p_T$ are the success probabilities in the control and treated groups respectively. The odds ratio is given by $\exp(\theta)$. The calculated odds ratio and its 95% CI are obtained by exponentiating respectively the estimated treatment difference for $\theta$ and its 95% confidence limits. Alternatively, $p_T$ can be calculated for a chosen value $p_C$ using the log-odds ratio. Here

$$p_T = \frac{p_C \exp(\theta)}{(1 - p_C) + p_C \exp(\theta)}. \tag{7.1}$$

The calculated probability and its 95% CI are obtained by substituting respectively the estimated treatment difference for $\theta$ and its 95% confidence limits in (7.1). If $(p_{TL}, p_{TU})$ is the 95% CI for $p_T$, then $(p_{TL} - p_C, p_{TU} - p_C)$ is a 95% CI for the difference in success probabilities. The estimate and CI for the difference in success probabilities will depend on the chosen value of $p_C$. One possibility is to calculate the overall proportion of successes in the control groups from all of the trials contributing to the meta-analysis. However, as the proportion of successes in the control group can often vary considerably from trial to trial, this may give rise to misleading information. In the context of the calculation of the 'number needed to treat' (Section 7.4.3), Smeeth *et al.* (1999) have argued that a better alternative is to use estimates obtained for specific patient populations. Alternatively, a graphical presentation of the results might be considered. For example, the curve of $100p_T$ against $100p_C$ may be produced, for $p_C$ taking values between 0 and 1 in (7.1) and with $\theta$ replaced by its estimate. In addition, the curves of the 95%

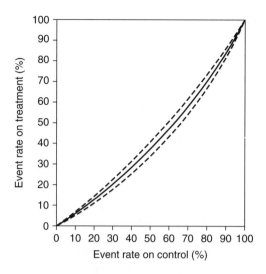

**Figure 7.9**   The event rate on treatment as a function of the event rate on control, calculated for a log-odds ratio of −0.535 with 95% confidence interval (−0.688, −0.383). The estimates of the event rate on treatment are indicated by the solid curve, and the 95% confidence limits by the dashed curves.

confidence limits for $100p_T$ could be included. Figure 7.9 demonstrates this for the Collins *et al.* data set. As presented in the first column of Table 4.3, the estimate of the log-odds ratio of a stroke on antihypertensive treatment relative to control is −0.535, with 95% CI (−0.688, −0.383). For specific values of the control event rate ($100p_C$), the estimate and CI for the treated event rate ($100p_T$) can be read off the graph. Instead of plotting ($100p_T$) on the $y$-axis, one may wish to plot $100(p_T - p_C)$.

Suppose that the chosen parameter for ordinal data is the log-odds ratio based on the proportional odds assumption. In this case $\theta$ is given by

$$\theta = \log\left\{\frac{Q_{kT}(1 - Q_{kC})}{Q_{kC}(1 - Q_{kT})}\right\}, \qquad k = 1, \ldots, m - 1,$$

where there are $m$ ordered categories, $Q_{kT}$ is the cumulative probability of a response in categories $1, \ldots, k$ in the treated group, and $Q_{kC}$ is defined similarly for the control group. The term $Q_{kT}$ is then calculated from a formula similar to (7.1):

$$Q_{kT} = \frac{Q_{kC}\exp(\theta)}{(1 - Q_{kC}) + Q_{kC}\exp(\theta)}. \tag{7.2}$$

For a particular value of $k$, $Q_{kT}$ can be considered as the probability of 'success' in the treated group. In this respect $Q_{kT}$ and $Q_{kC}$ can be treated in the same way as $p_T$ and $p_C$ above.

For survival data, consider the log-hazard ratio given by

$$\theta = \log[-\log\{S_T(t)\}] - \log[-\log\{S_C(t)\}],$$

where $S_C(t)$ and $S_T(t)$ are the survival probabilities at time $t$ in the control and treatment groups, respectively. Interest may lie in calculating the difference in survival probabilities between the two treatments at a specific timepoint, say $t_1$. Given a value of $S_C(t_1)$, the value of $S_T(t_1)$ may be calculated from the log-hazard ratio, $\theta$, as follows:

$$S_T(t_1) = \exp\{\exp(\theta) \log(S_C(t_1))\}. \tag{7.3}$$

The calculated survival probability and its 95% CI are obtained by substituting respectively the estimated treatment difference for $\theta$ and its 95% confidence limits in (7.3). A CI for the difference in survival probabilities can be obtained in the same way as for the difference in success probabilities. As the estimate and CI for the difference in survival probabilities will depend on $S_C(t_1)$, a suitable choice is needed for application to a specific patient population.

## 7.4.2   Probability of doing better on treatment than on control

On making a decision about the health care of a patient, one might ask whether the patient is likely to have a better response if given the new treatment than if given the control treatment. This question can be answered through the calculation of the probability of being better off on the new treatment, expressed in this or an alternative form. For example, a probability of 0.8 can be expressed as an 80% chance or odds of 4:1 of being better off on the new treatment than on the control treatment. It will usually be possible to calculate this probability from the overall estimate of treatment difference from the meta-analysis, and this is illustrated here for some typical parameterizations of treatment difference.

Suppose that $Y_T$ is the random variable associated with the response of a subject taking the new treatment and $Y_C$ that associated with a subject taking the control treatment. The probability that a person on the new treatment does better than one on the control treatment is $P(Y_T > Y_C)$.

Consider, first, continuous measurements which are assumed to be normally distributed. If $Y_T$ is normally distributed with mean $\mu_T$ and variance $\sigma^2$, and $Y_C$ is normally distributed with mean $\mu_C$ and variance $\sigma^2$, then $Y_T - Y_C$ is normally distributed with mean $\mu_T - \mu_C$ and variance $2\sigma^2$. So

$$P(Y_T > Y_C) = P\{(Y_T - Y_C) > 0\} = \Phi\left(\frac{\mu_T - \mu_C}{\sigma\sqrt{2}}\right),$$

where $\Phi$ is the standard normal distribution function.

If the absolute mean difference parameterization has been chosen for the meta-analysis, so that $\theta = \mu_T - \mu_C$, then

$$P(Y_T > Y_C) = \Phi \left( \frac{\theta}{\sigma\sqrt{2}} \right). \tag{7.4}$$

An estimate of $\sigma$ is required for the calculation. However, if the standardized mean difference has been chosen, so that $\theta = (\mu_T - \mu_C)/\sigma$, then

$$P(Y_T > Y_C) = \Phi \left( \frac{\theta}{\sqrt{2}} \right), \tag{7.5}$$

which can be calculated from the value of $\theta$ alone.
For binary data the log-odds ratio parameterization

$$\theta = \log \left\{ \frac{p_T(1 - p_C)}{p_C(1 - p_T)} \right\}$$

will be considered. The distributions of $Y_C$ and $Y_T$ are now discrete, whereas in the previous example they were continuous. For a pair of responses, one from a patient on the new treatment and one from a patient on the control treatment, there are only four possible outcomes: a success from the new treatment and a failure from the control; a success from the control and a failure from the new; a success from both; and a failure from both. Interest lies in the situation of success on one treatment and failure on the other. Given this scenario the probability that the success is on the new treatment can be calculated. Denoting a success by 1 and a failure by 0, a probability that expresses the chance of doing better on the new treatment is

$$P\{Y_T = 1 | Y_T + Y_C = 1\} = \frac{p_T(1 - p_C)}{p_T(1 - p_C) + p_C(1 - p_T)} = \frac{1}{1 + e^{-\theta}}. \tag{7.6}$$

Now consider ordinal data for which the assumption of proportional odds between treatments is made. The parameterization of treatment difference is the log-odds ratio, given by

$$\theta = \log \left\{ \frac{Q_{kT}(1 - Q_{kC})}{Q_{kC}(1 - Q_{kT})} \right\}, \qquad k = 1, \ldots, m - 1,$$

where $m$ is the number of categories. Generalization of formula (7.6) becomes more difficult in this case, because the number of potential outcomes is much larger. Instead we derive an expression in terms of the underlying latent variables, which were discussed in Section 5.4.1. This approach could also be applied to the binary case. In this context $Y_T$ and $Y_C$ will represent the continuous 'latent' variables for the treated and control groups, respectively. Under the proportional odds assumption, $Y_C$ and $Y_T$ can be considered to have logistic distributions, so that

$$P(Y_C \leqslant y) = \frac{1}{1 + e^{-y}}$$

and

$$P(Y_T \leqslant y) = \frac{1}{1 + e^{-(y+\theta)}}.$$

When categories are ordered with $C_1$ being the best to $C_m$ being the worst, it is $P(Y_C > Y_T)$ that is required. It can be shown that

$$P(Y_C > Y_T) = \frac{1 - e^{-\theta} - \theta e^{-\theta}}{\left(1 - e^{-\theta}\right)^2}. \tag{7.7}$$

For survival data or interval-censored survival data the log-hazard ratio is typically chosen to measure treatment difference. The variables $Y_C$ and $Y_T$ now represent survival times in the two treatment groups. Here $Y_C$ and $Y_T$ are assumed to have continuous distributions. Expressing the log-hazard ratio $\theta$ in terms of survivor functions, it can be seen that

$$\theta = \log[-\log\{S_T(t)\}] - \log[-\log\{S_C(t)\}],$$

where $S_T(t) = P(Y_T > t)$ and $S_C(t) = P(Y_C > t)$.

Under the proportional hazards assumption $Y_C$ and $Y_T$ are considered to have exponential distributions, so that

$$P(Y_C > t) = e^{-\lambda t}$$

and

$$P(Y_T > t) = e^{-\lambda \psi t},$$

where $\psi = e^{\theta}$. The required probability is given by

$$P(Y_T > Y_C) = \frac{1}{\psi + 1}. \tag{7.8}$$

In all cases, the calculated probability and its 95% CI are obtained by substituting respectively the estimated treatment difference for $\theta$ and its 95% confidence limits in the appropriate formula (7.4)–(7.8).

### 7.4.3   The number needed to treat

The number needed to treat (NNT) has become a popular way of reporting the results from both individual trials and meta-analyses. The NNT can be calculated when the response of interest is a binary outcome. It is defined as the number of patients who need to be treated with the new treatment rather than the control treatment for one additional patient to benefit. It is the inverse of the probability difference, NNT $= 1/(p_T - p_C)$, where $p_T$ and $p_C$ are the probabilities of success on new treatment and control, respectively. Its proponents claim that it is a more meaningful measure of treatment benefit than alternatives such as the probability difference or odds ratio. However, it does have some undesirable statistical properties. These will be explained below.

As the probability difference $p_T - p_C$ takes values between $-1$ and $1$, the NNT takes values between $-\infty$ and $-1$ and between $1$ and $\infty$. As the probability difference moves from a very small positive value through $0$ to a very small negative value, the NNT moves from $\infty$ to $-\infty$ without going through $0$. If some studies show a positive effect of the new treatment and some studies a negative effect, then the overall result from a meta-analysis based on the NNT parameterization may produce a nonsensical result. The scale of the NNT is not suitable for the calculations involved in a meta-analysis. This is shown in more detail by Lesaffre and Pledger (1999), who demonstrate that it is better to conduct the meta-analysis using the probability difference parameterization and then calculate the NNT from the overall estimate of the probability difference.

If the meta-analysis has been conducted using the probability difference, the NNT can be calculated as the inverse of the overall estimate of the probability difference. A CI for the NNT can also be calculated by taking the inverse of the limits of the CI for the probability difference. However, this latter calculation may be problematic. If the CI for the probability difference includes both positive and negative values, then its interpretation on the NNT scale is difficult. For example, a 95% CI on the probability difference scale of $(-0.05, 0.1)$ would correspond to a 95% CI on the NNT scale which comprises the two regions $(-\infty, -20)$ and $(10, \infty)$. In an attempt to present the disjoint CIs in a more meaningful way, Altman (1998) proposed using the notation NNTB and NNTH. The number of patients needed to be treated for one additional patient to benefit (to be harmed) is denoted NNTB (NNTH). The 95% CI on the NNT scale would then become (NNTH 20 to $\infty$ to NNTB 10). He suggests that a CI plot based on the probability difference, in which the $x$-axis is relabelled in terms of NNTB and NNTH, can be presented.

Given the problems surrounding the NNT, it is not at all clear why the NNT is thought to be easier to understand than the probability difference. As discussed by Hutton (2000), the probability difference can be given a simple interpretation in terms of numbers of patients. For example, $100(p_T - p_C)$ is the additional number of patients per 100 treated who benefit from the new treatment compared with control. Hutton argues that both the meta-analysis and the presentation of the results should be based on the probability difference.

The interpretation of the NNT runs into more difficulties if the most appropriate parameterization for the meta-analysis is the log-odds ratio or log-relative risk, as is very often the case. The NNT can be calculated from each of these parameters as follows. If the log-odds ratio has been used, the NNT can be calculated from the equation

$$\text{NNT} = \frac{p_C \left(e^\theta - 1\right) + 1}{p_C \left(1 - p_C\right) \left(e^\theta - 1\right)}, \tag{7.9}$$

where

$$\theta = \log\left\{ \frac{p_T \left(1 - p_C\right)}{p_C \left(1 - p_T\right)} \right\}.$$

If the log-relative risk has been used, the NNT calculation is based on the equation

$$\text{NNT} = \frac{1}{p_C \left(e^\theta - 1\right)}, \tag{7.10}$$

where $\theta = \log(p_T/p_C)$.

To produce an estimate of the NNT it is necessary to substitute the estimated treatment difference for $\theta$ in either (7.9) or (7.10). However, in addition it is also necessary to provide a value for $p_C$. If the log-odds ratio (log-relative risk) is approximately constant over a range of values of $p_C$, then the NNT will not be. Therefore, reporting the NNT in the absence of the value of $p_C$ can be potentially misleading. As discussed in Section 7.4.1, when making inferences about specific populations, it is advisable to use the estimate of $p_C$ which is relevant to that population. A CI for the NNT can be calculated by substituting the upper and lower limits of the 95% CI for the log-odds ratio in formula (7.9) or the log-relative risk in (7.10). However, there may still be the same problem with the CI for the NNT as discussed above.

In conclusion, there are difficulties in the calculation of the NNT estimate and its CI and plenty of scope for misinterpretation. Smeeth *et al.* (1999) comment that the NNT is no better understood than other parameterizations.

# 8

# *Selection Bias*

## 8.1  INTRODUCTION

When judging the reliability of the results of a meta-analysis, attention should focus on factors which might systematically influence the overall estimate of treatment difference. One important factor is the selection of studies for inclusion in the meta-analysis. In this regard, bias may be introduced in two different ways. One is by including studies which have themselves produced biased estimates of the treatment difference. The other is by selective exclusion of the results of some eligible studies, perhaps because relevant data are not available.

The first scenario is easier to handle, because sensitivity analyses can be conducted in which studies suspected of producing a biased estimate can be excluded. The main challenge is in identifying potential sources of bias. Bias may be introduced into the results of a study because of methodological flaws. In Section 2.6, the methodological quality of a trial was considered as a means of determining which trials should be included in the meta-analysis. In this case, trials which do not adhere to important methodological standards, such as unbiased allocation of patients to treatment groups, are omitted from the meta-analysis. Bias may also be introduced by the order in which studies are conducted. For example, large-scale clinical trials of a new treatment are often undertaken following promising results from small trials. In particular, in a drug development programme promising results from phase II studies will lead to phase III studies, whereas disappointing results will not. A meta-analysis may be undertaken in the former case, but is unlikely to be performed in the latter. Therefore, given that a meta-analysis is being undertaken, larger estimates of treatment difference are more likely from the small early studies than from the later larger studies. A meta-analysis can be performed which excludes the small early studies. Such a meta-analysis may be planned either as the main analysis or as a supporting sensitivity analysis. It should be noted that the inclusion of such studies in a meta-analysis will have little effect on the overall fixed effects estimate of treatment difference due to their small weights. However, if the difference between these studies and the later larger ones is sufficient to produce significant heterogeneity, the random effects estimate may alter substantially.

The second scenario causes difficulties because sensitivity analyses may require specific assumptions to be made about the extent of and reasons for data being missing. These assumptions cannot usually be validated. Therefore, although sensitivity analyses may provide some useful information on the reliability of the meta-analysis, they are unlikely to overcome the problem completely. One reason why relevant data are missing is *publication bias*. Publication bias may be encountered if a meta-analysis is restricted to the combination of results obtained from trials which have been published. Often, the decision to submit or accept a manuscript is influenced by whether or not statistical significance is achieved for a treatment comparison, so that studies with statistically significant results are more likely to be published than are those showing no significant difference. The direction of the treatment difference is also likely to be influential. For example, studies which indicate that a new treatment is worse than a standard or control treatment are less likely to be published than those indicating a benefit. Publication bias will result in overestimation of the benefit of the new treatment.

Publication bias has received much attention in the literature, and this chapter focuses on methods for detecting it and correcting for it. A meta-analysis concerning the effect of intravenous magnesium on mortality following acute myocardial infarction is introduced in Section 8.2 and will be used as an example. Section 8.3 considers the 'funnel plot' for the graphical detection of publication bias. Statistical methods for the detection and correction of publication bias are discussed in Section 8.4. In Section 8.5, the related problem of bias due to selective reporting within studies is addressed.

When using the methods of Sections 8.3 and 8.4 it should be borne in mind that other causes of bias may be confounded with publication bias. For example, it may be impossible to distinguish between the bias due to the overestimation of the treatment benefit in early small studies, as discussed earlier, and publication bias resulting in the lack of data from small negative studies. Sterne *et al.* (2001a) also note that studies with lower methodological quality tend to show larger treatment benefits and also tend to be small. Therefore, any bias detected by these methods should not automatically be ascribed to publication bias.

Another reason why relevant data might not be available is that different rating scales or methods of assessment may have been used across studies. If the meta-analysis is conducted only on trials using a common outcome measure, this may lead to selection bias, although this will not necessarily result in overestimation of the benefit of the new treatment. A related problem occurs when the times at which patients are assessed vary from trial to trial. Furthermore, even if the same outcome measure has been used in all studies, the way in which the results are presented in a published paper or report may vary from one study to another. This may make it difficult or impossible to extract the relevant data from all studies. Methods for combining different types of information are discussed in Chapter 9. An appropriate choice of one of these methods may be used as the basis for a sensitivity analysis.

## 8.2   AN INVESTIGATION OF PUBLICATION BIAS: INTRAVENOUS MAGNESIUM FOLLOWING ACUTE MYOCARDIAL INFARCTION

To illustrate the investigation of publication bias, a set of trials undertaken to investigate the effect on short-term mortality of giving intravenous magnesium to patients with acute myocardial infarction will be used. The data from 16 trials are presented in Table 8.1. The treatment difference is the log-odds ratio of mortality on magnesium relative to control, based on the binary yes/no outcome for mortality. The calculations are based on the efficient score and Fisher's information statistics from the conditional likelihood (formulae (3.5) and (3.6)). Teo and Yusuf (1993) reported the results of a fixed effects meta-analysis undertaken following the publication of the results of the LIMIT-2 study (Woods *et al.*, 1992). This meta-analysis (see Table 8.2) was based on the first ten clinical trials presented in Table 8.1. They noted a smaller effect in the LIMIT-2 study than in most of the smaller studies, but concluded that there was no statistical evidence of real differences between the trials, as the 95% confidence intervals of all trials overlapped (see Figure 8.1). If they had conducted a test for heterogeneity, they would have found that this almost reached statistical significance ($p = 0.07$, Table 8.2). A radial plot (Figure 8.2) suggests a possibility of heterogeneity, but does not provide strong evidence. However, the random effects estimate of the log-odds ratio is considerably larger than the fixed effects estimate, as it gives more weight to the smaller studies (Table 8.2). In a subsequent editorial, Yusuf *et al.* (1993) concluded: 'it appears that intravenous magnesium is a safe, effective, widely practicable, and inexpensive intervention that has the potential of making an important impact on the management of patients with MI in most countries throughout the world'. In 1995, the results from the large ISIS-4 trial (ISIS-4 Collaborative Group, 1995) showed that magnesium had no effect on mortality. Egger and Davey Smith (1995) considered possible reasons for the difference in the findings between the meta-analysis and the ISIS-4 study. One possibility was selective identification of positive studies for inclusion in the meta-analysis. Egger and Davey Smith conducted a more extensive search and discovered another five small studies (studies 11–15 in Table 8.1). However, all five studies indicated a beneficial effect of magnesium, two of them showing a statistically significant effect. Publication bias was considered as another possibility. Based on a funnel plot, they concluded that 'selective non-publication of negative trials seems to be a likely explanation for the discrepant findings of the magnesium meta-analysis'.

## 8.3   A FUNNEL PLOT

Light and Pillemer (1984) introduced the 'funnel plot' for the graphical detection of publication bias. The funnel plot is a bivariate scatter plot $(x, y)$ of the study sample size against the study estimate of treatment difference. It is based on the

**Table 8.1** Intravenous magnesium following acute myocardial infarction: study estimates of the log-odds ratio of mortality for intravenous magnesium relative to control, based on formulae (3.5) and (3.6)

| Study | Treated group | | Control group | | $\hat{\theta}_i$ | $w_i$ | $\hat{\theta}_i w_i$ | $\hat{\theta}_i^2 w_i$ |
|---|---|---|---|---|---|---|---|---|
| | Dead | Total | Dead | Total | | | | |
| 1 Morton (1984) | 1 | 40 | 2 | 36 | −0.795 | 0.73 | −0.58 | 0.46 |
| 2 Rasmussen (1986) | 9 | 135 | 23 | 135 | −0.989 | 7.08 | −7.00 | 6.92 |
| 3 Smith (1986) | 2 | 200 | 7 | 200 | −1.134 | 2.21 | −2.50 | 2.83 |
| 4 Abraham (1987) | 1 | 48 | 1 | 46 | −0.043 | 0.49 | −0.02 | 0.00 |
| 5 Feldstedt (1988) | 10 | 150 | 8 | 148 | 0.221 | 4.24 | 0.94 | 0.21 |
| 6 Shechter (1989) | 1 | 59 | 9 | 56 | −1.795 | 2.30 | −4.13 | 7.41 |
| 7 Ceremuzynski (1989) | 1 | 25 | 3 | 23 | −1.159 | 0.94 | −1.08 | 1.26 |
| 8 Singh (1990) | 6 | 76 | 11 | 75 | −0.673 | 3.80 | −2.56 | 1.72 |
| 9 Shechter and Hod (1991) | 2 | 89 | 12 | 80 | −1.669 | 3.22 | −5.37 | 8.96 |
| 10 Woods et al. (LIMIT-2) (1992) | 90 | 1159 | 118 | 1157 | −0.298 | 47.35 | −14.09 | 4.19 |
| 11 Bertschat (1989) | 0 | 22 | 1 | 21 | −2.048 | 0.25 | −0.51 | 1.05 |
| 12 Pereira (1990) | 1 | 27 | 7 | 27 | −1.728 | 1.74 | −3.00 | 5.18 |
| 13 Golf (1991) | 5 | 23 | 13 | 33 | −0.795 | 3.01 | −2.39 | 1.90 |
| 14 Thogersen (1991) | 4 | 130 | 8 | 122 | −0.764 | 2.87 | −2.19 | 1.67 |
| 15 Schechter and Hod (1995) | 4 | 107 | 17 | 108 | −1.356 | 4.76 | −6.45 | 8.74 |
| 16 ISIS-4 (1995) | 2216 | 29011 | 2103 | 29039 | 0.058 | 999.43 | 57.54 | 3.31 |
| Total (1–10) | 123 | 1981 | 194 | 1956 | | 72.35 | −36.39 | 33.98 |
| Total (1–15) | 136 | 2290 | 240 | 2267 | | 84.97 | −50.94 | 52.53 |
| Total (1–16) | 2352 | 31301 | 2343 | 31306 | | 1084.40 | 6.60 | 55.84 |

*Sources:* studies 1–9, Figure 1 in Teo and Yusuf (1993); 10, Woods *et al.* (1992); 11–15, Egger and Davey Smith (1995); 16, 1S1S-4 (1995).

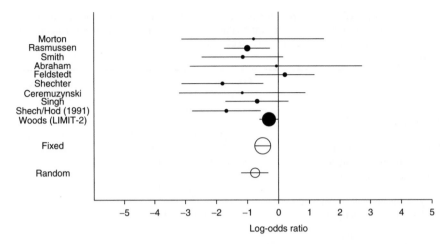

**Figure 8.1** Intravenous magnesium following acute myocardial infarction. Estimates and 95% confidence intervals of the log-odds ratio of mortality for intravenous magnesium relative to control.

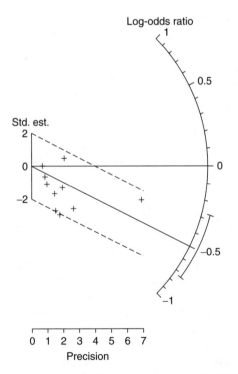

**Figure 8.2** Intravenous magnesium following acute myocardial infarction: radial plot of the 'standardized estimates' of the log-odds ratio of mortality for intravenous magnesium relative to control, against 'precision'.

**Table 8.2**   Intravenous magnesium following acute myocardial infarction: meta-analysis of the log-odds ratio of mortality for intravenous magnesium relative to control, applying the methods of Chapter 4 with the method of moments estimate of $\tau^2$ to the study estimates in Table 8.1

|  | Log-odds ratio | Std. error | 95% CI |
|---|---|---|---|
| Meta-analysis (studies 1–10) |  |  |  |
| Fixed effects estimate | −0.50 | 0.12 | −0.73, −0.27 |
| Random effects estimate | −0.75 | 0.22 | −1.19, −0.32 |
| Test for treatment difference ($\chi^2$), fixed effects model | 18.31; (1 df) $p < 0.001$ |  |  |
| Test for treatment difference ($\chi^2$), random effects model | 11.76; (1 df) $p < 0.001$ |  |  |
| Test for heterogeneity ($\chi^2$) | 15.67; (9 df) $p = 0.07$ |  |  |
| Meta-analysis (studies 1–15) |  |  |  |
| Fixed effects estimate | −0.60 | 0.11 | −0.81, −0.39 |
| Random effects estimate | −0.86 | 0.18 | −1.21, −0.51 |
| Test for treatment difference ($\chi^2$), fixed effects model | 30.54; (1 df) $p < 0.001$ |  |  |
| Test for treatment difference ($\chi^2$), random effects model | 22.88; (1 df) $p < 0.001$ |  |  |
| Test for heterogeneity ($\chi^2$) | 21.99; (14 df) $p = 0.08$ |  |  |
| Meta-analysis (all studies) |  |  |  |
| Fixed effects estimate | 0.01 | 0.03 | −0.05, 0.07 |
| Random effects estimate | −0.76 | 0.19 | −1.13, −0.39 |
| Test for treatment difference ($\chi^2$), fixed effects model | 0.04; (1 df) $p = 0.84$ |  |  |
| Test for treatment difference ($\chi^2$), random effects model | 15.86; (1 df) $p < 0.001$ |  |  |
| Test for heterogeneity ($\chi^2$) | 55.80; (15 df) $p < 0.001$ |  |  |

premise that the precision in estimating the treatment difference will increase as the sample size of the study increases. Usually, there is good correlation between the two. As an alternative, the reciprocal of the standard error of the estimate ('precision') of the treatment difference may be used instead of the study sample size. In the absence of any selection bias, the spread of results will be wide at the bottom of the graph where small studies are placed, and will become narrower as the studies become larger: the plot will resemble a symmetrical inverted funnel, as indicated in Figure 8.3. The funnel plot for the Collins *et al.* (1990) results from Table 4.2 is shown in Figure 8.4. The vertical dashed line is placed at the fixed effects estimate of the log-odds ratio. In Section 4.2.5 it was noted that there was little evidence of heterogeneity between the study estimates. It is possible to imagine where the funnel might be drawn, and there is no strong evidence of selection bias.

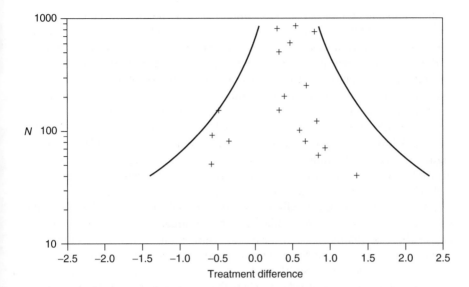

**Figure 8.3**    Funnel plot in the absence of selection bias.

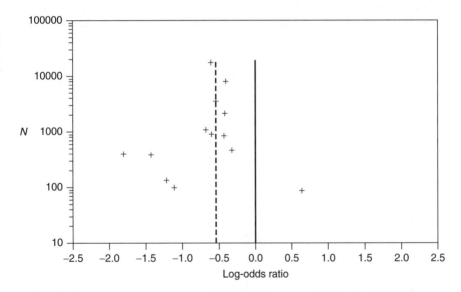

**Figure 8.4**    Stroke in hypertensive patients: funnel plot of sample size against the log-odds ratio of a stroke on antihypertensive treatment relative to control treatment. The dashed vertical line lies at the overall fixed effects estimate.

One plausible way in which publication bias may be introduced is as follows. First, the probability of selection increases as the one-sided *p*-value for testing the benefit of the new treatment decreases. This means that the magnitude of the bias in the estimate of treatment difference will increase as the sample size decreases. Second, the probability of selection increases with the size of the study. It is more likely that the results from a large study will be published than those from a small study, and this is especially true if the benefit from the new treatment is not statistically significant. This scenario will lead to an absence of small negative studies. A funnel plot of the ten studies from Teo and Yusuf (1993) is shown in Figure 8.5. For these studies there is a suggestion of heterogeneity (as discussed in Section 8.2). In the absence of selection bias, the presence of heterogeneity will affect the shape of the funnel plot by reducing the difference in the spread of results between large and small studies. However, selection bias will still result in an absence of small negative studies. Figure 8.5 suggests there may be selection bias as there is a blank space in the bottom right-hand corner of the funnel plot. However, the visual impact is dominated by the position of the LIMIT-2 study at the top. Egger and Davey Smith (1995) present a funnel plot for studies 1–15. The additional five trials all indicate a benefit from magnesium (Table 8.1), so that their funnel plot looks even more asymmetric. They conclude that the funnel plot is not symmetrical.

In Figure 8.4 it is possible to imagine where the funnel might be drawn. In other cases the position of the funnel would not be as obvious. An alternative

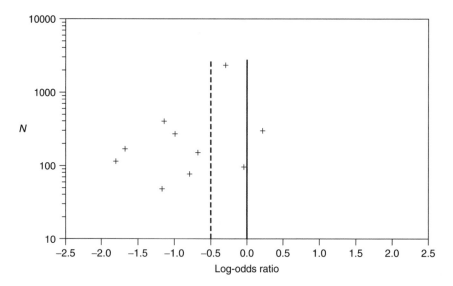

**Figure 8.5**   Intravenous magnesium following acute myocardial infarction: funnel plot of sample size against the log-odds ratio of mortality for intravenous magnesium relative to control. The dashed vertical line lies at the overall fixed effects estimate.

approach is to plot sample size against the 'standardized estimate' (as defined in Section 7.3.2). In the absence of selection bias and heterogeneity between the study estimates, the spread of results should be the same at all values of the sample size, whereas in the absence of small negative studies the spread would become narrower at small sample sizes. A second alternative is to use the radial plot, in which the 'standardized estimate' is plotted against 'precision'. In the absence of selection bias and heterogeneity between the study estimates, the spread of points around the regression line should be the same for all levels of precision, with points above and below the regression line for all levels of precision. Figure 8.2 shows that seven of the nine small studies lie below the regression line, whereas the LIMIT-2 study on the right-hand side of the plot lies above the line, indicating a difference in the size of effect between the small studies and the LIMIT-2 study.

## 8.4 STATISTICAL METHODS FOR THE DETECTION AND CORRECTION OF PUBLICATION BIAS

A number of methods for identifying and modelling publication bias have been proposed in the literature. Three particular methods are presented in detail in this section in order to illustrate the different types of approach taken. The reader is referred to Begg and Berlin (1988) and Begg (1994) for a more comprehensive coverage of the topic.

### 8.4.1 A test of funnel plot asymmetry

Egger *et al.* (1997) present a formal test for publication bias based on linear regression analysis. Although discussed in the context of a funnel plot, the $x$ and $y$ variables that they use for the linear regression are the same as those defined for the radial plot. Because it is an extension of the regression approach already presented for the radial plot, it is discussed here in the context of the radial plot.

The linear regression of the 'standardized estimate' on 'precision' was discussed in Section 7.3.2. In that section attention focused on fitting a regression line which passed through the origin. If the fixed effects model is appropriate, this calculated regression line will be a good fit to the data. If, however, the estimates of treatment difference from smaller studies differ systematically from those from larger trials, it will not be a good fit to the data. A more appropriate model would then include both intercept and slope parameters, and be given by

$$y_i = \alpha + \beta x_i + \varepsilon_i,$$

for $i = 1, \ldots, r$, where $r$ is the number of studies, $y_i$ is the 'standardized estimate' ($\hat{\theta}_i \sqrt{w_i}$), $x_i$ is the 'precision' ($\sqrt{w_i}$), and the error terms, $\varepsilon_i$, are realizations of normally distributed random variables with expected value 0 and variance 1.

A test of publication bias would be a test of the null hypothesis that $\alpha$ is equal to zero. The intercept, $\alpha$, provides a measure of funnel plot asymmetry: the larger its deviation from zero, the more pronounced the asymmetry. Suppose that positive values of $\theta$ are associated with a beneficial effect of the new treatment over control. If there are larger beneficial effects in the smaller studies than in the larger studies, the estimated slope, $\hat{\beta}$, will be less than the fixed effects estimate $\hat{\theta}$, and may even be negative. The estimated intercept will be greater than zero.

The least-squares estimates of $\alpha$ and $\beta$ are given by

$$\hat{\alpha} = \frac{\sum_{i=1}^{r}(\hat{\theta}_i - \hat{\beta})\sqrt{w_i}}{r}$$

and

$$\hat{\beta} = \frac{r\sum_{i=1}^{r}\hat{\theta}_i w_i - \left(\sum_{i=1}^{r}\sqrt{w_i}\right)\left(\sum_{i=1}^{r}\hat{\theta}_i\sqrt{w_i}\right)}{r\sum_{i=1}^{r} w_i - \left(\sum_{i=1}^{r}\sqrt{w_i}\right)^2}.$$

Under the fixed effects model (4.1), the variance of $\hat{\alpha}$ is given by

$$\mathrm{var}(\hat{\alpha}) = \frac{\sum_{i=1}^{r} w_i}{r\sum_{i=1}^{r} w_i - \left(\sum_{i=1}^{r}\sqrt{w_i}\right)^2}.$$

A test of the null hypothesis that the intercept is equal to zero can be conducted by comparing the statistic $\hat{\alpha}/\mathrm{se}(\hat{\alpha})$ with the standard normal distribution.

The parameter estimates $\hat{\alpha}$ and $\hat{\beta}$ can be obtained by performing a least-squares regression of $\hat{\theta}_i\sqrt{w_i}$ on $\sqrt{w_i}$ (see Section A.2 in the Appendix). Such an analysis can be performed in many packages, for example by using PROC GLM in SAS. These produce the correct estimates of the regression coefficients. However, the standard errors and test statistics computed by these packages are incorrect for the required model, because they assume that $\mathrm{var}(\varepsilon_i) = \sigma^2$, where $\sigma^2$ is to be estimated from the data, instead of equal to 1. To obtain the correct standard error for $\hat{\alpha}$, the standard error for the intercept given by the package should be divided by the square root of the residual (error) mean square. Alternatively, the correct standard error can be obtained as the square root of the first diagonal element of the matrix $(X'X)^{-1}$, where $X$ is the $r \times 2$ matrix of explanatory variables associated with $\alpha$ and $\beta$. Many packages, such as SAS PROC GLM, will present this matrix as an option (see Section 4.2.4). A confidence interval for the intercept is based on asymptotic normality and is given by $\hat{\alpha} \pm 1.96\mathrm{se}(\hat{\alpha})$.

For the Collins *et al.* data set of 13 studies, the estimate of the intercept was $-0.79$, with 95% CI $(-1.93, 0.34)$. As the CI includes zero, the null hypothesis that $\alpha = 0$ is not rejected. There is no strong evidence of a difference between the

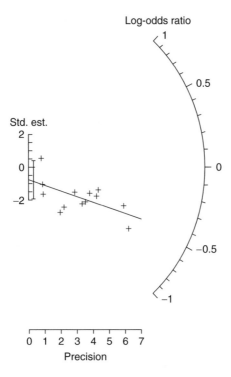

**Figure 8.6**    Stroke in hypertensive patients: radial plot with fitted regression line for the log-odds ratio of a stroke on antihypertensive treatment relative to control treatment. The 95% confidence interval for the intercept of the regression line is shown to the right of the vertical axis.

smaller and larger studies (Figure 8.6). This concurs with the visual inspection of the funnel plot (Figure 8.4).

The fitted regression line for the ten magnesium trials is shown in Figure 8.7, together with the 95% CI for the intercept. The estimate of the intercept was $-1.07$, with 95% CI $(-2.05, -0.09)$. This is significant evidence that $\alpha$ is not equal to 0. As a negative estimate of $\theta$ is associated with a benefit of magnesium, the negative estimate for the intercept shows that the smaller studies are associated with larger estimates of benefit than the larger one. Again, this concurs with the visual inspection of the funnel plot (Figure 8.5).

Another method associated with the funnel plot is the 'trim and fill' procedure proposed by Duval and Tweedie (2000a, 2000b). This consists of adding studies to a funnel plot until it becomes symmetrical. The procedure involves a number of steps. First, the number of studies in the asymmetric outlying part of the funnel is estimated. These studies are removed, or 'trimmed', and either a fixed or a random effects meta-analysis (whichever is considered to be the more appropriate) is performed on the remaining studies. The estimated treatment difference from this

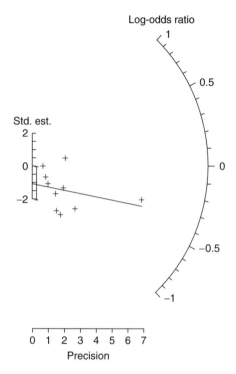

**Figure 8.7**   Intravenous magnesium following acute myocardial infarction: radial plot with fitted regression line for the log-odds ratio of mortality for intravenous magnesium relative to control. The 95% confidence interval for the intercept of the regression line is shown to the right of the vertical axis.

analysis provides an estimate of the true centre of the funnel. Each 'trimmed' study is then replaced together with its missing counterpart, which is its mirror image about the estimated centre of the funnel plot. The final estimate of the treatment difference is obtained from a meta-analysis which includes the 'filled' studies.

Although the 'trim and fill' procedure provides a simpler approach than using the selection models of Section 8.4.3, it has been shown in a simulation exercise to add studies in a substantial proportion of meta-analyses, even in the absence of publication bias (Sterne and Egger, 2000).

## 8.4.2   Rosenthal's file-drawer method

The method of Rosenthal (1979) is a very simple means of assessing the impact of missing studies on the overall estimate of treatment difference. It determines the number of unpublished studies with an average observed treatment difference of zero which would be needed to produce a test statistic for the overall treatment difference which just failed to reach statistical significance. The term 'file-drawer' is used because the results from unpublished studies are assumed to be hidden away in filing cabinets. The information required from each of the $r$ studies providing results is the one-sided significance level $p_{1i}$, $i = 1, \ldots, r$, for the null hypothesis that the new treatment is equal to the control versus the alternative that the new treatment is better. Let $u(p_{1i})$ be the upper $100p_{1i}$th percentage point of the standard normal distribution, that is,

$$u(p_{1i}) = \Phi^{-1}(1 - p_{1i}),$$

where $\Phi$ is the standard normal distribution function. Under the null hypothesis of no treatment difference in any study, the sum of the $u(p_i)$ values is normally distributed with mean 0 and variance $r$. To test the global hypothesis that there is no difference between the treatments against the one-sided alternative that the new treatment is better, the statistic

$$U_r = \frac{\sum_{i=1}^{r} u(p_{1i})}{\sqrt{r}}$$

is compared with the standard normal distribution. The null hypothesis is rejected at level $\alpha$ if $U_r > u(\alpha)$.
As $u(p_{1i})$ is equal to $\hat{\theta}_i \sqrt{w_i}$, an alternative form of the test statistic $U_r$ is given by

$$U_r = \frac{\sum_{i=1}^{r} \hat{\theta}_i \sqrt{w_i}}{\sqrt{r}}.$$

Suppose that $k$ is the number of additional studies required such that the statistic

$$U_{r,k} = \frac{\sum_{i=1}^{r} u(p_{1i})}{\sqrt{r+k}} < u(\alpha).$$

Then $k$ will satisfy

$$k > -r + \frac{\left\{\sum_{i=1}^{r} u(p_{1i})\right\}^2}{\{u(\alpha)\}^2} = -r + \frac{\left\{\sum_{i=1}^{r} \hat{\theta}_i \sqrt{w_i}\right\}^2}{\{u(\alpha)\}^2}.$$

Applying this method to the ten magnesium trials, and using a one-sided 2.5% significance level so that $\alpha = 0.025$ and $u(\alpha) = 1.96$, it can be seen that

$$k > -10 + \left(\frac{-14.765}{1.96}\right)^2 = 46.7.$$

This means that if there are 47 or more unpublished studies, with an average estimate of the treatment difference being zero, the apparent statistical significance of the meta-analysis would be lost. Whether or not such a figure is plausible must be judged within the context of the meta-analysis. In this case, the chance of such a large number of unpublished studies must be almost zero.

Although this method is simple, the assumption on which it is based may be unrealistic. It assumes that the average of the treatment difference parameters in the unpublished studies is equal to zero. Also, it ignores the size of the studies and is not influenced by differences in the estimates of treatment difference between small and large studies.

### 8.4.3 Models for the probability of selection

A number of authors (Lane and Dunlap, 1978; Hedges, 1984, 1992; Iyengar and Greenhouse, 1988; Dear and Begg, 1992; Copas, 1999) have proposed models for the probability of selection and used a conditional likelihood approach (sometimes referred to as *weighted distribution theory*) to adjust the meta-analysis for selection bias. The general approach is as follows. Suppose that the treatment difference parameter, $\theta$, is greater than zero if the new treatment is better than control. The estimate of treatment difference in study $i$, $\hat{\theta}_i$, is a realization of a random variable $Y_i$, which has density function $f_{Y_i}(y_i)$. The distribution of $Y_i$ will depend on the model chosen for the meta-analysis. For example, for the random effects model of Section 4.3.1 the distributional assumption is that $Y_i \sim N(\theta, w_i^{-1} + \tau^2)$. However, when selection bias is present the study estimate is not a random sample from this distribution: instead it is a random sample from the conditional distribution of $Y_i$ given that study $i$ has been selected. Let $S_i$ be the random variable associated with the selection of study $i$. Then $S_i$ has a Bernoulli distribution, taking the value 1 if study $i$ is selected and 0 otherwise. The conditional density function of $Y_i$ given that study $i$ has been selected is given by

$$f_{Y_i|S_i}(y_i|S_i = 1) = \frac{f_{Y_i}(y_i)P(S_i = 1|Y_i = y_i)}{\int_{-\infty}^{\infty} f_{Y_i}(u)P(S_i = 1|Y_i = u)\,du},$$

where $P(S_i = 1|Y_i = y_i)$ is the probability that study $i$ is selected for the meta-analysis given that the estimate of treatment difference is $y_i$. A likelihood function is constructed by taking the product of the individual study likelihood functions, that is, the $f_{Y_i|S_i}(y_i|S_i = 1)$, in which $y_i$ is replaced by $\hat{\theta}_i$. Maximum likelihood estimates of unknown parameters can then be obtained.

To calculate the likelihood function it is necessary to choose an appropriate model to define the conditional selection probability, $P(S_i = 1|Y_i = y_i)$. If the conditional selection probability is the same for all studies, then no bias is introduced. If it is small for estimates of treatment difference which are close to zero and large for those of greater magnitude the bias will be substantial. The simplest model was examined by Hedges (1984), following work by Lane and Dunlap (1978). It assumes that the study will only be selected if statistical significance is reached in the test of the treatment difference. If applied in the context of a one-sided alternative hypothesis ($\theta > 0$), with significance level $\alpha$, this model is defined by

$$P(S_i = 1 | Y_i = y_i) = \begin{cases} 1 & \text{if } y_i \geqslant C_{\alpha i}, \\ 0 & \text{otherwise}, \end{cases}$$

where $C_{\alpha i}$ is the critical value for the one-sided $\alpha$ test for study $i$. In this case the contribution to the likelihood function for study $i$ is

$$\frac{f_{Y_i}(\hat{\theta}_i)}{\int_{C_{\alpha i}}^{\infty} f_{Y_i}(u)\, du} \qquad \text{if } \hat{\theta}_i \geqslant C_{\alpha i},$$

and 0 otherwise. In the case of the random effects model of Section 4.3.1, the contribution to the likelihood function from study $i$ would be

$$L(\theta, \tau^2; \hat{\theta}_i) = \frac{1}{\sqrt{2\pi(w_i^{-1} + \tau^2)}} \exp\left\{\frac{-(\hat{\theta}_i - \theta)^2}{2(w_i^{-1} + \tau^2)}\right\}$$

$$\times \frac{1}{1 - \Phi\{(C_{\alpha i} - \theta)/\sqrt{(w_i^{-1} + \tau^2)}\}}, \qquad \text{if } \hat{\theta}_i \geqslant C_{\alpha i},$$

and 0 otherwise, where $\Phi$ is the standard normal distribution function.

In a later paper (Hedges, 1992), the model was generalized to allow the conditional probability of selection to depend on the $p$-value calculated for the study. As the $p$-value decreases the probability of selection increases. Alternative relationships between the probability of selection and $p$-values are given by Iyengar and Greenhouse (1998) and Dear and Begg (1992).

Copas (1999) increased the complexity of the model. In his approach study selection is associated with a normally distributed latent variable. Let $X_i$ be the latent variable for study $i$ which has mean $\gamma_0 + \gamma_1 \sqrt{n_i}$ and variance 1, where $n_i$ is the sample size of study $i$. The study is selected only if the realization of $X_i$ for study $i$ is greater than zero. That is, $S_i = 1$ if $x_i > 0$. In the absence of selection bias, the probability of selection for study $i$ is $\Phi(\gamma_0 + \gamma_1 \sqrt{n_i})$. Assuming that $\gamma_1$ is positive, large studies are more likely to be selected than small studies. Selection bias is modelled by assuming that the variables $X_i$ and the random variable $Y_i$ of which $\hat{\theta}_i$ is a realization have a bivariate normal distribution with correlation coefficient $\rho$. If $\rho = 0$ there is no selection bias. If, however, $\rho > 0$, the selected studies which have positive values of $x_i$ will tend to have positively biased values of $\hat{\theta}_i$. The conditional density function of $Y_i$ given that study $i$ has been selected is given by

$$f_{Y_i | X_i}(y_i | X_i > 0) = \frac{f_{Y_i}(y_i) P(X_i > 0 | Y_i = y_i)}{P(X_i > 0)} = \frac{f_{Y_i}(y_i) P(X_i > 0 | Y_i = y_i)}{\int_{-\infty}^{\infty} f_{Y_i}(u) P(X_i > 0 | Y_i = u)\, du}.$$

Consider the application to the random effects model of Section 4.3.1. From multivariate normal theory, the conditional distribution of $X_i$ given $Y_i$ is

$$X_i | Y_i \sim N\left(\gamma_0 + \gamma_1\sqrt{n_i} + \frac{\rho(Y_i - \theta)}{(w_i^{-1} + \tau^2)^{1/2}}, 1 - \rho^2\right).$$

The contribution to the likelihood function from study $i$ would be

$$L(\theta, \tau^2, \gamma_0, \gamma_1, \rho; \hat{\theta}_i) = \frac{1}{\sqrt{2\pi(w_i^{-1} + \tau^2)}} \exp\left\{\frac{-(\hat{\theta}_i - \theta)^2}{2(w_i^{-1} + \tau^2)}\right\} \frac{\Phi(a_i)}{\Phi(b_i)},$$

where

$$a_i = \frac{\gamma_0 + \gamma_1\sqrt{n_i} + \rho(\hat{\theta}_i - \theta)(w_i^{-1} + \tau^2)^{-1/2}}{(1 - \rho^2)^{1/2}}$$

and

$$b_i = \gamma_0 + \gamma_1\sqrt{n_i}.$$

Copas suggests that it will not be possible to estimate reliably more than three out of the five parameters $\theta$, $\tau^2$, $\gamma_0$, $\gamma_1$ and $\rho$. As $\gamma_0$ and $\gamma_1$ have a direct interpretation in terms of the probability of selection, they can be given fixed values, and ML estimates of the other three can be found. The sensitivity of $\hat{\theta}$ to the choice of values for $\gamma_0$ and $\gamma_1$ can then be explored and displayed in a contour plot.

Consider the application of the Copas model to the first 15 magnesium studies. The number of patients per study ranges from about 40 to 2300. If the probabilities of selection for studies of size 40 and 2300 are 0.1 and 0.9 respectively, then $\gamma_0 = -1.673$ and $\gamma_1 = 0.0616$. If the data set 'meta' contains the values of $\hat{\theta}_i$, $n_i$ and $w_i$ under the variable names 'y', 'n' and 'w', then the following SAS PROC NLMIXED program can be used to calculate ML estimates of $\theta$, $\tau^2$ and $\rho$.

```
PROC NLMIXED data =meta;
PARMS tausq = 1 rho theta =0;
BOUNDS tausq >= 0, -1 <= rho <=1;

gamma0 = -1.673;
gamma1 = 0.0616;
var = 1/w + tausq;
b = gamma0+gamma1*sqrt(n);
a = (b + rho*(y-theta)/sqrt(var))/sqrt(1-rho*rho);
phia = probnorm(a);
phib = probnorm(b);
ll = -0.5*log(var)-0.5*(y-theta)**2/var + log(phia)- log(phib);
MODEL y ~ general(ll);
```

When $\gamma_0 = -1.673$ and $\gamma_1 = 0.0616$, the estimates of $\theta$ and its standard error are $-0.43$ and $0.19$, respectively. Compared with the random effects estimate of

−0.86 which assumed no selection bias (Table 8.2), the treatment difference is reduced by about half. The estimate of $\rho$ is −0.55.

## 8.5 BIAS DUE TO SELECTIVE REPORTING WITHIN STUDIES

The models discussed in Section 8.4.3 consider only one outcome measure of interest. The probability that a study is selected for the meta-analysis is dependent on the significance level or magnitude of the estimate of treatment difference of that one outcome measure. However, bias can also be introduced via the selective reporting of results from a study. If a number of outcome variables have been analysed, only the ones showing a statistically significant benefit of the new treatment may be reported. Hutton and Williamson (2000) consider a model in which the outcome with the smallest significance level, out of a possible $p$ outcomes analysed, is the only one reported.

Subgroup analyses are often undertaken to investigate heterogeneity in a meta-analysis. A study can only be included in a subgroup analysis if the estimate of treatment difference and its standard error have been reported for the specific subgroup. Again, bias can be introduced due to selective reporting of subgroup analyses based on statistical significance. Hahn *et al.* (2000) perform a sensitivity analysis under the assumption that subgroup results have been selected for presentation when the $p$-value is less than 0.05.

# 9

# Dealing with Non-Standard Data Sets

## 9.1 INTRODUCTION

For some meta-analyses, the characteristics of the available data make it difficult or impossible to implement the methods described in Chapters 4 and 5. In this chapter, various commonly occurring problems are discussed and solutions suggested.

Section 9.2 considers the problem in which the outcome measure is a binary response and there are no 'successes' or no 'failures' in one or both of the treatment arms of individual trials. This situation is likely to arise when the event of interest has a low probability of occurring. In particular, it will be a common situation for rarely occurring adverse events.

A common problem which occurs in a retrospective meta-analysis is when different rating scales or methods of assessment have been used from one trial to the next. If the meta-analysis is conducted only on trials using a common outcome measure, this will lead to loss of power and the possibility of selection bias. Methods for combining the data from different rating scales are discussed in Section 9.3. A related problem, addressed in Section 9.4, occurs when the times at which patients are assessed vary from trial to trial.

Even if the same outcome measure has been used in all studies, the way in which the results are presented in a published paper or report may vary from one study to another. Section 9.5 considers ways of combining trials which report different summary statistics. Sometimes the estimate of the chosen measure of treatment difference and its variance are not directly reported, but may be computed from other available data. Ways in which this may be done are presented in Section 9.6.

It may be planned to perform a meta-analysis using individual patient data, but it may only be possible to obtain summary information from some studies. In this case there will be a need to combine estimates of treatment difference based on summary statistics with those based on individual patient data, and this is discussed in Section 9.7.

Finally, Section 9.8 considers methods for combining $p$-values when it is impossible to calculate estimates of treatment difference from individual studies.

## 9.2   NO EVENTS IN TREATMENT ARMS OF INDIVIDUAL TRIALS

In the stroke example described in Section 3.2.1, there were two studies (1 and 12) in which there was no occurrence of stroke in either treatment group, and one study (3) in which there was no occurrence of stroke in the treated group (Table 3.1). For the analysis of the stroke example described in Chapters 4 and 5, the three studies were excluded. In this section, the implications of this approach are discussed and other possibilities considered. The issues are discussed in relation to the log-odds ratio parameterization, although difficulties also arise with the other parameterizations which were discussed in Section 3.2.2.

The traditional meta-analysis methods presented in Chapter 4 involve the calculation of an overall estimate of treatment difference from a weighted average of individual study estimates. For the stroke example, the measure of treatment difference is the log-odds ratio of a stroke on antihypertensive treatment relative to control. In Section 3.2.2, four methods of estimating the log-odds ratio for an individual study were presented. These are maximum likelihood estimation and the approach using the efficient score and Fisher's information statistics, both of which can be based either on an unconditional or a conditional likelihood. Each of the four methods is discussed in turn below.

The unconditional ML estimate of the log-odds ratio (formula (3.1)) is undefined for studies 1, 3 and 12. In addition, the inverse variance of the estimate (3.2) is equal to 0, so that these studies would contribute nothing towards the overall estimate. However, Gart and Zweifel (1967) showed that adding 0.5 to the number of 'successes' and 'failures' in each treatment group improved the estimate of the log-odds ratio by reducing its bias. This also allows an estimate to be calculated in the case of zero cells in the $2 \times 2$ table. Formulae (3.1) and (3.2) now become

$$\hat{\theta} = \log \left\{ \frac{(s_T + 0.5)(f_C + 0.5)}{(s_C + 0.5)(f_T + 0.5)} \right\} \tag{9.1}$$

and

$$\text{var}(\hat{\theta}) = \frac{1}{(s_T + 0.5)} + \frac{1}{(s_C + 0.5)} + \frac{1}{(f_T + 0.5)} + \frac{1}{(f_C + 0.5)}. \tag{9.2}$$

Table 9.1 shows the results from a fixed effects meta-analysis in which formulae (9.1) and (9.2) have been used for all 16 studies. Although the estimates from studies 1, 3 and 12 are now included in the analysis, they have larger standard errors than the other studies and consequently smaller weight. For most of the other studies the impact of adding 0.5 to each of the cells has been slight (see Table 4.3). However, this is not the case for studies 7, 10 and 11 which have a small number of strokes. Nevertheless, the overall fixed effects estimate of $-0.532$ (standard error 0.077) has hardly changed.

**Table 9.1**   Fixed effects meta-analysis of the log-odds ratio of a stroke on antihypertensive treatment relative to control. Estimates with standard error in square brackets

| Study | Estimation method | |
|---|---|---|
| | Unconditional ML (adding 0.5 to all cells): (9.1), (9.2) | Conditional $Z$ and $V$: (3.5), (3.6) |
| 1 VA-NHLB1 | −0.008 [2.001] | − |
| 2 HDFP (Stratum I) | −0.400 [0.169] | −0.397 [0.167] |
| 3 Oslo | −2.480 [1.479] | −2.082 [0.897] |
| 4 ANBPS | −0.525 [0.346] | −0.528 [0.340] |
| 5 MRC | −0.604 [0.161] | −0.591 [0.155] |
| 6 VAII | −1.355 [0.492] | −1.240 [0.414] |
| 7 USPHS | −1.477 [0.912] | −1.439 [0.763] |
| 8 HDFP (Stratum II) | −0.414 [0.262] | −0.416 [0.260] |
| 9 HSCSG | −0.317 [0.231] | −0.319 [0.231] |
| 10 VAI | −0.957 [0.992] | −1.112 [1.016] |
| 11 WOLFF | 0.464 [1.055] | 0.620 [1.176] |
| 12 Barraclough | 0.000 [2.009] | − |
| 13 Carter | −1.079 [0.451] | −1.073 [0.435] |
| 14 HDFP (Stratum III) | −0.665 [0.295] | −0.657 [0.284] |
| 15 EWPHE | −0.421 [0.238] | −0.421 [0.235] |
| 16 Coope | −0.590 [0.281] | −0.580 [0.270] |
| $U$ (1 df) | 48.23; $p < 0.001$ | 53.33; $p < 0.001$ |
| $Q$ | 10.64; (15 df) | 12.35; (13 df) |
| | $p = 0.78$ | $p = 0.50$ |
| $\hat{\theta}$ [se($\hat{\theta}$)] | −0.532   [0.077] | −0.544   [0.075] |
| 95% CI | (−0.683, −0.382) | (−0.690, −0.398) |

The conditional ML estimate is also undefined for studies 1, 3 and 12 and the corresponding inverse variances are equal to 0. Using this approach, all three studies must be excluded from the meta-analysis.

The methods based on efficient score and Fisher's information statistics do allow study 3 to be included, but not studies 1 and 12. The meta-analysis using the Peto approach ((3.5) and (3.6)) is shown in Table 9.1. The inclusion of study 3, which indicates a large benefit from antihypertensive treatment, changes the overall estimate from −0.533 (Table 4.3) to −0.544.

In addition to the four methods of estimation, there is the Mantel–Haenszel estimate (Mantel and Haenszel, 1959), which is a weighted average of the individual study estimates of the odds ratio. If the odds ratio is denoted by $\psi$, where $\psi = \exp(\theta)$, each study estimate, $\hat{\psi}_i$, and weight, $w_i$, can be calculated as follows:

$$\hat{\psi}_i = \frac{s_{Ti} f_{Ci}}{s_{Ci} f_{Ti}} \tag{9.3}$$

and

$$w_i = \frac{s_{Ci} f_{Ti}}{n_i}. \tag{9.4}$$

The Mantel–Haenszel estimate is given by

$$\hat{\psi} = \frac{\sum_{i=1}^{r} \hat{\psi}_i w_i}{\sum_{i=1}^{r} w_i} = \frac{\sum_{i=1}^{r} (s_{Ti} f_{Ci}/n_i)}{\sum_{i=1}^{r} (s_{Ci} f_{Ti}/n_i)}. \tag{9.5}$$

The calculation of the Mantel–Haenszel estimate for the stroke example is shown in Table 9.2. Although the contributions to the numerator and denominator in (9.5) are defined for all 16 studies, studies 1 and 12 do not contribute to the overall estimate of the odds ratio, because for these studies both terms are zero. The same overall estimate is obtained when both studies are removed from the analysis. However, the results from study 3 do make a contribution.

Although the Mantel–Haenszel estimate has been shown to have good statistical properties, it is an estimate of the odds ratio rather than the log-odds ratio. As a result, it does not have a symmetric distribution, so that the assumption that $\hat{\psi}$ has arisen from a normal distribution with variance $(\sum_{i=1}^{r} w_i)^{-1}$ is inappropriate. Emerson (1994) recommends the use of the variance estimate due to Robins *et al.* (1986) for the log-odds ratio estimate to provide a confidence interval for the odds

**Table 9.2**   Mantel–Haenszel estimate of the odds ratio of a stroke on antihypertensive treatment relative to control treatment

| Study | Treated group | | Control group | | $s_{Ti} f_{Ci}/n_i$ | $s_{Ci} f_{Ti}/n_i$ |
|---|---|---|---|---|---|---|
| | Success (stroke) | Failure | Success (stroke) | Failure | | |
| 1 VA-NHLB1 | 0 | 508 | 0 | 504 | 0.00 | 0.00 |
| 2 HDFP (Stratum I) | 59 | 3844 | 88 | 3834 | 28.91 | 43.23 |
| 3 Oslo | 0 | 406 | 5 | 374 | 0.00 | 2.59 |
| 4 ANBPS | 13 | 1708 | 22 | 1684 | 6.39 | 10.96 |
| 5 MRC | 60 | 8640 | 109 | 8545 | 29.54 | 54.27 |
| 6 VAII | 5 | 181 | 20 | 174 | 2.29 | 9.53 |
| 7 USPHS | 1 | 192 | 6 | 190 | 0.49 | 2.96 |
| 8 HDFP (Stratum II) | 25 | 1023 | 36 | 968 | 11.79 | 17.95 |
| 9 HSCSG | 43 | 190 | 52 | 167 | 15.89 | 21.86 |
| 10 VAI | 1 | 67 | 3 | 60 | 0.46 | 1.53 |
| 11 WOLFF | 2 | 43 | 1 | 41 | 0.94 | 0.49 |
| 12 Barraclough | 0 | 58 | 0 | 58 | 0.00 | 0.00 |
| 13 Carter | 10 | 39 | 21 | 27 | 2.78 | 8.44 |
| 14 HDFP (Stratum III) | 18 | 516 | 34 | 495 | 8.38 | 16.50 |
| 15 EWPHE | 32 | 384 | 48 | 376 | 14.32 | 21.94 |
| 16 Coope | 20 | 399 | 39 | 426 | 9.64 | 17.60 |
| Total | | | | | 131.83 | 229.86 |

$\hat{\psi} = 131.83/229.86 = 0.574$
95% CI = (0.493, 0.667)

ratio. If $\hat{\theta}$ is the estimated log-odds ratio, where $\hat{\theta} = \log(\hat{\psi})$, then this variance estimate is given by

$$\text{var}(\hat{\theta}) = \frac{1}{2} \sum_{i=1}^{r} \left( \frac{A_i C_i}{C^2} + \frac{A_i D_i + B_i C_i}{CD} + \frac{B_i D_i}{D^2} \right), \quad (9.6)$$

where

$$A_i = \frac{s_{Ti} + f_{Ci}}{n_i}, \qquad B_i = \frac{s_{Ci} + f_{Ti}}{n_i}, \qquad C_i = \frac{s_{Ti} f_{Ci}}{n_i}, \qquad D_i = \frac{s_{Ci} f_{Ti}}{n_i},$$

$$C = \sum_{i=1}^{r} C_i, \qquad D = \sum_{i=1}^{r} D_i.$$

A 95% CI for the odds ratio is then given by

$$[\exp\{\hat{\theta} - 1.96\text{se}(\hat{\theta})\}, \exp\{\hat{\theta} + 1.96\text{se}(\hat{\theta})\}].$$

The Mantel–Haenszel estimate (95% CI) for the overall odds ratio in the stroke example is 0.574 (0.493, 0.667) (Table 9.2). These are similar to the values of 0.580 (0.502, 0.672) obtained by exponentiating the results from the Peto approach (Table 9.1). It should be noted that the Mantel–Haenszel test statistic is the $U$ statistic calculated from the Peto approach. Therefore, within the framework of the general fixed effects parametric approach presented in Section 4.2, the Mantel–Haenszel test statistic is connected with the Peto estimate rather than the Mantel–Haenszel estimate. Because the Mantel–Haenszel estimate does not fit into the general meta-analysis framework, it is difficult to see how a random effects model or meta-regression might be accommodated.

The Mantel–Haenszel test statistic, the Mantel–Haenszel estimate and 95% CI (using the Robins *et al.* method) can be obtained using PROC FREQ in SAS via the following statements:

```
PROC FREQ;
TABLES trial*treat*y/cmh2;
```

In the SAS output, the test statistic is referred to as the 'Cochran–Mantel–Haenszel Statistic', and the appropriate Mantel–Haenszel estimate is the odds ratio associated with the 'Case-Control' study. Also included in the output is what is termed the 'Logit' estimate of the odds ratio. This is calculated from the fixed effects meta-analysis using (3.1) and (3.2). However, studies which have no 'successes' or no 'failures', such as studies 1 and 12 in the stroke example, are omitted from the calculations, and for studies which have other types of occurrence of zero cells, such as study 3, (9.1) and (9.2) are used instead.

When fitting the meta-analysis models for binary data described in Chapter 5, care is needed if there are no 'successes' or no 'failures' in one or both treatment arms. If the $i$th trial has either no 'successes' or no 'failures' in both treatment arms then the estimate of the trial effect, $\beta_{0i}$, in model (5.4) will not be defined. When confronted with this problem, statistical packages will tend to produce a very large negative (no 'successes') or large positive (no 'failures') estimate of the trial effect, the magnitude depending on the largest value which can be stored. If all trials have at least one 'success' and one 'failure' then model (5.4) may be fitted and an overall fixed effects estimate of the log-odds ratio obtained. If, however, the $i$th trial has either no 'successes' or no 'failures' in one treatment arm, the estimate of the trial by treatment interaction term, $\beta_{1i}$, in model (5.6) will not be defined, and the same problem arises.

In summary, when there are studies with no 'successes' or no 'failures' in both treatment arms, the usual meta-analysis methods which stratify by study may not be appropriate. These methods effectively ignore the data from such studies. Depending on the method used, problems may also be encountered when a study has either no 'successes' or no 'failures' in one treatment arm. Although for the stroke example the exclusion of studies 1, 3 and 12 did not appear to alter the overall conclusion, this might not always be the case. For the situation in which there are very few events in any of the studies, an analysis which pools all the data and only includes the treatment effects in the model (for example, model (5.32)), may provide a sensible summary. In some cases, alternative stratification factors might be considered. For example, studies may be pooled together in homogeneous groups to form larger units, as is sometimes done with centres in a multicentre trial. Alternatively, a specific prognostic factor might be considered. In some situations exact methods may provide a solution (see, for example, Emerson, 1994).

## 9.3    DIFFERENT RATING SCALES OR METHODS OF ASSESSMENT ACROSS TRIALS

The use of rating scales to assess outcome is common in clinical trials. For example, they can be found in the assessment of quality of life, cognition and functional ability. For the situation in which there is no consensus on the most appropriate scale to use for a particular assessment, it is common to find a wide variety of alternatives. Therefore, when undertaking a retrospective meta-analysis on trials some of which were conducted in the more distant past, it is not unusual to find that there is no single scale which has been used in all of the relevant studies. If the meta-analysis is restricted to studies in which the same scale is used, then the power to detect a treatment difference will be reduced, but more importantly bias may be introduced into the overall estimate. To obtain an overall picture it is desirable to perform a meta-analysis which includes as many studies measuring the same therapeutic benefit or health outcome as possible. If a common scale has been used in the majority of studies, the main analysis may concern this scale alone, and the analysis involving all trials may be undertaken as a sensitivity analysis. However, if this is not the case, the latter may become the main analysis.

In order to combine the results from different rating scales, it is important to establish that the scales to be combined are measuring the same effect. Having established this, the type of meta-analysis which can be undertaken will be dependent on the characteristics of the scales. Three different scenarios are discussed here.

First, suppose that for each rating scale there is a clear ordering to the scale and that the clinical importance of a jump of $x$ units on the scale is the same throughout the scale. If, in addition, the data are approximately normally distributed, the meta-analysis may be conducted using the standardized mean difference as the measure of treatment difference.

As an illustration, consider a meta-analysis of selegiline versus placebo in the treatment of patients with Alzheimer's disease, presented in Wilcock *et al.* (2002). The outcome considered here is the effect on activities of daily living at approximately 3 months following the start of treatment. Data are available from seven trials, but five different rating scales have been used. These scales are the Blessed Dementia Scale (scores 0 to 84), the Dependence Scale (scores 1 to 7), the Gottfries–Brane–Steen scale (scores 0 to 36), the Nurses' Observation Scale for Inpatient Evaluation (scores 0 to 320), and the Physical and Instrumental Activities of Daily Living (scores 0 to 24). In all cases a low score is good. The summary data are presented in Table 9.3 in relation to the change from baseline at 3 months. A negative value indicates improvement. It can be seen that there is good agreement between the two estimates of standard deviation within each trial, but wide variation between trials. To a large extent this reflects the differences in the lengths of the rating scales. The standardized mean difference was calculated for each study using (3.29) and (3.30). Fixed and random effects meta-analyses were performed using the methods of Chapter 4, with the method of

**Table 9.3** Comparison between selegiline and placebo on activities of daily living for patients with Alzheimer's disease. For each rating scale, the outcome of interest is change from baseline at 3 months

| Trial | Rating Scale | Selegiline | | | Placebo | | |
|---|---|---|---|---|---|---|---|
| | | No. of patients | Mean | Standard deviation | No. of patients | Mean | Standard deviation |
| 1 | GBS | 9 | −0.73 | 6.24 | 9 | 0.62 | 6.42 |
| 2 | BDS | 15 | 0.13 | 0.64 | 15 | 0.23 | 1.08 |
| 3 | NOSIE | 79 | −0.84 | 6.28 | 77 | 0.43 | 6.64 |
| 4 | BDS | 59 | −1.90 | 3.47 | 49 | 1.04 | 3.52 |
| 5 | BDS | 62 | −2.02 | 2.44 | 46 | 0.63 | 2.59 |
| 6 | DS | 172 | −0.02 | 0.89 | 169 | 0.01 | 0.89 |
| 7 | PIADL | 25 | 0.88 | 2.82 | 24 | 0.08 | 2.83 |

**Table 9.4** Meta-analysis of the standardized mean difference (selegiline minus placebo), using formulae (3.29) and (3.30), and the methods of Chapter 4 with the method of moments estimate of $\tau^2$

| Trial | Standardized mean difference | Std. error | 95% CI |
|---|---|---|---|
| 1 | −0.20 | 0.47 | (−1.13, 0.72) |
| 2 | −0.11 | 0.37 | (−0.83, 0.61) |
| 3 | −0.20 | 0.16 | (−0.51, 0.12) |
| 4 | −0.84 | 0.20 | (−1.23, −0.44) |
| 5 | −1.05 | 0.21 | (−1.46, −0.64) |
| 6 | −0.03 | 0.11 | (−0.25, 0.18) |
| 7 | 0.28 | 0.29 | (−0.28, 0.84) |
| Fixed effects estimate | −0.27 | 0.07 | (−0.41, −0.13) |
| Random effects estimate | −0.33 | 0.18 | (−0.69, 0.03) |
| Test for heterogeneity ($\chi^2$) | 30.90; (6 df) $p < 0.001$ | | |

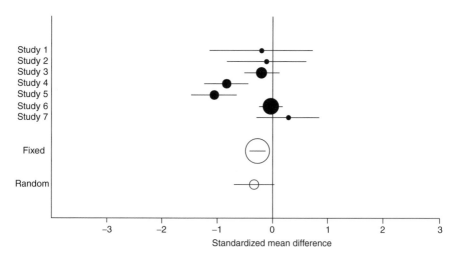

**Figure 9.1** Activities of daily living for patients with Alzheimer's disease. Estimates and 95% confidence intervals for the standardized mean difference (selegiline−placebo) on change from baseline at 3 months. Negative values indicate a benefit of selegiline.

moments estimate of the heterogeneity parameter, $\tau^2$ (Table 9.4 and Figure 9.1). The random effects estimate (95% CI) of the standardized mean difference is −0.33 (−0.69, 0.03), which just fails to reach statistical significance at the 5% level. The authors considered that the size of the effect was unlikely to be of clinical relevance. In order to interpret the overall results in terms of a particular rating scale one may multiply the overall standardized mean difference by a typical standard deviation for that rating scale.

Second, suppose that for each rating scale there is a clear ordering to the scale, but that the assumptions of equal spacing between consecutive scores and normality are not appropriate. If the rating scales have a small number of possible values, then the methods described for ordered categorical data may be used. If a rating scale has a large number of possible values, then the same methodology can be applied following the division of the scale into a small number of interval-based categories. Whitehead (1993) concludes that there is little to be gained in efficiency by creating more than five categories. To avoid bias in the estimate of treatment difference, the choice of cut-points should have a clinical rationale and not be based on the data. If individual patient data are available models such as the fixed effects meta-analysis model (5.8) may be used. This model assumes proportional odds between treatments, but stratifies by study. This means that the cut-points associated with the distribution of the latent variable for determining the response category are allowed to vary from study to study but are the same for both treatment groups within a study.

As an example, consider a set of eight trials conducted in patients suffering from arthritis. The trials were designed to investigate whether concurrent treatment with the synthetic prostaglandin, misoprostol, would prevent or at least reduce the degree of gastrointestinal damage without reducing the anti-inflammatory effect of non-steroidal anti-inflammatory drugs. The data for these eight trials can be found as studies 6–13 in Whitehead and Jones (1994) and are shown in Table 9.5. Amongst the eight trials, different schemes for classifying the extent of gastrointestinal damage detected by endoscopy had been used to create an ordinal response variable. Although the definition of category 1, for example, is not the same across studies, within each study there is an ordering of the response, so that category 1 is always clinically the best response. In study 10 sucralfate was given to the control group. As this study was included in the original meta-analysis, it is also included here. Misoprostol is apparently associated with better outcome than placebo/control in each trial. For each study, the ML estimate of the log-odds ratio was obtained by fitting a proportional odds model based on the number of categories used in that study. Fixed and random effect meta-analyses were performed using the methods of Chapter 4 (Figure 9.2). Results from the fixed effects analysis show a significant treatment effect, the log-odds ratio of 1.25 indicating a substantial benefit of misoprostol over control. The test for heterogeneity does not reach statistical significance, but the estimate of the heterogeneity parameter is greater than zero. The random effects analysis produces increased estimates of the log-odds ratio and its standard error.

Finally, for the situation in which it is not possible to estimate a common measure of treatment difference in all studies, one may have to resort to the methods of combining $p$-values, described in Section 9.8.

**Table 9.5**   Endoscopic classification in the misoprostol trials: meta-analysis of the log-odds ratio of being in a better category on misoprostol than on placebo from the proportional odds model, using the methods of Chapter 4 with the method of moments estimate of $\tau^2$

| Study | Treatment | Category 1 | 2 | 3 | 4 | 5 | Total | Log-odds ratio [se]* |
|---|---|---|---|---|---|---|---|---|
| 6 | Misoprostol | 93 | 5 | 3 | 1 | 1 | 103 | 1.176 |
|   | Placebo | 85 | 10 | 10 | 4 | 5 | 114 | [0.395] |
| 7 | Misoprostol | 61 | 12 | 0 |   |   | 73 | 1.193 |
|   | Placebo | 49 | 28 | 3 |   |   | 80 | [0.390] |
| 8 | Misoprostol | 45 | 1 | 0 |   |   | 46 | 1.840 |
|   | Placebo | 65 | 6 | 3 |   |   | 74 | [1.072] |
| 9 | Misoprostol | 138 | 1 |   |   |   | 139 | 2.965 |
|   | Placebo | 121 | 17 |   |   |   | 138 | [1.037] |
| 10 | Misoprostol | 126 | 2 |   |   |   | 128 | 2.487 |
|   | Sucralfate | 110 | 21 |   |   |   | 131 | [0.751] |
| 11 | Misoprostol | 30 | 1 | 1 |   |   | 32 | 2.567 |
|   | Placebo | 20 | 11 | 7 |   |   | 38 | [0.797] |
| 12 | Misoprostol | 56 | 12 | 8 | 0 |   | 76 | 0.647 |
|   | Placebo | 50 | 15 | 12 | 5 |   | 82 | [0.339] |
| 13 | Misoprostol | 12 | 3 | 1 | 0 |   | 16 | 1.112 |
|   | Placebo | 11 | 5 | 2 | 3 |   | 21 | [0.710] |

Fixed effects estimate $= 1.250$; se $= 0.186$; 95% CI $= (0.885, 1.614)$
Test for heterogeneity: $Q = 11.74$; (7 df) $p = 0.11$
$\hat{\tau}^2 = 0.207$ – method of moments estimate
Random effects estimate $= 1.428$; se $= 0.267$; 95% CI $= (0.906, 1.951)$

*From a proportional odds model for an individual study.

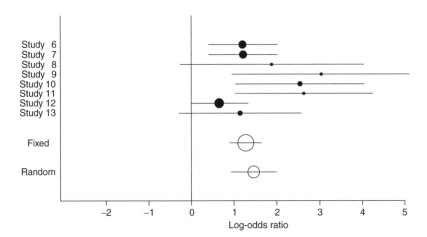

**Figure 9.2**   Endoscopic classification of gastrointestinal damage. Estimates and 95% confidence intervals for the log-odds ratio of being in a better category on misoprostol than on placebo.

## 9.4  DIFFERENT TIMES OF ASSESSMENT ACROSS TRIALS

In clinical trials which follow up subjects over a long period of time, it is common to find that the same assessment is carried out at a number of timepoints during the trial. For example, in the treatment of patients with Alzheimer's disease, cognitive function may be recorded prior to randomization and then every 3 months following the start of study treatment. If there is no consensus regarding the duration of the treatment period or the timing of repeated assessments, then a meta-analysis conducted at a specific timepoint may exclude some studies. In an attempt to obtain a fuller picture, one might wish to fit a model to the repeated assessments and choose an appropriate parameter to measure treatment difference.

As an example, consider the data from five trials comparing selegiline with placebo, for the treatment of Alzheimer's disease, in which the cognitive function was measured by the Mini-Mental State Examination. The MMSE takes integer values between 0 and 30, where 30 is good, and is considered here to be normally distributed. The five trials were of different duration, and without a common timepoint for post-treatment assessment across all trials. Table 9.6 shows summary

**Table 9.6**    Selegiline studies: summary statistics for MMSE across time

| Week | Study | Placebo | | | Selegiline | | |
|------|-------|---------|------|----------------------|------------|------|----------------------|
|      |       | Number | Mean | Standard deviation | Number | Mean | Standard deviation |
| 0  | 1 | 20  | 18.80 | 5.01 | 18  | 19.56 | 4.49 |
|    | 2 | 86  | 18.78 | 3.51 | 84  | 18.80 | 3.63 |
|    | 3 | 26  | 17.25 | 3.53 | 25  | 18.28 | 4.39 |
|    | 4 | 168 | 12.26 | 5.40 | 172 | 12.81 | 5.35 |
|    | 5 | 25  | 19.96 | 6.42 | 25  | 18.16 | 4.62 |
| 4  | 4 | 166 | 12.33 | 5.61 | 165 | 13.07 | 5.40 |
|    | 5 | 25  | 19.88 | 6.27 | 25  | 17.72 | 5.67 |
| 5  | 3 | 24  | 17.08 | 4.33 | 22  | 17.73 | 6.78 |
| 8  | 5 | 24  | 19.33 | 6.35 | 25  | 17.56 | 4.93 |
| 9  | 1 | 20  | 18.30 | 4.40 | 18  | 18.78 | 6.28 |
|    | 3 | 23  | 18.04 | 5.00 | 23  | 17.43 | 6.71 |
| 13 | 3 | 21  | 17.95 | 4.80 | 23  | 17.70 | 6.41 |
| 17 | 3 | 20  | 17.20 | 4.49 | 23  | 18.00 | 6.28 |
|    | 4 | 151 | 11.84 | 5.57 | 156 | 12.28 | 5.47 |
| 21 | 3 | 20  | 17.40 | 5.17 | 24  | 18.92 | 6.53 |
| 24 | 2 | 68  | 20.32 | 5.16 | 64  | 19.80 | 5.46 |
| 25 | 3 | 18  | 16.33 | 5.40 | 23  | 17.74 | 6.24 |
| 30 | 4 | 139 | 11.14 | 5.95 | 144 | 11.23 | 5.68 |
| 35 | 1 | 18  | 16.17 | 6.22 | 17  | 17.12 | 6.38 |
| 43 | 4 | 125 | 9.94  | 6.01 | 134 | 10.45 | 5.74 |
| 56 | 4 | 112 | 9.59  | 6.01 | 121 | 9.79  | 6.05 |
| 65 | 1 | 17  | 15.47 | 6.34 | 15  | 13.07 | 7.41 |

statistics for the MMSE for each treatment group in each study for each timepoint, with a corresponding plot of mean scores in Figure 9.3. The simplest model to fit is one assuming a linear trend over time. Alzheimer's disease is a progressive disease, and it is hoped that treatment would slow down the progression.

The meta-analysis may now be considered within the framework of a hierarchical model, in which there are three levels: study at the highest (level 3), patient

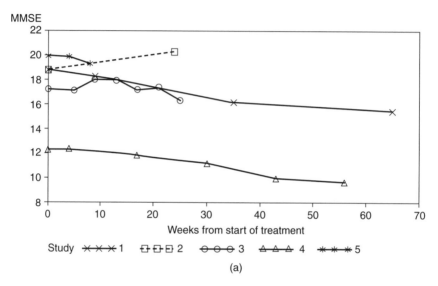

(a)

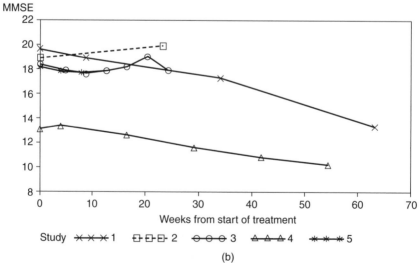

(b)

**Figure 9.3**  Selegiline studies: mean MMSE across time. (a) Placebo. (b) Selegiline.

at the next level down (level 2) and time at the lowest (level 1). The models of Chapter 5 can be extended to incorporate this additional level, and terms may be included as either fixed or random effects as appropriate. For example, consider the model in which there is a linear relationship for the MMSE scores over time, the intercept differs from study to study and the slope is dependent on study and treatment. Each patient's intercept and slope will be randomly distributed about the line described by the particular study and treatment group to which they belong. The model is given by

$$y_{ijk} = \alpha + \beta_{0i} + \beta_2 x_{2ijk} + \beta_{3i} x_{2ijk} + \beta_1 x_{1ijk} x_{2ijk} + v_{0ij} + v_{2ij} x_{2ijk} + \varepsilon_{ijk},$$

where $y_{ijk}$ denotes the response from patient $j$ in study $i$ at the $k$th timepoint, $x_{1ijk}$ is the treatment covariate, which takes the value 0 for the placebo group and 1 for the selegiline group, and $x_{2ijk}$ is the number of weeks post-treatment. The terms $v_{0ij}$ and $v_{2ij}$ are normally distributed random effects with mean 0, variances $\sigma_0^2$ and $\sigma_2^2$ respectively, and correlation coefficient $\rho$. The error terms $\varepsilon_{ijk}$ are normally distributed with 0 mean and variance $\sigma^2$, independently of the level 2 random effects. The model can be fitted using the following PROC MIXED statements:

```
PROC MIXED;
CLASS study;
MODEL mmse = study time study*time treat*time/ htype =1
              ddfm =kenwardroger solution;
RANDOM = int time/type = un subject = patient;
```

Table 9.7 shows estimated MMSE scores using the above model. There is reasonable agreement between these values and the observed means. The overall fixed effects estimate of the difference between selegiline and placebo at 8 weeks

**Table 9.7**  Selegiline studies: estimated MMSE scores at weeks 8 and 24 assuming a linear trend over time

| Study | Treatment | Week 8 | Week 24 |
|---|---|---|---|
| 1 | Placebo | 18.60 | 17.51 |
|   | Selegiline | 18.53 | 17.31 |
| 2 | Placebo | 19.22 | 20.10 |
|   | Selegiline | 19.15 | 19.89 |
| 3 | Placebo | 17.68 | 17.73 |
|   | Selegiline | 17.61 | 17.52 |
| 4 | Placebo | 12.34 | 11.35 |
|   | Selegiline | 12.27 | 11.14 |
| 5 | Placebo | 18.64 | 17.85 |
|   | Selegiline | 18.57 | 17.65 |
| Overall (selegiline − placebo) | | −0.07 [se = 0.05] | −0.21 [se = 0.16] |

post-treatment is $-0.07$ (standard error 0.05), and at 24 weeks is $-0.21$ (standard error 0.16), which do not reach statistical significance.

Clearly, this approach is dependent on the model chosen to reflect the relationship between the response and time. Provided an appropriate model is chosen, it provides a fuller picture than meta-analyses performed at specific timepoints on subsets of studies. As part of this consideration it is necessary to reach a decision regarding the handling of subjects who withdraw early or are lost to follow-up. Such subjects provide data at the early timepoints and these data may be included in the analysis. In the selegiline example, such data were included and there was no imputation of missing data for these subjects. This assumed that the linear relationship between the recorded MMSE scores for a subject at the start of the study period would not change after they had stopped taking study medication.

## 9.5 COMBINING TRIALS WHICH REPORT DIFFERENT SUMMARY STATISTICS

There is variation in the way summary statistics for a particular outcome measure are reported. This partly reflects differences between the methods of analysis which may have been undertaken. However, it can create a problem if the meta-analysis is based on summary information from published papers. The extent of the problem will depend on the type of outcome measure which is to be combined. For example, there is rarely a problem for a binary outcome, as sufficient information is usually available to enable the calculation of the number of patients in each of the two categories for each treatment group. On the other hand, for ordinal data with more than two categories, the number of patients in each category are rarely provided. This section focuses on ways of combining trials which report different summary statistics when the outcome measure is continuous, ordinal or a survival time.

### 9.5.1 Continuous outcomes

An outcome measured on a continuous quantitative scale is often treated as arising from a normal distribution. The summary statistics which are often presented in published papers are the number of patients, sample mean and standard deviation for each treatment group. However, the summary information from a continuous outcome can occasionally be reported as if it related to a binary outcome. For example, a patient can be classified as a responder if a particular value on the continuous scale is exceeded, and a non-responder otherwise. In order to combine summaries of binary outcomes with those of continuous outcomes one might chose the log-odds ratio as a common measure of treatment difference. Details of this methodology can be found in Whitehead *et al.* (1999). It is illustrated by a series of perinatal trials investigating the effect of prophylactic use of oxytocics on postpartum blood loss during labour. One of the meta-analyses presented in the paper concerned the combination of eight trials reporting binary outcomes and three reporting continuous outcomes, and this is considered here.

The binary outcome in the perinatal trials was whether or not a woman had a postpartum haemorrhage, usually defined by a blood loss of 500 ml or more in the first 24 hours following delivery of the baby. The continuous outcome was the actual amount of blood lost. The log-odds ratio of a postpartum haemorrhage on the oxytocic treatment relative to the control treatment is defined as

$$\theta = \log \left\{ \frac{p_T(1 - p_C)}{p_C(1 - p_T)} \right\},$$

where $p_T$ and $p_C$ are the probabilities of a haemorrhage in the oxytocic and control groups respectively. For studies in which summary information on the binary outcome was reported, the log-odds ratio and its variance were estimated from (3.1) and (3.2).

For the continuous outcome, the reported summary statistics were the number of patients, mean and standard deviation in each treatment group. Let $Y_T$ and $Y_C$ represent the continuous outcome variables in one trial for the oxytocic and control treatments, respectively. Individual patient observations are assumed to be normally distributed, with $y_{Tj} \sim N(\mu_T, \sigma^2)$, $j = 1, \ldots, n_T$, and $y_{Cj} \sim N(\mu_C, \sigma^2)$, $j = 1, \ldots, n_C$. Let $A$ be the cut-point value so that $p_T = P(Y_T > A)$ and $p_C = P(Y_C > A)$. The ML estimate of $p_T$ is $1 - \Phi(A_T)$, where $A_T = (A - \bar{y}_T)/\hat{\sigma}_M$ and $\Phi$ is the standard normal distribution function. The statistics $\bar{y}_T$ and $\hat{\sigma}_M$ are the ML estimates of $\mu_T$ and $\sigma^2$ respectively, as defined in Section 3.6.2. The estimate of $p_C$ is similarly defined. The ML estimate of $\theta$ is given by

$$\hat{\theta} = \log \left[ \frac{\Phi(A_C)\{1 - \Phi(A_T)\}}{\Phi(A_T)\{1 - \Phi(A_C)\}} \right].$$

The variance of $\hat{\theta}$ is obtained by the delta method and given by

$$\text{var}(\hat{\theta}) = \frac{\{\phi(A_T)\}^2(1/n_T + A_T^2/2n)}{[\Phi(A_T)\{1 - \Phi(A_T)\}]^2} + \frac{\{\phi(A_C)\}^2(1/n_C + A_C^2/2n)}{[\Phi(A_C)\{1 - \Phi(A_C)\}]^2}$$
$$- \frac{A_T A_C \phi(A_T)\phi(A_C)}{n\Phi(A_T)\Phi(1 - A_T)\Phi(A_C)\Phi(1 - A_C)},$$

where $n = n_T + n_C$, and $\phi$ is the standard normal density function.

The summary statistics from the 11 trials are given in Table 9.8. In all trials reporting binary outcomes, apart from trial 1, a postpartum haemorrhage was defined as a blood loss of 500 ml or more. In trial 1 a cut-point value of 20 oz was used, which converts to 568 ml. For the continuous outcomes, the standard deviation presented in the published papers was assumed to be the usual unbiased estimate rather than the ML estimate. For a trial consisting of more than one

**Table 9.8**   Prophylactic use of oxytocics on postpartum haemorrhage: summary statistics for each trial

(a) Binary outcomes

| Trial | Oxytocic | | Control | |
|---|---|---|---|---|
| | Haemorrhage | Total | Haemorrhage | Total |
| 1 | 45 | 490 | 80 | 510 |
| 2 | 1 | 150 | 5 | 50 |
| 3 | 14 | 591 | 4 | 177 |
| 5 | 24 | 963 | 25 | 470 |
| 9 | 34 | 346 | 42 | 278 |
| 11 | 50 | 846 | 152 | 849 |
| 12 | 0 | 10 | 1 | 15 |
| 13 | 14 | 705 | 60 | 724 |

(b) Continuous outcomes

| Trial | Oxytocic | | | Control | | |
|---|---|---|---|---|---|---|
| | Number | Mean | Standard deviation ($s_T$); df | Number | Mean | Standard deviation ($s_C$); df |
| 6 | 41 | 150.49 | 86.31; 35 | 10 | 305.00 | 59.86; 9 |
| 8 | 97 | 188.35 | 84.18; 95 | 43 | 213.65 | 119.35; 42 |
| 10 | 319 | 125.14 | 97.68; 317 | 122 | 233.20 | 107.40; 121 |

oxytocic group, the results were pooled to provide one oxytocic group. In the case of the continuous data, this meant assuming a common mean and variance for each oxytocic treatment. The denominator for the calculation of the pooled variance is shown as degrees of freedom (df) in the table.

Table 9.9 shows estimates of the percentage of women experiencing a haemorrhage and the log-odds ratio from each trial. It should be noted that in trial 12 the ML estimate could not be calculated because there were no haemorrhages in the oxytocic group. In order to include this trial in the analysis, an approximate ML estimate was obtained by adding 0.5 to all cells in the $2 \times 2$ table. Fixed and random effects meta-analyses were performed using the methods of Chapter 4 and the method of moments estimate of $\tau^2$. It can be seen that the estimates of the percentage of women experiencing a haemorrhage in the three trials reporting continuous summary statistics are generally much smaller than those in the other trials. This may be due to very few or no women actually experiencing more than 500 ml of blood loss in these trials. In order to present a measure of treatment difference, the authors may have resorted to reporting the continuous outcome. Two of the three log-odds ratio estimates have larger magnitude than those based on the binary outcomes. Although there may be

**Table 9.9**    Meta-analysis of the log-odds ratio of a haemorrhage on oxytocics relative to control, using the methods of Chapter 4 with the method of moments estimate of $\tau^2$

| Trial | Estimated % of women experiencing a haemorrhage | | Log-odds ratio | Std. error | 95% CI |
|---|---|---|---|---|---|
| | Oxytocic | Control | | | |
| 1 | 9.2 | 15.7 | −0.61 | 0.20 | (−1.00, −0.22) |
| 2 | 0.7 | 10.0 | −2.81 | 1.11 | (−4.98, −0.63) |
| 3 | 2.4 | 2.3 | 0.05 | 0.57 | (−1.08, 1.17) |
| 5 | 2.5 | 5.3 | −0.79 | 0.29 | (−1.36, −0.22) |
| 6 | <0.01 | 0.5 | −7.84 | 1.88 | (−11.52, −4.15) |
| 8 | 0.05 | 0.1 | −0.91 | 0.63 | (−2.13, 0.32) |
| 9 | 9.8 | 15.1 | −0.49 | 0.25 | (−0.97, −0.01) |
| 10 | <0.01 | 0.4 | −3.75 | 0.42 | (−4.58, −2.93) |
| 11 | 5.9 | 17.9 | −1.24 | 0.17 | (−1.58, −0.91) |
| 12 | 0.0 | 6.7 | −0.78 | 1.68 | (−4.07, 2.52) |
| 13 | 2.0 | 8.3 | −1.50 | 0.30 | (−2.09, −0.90) |
| Fixed effects estimate | | | −1.08 | 0.09 | (−1.26, −0.89) |
| Random effects estimate | | | −1.38 | 0.31 | (−1.99, −0.77) |
| Test for heterogeneity ($\chi^2$) | | | 74.79; (10 df) $p < 0.001$ | | |

some doubt over the magnitude of the treatment difference, the conclusion that may be drawn from the meta-analysis is that the routine use of oxytocic drugs is beneficial in reducing the risk of excessive bleeding in the third stage of labour (Figure 9.4).

One concern about including the trials reporting continuous data was the assumption of normality. Positive skewness would be expected under the likely scenario that a few women experience heavy blood loss compared with the rest who experience none or very little. This problem is not confined to the situation described here, but is of general concern when continuous outcomes are summarized. The lognormal distribution may be a more appropriate choice. Further details can be found in Whitehead *et al.* (1999).

### 9.5.2    Ordinal data

Ordinal data may be reported in many different ways. Sometimes an ordinal outcome is reported as if it were a binary outcome. For example, a 'success' may constitute a response in the best category or perhaps one of the best categories. The same ordinal outcome may be recorded in each study, but the definition of 'success' may vary from one study to another. If the numbers of patients in the 'success' and 'failure' categories are reported for each treatment group in each study, then the meta-analysis may be performed on the log-odds ratio. It should be noted that even meta-analyses based

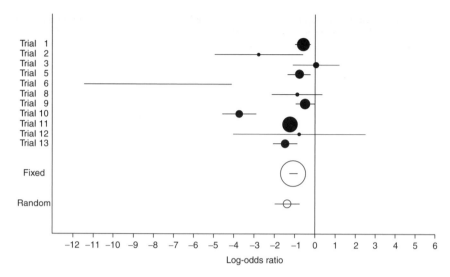

**Figure 9.4**    Prophylactic use of oxytocics on postpartum haemorrhage. Estimates and 95% confidence intervals for the log-odds ratio of a haemorrhage on oxytocic treatment relative to control.

only on binary data may be making an implicit assumption of proportional odds if the definition of a 'success' is not the same across all studies. If for some studies the numbers of responses in more than two categories are available for each treatment group, then the log-odds ratio can be calculated from a proportional odds model. Indeed, the meta-analysis may be performed in the same way as that for the misoprostol example described in Section 9.3.

Sometimes ordinal data are analysed as if they were continuous data arising from a normal distribution, and the same summary statistics as those described in Section 9.5.1 are presented. However, this is appropriate only if the difference between two consecutive scores is of equal clinical importance throughout the scale, and the data are approximately normally distributed. If this is the case, the approaches of Section 9.5.1 are appropriate. The need to combine studies some of which report binary summary statistics and others continuous summary statistics is likely to be frequent in the case of an ordinal outcome. The meta-analysis could proceed as for the oxytocic example. It might seem more appropriate to consider a logistic distribution rather than a normal distribution to model the continuous data. Although the two distributions are similar, the logistic distribution has the proportional odds property, which means that the log-odds ratio remains constant across all cut-points. However, extraction of relevant data pertaining to the logistic distribution is likely to be problematic.

### 9.5.3   Survival data

The log-hazard ratio is usually the parameter of interest for comparing two survival curves. Unfortunately, published reports do not often present the estimate of the log-hazard ratio and its standard error or variance. Sometimes the results are presented as the number of events in each treatment group before a fixed point in time. It is then possible to construct a $2 \times 2$ table as for binary data, in which 'failure' is associated with occurrence of the event within the defined time period and 'success' with being event-free at the fixed point in time. The number of 'successes' is usually calculated by subtracting the number of 'failures' from the number randomized, although some assumption has to be made about censoring. The methods of Section 3.4 can then be applied to obtain estimates of the log-hazard ratio and its variance, as this is an example of interval-censored survival data with one time interval.

## 9.6   IMPUTATION OF THE TREATMENT DIFFERENCE AND ITS VARIANCE

When the estimate of treatment difference and its variance (or standard error) are not presented in the published report of a trial, the challenge is to find ways of using the available data in order to compute them. Two specific measures of treatment difference which have received attention in the literature in this respect are the absolute mean difference for continuous outcomes and the log-hazard ratio for survival data. These are discussed below.

### 9.6.1   Absolute mean difference for continuous outcomes

A quantitative measurement on a continuous scale is often treated as following a normal distribution. Consequently, the summary statistics which are often presented include the number of patients, the sample mean and the standard deviation for each treatment group. Here, the number of patients refers to the number used in the calculation of the mean and standard deviation. In this case, an estimate of the absolute mean difference together with its variance can be calculated using the methods described in Section 3.6. That is,

$$\hat{\theta} = \bar{y}_T - \bar{y}_C,$$

and

$$\text{var}(\hat{\theta}) = s^2 \left( \frac{1}{n_T} + \frac{1}{n_C} \right),$$

where $\bar{y}_T$ and $\bar{y}_C$ are the sample means in the treated and control groups, $n_T$ and $n_C$ are the number of patients in the treated and control groups, and $s^2$ is the pooled sample variance.

When no variance estimates are reported, it may be possible to calculate a value for $\mathrm{var}(\hat{\theta})$ from other statistics presented. For example, if the $t$ statistic is provided, where

$$t = \frac{\bar{y}_{\mathrm{T}} - \bar{y}_{\mathrm{C}}}{\mathrm{se}(\bar{y}_{\mathrm{T}} - \bar{y}_{\mathrm{C}})},$$

then

$$\mathrm{var}(\hat{\theta}) = \left(\frac{\bar{y}_{\mathrm{T}} - \bar{y}_{\mathrm{C}}}{t}\right)^2. \tag{9.7}$$

Alternatively, if the two-sided $p$-value, $p_2$, for the $t$ statistic is provided, then

$$t \approx \begin{cases} F_{\nu}^{-1}(1 - p_2/2), & \text{if } \bar{y}_{\mathrm{T}} - \bar{y}_{\mathrm{C}} \geq 0, \\ -F_{\nu}^{-1}(1 - p_2/2), & \text{if } \bar{y}_{\mathrm{T}} - \bar{y}_{\mathrm{C}} < 0, \end{cases}$$

where $F_{\nu}(x)$ is the probability that a random variable, with a $t$ distribution on $\nu$ degrees of freedom, will be less than or equal to $x$. The degrees of freedom $\nu$ may be approximated by $n_{\mathrm{T}} + n_{\mathrm{C}} - 2$. This value of $t$ may be substituted into (9.7). As $\nu$ increases the $t$ distribution is approximated well by the normal distribution, enabling $F_{\nu}(x)$ to be approximated by $\Phi(x)$.

If $\hat{\theta}$ is reported with a two-sided $100(1 - \alpha)\%$ CI $(\theta_{\mathrm{L}}, \theta_{\mathrm{U}})$ instead of a variance, the variance can be calculated as

$$\mathrm{var}(\hat{\theta}) = \left(\frac{\theta_{\mathrm{U}} - \theta_{\mathrm{L}}}{2t_{\nu}(\alpha/2)}\right)^2, \tag{9.8}$$

where $t_{\nu}(\alpha/2)$ is the upper $(100\alpha/2)$th percentage point of the $t$ distribution. That is, $t_{\nu}(\alpha/2)$ is equal to $F_{\nu}^{-1}(1 - \alpha/2)$. For large $\nu$, $t_{\nu}(\alpha/2)$ can be approximated by $\Phi^{-1}(1 - \alpha/2)$. In the case of a 95% CI based on the normal distribution,

$$\mathrm{var}(\hat{\theta}) \approx \left(\frac{\theta_{\mathrm{U}} - \theta_{\mathrm{L}}}{4}\right)^2.$$

For some meta-analyses, the situation may arise in which a variance estimate, $s^2$, is available for some trials but not others. If it is reasonable to assume a common within-treatment group variance across all trials, then an estimate of this common variance may be obtained by pooling the variance estimates from those trials for which the correctly calculated values are available (see Section 4.2.9 for details). This pooled estimate, $s_{\mathrm{p}}^2$, is then used in the calculation of the variance of each of the individual study estimates of treatment difference.

Sometimes the outcome of interest is the change in the measurement between two timepoints. For example, the difference between a pre-treatment and a post-treatment assessment is often reported. However, some publications may report means and standard deviations for each timepoint, while others report means and standard deviations for the change between two timepoints. If the sample size is the same for both timepoints it is possible to calculate the mean change from the difference in the mean values at the two timepoints. However, if the sample sizes differ this calculation will only be approximate. Also, the variance of the change between two timepoints cannot be calculated just from the variances of the assessments at each timepoint. If $y_1$ and $y_2$ are the observations on one patient at the two timepoints, then

$$\text{var}(y_1 - y_2) = \text{var}(y_1) + \text{var}(y_2) - 2\,\text{cov}(y_1, y_2).$$

Usually no information is available on the covariance term. There is likely to be a positive correlation between two observations on the same patient, in which case the covariance term will be positive. A calculation which ignores the covariance term is, therefore, likely to lead to an overestimate. Only in the extremely unlikely event that there is zero correlation between the two sets of observations would such a calculation be correct. The approaches to this problem are similar to those described above. One is to calculate the appropriate variance from other statistics presented and another is to calculate a pooled estimate of the variance of the change between two assessment times from trials for which the correctly calculated values are reported. Further details can be found in Follmann *et al.* (1992).

## 9.6.2   The log-hazard ratio for survival data

Authors of publications of trials in which the outcome of interest is the time to an event often do not present the estimate of the log-hazard ratio and its standard error or variance. Instead, values need to be calculated from other statistics or from diagrams showing estimated survival curves. Parmar *et al.* (1998) present three methods of extracting the relevant information. Two of them are discussed in this section.

The first method can be used if the estimate of the log-hazard ratio and a CI are provided. In this case the variance of the log-hazard ratio can be calculated using (9.8), in which $t_\nu(\alpha/2)$ is replaced by $\Phi^{-1}(1 - \alpha/2)$.

However, as noted by Altman *et al.* (1995), the $p$-value for the log-rank test is frequently quoted. Therefore, the second method makes use of this information. The log-rank chi-squared statistic, $\chi^2$, is equal to $Z^2/V$, where $Z$ is the log-rank statistic and $V$ its null variance, as defined in (3.11) and (3.12). If the two-sided $p$-value, $p_2$, for the log-rank chi-squared statistic is reported, then

$$\chi^2 = \{\Phi^{-1}(1 - p_2/2)\}^2,$$

and

$$Z = \begin{cases} \Phi^{-1}(1 - p_2/2)\sqrt{V}, & \text{if the new treatment increases the risk of an event,} \\ -\Phi^{-1}(1 - p_2/2)\sqrt{V}, & \text{if the new treatment reduces the risk of an event.} \end{cases}$$

To complete the calculations, a value for $V$ is required. Three alternatives are given by

$$V = \frac{O}{4},$$ (9.9)

$$V = \frac{O_T O_C}{O}$$ (9.10)

and

$$V = \frac{O n_T n_C}{n^2},$$ (9.11)

where $O_T$ and $O_C$ are the total number of events in the treated and control groups, $n_T$ and $n_C$ are the number of patients in the treated and control groups, $O = O_T + O_C$ and $n = n_T + n_C$.

Formulae (9.9) and (9.10) are identical if there are an equal number of events in each treatment group, and formulae (9.9) and (9.11) are identical if there are equal sample sizes in both groups. If the treatment difference is fairly small and there is approximately equal allocation of patients to the two groups, then Formula (9.9) is a reasonable approximation. It can be shown that this approximation is always an overestimate of $V$, but the bias reduces as the amount of censoring increases. Collette *et al.* (1998) compared the three formulae in a simulation exercise of meta-analyses of ten trials. They concluded that all three performed well, but that (9.10) was the best when the amount of censoring is small, and in the case of unequal allocation to treatment group (9.11) is preferable.

The third method described by Parmar *et al.* (1998) involves extracting data from survival curves, and the reader is referred to the paper for further details. Tudur *et al.* (2001) apply all three methods to two meta-analysis data sets and highlight the problems involved. They also consider an extension of the third method to incorporate information reported on the numbers of patients at risk at various timepoints.

## 9.7  COMBINING SUMMARY STATISTICS AND INDIVIDUAL PATIENT DATA

A meta-analysis using individual patient data is likely to prove more reliable than one based on summary statistics from trial reports. However, the situation can arise in which individual patient data are not available for some of the eligible trials. Such trials may be incorporated into the meta-analysis provided that sufficient summary information is presented in the trial report. At the very least it will be desirable to perform such a meta-analysis as a sensitivity analysis, although in some cases this may become the primary meta-analysis.

In order to implement the meta-analysis methods of Chapter 4, it is necessary to calculate an estimate of the chosen parameter measuring treatment difference, together with an estimate of its variance. If these quantities are not directly available, the approaches described in Sections 9.3, 9.5 and 9.6 may be considered. For some data types (such as binary), there may be sufficient summary information to enable the methods of Chapter 5 to be implemented. For the specific case of normally distributed data, Goldstein *et al.* (2000) present a model for combining individual patient data with study-level data.

## 9.8 COMBINING *P*-VALUES

A typical meta-analysis involves the calculation of study estimates of treatment difference and an overall estimate. However, in some cases there may be insufficient data to enable these calculations to be undertaken, particularly if the only available information is that obtained from published papers. An alternative is to use methods developed during the 1930s for the combination of *p*-values, provided that these have been reported. This approach may also be taken if different outcome measures have been reported from one study to the next, and the assumptions required for either of the two approaches discussed in Section 9.3 are not met.

Methods which have been derived for summarizing *p*-values are based on one-sided *p*-values. As an illustration of the approach, consider the situation in which there is a common parameter, $\theta$, measuring the treatment difference in all studies. Suppose that $\theta$ equals 0 when the two treatments are equivalent and takes positive values if the new treatment is better than the control. Interest lies in testing the null hypothesis that $\theta$ equals 0 against the one-sided alternative that $\theta$ is greater than 0. The one-sided *p*-value is the probability of obtaining a test statistic at least as extreme as that calculated in favour of this one-sided alternative given that the null hypothesis is true. Let $p_{1i}$ be the one-sided *p*-value for study *i*. The *p*-value presented in a trial report or publication is not usually $p_{1i}$: it is more common to report $p_{2i}$, the *p*-value associated with the two-sided alternative that $\theta$ is not equal to 0. The value of $p_{1i}$ can be calculated from $p_{2i}$, but care is needed. First, it is necessary to check whether the estimate of $\theta$ is positive or negative. If the estimate is positive then $p_{1i} = p_{2i}/2$. However, if the estimate is negative then $p_{1i} = 1 - p_{2i}/2$. When the *p*-values from different outcome measures are to be combined, it is important to check that $p_{1i}$ relates to the one sided alternative that the new treatment is better than the control.

The methods for combining *p*-values also assume that the *p*-value is a continuous variable, that is, it can take all values between 0 and 1. Fisher (1932) derived a chi-squared statistic, based on the $p_{1i}$, for testing the global null hypothesis that the two treatments are equivalent against the one-sided alternative that in at least one study the new treatment is better than control. Under the null hypothesis, $p_{1i}$ is uniformly distributed between 0 and 1. Therefore, the statistic $T_i = -2\log(p_{1i})$

has a chi-squared distribution with two degrees of freedom. This can be shown as follows:

$$P(T_i > t) = P(-2\log(p_{1i}) > t) = P(p_{1i} < \exp(-t/2)) = \exp(-t/2).$$

As the $r$ studies are independent, if the null hypothesis is true for each study, then

$$P = \sum_{i=1}^{r} T_i$$

follows a chi-squared distribution with $2r$ degrees of freedom.

To test the global hypothesis that the two treatments are equivalent against the one-sided alternative that in at least one study the new treatment is worse than control, the test statistic

$$P^- = -2\sum_{i=1}^{r} \log(1 - p_{1i})$$

is compared with the chi-squared distribution with $2r$ degrees of freedom.

For the Canner (1987) data set discussed in Section 6.8, the parameter of interest, $\theta$, is the log-odds ratio for mortality on aspirin relative to control. In this case negative values indicate that aspirin is better than control, and interest lies in testing the global null hypothesis that $\theta$ equals 0 against the one-sided alternative that $\theta$ is negative. Table 9.10 shows the one-sided $p$-values for each study calculated from the Wald chi-squared statistic. Fisher's chi-squared statistic is equal to 26.32, and its associated degrees of freedom are 12, that is, twice the number of studies. The one-sided $p$-value of 0.01 indicates a statistically significant difference in favour of aspirin. One of the disadvantages of Fisher's method is that equal weight is given to each study. For the Canner example this means that the influence of study 6 is considerably downweighted relative to its influence in the traditional meta-analysis presented in Table 6.8.

**Table 9.10**   Fisher's combination of $p$-values applied to the Canner data set

| Study | Log-odds ratio* | Std. error | Wald $\chi^2$ | $p_{1i}$ | $T_i$ |
|-------|-----------------|------------|---------------|----------|-------|
| 1 | −0.329 | 0.197 | 2.78 | 0.048 | 6.09 |
| 2 | −0.385 | 0.203 | 3.59 | 0.029 | 7.08 |
| 3 | −0.216 | 0.275 | 0.62 | 0.216 | 3.07 |
| 4 | −0.220 | 0.143 | 2.35 | 0.063 | 5.54 |
| 5 | −0.225 | 0.188 | 1.44 | 0.115 | 4.33 |
| 6 | 0.125 | 0.098 | 1.62 | 0.898 | 0.21 |
| Total | | | | | 26.32 |
| $\chi^2 = 26.32$; (12 df) $p = 0.01$ | | | | | |

*Log-odds ratio of mortality on aspirin relative to placebo.

Methods related to that of Fisher are those of Tippett (1931) and Stouffer *et al.* (1949). Tippett's minimum $p$ test rejects the global null hypothesis that the two treatments are equivalent against the one-sided alternative that in at least one study the new treatment is better than control if any of the $p_{1i}$, $i = 1, \ldots, r$ is less than $\alpha^*$, where

$$\alpha^* = 1 - (1 - \alpha)^{1/r},$$

and $\alpha$ is the prespecified significance level for the combined significance test. The Stouffer *et al.* method was used as the basis for Rosenthal's file-drawer method, described in Section 8.4.2. The statistic $U_r$, given by

$$U_r = \frac{\sum_{i=1}^{r} u(p_{1i})}{\sqrt{r}},$$

where $u(p_{1i}) = \Phi^{-1}(1 - p_{1i})$, is compared with the standard normal distribution. If $U_r > u(\alpha)$, the global null hypothesis that the two treatments are equivalent is rejected at level $\alpha$ against the one-sided alternative. This method is also referred to as the 'sum of zs method' as $u(p_{1i})$ is often written as $z(p_{1i})$ because it is a standard normal deviate.

In common with Fisher's approach, these two methods have the disadvantage that equal weight is given to each study. Instead, it would seem more appropriate to give more accurate studies larger weights. Mosteller and Bush (1954) suggested a generalization of the Stouffer *et al.* method which allows each of the standard normal deviates $u(p_{1i})$ to be weighted. In this approach, the statistic $U_r$ is replaced by $U_{gr}$, where

$$U_{gr} = \frac{\sum_{i=1}^{r} g_i u(p_{1i})}{\sqrt{\sum_{i=1}^{r} g_i^2}},$$

and

$$\sum_{i=1}^{r} g_i^2 = 1.$$

$U_{gr}$ is compared with the standard normal distribution. This method is also referred to as the 'weighted sum of zs method'.

Consider now the choice of values for the weights $g_i$, $i = 1, \ldots, r$. If they are all set equal to $1/\sqrt{r}$, then $U_{gr} = U_r$. As an alternative, suppose that the same outcome measure has been recorded in each trial and that the parameter measuring treatment difference is also identically defined. If the $p_{1i}$ are calculated using the assumption that

$$\hat{\theta}_i \sim N(\theta, w_i^{-1}),$$

then $p_{1i} = 1 - \Phi(\hat{\theta}_i \sqrt{w_i})$ and $u(p_{1i}) = \hat{\theta}_i \sqrt{w_i}$. Setting $g_i = \sqrt{w_i}$ gives

$$U_{gr} = \frac{\sum_{i=1}^{r} \hat{\theta}_i w_i}{\sqrt{\sum_{i=1}^{r} w_i}}.$$

**Table 9.11** Mosteller and Bush method of combining $p$-values, with weights equal to the square root of the study sample size, applied to the Canner data set

| Study | $p_{1i}$ | $u(p_{1i})$ | $u(p_{1i})\sqrt{n_i}$ | $n_i$ |
|-------|----------|-------------|------------------------|-------|
| 1 | 0.048 | 1.67 | 58.70 | 1 239 |
| 2 | 0.029 | 1.90 | 74.11 | 1 529 |
| 3 | 0.216 | 0.79 | 19.67 | 626 |
| 4 | 0.063 | 1.53 | 62.90 | 1 682 |
| 5 | 0.115 | 1.20 | 41.91 | 1 216 |
| 6 | 0.898 | −1.27 | −85.49 | 4 524 |
| Total | | | 171.80 | 10 816 |

$U_{gr} = 171.80/\sqrt{10816} = 1.65; p_1 = 0.049$

In this case $U_{gr}^2$ is equal to the $U$ statistic defined in Section 4.2.2, that is, it is the test statistic for testing the treatment difference in a traditional fixed effects meta-analysis. Hall and Ding (2001) considered this approach for the specific case in which the efficient score and Fisher's information statistics are used. That is, $u(p_{1i}) = Z_i/\sqrt{V_i}$ and $g_i = \sqrt{V_i}$.

In the absence of information on $w_i$, a suitable choice for $g_i$ might be $\sqrt{n_i}$, where $n_i$ is the total number of patients in the two treatment groups. Using this weight for the Canner data set, the statistic $U_{gr}$ is equal to 1.65, which has a one-sided $p$-value equal to 0.049 (Table 9.11). Compared with the result from Fisher's approach, this result is in much closer agreement with that from the fixed effects meta-analysis presented in Table 6.8. It can be seen that the value of 2.73 for $U_{gr}^2$ is close to the value of 2.52 for $U$. It should be noted that the $p$-value of 0.11 associated with $U$ is a two-sided $p$-value. The one-sided $p$-value is 0.055. For this data set, the same outcome measure was used in all trials, and, therefore, weighting by the square root of the sample size is a reasonable approach. This weighting scheme may not be appropriate if different outcome measures have been used across the studies.

Numerous other methods have been derived for combining $p$-values, most of which are straightforward to implement. For a comprehensive coverage of the topic, the reader is referred to Becker (1994). In comparison with the meta-analysis approach based on combining study estimates of treatment difference, methods for combining $p$-values are much less informative and are easier to misinterpret.

# 10

# *Inclusion of Trials with Different Study Designs*

## 10.1  INTRODUCTION

In Chapters 3–5, methods for conducting a meta-analysis were described in detail for the situation in which each trial has a parallel group design. The focus was on the comparison of two treatments, each of which were studied in each trial. Only the data pertaining to the two treatments were included in the meta-analysis. In this chapter, other scenarios are considered.

It is often the case that more than two treatment groups have been included in some or all of the studies to be combined in a meta-analysis. For example, a new treatment may have been compared with both an active standard therapy and placebo. There may be interest in making a comparison of the new treatment with both the active comparator and placebo. A straightforward approach would be to perform a separate meta-analysis for each pairwise comparison, using only the subset of the data which pertains to that specific comparison. A more informative analysis would be to estimate both parameters of treatment difference simultaneously. Even if the interest lies in one particular pairwise comparison, a more precise estimate of the treatment difference may be obtained by including data from other treatment comparisons. This topic is discussed in Section 10.2.

It may be the case that a new treatment has been tested at several different dose levels. Indeed, this is a common occurrence in the development of a new drug. If the drug shows signs of activity, then the magnitude of the effect will depend on the dose administered. Therefore, performing a meta-analysis in which all dose groups are pooled together will usually not be very informative. Instead, it will be of interest to explore the dose–response relationship and to determine the optimum dose. Section 10.3 considers this special case.

Frequently, some of the studies to be combined in a meta-analysis are multicentre trials. The question then arises as to how the centre effect should be handled in the meta-analysis. This issue is discussed in Section 10.4.

In a cross-over trial, subjects receive two or more treatments in a sequence so that information concerning the treatment difference is obtained from within-subject comparisons. The fact that a study has been designed as a cross-over study is not a reason in itself to exclude it from a meta-analysis, and Section 10.5 considers the incorporation of data from such studies into a meta-analysis.

Sequential designs are now a familiar part of clinical trial methodology. Such designs allow for successive interim analyses of the accumulating data, with stopping rules for study termination which are dependent on the observed treatment difference. Section 10.6 considers the incorporation of data from sequential trials into a meta-analysis.

## 10.2   MORE THAN TWO TREATMENT GROUPS

This section extends the models for individual patient data described in Chapter 5 to deal with more than two treatment groups, illustrating the approach specifically for the case of three treatments.

### 10.2.1   A fixed effects meta-analysis model

The meta-analysis model for more than two treatment groups is developed here for the case of normally distributed responses. Model (5.1), which is the fixed effects meta-analysis model for two treatments, will be extended. The approach may also be used for the other data types presented in this book. An example based on binary data is discussed in Section 10.2.4.

Model (5.1) can be written as $\mu_{ij} = \alpha + \eta_{ij}$. The term $\eta_{ij}$ includes study and treatment as covariates, and is defined as

$$\eta_{ij} = \beta_{0i} + \beta_1 x_{1ij},$$

where $x_{1ij}$ takes the value 0 for the control group and 1 for the treated group. Suppose now that there are three treatment groups, denoted by A, B and C. It is necessary to include two indicator variables instead of one, so that the model becomes

$$\eta_{ij} = \beta_{0i} + \beta_{11} x_{11ij} + \beta_{12} x_{12ij}. \tag{10.1}$$

If, for example, $x_{11ij}$ takes the value 1 for treatment A and 0 otherwise, and $x_{12ij}$ takes the value 1 for treatment B and 0 otherwise, then $\beta_{11}$ represents the absolute mean difference A − C, and $\beta_{12}$ the absolute mean difference B − C. The absolute mean difference A − B is given by $\beta_{11} - \beta_{12}$. Studies which include all three treatments contribute information on all three pairwise comparisons. However, it is not necessary for each study to include all three treatment groups.

If a study compares two of the treatments, then it will contribute information on that particular treatment comparison. A meta-analysis which includes the two-treatment studies as well as the three-treatment studies is similar to the analysis of an incomplete block design, in which 'study' plays the role of 'block' (see, for example, Cochran and Cox, 1957).

For $t$ treatment groups, it is necessary to include $t - 1$ indicator variables, $x_{11ij}, \ldots, x_{1(t-1)ij}$, where, for example, $x_{1hij} = 1$ if the patient is in treatment group $h$ and 0 otherwise. Models with three or more treatment groups can be fitted by many statistical packages. In particular, they can be fitted using the GLM and GENMOD procedures in SAS by including 'treat' in the CLASS statement (see Sections 5.2.1 and 5.2.2). For the PHREG and NLMIXED procedures, however, each indicator variable must be calculated and entered into the appropriate model statement. Studies which compare a subset of the $t$ treatments may be included in the meta-analysis.

Study by treatment interaction terms can be included in model (10.1) to give

$$\eta_{ij} = \beta_{0i} + \beta_{11i}x_{11ij} + \beta_{12i}x_{12ij}. \tag{10.2}$$

The test of the study by treatment interaction term involves a comparison between model (10.2) and model (10.1). In the case of normally distributed responses, model (10.2) can be fitted by including a 'study*treat' interaction term in the MODEL statement (see Section 5.2.3). The appropriate $F$ statistic is that associated with the 'study*treat' term. Care should be taken if the LSMEANS statement is used when fitting an interaction term. In this case, the overall estimates of treatment difference are obtained by giving equal weight to each study, instead of weighting by precision.

### 10.2.2   A random effects meta-analysis model

The random effects model (5.23) can be extended to incorporate the three treatment groups A, B and C. This model is given by

$$\eta_{ij} = \beta_{0i} + \beta_{11}x_{11ij} + \beta_{12}x_{12ij} + v_{11i}x_{11ij} + v_{12i}x_{12ij}, \tag{10.3}$$

where $v_{11i}$ and $v_{12i}$ are level 2 random effects which are normally distributed with mean 0 and variances $\tau_1^2$ and $\tau_2^2$, respectively. It is also necessary to consider the correlation between the two random effects from the same study, which will be denoted by $\rho_1$.

The three variance components describe the degree of heterogeneity between the three pairwise treatment comparisons. Let $\gamma_{ACi}$, $\gamma_{BCi}$ and $\gamma_{ABi}$ represent the absolute mean difference parameters for $A - C$, $B - C$, and $A - B$ in the $i$th study.

Using the coding for $x_{11ij}$ and $x_{12ij}$ as presented in Section 10.2.1,

$$\text{var}(\gamma_{ACi}) = \text{var}(v_{11i}) = \tau_1^2,$$

$$\text{var}(\gamma_{BCi}) = \text{var}(v_{12i}) = \tau_2^2,$$

$$\text{var}(\gamma_{ABi}) = \text{var}(v_{11i} - v_{12i}) = \text{var}(v_{11i}) + \text{var}(v_{12i}) - 2\text{cov}(v_{11i}, v_{12i})$$

$$= \tau_1^2 + \tau_2^2 - 2\rho_1\tau_1\tau_2.$$

In order to simplify the model, it may be appropriate to assume that each pairwise treatment comparison has the same amount of heterogeneity. In this case, let $\tau_1^2$ and $\tau_2^2$ equal $\tau^2$. For this particular coding of the treatment indicator variables, this means that $\rho_1$ must equal $\frac{1}{2}$, as discussed by Higgins and Whitehead (1996).

As the number of treatments increases, the number of variance components will increase, and it may be impractical to fit separate variance and covariance terms for each pairwise comparison. Again, the model may be simplified by assuming the same amount of heterogeneity for each pairwise treatment comparison. If there are t treatments and the indicator variables are defined as in Section 10.2.1, then all variance terms can be set to $\tau^2$ and all correlation coefficients to $\frac{1}{2}$. Most statistical packages do not allow the user to enter this particular structure for the variance matrix. However, they often permit the models to be fitted if they are expressed as mixed effects linear models. For example, for normally distributed responses, the SAS statements presented in Section 5.8.4 may be used. In the SAS output the difference between the least-squares means of any two treatments provides an estimate of that particular treatment difference. As before, the estimate alongside the covariance parameter 'study*treat' is an estimate of $\tau^2/2$. As was the case for the fixed effects meta-analysis, it is possible to incorporate studies which only compare a subset of the treatments.

## 10.2.3  Random study effects

Random study effects may be incorporated into model (10.3), in a similar way to that described in Section 5.11. When there are more than two treatment groups, it is usually easier to fit the model by expressing it as a traditional mixed effects linear model, in which all random effects are uncorrelated. For normally distributed responses, the model can be fitted using the SAS statements presented in Section 5.8.4, but with the MODEL and RANDOM statements altered as follows:

```
MODEL y = treat / htype = 1 ddfm = kenwardroger;
RANDOM study study*treat;
```

Again, it is possible to incorporate studies which only compare a subset of the treatments. When there are more than two treatments to compare and not all of the treatments are included in each study, it is possible to recover between-study information about treatment differences by including study as a random rather than a fixed effect. This is analogous to the recovery of inter-block information from incomplete block designs, discussed by Yates (1940) in the case of balanced incomplete blocks.

## 10.2.4    Example: First bleeding in cirrhosis

The example considered in this section relates to three treatment groups and a binary response. Therefore, the models presented in Sections 10.2.1–10.2.3 will be applied within the binary context.

Pagliaro *et al.* (1992) investigated the use of beta-blockers and sclerotherapy for the prevention of first bleeding in cirrhosis. There were 26 trials in total, of which 7 involved a comparison between beta-blockers and the control treatment, 17 a comparison between sclerotherapy and control, and 2 a comparison between all three treatments (Table 10.1). Whilst direct comparisons between beta-blockers and control and between sclerotherapy and control can be made from 9 and 19 trials respectively, there are only two trials providing a direct comparison of beta-blockers with sclerotherapy. In the following analyses, beta-blockers, sclerotherapy and control treatment are denoted as treatments A, B and C, respectively.

In Pagliaro *et al.* (1992) the two pairwise comparisons involving the control treatment were presented. The study estimates of the log-odds ratio of bleeding on experimental treatment relative to control were combined using efficient score and Fisher's information statistics (formulae (3.5) and (3.6)), and based on the fixed effects model of Chapter 4. Both experimental treatments were shown to be significantly better than control. Although the test for heterogeneity was statistically significant in both cases, no random effects meta-analysis was performed. Table 10.1 shows fixed and random effects estimates for each of the three two-treatment comparisons, in which the trial log-odds ratio and its variance were estimated from (3.5) and (3.6) and the method of moments estimate of the heterogeneity parameter was used. From the meta-analyses based on the comparison of beta-blockers with control and of sclerotherapy with control, both experimental treatments appear to be better than control, with beta-blockers showing a slightly larger treatment advantage than sclerotherapy, although there is not much in it.

The two studies in which beta-blockers can be compared directly with sclerotherapy provide estimates of the log-odds ratio of bleeding on beta-blockers relative to sclerotherapy of $-1.472$ (standard error $0.643$) and $-0.011$ (standard error $0.440$). Both fixed and random effects estimates can be calculated from these two studies, although the latter may be considered an inappropriate summary due to the lack of information about the heterogeneity parameter. The random effects estimate is larger than the fixed effects estimate, but neither is statistically

**Table 10.1** Randomized trials of treatment of first bleeding in cirrhosis. The log-odds ratio and its standard error from each trial are based on formulae (3.5) and (3.6). Fixed and random effects meta-analyses are conducted on each pairwise comparison using the methods of Chapter 4

| Trial | Number of patients | | | Treatment comparison | Log-odds ratio | Std. error |
|---|---|---|---|---|---|---|
| | Beta-blockers (A) bled/total | Sclerotherapy (B) bled/total | Control (C) bled/total | | | |
| 1 | 2/43 | 9/42 | 13/41 | A − B | −1.472 | 0.643 |
| | | | | A − C | −1.823 | 0.567 |
| | | | | B − C | −0.521 | 0.494 |
| 2 | 12/68 | 13/73 | 13/72 | A − B | −0.011 | 0.440 |
| | | | | A − C | −0.028 | 0.440 |
| | | | | B − C | −0.017 | 0.431 |
| 3 | 4/20 | | 4/16 | A − C | −0.281 | 0.796 |
| 4 | 20/116 | | 30/111 | A − C | −0.567 | 0.320 |
| 5 | 1/30 | | 11/49 | A − C | −1.465 | 0.642 |
| 6 | 7/53 | | 10/53 | A − C | −0.416 | 0.527 |
| 7 | 18/85 | | 31/89 | A − C | −0.671 | 0.336 |
| 8 | 2/51 | | 11/51 | A − C | −1.571 | 0.591 |
| 9 | 8/23 | | 2/25 | A − C | 1.590 | 0.704 |
| 10 | | 4/18 | 0/19 | B − C | 2.242 | 1.045 |
| 11 | | 3/35 | 22/36 | B − C | −2.271 | 0.493 |
| 12 | | 5/56 | 30/53 | B − C | −2.167 | 0.409 |
| 13 | | 5/16 | 6/18 | B − C | −0.092 | 0.724 |
| 14 | | 3/23 | 9/22 | B − C | −1.393 | 0.667 |
| 15 | | 11/49 | 31/46 | B − C | −1.803 | 0.411 |
| 16 | | 19/53 | 9/60 | B − C | 1.109 | 0.435 |
| 17 | | 17/53 | 29/60 | B − C | −0.473 | 0.387 |
| 18 | | 10/71 | 29/69 | B − C | −1.381 | 0.376 |
| 19 | | 12/41 | 14/41 | B − C | −0.223 | 0.472 |
| 20 | | 0/21 | 3/20 | B − C | −2.158 | 1.185 |
| 21 | | 13/33 | 14/35 | B − C | −0.025 | 0.492 |
| 22 | | 31/143 | 23/138 | B − C | 0.322 | 0.302 |
| 23 | | 20/55 | 19/51 | B − C | −0.038 | 0.401 |
| 24 | | 3/13 | 12/16 | B − C | −2.008 | 0.734 |
| 25 | | 3/21 | 5/28 | B − C | −0.256 | 0.773 |
| 26 | | 6/22 | 2/24 | B − C | 1.290 | 0.770 |

| | | | |
|---|---|---|---|
| Fixed effects estimate | A − B | −0.477 | 0.363 |
| Random effects estimate (method of moments $\hat{\tau}^2$ =0.76) | A − B | −0.666 | 0.727 |
| Fixed effects estimate | A − C | −0.612 | 0.159 |
| Random effects estimate (method of moments $\hat{\tau}^2$ =0.39) | A − C | −0.611 | 0.273 |
| Fixed effects estimate | B − C | −0.552 | 0.111 |
| Random effects estimate (method of moments $\hat{\tau}^2$ =0.96) | B − C | −0.546 | 0.260 |

significant. In an attempt to improve the inference which can be made about the treatment difference, an analysis which uses all of the data from the 26 trials was undertaken.

In fitting a fixed effects model for the three treatment groups, the binary observation, $y_{ij}$ for patient $j$ in trial $i$, takes the value 1 if bleeding occurs and 0 otherwise. The model, which is based on model (10.1), is given by

$$\log\left(\frac{p_{ij}}{1 - p_{ij}}\right) = \alpha + \beta_{0i} + \beta_{11i}x_{11ij} + \beta_{12i}x_{12ij}, \tag{10.4}$$

and can be fitted using PROC GENMOD in SAS with the following statements:

```
PROC GENMOD;
CLASS trial treat;
MODEL y = trial treat/ type1 dist=bin link=logit;
LSMEANS treat/pdiff cl;
```

The results are presented in the first row of Table 10.2. The estimate of the log-odds ratio of bleeding on beta-blockers relative to sclerotherapy is $-0.117$, considerably smaller than the estimate of $-0.477$ in Table 10.1. On the other hand, the estimates of the log-odds ratios of each of these treatments relative to control have not changed much.

In order to take account of the heterogeneity between trials, a random effects model with a common heterogeneity parameter was fitted using MLwiN. In Section 5.9.2, a set of MLn commands was provided for fitting model (5.27), a random effects model for binary data in the case of two treatments. In Section 5.8.4, the relationship between the multilevel model and the traditional mixed effects linear model was discussed for the case of normally distributed responses. This

**Table 10.2** Log-odds ratio for first bleeding in cirrhosis. Estimates with standard error in square brackets

| Model | Test of treatment differences | $\hat{\tau}^2$ | Treatment comparison | | |
|---|---|---|---|---|---|
| | | | A − B | A − C | B − C |
| Fixed study | $\chi^2 = 39.31$; | – | −0.117 | −0.670 | −0.553 |
| Fixed treatment | (2 df) | | [0.189] | [0.161] | [0.113] |
| | $p < 0.001$ | | $p = 0.54$ | $p < 0.001$ | $p < 0.001$ |
| Fixed study | $\chi^2 = 6.81$; | 1.17 | −0.162 | −0.737 | −0.574 |
| Fixed treatment | (2 df) | | [0.469] | [0.403] | [0.283] |
| Random study by treatment | $p = 0.03$ | | $p = 0.73$ | $p = 0.07$ | $p = 0.04$ |
| Random study | $\chi^2 = 10.84$; | 0.92 | −0.526 | −0.981 | −0.455 |
| Fixed treatment | (2 df) | | [0.328] | [0.312] | [0.239] |
| Random study by treatment | $p = 0.004$ | | $p = 0.11$ | $p = 0.002$ | $p = 0.06$ |

approach may also be taken for other data types. In the case of binary responses, model (5.25) becomes

$$\log\left(\frac{p_{ihj}}{1 - p_{ihj}}\right) = \mu + s_i + t_h + (st)_{ih}. \tag{10.5}$$

Model (5.27), the random effects meta-analysis model for binary responses, may be written as model (10.5), in which $(st)_{ih}$ is normally distributed with mean 0 and variance $\sigma_\tau^2$.

Model (10.5) may be fitted in MLn by introducing treatment as an additional level in the hierarchy. In this case patient is at the lowest level (level 1), nested within treatment at the middle level (level 2), which is nested in turn within study at the highest level (level 3). The first set of commands presented in Section 5.9.2 would need to be changed as follows:

```
DINPUT c1-c8
meta.dat
NAME c1 'subject' c2 'trtmnt' c3 'study' c4 'treat' c5 'y'
c6 'cons' c7 'bcons' c8 'denom'
RESP 'y'
IDEN 1 'subject' 2 'trtmnt' 3 'study'
EXPL 'treat' 'cons' 'bcons'
FPAR 'bcons'
SETV 2 'cons'
LINK 'bcons' G9
SETV 1 'bcons'
DUMM 'study' c9-c16
EXPL c9-c16
```

The data set needs to include an extra variable 'trtmnt', which contains a unique number for each treatment. The first SETV command requests that the study by treatment interaction term is random. As was the case with PROC MIXED, the variance component at the treatment level is $\sigma_\tau^2$, which is equal to $\tau^2/2$. The parameter associated with 'treat' is $\beta_1$.

This new set of commands can be used for the Pagliaro *et al.* data set, with the exception that there would need to be two treatment indicator variables instead of 'treat', and the number of studies would need to be increased to 26.

The results from fitting the random effects model, using first-order penalized quasi-likelihood estimates under restrictive generalized least squares, are shown in the second row of Table 10.2. Compared with the first row, the log-odds ratio estimates have changed, but not substantially. However, the standard errors have increased substantially due to the between-trial heterogeneity.

The inclusion of the trial effect as random rather than fixed allows the recovery of between-trial treatment information, which is likely to be substantial for the comparison between beta-blockers and sclerotherapy. This model may be fitted by removing the study effects from the fixed part of the model and including them as random effects by issuing the command

```
SETV 3 'cons'
```

The log-odds ratio estimates from this model, shown in the last row of Table 10.2, are substantially different from the previous row. They indicate a larger beneficial effect of beta-blockers relative to sclerotherapy, although this does not reach statistical significance. The standard errors of all three estimates are smaller, in particular the beta-blockers versus sclerotherapy comparison, illustrating the amount of information which has been recovered. However, even with the additional information there is insufficient evidence to draw any conclusions about the comparison between beta-blockers and sclerotherapy.

The GLIMMIX macro discussed in Section 5.9.2 could also be used to fit the random effects model by changing the CLASS, MODEL and RANDOM statements in the program presented in that section to

```
CLASS trial treat;
MODEL y = trial treat/htype = 1 solution;
RANDOM trial*treat;
```

The model which includes trial as a random rather than a fixed effect can also be fitted by changing the MODEL and RANDOM statements to

```
MODEL y = treat/htype = 1 solution;
RANDOM trial trial*treat;
```

## 10.3   DOSE–RESPONSE RELATIONSHIPS

This section deals with the situation in which the treatment groups represent different doses of the same compound. If each dose is considered as a separate treatment, then the methods described in Section 10.2 can be applied and pairwise comparisons made. In addition, a model describing the dose–response relationship may be fitted, using an extension of the methods described in Section 6.7.

Sometimes the studies to be combined in the meta-analysis will include the same selection of doses. However, it is more likely that the selected doses will vary from one trial to the next. In this latter case the dose–response relationship will describe a mixture of between-trial and within-trial relationships and care needs to be taken with the interpretation.

In this section, data from the tacrine studies described in Section 3.5.1 are used to illustrate the methods. For simplification, the Clinical Global Impression of Change scale is dichotomized, so that categories 1–3 represent a 'success' and categories 4–7 a 'failure'. As discussed in Section 6.6.1, in most studies the dose for each patient was titrated to or selected to be the patient's best dose. However, the analysis shown in this section would require each patient to be *randomized* to one of the selection of six doses in order to be valid. This analysis is thus for illustrative purposes only, and not a recommendation of how to analyse the tacrine data set.

The studies together included six doses: 0, 20, 40, 80, 120 and 160 mg/day of tacrine. Table 10.3 shows the number and percentage of successes in each treatment group in each study. All studies include a placebo (0 mg/kg) group and four include the 80 mg/kg group. Data on the other dose groups occur in only one or two studies, although they do occur with several other doses within the same study. Estimates of the log-odds ratio of success for each dose group relative to placebo are presented in Table 10.4. These were calculated separately for each study using the following SAS statements:

```
PROC GENMOD;
CLASS dose;
MODEL y = dose/ type1 dist=bin link=logit;
LSMEANS dose/pdiff cl;
BY study;
```

There appears to be some evidence of an increasing effect with increasing dose. The fixed effects model (10.4), extended to include six treatment groups, was fitted using the SAS statements

```
PROC GENMOD;
CLASS study dose;
MODEL y = study dose/ type1 dist=bin link=logit;
LSMEANS dose/pdiff cl;
```

**Table 10.3** Global impression of change in Alzheimer's disease. Number (percentage) of successful responses in each tacrine dose group

| Dose (mg) | Study | | | | |
|---|---|---|---|---|---|
| | 1 | 2 | 3 | 4 | 5 |
| 0 | 24/110 (21.8) | 23/72 (31.9) | 23/53 (43.4) | 32/170 (18.2) | 15/41 (36.6) |
| 20 | – | 53/152 (34.9) | – | – | – |
| 40 | 27/96 (28.1) | 47/147 (32.0) | – | – | – |
| 80 | – | 33/74 (44.6) | 33/68 (48.5) | 16/50 (32.0) | 17/39 (43.6) |
| 120 | – | – | – | 50/144 (34.7) | – |
| 160 | – | – | – | 61/187 (32.6) | – |

**Table 10.4**    Global impression of change in Alzheimer's disease. Log-odds ratio of success for each tacrine dose group relative to placebo. Study estimates are shown with standard error in square brackets

| Dose (mg) | Study | | | | |
|---|---|---|---|---|---|
| | 1 | 2 | 3 | 4 | 5 |
| 20 | – | 0.132 [0.305] | – | – | – |
| 40 | 0.338 [0.324] | 0.001 [0.309] | – | – | – |
| 80 | – | 0.539 [0.344] | 0.207 [0.368] | 0.708 [0.361] | 0.292 [0.458] |
| 120 | – | – | – | 0.830 [0.263] | – |
| 160 | – | – | – | 0.736 [0.251] | – |

This indicated a statistically significant difference amongst the doses ($\chi^2 = 16.55$, 5 df, $p = 0.005$), with the three highest doses being better than placebo (Table 10.5). A test of the study by dose interaction was undertaken by changing the MODEL statement above to

```
MODEL y = study dose study*dose / type1 dist=bin link=logit;
```

This was not statistically significant ($\chi^2 = 1.95$, 4 df, $p = 0.74$), although it is based mainly on the 80 mg/kg dose.

The random effects model in which the dose was considered as a factor with six levels was fitted using MLwiN. This produced almost identical results to the fixed effects model because the heterogeneity parameter was estimated to be zero (Table 10.5). Inclusion of a random instead of a fixed study effect has had a small effect on the estimates of the log-odds ratios, and an even smaller effect on their precision. The relative rankings of the dose groups remain unchanged. From these analyses it appears that the dose of 120 mg/day provides the best efficacy result, although it should be noted that study 4 is the only study which provides data on this dose.

The simplest form of dose–response relationship which can be fitted is a straight line. This is easily fitted within any of the fixed or random effects models by treating dose as a continuous covariate rather than a factor. Here, the model which has a fixed linear dose response and a random study effect was fitted. This model is given by

$$\log\left(\frac{p_{ij}}{1 - p_{ij}}\right) = \alpha + v_{0i} + \beta_1 d_{ij}, \tag{10.6}$$

**Table 10.5** Global impression of change in Alzheimer's disease. Log-odds ratio of success for each dose group relative to placebo. Overall estimates are shown with standard error in square brackets

| Model | Test of treatment differences | $\hat{\tau}^2$ | Treatment comparison relative to placebo | | | | |
|---|---|---|---|---|---|---|---|
| | | | 20 | 40 | 80 | 120 | 160 |
| Fixed study Fixed treatment | $\chi^2 = 16.55$; (5 df) $p = 0.005$ | — | 0.174 [0.245] $p = 0.48$ | 0.111 [0.206] $p = 0.59$ | 0.498 [0.184] $p = 0.007$ | 0.770 [0.245] $p = 0.002$ | 0.676 [0.232] $p = 0.004$ |
| Fixed study Fixed treatment Random study by treatment | $\chi^2 = 15.91$; (5 df) $p = 0.007$ | 0 | 0.174 [0.245] $p = 0.48$ | 0.111 [0.206] $p = 0.59$ | 0.498 [0.184] $p = 0.007$ | 0.770 [0.245] $p = 0.002$ | 0.676 [0.232] $p = 0.004$ |
| Random study Fixed treatment Random study by treatment | $\chi^2 = 16.11$; (5 df) $p = 0.007$ | 0 | 0.200 [0.239] $p = 0.40$ | 0.112 [0.199] $p = 0.57$ | 0.550 [0.181] $p = 0.002$ | 0.695 [0.236] $p = 0.003$ | 0.600 [0.222] $p = 0.007$ |

where $d_{ij}$ is the dose of tacrine (mg/kg) and $\beta_1$ now represents the change in the log-odds of success with each 1 mg/kg increase in dose. The model can be fitted in MLwinN as a two-level hierarchical model, the levels being study and patient. The estimate of $\beta_1$ was 0.004 55 (standard error 0.001 26), producing a log-odds ratio relative to placebo of 0.546 at 120 mg/kg and 0.728 at 160 mg/kg. The linear dose–response relationship is not satisfactory, because it predicts an increasing effect with increasing dose. Therefore, a quadratic dose–response curve was considered. The model is given by

$$\log \left( \frac{p_{ij}}{1 - p_{ij}} \right) = \alpha + v_{0i} + \beta_1 d_{ij} + \beta_2 d_{ij}^2. \qquad (10.7)$$

Estimates of $\beta_1$ and $\beta_2$ were calculated to be 0.008 73 (standard error 0.003 71) and 0.000 030 5 (standard error 0.000 025 3) respectively, resulting in an optimum dose of 143 mg/kg.

## 10.4   MULTICENTRE TRIALS

When multicentre trials are to be included in a meta-analysis, consideration needs to be given to the handling of the centre effects. When the available data consist of summary statistics from published papers there may be no choice. However, when individual patient data are available there are numerous possibilities to consider. Some of the various options are discussed in this section.

One option is to use the methods of Chapter 4 to combine study estimates of treatment difference. This means that study would remain the stratifying factor for the meta-analysis. There is then a decision to be made regarding the calculation of the study estimate from the multicentre trial. Should the study estimate be stratified by centre or not? To some extent this will depend on the analysis which was planned for the multicentre trial. The model which is commonly used for the analysis of a multicentre trial is the fixed effects meta-analysis model of Chapter 5, in which 'centre' plays the role of 'study' (see Section 5.12). This leads to an estimate stratified by centre, and so for consistency it is this estimate which should be used in the meta-analysis. An alternative approach is to combine the estimates from each centre using the fixed effects model of Chapter 4. Some multicentre trials consist of a large number of centres with few patients per centre. In this case, stratifying by centre may result in too much loss of power. Instead, centres may be pooled together in homogeneous groups, perhaps by geographical location, to form larger units for stratification. If this is not possible then there should be no stratification.

A second option is to use the methods of Chapter 4, but make centre the stratifying factor. Then estimates from each centre would act as separate studies in the meta-analysis. This might have a dramatic effect on the number of 'studies' in the meta-analysis. However, if the centre estimates are reasonably homogeneous this is unlikely to produce results which are very different from the approach in the previous paragraph. On the other hand, if there is heterogeneity between centres within studies the results from the two approaches may differ, as the first approach ignores this.

When individual patient data are available, the models of Chapter 5 can be used with centres acting as separate studies. As another option, an additional level may be introduced into the hierarchical model: study at the highest level (level 3), centre at the next level down (level 2) and patient at the lowest level (level 1).

## 10.5   CROSS-OVER TRIALS

In a parallel group trial, subjects are randomized to receive one of the set of treatments being compared. By contrast, a cross-over trial is one in which subjects receive two or more of the treatments, with randomization being to one of the set of treatment sequences. In many of the cross-over trials undertaken, each subject receives each of the treatments being compared. Their use is limited in practice because they are only suitable if the disease or condition under study is chronic and stable.

The advantage that cross-over trials have over parallel group trials is that they can lead to a saving in resources. This is because the same number of observations can be obtained from fewer subjects and also fewer observations are needed to obtain the same precision in the estimate of treatment difference. The disadvantage is that there are potential problems which may arise because of the nature of the design. One of these is the carry-over effect from one treatment period into the next, the magnitude of which depends on the treatment received in the earlier period. Cross-over designs need to include sufficiently long washout periods between the treatment periods in order to allow the effect of the previous treatment to disappear. A second problem occurs if a number of the subjects drop out of the trial before providing data from each treatment period. This can lead to complications of the analysis and interpretation of the results.

The cross-over trial has a hierarchical structure, in which there are two levels: patient at the higher level (level 2) and treatment period at the lower level (level 1). Information concerning the treatment comparisons is mainly obtained from the lower level. In some respects, the analysis of a cross-over study can be viewed in the same light as the analysis of a multicentre trial or a meta-analysis, where 'subject' plays the role of 'centre' or 'study'. The subject effects can be treated as fixed or random. However, the treatment effect is usually considered as fixed, with no subject by treatment interaction terms. Often, adjustment is made for period effects. For details of the analysis of a cross-over trial, the reader is referred to Senn (1993) or Brown and Prescott (1999).

If individual patient data are available from a cross-over trial, the data from all treatment periods can be used to provide estimates of the treatment difference and its standard error. If the data from the later treatment periods are considered to be unreliable because, for example, the washout period is too short, it may be necessary to use the data from the first period only. In this case the analysis is identical to that for a parallel group study. Estimates from both parallel group studies and cross-over trials may be combined in the same meta-analysis using the methods of Chapter 4.

Difficulties may arise if the only data available from a cross-over study are summary statistics from a published paper. In particular, caution is needed if the reported statistics are the mean and standard deviation for each treatment. These standard deviations relate to the variability between patients and not between periods for the same patient. It is the latter which is required for the meta-analysis. This is similar to the problem discussed in Section 9.6.1 when the outcome of interest was the change in measurement between two timepoints.

If the trials to be included in a meta-analysis have a variety of designs, it may be possible to combine the data using a hierarchical model. Frost *et al.* (1999) consider this approach for investigating the effect on blood cholesterol of changes in intake of various dietary lipids. Parallel group, cross-over and Latin square designs were amongst the study designs included.

## 10.6  SEQUENTIAL TRIALS

In a non-sequential study with a fixed sample size, there will be one analysis at the end of the study when all of the data have been collected. In this case, frequentist point estimates, confidence intervals and $p$-values are based on an imaginary infinite number of repetitions of the same study with the same sample size. However, in a sequential study the data are examined repeatedly in a way which might lead to early stopping, and so the fixed sample size analysis will not be valid. Without adjustment, repeated significance tests using a fixed sample size analysis will result in an excessive number of false positive conclusions when no treatment difference exists and the conventional estimate of treatment difference will be biased.

If a study is to incorporate a series of interim analyses, then these should follow some predetermined sequential design. Once the study has been stopped, frequentist analyses should concern infinite repetitions of that design. In this way, estimates and confidence intervals can be constructed which have desirable properties. Data from trials which have been stopped due to an interim analysis, without any predetermined design, are far more difficult to interpret.

There are two main types of sequential procedure which are implemented in practice. The first is derived from a boundaries approach, in which the test statistics $Z$ and $V$ discussed in Chapter 3 are plotted against one another until certain stopping boundaries are crossed. The second is a repeated significance test approach, in which a series of conventional analyses are performed with significance levels adjusted to allow for the repetition. Further details can be found in J. Whitehead (1997) and Jennison and Turnbull (2000). Computer programs are available to provide valid analyses, including estimates of the treatment difference which are either unbiased or median unbiased – see, for example, PEST 4 EaSt (website at http://www.cytel.com) and S-Plus SeqTrial (website at http://www.insightful.com/products/addons.asp).

Suppose that one of the studies to be included in a meta-analysis has been conducted using a predetermined sequential design. The meta-analysis methods of Chapter 4 assume that the estimate of the treatment difference from each study is normally distributed. The overall fixed effects estimate is then calculated as a weighted average of the individual study estimates in which the weights are the inverse variances of these estimates. An obvious choice for the estimate of treatment difference from the sequential trial is a bias-adjusted maximum likelihood estimate. However, such an estimate is not normally distributed and also does not have a symmetrical distribution. Therefore, it is not clear what weight should be attached to it.

Todd (1997) presented the results of a simulation exercise, in which sequential trials are incorporated into a fixed effects meta-analysis, using the $Z$ and $V$ statistics calculated at the termination of the study. For a fixed sample size design, $Z/V$ is an approximate ML estimate of the treatment difference parameter, $\theta$. The bias of this estimate is small for small values of $\theta$, but increases with increasing values of $\theta$. For a sequential design, an additional source of bias is introduced due to the nature of the design. Todd considered the scenario in which the meta-analysis includes five trials, of which between one and four are sequential trials whilst the remainder have a fixed sample size design. Binary outcome data were generated. The triangular test (J. Whitehead, 1997) and the O'Brien and Fleming design (O'Brien and Fleming, 1979) were the chosen sequential procedures, each investigated separately. The triangular test allows early stopping either when the new treatment is shown to be better than the control or when it is shown to offer no advantage. With the O'Brien and Fleming design, early stopping is unlikely, and the number of subjects is similar to the equivalent fixed sample size design. Therefore, the bias after using the O'Brien and Fleming design is expected to be less than that after using the triangular test. Todd showed that the bias inherent in a single sequential study was not carried through into a meta-analysis. This is probably because a sequential trial which stops early, giving a large, often biased estimate of treatment difference, has a relatively small weight in the meta-analysis. Sequential trials which continue for longer, lead to less biased estimates, and their larger weight in the meta-analysis is not a problem.

Previously, Green *et al.* (1987) had considered the effect of including in a meta-analysis studies which had been stopped early using inappropriate stopping rules. In a simulation exercise, studies with survival time as the primary measure were stopped early whenever the $p$-value for the log-rank test statistic reached 0.05 or less. It was assumed that studies which had stopped early were only a minority of those to be included in the meta-analysis. Green *et al.* concluded that inclusion of the unadjusted results from such studies had little effect on the $p$-value of the test of treatment difference in a meta-analysis. They also found this to be the case for correctly designed sequential trials. The designs considered were those based on repeated significance testing, which included the O'Brien and Fleming design. They concluded that publication bias was likely to have a greater effect on the *p*-value.

Hughes *et al.* (1992) considered the impact of sequential trials on the amount of heterogeneity in a meta-analysis. They considered sequential designs based on repeated significance testing, and normally distributed subject responses. Like the earlier authors, they observed that the inclusion of the unadjusted results from sequential trials had little effect on the *p*-value of the test of treatment difference in a fixed effects meta-analysis. However, they found that if the true treatment difference was small, then artificial heterogeneity was introduced, increasing the *p*-value for the test for heterogeneity, whereas if the true treatment difference was large, then the heterogeneity may be underestimated. An overestimate of the heterogeneity parameter in a random effects meta-analysis leads to a larger weight being given to smaller trials. In this case, the sequential trials which stop early become more influential, leading to a biased random effects estimate of treatment difference.

The approach discussed by Hall and Ding (2001) for combining *p*-values, based on efficient score and Fisher's information statistics (see Section 9.8), may provide a means of combining results from sequential trials and non-sequential trials. In this approach, the test of the null hypothesis of no treatment difference is conducted by comparing the statistic

$$U_{gr} = \frac{\sum_{i=1}^{r} g_i u(p_{1i})}{\sqrt{\sum_{i=1}^{r} g_i^2}}$$

with the standard normal distribution. For all trials, the weight $g_i = \sqrt{V_i}$. For non-sequential trials, $u(p_{1i}) = Z_i / \sqrt{V_i}$, and for sequential trials $u(p_{1i}) = \Phi^{-1}(1 - p_{1i})$, where $p_{1i}$ is the correctly calculated one-sided *p*-value, taking account of the interim analyses. In this case, $U_{gr}^2$ is analogous to the $U$ statistic defined in Section 4.2.2 for testing the treatment difference in a traditional fixed effects meta-analysis.

# 11

# A Bayesian Approach to Meta-Analysis

## 11.1 INTRODUCTION

The statistical procedures presented so far in this book have been derived from a classical or frequentist approach, in which point estimates, confidence intervals and hypothesis tests are prominent features. The frequentist approach is concerned with an imagined infinite number of repetitions of the same inferential problem for fixed values of the unknown parameters. For example, consider inferences about the treatment difference parameter, $\theta$, based on data collected during a clinical trial. A one-sided $p$-value, for a test of the null hypothesis that $\theta$ is zero against the alternative that $\theta$ is greater than zero, is the proportion of such infinite repetitions when $\theta$ is zero in which the test statistic is greater than or equal to its calculated value. A 95% CI, $(\theta_L, \theta_U)$, has the property that in 95% of repetitions it will include the true value of $\theta$. This is not the same as saying '$\theta$ has a 95% chance of falling in the interval $(\theta_L, \theta_U)$', as $\theta$ is fixed and not a random variable.

The Bayesian philosophy is fundamentally different from the frequentist, although it can lead to methods which are numerically very similar. In the Bayesian approach, all unknown parameters, such as $\theta$, are treated as random variables, and these have a joint probability distribution specified prior to observation of data. In principle, these prior distributions are reflections of subjective opinion. The updating of the prior distribution in the light of the data, governed by Bayes' theorem, leads to the posterior distribution. Bayesian inference is based on this posterior distribution. From it can be calculated such quantities as $P(\theta < 0)$, the probability that $\theta$ is less than zero. The analogue of a frequentist confidence interval is the credibility interval. The 95% credibility interval, $(\theta_L, \theta_U)$, has the property that the Bayesian is 95% certain that $\theta$ lies within it.

The Bayesian approach has two important aspects. The first is the expression of subjective opinion as the prior distribution. As the posterior distribution is influenced by the choice of the prior distribution it is also subjective. The choice of a prior distribution is therefore important and often controversial. In a meta-analysis, the two main parameters are the treatment difference, $\theta$, and the heterogeneity, $\tau^2$. In this chapter only non-informative prior distributions are considered for θ. Usually, the amount of information from the trials considered in a meta-analysis would overwhelm any prior information about θ, so that the choice of prior distribution is not crucial. On the other hand, when there are only a small number of trials, the estimate of $\tau^2$ from the data is usually imprecise. In addition to non-informative prior distributions, consideration is given to empirical prior distributions for $\tau^2$. The second important aspect of the Bayesian approach is the method of combining and updating evidence. Because all unknown parameters are treated as random variables, the combination of diverse information is facilitated. The recent development of software, such as BUGS, to deal with the intensive computations makes it possible to implement these methods quite easily.

An important advantage of the Bayesian approach is the ability to account for uncertainty of all relevant sources of variability in the model. In a Bayesian analysis, the posterior density is fully evaluated and exact posterior standard deviations and credibility intervals can be obtained from the posterior distributions for each model parameter. By contrast, in the frequentist approach, the standard errors and CIs are often computed using formulae which assume that the variance components are known.

It is not the intention here to provide a detailed account of the Bayesian approach. There are a number of books which provide this (see, for example, Lee, 1989; Bernado and Smith, 1993; O'Hagan 1994). In this chapter, the focus is on describing some of the Bayesian techniques which are of relevance to a meta-analysis, together with their implementation. The software package BUGS is used to implement the methods.

In this chapter, a number of the meta-analysis models presented in earlier chapters within a frequentist framework will be discussed within a Bayesian framework. To facilitate the comparison with the frequentist approach, the models will be referred to by the names given to them within the frequentist setting. Within the Bayesian setting, the 'fixed effect' parameters will be treated as random, and will usually be given non-informative prior distributions.

In Section 11.2 the Bayesian formulation is introduced in relation to the random effects meta-analysis model, for which the data consist of the study estimates of treatment difference. The choice of prior distributions is discussed in Section 11.3, and the implementation of the method using BUGS is presented in Section 11.4. In Sections 11.5 and 11.6 the model is extended to allow for study-level covariates and individual patient data, respectively.

External information from related trials can be incorporated into the model to provide more precise posterior distributions for the parameters of interest. In Sections 11.7 and 11.8, two ways of incorporating external information are discussed. The first uses data from trials comparing one of the treatments in the treatment comparison of interest with a common third treatment to improve the inference on both heterogeneity and the treatment difference. This topic was discussed within the frequentist setting in Section 10.2. The second uses data from previous meta-analyses in the same therapeutic area to formulate a prior distribution for the heterogeneity parameter.

Other examples of the application of a Bayesian approach to meta-analysis may be found in Eddy *et al.* (1992) and Stangl and Berry (2000).

## 11.2    A BAYESIAN APPROACH TO THE RANDOM EFFECTS MODEL FOR STUDY ESTIMATES

This section considers a Bayesian approach to the random effects meta-analysis model described in Chapter 4 within the frequentist setting. In the Bayesian approach, parameters such as $\theta_i$ become random variables, and a hierarchical model, which has similarities with the model described in Section 4.3, is considered. The data consist of study estimates of treatment difference, $\hat{\theta}_i$, $i = 1, \ldots, r$, where

$$\hat{\theta}_i \sim N(\theta_i, \xi_i^2). \tag{11.1}$$

The parameter $\theta_i$ is given the prior distribution

$$\theta_i \sim N(\theta, \tau^2). \tag{11.2}$$

In this model, it is assumed that the $\theta_i$ are exchangeable, that is, they may be expected to be different, but there is no prior belief about their ordering. For consistency with the frequentist approach, it is assumed that $\xi_i^2$ is known and is replaced by the calculated value $w_i^{-1}$, $i = 1, \ldots, r$. The vector of study estimates, $\hat{\theta}_i$, is denoted by $y$, the corresponding vector of parameters, $\theta_i$, by $\psi$, the joint density (likelihood) function for the data by $f(y|\psi)$ and the prior distribution for $\psi$ by $p(\psi|\theta, \tau^2)$.

As a simple example of the Bayesian approach, consider the situation in which $\theta$ and $\tau^2$ are both known. In this case the posterior distribution for $\psi$, obtained using Bayes' theorem, would be given by

$$p(\psi|y, \theta, \tau^2) = \frac{p(y, \psi|\theta, \tau^2)}{p(y|\theta, \tau^2)} = \frac{f(y|\psi)p(\psi|\theta, \tau^2)}{\int f(y|u)p(u|\theta, \tau^2)\,du}, \tag{11.3}$$

where

$$\int f(y|u)p(u|\theta, \tau^2)\,du = \iint \ldots \int f(y|u)p(u|\theta, \tau^2)\,du_1\,du_2 \ldots du_r.$$

As $\theta$ and $\tau^2$ are both known, they can both be suppressed in the notation, and equation (11.3) can be expressed in a more shortened form, as

$$p(\psi|y) \propto f(y|\psi)p(\psi), \tag{11.4}$$

that is, the posterior is proportional to the likelihood multiplied by the prior. Substituting the appropriate normal density functions into the right-hand side of (11.4) gives

$$p(\psi|y) \propto \exp\left[-\frac{1}{2}\left\{\sum_{i=1}^{r} w_i(\hat{\theta}_i - \theta_i)^2 + \frac{\sum_{i=1}^{r}(\theta_i - \theta)^2}{\tau^2}\right\}\right].$$

It can be shown that this posterior distribution is multivariate normal, with means and variances of the $\theta_i$ given by

$$E(\theta_i|y) = \frac{\hat{\theta}_i\tau^2 + \theta w_i^{-1}}{\tau^2 + w_i^{-1}} = \frac{\hat{\theta}_i w_i + \theta\tau^{-2}}{w_i + \tau^{-2}}$$

and

$$\mathrm{var}(\theta_i|y) = \frac{\tau^2 w_i^{-1}}{\tau^2 + w_i^{-1}}.$$

The prior information is worth extra data with mean $\theta$ and weight $\tau^{-2}$ in the $i$th study. The estimate of treatment difference in the $i$th study is 'shrunk' towards the value of $\theta$. If $\tau^2 = 0$, then the $\theta_i$ are all assumed to be equal to $\theta$, and if $\tau^2 = \infty$, then the studies are assumed to be unrelated, so the individual study estimates remain unchanged. For other values of $\tau^2$, the amount of shrinkage depends on $w_i$, decreasing as $w_i$ increases.

In practice one may want to consider $\theta$ and $\tau^2$ as hyperparameters, and to give them prior distributions. For example, $\theta$ and $\tau^2$ may have independent prior distributions represented by a normal distribution and inverse gamma distribution respectively, so that

$$\theta \sim N(\theta_0, \sigma_0^2), \tag{11.5}$$

and

$$\tau^2 \sim IG(\alpha, \lambda). \tag{11.6}$$

The inverse gamma distribution with parameters $\alpha$ and $\lambda$ has density of the form

$$p(x) = \frac{\lambda^\alpha}{\Gamma(\alpha)} x^{-\alpha-1} \exp\left(\frac{-\lambda}{x}\right),$$

where

$$\Gamma(\alpha) = \int_0^\infty x^{\alpha-1} \exp(-x)\,dx$$

for $\alpha > 0$.

The parameters of these prior distributions could also be given prior distributions (and this process could continue indefinitely), although this possibility will not be considered here.

The unknown parameters now consist of $\psi$, $\theta$ and $\tau^2$, and their joint posterior distribution, using Bayes' theorem, is given by

$$p(\psi, \theta, \tau^2 | y) \propto f(y|\psi)p(\psi|\theta, \tau^2)p(\theta)p(\tau^2), \tag{11.7}$$

where $p(\theta)$ and $p(\tau^2)$ are the prior distributions for $\theta$ and $\tau^2$, such as those given in (11.5) and (11.6).

Inference about each parameter may be made by integrating over the other parameters. It can be shown (Higgins, 1997) that the marginal posterior distributions of the parameters given the data are given by

$$p(\theta|y) = \int \frac{f(y|\theta, \tau^2)p(\theta)p(\tau^2)}{\int f(y|\theta, \tau^2)p(\theta)\,d\theta}\,d\tau^2, \tag{11.8}$$

$$p(\tau^2|y) = \int \frac{f(y|\theta, \tau^2)p(\theta)p(\tau^2)}{\int f(y|\theta, \tau^2)p(\tau^2)\,d\tau^2}\,d\theta, \tag{11.9}$$

$$p(\psi|y) = \iint \frac{f(y|\psi)p(\psi|\theta, \tau^2)p(\theta)p(\tau^2)}{f(y|\theta, \tau^2)}\,d\theta\,d\tau^2. \tag{11.10}$$

Unless the prior distributions are very simple, these integrals cannot be calculated in closed form. This is a general problem with the Bayesian approach which has restricted its use in practice until recently. Solutions to the problem include the use of asymptotic methods to obtain analytical approximations to the posterior density, numerical integration and simulation. In the latter category, Markov chain Monte Carlo methods such as the Gibbs sampler provide a way of approximating posterior distributions, by sampling large numbers of observations from them. As its name suggests, the software package BUGS (Bayesian inference Using Gibbs Sampling), uses the Gibbs sampling approach. For details of other approaches, see, for example, Carlin and Louis (1996).

## 11.3   CHOICE OF THE PRIOR DISTRIBUTION

It is computationally convenient to choose a distribution for the prior which is conjugate to the likelihood function, that is, one that produces a posterior distribution of the same type as the prior. In the case of a normal likelihood, the

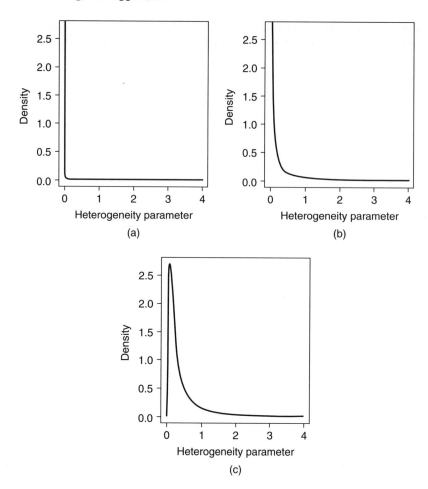

**Figure 11.1** Densities of prior distributions for $\tau^2$: (a) $IG(0.001, 0.001)$; (b) $IG(0.5, 0.005)$; (c) $IG(1.0, 0.2)$. Reproduced from Higgins and Whitehead, 1996 (Figure 1) by permission of John Wiley & Sons, Ltd.

conjugate prior for the mean is a normal distribution and for the variance an inverse gamma distribution.

A prior normal distribution with a very large variance for $\theta$ will have little influence on the eventual posterior. Similarly, an inverse gamma prior distribution with parameters close to zero for $\tau^2$ will have little effect. Thus choices such as $N(0, 10^4)$ and $IG(0.001, 0.001)$ respectively are often used. Such prior distributions are referred to as *non-informative*. The $IG(0.001, 0.001)$ distribution is shown in Figure 11.1(a). In this chapter only non-informative prior distributions are considered for $\theta$. For $\tau^2$ both non-informative and databased prior distributions are considered.

## 11.4 IMPLEMENTATION USING THE BUGS SOFTWARE

The BUGS software allows the user to specify the model via a graphical structure, in which nodes in the graph represent the data and parameters of the model. Figure 11.2 shows the graphical model for the random effects meta-analysis model of Section 11.2. There are three types of node: stochastic nodes for parameters and observed variables (such as $\theta$, $\tau^2$, $\theta_i$, $\hat{\theta}_i$), fixed value nodes for known constants and covariates (such as $w_i$), and deterministic nodes for logical functions of other nodes. In this example there are no deterministic nodes. An example of a deterministic node is given in Section 11.4.1. Directed links are drawn from *parent* nodes to *children* nodes. These links may indicate either a stochastic dependence or a logical function. In order to specify the model fully, it is only necessary to provide the parent–child distributions. The full joint probability distribution of all of the parameters and observed variables has a simple factorization in terms of the conditional distribution of each node given its parents. For our particular model the factorization is given by

$$p(\psi, \theta, \tau^2, y) = f(y|\psi)p(\psi|\theta, \tau^2)p(\theta)p(\tau^2).$$

It can be shown that this factorization leads to the posterior distributions defined by (11.7)–(11.10).

The sampling distributions required for the Gibbs sampling algorithm are set up by BUGS, following the specification of the model. The basis of the Gibbs sampler algorithm is as follows. Suppose that there are $k$ parameters in the model, denoted by $\phi_1, \ldots, \phi_k$, and that the conditional distributions $p(\phi_i|\phi_{j \neq i}, y)$, $i = 1, \ldots, k$, are available for sampling. Then given a set of starting values $(\phi_1^{(0)}, \ldots, \phi_k^{(0)})$, for the

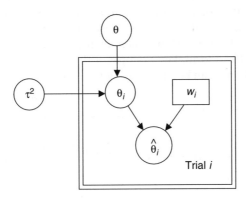

**Figure 11.2** Graphical model for random effects meta-analysis using study estimates of treatment difference.

first iteration one samples

$$\phi_1^{(1)} | y \text{ from } p(\phi_1 | \phi_2^{(0)}, \ldots, \phi_k^{(0)}, y),$$

$$\phi_2^{(1)} | y \text{ from } p(\phi_2 | \phi_1^{(1)}, \phi_3^{(0)}, \ldots, \phi_k^{(0)}, y),$$

$$\vdots$$

$$\phi_k^{(1)} | y \text{ from } p(\phi_k | \phi_1^{(1)}, \ldots, \phi_{k-1}^{(1)}, y).$$

The process continues until after $n$ iterations a sample $(\phi_1^{(n)}, \ldots, \phi_k^{(n)})$ is obtained. The iterative process follows a Markov chain, which converges to its stationary distribution, that being the joint posterior distribution of the $k$ parameters. The marginal posterior distribution for $\phi_i$ is estimated from sampled values of that parameter or can be smoothed using kernel density estimation. Usually there is an initial period, referred to as the *burn-in* period, during which the output chain converges to its stationary distribution. It is advisable to exclude sampled values collected during the burn-in period.

For every node it is therefore necessary to define the full conditional distribution given all other nodes. These are obtained by exploiting the factorization of the full joint probability distribution. The required conditional distribution of a parameter is proportional to the terms in the factorization which contain that parameter. For our example, it can be seen that

$$p(\theta | \tau^2, \psi, y) \propto p(\psi | \theta, \tau^2) p(\theta),$$

$$p(\tau^2 | \psi, \theta, y) \propto p(\psi | \theta, \tau^2) p(\tau^2)$$

and

$$p(\psi | \theta, \tau^2, y) \propto f(y | \psi) p(\psi | \theta, \tau^2).$$

More generally, the full conditional distribution of any node depends only on the values of its parents, children and co-parents, through the parent–child prior distributions and likelihood components arising from each of its children.

For many hierarchical models with conjugate priors, the sampling distributions are available in closed form. For example, if the prior distributions (11.5) and (11.6) are used, then it can be shown (Higgins, 1997) that

$$p(\theta | \tau^2, \psi, y) \sim N\left( \frac{\sigma_0^2 \sum_{i=1}^r \theta_i + \mu_0 \tau^2}{r \sigma_0^2 + \tau^2}, \frac{\sigma_0^2 \tau^2}{r \sigma_0^2 + \tau^2} \right),$$

$$p(\tau^2 | \psi, \theta, y) \sim IG\left( \alpha + \frac{r}{2}, \frac{\sum_{i=1}^r (\theta_i - \theta)^2}{2} + \lambda \right),$$

and

$$p(\psi |, \theta, \tau^2, y) \sim N\left( \frac{\tau^2 \hat{\theta}_i + w_i^{-1} \theta}{\tau^2 + w_i^{-1}}, \frac{\tau^2 w_i^{-1}}{\tau^2 + w_i^{-1}} \right).$$

There are a number of different methods for checking the convergence of the output chain, ranging from inspection of graphical output to complicated techniques based on time series analysis (see, for example, Brooks and Gelman, 1998; Gewecke, 1992). Some of these methods have been incorporated into a menu-driven set of S-Plus functions under the name CODA (Best *et al.*, 1995). CODA computes convergence diagnostics and statistical and graphical summaries for the samples produced by the Gibbs sampler, from BUGS or other programs.

For the examples in this and the following sections, the interactive Windows version of BUGS, WinBUGS, was used. WinBUGS provides a graphical interface called DoodleBUGS to assist the user in constructing the model. Model statements can be generated from the DoodleBUGS diagram or can be written directly. There are menu-driven windows for controlling the analysis and graphical tools for monitoring convergence of the simulation. All the results presented are based on 50 000 iterations following a burn-in of 10 000.

## 11.4.1   Example: Recovery time after anaesthesia

The anaesthetic study described in Section 3.6.1 and used to illustrate many of the frequentist methods is revisited to illustrate the Bayesian random effects meta-analysis. The graphical model for this analysis is shown in Figure 11.2. The following programming statements were written to perform the analysis:

```
model
{
  for (i in 1:r)
    {
     y[i] ~ dnorm(psi[i],w[i])
     psi[i] ~ dnorm(theta,t)
    }
  theta ~ dnorm(0,1.0E-4)
  t ~ dgamma(0.001,0.001)
  tausq <- 1/t
}
list(y = c(0.864, 0.646, 0.272, 0.916, 0.867, 0.819, 0.809, 1.212, -0.273),
       w = c(4.40, 9.89, 16.81, 8.38, 8.15, 10.36, 10.79, 4.40, 15.95), r = 9)

list(theta = 0, t = 1, psi = c(0,0,0,0,0,0,0,0,0))
```

The observed data consist of the centre estimates of the absolute mean difference in the log-recovery time between treatments A and B (Table 4.30). These study estimates become the elements of the vector $y$, and their calculated inverse variances, $w_i$, become the elements of the vector $w$. In the WinBUGS code, the likelihood function for the data $y$, $f(y|\psi)$, and the prior distribution for $\psi$, $p(\psi|\theta, \tau^2)$, are both specified as normal distributions. It should be noted that WinBUGS parameterizes the normal distribution in terms of precision, that is, the inverse variance as opposed to the variance itself. This introduces an additional parameter, $t$, which is the inverse of $\tau^2$. However, as interest lies in $\tau^2$, a logical

**Table 11.1**   A Bayesian random effects analysis of the anaesthetic study, based on centre estimates of absolute mean difference (treatment A − treatment B) from Table 4.30

| Parameter | Mean (median) | Standard deviation | 95% credibility interval |
|-----------|---------------|--------------------|--------------------------|
| $\theta$ | 0.600 (0.592) | 0.169 | (0.285, 0.957) |
| $\tau^2$ | 0.138 (0.093) | 0.164 | (0.002, 0.548) |
| $\theta_1$ | 0.675 (0.651) | 0.292 | (0.139, 1.313) |
| $\theta_2$ | 0.612 (0.604) | 0.229 | (0.172, 1.088) |
| $\theta_3$ | 0.408 (0.419) | 0.204 | (−0.017, 0.785) |
| $\theta_4$ | 0.726 (0.705) | 0.257 | (0.273, 1.278) |
| $\theta_5$ | 0.703 (0.684) | 0.255 | (0.243, 1.252) |
| $\theta_6$ | 0.693 (0.677) | 0.236 | (0.266, 1.196) |
| $\theta_7$ | 0.690 (0.674) | 0.233 | (0.270, 1.180) |
| $\theta_8$ | 0.779 (0.740) | 0.316 | (0.250, 1.487) |
| $\theta_9$ | 0.113 (0.118) | 0.277 | (−0.438, 0.613) |

function link is created between $t$ and $\tau^2$, to enable the posterior distribution of $\tau^2$ to be simulated. Here $\tau^2$ is a deterministic node. A non-informative $IG(0.001, 0.001)$ prior distribution is used for $t$, and a non-informative $N(0, 10^4)$ prior distribution for $\theta$. The data to be used in fitting the model are provided in the first list statement, and the initial values for the parameters for the Gibbs sampler are provided in the second list statement.

The treatment difference parameter, $\theta$, has a posterior mean of 0.600 (Table 11.1), slightly smaller than the residual (restricted) maximum likelihood estimate of 0.615 (Table 4.33). Its posterior standard deviation of 0.169 is slightly larger than the value of 0.162 obtained from the REML analysis. It will usually be the case that the posterior standard deviation is larger than the REML estimate because full allowance is being made for uncertainty in the estimation of the heterogeneity parameter, $\tau^2$, in the former but not the latter approach. The posterior distribution of $\tau^2$ is skewed, with a median of 0.093 and a 95% credibility interval from 0.002 to 0.548. Comparison of the centre estimates of treatment difference (Table 4.30) with the posterior means shows the amount of shrinkage which has taken place. All values have shrunk towards the posterior mean of $\theta$. The amount of shrinkage depends on $w_i$. Centres with a small value of $w_i$, such as centre 1, have shrunk more than those with larger values, such as centre 6. In fact, centres 1 and 6 are reversed in terms of their relative magnitudes.

## 11.5   BAYESIAN META-REGRESSION

It is relatively straightforward to introduce a trial-level covariate into the analysis. The prior distribution for $\theta_i$, given by (11.2), is now extended to give

$$\theta_i \sim N(\mu_i, \tau^2),$$

where

$$\mu_i = \beta_1 + \eta_i$$

and $\beta_1$ and $\eta_i$ are as defined in Section 6.6.

The approach is illustrated by the anaesthetic study in which the covariate is the premedication drug, as discussed in Section 6.6.2. In this case $\eta_i = \beta_2 x_{2i}$, where $x_{2i}$ takes the value 0 for centres 1–8, at which premedication 1 is used, and 1 for centre 9 at which premedication 2 is used. Figure 11.3 shows the graphical model for the analysis. This is similar to Figure 11.2, with the exception that the node $\theta$ is replaced by the node $\mu_i$, which is dependent on the two parameters $\beta_1$ and $\beta_2$. Non-informative prior distributions of $N(0, 10^4)$ are given to $\beta_1$ and $\beta_2$. The covariate $x_{2i}$ enters as a fixed value node. The programming statements are as follows:

```
model
{
   for (i in 1: r)
   {
     y[i] ~ dnorm(psi[i],w[i])
     psi[i] ~ dnorm(mu[i],t)
     mu[i] <- beta1 + beta2 * x2[i]
   }
   beta1 ~ dnorm(0.0,1.0E-4)
   beta2 ~ dnorm(0.0,1.0E-4)
   t ~ dgamma(0.001,0.001)
   tausq <- 1/t
   premed2 <- beta1 + beta2
}

list(y = c(0.864, 0.646, 0.272, 0.916, 0.867, 0.819, 0.809, 1.212, -0.273),
     w = c(4.40, 9.89, 16.81, 8.38, 8.15, 10.36, 10.79, 4.40, 15.95),
     x2 = c(0,0,0,0,0,0,0,0,1), r = 9)

list(beta1 = 0, beta2 = 0, t = 1, psi = c(0,0,0,0,0,0,0,0,0))
```

A logical function link has been created between 'premed2' and the parameters 'beta1' and 'beta2' to enable the distribution of the treatment difference for the second premedication to be simulated. The treatment difference for the first medication is given by 'beta1'.

The posterior distribution for the treatment difference has a mean of 0.725 when premedication 1 is used and $-0.274$ when premedication 2 is used (Table 11.2). These are similar to the values of 0.711 and $-0.273$ from Table 6.5. The posterior standard deviations of 0.134 and 0.310 are larger than those of 0.117 and 0.250 given in Table 6.5. This is because $\tau^2$ is given the value 0 in Table 6.5, whereas in the Bayesian analysis $\tau^2$ takes a small positive value and allowance is made for the uncertainty in its estimation. Posterior means for the treatment difference at each centre are different from those in Table 11.1. In Table 11.2 those for centres 1–8 are now closer together, whereas centre 9 has not been shrunk at all.

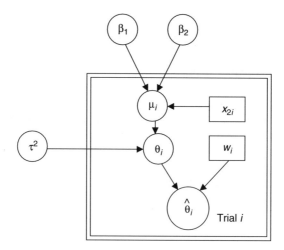

**Figure 11.3**  Graphical model for meta-regression using study estimates of treatment difference.

**Table 11.2**  A Bayesian random effects analysis of the anaesthetic study, based on centre estimates of absolute mean difference (treatment A − treatment B) from Table 4.30, with type of premedication as a centre covariate

| Parameter | Mean (median) | Standard deviation | 95% credibility interval |
|---|---|---|---|
| Premedication 1 ($\beta_1$) | 0.725  (0.721) | 0.134 | (0.469, 0.993) |
| Premedication 2 ($\beta_1 + \beta_2$) | −0.274 (−0.272) | 0.310 | (−0.878, 0.330) |
| $\tau^2$ | 0.032  (0.011) | 0.061 | (0.001, 0.185) |
| $\theta_1$ | 0.737  (0.729) | 0.190 | (0.382, 1.151) |
| $\theta_2$ | 0.709  (0.708) | 0.167 | (0.374, 1.041) |
| $\theta_3$ | 0.615  (0.631) | 0.177 | (0.211, 0.921) |
| $\theta_4$ | 0.752  (0.741) | 0.179 | (0.429, 1.146) |
| $\theta_5$ | 0.743  (0.734) | 0.177 | (0.412, 1.122) |
| $\theta_6$ | 0.737  (0.731) | 0.169 | (0.416, 1.089) |
| $\theta_7$ | 0.736  (0.729) | 0.167 | (0.422, 1.091) |
| $\theta_8$ | 0.770  (0.751) | 0.200 | (0.424, 1.234) |
| $\theta_9$ | −0.273 (−0.272) | 0.253 | (−0.771, 0.216) |

## 11.6  A BAYESIAN RANDOM EFFECTS MODEL BASED ON INDIVIDUAL PATIENT DATA

When individual patient data are available the Bayesian hierarchical model can be based on the models described in Chapter 5, which take account of the underlying distribution of the patient's response. This involves replacing the distribution presented in (11.1) by the appropriate distribution specific to the type of data. This section presents the approach for three different data types. The extension of the models to include covariates is discussed, as is the inclusion of the study effects as a random sample from an overall population.

## 11.6.1   Normally distributed data

Let $y_{ij}$ be the normally distributed response from patient $j$ in study $i$. The random effects model of Section 5.8.1 can be presented in the Bayesian framework in the following way:

$$y_{ij} \sim N(\mu_{ij}, \sigma^2), \tag{11.11}$$

where

$$\mu_{ij} = \beta_{0i} + \gamma_{1i} x_{1ij},$$

and

$$\gamma_{1i} \sim N(\beta_1, \tau^2). \tag{11.12}$$

In this subsection, the intercept term $\alpha$ in model (5.24) is set to zero so that $\beta_{0i}$ now represents the effect in the control group in study $i$. The treatment difference parameter is $\beta_1$, and $\gamma_{1i}$ represents the treatment difference in study $i$. The distributions (11.11) and (11.12) now replace (11.1) and (11.2). Compared with the model of Section 11.2, there are additional parameters, namely the within-study variance component, $\sigma^2$, and the study effects, $\beta_{0i}$. These can be given non-informative inverse gamma and independent normal prior distributions, respectively.

The graphical model is presented in Figure 11.4. The following programming statements were used in connection with the anaesthetic study:

```
model
{
  for (i in 1:r)
   {
    for(j in n[i]+1:n[i+1])
     {
        y[j] ~ dnorm(mu[j],s)
        mu[j] <- beta0[i] + gamma1[i] * x1[j]
     }
     gamma1[i] ~ dnorm(beta1,t)
     beta0[i] ~ dnorm(0,1.0E-4)
   }
   beta1 ~ dnorm(0,1.0E-4)
   s ~ dgamma(0.001,0.001)
   t ~ dgamma(0.001,0.001)
   sigmasq <- 1/s
```

```
 tausq <- 1/t
}
list(r = 9, n = c(0,9,29,63,80,97,118,140,149,182))
x1[] y[]
 0.5 1.79176
 0.5 0.69315
 . . .

list(beta1= 0, s = 1, t = 1, beta0 = c(0,0,0,0,0,0,0,0,0), gamma1 =
c(0,0,0,0,0,0,0,0,0) )
```

The data are provided in the first list statement. The individual patient data on the treatment covariate and observed response are entered as a rectangular array. Note that for this example the treatment covariate is coded '0.5' for treatment A and '−0.5' for treatment B, as this data file will also be used for fitting the model in which the centre effects are randomly distributed with a common mean (see Section 5.11). The data are sorted by centre and the vector $n$ contains the row numbers of the last patient in each centre. The second list file contains the initial values for the Gibbs sampler.

The results of the analysis are presented in Table 11.3. There is very close agreement between the estimates in this table and those in Table 11.1 (note that $\beta_1$ should be compared with $\theta$ and $\gamma_{1i}$ with $\theta_i$). This is to be expected as the individual patient data are treated as being normally distributed. The standard

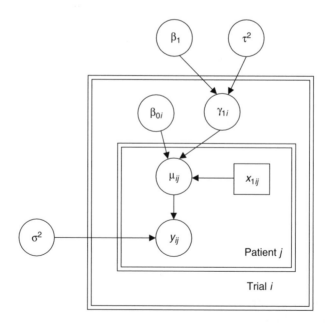

**Figure 11.4**  Graphical model for a random effects meta-analysis using normally distributed individual patient data.

**Table 11.3**   A Bayesian random effects analysis of the anaesthetic study, based on individual patient data and assuming a common $\sigma^2$ across all centres

| Parameter | Mean (median) | Standard deviation | 95% credibility interval |
|---|---|---|---|
| $\beta_1$ | 0.600 (0.593) | 0.171 | (0.283, 0.957) |
| $\sigma^2$ | 0.515 (0.510) | 0.058 | (0.414, 0.639) |
| $\tau^2$ | 0.139 (0.092) | 0.168 | (0.002, 0.553) |
| $\gamma_1$ | 0.671 (0.648) | 0.291 | (0.137, 1.306) |
| $\gamma_2$ | 0.612 (0.605) | 0.232 | (0.169, 1.086) |
| $\gamma_3$ | 0.411 (0.421) | 0.207 | (−0.020, 0.788) |
| $\gamma_4$ | 0.725 (0.705) | 0.257 | (0.269, 1.277) |
| $\gamma_5$ | 0.704 (0.685) | 0.256 | (0.242, 1.253) |
| $\gamma_6$ | 0.693 (0.676) | 0.237 | (0.265, 1.197) |
| $\gamma_7$ | 0.690 (0.676) | 0.235 | (0.257, 1.180) |
| $\gamma_8$ | 0.778 (0.740) | 0.315 | (0.243, 1.488) |
| $\gamma_9$ | 0.115 (0.118) | 0.281 | (−0.445, 0.625) |

deviations in Table 11.3 are slightly larger than those in Table 11.1, due to the estimation of $\sigma^2$.

There is a connection between the Bayesian approach and the REML approach described in Section 5.8.2. Suppose that within the Bayesian context the variance components (in this case $\tau^2$ and $\sigma^2$) are assumed fixed and unknown and that the 'fixed effects parameters' (in this case $\beta_{0i}$, $i = 1, \ldots, r$, and $\beta_1$) are given independent uniform prior distributions. Integrating over all parameters in the joint posterior distribution which are not variance components (in this case $\beta_{0i}$, $\gamma_{1i}$, $i = 1, \ldots, r$, and $\beta_1$), leads to a posterior distribution for the variance components which is the same as the REML likelihood. Details may be found in Searle *et al.* (1992).

## 11.6.2   Binary data

If $y_{ij}$ is a binary observation, it takes the value 1 if the patient response is a success and 0 if the response is a failure. The distribution in (11.11) is therefore replaced by

$$y_{ij} \sim Bin(p_{ij}, n_{ij}), \tag{11.13}$$

where

$$\log\left(\frac{p_{ij}}{1 - p_{ij}}\right) = \beta_{0i} + \gamma_{1i}x_{1ij}.$$

In order to run the model in WinBUGS, the code in the fourth and fifth lines of the program in Section 11.6.1 need to be replaced as follows:

```
y[j] ~ dbin(p[j], ni[j]);
logit(p[j]) <- beta0[i] + gamma1[i] * x1[j];
```

If each subject's data are entered individually then $n_{ij} = 1$. However, the program will run more efficiently if the data are entered in binomial form – one line for each treatment group in each study, with $y_{ij}$ equal to the total number of successes and $n_{ij}$ the total number of patients in that treatment group and study.

Table 11.4 shows the results from the Bayesian analysis of the pre-eclampsia data set described in Section 5.9.3. The parameter of interest is the log-odds ratio of pre-eclampsia on diuretic treatment versus control during pregnancy. Also given are the results from a Bayesian analysis based on the study estimates of the log-odds ratio from Table 5.16 using the approach in Section 11.2. Estimates of the log-odds ratio are similar in both cases, although the standard deviation based on the binary model is slightly larger. Estimates of $\tau^2$ are not so close. In comparison with the random effects models fitted in Chapter 5 (Table 5.17), estimates of the log-odds ratio from the Bayesian approaches are similar, but have larger standard errors.

## 11.6.3   Ordinal data

For an ordinal response with $m$ categories the observation $y_{ij}$ takes the value $k$ if subject $j$ in study $i$ has a response in category $k$, $k = 1, \ldots, m$. The parameter $p_{ijk}$ is the probability that patient has a response in the $k$th category, and $Q_{ijk}$ is the cumulative probability of a response in category $k$ or better, that is, $Q_{ijk} = p_{ij1} + \cdots + p_{ijk}$ and $Q_{ijm} = 1$. For a Bayesian analysis comparable with the stratified proportional odds model defined in (5.28), the following relationship holds:

$$\log\left(\frac{Q_{ijk}}{1 - Q_{ijk}}\right) = \alpha_{ik} + \gamma_{1i}x_{1ij}, \qquad k = 1, \ldots, m - 1.$$

The following WinBUGS code can be used to perform the analysis of the tacrine data set described in Section 3.5.1:

**Table 11.4**   A Bayesian random effects analysis of the pre-eclampsia data set: comparison between one based on individual patient data and the other based on study estimates from Table 5.16

| Parameter | | Individual patient data | Study estimates |
|---|---|---|---|
| $\beta_1\ (\theta)$ | Mean | −0.510 | −0.506 |
| | Median | −0.507 | −0.500 |
| | Standard deviation | 0.258 | 0.242 |
| | 95% credibility interval | (−1.035, 0.009) | (−1.000, −0.022) |
| $\tau^2$ | Mean | 0.447 | 0.381 |
| | Median | 0.317 | 0.265 |
| | Standard deviation | 0.476 | 0.416 |
| | 95% credibility interval | (0.030, 1.643) | (0.0013, 1.443) |

```
model
{
 for (i in 1:r)
  {
   for(j in n[i]+1:n[i+1])
    {
       y[j] ~ dcat(p[j, ])
       p[j,1] <- Q[j,1]
       for (k in 2:mminus1)
        {
          p[j,k] <- Q[j,k] - Q[j,k-1]
        }
        p[j,mminus1+1]<- 1 - Q[j,mminus1]
        for (k in 1:mminus1)
        {
        logit(Q[j,k]) <- a[i,k] + gamma1[i]*x1[j]
        }
    }
   gamma1[i] ~ dnorm(beta1, t)
   a[i,1] ~ dnorm(0,1.0E-4)I ( , a[i,2])
   a[i,2] ~ dnorm(0,1.0E-4)I(a[i,1], a[i,3])
   a[i,3] ~ dnorm(0,1.0E-4)I(a[i,2], a[i,4])
   a[i,4] ~ dnorm(0,1.0E-4)I(a[i,3], )
  }
 beta1 ~ dnorm(0,1.0E-4)
 t ~ dgamma(0.001,0.001)
 tausq <- 1/t
}

list(r = 5, mminus1 = 4, n = c(0,206,651,772,852,1403))
x1[] y[]
0 3
1 3
. . .

list(beta1 = 0, t = 1, gamma1 = c(0,0,0,0,0), a = structure(.Data =
c(0,1,2,3,0,1,2,3,0,1,2,3,0,1,2,3,0,1,2,3), .Dim = c(5,4)))
```

The intercept terms $\alpha_{ik}$ are constrained to be ordered within each study and given non-informative $N(0, 10^4)$ prior distributions. In the program above, the data are entered as one line per subject. However, the program will run more efficiently if the data are entered in multinomial form, with one line for each treatment group in each study. The data required in each line are the number of responses in each category and the total number of subjects. The fourth line of the code should be replaced by

```
y[j, 1:mminus1+1] ~ dmulti(p[j,], ni[j])
```

and the data set by

```
list(r = 5, mminus1 = 4, n = c(0,2,4,6,8,10))
x1[] y[ ,1] y[ , 2] y[ ,3] y[ ,4] y[ ,5] ni[]
```

```
1  4  23  45  22  2  96
0  2  22  54  29  3  110
. . .
```

The results from the Bayesian analysis of the Tacrine data set using individual patient data are presented in Table 11.5, together with those based on the study estimates of the log-odds ratio from Table 4.16. The results are very similar. In comparison with the random effects models fitted in Chapters 4 and 5 (Tables 4.32 and 5.18), the estimates of the log-odds ratio from the Bayesian approach are similar, but have larger standard errors.

### 11.6.4   Study-level and patient-level covariates

The inclusion of covariates in the meta-analysis models based on individual patient data was discussed in Section 6.7. These same models can be used within a Bayesian approach. In the Bayesian approach it is necessary to provide prior distributions for all of the parameters associated with these covariate terms.

### 11.6.5   Random study effects

In this subsection, the anaesthetic study is used to illustrate the Bayesian approach to fitting the model which contains random study and random study by treatment effects. Within the Bayesian framework, model (5.31) becomes

$$y_{ij} \sim N(\mu_{ij}, \sigma^2),$$

where

$$\mu_{ij} = \gamma_{0i} + \gamma_{1i}x_{1ij}$$

**Table 11.5**  A Bayesian random effects analysis of the tacrine studies: comparison between one based on individual patient data and the other based on study estimates from Table 4.29

| Parameter | | Individual patient data | Study estimates |
|---|---|---|---|
| $\beta_1$ ($\theta$) | Mean | 0.479 | 0.473 |
| | Median | 0.484 | 0.478 |
| | Standard deviation | 0.165 | 0.164 |
| | 95% credibility interval | (0.141, 0.782) | (0.137, 0.779) |
| $\tau^2$ | Mean | 0.063 | 0.066 |
| | Median | 0.020 | 0.021 |
| | Standard deviation | 0.171 | 0.200 |
| | 95% credibility interval | (0.0008, 0.369) | (0.0008, 0.392) |

and

$$\begin{pmatrix} \gamma_{0i} \\ \gamma_{1i} \end{pmatrix} \sim N\left( \begin{pmatrix} \beta_0 \\ \beta_1 \end{pmatrix}, \begin{pmatrix} \zeta^2 & \rho\zeta\tau \\ \rho\zeta\tau & \tau^2 \end{pmatrix} \right). \tag{11.14}$$

In contrast to the model described in Section 11.6.1, the prior distribution (11.14) specifies that the study effects are no longer independent of one another. Additionally, the study effects are no longer independent of the treatment difference effects. The parameters $\beta_0$ and $\beta_1$ are given non-informative normal prior distributions, and the variance matrix

$$\begin{pmatrix} \zeta^2 & \rho\zeta\tau \\ \rho\zeta\tau & \tau^2 \end{pmatrix}$$

is given a non-informative *Wishart*($R$, 2) distribution. The degrees for the Wishart distribution have been set to 2, the rank of the variance matrix. Values assigned to the scale matrix $R$ are an assessment of the order of magnitude of the variance matrix.

The following WinBUGS code can be used to fit this model to the anaesthetic study:

```
model
{
  for (i in 1:r)
   {
    for(j in n[i] +1:n[i+1])
      {
         y[j] ~ dnorm(mu[j],s);
         mu[j] <- delta[i, 1] + delta[i, 2] * x1[j]
      }
    delta[i, 1:2] ~ dmnorm(b[], t[,])
    gamma0[i] <- delta[i,1]
    gamma1[i] <- delta[i,2]
   }
  b[1] ~ dnorm(0,1.0E-4)
  b[2] ~ dnorm(0,1.0E-4)
  s ~ dgamma(0.001,0.001)
  t[1:2, 1:2] ~ dwish(R[,], 2)
  R[1,1] <- 1.0
  R[1,2] <- 0.0
  R[2,1] <- 0.0
  R[2,2] <- 0.1
  beta0 <- b[1]
  beta1 <- b[2]
  sigmasq <- 1/s
  for (i in 1:2)
    {
     for (j in 1:2)
       {
        omega[i, j] <- inverse(t[, ], i,j)
       }
    }
```

```
zetasq <- omega[1,1]
tausq <-  omega[2,2]
covar <-  omega[1,2]
rho <- omega[1,2]/(sqrt(omega[1,1])*sqrt(omega[2,2]))
  }
```

```
list( s = 1, b=c(0,0), t = structure(.Data = c(1,0,0,1), .Dim =
c(2,2)), delta = structure(.Data =
c(0,0,0,0,0,0,0,0,0,0,0,0,0,0,0,0,0,0), .Dim = c(9,2)) )
```

The data set described in Section 11.6.1 can be used with this program.

For the model in which $\rho = 0$, the multivariate normal distribution described by (11.14) is replaced by

$$\gamma_{0i} \sim N(\beta_0, \zeta^2)$$

and

$$\gamma_{1i} \sim N(\beta_1, \tau^2), \tag{11.15}$$

and the programming statements are changed as follows:

```
  mu[j] <- gamma0[i] + gamma1[i] * x1[j]
  }
gamma0[i] ~ dnorm(beta0, t0)
gamma1[i] ~ dnorm(beta1, t)
  }
beta0 ~ dnorm(0,1.0E-4);
beta1 ~ dnorm(0,1.0E-4);
s ~ dgamma(0.001, 0.001);
t0 ~ dgamma(0.001, 0.001);
```

**Table 11.6**  A Bayesian model equivalent to the mixed model (5.31) for the anaesthetic study, based on individual patient data and assuming a common $\sigma^2$ across all centres, with $\rho$ set equal to 0 and $\rho$ estimated

| Parameter | Mean (median) | | Standard deviation | 95% credibility interval |
|---|---|---|---|---|
| $\rho = 0$ | | | | |
| $\beta_1$ | 0.611 | (0.603) | 0.174 | (0.288, 0.978) |
| $\sigma^2$ | 0.515 | (0.511) | 0.058 | (0.414, 0.639) |
| $\zeta^2$ | 0.386 | (0.309) | 0.307 | (0.109, 1.114) |
| $\tau^2$ | 0.148 | (0.100) | 0.174 | (0.002, 0.586) |
| $\rho$ included as a parameter | | | | |
| $\beta_1$ | 0.609 | (0.605) | 0.168 | (0.288, 0.953) |
| $\sigma^2$ | 0.513 | (0.509) | 0.057 | (0.413, 0.636) |
| $\zeta^2$ | 0.483 | (0.402) | 0.321 | (0.166, 1.279) |
| $\rho\zeta\tau$ | −0.077 | (−0.058) | 0.134 | (−0.389, 0.128) |
| $\tau^2$ | 0.136 | (0.101) | 0.127 | (0.022, 0.461) |

```
t ~ dgamma(0.001, 0.001)
sigmasq <- 1/s
zetasq <- 1/t0
tausq <- 1/t
}
```

```
list( s = 1, t0 = 1, t = 1, beta0 = 0, beta1 = 0, gamma0 =
c(0,0,0,0,0,0,0,0,0), gamma1 = c(0,0,0,0,0,0,0,0,0))
```

The results of the Bayesian analyses, the first of which assumes that $\rho = 0$ and the second of which estimates $\rho$, are presented in Table 11.6. Estimates of the treatment difference are similar, and both slightly smaller than those calculated from the frequentist analysis (Table 5.19). The standard errors in Table 11.6 are slightly larger than those in Table 5.19.

## 11.7 INCORPORATING DATA FROM OTHER TREATMENT COMPARISONS

The Pagliaro *et al.* (1992) data set described in Section 10.2.4 is used here for illustrative purposes. This data set consists of 26 studies, 7 of which involve a comparison between beta-blockers and control treatment, 17 a comparison between sclerotherapy and control, and 2 a comparison between all three treatments. In Section 10.2.4, data from all studies were combined in a meta-analysis in order to improve the inference concerning the treatment difference parameters. In this section, a Bayesian approach to the problem is presented. This is based on the work by Higgins and Whitehead (1996) which focuses on the inference about the difference in effect between beta-blockers and sclerotherapy.

The 26 trials fall into three groups. Group 1 contains trials 1 and 2, which compare all three treatment groups, group 2 contains trials 3–9, which compare beta-blockers with control, and group 3 contains trials 10–26, which compare sclerotherapy with control. Assuming a common heterogeneity parameter for the three pairwise treatment comparisons, the random effects model from Section 11.6.2 can be extended to accommodate the three groups of trials as follows. As in Section 10.2.4, $x_{11ij}$ takes the value 1 for the beta-blocker treatment and 0 otherwise, and $x_{12ij}$ takes the value 1 for the sclerotherapy treatment and 0 otherwise. For group 1,

$$\log\left(\frac{p_{ij}}{1 - p_{ij}}\right) = \beta_{0i} + \gamma_{11i}x_{11ij} + \gamma_{12i}x_{12ij},$$

where

$$\begin{pmatrix} \gamma_{11i} \\ \gamma_{12i} \end{pmatrix} = N\left(\begin{pmatrix} \beta_{11} \\ \beta_{12} \end{pmatrix}, \begin{pmatrix} \tau^2 & \tau^2/2 \\ \tau^2/2 & \tau^2 \end{pmatrix}\right).$$

For group 2,

$$\log\left(\frac{p_{ij}}{1-p_{ij}}\right) = \beta_{0i} + \gamma_{11i}x_{11ij},$$

where

$$\gamma_{11i} \sim N(\beta_{11}, \tau^2).$$

For group 3,

$$\log\left(\frac{p_{ij}}{1-p_{ij}}\right) = \beta_{0i} + \gamma_{12i}x_{12ij},$$

where

$$\gamma_{12i} \sim N(\beta_{12}, \tau^2).$$

The study effects, $\beta_{0i}$, and the treatment difference parameters, $\beta_{11}$ and $\beta_{12}$, are given non-informative normal prior distributions, and the variance component, $\tau^2$, a non-informative inverse gamma distribution.

The following WinBUGS code can be used to perform the analysis:

```
model
{
 for (i in set[1] +1: set[2]) {
    for(j in n[i] + 1: n[i+1]) {
       y[j] ~ dbin(p[j], ni[j])
       logit(p[j]) <- b0abc[i] + g[i,1] * x11[j] + g[i,2] * x12[j]
 }
 g[i, 1] ~ dnorm(beta1ac, ts)
 mubc[i] <- beta1bc + 0.5*(g[i,1] - beta1ac)
 g[i, 2] ~ dnorm(mubc[i], precbc)
 gam1ab[i] <- g[i,1] - g[i,2]
 b0abc[i] ~ dnorm(0,1.0E-4)
 }
 varbc <- 0.75/ts
 precbc <- 1/varbc

  for (i in set[2] +1: set[3]) {
     for(j in n[i] + 1: n[i+1]) {
        y[j] ~ dbin(p[j], ni[j])
        logit(p[j]) <- b0ac[i-set[2]] + gam1ac[i-set[2]] * x11[j]
 }
 gam1ac[i -set[2]] ~ dnorm(beta1ac, ts)
 b0ac[i-set[2]] ~ dnorm(0,1.0E-4)
 }

 for (i in set[3]+1: set[4]) {
     for(j in n[i] + 1: n[i+1]) {
        y[j] ~ dbin(p[j], ni[j])
        logit(p[j]) <- b0bc[i-set[3]] + gam1bc[i -set[3]] * x12[j]
 }
 gam1bc[i - set[3]] ~ dnorm(beta1bc, ts)
 b0bc[i-set[3]] ~ dnorm(0,1.0E-4)
 }
```

```
beta1ac ~ dnorm(0,1.0E-4)
beta1bc ~ dnorm(0,1.0E-4)
beta1ab <- beta1ac - beta1bc
ts ~dgamma(0.001,0.001)
tausq <- 1/ts

}
list( ts = 1, beta1ac= 0, beta1bc = 0, b0abc = c(0,0), b0ac =
c(0,0,0,0,0,0,0), b0bc= c(0,0,0,0,0,0,0,0,0,0,0,0,0,0,0,0,0,0),
g = structure(.Data = c(0,0,0,0), .Dim = c(2,2)), gam1bc=
c(0,0,0,0,0,0,0,0,0,0,0,0,0,0,0,0,0,0), gam1ac = c(0,0,0,0,0,0,0))

list(set = c(0,2,9,26), n =
c(0,3,6,8,10,12,14,16,18,20,22,24,26,28,30,32,34,36,38,40,42,44,46,48
,50,52,54))
x11[] x12[] y[] ni[]
1 0 2 43
0 1 9 42
0 0 13 41
. . .
```

The bivariate normal distribution for $\gamma_{11i}$ and $\gamma_{12i}$ is specified as two independent univariate normal distributions, one for $\gamma_{11i}$ given by

$$\gamma_{11i} \sim N(\beta_{11}, \tau^2),$$

and one for $\gamma_{12i}$ conditional on $\gamma_{11i}$ given by

$$\gamma_{12i}|\gamma_{11i} \sim N(\beta_{12} + 0.5(\gamma_{11i} - \beta_{11}), 0.75\tau^2).$$

The results of the analysis (Table 11.7) are similar to those from the frequentist analysis (second row of Table 10.2).

**Table 11.7**   A Bayesian random effects meta-analyses of the Pagliaro *et al.* data set, based on data from all 26 studies, using a non-informative prior distribution of $IG(0.001, 0.001)$ and an empirical prior distribution of $IG(1.0, 0.35)$ for the heterogeneity parameter $\tau^2$

| Parameter | Mean (median) | Standard deviation | 95% credibility interval |
|---|---|---|---|
| Non-informative prior distribution | | | |
| log-odds ratio (A−B) | −0.185 (−0.183) | 0.515 | (−1.214, 0.836) |
| log-odds ratio (A−C) | −0.784 (−0.782) | 0.442 | (−1.664, 0.082) |
| log-odds ratio (B−C) | −0.599 (−0.599) | 0.312 | (−1.213, 0.018) |
| $\tau^2$ | 1.46   (1.33) | 0.64 | (0.60, 3.03) |
| Empirical prior distribution | | | |
| log-odds ratio (A−B) | −0.176 (−0.175) | 0.489 | (−1.147, 0.784) |
| log-odds ratio (A−C) | −0.775 (−0.772) | 0.419 | (−1.612, 0.051) |
| log-odds ratio (B−C) | −0.599 (−0.600) | 0.297 | (−1.183, −0.011) |
| $\tau^2$ | 1.29   (1.19) | 0.55 | (0.54, 2.64) |

## 11.8    AN EMPIRICAL PRIOR DISTRIBUTION FOR THE HETEROGENEITY PARAMETER

The heterogeneity parameter is typically included in the meta-analysis model to allow for unexplained variation in the treatment difference between trials. However, when there are only a small number of trials in the meta-analysis, the estimate of heterogeneity calculated from them will be imprecise. In this case, trials of treatments for similar interventions might provide useful information on the likely amount of variation to expect in the current meta-analysis. Such information can then be used to create a prior distribution for $\tau^2$.

Smith (1995) formed a prior distribution from method of moments estimates of $\tau^2$, obtained from 30 meta-analyses in a variety of indications. Calculation of the empirical cumulative distribution function and use of kernel density estimation led to the choice of an $IG(0.5, 0.005)$ distribution (Figure 11.1(b)). When applied to a meta-analysis of 22 randomized trials, she found little difference in the results based on this prior distribution and the non-informative prior distribution. However, it is likely that the information contained in the 22 trials overwhelmed that contained in the prior distribution. When there are only a small number of trials to be included in the meta-analysis this will not be the case.

Higgins and Whitehead (1996) considered an approach based on combining the data from previous meta-analyses, conducted on therapies used in similar indications to that in the current meta-analysis, in one large Bayesian meta-analysis of meta-analyses. In this approach, the treatment difference parameter in the $i$th study of the $j$th meta-analysis was denoted by $\theta_{ij}$, where $i = 1, \ldots, r_j$ and $j = 1, \ldots, m$, and prior distributions were specified as follows:

$$\theta_{ij} \sim N(\theta_j, \tau_j^2)$$

$$\theta_j \sim N(0, 10^3),$$

$$\tau_j^2 \sim IG(\alpha, \lambda),$$

$$\alpha \sim Gamma(0.001, 0.001),$$

$$\lambda \sim Gamma(0.001, 0.001).$$

The predictive distribution of a 'new' heterogeneity parameter, $\tau_{new}^2$, provides a prior distribution for $\tau^2$ in the current meta-analysis. This predictive distribution may be specified as follows:

$$\tau_{new}^2 \sim IG(\alpha, \lambda).$$

As it will be necessary to approximate this predictive distribution by a parametric distribution, an alternative simpler approach is to use, say, the median values of $\alpha$ and $\lambda$ from their posterior distributions. The prior distribution for $\tau^2$ would then be given by $IG(\hat{\alpha}, \hat{\lambda})$. However, in cases in which the credibility intervals for $\alpha$ and $\lambda$ are wide, this approach is not recommended.

Higgins and Whitehead illustrated the approach using the Pagliaro *et al.* data set described in Section 10.2.4. Their main focus was on the comparison between beta-blockers and sclerotherapy. If the only data available are the results from the beta-blocker and sclerotherapy treatments in the first two studies, then there is very little information about $\tau^2$. To overcome this problem, Higgins and Whitehead undertook a literature search of trials in gastroenterology. This produced 18 sets of very similar types of study, all investigating the occurrence or reoccurrence of gastrointestinal bleeding following treatment. A prior distribution could be formulated for $\tau^2$ based on these 18 meta-analyses.

First, they calculated the method of moments estimates of $\tau^2$ from each of the 18 meta-analysis data sets. The closest-fitting inverse gamma distribution to the empirical cumulative distribution function of these estimates was found to be one with parameters $\alpha = 1.0$ and $\lambda = 0.2$ (Figure 11.1(c)). As its parameters are larger than those used by Smith, it is a more influential prior distribution.

Second, they calculated a prior distribution for $\tau^2$ by performing a Bayesian meta-analysis of meta-analyses. The predictive distribution for $\tau^2$ was found to have a posterior median of 0.42 and a 95% credibility interval (0.05, 7.1). The kernel density estimate of this distribution is illustrated in Figure 11.5(a). A close-fitting inverse gamma distribution was found to have parameters $\alpha = 1.0$ and $\lambda = 0.35$ (Figure 11.5(b)), which agreed reasonably with those obtained by the simpler first method. A repeat of the exercise, with the $\tau_j^2$ assumed to be equal across all studies, led to a very narrow predictive distribution for $\tau^2$ (Figure 11.5(c)). Indeed, half of the individual method of moments estimates lie outside the 95% credibility interval. The random effects model for the $\tau_j^2$ was therefore felt to be more appropriate than the fixed effects model.

To see the effect of using an empirical prior distribution for $\tau^2$, two analyses were performed based on the data from the sclerotherapy and beta-blocker treatment groups from the first two studies. Using the approach of Section 11.6.2, the first was an attempt to fit a Bayesian random effects model, in which an $IG(0.001, 0.001)$ distribution was used as the prior distribution for $\tau^2$. This did not give a satisfactory convergent chain, even after many iterations, mainly because of the lack of information regarding the heterogeneity parameter. The analysis was repeated using an $IG(1.0, 0.35)$ prior distribution for $\tau^2$, and in this case convergence diagnostic tests were passed. The posterior mean (95% credibility interval) for the log-odds ratio of bleeding on beta-blockers relative to sclerotherapy was $-0.74$ ($-2.61, 0.95$). The posterior mean (95% credibility interval) of the log-odds ratio from trials 1 and 2 was $-1.28$ ($-2.85, -0.05$) and $-0.21$ ($-1.08, 0.65$), respectively.

With regard to the analysis of the complete data set from the 26 trials, the effect of using an $IG(1.0, 0.35)$ prior distribution for $\tau^2$ was less dramatic (Table 11.7). This was to be expected as the data set itself provides a lot of information about $\tau^2$. The effect has been to tighten the posterior distributions for all parameters,

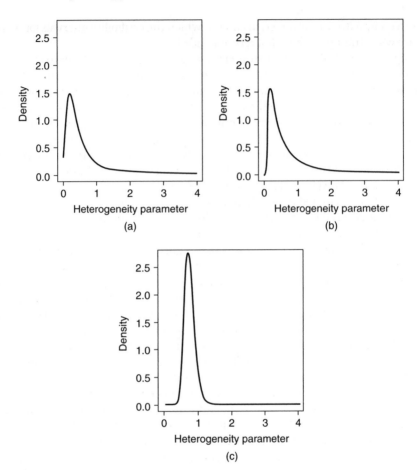

**Figure 11.5**   Kernel density estimates of posterior distributions following meta-analysis of 18 meta-analysis data sets: (a) assuming random effects for heterogeneity parameters, 15 000 iterations of the Gibbs sampler following a burn-in of 1000; (b) a parametric approximation to (a), $IG(1.0, 0.35)$; (c) assuming equal heterogeneity parameter in all meta-analyses, 15 000 iterations following a burn-in of 1000. Reproduced from Higgins and Whitehead, 1996 (Figure 2) by permission of John Wiley & Sons, Ltd.

resulting in a 95% credibility interval for the comparison of sclerotherapy with control which excludes zero.

In principle it should be possible to incorporate the information about $\tau^2$ from previous meta-analyses within a frequentist meta-analysis. However, the lack of a prescribed procedure and suitable software makes implementation difficult. As the models become more complicated, the Bayesian approach offers advantages.

# 12

# Sequential Methods for Meta-Analysis

## 12.1  INTRODUCTION

Sometimes meta-analyses are repeated following completion of further studies addressing the same question. Indeed, this is encouraged within the Cochrane Collaboration, to enable the information in the Cochrane Database of Systematic Reviews to be kept up to date. The term 'cumulative meta-analysis' has been used to define the technique of conducting a new meta-analysis every time the results of a new trial become available. In this chapter the term will be used more generally to include an updating based on additional data, whether it be from one or more ongoing or completed studies. A 'cumulative meta-analysis' may also be performed retrospectively in order to determine the date at which sufficient evidence was available to demonstrate a beneficial treatment effect. Even though the latter process is retrospective, the same statistical issues arise as for the prospective updating of a meta-analysis.

Typically, each meta-analysis in the course of this cumulative procedure is conducted without any of the allowances for the issues of multiple testing and biased estimation which have become an accepted part of the conduct of interim analyses for an individual clinical trial. Chalmers and Lau (1993) question the need to correct for multiple looks within a cumulative meta-analysis. One of the reasons which they give is that the decision to stop is not being made by the meta-analyst. However, the absence of a formal stopping rule does not remove the multiple-looks problem. When there is no difference between two treatments, a cumulative meta-analysis which continues to add studies will eventually show a statistically significant treatment difference. Repeated significance tests, each of which have a fixed significance level of 5%, will approach a cumulative level of 100% as the number of trials gets very large. This point was also appreciated by Pogue and Yusuf (1997), who proposed the use of sequential monitoring procedures which allow for repeated analyses.

Cumulative meta-analyses are usually conducted in a reactive way, in that the meta-analyst has no influence on the decision to undertake new studies. However, in some situations it may be possible to conduct a cumulative meta-analysis in a proactive way, by prospectively determining and applying a suitable stopping rule. This situation might arise within a pharmaceutical company, when it is advantageous to obtain an answer as quickly as possible on one of the outcomes measured, perhaps the primary efficacy variable. For example, in the evaluation of a drug for relieving an unwanted effect resulting from chemotherapy given to cancer patients, different studies may deal with patients having cancers at different sites. However, all recruited patients would have the unwanted effect, and the primary efficacy variable, which is the elimination of the unwanted effect, is the same in all studies. Alternatively, the outcome of interest may be a safety variable such as the occurrence of a serious side-effect. In such cases individual fixed sample size studies may be designed for the primary efficacy variable, but the safety variable would be analysed according to a sequential design with stopping boundaries. Significant evidence demonstrating that the new treatment was harmful could then lead to the stopping of all current studies. Another scenario would be when a particular assessment is undertaken on a subset of the patients, possibly because it is expensive or time-consuming, or because there is a secondary question to answer which concerns only some of the patients. Individual fixed sample size studies may be designed for the primary efficacy variable. If the secondary variable is analysed sequentially then once a stopping boundary is crossed, data collection on this variable can be stopped.

Section 12.2 considers the proactive cumulative meta-analysis, and discusses the methodological aspects of implementing a formal stopping rule. Section 12.3 then considers the reactive cumulative meta-analysis, in which the decision to stop is not governed completely by the evidence from the accumulating data. In this case the meta-analyst may utilize a sequential design, but updating of the meta-analysis is less clear-cut.

## 12.2   A PROACTIVE CUMULATIVE META-ANALYSIS

Suppose that a series of studies is to be conducted, following broadly similar protocols, comparing a new treatment with a control treatment. A cumulative meta-analysis is to be conducted on one chosen outcome variable. The choice of the sequential design will depend on whether the outcome variable is a measure of efficacy or safety and on the situations in which it is desirable to stop. The choice of design is discussed in Section 12.2.1.

In a typical cumulative meta-analysis, an interim meta-analysis is undertaken following completion of a further study or group of studies. However, it is not necessary to wait until a study is completed before including it. It can be planned to include all currently available data from all studies at each meta-analysis. Although for administrative reasons it may be helpful to plan the interim meta-analyses in advance, it is not mathematically necessary to specify the number and timing of such analyses. Also, the analyses do not need to be conducted at regular intervals. The important point is that the timing of the analyses should not depend on the apparent magnitude of the treatment difference as this will introduce bias.

If it is assumed that the measure of treatment difference is the same across all studies, then the interim meta-analyses will be based on a fixed effects model. If allowance is to be made for differences in the magnitude of the treatment difference amongst studies, then the interim meta-analyses will be based on a random effects model. The fixed and random effects approaches, as discussed by A. Whitehead (1997), are presented in Sections 12.2.2 and 12.2.3 respectively, and illustrated by an example in Section 12.2.4. One particular problem which arises for the random effects model is the estimation of the heterogeneity parameter, $\tau^2$. This issue is discussed in Section 12.2.5.

## 12.2.1   Choice of a sequential design

For a sequential design, as for a fixed sample size design, it is necessary to specify the clinically important treatment difference, the power required to detect it and the overall significance level. For an individual trial, the overall significance level is frequently set at 5% (two-sided alternative), and the power at 80% or 90%. This may be a suitable choice for some cumulative meta-analyses. However, if the objective is to obtain a result which is as close to definitive as possible, then a lower significance level (1% or 0.1%) and a higher power (95% or 97.5%) may be desirable.

The next stage is to select an appropriate sequential design. As discussed in Section 10.6, there are two main types of sequential procedure which are implemented in practice. Here we consider the boundaries approach described by J. Whitehead (1997), because it is based on the test statistics $Z$ and $V$, which have been introduced into the meta-analysis framework in Chapter 3. In the boundaries approach, $Z$ and $V$ are plotted against one another until certain stopping boundaries are crossed. Four types of sequential design are considered in this section, and the scenarios in which each are appropriate are discussed. For details of other designs the reader is referred to J. Whitehead (1997) and Jennison and Turnbull (2000). The designs and examples presented in this chapter have been implemented using the package PEST 4.

To aid the comparison between the different designs, they are illustrated for the case in which the response is binary and there is to be a 5% significance level and 90% power to detect a change in the success rate from 50% to 70%, corresponding to a log-odds ratio of 0.847. For binary data it is the log-odds ratio which is used as the measure of treatment difference, $\theta$, and the corresponding $Z$ and $V$ statistics are those defined by formulae (3.3) and (3.4).

The triangular test (Figure 12.1) has been widely used for individual clinical trials. It has the property that it will stop early if there is sufficient evidence to declare that the new treatment is significantly better than the control treatment. It will also stop early for futility, that is, when there is very little chance that

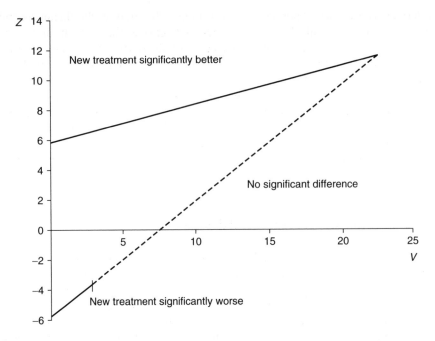

**Figure 12.1**  The triangular test designed for detecting a log-odds ratio of 0.847 (70% success rate on a new treatment versus 50% success rate on control treatment) with 90% power using a global two-sided 5% significance level.

the new treatment will be shown to be better than control. There will not be a continuation just to determine whether the new treatment is no different from the control treatment or is significantly worse. The triangular test may be appropriate for an efficacy variable, when interest lies in the superiority of the new treatment.

The restricted procedure (Figure 12.2) is designed to stop early only if one treatment is substantially superior to the other. It will not stop early for futility: if no treatment difference becomes apparent, then continuation will be to the planned maximum size. The maximum sample size of the restricted procedure is a little larger than the equivalent fixed sample size as a consequence of the early stopping option. The choice of horizontal upper and lower stopping boundaries leads to the O'Brien and Fleming design (O'Brien and Fleming, 1979). The restricted procedure may be used for either efficacy or safety outcomes, and is appropriate if the full sample is required for the study of the other measured outcomes. If the design is to be used for a safety outcome measure, it is desirable that the maximum sample size be large enough to ensure that the power requirement of the primary efficacy measure is met.

The double triangular test (Figure 12.3) consists of combining a triangular test with a reverse triangular test. By itself, the reverse triangular test has a high power of detecting inferiority. In terms of the example, it has a 90% power to

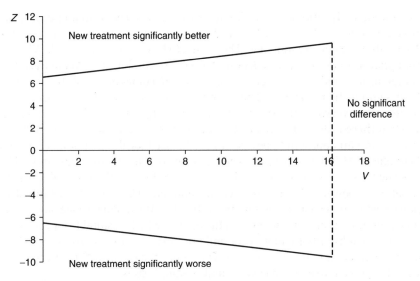

**Figure 12.2** The restricted procedure designed for detecting a log-odds ratio of 0.847 (70% success rate on new treatment versus 50% success rate on control treatment) or −0.847 (30% success rate on new treatment versus 50% success rate on control treatment) with 90% power using a global two-sided 5% significance level.

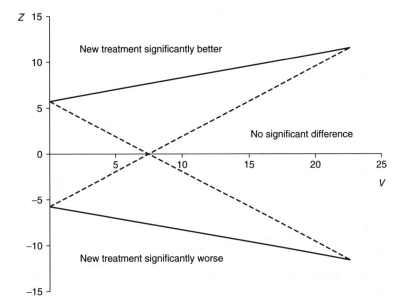

**Figure 12.3** The double triangular test designed for detecting a log-odds ratio of 0.847 (70% success rate on new treatment versus 50% success rate on control treatment) or −0.847 (30% success rate on new treatment versus 50% success rate on control treatment) with 90% power using a global two-sided 5% significance level.

detect a log-odds ratio of −0.847, which would correspond to a change in the success rate from 50% to 30%. It will also stop early when there is very little chance that the new treatment will be shown to be worse than control. When the triangular test and the reverse triangular test are combined to create the double triangular test, and the study continues until *both* component tests have stopped, the design has high power to detect both superiority and inferiority. In contrast to the restricted procedure, the double triangular test stops early for futility, that is, when there is little chance of showing that the two treatments are different. By choosing an appropriate power, it may be used for determining equivalence (Whitehead, 1996). For example, suppose that equivalence may be claimed if the two-sided 95% confidence interval for θ is contained in the interval $(-\theta_R, \theta_R)$. By setting a power of 97.5% to detect a treatment difference of $\theta_R$, equivalence may be claimed as soon as the sample path enters the middle wedge-shaped area indicating no significant difference. This design, which is suitable for an efficacy measure, is substantially more economic than the restricted procedure when θ lies in the interval $(-\theta_R, \theta_R)$. Only for values of θ well outside this interval is the restricted procedure likely to lead to smaller sample sizes.

A design specifically intended for a safety outcome is the safety monitoring procedure described by Bolland and Whitehead (2000). This procedure (Figure 12.4)

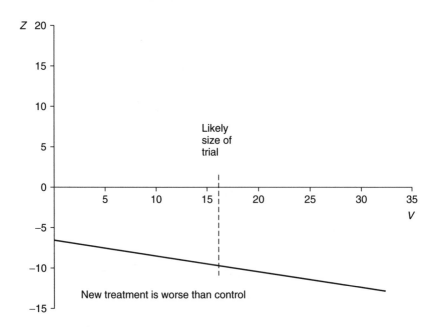

**Figure 12.4** The safety monitoring procedure designed so that there is a 90% chance of stopping at or before 270 patients have provided data if the log-odds ratio is −0.847 (70% adverse event rate on new treatment versus 50% adverse event rate on control treatment), and a 2.5% chance if the log-odds ratio is 0 (50% adverse event rate on each treatment).

recommends stopping as soon as there is sufficient evidence that the new treatment is worse than the control. If the new treatment is not worse than the control, then it is desirable that recruitment should continue until the sample size is large enough to ensure that the power requirement of the primary efficacy measure is met. The safety monitoring procedure has an advantage over the restricted procedure in that there is no maximum sample size at which the monitoring stops. Instead, the properties of the safety procedure are described by the probability of stopping at or before the data from $n$ subjects have been included when the true treatment difference is $\theta$. In the specification of the design, attention is focused on $n = n^*$, where $n^*$ is the sample size required for primary efficacy.

## 12.2.2   A fixed effects model

Suppose that there are a total of $r$ studies to be conducted, each of which compares the new treatment with the control treatment. Under the fixed effects model, it is assumed that the treatment difference parameter takes the same value in each study. Each time an interim meta-analysis is conducted, the $Z$ and $V$ statistics are calculated for each study and combined according to the fixed effects approach of Chapter 4. Studies with no available data do not contribute to the analysis: the $Z$ and $V$ statistics are equal to zero.

Let the cumulative efficient score and Fisher's information for the $i$th study, $i = 1, \ldots, r$, at the $a$th interim analysis be given by $Z_{ia}$ and $V_{ia}$. Suppose that at the $a$th inspection the first $h_a$ studies have started. The combined cumulative efficient score and Fisher's information for plotting on the sequential design are given by $Z_a$ and $V_a$ respectively, where

$$Z_a = \sum_{i=1}^{h_a} Z_{ia}$$

$$V_a = \sum_{i=1}^{h_a} V_{ia}.$$

The estimate of $\theta$ from the $i$th study at the $a$th inspection, $\hat{\theta}_{ia}$, is given by

$$\hat{\theta}_{ia} = \frac{Z_{ia}}{V_{ia}}.$$

The overall estimate of $\theta$, at the $a$th inspection, $\hat{\theta}_a$, is given by

$$\hat{\theta}_a = \frac{\sum_{i=1}^{h_a} \hat{\theta}_{ia} V_{ia}}{\sum_{i=1}^{h_a} V_{ia}} = \frac{Z_a}{V_a}.$$

### 12.2.3 A random effects model

For the random effects model it is assumed that the treatment difference parameters from the $r$ studies $(\theta_1, \ldots, \theta_r)$ are a sample of independent observations from $N(\theta, \tau^2)$. In a random effects meta-analysis based on the efficient score and Fisher's information statistics, the fixed effects $Z_i$ and $V_i$ are simply replaced by their random counterparts $Z_i^*$ and $V_i^*$, where $V_i^* = (V_i^{-1} + \hat{\tau}^2)^{-1}$ and $Z_i^* = \hat{\theta}_i V_i^*$. It is tempting to make the same substitution in the sequential setting, although the mathematical correctness of this has not been established.

In the sequential setting, $\hat{\theta}_{ia} \sim N(\theta, V_{ia}^{-1} + \tau^2)$ and the estimate of $\theta$ at the $a$th inspection is given by $\hat{\theta}_a^*$, where

$$\hat{\theta}_a^* = \frac{\sum_{i=1}^{h_a} \hat{\theta}_{ia} V_{ia}^*}{\sum_{i=1}^{h_a} V_{ia}^*},$$

$$V_{ia}^* = (V_{ia}^{-1} + \hat{\tau}_a^2)^{-1}$$

and $\hat{\tau}_a^2$ is an estimate of $\tau^2$. Setting

$$Z_{ia}^* = \hat{\theta}_{ia} V_{ia}^*,$$

$$Z_a^* = \sum_{i=1}^{h_a} Z_{ia}^*,$$

$$V_a^* = \sum_{i=1}^{h_a} V_{ia}^*,$$

then

$$\hat{\theta}_a^* = \frac{Z_a^*}{V_a^*}$$

and

$$Z_a^* \sim N(\theta V_a^*, V_a^*).$$

The heterogeneity parameter, $\tau^2$, may be estimated using either the method of moments (see Section 4.3.3) or likelihood methods (see Section 4.3.8). If the method of moments is used, then $\hat{\tau}_a^2$ is given by

$$\hat{\tau}_a^2 = \frac{Q_a - (h_a - 1)}{\sum_{i=1}^{h_a} V_{ia} - \left(\sum_{i=1}^{h_a} V_{ia}^2\right) \Big/ \sum_{i=1}^{h_a} V_{ia}}.$$

Here, $Q_a$ is the homogeneity test statistic at the $a$th inspection given by

$$Q_a = \sum_{i=1}^{h_a} V_{ia}(\hat{\theta}_{ia} - \hat{\theta}_a)^2 = \sum_{i=1}^{h_a} \frac{Z_{ia}^2}{V_{ia}} - \frac{\left(\sum_{i=1}^{h_a} Z_{ia}\right)^2}{\sum_{i=1}^{h_a} V_{ia}}.$$

If $\hat{\tau}_a^2 \leqslant 0$ then the estimate is set to 0 so that the fixed effects statistics are used.

In the random effects analysis, $Z_a^*$ is plotted against $V_a^*$ on the sequential design. Notice that $V_a^*$ will be smaller than $V_a$ when $\hat{\tau} > 0$ and will decrease as $\hat{\tau}$ increases.

A. Whitehead (1997) showed in a simulation exercise that the random effects meta-analysis model used with the triangular test achieves the specified error probabilities with reasonable accuracy provided that the heterogeneity parameter is relatively small. Ignoring the random effect when it is present and using a fixed effects meta-analysis model instead leads to increased error probabilities.

### 12.2.4  Example: The triangular test for a primary efficacy outcome

A. Whitehead (1997) presents a simulated example to illustrate the random effects cumulative meta-analysis, and this is described briefly in this subsection. The example concerns the use of the triangular test (Figure 12.1) for a primary efficacy outcome. The power requirement was that defined in Section 12.2.1, that is, a 90% power to detect a change in the success rate from 50% to 70%. For this design, the maximum sample size under a fixed effects model is 380 subjects. The equivalent fixed sample size would be 244. Ten parallel group trials, comparing the new treatment with the control treatment, were each planned to recruit 50 patients. Therefore, each study had an 80% power to detect a change in the success rate from 50% to 85%. The maximum sample size of 500 was chosen to provide a high probability that a stopping boundary is crossed before all of the subjects have completed.

The upper and lower boundaries of the triangular test are given by

$$Z = 5.823 + 0.2573V$$

and

$$Z = -5.823 + 0.7718V.$$

A random effects model was chosen to allow for some heterogeneity between the trials. Four inspections of the data were planned to occur after approximately every 125 completed subjects. To preserve the overall error rates, a correction for discrete monitoring, referred to as the 'Christmas tree correction', was applied to the boundaries. This leads to stopping if

$$Z_a^* \geqslant 5.823 + 0.2573\, V_a^* - 0.583\sqrt{V_a^* - V_{a-1}^*}$$

or if

$$Z_a^* \leqslant -5.823 + 0.7718\, V_a^* + 0.583\sqrt{V_a^* - V_{a-1}^*},$$

for $a = 1, \ldots, 4$ and $V_0^* = 0$.

Individual binary outcomes were simulated, and the data for the first interim analysis are summarized in Table 12.1. At this analysis data are only available from the first six studies. The log-odds ratio for the $i$th study, $\theta_i$, is estimated by $Z_{i1}/V_{i1}$, and $Z_{i1}^2/V_{i1}$ is the score statistic which in a fixed sample size analysis would follow the chi-squared distribution with one degree of freedom if $\theta_i$ were equal to 0. From Table 12.1 it can be seen that study 4 already shows a significant effect ($Z_{41}^2/V_{41} = 4.750; p = 0.03$), when sequential monitoring and multiplicity are not allowed for. Studies 1, 2 and 5 are positive. Studies 3 and 6 show negative effects, although study 6 has few patients.

The homogeneity test statistic, $Q_1$, is equal to 7.125, which compared with the chi-squared distribution with five degrees of freedom is not significant ($p = 0.21$). The method of moments estimate, $\hat{\tau}_1^2$, is equal to 0.417. The resulting statistics for plotting on the sequential design are $Z_1^* = 3.758$ and $V_1^* = 4.217$ (Figure 12.5). Using the Christmas tree correction, the upper and lower critical values for $Z_1^*$ are 5.71 and $-1.371$. As $Z_1^*$ lies between these, the trials all continue to the second interim analysis.

The data from the second interim analysis are also shown in Table 12.1. Study 4 remains significantly positive. Study 6 remains negative. Now $Q_2$ is equal to 9.932, which compared with the chi-squared distribution with nine degrees of freedom

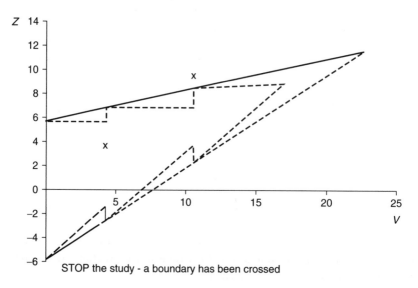

STOP the study - a boundary has been crossed

**Figure 12.5** Simulated example of a proactive meta-analysis, using the triangular test from Figure 12.1.

**Table 12.1** Simulated example of a proactive cumulative meta-analysis, using the triangular test for a primary efficacy outcome

First interim analysis

| Trial | New treatment | | Control | | $V_{i1}$ | $Z_{i1}$ | $Z_{i1}/V_{i1}$ | $Z_{i1}^2/V_{i1}$ | $V_{i1}^*$ | $Z_{i1}^*$ |
|---|---|---|---|---|---|---|---|---|---|---|
| | Success | Failure | Success | Failure | | | | | | |
| 1 | 13 | 2 | 9 | 5 | 1.373 | 1.621 | 1.180 | 1.913 | 0.873 | 1.031 |
| 2 | 8 | 5 | 5 | 7 | 1.622 | 1.240 | 0.764 | 0.948 | 0.968 | 0.740 |
| 3 | 8 | 4 | 9 | 3 | 1.293 | −0.500 | −0.387 | 0.193 | 0.840 | −0.325 |
| 4 | 10 | 0 | 6 | 4 | 0.842 | 2.000 | 2.375 | 4.750 | 0.623 | 1.480 |
| 5 | 6 | 1 | 3 | 5 | 0.960 | 1.800 | 1.875 | 3.375 | 0.686 | 1.285 |
| 6 | 2 | 1 | 3 | 0 | 0.250 | −0.500 | −2.000 | 1.000 | 0.226 | −0.453 |
| Total | 47 | 13 | 35 | 24 | 6.341 | 5.661 | | 12.179 | 4.217 | 3.758 |

Second interim analysis

| Trial | New treatment | | Control | | $V_{i2}$ | $Z_{i2}$ | $Z_{i2}/V_{i2}$ | $Z_{i2}^2/V_{i2}$ | $V_{i2}^*$ | $Z_{i2}^*$ |
|---|---|---|---|---|---|---|---|---|---|---|
| | Success | Failure | Success | Failure | | | | | | |
| 1 | 21 | 3 | 16 | 7 | 2.010 | 2.106 | 1.048 | 2.207 | 1.703 | 1.785 |
| 2 | 10 | 6 | 6 | 10 | 2.065 | 2.000 | 0.969 | 1.938 | 1.742 | 1.688 |
| 3 | 15 | 5 | 14 | 5 | 1.907 | 0.128 | 0.067 | 0.009 | 1.629 | 0.110 |
| 4 | 19 | 0 | 13 | 0 | 1.473 | 3.410 | 2.316 | 7.897 | 1.301 | 3.013 |
| 5 | 11 | 3 | 8 | 6 | 1.583 | 1.500 | 0.947 | 1.421 | 1.387 | 1.314 |
| 6 | 8 | 3 | 9 | 1 | 0.848 | −0.905 | −1.067 | 0.965 | 0.788 | −0.841 |
| 7 | 5 | 3 | 4 | 3 | 0.960 | 0.200 | 0.208 | 0.042 | 0.884 | 0.184 |
| 8 | 7 | 0 | 4 | 3 | 0.6635 | 1.500 | 2.364 | 3.545 | 0.600 | 1.419 |
| 9 | 4 | 0 | 4 | 1 | 0.247 | 0.444 | 1.800 | 0.800 | 0.242 | 0.435 |
| 10 | 3 | 0 | 2 | 1 | 0.250 | 0.500 | 2.000 | 1.000 | 0.245 | 0.489 |
| Total | 103 | 23 | 80 | 44 | 11.997 | 10.885 | | 19.824 | 10.521 | 9.596 |

Reproduced from Whitehead, 1997 (Table IV) by permission of John Wiley & Sons, Ltd.

is not statistically significant ($p = 0.36$). The method of moments estimate, $\hat{\tau}_2^2$, is equal to 0.090. The resulting statistics for plotting on the sequential design are $Z_2^* = 9.596$ and $V_2^* = 10.521$. The upper and lower critical values for $Z_2^*$ are 7.066 and 3.761 (Figure 12.5). As $Z_2^*$ is greater than the upper critical value, there is sufficient evidence to declare that the new treatment is superior to the control treatment.

In cases such as this where the outcome of interest is the primary efficacy variable, it is envisaged that patient recruitment would stop once a stopping boundary has been crossed. A final analysis conducted using PEST 4, allowing for the previous interim analysis, gives a $p$-value of 0.005 (two-sided). A median unbiased estimate of the log-odds ratio is 0.905, with 95% CI (0.289, 1.512). If it is considered to be more likely that study 6 produced a random poor result than that the new treatment does not work for the type of patients in study 6, then the overall positive result is an appropriate summary.

### 12.2.5   Estimation of the heterogeneity parameter

Whilst the methodology for conducting a fixed effects cumulative meta-analysis has a solid foundation, that for conducting the random effects cumulative meta-analysis is tentative. Methodological issues which still need to be addressed are ones connected with the estimation of the heterogeneity parameter. Three particular problems are described in this section.

First, if based only on a small subset of the trials, the parameter estimate of $\tau^2$ will be unreliable. If practical, it may be better to postpone the first interim analysis until the majority of the studies can provide patient data. Alternatively, an empirical prior distribution for $\tau^2$ may be utilized, as discussed in Section 11.8. At the first interim analysis, the mean of this prior distribution can be used in the calculation of the $Z$ and $V$ statistics, and a posterior distribution for $\tau^2$ can be determined. This posterior distribution can be used as the prior distribution for the second interim analysis, and so on.

The second problem is that if the estimate of $\tau^2$ changes at each interim analysis, it is possible for the sample path to go backwards. The interpretation of such an event is that because of new evidence indicating larger heterogeneity than previously believed, there is less information in the data about the treatment difference than at the previous analysis. Higgins (1997) has suggested possible ways of avoiding this problem, although none has yet been investigated. These include adapting the parameter estimation of $\tau^2$ to avoid large changes, and altering the boundaries so that they incorporate the current estimate. This problem will be illustrated in the context of a reactive cumulative meta-analysis in Section 12.3.1 (see Figure 12.9).

The third problem is that of bias in the estimation of $\tau^2$ at the final analysis. If by chance $\hat{\tau}_a^2$ is smaller than the true parameter, then a stopping boundary is more likely to be crossed. This is because $Z_a^*$ and $V_a^*$ will be larger than they would be if calculated using the true parameter value. Therefore, at the point when a boundary is crossed, $\hat{\tau}_a^2$ will on average be an underestimate. This means that the estimate of treatment difference, even when corrected for interim inspections, will on average be an overestimate. Possible solutions, which have not yet been investigated include altering the boundaries and adapting the parameter estimation of $\tau^2$ (Higgins, 1997).

## 12.3   A REACTIVE CUMULATIVE META-ANALYSIS

In a reactive cumulative meta-analysis, the meta-analyst usually has little or no influence on the number and size of studies which are available for inclusion. Instead, the decision to undertake a new study is likely to be made by a group of clinical investigators, using different criteria from those which might be used for a formal stopping rule. Chalmers and Lau (1993) stress the importance of conducting a meta-analysis before undertaking a new study, so that investigators can evaluate the number of patients and data items required to answer the clinical question. The availability of results from a cumulative meta-analysis could influence their decision-making.

A reactive cumulative meta-analysis is more likely to be undertaken for a new treatment with promising early results than for one which does not. Often, if a new treatment does not show promising results in the initial studies, no further studies are undertaken. As a consequence there never arises a need for a cumulative meta-analysis. On the other hand, if the initial studies indicate some useful clinical benefit, further studies will be initiated. There may then be an interest in performing a cumulative meta-analysis. This introduces selection bias, as discussed in Section 8.1. If these early results are included in the cumulative meta-analysis, it is especially important to adjust for the multiple inspections of the data in order to minimize the number of false positives.

In Section 12.3.1, an example of how a sequential design may be used for a retrospective cumulative meta-analysis is discussed, together with the practical aspects of its implementation. Alternative procedures which do not have a formal stopping rule are discussed in Section 12.3.2.

### 12.3.1   Example: Endoscopic haemostasis for bleeding peptic ulcers

Sacks *et al.* (1990) present the data from 23 trials comparing endoscopic haemostasis with a control treatment in the treatment of bleeding peptic ulcers. The outcome variable of interest is the occurrence of bleeding following treatment. In this section, the measure of treatment difference is taken to be the log-odds ratio of no bleeding (endoscopic haemostasis relative to control). Therefore, a positive log-odds ratio indicates the superiority of endoscopic haemostasis. The $Z$ and $V$ statistics (formulae (3.3) and (3.4)) are presented for each study in Table 12.2. Studies are ordered by publication date, and the last column of the table shows the study estimates of the log-odds ratio. The CI plot indicates heterogeneity between the study estimates (Figure 12.6). Indeed, the test for heterogeneity based on all 23 studies is highly significant ($p < 0.001$).

This data set was also discussed in the context of a cumulative meta-analysis by Chalmers and Lau (1993). They present the results of both a fixed and a random effects cumulative meta-analysis, but with no allowance made for multiple looks. Although they acknowledge that the $p$-values are not corrected for multiple looks, they still base their conclusions on them. In this section a formal sequential procedure is considered.

Suppose that it had been planned to conduct a cumulative meta-analysis, with interim analyses after the results of each study had been published. The

**Table 12.2**   Randomized trials of bleeding peptic ulcers: log-odds ratio of no bleeding (endoscopic haemostasis relative to control)

| Trial | Haemostasis | | Control | | $V_i$ | $Z_i$ | $Z_i/V_i$ |
|---|---|---|---|---|---|---|---|
| | Bled | Total | Bled | Total | | | |
| 1. Vallon 1980 | 20 | 68 | 23 | 68 | 7.35 | 1.50 | 0.20 |
| 2. Swain 1981 | 11 | 36 | 17 | 40 | 4.41 | 2.26 | 0.51 |
| 3. Papp 1982 | 1 | 16 | 13 | 16 | 1.97 | 6.00 | 3.05 |
| 4. Rutgeerts 1982 | 5 | 52 | 19 | 54 | 4.64 | 6.77 | 1.46 |
| 5. MacLeod 1983 | 6 | 21 | 8 | 24 | 2.40 | 0.53 | 0.22 |
| 6. Jensen 1984 | 2 | 7 | 7 | 9 | 0.97 | 1.94 | 2.00 |
| 7. Kernohan 1984 | 9 | 21 | 7 | 24 | 2.57 | −1.53 | −0.60 |
| 8. Goudie 1984 | 7 | 21 | 5 | 25 | 2.20 | −1.52 | −0.69 |
| 9. Freitas 1985 | 7 | 36 | 17 | 42 | 4.13 | 4.08 | 0.99 |
| 10. Swain 1986 | 7 | 69 | 27 | 68 | 6.39 | 10.12 | 1.58 |
| 11. O'Brien 1986 | 17 | 101 | 34 | 103 | 9.56 | 8.25 | 0.86 |
| 12. Krejs 1987 | 19 | 85 | 18 | 89 | 7.28 | −0.93 | −0.13 |
| 13. Brearley 1987 | 6 | 20 | 8 | 21 | 2.30 | 0.83 | 0.36 |
| 14. Moreto 1987 | 1 | 16 | 11 | 21 | 1.99 | 4.19 | 2.11 |
| 15. Laine 1987 | 0 | 10 | 12 | 14 | 1.46 | 5.00 | 3.43 |
| 16. Panes 1987 | 3 | 55 | 25 | 58 | 5.26 | 10.63 | 2.02 |
| 17. Chung 1987 | 0 | 34 | 34 | 34 | 4.25 | 17.00 | 4.00 |
| 18. Balanzo 1988 | 7 | 36 | 15 | 36 | 3.82 | 4.00 | 1.05 |
| 19. Fellerton 1989 | 0 | 20 | 5 | 23 | 1.10 | 2.33 | 2.12 |
| 20. Angerinas 1989 | 7 | 33 | 4 | 32 | 2.28 | −1.42 | −0.62 |
| 21. Rutgeerts 1989 | 10 | 40 | 12 | 20 | 3.10 | 4.67 | 1.51 |
| 22. Chiozzini 1989 | 4 | 34 | 5 | 19 | 1.72 | 1.77 | 1.03 |
| 23. Laine 1989 | 7 | 38 | 15 | 37 | 3.89 | 4.15 | 1.07 |

sequential design to be considered is the O'Brien and Fleming design (or restricted procedure with boundary slope zero – Figure 12.7). The design has an overall significance level of 1% (two-sided alternative) and a 90% power to detect an odds ratio of 2 (log-odds ratio of 0.693). This design will allow early stopping only if one treatment is substantially superior to the other. In practice, the design and clinically relevant difference would need to be carefully thought out by a group of experts.

First, consider a cumulative meta-analysis based on a fixed effects model. The sample path is plotted (Figure 12.8) using the values of $Z_a$ and $V_a$, $a = 1, \ldots, 23$, from Table 12.3. It can be seen that the upper stopping boundary is crossed at the fourth inspection, indicating that endoscopic haemostasis is better than the control treatment. An analysis conducted using PEST 4, allowing for the previous inspections, gives a $p$-value of 0.0001 (two-sided). A median unbiased estimate of the log-odds ratio is 0.897, with 95% CI (0.438, 1.356).

However, to allow for possible heterogeneity between the studies, it would be preferable to use the random effects model. This is also likely to be the preferred choice in practice, because if the cumulative meta-analysis is planned

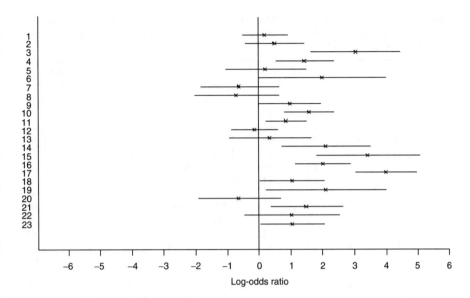

**Figure 12.6** Randomized trials of bleeding peptic ulcers. Estimates and 95% confidence intervals of the log-odds ratio of no bleeding (endoscopic haemostasis versus control).

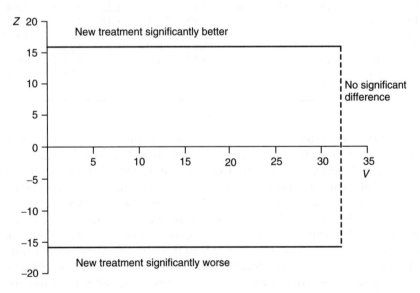

**Figure 12.7** The O'Brien and Fleming design for the bleeding peptic ulcer data set. The design has a 90% power to detect a log-odds ratio of 0.693 (odds ratio of 2) using a global two-sided 1% significance level.

**Table 12.3**  Randomized trials of bleeding peptic ulcers: log-odds ratio of no bleeding (endoscopic haemostasis relative to control). Cumulative Z and V statistics for both fixed and random effects models

| Trial | Haemostasis | | Control | | Cumulative (fixed effects) | | $\hat{\tau}_a^2$ | Cumulative (random effects) | |
|---|---|---|---|---|---|---|---|---|---|
| | Bled | Total | Bled | Total | $V_a$ | $Z_a$ | | $V_a^*$ | $Z_a^*$ |
| 1 | 20 | 68 | 23 | 68 | 7.35 | 1.50 | – | 7.35 | 1.50 |
| 2 | 11 | 36 | 17 | 40 | 11.76 | 3.76 | 0.00 | 11.76 | 3.76 |
| 3 | 1 | 16 | 13 | 16 | 13.73 | 9.76 | 1.34 | 1.86 | 2.12 |
| 4 | 5 | 52 | 19 | 54 | 18.37 | 16.54 | 0.91 | 3.44 | 4.11 |
| 5 | 6 | 21 | 8 | 24 | 20.77 | 17.07 | 0.75 | 4.86 | 4.90 |
| 6 | 2 | 7 | 7 | 9 | 21.74 | 19.01 | 0.71 | 5.60 | 6.20 |
| 7 | 9 | 21 | 7 | 24 | 24.30 | 17.47 | 0.81 | 5.94 | 5.21 |
| 8 | 7 | 21 | 5 | 25 | 26.50 | 15.95 | 0.86 | 6.46 | 4.49 |
| 9 | 7 | 36 | 17 | 42 | 30.63 | 20.03 | 0.71 | 8.47 | 6.14 |
| 10 | 7 | 69 | 27 | 68 | 37.02 | 30.15 | 0.68 | 9.83 | 8.14 |
| 11 | 17 | 101 | 34 | 103 | 46.59 | 38.40 | 0.52 | 13.48 | 11.17 |
| 12 | 19 | 85 | 18 | 89 | 53.87 | 37.48 | 0.54 | 14.59 | 10.68 |
| 13 | 6 | 20 | 8 | 21 | 56.17 | 38.31 | 0.50 | 16.47 | 11.63 |
| 14 | 1 | 16 | 11 | 21 | 58.16 | 42.50 | 0.53 | 16.70 | 13.17 |
| 15 | 0 | 10 | 12 | 14 | 59.62 | 47.50 | 0.69 | 14.70 | 13.60 |
| 16 | 3 | 55 | 25 | 58 | 64.88 | 58.13 | 0.73 | 15.16 | 15.26 |
| 17 | 0 | 34 | 34 | 34 | 69.13 | 75.13 | 1.27 | 10.62 | 12.90 |
| 18 | 7 | 36 | 15 | 36 | 72.95 | 79.13 | 1.18 | 11.95 | 14.37 |
| 19 | 0 | 20 | 5 | 23 | 74.05 | 81.45 | 1.17 | 12.57 | 15.56 |
| 20 | 7 | 33 | 4 | 32 | 76.33 | 80.04 | 1.20 | 12.86 | 14.80 |
| 21 | 10 | 40 | 12 | 20 | 79.43 | 84.70 | 1.15 | 14.03 | 16.37 |
| 22 | 4 | 34 | 5 | 19 | 81.15 | 86.48 | 1.11 | 15.02 | 17.43 |
| 23 | 7 | 38 | 15 | 37 | 85.03 | 90.62 | 1.04 | 16.53 | 19.08 |

prospectively, the amount of heterogeneity will be unknown at the start. The sample path is now plotted using the values $Z_a^*$ and $V_a^*$ from Table 12.3. In the calculation of these values, the heterogeneity parameter, $\tau^2$, has been estimated using the method of moments. Because of the amount of heterogeneity present, the values of $V_a^*$ are generally much smaller than the corresponding values of $V_a$. When using the random effects model, a decision has to be taken regarding the timing of the first interim analysis. In the absence of prior information on $\tau^2$, it is perhaps reasonable to delay this until at least three trials have been published.

Figure 12.9 shows the sample path based on the random effects model The first point represents the results from the first three trials. Thereafter, the sample path is plotted after each additional study. It can be seen that information increases with each additional study until trial 15 is included. The values of $V_{14}^*$ and $V_{15}^*$ are 16.70 and 14.70 respectively, that is, the sample path goes backwards. This is an illustration of the problem mentioned in Section 12.2.5. In this situation, PEST 4 automatically replaces the value of V by the maximum value recorded so

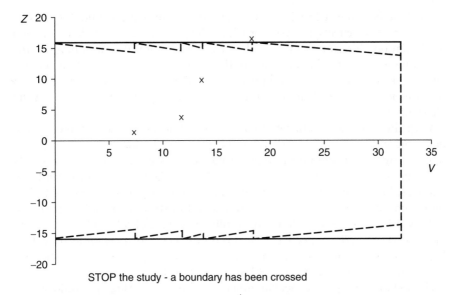

**Figure 12.8**    Randomized trials of bleeding peptic ulcers. Fixed effects cumulative meta-analysis using the $Z_a$ and $V_a$ values from Table 12.3.

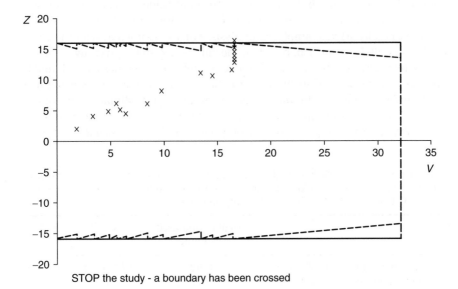

**Figure 12.9**    Randomized trials of bleeding peptic ulcers. Random effects cumulative meta-analysis using the $Z_a^*$ and $V_a^*$ values from Table 12.3.

far, so that the value at 15 trials is set to 16.70. The rationale behind this decision is that for a fixed effects analysis, for which the package is designed, a reduction in $V$ from one interim analysis to the next is very rare. If it does happen, the reduction in $V$ will tend to be small. In that context, the approximation adopted by PEST 4 is likely to be a reasonable one. In the present setting it is not clear that this is so. Neither is it clear that the calculated value of 14.70 is a valid alternative.

With this particular data set, it can be seen that the amount of information never increases beyond 16.70. When all values of $V_a^*$ for $a = 15, \ldots, 21$ are replaced by 16.70, the upper stopping boundary is crossed after 21 trials. At this point analysis can be conducted using PEST 4, allowing for previous interim analyses, but because the sample path has gone backwards its validity will be uncertain. For comparative purposes the results from three approaches are shown in Table 12.4. The first row shows the results based on final values of $Z$ and $V$ given by 16.37 and 16.70, respectively. As it is now difficult to allow for *increments* in $V$ between interim analyses, a continuous monitoring approximation is specified by setting the penultimate value of $V$ to be very close to the final value of 16.70, such as 16.69. This gives a median unbiased estimate of the log-odds ratio of 0.92 with CI (0.44, 1.40). The second row shows the results based on final values of $Z$ and $V$ given by 16.37 and 14.03, respectively. That is, the calculated value $V_{21}^*$ is used. Continuous monitoring is again specified by setting the penultimate value of $V$ to be smaller but very close to the final value. As expected, this gives a larger estimate of the log-odds ratio of 1.10, with a CI which is also shifted upwards. Finally, a fixed sample size analysis, which does not adjust for the interim analyses at all, is performed, based on the values of $Z$ and $V$ given by 16.37 and 14.03, respectively. This analysis is based on the score statistics $Z$ and $V$ and the approximate $N(\theta V, V)$ distribution for $Z$. Because no adjustment is being made for the interim analyses, this method produces the largest estimate of the log-odds ratio at 1.17. The three approaches have produced estimates which do not differ markedly, and there appears to be strong evidence that endoscopic haemostasis

**Table 12.4** Random effects cumulative meta-analysis of the randomized trials of bleeding peptic ulcers: estimates of the log-odds ratio of no bleeding (endoscopic haemostasis relative to control) following the crossing of a stopping boundary

|  | Median unbiased estimate | 95% CI | $p$-value |
|---|---|---|---|
| Using the maximum value of $V$ and assuming continuous monitoring | 0.92 | (0.44, 1.40) | 0.000 2 |
| Using the actual final value of $V$ and assuming continuous monitoring | 1.10 | (0.58, 1.63) | 0.000 04 |
| Using the actual final value of $V$ and performing a fixed sample size analysis | 1.17 | (0.64, 1.69) | 0.000 01 |

reduces the odds of bleeding for patients with a bleeding peptic ulcer compared with the control treatment.

## 12.3.2　Alternative approaches to a formal stopping rule

For the sequential designs which have been presented so far, it has been assumed that once a stopping boundary has been crossed data accrual ends. However, in a reactive cumulative meta-analysis, the meta-analyst may specify a stopping rule, but additional studies may be undertaken after a stopping boundary has been crossed. A sequential procedure which accounts for the multiple looks but which does not involve stopping boundaries would be attractive.

Repeated confidence intervals, developed by Jennison and Turnbull (1989), are a sequence of intervals $(\theta_{La}, \theta_{Ua})$, with the property that

$$P\{\theta \in (\theta_{La}, \theta_{Ua}) \text{ for all } a = 1, 2, \ldots\} = 1 - \alpha.$$

At the $a$th interim analysis, the interval $(\theta_{La}, \theta_{Ua})$ is calculated from the available data, adjusting for the multiple looks. Each of these intervals will be wider than the $100(1 - \alpha)\%$ fixed sample size CI. For this procedure it is necessary to specify the maximum information, $V_{max}$. Alternatively, the number and timings of the interim analyses can be specified.

Repeated confidence intervals are closely related to sequential testing procedures. For example, if $\ell_1, \ell_2, \ldots$ and $u_1, u_2, \ldots$ are the sequences of lower and upper stopping limits for the restricted procedure, then

$$\theta_{La} = \frac{Z_a - u_a}{V_a}$$

and

$$\theta_{Ua} = \frac{Z_a - \ell_a}{V_a}$$

for $a = 1, 2, \ldots$, form a $100(1 - \alpha)\%$ confidence sequence for $\theta$. Crossing the upper or lower boundary of the restricted procedure is then equivalent to the current repeated confidence interval excluding zero.

Repeated confidence intervals can be reported following each interim analysis. Early stopping is not a formal part of their formulation. Their defining property holds provided that data are accrued until $V = V_{max}$. If the cumulative meta-analysis is stopped before this point, the intervals will be conservative. If the cumulative meta-analysis continues beyond this point, the repeated confidence interval calculated at $V_{max}$ is the last valid member of the sequence.

The confidence sequence, an antecedent of repeated confidence intervals, introduced by Robbins (1970), allows the number of interim analyses to be left open. A $(1 - \alpha)$-level confidence sequence is a continuous sequence of intervals $(\theta_L(V), \theta_U(V))$, with the property that

$$P\{\theta \in (\theta_L(V), \theta_U(V)) \text{ for all } V \geqslant 0\} = 1 - \alpha.$$

However, because the sequence contains the true value of $\theta$ with probability $1 - \alpha$ for all values of $V$ from zero to infinity, these intervals tend to be wider than the repeated confidence intervals.

Within a Bayesian framework, a cumulative meta-analysis may be undertaken without the concern about repeated significance tests. Unlike the frequentist confidence interval, the Bayesian credibility interval at any interim analysis does not depend on the sampling scheme used to obtain the data. With each interim analysis the Bayesian meta-analyst would update his/her beliefs about the treatment difference. The posterior distribution of the model parameters from the first interim analysis would become the prior distribution for the second interim analysis and so on. If between-trial heterogeneity increases during the process, the credibility interval may become wider, but this causes no problem.

Bayesian stopping rules for individual clinical trials have been proposed by various authors (see, for example, Berry, 1985; Freedman and Spiegelhalter, 1989). The following rules provide a simple example: stop and recommend the new treatment if

$$P(\theta > \theta_A | \text{data}) > 1 - \delta;$$

stop and reject the new treatment if

$$P(\theta < \theta_B | \text{data}) > 1 - \varepsilon.$$

If $\theta_A$ and $\theta_B$ were both zero and $\delta$ and $\varepsilon$ were both 0.025, then stopping would occur when the 95% credibility interval excluded zero.

As the sequential design does not affect the Bayesian inference, the credibility interval at any interim analysis is not corrected for multiple looks. However, Bayesian monitoring procedures can have very poor frequentist properties, as discussed by Jennison and Turnbull (2000). In particular, the overall significance level is not controlled and can be greatly inflated. Spiegelhalter *et al.* (1994) consider the use of 'pragmatic Bayes' prior distributions in order to control the frequentist properties of a Bayesian monitoring system.

In conclusion, the methodology for conducting a reactive cumulative meta-analysis is still in its infancy. None of the methods which have been discussed yet provides an ideal solution, and further research is needed in this area.

# Appendix: Methods of Estimation and Hypothesis Testing

## A.1 INTRODUCTION

This appendix gives a summary of the main methods of estimation and hypothesis testing which are used in individual trials, focusing primarily on those which can be extended to the meta-analysis of all of the trials when individual patient data are available. The model for a single trial and the model for a fixed effects meta-analysis based on individual patient data are both examples of fixed effects models. With the inclusion of random effects, the meta-analysis model becomes a mixed model.

The first part of the appendix deals with fixed effects models. In Section A.2 fixed effects models for normally distributed data are considered within the framework of a general linear model. Parameter estimates are obtained using the method of least squares. The extension to a weighted least-squares procedure is described in Section A.3, as this procedure can be utilized for the combination of study estimates of a treatment difference. For other data types, maximum likelihood (ML) estimation can be used. A general description of iterative ML estimation is given in Section A.4. An approach which is related to, but simpler than, the ML approach is that based on efficient score and Fisher's information statistics. This simpler approach has been widely used for the calculation of study estimates of a treatment difference prior to their combination in a meta-analysis. The relationship between the two approaches is presented in Section A.5 in the context of an individual trial. In Section A.6 the fixed effects models for binary data and interval-censored survival data are considered within the framework of a generalized linear model, and it is shown that ML estimates can be obtained via an iteratively weighted least-squares procedure.

The second part of the appendix deals with mixed models. For normally distributed data the meta-analysis models containing random effects are considered within the framework of a general linear mixed model. Parameter estimates of both the fixed effect parameters and the variance components can be obtained using methods based on ML or residual (restricted) maximum likelihood (REML). These approaches are described in Section A.7. For other data types it is traditional to assume that the random effects have a multivariate normal distribution. A joint marginal distribution for the observations can be obtained by integrating the likelihood function over the variance components. A full ML analysis based on the joint marginal distribution requires numerical integration techniques for calculation of the log-likelihood, efficient score and information matrix. Because of the computational complexity, this approach is not considered further here. However, approximate methods based on either a marginal quasi-likelihood approach or a penalized quasi-likelihood approach are available in some of the mainstream packages. In Section A.8 the method of iterative generalized least squares, as proposed by Goldstein (1986) and used in the MLn software, is described in the context of normally distributed data. Its extension to other data types is considered in Section A.9.

## A.2   THE METHOD OF LEAST SQUARES

The general linear model is the basis of many of the most frequently used statistical techniques, including simple linear regression and multiple regression analysis, analysis of variance and analysis of covariance. The model takes the general form

$$y = X\beta + \varepsilon,$$

where $y$ is the vector of observations of length $n$, $X$ is the $n \times q$ matrix of explanatory variables associated with the fixed effects, $\beta$ is the vector of fixed effect parameters of length $q$, and $\varepsilon$ is a vector of errors of length $n$. In this and other models presented in this appendix, the dummy covariates associated with the intercept terms are included in the $X$ matrix and their parameters in the $\beta$ vector. The error terms are assumed to be realizations of independent normally distributed random variables with expected value 0 and variance $\sigma^2$. If $Y$ is the vector of random variables associated with $y$, then $Y$ has a multivariate normal distribution with expected value $X\beta$ and variance $\Lambda = \sigma^2 I_n$, where $I_n$ is the $n \times n$ identity matrix.

The least-squares estimates $\hat{\beta}$ of the parameters $\beta$ are those which minimize the residual sum of squares

$$\sum_{i=1}^{n} \left( y_i - \sum_{j=1}^{q} \hat{\beta}_j x_{ij} \right)^2.$$

Written in matrix notation, the residual sum of squares is given by

$$(y - X\hat{\beta})'(y - X\hat{\beta}),$$

and the least squares estimates of $\beta$ by

$$\hat{\beta} = (X'X)^{-1}X'y, \tag{A.1}$$

with variance (dispersion) matrix

$$D(\hat{\beta}) = \sigma^2(X'X)^{-1}. \tag{A.2}$$

An unbiased estimate of the variance component $\sigma^2$ is given by $s^2$, where

$$s^2 = (n-q)^{-1}(y - X\hat{\beta})'(y - X\hat{\beta}).$$

The estimate $s^2$ is called the residual mean square. The degrees of freedom associated with estimating $\sigma^2$ are $n - q$. The variance matrix of the fixed effect parameters is calculated by substituting $s^2$ for $\sigma^2$ in equation (A.2). The standard errors of the parameter estimates can be obtained as the square roots of the diagonal elements of $s^2(X'X)^{-1}$.

Models are compared on the basis of the residual sum of squares. Suppose that a model with $q$ parameters is to be compared with a model which includes these $q$ parameters and an additional $p$ parameters. Let RSS(1) and RSS(2) be the residual sums of squares on fitting the two models, which have $n - q$ and $n - q - p$ degrees of freedom, respectively. Then under the null hypothesis that all of the additional $p$ parameters are equal to 0,

$$\frac{\{RSS(1) - RSS(2)\}/p}{RSS(2)/(n - p - q)}$$

follows an $F$ distribution with $p$ and $n - q - p$ degrees of freedom.

Confidence intervals for single parameters or a linear combination of parameters from a model with $n - q$ degrees of freedom associated with the residual sum of squares can be calculated using the $t$ distribution with $n - q$ degrees of freedom. If the linear combination of parameters given by $A'\beta$ can be estimated from the model, then

$$D(A'\hat{\beta}) = \sigma^2 A'(X'X)^{-1}A$$

and the two-sided $100(1 - \alpha)\%$ confidence interval for $A'\beta$ is given by

$$A'\hat{\beta} \pm t_{\alpha/2}\sqrt{D(A'\hat{\beta})},$$

where $t_{\alpha/2}$ is the upper $(100\alpha/2)$th percentage point of the $t$ distribution with $n - q$ degrees of freedom. The estimated variance $s^2$ is substituted for $\sigma^2$.

Further details of the methodology in this section can be found in Searle (1971).

## A.3   THE METHOD OF WEIGHTED LEAST SQUARES

If instead of a common variance $\sigma^2$, the error terms $\varepsilon_i, i = 1, \ldots, n$, have a variance of the form $\sigma^2/w_i$, where $w_i$ is known, then the method of weighted least squares can be used. In this case the quantity to be minimized is the weighted residual sum of squares,

$$\sum_{i=1}^{n} w_i \left( y_i - \sum_{j=1}^{q} \hat{\beta}_j x_{ij} \right)^2.$$

The weighted least-squares estimates $\hat{\beta}$ of $\beta$ are given by

$$\hat{\beta} = (X'WX)^{-1} X'Wy,$$

with variance

$$D(\hat{\beta}) = \sigma^2 (X'WX)^{-1}, \tag{A.3}$$

where $W$ is a diagonal matrix with diagonal elements $w_i$.

An unbiased estimate of the variance component $\sigma^2$ is given by the residual mean square $s^2$, where

$$s^2 = (n - q)^{-1}(y - X\hat{\beta})'W(y - X\hat{\beta}).$$

The degrees of freedom associated with estimating $\sigma^2$ are $n - q$. The variance matrix of the fixed effect parameters is calculated by substituting $s^2$ for $\sigma^2$ in (A.3). The standard errors of the parameter estimates can be obtained as the square roots of the diagonal elements of $s^2 (X'WX)^{-1}$. Standard tests of significance and methods for calculating confidence intervals as described in the previous section can be used.

## A.4   ITERATIVE MAXIMUM LIKELIHOOD ESTIMATION

In the context of this section $\beta$ is taken as the vector of fixed effect parameters associated with the explanatory variables and intercept terms, and is of length $q$. However, the results presented here are valid for any vector of parameters, which might include nuisance parameters such as $\sigma^2$ in the case of normally distributed data. The vector of observations is denoted by $y$ and is of length $n$. The likelihood function will be denoted by $L(\beta; y)$ and the log-likelihood function by $\ell(\beta) \equiv \log L(\beta; y)$. Let $\ell_\beta(\beta)$ and $\ell_{\beta\beta}(\beta)$ denote respectively the first and second derivatives of $\ell(\beta)$ with respect to $\beta$, so that $\ell_\beta(\beta)$ is a vector of length $q$ with $i$th component $\partial \ell(\beta) / \partial \beta_i$, and $\ell_{\beta\beta}(\beta)$ is a $q \times q$ matrix with $(i, j)$th element $\partial^2 \ell(\beta) / \partial \beta_i \partial \beta_j$. The vector comprising the $q$ derivatives of the log-likelihood function with respect to $\beta_1, \ldots, \beta_q$ is known as the *efficient score*. The matrix $\ell_{\beta\beta}(\beta)$ containing the observed second derivatives is known as the *Hessian* matrix. The matrix $-\ell_{\beta\beta}(\beta)$ is known as the *observed Fisher's information* matrix.

Let $\hat{\beta}$ be the ML estimate of $\beta$. Using a Taylor series to expand $\ell_\beta(\hat{\beta})$ about $\ell_\beta(\beta^*)$, where $\beta^*$ is close to $\hat{\beta}$, it can be seen that

$$\ell_\beta(\hat{\beta}) \approx \ell_\beta(\beta^*) + \ell_{\beta\beta}(\beta^*)(\hat{\beta} - \beta^*). \tag{A.4}$$

The ML estimates of the $\beta$s must satisfy the equations

$$\left. \frac{\partial \ell(\beta)}{\partial \beta_i} \right|_{\hat{\beta}} = 0,$$

for $i = 1, \ldots, q$, so that $\ell_\beta(\hat{\beta}) = 0$. It follows from (A.4) that

$$\hat{\beta} \approx \beta^* - \{\ell_{\beta\beta}(\beta^*)\}^{-1} \ell_\beta(\beta^*).$$

The Newton–Raphson procedure utilizes this approximation in an iterative scheme for calculating the ML estimate of the $\beta$s. In this scheme the estimate of $\beta$ at the $(t+1)$th cycle of the iteration is given by

$$\hat{\beta}_{t+1} = \hat{\beta}_t - \left\{ \ell_{\beta\beta} \left( \hat{\beta}_t \right) \right\}^{-1} \ell_\beta(\hat{\beta}_t)$$

for $t = 0, 1 \ldots$, where $\hat{\beta}_0$ is a vector of initial estimates of $\beta$. As $t \to \infty$, $\hat{\beta}_t \to \hat{\beta}$, the ML estimate of $\beta$.

The variance of $\hat{\beta}$ is given by

$$D(\hat{\beta}) = - \left\{ \ell_{\beta\beta} \left( \hat{\beta} \right) \right\}^{-1}.$$

The standard errors of the parameter estimates can be obtained as the square roots of the diagonal elements of $-\{\ell_{\beta\beta}(\hat{\beta})\}^{-1}$.

An alternative procedure is Fisher's method of scoring, in which the expected Fisher's information matrix, $I(\beta)$, whose $(i, j)$th element is $-E\{\partial^2 \ell(\beta)/\partial\beta_i\partial\beta_j\}$, is used instead of the observed Fisher's information matrix. In this scheme the estimate of $\beta$ at the $(t+1)$th cycle of the iteration is given by

$$\hat{\beta}_{t+1} = \hat{\beta}_t + \left\{ I \left( \hat{\beta}_t \right) \right\}^{-1} \ell_\beta(\hat{\beta}_t). \tag{A.5}$$

A corresponding alternative estimate of the variance of $\hat{\beta}$ is given by

$$D(\hat{\beta}) = \left\{ I \left( \hat{\beta} \right) \right\}^{-1}, \tag{A.6}$$

and the standard errors of the parameter estimates can be obtained as the square roots of the diagonal elements of $\{I(\hat{\beta})\}^{-1}$.

Models are compared by means of the likelihood ratio test statistic. Suppose that a model with $q$ parameters $\beta_1, \ldots, \beta_q$ is to be compared with a model which includes these $q$ parameters and an additional $p$ parameters, that is, it contains the parameters $\beta_1, \ldots, \beta_q, \beta_{q+1}, \ldots, \beta_{q+p}$. Let $\hat{\beta}_{(q)}$ denote the vector of ML estimates for the model with the $q$ parameters $\beta_1, \ldots, \beta_q$, and $\hat{\beta}_{(q+p)}$ the vector of ML estimates for the model with all $q + p$ parameters. The likelihood ratio test of the null hypothesis that all of the additional $p$ parameters are equal to 0 is based on the statistic

$$-2\left\{\ell\left(\hat{\beta}_{(q)}\right) - \ell\left(\hat{\beta}_{(q+p)}\right)\right\}.$$

For large samples this likelihood ratio test statistic follows the chi-squared distribution with $p$ degrees of freedom under the null hypothesis.

The score test (Rao, 1948) and the Wald test (Wald, 1943) are approximations to the likelihood ratio test. The score test statistic is given by

$$[\ell_\beta(\hat{\beta}_{(q)})]'[D(\hat{\beta}_{(q)})][\ell_\beta(\hat{\beta}_{(q)})].$$

The Wald test statistic is given by

$$[\hat{\beta}_{(q+p)}]'[D(\hat{\beta}_{(q+p)})]^{-1}[\hat{\beta}_{(q+p)}].$$

Both of these test statistics can be calculated using either the observed or expected Fisher's information matrix. Under the null hypothesis they have an asymptotic chi-squared distribution with $p$ degrees of freedom.

Confidence intervals for single parameters or a linear combination of parameters from a model can be calculated based on the asymptotic normal distribution of the ML estimates. If the linear combination of parameters given by $A'\beta$ can be estimated from the model, then

$$D(A'\hat{\beta}) = A'\{D(\hat{\beta})\}A,$$

and the two-sided $100(1 - \alpha)\%$ confidence interval for $A'\beta$ is given by

$$A'\hat{\beta} \pm u_{\alpha/2}\sqrt{D(A'\hat{\beta})},$$

where $u_{\alpha/2}$ is the upper $(100\alpha/2)$th percentage point of the standard normal distribution.

Further details of ML estimation can be found in Azzalini (1996), Lindsey (1996) and Cox and Hinkley (1974).

## A.5    LIKELIHOOD, EFFICIENT SCORE AND FISHER'S INFORMATION

This section concerns the estimation of the parameter measuring treatment difference, $\theta$, from an individual study. Suppose that the individual patient data collected from one study are represented by $y$. The model being used to describe the behaviour of $y$ will be known apart from the values of a certain number of parameters, one of these being the scalar parameter of interest $\theta$ and the others forming a vector $\phi$ of length $b$ of nuisance parameters. So the vector of fixed effect parameters, $\beta$, from the previous section is partitioned into two components $\theta$ and $\phi$. The likelihood of $\theta$ and $\phi$ based on the data $y$ will be known. The likelihood will be denoted by $L(\theta, \phi; y)$ and the log-likelihood by $\ell(\theta, \phi) \equiv \log L(\theta, \phi; y)$.

When nuisance parameters have to be estimated, it is often useful to work with the profile log-likelihood of $\theta$, in which $\phi$ is replaced by the ML estimate of $\phi$ for a given true value of $\theta$. In particular, efficient score and Fisher's information statistics can be calculated from the profile log-likelihood.

The likelihood ratio test of the null hypothesis that $\theta = 0$ is based on the statistic

$$-2\{\ell(0, \hat{\phi}_0) - \ell(\hat{\theta}, \hat{\phi})\},$$

where $\hat{\theta}$ and $\hat{\phi}$ are ML estimates, and $\hat{\phi}_0$ is the ML estimate of $\phi$ under the constraint that $\theta = 0$. For large sample sizes, it follows the chi-squared distribution with one degree of freedom under the null hypothesis.

Let $\ell_\theta(\theta, \phi)$ and $\ell_{\theta\theta}(\theta, \phi)$ denote respectively the first and second derivatives of $\ell(\theta, \phi)$ with respect to $\theta$, and let $\ell_\phi(\theta, \phi)$ and $\ell_{\phi\phi}(\theta, \phi)$ denote respectively the first and second derivatives of $\ell(\theta, \phi)$ with respect to $\phi$; $\ell_{\theta\phi}(\theta, \phi)$ will denote the mixed derivative. As $\phi$ is a vector with components $\phi_1, \ldots, \phi_b$, $\ell_\phi(\theta, \phi)$ will be a vector with $i$th component $\partial\ell(\theta, \phi)/\partial\phi_i$, $\ell_{\phi\phi}(\theta, \phi)$ will be a matrix with $(i, j)$th element $\partial^2\ell(\theta, \phi)/\partial\phi_i\partial\phi_j$ and $\ell_{\theta\phi}(\theta, \phi)$ will be a vector with $i$th component $\partial^2\ell(\theta, \phi)/\partial\theta\partial\phi_i$.

Asymptotically,

$$\begin{pmatrix} \hat{\theta} \\ \hat{\phi} \end{pmatrix} \sim N\left( \begin{pmatrix} \theta \\ \phi \end{pmatrix}, \begin{pmatrix} i_{\theta\theta}(\theta, \phi) & i_{\theta\phi}(\theta, \phi) \\ i_{\theta\phi}(\theta, \phi) & i_{\phi\phi}(\theta, \phi) \end{pmatrix}^{-1} \right),$$

where $i_{\theta\theta}(\theta, \phi) = -\mathrm{E}(\ell_{\theta\theta}(\theta, \phi))$, etc. and the matrix of $i$-values is the expected Fisher's information matrix. Also, asymptotically

$$\hat{\theta} \sim N(\theta, i^{\theta\theta}(\theta, \phi)),$$

where

$$\{i^{\theta\theta}(\theta, \phi)\}^{-1} = i_{\theta\theta}(\theta, \phi) - \{i_{\theta\phi}(\theta, \phi)\}'\{i_{\phi\phi}(\theta, \phi)\}^{-1}i_{\theta\phi}(\theta, \phi).$$

The variance of $\hat{\theta}$ is estimated by $i^{\theta\theta}(\hat{\theta}, \hat{\phi})$.

An alternative approximation to the variance of $\hat{\theta}$ can be based on the observed second derivatives and is given by $\{-\ell^{\theta\theta}(\theta, \phi)\}$, where

$$\{\ell^{\theta\theta}(\theta, \phi)\}^{-1} = \ell_{\theta\theta}(\theta, \phi) - \{\ell_{\theta\phi}(\theta, \phi)\}'\{\ell_{\phi\phi}(\theta, \phi)\}^{-1}\ell_{\theta\phi}(\theta, \phi).$$

The variance estimate is $\{-\ell^{\theta\theta}(\hat{\theta}, \hat{\phi})\}$.

The score test is based on two statistics $Z$ and $V$, where $Z$ is the efficient score for $\theta$ evaluated under the null hypothesis that $\theta = 0$ and $V$ is the observed Fisher's information also evaluated at $\theta = 0$:

$$Z = \ell_\theta(0, \hat{\phi}_0)$$

$$V = \left(-\ell^{\theta\theta}(0, \hat{\phi}_0)\right)^{-1}.$$

When $\theta$ is small, the approximate distributional result $Z \sim N(\theta V, V)$ can be used. The ratio $Z/V$ is an approximate ML estimate for $\theta$. The estimate $Z/V$ is sometimes referred to as the 'one-step estimate' because it is obtained on the first step of a Newton–Raphson procedure to maximize the profile log-likelihood function when the starting value for $\theta$ is 0. Although this estimate is asymptotically unbiased under the null hypothesis that $\theta = 0$, it becomes increasingly biased the further that $\theta$ moves from 0. An estimate of the variance of $\hat{\theta}$ is given by $1/V$. The score test statistic $Z^2/V$ is an approximate likelihood ratio test statistic. For further details, see Chapter 3 of J. Whitehead (1997). The approach based on the $Z$ and $V$ statistics has the advantage that it does not require iterative calculations to implement.

In certain circumstances it is preferable to use a marginal or conditional likelihood instead of the full likelihood. Often this will remove dependence on nuisance parameters, so their estimation becomes unnecessary. In the case of a proportional hazards model for survival data it is the partial likelihood (Cox, 1975) that is generally used.

## A.6    ITERATIVELY WEIGHTED LEAST SQUARES

The generalized linear model, introduced by Nelder and Wedderburn (1972), was originally developed for distributions of the exponential family, such as the binomial distribution. In a generalized linear model, $y$, the vector of observations, is assumed to be a realization of a vector of random variables, $Y$, independently distributed with the vector of expected values given by $\mu$, and diagonal variance matrix $\Lambda$. The diagonal element of $\Lambda$, $\lambda_i$, is a function of the expected value $\mu_i$, $i = 1, \ldots, n$. The dependence of $\mu$ on explanatory variables is modelled via a transformation $g(\mu)$. If $\eta$ is the linear predictor based on the explanatory variables and any intercept terms, so that

$$\eta = X\beta,$$

then $\eta = g(\mu)$. The transformation $g(\mu)$ is known as the link function because it links the systematic and random components of the model.

It can be shown that for a generalized linear model Fisher's method of scoring is equivalent to using an iteratively weighted least-squares procedure. In this weighted regression the dependent variable at the $(t+1)$th iteration is $y_t^*$, a vector of length $n$ with $i$th component $\hat{\eta}_{it} + (y_i - \hat{\mu}_{it})g'(\hat{\mu}_{it})$, where

$$g'(\hat{\mu}_{it}) = \frac{\partial \eta_i}{\partial \mu_i},$$

with

$$\mu_i = \hat{\mu}_{it}, \qquad \hat{\mu}_{it} = g^{-1}(\hat{\eta}_{it}), \qquad \hat{\eta}_{it} = \sum_{j=1}^{q} \hat{\beta}_{jt} x_{ij}.$$

The weight matrix is denoted by $W_t$, an $n \times n$ diagonal matrix with diagonal elements $w_{it}$, where

$$w_{it} = \left[ \lambda_{it} \left\{ g'\left(\hat{\mu}_{it}\right) \right\}^2 \right]^{-1}$$

and $\lambda_{it}$ is the variance of $y_i$, a function of $\mu_i$, with $\mu_i = \hat{\mu}_{it}$.

The estimate of $\beta$ at the $(t+1)$th iteration is

$$\hat{\beta}_{t+1} = (X'W_tX)^{-1}X'W_ty_t^*, \tag{A.7}$$

which is identical to that obtained from (A.5). As $t \to \infty$, $\hat{\beta}_t \to \hat{\beta}$, the ML estimate of $\beta$. The variance of $\hat{\beta}$ is given by

$$D(\hat{\beta}) = (X'WX)^{-1}. \tag{A.8}$$

which is identical to that obtained from (A.6). The standard errors of the parameter estimates can be obtained as the square roots of the diagonal elements of $(X'WX)^{-1}$.

It can be seen that in the case of the general linear model based on normally distributed data, equation (A.7) reduces to (A.1) and equation (A.8) reduces to (A.2), as in this case $\eta_i = \mu_i$, $\partial \eta_i / \partial \mu_i = 1$, and $\lambda_i = \sigma^2$.

Further details about generalized linear models can be found in McCullagh and Nelder (1989).

## A.7    MAXIMUM LIKELIHOOD METHODS FOR GENERAL LINEAR MIXED MODELS

The general linear mixed model contains both fixed and random effects and is an extension of the general linear model presented in Section A.2. The general linear mixed model assumes that the random effects have a multivariate normal distribution, whose variance components need to be estimated from the data. It has the equation

$$y = X\beta + Mv + \varepsilon,$$

where $M$ is the $n \times p$ matrix of constants associated with the random effects, and $v$ is the vector of random effects of length $p$.

Let the variance matrix of the random variables associated with the vector of errors, $\varepsilon$, be denoted by $R$, and the one associated with the $v$ terms by $G$. Assuming that the random effects, $v$, and the error terms, $\varepsilon$, are uncorrelated, then $Y$, the vector of random variables associated with $y$, has a multivariate normal distribution with expected value $X\beta$ and variance $\Lambda = MGM' + R$. Let $\Omega$ be the vector of length $h$ containing the variance components which appear in the $G$ and $R$ matrices. In model (5.24), $\Omega$ would be a vector with two components, namely $\sigma^2$ and $\tau^2$.

If the variance matrix $\Lambda$ is known, then the estimates $\hat{\beta}$ of $\beta$ can be obtained using generalized least squares, and are given by

$$\hat{\beta} = (X'\Lambda^{-1}X)^{-1}X'\Lambda^{-1}y,$$

with variance

$$D(\hat{\beta}) = (X'\Lambda^{-1}X)^{-1}.$$

If $\Lambda$ contains variance components which need to be estimated, then iterative generalized least squares is required. In this scheme the estimate of $\beta$ at the $(t + 1)$th cycle of the iteration is given by

$$\hat{\beta}_{t+1} = (X'\hat{\Lambda}_t^{-1}X)^{-1}X'\hat{\Lambda}_t^{-1}y, \tag{A.9}$$

for $t = 0, 1, \ldots$, where $\hat{\Lambda}_0$ contains the initial estimates of $\Omega$.

Maximum likelihood estimates of $\Omega$ can then be calculated by maximizing the log-likelihood in which the estimates $\hat{\beta}_{t+1}$ are inserted in place of $\beta$ in the log-likelihood function. The form of this log-likelihood function is

$$\ell(\Omega; y, \hat{\beta}_{t+1}) = \text{constant} - \tfrac{1}{2}\log|\Lambda| - \tfrac{1}{2}(y - X\hat{\beta}_{t+1})'\Lambda^{-1}(y - X\hat{\beta}_{t+1}). \tag{A.10}$$

However, this procedure takes no account of the information used in estimating the fixed effects and so leads to downwardly biased estimates of $\Omega$. Residual (restricted) maximum likelihood takes account of this loss of information by modifying the likelihood equation to exclude the contribution from fixed effects. The REML log-likelihood function is based on the residual terms $(y - X\hat{\beta}_{t+1})$ instead of the observations $y$, and is given by

$$\ell_R(\Omega; y - X\hat{\beta}_{t+1}) = \text{constant} - \tfrac{1}{2} \log |\Lambda| - \tfrac{1}{2}(y - X\hat{\beta}_{t+1})'\Lambda^{-1}(y - X\hat{\beta}_{t+1})$$

$$+ \tfrac{1}{2} \log |X'\Lambda^{-1}X|^{-1}. \tag{A.11}$$

Estimation using REML proceeds in an iterative manner as for the ML procedure but with equation (A.11) replacing equation (A.10). The Newton–Raphson procedure as described in Section A.4 can be utilized to obtain either ML or REML estimates for the variance components. The standard errors of these estimates can be obtained as the square roots of the diagonal elements of the observed Fisher's information matrix.

When there is only one variance component, that is $\Omega = \sigma^2$, as defined for the general linear model, the procedure using REML is identical to the method of least squares described in Section A.2. Therefore, $s^2$ is the REML estimator.

The variance of $\hat{\beta}$ is given by

$$D(\hat{\beta}) = (X'\hat{\Lambda}^{-1}X)^{-1}. \tag{A.12}$$

The standard errors of the fixed effect parameter estimates can be obtained as the square roots of the diagonal elements of $(X'\hat{\Lambda}^{-1}X)^{-1}$.

Random effects are estimated using shrinkage estimators. The estimates of $v$ are given by

$$\hat{v} = \hat{G}M'\hat{\Lambda}^{-1}(y - X\hat{\beta}).$$

The variance matrix for $\hat{v}$ is given by

$$D(\hat{v}) = \hat{G}M'\hat{\Lambda}^{-1}M\hat{G} - \hat{G}M'\hat{\Lambda}^{-1}X(X'\hat{\Lambda}^{-1}X)^{-1}X'\hat{\Lambda}^{-1}M\hat{G}.$$

If $\Omega$ is known, $\hat{\beta}$ is the best linear unbiased estimator of $\beta$ (see, for example Robinson, 1991). In addition, substitution of $\hat{\beta}$ and $\hat{v}$ into a linear combination of these parameters would provide the best linear unbiased predictor. In practice, the components of $\Omega$ will usually have to be estimated.

When the variance components are estimated, the variance and covariance terms for $\hat{\beta}$ and $\hat{v}$ tend to underestimate the true sampling variability for $\hat{\beta}$ and $\hat{v}$ because no account is made for the uncertainty in estimating $\Omega$.

Likelihood ratio tests can be performed for the variance components, based on either ML or REML methods. However, the results should be interpreted with caution when estimates of the variance components are close to zero. Although valid for large samples, the Wald test can be unreliable due to the skewed and bounded nature of the sampling distribution for a variance component (Brown and Kempton, 1994).

The Wald test statistic for the fixed effect parameters based on the variance matrix given in (A.12) asymptotically has a chi-squared distribution under the null hypothesis when the variance components are known. However, when the variance components are estimated, account needs to be taken of this. One option is to compare the Wald test statistic with the $F$ distribution. Usually this statistic only approximately follows the $F$ distribution and the denominator degrees of freedom must be estimated. Satterthwaite's (1941) procedure may be used to obtain an estimate for the denominator degrees of freedom. Kenward and Roger (1997) consider a scaled Wald statistic together with an $F$ approximation to its sampling distribution. Likelihood ratio tests may be performed for the fixed effect parameters. However, the $(-2\times)$ log-likelihood values used in the comparison should be obtained from the ML procedure as the penalty term associated with REML depends on the fixed effect terms in the model. Welham and Thompson (1997) consider a likelihood ratio test statistic based on modified REML log-likelihoods.

Further details of the methodology in this section can be found in Searle *et al.* (1992) and Brown and Prescott (1999).

## A.8    ITERATIVE GENERALIZED LEAST SQUARES FOR NORMALLY DISTRIBUTED DATA

For normally distributed data the iterative generalized least-squares (IGLS) estimation procedure (Goldstein, 1986) and the restricted iterative generalized least-squares (RIGLS) estimation procedure (Goldstein, 1989) are equivalent to ML and REML, respectively.

In the IGLS procedure, (A.9) is used to update the estimates of the fixed effect parameters. A generalized least-squares procedure is then used to estimate the variance components, $\Omega$. If $\beta$ is known,

$$E\{(Y - X\beta)(Y - X\beta)'\} = \Lambda.$$

In the generalized least-squares procedure the dependent variable at the $(t + 1)$th iteration is $y_{t+1}^{**}$, a vector of length $n^2$ created from stacking the columns of the matrix

$$(y - X\hat{\beta}_{t+1})(y - X\hat{\beta}_{t+1})' \tag{A.13}$$

underneath each other. The matrix of explanatory variables for the variance components is given by $M^*$, which is an $n^2 \times h$ matrix. The weight matrix is the inverse of the $n^2 \times n^2$ matrix $\hat{\Lambda}_t^*$ given by

$$\hat{\Lambda}_t^* = \hat{\Lambda}_t^* \otimes \hat{\Lambda}_t^*,$$

where $\otimes$ is the Kronecker product. Note that if $A$ is an $r \times c$ matrix and $B$ an $s \times d$ matrix, then $A \otimes B$ is an $rs \times cd$ matrix given by

$$
\begin{bmatrix}
a_{11}B & a_{12}B & \cdots & a_{1c}B \\
a_{21}B & a_{22}B & \cdots & a_{2c}B \\
\cdots & \cdots & \cdots & \cdots \\
a_{r1}B & a_{r2}B & \cdots & a_{rc}B
\end{bmatrix}.
$$

The estimate of $\Omega$ is given by

$$
\hat{\Omega}_{t+1} = \left\{ M^{*'} \left( \hat{\Lambda}_t^* \right)^{-1} M^* \right\}^{-1} M^{*'} \left( \hat{\Lambda}_t^* \right)^{-1} y_{t+1}^{**}. \tag{A.14}
$$

The variance of $\hat{\Omega}$ is given by

$$
D(\hat{\Omega}) = \left\{ M^{*'} \left( \hat{\Lambda}^* \right)^{-1} M^* \right\}^{-1} M^{*'} \left( \hat{\Lambda}^* \right)^{-1}
$$

$$
\operatorname{cov}\left( y^{**} \right) \left( \hat{\Lambda}^* \right)^{-1} M^* \left\{ M^{*'} \left( \hat{\Lambda}^* \right)^{-1} M^* \right\}^{-1},
$$

which reduces to $2 \left\{ M^{*'} \left( \hat{\Lambda}^* \right)^{-1} M^* \right\}^{-1}$.

For the RIGLS procedure, (A.9) is used to update the estimates of the fixed effect parameters. The generalized least-squares procedure then used to estimate the variance components is identical to (A.14), except that the dependent variable now includes a bias correction term. Instead of the matrix defined in (A.13) the following matrix is used:

$$
(y - X\hat{\beta}_{t+1})'(y - X\hat{\beta}_{t+1}) + X(X'\hat{\Lambda}_t^{-1}X)^{-1}X'.
$$

Further details can be found in Goldstein (1995).

## A.9   MARGINAL QUASI-LIKELIHOOD AND PENALIZED QUASI-LIKELIHOOD METHODS FOR DISCRETE DATA

Marginal quasi-likelihood is the name given to the procedure proposed by Goldstein (1991) as an extension of his work on multilevel modelling to generalized linear models. Suppose that $y$ is the vector of observations, $X$ is the $n \times q$ matrix of explanatory variables and intercept terms associated with the fixed effects, $\beta$ is the vector of fixed effect parameters of length $q$, $M$ is the $n \times p$ matrix of constants associated with the random effects, and $\nu$ is the vector of random effects of length $p$. The vector of observations, $y$, is assumed to be a realization of a vector of random variables $Y$ with variance matrix $\Lambda$. The expected value of $Y$ conditional on the random effects is modelled by

$$E(Y|v) = \mu(v) = f(X\beta + Mv). \tag{A.15}$$

In the case of the generalized linear mixed model, the function $f$ would be the inverse of the link function $g$ described in Section A.6. In this case the linear predictor $\eta$ is given by

$$\eta = g(\mu(v)) = f^{-1}(\mu(v)) = X\beta + Mv.$$

The marginal model concerns the marginal mean given by

$$E(Y) = \mu = f(X\beta), \tag{A.16}$$

which, unless the link function is the identity, will not usually be equal to the marginal mean calculated from (A.15). As discussed by Breslow and Clayton (1993), (A.16) can be thought of as a crude first-order approximation to (A.15), valid in the limit as the variance components approach 0.

The random effects $v$ are assumed to have a multivariate normal distribution with expected value 0 and variance matrix $G$. An approximation for $\Lambda$ is obtained as follows. Writing the model in the form

$$y_i = \mu_i(v) + \varepsilon_i,$$

where $\mu_i(v) = f(x_i'\beta + m_i'v)$,

$$X = \begin{pmatrix} x_1' \\ \vdots \\ x_n' \end{pmatrix}, \qquad M = \begin{pmatrix} m_1' \\ \vdots \\ m_n' \end{pmatrix}, \qquad \varepsilon = \begin{pmatrix} \varepsilon_1 \\ \vdots \\ \varepsilon_n \end{pmatrix},$$

and $R$ is the variance matrix associated with $\varepsilon$, and using the first-order Taylor expansion for $f(x_i'\beta + m_i'v)$ about $f(x_i'\beta)$ given by

$$f(x_i'\beta + m_i'v) \approx f(x_i'\beta) + f'(x_i'\beta)m_i'v, \tag{A.17}$$

$y_i$ can be approximated by

$$f(x_i'\beta) + f'(x_i'\beta)m_i'v + \varepsilon_i.$$

The first-order variance approximation for $Y$ is given by

$$\Lambda = \Delta MGM'\Delta + R, \tag{A.18}$$

where $\Delta$ is an $n \times n$ diagonal matrix with diagonal elements $f'(x_i'\beta)$. The IGLS or RIGLS approach of Section A.8 is used, in which $y$, $X$ and $\hat{\Lambda}_t$ are replaced as follows.

The estimate of $\beta$ at the $(t+1)$th cycle of the iteration is given by equation (A.9), in which $y_i$ is replaced by $y_{it}^+$, where

$$y_{it}^+ = y_i - f(x_i'\hat{\beta}_t) + f'(x_i'\hat{\beta}_t)x_i'\hat{\beta}_t, \qquad (A.19)$$

the $X$ matrix is replaced by $X_t^+$, with $i$th row given by $f'(x_i'\hat{\beta}_t)x_i'$, and $\hat{\Lambda}_t$ is equal to the right-hand side of (A.18), evaluated at the $t$th iteration.

The variance components $\Omega$ are then estimated from (A.14), in which $y_{t+1}^{**}$ is created from the matrix

$$(y - f(X\hat{\beta}_{t+1}))(y - f(X\hat{\beta}_{t+1}))'$$

where $f(X\hat{\beta}_{t+1})$ is a vector with $i$th element $f(x_i'\hat{\beta}_{t+1})$, and $M^*$ is replaced by $M_{t+1}^+$, the latter being the matrix of explanatory variables for the variance components contained in the matrix $\Lambda = \Delta MGM'\Delta + R$.

A second-order Taylor expansion may be used in place of (A.17) in order to improve the estimates. Its inclusion defines further terms for (A.18) and (A.19). Details can be found in Goldstein (1995).

In the penalized quasi-likelihood model the random effect terms are incorporated into the linear predictor so that the working dependent vector $y_{it}^+$ now becomes

$$y_{it}^+ = y_i - f(x_i'\hat{\beta}_t + m_i'\hat{v}_t) + f'(x_i'\hat{\beta}_t + m_i'\hat{v}_t)(x_i'\hat{\beta}_t + m_i'\hat{v}_t),$$

and the variance matrix is modified. Again either first- or second-order Taylor expansions can be used with the random terms. Further details are found in Goldstein (1995).

# References

Chapters in which the references are cited are shown in parentheses.

Altman, D.G. (1998). Confidence intervals for the number needed to treat. *British Medical Journal*, **317**, 1309–1312. (7)

Altman, D.G. (2000). Statistics in medical journals: some recent trends. *Statistics in Medicine*, **19**, 3275–3289. (1)

Altman, D.G., De Stavola, B.L., Love, S.B. and Stepnieweska, K.A. (1995). Review of survival analyses published in cancer journals. *British Journal of Cancer*, **72**, 511–518. (9)

Azzalini, A. (1996). *Statistical Inference Based on the Likelihood*. London: Chapman & Hall. (3, Appendix)

Bartlett, M.S. (1937). Properties of sufficiency and statistical tests. *Proceedings of the Royal Society of London, Series A*, **160**, 268–282. (4, 5)

Becker, B.J. (1994). Combining significance levels. In H. Cooper and L.V. Hedges (eds), *The Handbook of Research Synthesis*. New York: Russell Sage. (9)

Begg, C.B. (1994). Publication bias. In H. Cooper and L.V. Hedges (eds), *The Handbook of Research Synthesis*. New York: Russell Sage. (8)

Begg, C.B. and Berlin, J.A. (1988). Publication bias: a problem in interpreting medical data. *Journal of the Royal Statistical Society, Series A*, **151**, 419–463. (8)

Begg, C., Cho, M., Eastwood, S., Horton, R., Moher, D., Olkin, I., Pitkin, R., Rennie, D., Schulz, K.F., Simel, D. and Stroup, D.F. (1996). Improving the quality of reporting of randomized controlled trials: the CONSORT statement. *Journal of the American Medical Association*, **276**, 637–639. (7)

Berkey, C.S., Hoaglin, D.C., Mosteller, F. and Colditz, G.A. (1995). A random-effects regression model for meta-analysis. *Statistics in Medicine*, **14**, 395–411. (6)

Bernado, J.M. and Smith, A.F.M. (1993). *Bayesian Theory*. Chichester: Wiley. (11)

Berry, D.A. (1985). Interim analyses in clinical trials: classical vs. Bayesian approaches. *Statistics in Medicine*, **4**, 521–526. (12)

Best, N.G., Cowles, M.K. and Vines, S.K. (1995). *CODA: Convergence Diagnostics and Output Analysis Software for Gibbs Sampler Output, Version 0.3*. Cambridge: MRC Biostatistics Unit. (11)

Bolland, K. and Whitehead, J. (2000). Formal approaches to safety monitoring of clinical trial in life-threatening conditions. *Statistics in Medicine*, **19**, 2899–2917. (12)

Breslow, N.E. (1974). Covariance analysis of censored survival data. *Biometrics*, **30**, 89–100. (3)

Breslow, N.E. and Clayton, D. (1993). Approximate inference in generalized linear mixed models. *Journal of the American Statistical Association*, **88**, 9–25. (Appendix)

Brooks, S.P. and Gelman, A. (1998). Alternative methods for monitoring convergence of iterative simulations. *Journal of Computational and Graphical Statistics*, **7**, 434–455. (11)

Brown, H.K. and Kempton, R.A. (1994). The application of REML in clinical trials. *Statistics in Medicine*, **13**, 1601–1617. (Appendix)

Brown, H. and Prescott, R. (1999). *Applied Mixed Models in Medicine*. Chichester: Wiley. (4, 5, 10, Appendix)

Canner, P.L. (1987). An overview of six clinical trials of aspirin in coronary heart disease. *Statistics in Medicine*, **6**, 255–263. (6, 9)

Carlin, B.P. and Louis, T.A. (1996). *Bayes and Empirical Bayes Methods for Data Analysis*. London: Chapman & Hall. (11)

Chalmers, T.C. and Lau, J. (1993). Meta-analytic stimulus for changes in clinical trials. *Statistical Methods in Medical Research*, **2**, 161–172. (1, 12)

Cholesterol Treatment Trialists' Collaboration (1995). Protocol for a prospective collaborative overview of all current and planned randomized trials of cholesterol treatment regimens. *American Journal of Cardiology*, **75**, 1130–1134. (1)

Clarke, M. and Oxman, A.D. (eds) (2001). *Cochrane Reviewers' Handbook 4.1.4* [updated October 2001]. In *The Cochrane Library, Issue 4*. Oxford: Update Software. Updated quarterly (http://www.cochrane.org/cochrane/hbook.htm, accessed 9 January 2002). (2, 7)

Cochran, W.G. (1954). The combination of estimates from different experiments. *Biometrics*, **10**, 101–129. (4)

Cochran, W.G. and Cox, G.M. (1957). *Experimental Designs* (2nd edn). New York: Wiley. (10)

Collett, D. (1991). *Modelling Binary Data*. London: Chapman & Hall. (5)

Collett, D. (1994). *Modelling Survival Data in Medical Research*. London: Chapman & Hall. (3, 5)

Collette, L., Suciu, S., Bijnens, L. and Sylvester, R. (1998). Including literature data in individual patient data meta-analyses for time-to-event endpoints. In *First Symposium on Systematic Reviews: Beyond the Basics*. Oxford: Centre for Statistics in Medicine (http://www.ihs.ox.ac.uk/csm/sympabs.html, accessed 22 January 2002). (9)

Collins, R., Peto, R., MacMahon, S., Herbert, P., Fiebach, N.H., Eberlein, K.A., Godwin, J., Qizilbash, N., Taylor, J.O. and Hennekens, C.H. (1990). Blood pressure, stroke, and coronary heart disease. Part 2. Short-term reductions in blood pressure: overview of randomised drug trials in their epidemiological context. *Lancet*, **335**, 827–838. (3, 6, 7, 8)

Committee for Proprietary Medicinal Products (2001). *Points to Consider on Application with 1. Meta-analyses; 2. One Pivotal Study*, CPMP/EWP/2330/99. London: European Agency for the Evaluation of Medicinal Products (http://www.emea.eu.int/pdfs/human/ewp/233099en.pdf, accessed 9 January 2002). (1)

Cook, D.J., Sackett, D.L. and Spitzer, W.O. (1995). Methodologic guidelines for systematic reviews of randomized control trials in health care from the Potsdam consultation on meta-analysis. *Journal of Clinical Epidemiology*, **48**, 167–171. (2)

Cooper, H. and Hedges, L.V. (eds) (1994). *The Handbook of Research Synthesis*. New York: Russell Sage Foundation. (2)

Copas, J. (1999). What works? Selectivity models and meta-analysis. *Journal of the Royal Statistical Society, Series A*, **162**, 95–109. (8)

Cox, D.R. (1972). Regression models and life-tables. *Journal of the Royal Statistical Society, Series B*, **34**, 187–202. (3, 5)

Cox, D.R. (1975). Partial likelihood. *Biometrika*, **62**, 269–276. (Appendix)

Cox, D.R. and Hinkley, D.V. (1974). *Theoretical Statistics*. London: Chapman & Hall. (Appendix)

Dear, K.B.G. and Begg, C.B. (1992). An approach for assessing publication bias prior to performing a meta-analysis. *Statistical Science*, **7**, 237–245. (8)

Deeks, J., Glanville, J. and Sheldon, T. (1996). *Undertaking Systematic Reviews of Research on Effectiveness: CRD Guidelines for Those Carrying out or Commissioning Reviews*, CRD Research Report No. 4. York: Centre for Reviews and Dissemination. (2, 7)

DerSimonian, R. and Laird, N. (1986). Meta-analysis in clinical trials. *Controlled Clinical Trials*, **7**, 177–188. (4)

Diggle, P.J., Liang, K.Y. and Zeger, S.L. (1994). *Analysis of Longitudinal Data*. Oxford: Clarendon Press. (5)

Duval, S. and Tweedie, R. (2000a). A nonparametric 'trim and fill' method of accounting for publication bias in meta-analysis. *Journal of the American Statistical Association*, **95**, 89–98. (8)

Duval, S. and Tweedie, R. (2000b). Trim and fill: a simple funnel-plot-based method of testing and adjusting for publication bias in meta-analysis. *Biometrics*, **56**, 455–463. (8)

Early Breast Cancer Trialists' Collaborative Group (1988). Effects of adjuvant tamoxifen and cytotoxic therapy on mortality in early breast cancer: an overview of 61 randomised trials among 28 896 women. *New England Journal of Medicine*, **319**, 1681–1692. (1)

Early Breast Cancer Trialists' Collaborative Group (1990). *Treatment of Early Breast Cancer: Volume 1. Worldwide Evidence 1985–1990*. Oxford: Oxford University Press. (4, 6)

Eddy, D.M., Hasselblad, V. and Shachter, R. (1992). *Meta-analysis by the Confidence Profile Method*. San Diego, CA: Academic Press. (11)

Efron, B. (1977). The efficiency of Cox's likelihood function for censored data. *Journal of the American Statististical Association*, **76**, 312–319. (3)

Efron, B. and Tibshirani R.J. (1993). *An Introduction to the Bootstrap*. New York: Chapman & Hall. (5)

Egger, M. and Davey Smith, G. (1995). Misleading meta-analysis. *British Medical Journal*, **310**, 752–754. (8)

Egger, M., Davey Smith, G., Schneider, M. and Minder, C. (1997). Bias in meta-analysis detected by a simple, graphical test. *British Medical Journal*, **315**, 629–634. (8)

Egger, M., Sterne, J.A.C., Davey Smith, G. (1998). Meta-analysis software. http://www.bmj.com/archive/7126/7126ed9.htm (accessed 9 January 2002). (1)

Egger, M., Davey Smith, G. and Altman, D.G. (eds) (2001). *Systematic Reviews in Health Care: Meta-analysis in Context*. London: BMJ Publishing Group. (1)

Emerson, J.D. (1994). Combining estimates of the odds ratio: the state of the art. *Statistical Methods in Medical Research*, **3**, 157–178. (9)

Fisher, L.D.(1999). One large, well-designed, multicenter study as an alternative to the usual FDA paradigm. *Drug Information Journal*, **33**, 265–271. (1)

Fisher, R.A. (1932). *Statistical Methods for Research Workers* (4th edn). London: Oliver and Boyd. (1, 9)

Follmann, D., Elliot, P., Suh, I. and Cutler, J (1992). Variance imputation for overviews of clinical trials with continuous response. *Journal of Clinical Epidemiology*, **45**, 769–773. (9)

Folstein, M.F., Folstein, S.E. and McHugh, P.R. (1975). Mini-mental state: A practical method for grading the cognitive state of patients for the clinician. *Journal of Psychiatric Research*, **12**, 189–198. Available at http://www.minimental.com/article.hmtl (accessed 17 December 2001). (6)

Freedman, L.S. and Spiegelhalter, D.J. (1989). Comparison of Bayesian with group sequential methods for monitoring clinical trials. *Controlled Clinical Trials*, **10**, 357–367. (12)

Frost, C., Clarke, R. and Beacon, H. (1999). Use of hierarchical models for meta-analysis: experience in the metabolic ward studies of diet and blood cholesterol. *Statistics in Medicine*, **18**, 1657–1676. (10)

Galbraith, R.F. (1988). A note on graphical presentation of estimated odds ratios from several trials. *Statistics in Medicine*, **7**, 889–894. (7)

Gart, J.J. and Zweifel, J.R. (1967). On the bias of various estimators of the logit and its variance with applications to quantal bioassay. *Biometrika*, **54**, 181–187. (9)

Geweke, J. (1992). Evaluating the accuracy of sampling-based approaches to the calculation of posterior moments. In J.M. Bernado, J.O. Berger, A.P. Dawid and A.F.M. Smith (eds), *Bayesian Statistics 4*. Oxford: Oxford University Press. (11)

Glass, G.V. (1976). Primary, secondary and meta-analysis of research. *Educational Researcher*, **5**, 3–8. (1, 3)

Goldstein, H. (1986). Multilevel mixed linear model analysis using iterative generalized least squares. *Biometrika*, **73**, 43–56. (5, Appendix)

Goldstein, H. (1989). Restricted unbiased iterative generalized least-squares estimation. *Biometrika*, **76**, 622–623. (5, Appendix)

Goldstein, H. (1991). Non-linear multilevel models with an application to discrete response data. *Biometrika*, **78**, 43–51. (Appendix)

Goldstein, H. (1995). *Multilevel Statistical Models*, (2nd edn). London: Arnold. (5, Appendix)

Goldstein, H., Yang, M., Omar, R., Turner, R. and Thompson, S. (2000). Meta-analysis using multilevel models with an application to the study of class size effects. *Applied Statistics*, **49**, 399–412. (9, 10)

Green, S.J., Fleming, T.R. and Emerson, S. (1987). Effects on overviews of early stopping rules for clinical trials. *Statistics in Medicine*, **6**, 361–367. (10)

Greenland, S. and Salvan, A. (1990). Bias in the one-step method for pooling study results. *Statistics in Medicine*, **9**, 247–252. (3, 4)

Hahn, S., Williamson, P.R., Hutton, J.L., Garner, P. and Flynn, E.V. (2000). Assessing the potential for bias in meta-analysis due to selective reporting of subgroup analyses within studies. *Statistics in Medicine*, **19**, 3325–3336. (8)

Hall, W.J. and Ding, K. (2001). Sequential tests and estimates after overrunning based on *p*-value combination. Technical report 01/06. Department of Biostatistics, University of Rochester. (9, 10)

Halvorsen, K.T. (1994). The reporting format. In H. Cooper and L.V. Hedges (eds), *The Handbook of Research Synthesis*. New York: Russell Sage. (7)

Hardy, R.J. and Thompson, S.G. (1996). A likelihood approach to meta-analysis with random effects. *Statistics in Medicine*, **15**, 619–629. (4)

Hardy, R.J. and Thompson, S.G. (1998). Detecting and describing heterogeneity in meta-analysis. *Statistics in Medicine*, **17**, 841–856. (6)

Hartung, J. (1999). An alternative method for meta-analysis. *Biometrical Journal*, **41**, 901–916. (4)

Hedeker, D. and Gibbons, R.D. (1994). A random effects ordinal regression model for multilevel analysis. *Biometrics*, **40**, 393–408. (5)

Hedges, L.V. (1984). Estimation of effect size under nonrandom sampling: the effect of censoring studies yielding statistically insignificant mean differences. *Journal of Education Studies*, **9**, 61–85. (8)

Hedges, L.V. (1992). Modelling publication selection effects in meta-analysis. *Statistical Science*, **7**, 246–255. (8)

Hedges, L.V. (1994). Fixed effects models. In H. Cooper and L.V. Hedges (eds), *The Handbook of Research Synthesis*. New York: Russell Sage. (6)

Hedges, L.V. and Olkin, J. (1985). *Statistical Methods for Meta-Analysis*. Orlando, FL: Academic Press. (3)

Higgins, J.P.T. (1997). Exploiting information in random effects meta-analysis. Ph.D thesis, University of Reading. (11, 12)

Higgins, J.P.T. and Whitehead, A. (1996). Borrowing strength from external trials in a meta-analysis. *Statistics in Medicine*, **15**, 2733–2749. (10, 11)

Higgins, J.P.T., Whitehead, A., Turner, R.M., Omar, R.Z. and Thompson, S.G. (2001). Meta-analysis of continuous outcome data from individual patients. *Statistics in Medicine*, **20**, 2219–2241. (5)

Hughes, M.D., Freedman, L.S. and Pocock, S.J. (1992). The impact of stopping rules on heterogeneity of results in overviews of clinical trials. *Biometrics*, **48**, 41–53. (10)

Hutton, J.L. (2000). Number needed to treat: properties and problems. *Journal of the Royal Statistical Society, Series A*, **163**, 403–419. (7)

Hutton, J.L. and Williamson, P.R. (2000). Bias in meta-analysis due to outcome variable selection within studies. *Applied Statistics*, **49**, 359–370. (8)

International Conference on Harmonisation of Technical Requirements for Registration of Pharmaceuticals for Human Use (1998). *ICH Topic E9: Statistical Principles for Clinical Trials.* http://www.emea.eu.int/pdfs/human/ich/036396en.pdf (accessed 9 January 2002). (1, 2)

ISIS-4 (Fourth International Study of Infarct Survival) Collaborative Group (1995). ISIS-4: A randomised factorial trial assessing early oral captopril, oral mononitrate, and intravenous magnesium sulphate in 58050 patients with suspected acute myocardial infarction. *Lancet*, **345**, 669–685. (8)

Iyengar, S. and Greenhouse, J.B. (1988). Selection models and the file drawer problem. *Statistical Science*, **3**, 109–117. (8)

Jennison, C. and Turnbull, B.W. (1989). Interim analyses: the repeated confidence interval approach. *Journal of the Royal Statistical Society, Series B*, **51**, 305–361. (12)

Jennison, C. and Turnbull, B.W. (2000). *Group Sequential Methods with Applications to Clinical Trials.* Boca Raton, FL: Chapman & Hall/CRC. (10, 12)

Jones, D.R. and Whitehead, J. (1979). Sequential forms of the log rank and modified Wilcoxon tests for censored data. *Biometrika*, **66**, 105–113. Correction (1981), *Biometrika*, **68**, 576. (3)

Kallen, A. (1997). Treatment-by-center interaction: what is the issue? *Drug Information Journal*, **31**, 927–936. (5)

Kenward, M.G. and Roger, J.H. (1997). Small sample inference for fixed effects from restricted maximum likelihood. *Biometrics*, **53**, 983–997. (5, Appendix)

Lane, D.M. and Dunlap, W.P. (1978). Estimating effect-size bias resulting from the significance test criterion in editorial decisions. *British Journal of Mathematical and Statistical Psychology*, **31**, 107–112. (8)

Lee, P.M. (1989). *Bayesian Statistics: An Introduction.* London: Edward Arnold. (11)

Lesaffre, E. and Pledger, G. (1999). A note on the number needed to treat. *Controlled Clinical Trials*, **20**, 439–447. (7)

Lewis, S. and Clarke, M. (2001). Forest plots: trying to see the wood and the trees. *British Medical Journal*, **322**, 1479–1480. (7)

Light, R.J. and Pillemer, D.B. (1984). *Summing Up: The Science of Reviewing Research.* Cambridge, MA: Harvard University Press. (8)

Lindsey, J.K. (1996) *Parametric Statistical Inference.* Oxford: Clarendon Press (Appendix)

Little, R.J.A. (1995). Modelling the drop-out mechanism in longitudinal studies. *Journal of the American Statistical Association*, **90**, 1112–1121. (2)

Little, R.J.A. and Rubin, D.B. (1987). *Statistical Analysis with Missing Data.* New York: Wiley. (2)

Mann, H.B. and Whitney, D.R. (1947). On a test of whether one of two random variables is stochastically larger than the other. *Annals of Mathematical Statistics*, **18**, 50–60. (3)

Mantel, N. and Haenszel, W. (1959). Statistical aspects of the analysis of data from retrospective studies of disease. *Journal of the National Cancer Institute*, **22**, 719–748. (9)

McCullagh, P. (1978). A class of parametric models for the analysis of square contingency tables with ordered categories. *Biometrika*, **65**, 413–415. (3)

McCullagh, P. (1980). Regression models for ordinal data. *Journal of the Royal Statistical Society, Series B*, **42**, 109–142. (3)

McCullagh, P. and Nelder, J.A. (1989). *Generalized Linear Models* (2nd edn). London: Chapman & Hall. (5, Appendix)

Moher, D., Jadad, A.R., Nichol, G., Penman, M., Tugwell, P. and Walsh, S. (1995). Assessing the quality of randomised controlled trials: an annotated bibliography of scales and checklists. *Controlled Clinical Trials*, **16**, 62–73. (2)

Moher, D., Cook, D.J., Eastwood, S., Olkin, I., Rennie, D. and Stroup, D.F. for the QUOROM Group (1999). Improving the quality of reports of meta-analyses of randomised controlled trials: the QUOROM statement. *Lancet*, **354**, 1896–1900. (1, 7)

Morrell, C.H. (1998). Likelihood ratio testing of variance components in the linear mixed-effects model using restricted maximum likelihood. *Biometrics*, **54**, 1560–1568. (5)

Mosteller, F. and Bush, R.R. (1954). Selected quantitative techniques. In G. Lindsey (ed), *Handbook of Social Psychology: Vol. 1. Theory and Method*. Cambridge, MA: Addison-Wesley. (9)

Multicenter Diltiazem Postinfarction Trial Research Group (1988). The effect of diltiazem on mortality and reinfarction after myocardial infarction. *New England Journal of Medicine*, **319**, 385–392. (3)

Nelder, J.A. and Wedderburn, R.W.M. (1972). Generalized linear models. *Journal of the Royal Statistical Society, Series A*, **135**, 370–384. (Appendix)

Normand, S.-L.T. (1999). Tutorial in biostatistics. Meta-analysis: formulating, evaluating, combining, and reporting. *Statistics in Medicine*, **18**, 321–359. (4)

O'Brien, P.C. and Fleming, T.R. (1979). A multiple testing procedure for clinical trials. *Biometrics*, **48**, 41–53. (10 ,12)

O'Hagan, A. (1994). *Bayesian Inference*. London: Edward Arnold. (11)

Pagliaro, L., D'Amico, G., Sorensen, T., Lebrec, D., Burroughs, A.K., Morabito, A., Tine, F., Politi, F. and Traina, M. (1992). Prevention of first bleeding in cirrhosis: a meta-analysis of randomized trials of nonsurgical treatment. *Annals of Internal Medicine*, **117**, 59–70. (10, 11)

Parmar, M.K.B., Torri, V., Stewart, L. (1998). Extracting summary statistics to perform meta-analyses of the published literature for survival endpoints. *Statistics in Medicine*, **17**, 2815–2834. (9)

Pearson, K. (1904). Report on certain enteric fever inoculations. *British Medical Journal*, **2**, 1243–1246. (1)

Pogue, J.M. and Yusuf, S. (1997). Cumulating evidence from randomized trials: utilizing sequential monitoring boundaries for cumulative meta-analysis. *Controlled Clinical Trials*, **18**, 580–593. (12)

Qizilbash, N., Whitehead, A., Higgins, J., Wilcock, G., Schneider, L. and Farlow, M., on behalf of the Dementia Trialists' Collaboration (1998). Cholinesterase inhibition for Alzheimer disease: a meta-analysis of the tacrine trials. *Journal of the American Medical Association*, **280**, 1777–1782. (3)

Rao, C.R. (1948). Large sample tests of statistical hypotheses concerning several parameters with applications to problems of estimation. *Proceedings of the Cambridge Philosophical Society*, **44**, 50–57. (Appendix)

Robbins, H. (1970). Statistical methods related to the law of the iterated logarithm. *Annals of Mathematical Statistics*, **41**, 1397–1409. (12)

Robins, J., Greenland, S. and Breslow, N. (1986). A general estimator for the variance of the Mantel–Haenszel odds ratio. *American Journal of Epidemiology*, **124**, 719–723. (9)

Robinson, G.K. (1991). That BLUP is a good thing. *Statistical Science*, **6**, 15–51. (Appendix)

Rosenthal, R. (1979). The 'file-drawer problem' and tolerance for null results. *Psychological Bulletin*, **86**, 638–641. (8)

Rubin, D.B. (1987). *Multiple Imputation for Nonresponse in Surveys*. New York: Wiley. (2)

Sackett, D.L., Richardson, W.S., Rosenberg, W. and Haynes, R.B. (1997). *Evidence-Based Medicine. How to Practice and Teach EBM*. London: Churchill-Livingstone. (1)

Sacks, H.S., Chalmers, T.C., Blum, A.L., Berrier, J. and Pagano, D. (1990). Endoscopic hemostasis: an effective therapy for bleeding peptic ulcers. *Journal of the American Medical Association*, **264**, 494–499. (12)

Satterthwaite, F.F. (1941). Synthesis of variance. *Psychometrika*, **6**, 309–316. (5, Appendix)

Scheffé, H. (1959). *The Analysis of Variance*. Wiley: New York. (4, 5)

Searle, S.R. (1971). *Linear Models*. Wiley: New York. (5, Appendix)

Searle, S.R., Casella, G. and McCulloch, C.E. (1992). *Variance Components*. Wiley: New York. (3, 11, Appendix)

Senn, S. (1993). *Cross-over Trials in Clinical Research*. Chichester: Wiley. (10)

Senn, S. (1997). *Statistical Issues in Drug Development*. Chichester: Wiley. (5)

Senn, S. (2000). The many modes of meta. *Drug Information Journal*, **34**, 535–549. (1, 5)

Shrewsbury, S., Pyke, S. and Britton, M. (2000). Meta-analysis of increased dose of inhaled steroid or addition of salmeterol in symptomatic asthma (MIASMA). *British Medical Journal*, **320**, 1368–1373. (2, 7)

Smeeth, L., Haines, A. and Ebrahim, S. (1999). Numbers needed to treat derived from meta-analyses – sometimes informative, usually misleading. *British Medical Journal*, **318**, 1548–1551. (7)

Smith, T.C. (1995). Interpreting evidence from multiple randomised and non-randomised studies. Ph.D. thesis, University of Cambridge. (11)

Spiegelhalter, D.J., Freedman, L.S. and Parmar, M.K.B. (1994). Bayesian approaches to randomized trials. *Journal of the Royal Statistical Society, Series A*, **157**, 357–416. (12)

Sprott, D.A. (1973). Normal likelihoods and their relation to large sample theory of estimation. *Biometrika*, **60**, 457–465. (3)

Stangl, D.K. and Berry, D.A. (eds) (2000). *Meta-Analysis in Medicine and Health Policy*. New York: Marcel Dekker. (1, 11)

Sterne, J.A.C. and Egger, M. (2000). High false positive rate for trim and fill method. http://www.bmj.com/cgi/eletters/320/7249/1574#EL1 (accessed 9 January 2002). (8)

Sterne, J.A.C., Egger, M. and Davey Smith, G. (2001a). Investigating and dealing with publication and other biases. In M. Egger, G. Davey Smith and D.G. Altman (eds), *Systematic Reviews in Health Care: Meta-analysis in Context*, (2nd edn) London: BMJ Books. (8)

Sterne, J.A.C., Egger, M. and Sutton, A.J. (2001b). Meta-analysis software. In M. Egger, G. Davey Smith and D.G. Altman (eds), *Systematic Reviews in Health Care: Meta-analysis in Context* (2nd edn) London: BMJ Books. (1)

Stewart, L.A. and Clarke, M.J. on behalf of the Cochrane working group on meta-analysis using individual patient data (1995). Practical methodology of meta-analyses (overviews) using updated individual patient data. *Statistics in Medicine*, **14**, 2057–2079. (1, 2)

Stouffer, S.A., Suchman, E.A., DeVinney, L.C., Star, S.A. and Williams, R.M., Jr. (1949). *The American Soldier: Adjustment during Army Life, Vol. 1*. Princeton, NJ: Princeton University Press. (9)

Sutton, A.J., Abrams, K.R., Jones, D.R., Sheldon, T.A. and Song, F. (2000). *Methods for Meta-analysis in Medical Research*. Chichester: Wiley. (1)

Teo, K.K. and Yusuf, S. (1993). Role of magnesium in reducing mortality in acute myocardial infarction. *Drugs*, **46**, 347–359. (8)

Thompson, S.G. (1994). Why sources of heterogeneity in meta-analysis should be investigated. *British Medical Journal*, **309**, 1351–1355. (1)

Thompson, S.G. and Sharp, S.J. (1999). Explaining heterogeneity in meta-analysis: a comparison of methods. *Statistics in Medicine*, **18**, 2693–2708. (6)

Tippett, L.H.C. (1931). *The Methods of Statistics*. London: Williams and Norgate. (1, 9)

Todd, S. (1997). Incorporation of sequential trials into a fixed effects meta-analysis. *Statistics in Medicine*, **16**, 2915–2925. (10)

Tudur, C., Williamson, P.R., Khan, S. and Best, L.Y. (2001). The value of the aggregate data approach in meta-analysis with time-to-event outcomes. *Journal of the Royal Statistical Society, Series A*, **164**, 357–370. (9)

Turner, R.M., Omar, R.Z., Yang, M., Goldstein, H. and Thompson, S.G. (2000). A multilevel model framework for meta-analysis of clinical trials with binary outcomes. *Statistics in Medicine*, **19**, 3417–3432. (5)

Wald, A. (1943). Tests of statistical hypotheses concerning several parameters when the number of observations is large. *Transactions of the American Mathematical Society*, **54**, 426–482. (Appendix)

Welham, S.J. and Thompson, R. (1997). Likelihood ratio tests for fixed model terms using residual maximum likelihood. *Journal of the Royal Statistical Society, Series B*, **59**, 701–714. (5, Appendix)

Whitehead, A. (1997). A prospectively planned cumulative meta-analysis applied to a series of concurrent clinical trials. *Statistics in Medicine*, **16**, 2901–2913. (12)

Whitehead, A. and Jones, N.M.B. (1994). A meta-analysis of clinical trials involving different classifications of response into ordered categories. *Statistics in Medicine*, **13**, 2503–2515. (9)

Whitehead, A. and Whitehead, J. (1991). A general parametric approach to the meta-analysis of randomised clinical trials. *Statistics in Medicine*, **10**, 1665–1677. (1, 4)

Whitehead, A., Bailey, A. and Elbourne, D. (1999). Combining summaries of binary outcomes with those of continuous outcomes in a meta-analysis. *Journal of Biopharmaceutical Statistics*, **9**, 1–16. (9)

Whitehead, A., Omar, R.Z., Higgins, J.P.T., Savaluny, E., Turner, R.M. and Thompson, S.G. (2001). Meta-analysis of ordinal outcomes using individual patient data. *Statistics in Medicine*, **20**, 2243–2260. (5)

Whitehead, J. (1989). The analysis of relapse clinical trials, with application to a comparison of two ulcer treatments. *Statistics in Medicine*, **8**, 1439–1454. (3, 5)

Whitehead, J. (1993). Sample size calculations for ordered categorical data. *Statistics in Medicine*, **12**, 2257–2271. (9)

Whitehead, J. (1996). Sequential designs for equivalence studies. *Statistics in Medicine*, **15**, 2703–2715. (12)

Whitehead, J. (1997). *The Design and Analysis of Sequential Clinical Trials* (rev. 2nd edn). Chichester: Wiley. (6, 10, 12, Appendix)

Wilcock, G.K., Birks, J., Whitehead, A. and Grimley Evans, J. (2002). The effect of selegiline in the treatment of people with Alzheimer's disease: a meta-analysis of published trials. *International Journal of Geriatric Psychiatry*, **17**, 175–183. (9)

Wolfinger, R. and O'Connell, M. (1993). Generalized linear mixed models: a pseudo-likelihood approach. *Journal of Statistical Computation and Simulation*, **48**, 233–243. (5)

Woods, K.L., Fletcher, S., Roffe, C. and Haider, Y. (1992). Intravenous magnesium sulphate in suspected acute myocardial infarction: results of the second Leicester Intravenous Magnesium Intervention Trial (LIMIT-2). *Lancet*, **339**, 1553–1558. (8)

Yang, M., Goldstein, H. and Rasbash, J. (1996). *MLn Macros for Advanced Multilevel Modelling, V1.1.* London: Institute of Education, University of London. (5)

Yates, F. (1940). The recovery of inter-block information in balanced incomplete block designs. *Annals of Eugenics*, **10**, 317–325. (10)

Yates, F. and Cochran, W.G. (1938). The analysis of groups of experiments. *Journal of Agricultural Science*, **28**, 556–580. (1)

Yusuf, S., Peto, R., Lewis, J., Collins, R. and Sleight, P. (1985). Beta-blockade during and after myocardial infarction: an overview of the randomized trials. *Progress in Cardiovascular Diseases*, **27**, 335–371. (1, 3)

Yusuf, S., Teo, K. and Woods, K. (1993). Intravenous magnesium in acute myocardial infarction: An effective, safe, simple, and inexpensive intervention. *Circulation*, **87**, 2043–2046. (8)

# Index

# Index of examples

*For each illustrative example used in the book the chapter is given followed by the page numbers in parentheses*

# *Statistics in Practice*

*Human and Biological Sciences*

Brown and Prescott – Applied Mixed Models in Medicine
Ellenberg, Fleming and DeMets – Data Monitoring in Clinical Trials: A Practical Perspective
Marubini and Valsecchi – Analysing Survival Data from Clinical Trials and Observation Studies
Parmigiani – Modeling in Medical Decision Making: A Bayesian Approach
Senn – Cross-over Trials in Clinical Research
Senn – Statistical Issues in Drug Development
A. Whitehead – Meta-analysis of Controlled Clinical Trials
J. Whitehead – The Design and Analysis of Sequential Clinical Trials, Revised Second Edition

*Earth and Environmental Sciences*

Buck, Cavanagh and Litton – Bayesian Approach to Interpreting Archaeological Data
Webster and Oliver – Geostatistics for Environmental Scientists

*Industry, Commerce and Finance*

Aitken – Statistics and the Evaluation of Evidence for Forensic Scientists
Lehtonen and Pahkinen – Practical Methods for Design and Analysis of Complex Surveys
Ohser and Mücklich – Statistical Analysis of Microstructures in Materials Science